ALL CATS GO TO HEAVEN

All Cats Go to Heaven

AN ANTHOLOGY OF STORIES ABOUT CATS

SELECTED BY BETH BROWN

ILLUSTRATED BY PEGGY BACON

PUBLISHERS Grosset & Dunlap NEW YORK

Acknowledgments

I deeply appreciate the cooperation of the following authors, publishers, and literary representatives for their kind permission to reprint the stories in this collection:

GEORGE ALLEN & UNWIN, LTD. for "The Immortal Cat" from *I Had a Cat and a Dog* by Karel Capek.

WILHELMINA C. ANDREWS for "Lord Jitters" by Roy Chapman Andrews selected from *Natural History Magazine.*

PEGGY BACON for "The Queen's Cat" from *The True Philosopher and Other Cat Tales* by Peggy Bacon.

HELEN DORE BOYLSTON for "The Stuff of Dreams" by Helen Dore Boylston. Copyright 1936, by The Atlantic Monthly Company. Reprinted by permission of Brandt & Brandt.

THE CATHOLIC WORLD for "The Cat That Was Fey" by Arthur Stanley Riggs. Originally published in *The Catholic World,* July, 1951.

CHILTON COMPANY for "Biography" by Era Zistel, from *A Treasury of Cat Stories* edited by Era Zistel, copyright 1944, Chilton Company.

THOMAS Y. CROWELL COMPANY and CASSELL & COMPANY, LTD. for "My First Tiger" from *My Five Tigers* by Lloyd Alexander. Reprinted by permission of Thomas Y. Crowell Company and Cassell & Company, Ltd.

CURTIS BROWN, LTD. for "Mister Youth" by Sophie Kerr, copyright © 1927 by *Delineator Magazine.* Reprinted by permission of the Author.

CURTIS BROWN, LTD. for "The Cat and the Cobra" by A. W. Smith. Copyright © 1933 by Harper & Brothers. Reprinted by permission of the Author.

MAZO DE LA ROCHE for her stories "The Ninth Life" and "Cat's Cruise." Reprinted by permission of the Author and The Macmillan Company of Canada Limited.

DOUBLEDAY AND COMPANY, INC. and A. P. WATT & SON for "The Cat That Walked by Himself" from *Just So Stories* by Rudyard Kipling.

FARRAR, STRAUS & CUDAHY, INC. for "Tobias" from *Phudd Hill* by Alan Devoe, copyright 1937 by Alan Devoe. Used by permission of the publishers, Farrar, Straus & Cudahy, Inc.

FARRAR, STRAUS & CUDAHY, INC. and MARTIN SECKER & WARBURG, LTD. for "The Long-Cat" from *Creatures Great and Small* by Colette, copyright 1904 by Colette Willy, translated by Enid McLeod.

HARCOURT, BRACE AND COMPANY, INC. for "The Fat of the Cat" from *The Fat of the Cat and Other Stories* by Gottfried Keller, adapted and translated by Louis Untermeyer, copyright 1925 by Harcourt, Brace and Company, Inc., renewed, 1953 by Louis Untermeyer. Reprinted by permission of the publishers.

iv

HARPER AND BROTHERS for "The Cat" from *Understudies* by Mary E. Wilkins. Reprinted by permission of Harper & .Brothers.

D. C. HEATH AND COMPANY for "Puss in Boots" from *The Tales of Mother Goose* by Charles Perrault, translated by Charles Welsh.

HENRY HOLT AND COMPANY, INC. and BARTHOLD FLES LITERARY AGENCY for "Birl Forms a Friendship" from *The Stout-Hearted Cat* by Alexander M. Frey, copyright 1947 by Henry Holt and Company, Inc.

HOUGHTON MIFFLIN COMPANY for "Calvin" from *My Summer in a Garden* by Charles Dudley Warner.

HUTCHINSON & COMPANY, LTD. for "Hurrli, Bold, Proud and Amiable Master of the Elk House" from *My Cats and I* by Paul Eipper.

INTERCULTURAL PUBLICATIONS INC. and ADRIAAN MORRIEN for his story "The Cats" which appeared in *The Atlantic Monthly*, April, 1954, from *Perspective of Holland and Belgium,* copyright 1954 by Intercultural Publications, Inc.

ALFRED A. KNOPF, INC. for "Feathers" from *Sacred and Profane Memories* by Carl Van Vechten. Copyright 1952 by Carl Van Vechten.

ALFRED A. KNOPF, INC. and HAROLD OBER ASSOCIATES INCORPORATED for "Jennie's Lesson to Peter on How to Behave Like a Cat" from *The Abandoned* by Paul Gallico. Copyright 1950 by Paul Gallico. I am grateful to Brandt Aymar and Crown Publishers for their permission to use the title and editor's note to the selection, as reprinted in their anthology, *The Personality of the Cat.*

ALFRED A. KNOPF, INC. and THE SOCIETY OF AUTHORS for "Broomsticks" by Walter de la Mare. Reprinted by permission of the Literary Trustees of Walter de la Mare and The Society of Authors as their representative.

J. B. LIPPINCOTT COMPANY for "Lillian" from *Guys and Dolls* by Damon Runyon. Copyright 1930, 1957 by Damon Runyon, Jr. and Mary Runyon McCann. Published by J. B. Lippincott Company.

LONGMANS, GREEN AND CO., INC. and MARTIN SECKER & WARBURG, LTD. for "James Goes Serenading" from *James and Macarthur* by Jennie Laird, copyright 1951 by Longmans, Green & Co., Inc.

THE MACMILLAN COMPANY for "Alice and the Cheshire Cat" from *Alice in Wonderland* by Lewis Carroll.

NISHINOMIYA & HASEGAWA, INC. for "The Boy Who Drew Cats" from *Japanese Fairy Tales* by Lafcadio Hearn, copyrighted, owned and published by Nishinomiya & Hasegawa, Inc., 17 Kami Negishi, Tokyo, Japan.

HAROLD OBER ASSOCIATES INCORPORATED for "My Boss the Cat" by Paul Gallico. Copyright © 1952 by Crowell-Collier Publishing Company. Reprinted by permission of Harold Ober Associates Incorporated.

DONALD CULROSS PEATTIE for "Plutarch's Lives" by Donald & Louise Peattie. Copyright © 1927 by The Curtis Publishing Company. Reprinted by permission of the Author and James Brown Associates, Inc.

EDEN PHILLPOTTS for "Corban" by Eden Phillpotts.

G. P. PUTNAM'S SONS for "Nellie & Tom" from *Pussy and Her Language* by Marvin R. Clark, and for "The Mysterious Ra" from *The Soul of a Cat and Other Stories* by Margaret Benson.

GEO. H. RICHMOND & SON for "The Paradise of Cats" from *Stories for Ninon* by Emile Zola, translated by Edward Vizetelly.

RINEHART & COMPANY, INC. for Chapters IV & V of *The Fur Person* by May Sarton. Copyright 1957 by Mary Sarton and reprinted by permission of Rinehart & Company, Inc.

MARY-CARTER ROBERTS and HARPER'S BAZAAR for "Tom Ivory, the Cat" by Mary-Carter Roberts. By permission of Russell & Volkening, Inc.

CHARLES SCRIBNER'S SONS for "The Slum Cat" from *Animal Heroes* by Ernest Thompson Seton. Copyright 1904 by The Curtis Publishing Company, renewal copyright 1932. Reprinted with the permission of Charles Scribner's Sons.

ELEANOR BOOTH SIMMONS, editor of *Cats and Their Care* in *The New York Sun,* for "Sukey."

THE SOCIETY OF AUTHORS for "The White Cat" and "A Black Affair" by W. W. Jacobs. Permission was granted by the Society of Authors as the literary representative of the Estate of the late W. W. Jacobs.

EMMA-LINDSAY SQUIER and GOOD HOUSEKEEPING MAGAZINE for "The Totem of Amarillo" by Emma-Lindsay Squier.

THE FREDERICK A. STOKES COMPANY for "A Black Affair" from *Many Cargoes* by W. W. Jacobs.

THIS WEEK MAGAZINE for "The Fat Cat" by Q. Patrick. Copyright © 1945 by Q. Patrick. Reprinted by permission of Curtis Brown, Ltd.

THE VIKING PRESS, INC. and THE BODLEY HEAD, LTD. for "Tobermory" from *The Short Stories of Saki* by H. H. Munro. Copyright 1930 by The Viking Press, Inc. and reprinted by their permission.

SYLVIA TOWNSEND WARNER and THE VIKING PRESS, INC. for "The Best Bed" from *The Salutation* by Sylvia Townsend Warner. Copyright 1932, 1960 by The Viking Press, Inc. and reprinted by their permission.

PEGGY WOOD for "The Far-Sighted Cat" by John V. A. Weaver and Peggy Wood. Copyright 1928 by The Curtis Publishing Company.

THE WORLD PUBLISHING COMPANY and A. M. HEATH & COMPANY, LTD. for Chapter 9 and the Epilogue from *Little White King* by Marguerite Steen. Copyright © 1956 by Marguerite Steen.

FREDERICK STUART GREENE for "The Cat of the Cane-Brake" by Frederick Stuart Greene.

CHARLES G. D. ROBERTS for "How a Cat Played Robinson Crusoe" from *Neighbors Unknown* by Charles G. D. Roberts.

A careful effort has been made to trace the ownership of stories included in this anthology in order to secure permission to reprint copyright material and to make full acknowledgment of their use. If any error of omission has occurred, it is purely inadvertent and will be corrected in subsequent editions, provided written notification is made to the publisher, Grosset & Dunlap, Inc., 1107 Broadway, New York 10, N. Y.

To
SAMUEL L. BLUMENFELD
for his counsel wise and warm

Preface

When my book *All Dogs Go to Heaven* was published, I invoked the wrath of millions of cat owners.

Was I by any chance insinuating that cats were excluded from entering the Pearly Gates of the Animal Hereafter? In my estimation, were cats inferior to dogs (an argument which will go on for Eternity)?

Did I own a cat or two or three—with all the accruing benefits of the cat fancier?

The answer was no.

Dogs were always my one great love. I began my career with a canine named Hobo who moved into my heart and home and became my collaborator. Four dog books were born of that warm companionship. I made no bones about it. All dogs were my people.

I never dreamed I could ever learn to care for a cat or two on my hearth. What could a cat contribute to the busy life of an author? Loyalty? Admiration? Obedience? I knew better than that. I knew that while I was the one who chose a dog and made a menial of him, the cat—in her ancient role of independence was the Queen who chose me—and not without first judging my house and my household before she deigned to bestow her regal presence on the place.

And no wonder the cat has remained proud, independent, inscrutable and aloof, wearing an air of royalty and stalking through life like a sage.

The cat has earned these honors. She has carved a niche for herself in the halls of antiquity. True, nowhere in the Old Testament is there any mention made of cats. Yet the scientists insist that cats inhabited the earth from the very beginning of time.

According to an old legend, the cat first came into being when Noah's Ark was floating on the waters of the earth. There was trouble within. The Ark was infested with rats and mice which multiplied at an alarming rate. They made life miserable for the odd assortment of passengers. The food stocks were threatened. Noah was at the end of his wits. Nothing but a miracle could save the situation.

Then, in answer to prayer, a cat sprang to life out of the head of the lioness. She fell to work at once, destroying all the rodents with the exception of a single pair—as specified in the Bible.

So proud was the cat of this achievement that when the Ark reached dry land, she insisted on being the first to alight in order to lead the parade of animals which followed at her heels.

Pride has remained her perogative from that day to this. Man has worshipped the cat all through the ages. Cats have been used in religious rites. In the early Roman household, when the house-cat died, the entire family shaved its eyebrows as a sign of mourning.

The female of the species were venerated as goddesses of love. Egyptian tombs, opened in recent years, have revealed a most interesting facet. The Egyptians not only buried mummified felines but thoughtfully enough included a few mummified mice as well!

All this, Dear Reader, no doubt you have known for years. I had to learn it, both out of books and out of the pages of life. The study of cats was a difficult one for me while I lived in the city. All I met were the strays on the sidewalks and a single Siamese duchess who lived across the lobby but seldom said good morning.

Then my daughter Betty acquired a kitten, which she found in the driveway, deserted by the human world.

We took her in. We christened her Inky. We fed her. We bought a basket for her as well as numerous toys.

But our apartment was twelve stories up from the street. Inky had a penchant for climbing out of the windows. The windows had no window sills. She insisted on exploring the brick face of the house while we held our breaths in anguish. Finally, in the cause of safety, we gave Inky away to our maid Jeanette. The kitten's life, on the ground floor apartment, became placid and peaceful, and zestful with liver. Neither Jeanette nor her husband Paddy have gone away on vacation since!

Subsequently, no meow ever came to our door in New York.

But once I moved out to the country, I found I had all sorts of four-legged brothers. There were rabbits and squirrels, chipmunks and deer down in the pasture lands. There were otters in the pond. But along the street, a number of wise old cats stalked by, inspecting the new house on the hill being built much too slowly to suit them.

Middle-aged cats now appeared, waiting impatiently for the new garbage cans to take their place at the kitchen door. Young cats leaped out of thin air, landed on my lawns and sunned themselves quite openly upon my favorite rocks.

Then, one day, under the porch, I found a new litter. I decided to

wait a little while till the infants grew up and, then, I promised myself, I would telephone around and distribute the gifts of black and
white beauty.

The weeks merged into months and when the winter came, the
kittens were cats on my hearth. I no longer had the heart to give
them away—not even to my most intimate friends. Besides, these
cats had become my textbooks.

I never dreamed that watching a cat would give me so much
pleasure or teach me so many lessons in patience, repose and dignity.
I began to fall in love with the feline of the species, and the dog
books on my bookshelves were shoved to one side to make room for
the cat books which I borrowed and bought and sometimes read
aloud to an appreciative audience of fur people.

Then, one day, Mr. Sam Blumenfeld, my Editor at Grosset and
Dunlap, to whom I owe a deep debt of gratitude for his non-edi-
torial attitude of patience, repose and dignity (acquired by *his* admiration for cats), invited me out to lunch. Would I, the so-called
dog authority, do a cat anthology for Grosset? I accepted, of course.

What I thought would be a chore turned into a joyous labor of
love—with cats now my collaborators. I began my search for stories
—cat stories—both in print and out of print. I spent my winter with
cats on the hearth, cats in my belfry, cats on my typewriter and cat
books in bed.

And here, between these covers, is the result. Every sort of cat—
for every sort of house—for every season of reading—in the hope
that you will enjoy meeting these mutual friends of ours—who lead
as we follow them in the procession across the arena of life.

And, speaking for myself, I shudder to think of all the years I
wasted without a cat in my life. So, in the cause of restitution, please
accept with apology my cat anthology—including two stories of my
own to assure you that dogs are not the ONLY CHOSEN.

You were right from the start, Dear Reader. All Cats Go to
Heaven!

Beth Brown

Contents

ALL CATS GO TO HEAVEN

All Cats Go to Heaven

BETH BROWN

IT HAPPENED so suddenly.

One moment ago, she was there. And now she was here.

She had felt no pain, no fear, just the slightest twinge as her shoulders sprouted into wings and the wings lifted her up from the city street, carried her like an autumn leaf high into the sky, sent her whirling through a long, strange tunnel—and now settled her down in this unfamiliar place, her four paws planted in fog.

There was fog all around her like a sea of surging gray, fearful yet wonderful to her aching senses, particularly to the broken bones in her body.

She drew a deep breath. Was this death, she wondered, a matter the cats often discussed as they gathered in the gutters of an evening? Was she finished with life forever?

Where was she? She had never felt so lonely. She had never heard silence so loud.

Then, off in the distance, the mist began lifting, cleaving the blue sky from the green earth. An eerie glow filled the firmament. And, suddenly, the blaze of morning lighted the universe and Tatters found herself standing before two immense bronze gates leading to another world, mysterious beyond measure.

She caught a glimpse of blooming tree tops. The heavenly odor of new-cut grass perfumed the air. Perhaps these were the green pastures of promise beside the still waters for those who passed on.

No sound came to her ears. Not a sign of life stirred anywhere.

Yet reality was everywhere. The gates were real. The sky was sky. And the earth had become brown and solid underfoot. Brown and solid also was the bronze tablet framed over the bronze entrance. The sun struck it with an arrow of light and Tatters spelled out the inscription.

WELCOME

THE ST. FRANCIS DOG CEMETERY

Beneath it, a small white placard fluttered in the breeze. She read that, too. It said:

NO VACANCIES

"Welcome!" she echoed. "How nice!" She took a step forward. "A dog cemetery! How odd!" She took another step. "No vacancies!" Not unusual, she mused. Even here there was no room for her. All her life not being wanted was all she ever knew.

What now? Where now? Why not go back?

She looked behind her. Cerulean blue immensity—a void of air and nothingness—stretched out to the South. Retreat was out of the question. Besides, as she stood debating her fate, she felt the two white wings at her shoulders shrink down to twin feathers and flutter to the ground at her feet.

Now there was no alternative for Tatters except to face the fearful challenge of her new destiny, taking the same sort of pot luck here as she had on earth where no home had ever invited her and no love had shared its loaf.

She approached the gates and peered in through the bars.

A curious sight greeted her eyes. She saw a giant patchwork quilt spread out in all directions. The lawns were dotted by hundreds of neat beds, some of them trimmed with fringes of white sea shells, others canopied by blooming apple, lilac and locust.

Each little grave had a headstone propped up like a pillow as if for those sleepers who liked to sit up late and read awhile in bed. The reading matter was profuse. There were rhymes inscribed in black on white and poetry written in silver and gold.

The well-tailored paths led to a little white chapel, its doors and windows locked tight in sleep, perhaps eternal sleep. How odd this world so deep asleep under its spell of enchantment! The gate was locked. That was odd, too.

Then she saw the bell. Good thing it was low enough to ring. She reached up and she pulled the cord.

Tatters expected a tinkle, a jangle at most. But the sound was enough to wake the dead—and it did! The gates opened wide as if by magic. The earth shook. The air trembled. A tornado split the horison.

She had never seen such a sight. Grassy blankets were tossed back right and left and a mad brigade of bodies leaped out of bed. She had never heard such barking and baying. The cacophony was deafening. A thousand dogs, it seemed, began bearing down toward Tatters at the gate.

The noise was enough to make the hair stand upright on her thin, black body and the bones of her legs curve inward and her heart drop out of her ribs. Then, all at once, as if on signal, the dogs slid to a stop. Not one of them ventured over the invisible threshold. Not one inched over the line to attack her.

Instead, she faced an audience of a thousand amazed expressions, the tumble of a thousand eager questions, volleyed like a ball and tossed back into their midst to be volleyed out again.

"A newcomer!"

"A newcomer!"

"Who is it?"

"Well, I'll be ossified!"

"What is it?"

"It's a cat."

"A cat?"

"Yes, you've got eyes. Can't you see?"

"Hey! Move over, Fatso! Let me have a look!"

"You're right. It's a cat all right. Something's wrong all right! Now what could a cat be doing here in a dog cemetery?"

A lean, amber-colored Whippet stepped forward. "There's been a mistake, I'm sure."

"Hello!" growled a formidable Boxer.

"Hello," answered Tatters tremulously.

"How did you get here?"

"I don't know."

"Let's see your ticket of admission—"

"I don't have any."

"Maybe she got in on a pass."

"Well, she's not in yet, not by a long shot. She's still an outsider out there!"

"This needs looking into, that's for sure!"

Now a small, black and white Terrier advanced his personal theory. "Maybe we're just imagining things. Maybe we just think we're seeing a cat."

"Maybe you're right. It's been over a hundred years since I last saw one—"

"Hey, Hemo!"

A pompous Bloodhound jostled his way through the crowd and

stood there studying Tatters out of keen, judicial eyes. "Friends and neighbors," he began, "sleepers and snorers!" He raised his paw for silence. "As you know, my testimony is accepted in a court of law. Therefore, I herewith testify to the fact that we do indeed have a cat in our midst, the disposition of which is a matter for legal procedure." Hemo paused briefly to scratch his tired brain. He pointed his paw at Tatters. "Would you care to take the stand in your defense?"

Tatters did not answer. She did not move. She did not venture a single step across the forbidden threshold. Dogs, she had decided long ago, were not to be trusted.

The dogs waited impatiently for some sign of submission. She gave no sign. She made no sound. She held her own—one small cat against a hostile horde of dogs.

Hemo sighed audibly. Finally, he briefed it up. "This, Ladies and Gentlemen of the Jury, is beyond my judicial offices. We better send for Old Adam. Wisdom—"

A Whippet stepped out. "At your service, Hemo!"

"Good! Go get Adam. Tell him it's an emergency. Have him bring his records."

"Righto!" And Wisdom streaked out of sight.

Silence settled again like a thick, lined curtain between Tatters and the crowd of onlookers. Not a word broke the tension. Suddenly, Tatters sat down. The dogs, alert to her every move, found themselves seating themselves. A solemn gravity pervaded the session.

It was Tatters who broke the silence. "You seem to be so alive," she ventured. "Yet you're dead—all of you—aren't you?"

"Who says we're dead?"

"I do." She went on bravely. "I must be dead, too, or I wouldn't be here, would I? This is the end, isn't it? I'll never see the world again, will I?"

"Yes and no," came the answering chorus. "No and yes."

"Well, which is it?"

A Pointer stepped forward. "See my tail wag?"

"I see."

A Poodle stood up. "I can speak. Hear me bark?"

"I hear."

"And our eyes—are they open—or closed?"

"They're open."

"Then what makes you say we're dead?"

"I don't know. I guess because of what happened to me down

there—and coming through the tunnel here to this place. I never had such an experience. I never wore a pair of wings before."

"Well, you couldn't get here otherwise."

She aimed her next question at Hemo. "What's going to happen to me now?"

"I don't know. Your fate, my dear defendant, is up to Old Adam."

"Old Adam?" she echoed in a hollow tone. "What's a human being doing here in a dog cemetery?"

"He used to be a dog catcher on earth."

"Oh!" And Tatters swallowed hard. Once on a time, a long time ago, she had the displeasure of meeting with a dog catcher. She recalled the cold strength of his hands. She remembered the tight, hot cage of wire and the all-night wailing and meowing.

A little white Spaniel interrupted her reverie. "What's your name?"

"Tatters." She tried to curl a drooping whisker. "I guess I look it, don't I?"

"It doesn't matter," he assured her. "It's the wind that does it enroute. In time, your fur will be just like silk—just like mine."

"That's if Old Adam decides to admit her. Don't raise her hopes, Hopscotch!"

"I'm merely trying to be civil to a stranger. There's no rule against being polite." Hopscotch turned his back on Hemo. Now his tone had an unmistakable note of warmth. "What happened to you, Tatters, that would bring you here?"

"I'd rather not talk about it."

"Do you good to get it off your chest. We always go over our pasts, both the good and the bad—all of it. And we always feel better for it. Talking things out seems like sweeping it out. It leaves you empty inside, empty and clean and fresh, and ready for the future."

"That'll be enough!" counseled Hemo. "It's up to Old Adam—not you—to map out her future—one way or the other."

"Well, while we're waiting for him, Tatters and I can become friends, can't we, Tatters? There's no law in your law books against it, is there, Hemo?"

"No. I guess not."

"Go on," invited Hopscotch warmly, "tell us something about yourself."

"What would you like to know?"

"Where were you born? Where did you live? Who was your mother? Etcetera."

"What's etcetera?" echoed Tatters bewildered.

"It's the trimmings," Hemo informed her. "All the fancy trimmings, Tatters, the big banquets and the little kitchen tidbits. How you lived—and how you lost your life."

"You mean her nine lives, don't you?" corrected a lively little Beagle.

"Begin at the beginning," prompted Hopscotch.

"Leave nothing out!" cued Hemo.

"Well," reminisced Tatters, "I was born in an old red barn. It was a beautiful day. I could smell the hay in the loft and the new-cut grass in the pasture. I could taste the air of Spring. My mother's milk was sweet."

"And then?"

"And then I felt a pair of human hands—"

"What happened?"

"They tossed me into a sack. They tossed the sack into a brook. Somehow I made my way to freedom. Then a small boy picked me up and sold me to a grocer. The grocer threw me down into a cellar." Tatters paused in the telling, then went on and on, living life after life, losing life after life at the whim of human hands.

Not one of her lives had been a happy one. The last of her lives was full of dark terror. She was sunning herself on the roof of an old brownstone tenement when the four boys came up through the bulkhead.

"The four of them saw me and I saw them. I knew in a flash what was in their minds. The chase began. I raced back and forth—up and down across that hot, tin roof. Finally they had me cornered at the light shaft. I thought I could make it to the house next door. I must have misjudged the distance."

She went on.

"I don't remember too much of what happened after that. I felt myself spinning through space. Then I struck the sidewalk. Hard!"

"Poor Tatters!"

"No, Hopscotch. Please don't feel sorry for me."

"Why not?"

"Well, just because—"

"Because why?"

"Because something wonderful happened." She closed her eyes at the memory. Yes, something wonderful had happened, something she had never known in all her life.

She heard a soft voice. The pendulum of a human heart beat against her body. She felt a soft pair of velvet hands bestowing human love upon her.

Then everything faded out and she knew no more until she found herself carried like an autumn leaf high in the sky, lifted then dropped down to earth before the astral majesty of these bronze gates.

A hue and a cry sounded off in the distance.

"Old Adam must be coming this way—"

Tatters trembled from head to tail. The approach of a man, any man, always made her heart contract. She began to shudder with fear. Her hair rippled to a crust of defense on her body. She arched her back ever so slightly.

Wisdom was now in their midst. He was trying to tell her something, his tail wagging hard, his words rushing over each other in a mad scramble to be done with the matter before Old Adam arrived.

According to Wisdom, although Old Adam was a dog catcher while on earth, he never disposed of an animal. He never put an animal to sleep. Instead, he brought them home to his house and put them away for safekeeping in the big white barn under the elms. And, when the time came for him to die, he asked to come here so he could go on being their keeper and guardian.

At this, Tatters regarded the approaching little man with a new and acute interest. The dog catcher, she observed, walked with a limp and a cane. He was small and stout. His nose was a bulb of rosy red set into a face lined with the centuries. He wore a round cap of hair as white as snow on a stone. A little dog danced in his way. Both arms were full with the weight of a tremendous black book. It seemed to be some sort of ledger. He puffed hard under his burden.

"Hello," he greeted. "What's this I hear about a cat?"

"You can see for yourself," opined Hemo.

"I see." Then he rested the book against a rock and opened its pages wide. "It's all here," he began. "It's all in the records."

"Good thing!" declared Hemo. "Records are positive proof in court."

Old Adam ran a fat finger down a long list of names. "There's Apple and Snoopy and Sheba. They've all been admitted as of yesterday—all safe and sound and still sleeping off the first shock of the crossing." He placed a pair of silver-rimmed specs on his nose and squinted through their rosy color at Tatters. "What do you call yourself?"

"Tatters—"

He guided his gaze to the bottom of the page, then turned the leaf and read three more names aloud. "Soybean—Tangerine—Tubby. Yes, here it is. *Tatters*. The same name, true, but not the same specie." Old Adam continued to read. "Tatters—an English Bull-dog. Three years of age. Poisoned when trees were sprayed in the park. Under ether at the Laura Speyer Hospital. Better make up his bed. Have it ready on Monday. N.S.G." Old Adam looked up. "That stands for not-so-good. And this is not so good either!" he reflected. "A cat in a dog cemetery. Someone's made a mistake somewhere."

"A whopper of one, if you ask me," observed Fatso.

"How in the world could such an error take place?" inquired Hemo loftily. "Such a thing has never happened in the two hundred years I've been here."

"I don't know," reflected Old Adam. "Might have been due to mixed signals. Light ray might have gone out. Somebody's tampered with something or someone down there is sending up prayer too powerful to handle up here." He threw the next question at Tatters. "Anyone praying for you?"

"No one I know of—"

"Is your thought down there?"

"Don't know what you're talking about," parried Tatters.

"Oh, yes, you do!" Old Adam shook his head knowingly. "I can read your aura, Tatters, and I see the bond streaming from it. You've made an attachment below—as strong as any power above." He closed the ledger softly. "We have room for one Tatters. Which one will it be?"

"If I may put a word in edgewise—"

"Yes, Hemo?"

"I'd like to see the little cat here—behind the bars." But he said it smilingly.

"Yes," agreed Old Adam. "That's a solution. If she likes—our Tatters could stay right here—a cat in a dog heaven. I could send the other Tatters to St. Vincent's—a dog in a cat heaven. A switch like that might be nice for a change. What do you think, Boys and Girls?"

"We'd love to have her here," barked Hopscotch happily. "Won't you stay and be our mascot?"

Tatters did not answer. She was too surprised for words. She looked from one to the other of those eager, friendly faces. It was hard to speak. It was hard to breathe. It was hard to keep from crying. At last, she belonged somewhere. At last, she was wanted. At last, she had finally come home.

Old Adam was saying: "The decision is not ours, Tatters. The decision, Little One, is yours. There's been a mistake which the upper realm must rectify. You're invited to stay. You are free to return."

"You mean I can go back to earth?"

"Yes. What's more, you'll be granted an extra life."

"How unique!" declared Hemo. "The only cat in the world with ten lives to live."

"Yes," said Old Adam. "And here's wishing you at least one happy one!"

"Thank you, Old Adam. Thank you."

"But, Tatters, you're not going, are you?" pleaded Hopscotch. "You're not going back to that place where so many terrible things happened to you, are you?" Hopscotch groaned loudly. "The brook and the boys and all the rest of it—the ache and the anguish and agony—"

Hemo cleared his throat. "The evidence is all against your going back, Tatters. If you stay, I will always defend you."

"Oh, Tatters. Make your home here. It's wonderful here."

Yes, Tatters now knew how wonderful it was here in this new world where hunger could never touch her again or fear would find her fighting for her life or cold could make her huddle for warmth deep in a city cellar.

Wisdom was saying. "We're never sick or unhappy. What's more, we never die."

"I know."

"Look at that apple tree. It never stops blooming."

"It is beautiful," she conceded. "Beautiful."

"The sun shines all year round."

"I know it's nice and warm."

"It's more than that—much more."

Now Hemo began to cross-examine her. "Are you hungry?"

"No."

"Thirsty?"

"No."

"Frightened?"

"No."

"Now isn't it better here than it was there?"

"Yes," she granted slowly, "yes and no."

"Well, what else?"

"Yes, is there something else there that you won't find here?"

"I don't know till I go back," she answered, almost in a whisper. "It may not be there at all," she murmured. "It may not be there anymore."

"It's there," acknowledged Old Adam regretfully. "It's the only thing we don't have here." He smiled enigmatically at Tatters.

"I knew it right from the start. It wasn't the light ray, was it?"

"No, Old Adam."

"A bond of the inner spirit is holding you to earth, isn't it?"

"Yes, Old Adam."

"Well, as long as it does—and because it's so strong, Tatters, you must look in your heart for the answer."

"In that case," she decided, "I'm going back. You understand, don't you, Old Adam?"

"I understand," he answered. "I was a human once." He turned to his charges. "You mustn't keep her. You must let her go. You mustn't want her. That would make her stay. Let her go, Boys and Girls. Let her go—"

"Yes, let me go."

Two big tears came into her eyes. They dropped to the ground at her feet. And in their place on her shoulders, two wings began sprouting again and rustling for her to be rising. Yet she remained rooted here to the earth. Her eyes were fixed on the hundreds of faces all shining with kindness. Old Adam was beaming with warmth. Was it wrong that she go? Was it right that she stay?

Perhaps she would not find what she was going back to seek. Perhaps she was gambling the extra life she had been given on the chance that the bond still held.

She looked at the sky with its big white clouds and she looked at the trees with their billowy white bloom and she looked at the beds, so neat and so prim with the sheets tucked out of sight. She looked at all of it with her inner third eye as if to remember it always.

She smiled at her friends for the last time. For the last time, she lifted her paw and she waved it. She nodded at their last goodby. She wheeled around in a burst of weeping. She dared not look back. She might stay if she did.

In a flash, she felt herself being lifted like a leaf in the autumn wind. The eerie new world became a blur. She found herself whirling through the tunnel at a speed too incredible for words. The cerulean blue faded behind her. The light of the city loomed up ahead. She was back again. She was here again in the old world of unhappiness and reality.

She heard a man's voice saying: "She's coming back to life."

She heard a woman's voice saying: "What a plucky little cat! I'm so glad I picked her up. I suppose you must lose your life to find it."

And then Tatters felt the velvet hands of a human being enfold her like a benediction in their love.

The Boy Who Drew Cats

LAFCADIO HEARN

A LONG, long time ago, in a small country village in Japan, there lived a poor farmer and his wife, who were very good people. They had a number of children, and found it hard to feed them all. The elder son was strong enough when only fourteen years old to help his father; and the little girls learned to help their mother almost as soon as they could walk.

But the youngest child, a little boy, did not seem to be fit for hard work. He was very clever,—cleverer than all his brothers and sisters; but he was quite weak and small, and people said he could never grow very big. So his parents thought it would be better for him to become a priest than to become a farmer. They took him with them to the village temple one day, and asked the good old priest who lived there, if he would have their little boy for his acolyte, and teach him all that a priest ought to know.

The old man spoke kindly to the lad, and asked him some hard questions. So clever were the answers that the priest agreed to take the little fellow into the temple as an acolyte, and to educate him for the priesthood.

The boy learned quickly what the old priest taught him, and was very obedient in most things. But he had one fault. He liked to draw cats during study-hours, and to draw cats when cats ought not to have been drawn at all.

Whenever he found himself alone, he drew cats. He drew them on the margins of the priest's books, and on all the screens of the temple, on the walls, and on the pillars. Several times the priest told him this was not right; but he did not stop drawing cats. He drew them because he could not really help it. He had what is called "the genius of an *artist*," and just for that reason he was not quite fit to be an acolyte;—a good acolyte should study books.

One day after he had drawn some very clever pictures of cats upon a paper screen, the old priest said to him severely—My boy, you must go away from this temple at once. You will never make a good priest, but perhaps you will become a great artist. Now let me give you a last piece of advice, and be sure you never forget it. *"Avoid large places at night;—keep to small!"*

The boy did not know what the priest meant by saying, *"Avoid large places;—keep to small!"* He thought and thought, while he was tying up his little bundle of clothes to go away; but he could not understand those words, and he was afraid to speak to the priest any more, except to say goodbye.

He left the temple very sorrowfully, and began to wonder what he should do. If he went straight home he felt his father would punish him for having been disobedient to the priest: so he was afraid to go home. All at once he remembered that at the next village, twelve miles away, there was a very big temple. He had heard there were several priests at that temple; and he made up his mind to go to them and ask them to take him for their acolyte.

Now that big temple was closed up but the boy did not know this fact. The reason it had been closed up was that a goblin had frightened the priests away, and had taken possession of the place. Some brave warriors had afterward gone to the temple at night to kill the goblin; but they had never been seen alive again. Nobody had ever told these things to the boy;—so he walked all the way to the village hoping to be kindly treated by the priests.

When he got to the village it was already dark, and all the people were in bed; but he saw the big temple on a hill on the other end of the principal street, and he saw there was a light in the temple. People who tell the story say the goblin used to make that light, in order to tempt lonely travellers to ask for shelter. The boy went at once to the temple, and knocked. There was no sound inside. He knocked and knocked again; but still nobody came. At last he pushed gently at the door, and was glad to find that it had not been fastened. So he went in and saw a lamp burning,—but no priest.

He thought that some priest would be sure to come very soon, and he sat down and waited. Then he noticed that everything in the temple was grey with dust, and thickly spun over with cobwebs. So he thought to himself that the priests would certainly like to have an acolyte, to keep the place clean. He wondered why they had allowed the place to get so dusty. What most pleased him, however, were some big white screens, good to paint cats upon. Though he was tired, he looked at once for a writing-box, and found one, and ground some ink, and began to paint cats.

He painted a great many cats upon the screens; and then he began

to feel very, very sleepy. He was just on the point of lying down to
sleep beside one of the screens, when he suddenly remembered the
words: *"Avoid large places—keep to small!"*

The temple was very large; he was alone; and as he thought of
these words,—though he could not quite understand them—he began to feel for the first time a little afraid; and he resolved to look for
a *small place* in which to sleep. He found a little cabinet, with a sliding door, and went into it and shut himself up. Then he lay down and
fell fast asleep.

Very late in the night he was awakened by a most terrible noise,—a
noise of fighting and screaming. It was so dreadful that he was afraid
even to look through a chink of the little cabinet; he lay very still,
holding his breath for fright.

The light that had been in the temple went out; but the awful
sounds continued, and became more awful, and all the temple shook.
After a long time silence came; but the boy was still afraid to move.
He did not move until the light of the morning sun shone into the
cabinet through the chinks of the little door.

Then he got out of his hiding-place very cautiously, and looked
about. The first thing he saw was that all the floor of the temple was
covered with blood. And then he saw, lying dead in the middle of it,
an enormous monstrous rat—a goblin-rat,—bigger than a cow!

But who or what could have killed it? There was no man or other creature to be seen. Suddenly the boy observed that the mouths of all the cats he had drawn the night before, were red and wet with blood. Then he knew that the goblin had been killed by the cats which he had drawn. And then also, for the first time, he understood why the wise old priest had said to him:—"*Avoid large places at night;—keep to small.*". . .

Afterward that boy became a very famous artist. Some of the cats which he drew are still shown to travellers in Japan.

Lord Jitters

ROY CHAPMAN ANDREWS

The true story of an aristocrat of the cat world who, though born to a soundless existence, epitomizes the ever-fascinating qualities of his ancient tribe.

LORD JITTERS walked deliberately down the stairs from his bedroom. I was in a hurry so I gave a gentle push to his lordly rear. He turned, withering me with an indignant look, and stalked into the living room to seat himself on the couch beside a vase of tulips. He sniffed delicately at each of the blossoms and stood off to criticize their arrangement.

"Not so good, if you ask me. Much too massed. A little more separation would make them much easier to smell." Quite evidently that's what he thought, although as a rule he keeps his opinions to himself.

"Now these on the piano. Much better. You see I have no difficulty in inhaling the odor from each separate flower without disarranging my hair. Yes, this is quite satisfactory. I shall remain here and let the perfume drift over me. As a matter of fact if I close my eyes I can imagine that I am in the rock garden at my country estate . . . that it is summer . . . and the sun is shining . . . and there are butterflies to catch and crickets . . . and leaves to chase across the lawn . . . all sorts of exciting things to do . . . and warm smelly earth to snuggle into when I am tired . . . and want to sleep . . . to go to sleep . . ."

I forgot to say that Lord Jitters is a white Persian cat. He got the last part of his name when he was only a fluffy ball of fur because he was never still. Elevation to the Peerage came by divine right at the age of four months; at that time he assumed his seat in the House of Lords. His inheritance included me, my wife Billie, an automobile, an apartment in New York, and a place in the country. For a cat he

15

has done very well for himself. He, however, does not consider that to be so. There are certain annoyances in his life which he bears as a cross; to wit, a black Persian cat, Poke-Poke, and a Llewellyn setter dog, name of Queen. But more of these anon.

Lord Jitters has an infirmity which he endeavors, catfully, to conceal from the public. He is stone-deaf. Not a sound can penetrate his eardrums. Were he consulted on the subject by a psychoanalyst, I am sure he would maintain that deafness is an asset. His thoughts are not disturbed by sounds which could hardly fail to be of less importance. It enables him to live in a world of his own.

Lord Jitters was a precocious child; I might even say, an infant prodigy. Still, he could not entirely escape the intrusion of certain inherited instincts which at his early age it was impossible to understand or analyze. One of these was the desire to watch a hole. His New York apartment does not abound in holes. After diligent search, the only one he could discover was the drain pipe in the bathtub. He very shortly made it evident to Billie and me that it displeased him to have the rubber plug left in the pipe. Then he settled down to prolonged concentration upon the hole. I do not think that he was clear in his mind as to what might possibly emerge from the cavity. Nevertheless, it was a place to be watched and a duty to be done.

His Lordship's bath

Being pure white, Lord Jitters accumulates a vast amount of soot during his excursions on the roof garden of his New York apartment. He just has to be washed with soap and water. Talcum and brushing only change the black to a dirty gray. In regard to baths, he has informed us as follows: "I admit that I like to be clean. Being scrubbed and soaked is not my idea of fun, still I will not object if you perfume the water with bath salts and use sandalwood soap." Ferdinand the Bull has nothing on Lord Jitters when it comes to appreciating pleasant odors. Also when it is all over and he is white as an Arctic fox, he spends hours admiring himself before a mirror.

I regret to have to admit that Lord Jitters is exceedingly vain and laps up admiration with more avidity than he does cream. When we have guests, he waits for the proper moment to make a stage entrance. Stalking into the room, his white plume waving, he introduces himself to each guest in turn. With gentle dignity he will allow himself to be stroked, purring in response. Then he selects a spot on a green stool, the back of a sofa or a yellow satin lama coat where he can pose in full view of the room. While he will court the attention of strangers, Billie and I or any of the maids are not allowed to pick him up except when we are in the motorcar.

We have often discussed this matter with him. His viewpoint is logical.

"I have a lovely apartment," says he. "I am decorative as everyone knows. I also am host. Therefore it is my duty to be gracious to our guests and to enhance the beauty of our surroundings by showing myself to the best advantage. This, however, does not mean that I have to submit myself to being pawed after the guests are gone. I do not like to be touched as you well know."

An ultimatum about "Spooky"

Once we made a great mistake by agreeing to care for a tiny monkey belonging to one of our friends. Its body was only about eight inches long. The little beast, which rejoiced in the name of "Spooky," was as near perpetual motion and chain lightning as any living thing I have ever seen. Lord Jitters was absolutely outraged at the presence of the animal in the house. The limit of his endurance was passed when Spooky one day made a flying leap from the curtain pole, landed on Jitters' back, tweaked his tail and disappeared behind a chair.

The Lord delivered an ultimatum to Billie and me. "I have endured the presence in my home of this distasteful creature," it ran. "I have endeavored to overlook the undignified conduct of both of you in the traffic you have had with it. I will not, however, be subjected to such personal attacks as that which you have just witnessed. I intend to retire to the rock garden, and I refuse to enter this house again until that objectionable animal has been permanently removed."

Out in the garden he went, and there he remained for two days. Even though it rained Lord Jitters preferred to crouch under a bush (where we could witness his misery, of course) rather than capitulate. That broke us down and the monkey was sent away.

At the age of seven months, Lord Jitters was taken in a motorcar to inspect his country estate, Pondwood Farm, at Colebrook, Conn. Not being entirely sure as to his reactions to such transport, his guardians, Billie and I, deemed it advisable to ensure his safety by purchasing for him at the most exclusive shop in New York a beautiful green leather harness. Lord Jitters, however, would have none of it. In a language of his own, which Billie and I understand perfectly, he said: "I will not be trussed up like a street dog and led about on a leash. If you persist in foisting this indignity on me, I shall not get to my feet. My decision is final."

His deportment in the car, of course, was exemplary as we should have known it would be. Stretching out on the top of the driver's seat, he watched the passing show interestedly until such time as he decided it had received enough of his attention. Then he settled in Billie's lap to sleep away the hours before out arrival at his country seat.

Pondwood Farm, however, offered so much that was new and unexpected that for the first time we saw his dignity shaken. Grass in the orchard was three feet high, interspersed with daisies, black-eyed Susans, and lesser flowers. Each one must be sniffed and investigated. Almost before he knew it he had ventured far into what to him was an unknown jungle. Great stems of grass stretched far above his head; enormous branching weeds cut off his view of the sky; a tangle of creepers made it well nigh impossible to walk. He could hear nothing, see nothing. He was lost—hopelessly lost. For the first time in his life, fear descended upon him like an enveloping cloud. Gathering all the breath his lungs would hold, he wailed in terror. Billie and I heard the first shriek and waded through the grass to his assistance. We found him crouching at the base of a huge milkweed, his little face contorted with fright. Into Billie's arms he came with a soft croon of happiness, clasping both paws tightly about her neck. Then in a series of "pur-r-r-ups" he related the terrifying experience through which he had passed.

What goes up must come down

The great maple trees in the yard offered the next adventure. His sharp claws clung easily to the rough bark, and before he realized it he was sitting in a crotch twelve feet from the ground. It was wonderful up there in the leaves and swaying branches. He had a feeling of exhilaration and achievement such as he had never known before. For an hour he stayed until a certain discomfort in the region of his tummy told him it was dinner time. All right, he'd come down—but how? It was easy enough to go up head first, but that didn't work on the down trip. Finally he gave up and sent out an S.O.S. Billie came on the run, as he knew she would, and stretched up her arms. That must mean she wanted him to jump, so jump he did. Lord Jitters landed on the top of her head clinging desperately to her thick blond hair and slid down to a seat on her shoulder, leaving several claw marks on her face.

I had viewed the performance with disapproval. "No cat of mine," said I, "shall go for another hour without learning how to come down a tree."

Therefore after his heart had regained its normal rate, we gave him the first lesson. In a few minutes he had learned how to switch his rear end about while hanging on with his front claws and to come down backward. This was a turning point in Lord Jitters' life for it opened up to him the World of Trees.

Setting his mental compass

To go on a walk with us through the woods of his estate is a delight. Trotting along at our heels, mile after mile, splashing through mud in the swamps or climbing over great glacial boulders, he finds it a most exciting adventure. When we stop, he settles down comfortably on a log and purrs in contentment. At first he often got lost in the underbrush and ferns, but he soon learned a trick which helps him out. Since he can't hear, he has to depend entirely on sight. Now when we have disappeared, he climbs the nearest tree, looks about until he has located us, sets his mental compass, and makes a beeline through the ferns, yowling for us to wait.

Lord Jitters distributes his affection equally between us and obviously feels that our safety is in his keeping. If we separate while in the woods, he is in a terrible quandary. He runs frantically from one to the other, trying to keep us both in sight, and finally sits down and howls miserably. If I go out of the house, and my wife remains indoors, Jitters is most unhappy for he can't decide where his duty lies. Running to the end of the porch he pleads, "Please come back and get Billie. I want to go with you but she mustn't be left alone. No one can tell what will happen to her."

Strangely enough, he rather likes water. Unless it is absolutely pouring, rain does not drive him indoors. One day he was with us in the canoe on the pond. We landed, but he remained playing with a bug. The canoe floated off ten feet or more before Jitters discovered that he was adrift and all alone. Without the least hesitation he jumped overboard, swam to shore, shook himself, and continued about his affairs.

As a hunter, Jitters rather fancies himself, but really he is not so hot. Being white, deaf, and wearing a bell are handicaps. To date he has caught six field mice, two shrews, one mole, and a six-inch garter snake. All of these are presented to us most proudly. Billie doesn't mind live mice, but she hates dead ones. Jitters doesn't appreciate this fact and insists upon placing his catch in her lap.

He always sleeps on our bed, but one night we put him out about eleven o'clock. At first he could not believe that I really meant he had to go. Then with the greatest dignity he stalked down the stairs, giving me what could only be called a "dirty look." At two o'clock in the morning a scratching and howling at the door waked both of us. There was Jitters with a mouse. He jumped on the bed and deposited the limp rodent on Billie's pillow. "You show me out of my room," said he. "I return good for evil. I rid the house of mice while you sleep."

Having delivered himself of this reproof, he walked sedately out of the door. For two nights he punished us by refusing to come into the bedroom.

"My property"

Lord Jitters had never seen a dog until a week or so after he went into residence on his country estate. One of our neighbors came on the lawn followed by his Irish setter, Cob. Jitters was in the garden sniffing the flowers. He looked up, saw us fondling the big red animal, and every hair on his body stood straight up. He crept toward us, eyes blazing, and suddenly flew at Cob like a white demon. The setter yelped in fright and legged it for the road. Lord Jitters followed to the gate and stopped, glaring. Then he paraded up and down the stone wall to make sure that the dog did not venture again upon his property. Moreover, we got a lecture upon what would happen if he ever saw us touching that red animal again.

Billie and I wanted a black Persian kitten and a setter dog. For a long time we debated whether or not we dared introduce them into our household. At last, we decided we could not continue to be ruled by a cat and keep our self-respect. The setter and the kitten arrived. Lord Jitters was indignant at first, but, when he learned that the arrangement was permanent, he did what we might have known he would do—brought them also under his authority. He still remains undisputed autocrat of the Andrews family.

Tobias

ALAN DEVOE

It was a little after two o'clock this morning when Tobias wakened me. Tobias is a tiger tomcat who, despite the brushed gloss of his fur and the neatness of his arrogant whiskers, belongs to no one. His home is wherever the tamarack may be paw-patted into a bed, or wherever a deserted rabbit burrow may be scratched out from beneath the withered leaves.

Behind our farmhouse rises a little mountain, and in many a spot on it I have found the place of Tobias's day-sleeping hours. Once I found a deep curved depression under a cedar tree, with Tobias's droppings near it and a chipmunk skull half hidden in a clump of yellow violets close by. Another day I came upon signs that Tobias had been tenanting a woodchuck hole, and once, when we were making a clearing, we found his spoor deep in a thorny tangle of wild blackberry.

It is irresistible to use such words as "spoor" in speaking of Tobias, just as I have always thought of those day-sleeping places of his as "lairs." Masterless and homeless probably from kittenhood, this midnight stalker of white-footed mice has become as crafty as any lynx or panther, as arrogant and mistrustful of mankind.

Like any of his wild feline cousins, whose coats are of a yellower shade but whose spirits would find their duplicate in Tobias's own, he chose the night hours, and those hours only, to "roar after his prey and seek his meat from God." Once or twice, walking over the hills in the dusk, I have caught a glimpse of his long lithe body, stretched concealingly in the tall meadow grass and yarrow. At such times as this I have seen Tobias's yellow eyes turned upon me, for the split second before he whisked noiselessly into the underbrush, and I have been glad to be a man and not a mole.

Quite early in May, about the time when the earliest bloodroots were beginning to flower in hidden places, I surprised Tobias close to our rain barrel one night. I have forgotten for what reason I was prowling outdoors with my flashlight; as I stepped suddenly around the angle of the old stone wall, there was Tobias. He was not more than ten feet from me; I had never before been so close to him. I could see the small black lynx-tips at the points of his ears, and I marveled to see that he kept himself as satiny and immaculate as any house pet. He had a tiny russet field mouse in his jaws, and, for the few seconds of his hypnosis in the beam of my light, he crouched perfectly motionless, glaring at me and making a deep, steady growling noise in his throat. Then he turned and was gone. The ground was layered with the crackle-dry maple leaves of last autumn, but he did not make a sound.

It was about two o'clock this morning when I awoke with Tobias's yowling in my ears. During the winter and the spring we have often heard him at night—especially in the winter, when his cries would seem particularly penetrating in the still, frosty air—and on my morning walks I used sometimes to find in the light snow indications that starvation had driven him to filch the dry crusts of bread from my bird tray. But he had never made sufficient clamor to awaken me thus from sound sleep.

I got out of bed and went to the north window and looked out. There was bright moonlight, and I could see the white trunks of our young birches gleaming where it touched them, and across the pasture I could see the glimmer of it in the brook. But I could not see Tobias. And then he cried out again and I followed the sound and saw him. He was crouching close beside the kitchen door, and he was snuffing and sniffing at the sill of it and rasping the screen with his powerful claws. How like a tiger he looked—an old tiger that had grown overbold and craved the taste of a new meat. For it was plain that his keen nostrils had caught a fresh and thrilling scent—the scent of a caged canary on the other side of that kitchen door. Tobias, Tobias, I thought, be those curving claws of yours however sharp, they are no match for galvanized wire, and I went back to bed.

But it was not the smell of a new bird's blood that had brought Tobias here. This morning when I opened the door and looked out into the misty sunlight and saw that Tobias was still there—his lithe striped body stretched on the stone step, one keen curved claw still caught in the screen's mesh—I could guess the truth.

I could guess what extremity of pain had come to him in his lonely world among the tamaracks, and I could guess how, in the hour of his death, there had recurred in that furry skull of his some misty memory from very long ago—some memory, perhaps, of the rubbing of friendly human fingers under his chin, some memory of a quiet bowl of milk.

The White Cat

W. W. JACOBS

THE TRAVELLER stood looking from the taproom window of the *Cauli-flower* at the falling rain. The village street below was empty, and everything was quiet with the exception of the garrulous old man smoking with much enjoyment on the settle behind him.

"It'll do a power o' good," said the ancient, craning his neck round the edge of the settle and turning a bleared eye on the window. "I ain't like some folk; I never did mind a drop o' rain."

The traveller grunted and, returning to the settle opposite the old man, fell to lazily stroking a cat which had strolled in attracted by the warmth of the small fire which smouldered in the grate.

"He's a good mouser," said the old man, "but I expect that Smith the landlord would sell 'im to anybody for arf a crown; but we 'ad a cat in Claybury once that you couldn't ha' bought for a hundred golden sovereigns."

The traveller continued to caress the cat.

"A white cat, with one yaller eye and one blue one," continued the old man. "It sounds queer, but it's as true as I sit 'ere wishing that I 'ad another mug o' ale as good as the last you gave me."

The traveller, with a start that upset the cat's nerves, finished his own mug, and then ordered both to be refilled. He stirred the fire into a blaze, and, lighting his pipe and putting one foot on to the hob, prepared to listen.

It used to belong to old man Clark, young Joe Clark's uncle, said the ancient, smacking his lips delicately over the ale and extending a tremulous claw to the tobacco-pouch pushed towards him; and he was never tired of showing it off to people. He used to call it 'is blue-eyed darling, and the fuss 'e made o' that cat was sinful.

Young Joe Clark couldn't bear it, but being down in 'is uncle's will for five cottages and a bit o' land bringing in about forty pounds a year, he 'ad to 'ide his feelings and pretend as he loved it. He used to take it little drops o' cream and tid-bits o' meat, and old Clark was so pleased that 'e promised 'im that he should 'ave the cat along with all the other property when 'e was dead.

Young Joe said he couldn't thank 'im enough, and the old man, who 'ad been ailing a long time, made 'im come up every day to teach 'im 'ow to take care of it arter he was gone. He taught Joe 'ow to cook its meat and then chop it up fine; 'ow it liked a clean saucer every time for its milk; and 'ow he wasn't to make a noise when it was asleep.

"Take care your children don't worry it, Joe," he ses one day, very sharp. "One o' your boys was pulling its tail this morning, and I want you to clump his 'ead for 'im."

"Which one was it?" ses Joe.

"The slobbery-nosed one," ses old Clark.

"I'll give 'im a clout as soon as I get 'ome," ses Joe, who was very fond of 'is children.

"Go and fetch 'im and do it 'ere," ses the old man; "that'll teach 'im to love animals."

Joe went off 'ome to fetch the boy, and arter his mother 'ad washed his face, and wiped his nose, an' put a clean pinneyfore on 'im, he took 'im to 'is uncle's and clouted his 'ead for 'im. Arter that Joe and 'is wife 'ad words all night long, and next morning old Clark, coming in from the garden, was just in time to see 'im kick the cat right acrost the kitchen.

He could 'ardly speak for a minute, and when 'e could Joe see plain wot a fool he'd been. Fust of all 'e called Joe every name he could think of—which took 'im a long time—and then he ordered 'im out of 'is house.

"You shall 'ave my money wen your betters have done with it," he ses, "and not afore. That's all you've done for yourself."

Joe Clark didn't know wot he meant at the time, but when old Clark died three months arterwards 'e found out. His uncle 'ad made a new will and left everything to old George Barstow for as long as the cat lived, providing that he took care of it. When the cat was dead the property was to go to Joe.

The cat was only two years old at the time, and George Barstow, who was arf crazy with joy, said it shouldn't be 'is fault if it didn't live another twenty years.

The funny thing was the quiet way Joe Clark took it. He didn't seem to be at all cut up about it, and when Henery Walker said it was a shame, 'e said he didn't mind, and that George Barstow was a old man, and he was quite welcome to 'ave the property as long as the cat lived.

"It must come to me by the time I'm an old man," he ses, "and that's all I care about."

Henery Walker went off, and as 'e passed the cottage where old Clark used to live, and which George Barstow 'ad moved into, 'e spoke to the old man over the palings and told 'im wot Joe Clark 'ad said. George Barstow only grunted and went on stooping and prying over 'is front garden.

"Bin and lost something?" ses Henery Walker, watching 'im.

"No; I'm finding," ses George Barstow, very fierce, and picking up something. "That's the fifth bit o' powdered liver I've found in my garden this morning."

Henery Walker went off whistling, and the opinion he'd 'ad o' Joe Clark began to improve. He spoke to Joe about it that arternoon, and Joe said that if 'e ever accused 'im o' such a thing again he'd knock 'is 'ead off. He said that he 'oped the cat 'ud live to be a hundred, and that 'e'd no more think of giving it poisoned meat than Henery Walker would of paying for 'is drink so long as 'e could get anybody else to do it for 'im.

They 'ad bets up at this 'ere *Cauliflower* public-'ouse that evening as to 'ow long that cat 'ud live. Nobody gave it more than a month, and Bill Chambers sat and thought o' so many ways o' killing it on the sly that it was wunnerful to hear 'im.

George Barstow took fright when he 'eard of them, and the care 'e took o' that cat was wunnerful to behold. Arf its time it was shut up in the back bedroom, and the other arf George Barstow was fussing arter it till that cat got to hate 'im like pison. Instead o' giving up work as he'd thought to do, 'e told Henery Walker that 'e'd never worked so 'ard in his life.

"Wot about fresh air and exercise for it?" ses Henery.

"Wot about Joe Clark?" ses George Barstow. "I'm tied 'and and foot. I dursent leave the house for a moment. I ain't been to the *Cauliflower* since I've 'ad it, and three times I got out o' bed last night to see if it was safe."

"Mark my words," ses Henery Walker; "if that cat don't 'ave exercise, you'll lose it."

"I shall lose it if it does 'ave exercise," ses George Barstow, "that I know."

He sat down thinking arter Henery Walker 'ad gone, and then he 'ad a little collar and chain made for it, and took it out for a walk.

Pretty nearly every dog in Claybury went with 'em, and the cat was in such a state o' mind afore they got 'ome he couldn't do anything with it. It 'ad a fit as soon as they got indoors, and George Barstow, who 'ad read about children's fits in the almanac, gave it a warm bath. It brought it round immediate, and then it began to tear round the room and up and down stairs till George Barstow was afraid to go near it.

It was so bad that evening, sneezing, that George Barstow sent for Bill Chambers, who'd got a good name for doctoring animals, and asked 'im to give it something. Bill said he'd got some powders at 'ome that would cure it at once, and he went and fetched 'em and mixed one up with a bit o' butter.

"That's the way to give a cat medicine," he ses; "smear it with butter and then it'll lick it off, powder and all."

He was just going to rub it on the cat when George Barstow caught 'old of 'is arm and stopped 'im.

"How do I know it ain't pison?" he ses. "You're a friend o' Joe Clark's, and for all I know he may ha' paid you to pison it."

"I wouldn't do such a thing," ses Bill. "You ought to know me better than that."

"All right," ses George Barstow; "you eat it then, and I'll give you two shillings instead o' one. You can easy mix some more."

"Not me," ses Bill Chambers, making a face.

"Well, three shillings, then," ses George Barstow, getting more and more suspicious like; "four shillings—five shillings."

Bill Chambers shook his 'ead, and George Barstow, more and more certain he 'ad caught 'im trying to kill 'is cat and that 'e wouldn't eat the stuff, rose 'im up to ten shillings.

Bill looked at the butter and then 'e looked at the ten shillings on the table, and at last he shut 'is eyes and gulped it down and put the money in 's pocket.

"You see, I 'ave to be careful, Bill," ses George Barstow, rather upset.

Bill Chambers didn't answer 'im. He sat there as white as a sheet, and making such extraordinary faces that George was arf afraid of 'im.

"Anything wrong, Bill?" he ses at last.

Bill sat staring at 'im, and then all of a sudden he clapped 'is 'andkerchief to 'is mouth and, getting up from his chair, opened the door and rushed out. George Barstow thought at fust that he 'ad eaten pison for the sake o' the ten shillings, but when 'e remembered that Bill Chambers 'ad got the most delikit stummick in Claybury he altered 'is mind.

The cat was better the next morning, but George Barstow had 'ad such a fright about it 'e wouldn't let it go out of 'is sight, and Joe Clark began to think that 'e would 'ave to wait longer for that property than 'e had thought, arter all. To 'ear 'im talk anybody'd ha' thought that 'e loved that cat. We didn't pay much attention to it up at the *Cauliflower* 'ere, except maybe to wink at 'im—a thing he couldn't a bear—but at 'ome, o' course, his young 'uns thought as everything he said was Gospel; and one day, coming 'ome from work, as he was passing George Barstow's he was paid out for his deceitfulness.

"I've wronged you, Joe Clark," ses George Barstow, coming to the door, "and I'm sorry for it."

"Oh!" ses Joe, staring.

"Give that to your little Jimmy," ses George Barstow, giving 'im a shilling. "I've give 'im one, but I thought arterwards it wasn't enough."

"What for?" ses Joe, staring at 'im agin.

"For bringing my cat 'ome," ses George Barstow. "'Ow it got out I can't think, but I lost it for three hours, and I'd about given it up when your little Jimmy brought it to me in 'is arms. He's a fine little chap and 'e does you credit."

Joe Clark tried to speak, but he couldn't get a word out, and Henery Walker, wot 'ad just come up and 'eard wot passed, took hold of 'is arm and helped 'im home. He walked like a man in a dream, but arf-way he stopped and cut a stick from the hedge to take 'ome to little Jimmy. He said the boy 'ad been asking him for a stick for some time, but up till then 'e'd always forgotten it.

At the end o' the fust year that cat was still alive, to everybody's surprise; but George Barstow took such care of it 'e never let it out of 'is sight. Every time 'e went out he took it with 'im in a hamper, and, to prevent its being pisoned, he paid Isaac Sawyer, who 'ad the biggest family in Claybury, sixpence a week to let one of 'is boys taste its milk before it had it.

The second year it was ill twice, but the horse-doctor that George Barstow got for it said that it was as 'ard as nails, and with care it might live to be twenty. He said that it wanted more fresh air and exercise; but when he 'eard 'ow George Barstow come by it he said that p'rhaps it would live longer indoors arter all.

At last one day, when George Barstow 'ad been living on the fat o' the land for nearly three years, that cat got out agin. George 'ad raised the front-room winder two or three inches to throw something outside, and, afore he knew wot was 'appening, the cat was outside and going up the road about twenty miles an hour.

George Barstow went arter it, but he might as well ha' tried to catch the wind. The cat was arf wild with joy at getting out agin, and he couldn't get within arf a mile of it.

He stayed out all day without food or drink, follering it about until it came on dark, and then, o' course, he lost sight of it, and, hoping against 'ope that it would come home for its food, he went 'ome and waited for it. He sat up all night dozing in a chair in the front room with the door left open, but it was all no use; and arter thinking for a long time wot was best to do, he went out and told some o' the folks it was lost and offered a reward of five pounds for it.

You never saw such a hunt then in all your life. Nearly every man, woman, and child in Claybury left their work or school and went to try and earn that five pounds. By the arternoon George Barstow made it ten pounds provided the cat was brought 'ome safe and sound, and people as was too old to walk stood at their cottage doors to snap it up as it came by.

Joe Clark was hunting for it 'igh and low, and so was 'is wife and the boys. In fact, I b'lieve that everybody in Claybury excepting the parson and Bob Pretty was trying to get that ten pounds.

O' course, we could understand the parson—'is pride wouldn't let 'im; but a low, poaching, thieving rascal like Bob Pretty turning up 'is nose at ten pounds was more than we could make out. Even on the second day, when George Barstow made it ten pounds down and a shilling a week for a year besides, he didn't offer to stir; all he did was to try and make fun o' them as *was* looking for it.

"Have you looked everywhere you can think of for it, Bill?" he ses to Bill Chambers.

"Yes, I 'ave," ses Bill.

"Well, then, you want to look everywhere else," ses Bob Pretty. "I know where I should look if I wanted to find it."

"Why don't you find it, then?" ses Bill.

"Cos I don't want to make mischief," ses Bob Pretty. "I don't want to be unneighbourly to Joe Clark by interfering at all."

"Not for all that money?" ses Bill.

"Not for fifty pounds," ses Bob Pretty; "you ought to know me better than that, Bill Chambers."

"It's my belief that you know more about where that cat is than you ought to," ses Joe Gubbins.

"You go on looking for it, Joe," ses Bob Pretty, grinning; "it's good exercise for you, and you've only lost two days' work."

"I'll give you arf a crown if you let me search your 'ouse, Bob," ses Bill Chambers, looking at 'im very 'ard.

"I couldn't do it at the price, Bill," ses Bob Pretty, shaking his 'ead. "I'm a pore man, but I'm very partikler who I 'ave come into my 'ouse."

O' course, everybody left off looking at once when they heard about Bob—not that they believed that he'd be such a fool as to keep the cat in his 'ouse; and that evening, as soon as it was dark, Joe Clark went round to see 'im.

"Don't tell me as that cat's found, Joe," ses Bob Pretty, as Joe opened the door.

"Not as I've 'eard of," said Joe, stepping inside. "I wanted to speak to you about it; the sooner it's found the better I shall be pleased."

"It does you credit, Joe Clark," ses Bob Pretty.

"It's my belief that it's dead," ses Joe, looking at 'im very 'ard; "but I want to make sure afore taking over the property."

Bob Pretty looked at 'im and then he gave a little cough. "Oh, you want it to be found dead," he ses. "Now, I wonder whether that cat's worth most dead or alive?"

Joe Clark coughed then. "Dead, I should think," he ses at last.

"George Barstow's just 'ad bills printed offering fifteen pounds for it," ses Bob Pretty.

"I'll give that or more when I come into the property," ses Joe Clark.

"There's nothing like ready-money, though, is there?" ses Bob.

"I'll promise it to you in writing, Bob," ses Joe, trembling.

"There's some things that don't look well in writing, Joe," ses Bob Pretty, considering; "besides, why should you promise it to *me?*"

"O' course, I meant if you found it," ses Joe.

"Well, I'll do my best, Joe," ses Bob Pretty; "and none of us can do no more than that, can they?"

They sat talking and argufying over it for over an hour, and twice Bob Pretty got up and said 'e was going to see whether George Barstow wouldn't offer more. By the time they parted they was as thick as thieves, and next morning Bob Pretty was wearing Joe Clark's watch and chain, and Mrs. Pretty was up at Joe's 'ouse to see whether there was any of 'is furniture as she 'ad a fancy for.

She didn't seem to be able to make up 'er mind at fust between a chest o' drawers that 'ad belonged to Joe's mother and a grandfather clock. She walked from one to the other for about ten minutes, and then Bob, who'd come to 'elp her, told 'er to 'ave both.

"You're quite welcome," he ses; "ain't she, Joe?"

Joe Clark said "Yes," and arter he 'ad helped them carry 'em 'ome the Prettys went back and took the best bedstead to pieces, cos Bob said as it was easier to carry that way. Mrs. Clark 'ad to go and sit down at the bottom o' the garden with the neck of 'er dress undone to give herself air, but when she saw the little Prettys each walking 'ome with one of 'er best chairs on their 'eads she got up and walked up and down like a mad thing.

"I'm sure I don't know where we are to put it all," ses Bob Pretty to Joe Gubbins, wot was looking on with other folks, "but Joe Clark is that generous he won't 'ear of our leaving anything."

"Has 'e gorn mad?" ses Bill Chambers, staring at 'im.

"Not as I knows on," ses Bob Pretty. "It's 'is good-'artedness, that's all. He feels sure that that cat's dead, and he'll 'ave George Barstow's cottage and furniture. I told 'im he'd better wait till he'd made sure, but 'e wouldn't."

Before they'd finished the Prettys 'ad picked that 'ouse as clean as a bone, and Joe Clark 'ad to go and get clean straw for his wife and children to sleep on; not that Mrs. Clark 'ad any sleep that night, nor Joe neither.

Henery Walker was the fust to see what it really meant, and he went rushing off as fast as 'e could run to tell George Barstow. George couldn't believe 'im at fust, but when 'e did he swore that if a 'air of that cat's 'ead was harmed 'e'd 'ave the law o' Bob Pretty, and arter Henery Walker 'ad gone 'e walked round to tell 'im so.

"You're not yourself, George Barstow, else you wouldn't try and take away my character like that," ses Bob Pretty.

"Wot did Joe Clark give you all them things for?" ses George, pointing to the furniture.

"Took a fancy to me, I s'pose," ses Bob. "People do sometimes. There's something about me at times that makes 'em like me."

"He gave 'em to you to kill my cat," ses George Barstow. "It's plain enough for anybody to see."

Bob Pretty smiled. "I expect it'll turn up safe and sound one o' these days," he ses, "and then you'll come round and beg my pardon. P'r'aps—"

"P'r'aps wot?" ses George Barstow, arter waiting a bit.

"P'r'aps somebody 'as got it and is keeping it till you've drawed the fifteen pounds out o' the bank," ses Bob, looking at 'im very hard.

"I've taken it out o' the bank," ses George, starting; "if that cat's alive, Bob, and you've got it, there's the fifteen pounds the moment you 'and it over."

"Wot d'ye mean—me got it?" ses Bob Pretty. "You be careful o' my character."

"I mean if you know where it is," ses George Barstow trembling all over.

"I don't say I couldn't find it, if that's wot you mean," ses Bob. "I can gin'rally find things when I want to."

"You find me that cat, alive and well, and the money's yours, Bob," ses George, 'ardly able to speak, now that 'e fancied the cat was still alive.

Bob Pretty shook his 'ead. "No; that won't do," he ses. "S'pose I did 'ave the luck to find that pore animal, you'd say I'd had it all the time and refuse to pay."

"I swear I wouldn't, Bob," ses George Barstow, jumping up.

"Best thing you can do if you want me to try and find that cat," ses Bob Pretty, "is to give me the fifteen pounds now, and I'll go and look for it at once. I can't trust you, George Barstow."

"And I can't trust you," ses George Barstow.

"Very good," ses Bob, getting up; "there's no 'arm done. P'r'aps Joe Clark'll find the cat is dead and p'r'aps you'll find it's alive. It's all one to me."

George Barstow walked off 'ome, but he was in such a state o' mind 'e didn't know wot to do. Bob Pretty turning up 'is nose at fifteen pounds like that made 'im think that Joe Clark 'ad promised to pay 'im more if the cat was dead; and at last, arter worrying about it for a couple o' hours, 'e came up to this 'ere *Cauliflower* and offered Bob the fifteen pounds.

"Wot's this for?" ses Bob.

"For finding my cat," ses George.

"Look here," ses Bob, handing it back, "I've 'ad enough o' your insults; I don't know where your cat is."

"I mean for trying to find it, Bob," ses George Barstow.

"Oh, well, I don't mind that," ses Bob, taking it. "I'm a 'ard-working man, and I've got to be paid for my time; it's on'y fair to my wife and children. I'll start now."

He finished up 'is beer, and while the other chaps was telling George Barstow wot a fool he was Joe Clark slipped out arter Bob Pretty and began to call 'im all the names he could think of.

"Don't you worry," ses Bob; "the cat ain't found yet."

"Is it dead?" ses Joe Clark, 'ardly able to speak.

" 'Ow should I know?" ses Bob; "that's wot I've got to try and find out. That's wot you gave me your furniture for, and wot George Barstow gave me the fifteen pounds for, ain't it? Now, don't you stop me now, 'cos I'm goin' to begin looking."

He started looking there and then, and for the next two or three days George Barstow and Joe Clark see 'im walking up and down with his 'ands in 'is pockets looking over garden fences and calling "Puss." He asked everybody 'e see whether they 'ad seen a white cat with one blue eye and one yaller one, and every time 'e came into the *Cauliflower* he put 'is 'ead over the bar and called "Puss," 'cos, as 'e said, it was as likely to be there as anywhere else.

It was about a week after the cat 'ad disappeared that George Barstow was standing at 'is door talking to Joe Clark, who was saying the cat must be dead and 'e wanted 'is property, when he sees a man coming up the road carrying a basket stop and speak to Bill Chambers. Just as 'e got near them an awful "miaow" come from the basket and George Barstow and Joe Clark started as if they'd been shot.

"He's found it!" shouts Bill Chambers, pointing to the man.

"It's been living with me over at Ling for a week pretty nearly," ses the man. "I tried to drive it away several times, not knowing that there was fifteen pounds offered for it."

George Barstow tried to take 'old of the basket.

"I want that fifteen pounds fust," ses the man.

"That's on'y right and fair, George," ses Bob Pretty, who 'ad just come up. "You've got all the luck, mate. We've been hunting 'igh and low for that cat for a week."

Then George Barstow tried to explain to the man and call Bob Pretty names at the same time; but it was all no good. The man said it 'ad nothing to do with 'im wot he 'ad paid to Bob Pretty; and at last they fetched Policeman White over from Cudford, and George Barstow signed a paper to pay five shillings a week till the reward was paid.

George Barstow 'ad the cat for five years arter that, but he never let it get away agin. They got to like each other in time and died within a fortnight of each other, so Joe Clark got 'is property arter all.

My Boss the Cat

PAUL GALLICO

IF YOU are thinking of acquiring a cat at your house and would care for a quick sketch of what your life will be like under *Felis domesticus,* you have come to the right party. I have figured out that, to date, I have worked for—and I mean *worked for*—39 of these four-legged characters, including one memorable period when I was doing the bidding of some 23 assorted resident felines all at the same time.

Cats are, of course, no good. They're chiselers and panhandlers, sharpers and shameless flatterers. They're as full of schemes and plans, plots and counterplots, wiles and guiles as any confidence man. They can read your character better than a $50-an-hour psychiatrist. They know to a milligram how much of the old oil to pour on to break you down. They are definitely smarter than I am, which is one reason why I love 'em.

Cat-haters will try to floor you with the old argument, "If cats are so smart, why can't they do tricks, the way dogs do?" It isn't that cats can't do tricks; it's that they *won't.* They're far too hep to stand up and beg for food when they know in advance you'll give it to them anyway. And as for rolling over, or playing dead, or "speaking," what's in it for pussy that isn't already hers?

Cats, incidentally, are a great warm-up for a successful marriage— they teach you your place in the household. The first thing Kitty does is to organize your home on a comfortable basis—*her* basis. She'll eat when she wants to; she'll go out at her pleasure. She'll come in when she gets good and ready, if at all.

She wants attention when she wants it and darned well means to be let alone when she has other things on her mind. She is jealous; she won't have you showering attentions or caresses on any other minxes, whether two- or four-footed.

She gets upset when you come home late and when you go away on a business trip. But when *she* decides to stay out a couple of nights, it is none of your darned business where she's been or what she's been up to. Either you trust her or you don't.

She hates dirt, bad smells, poor food, loud noises and people you bring home unexpectedly to dinner.

Kitty also has her share of small-child obstinacy. She enjoys seeing you flustered, fussed, red in the face and losing your temper. Sometimes, as she hangs about watching, you get the feeling that it is all she can do to keep from busting out laughing. And she's got the darndest knack for putting the entire responsibility for everything on *you*.

For instance, Kitty pretends that she can neither talk nor understand you, and that she is therefore nothing but a poor helpless dumb animal. What a laugh! Any self-respecting racket-working cat can make you understand at all times exactly what she wants. She has one voice for "Let's eat," another for wanting out, still a third for "You don't happen to have seen my toy mouse around here, the one with the tail chewed off?" and a host of other easily identifiable speeches. She can also understand you perfectly, if she thinks there's profit in it.

I once had a cat I suspected of being able to read. This was a gent named Morris, a big tabby with topaz eyes who lived with me when I was batching it in a New York apartment. One day I had just finished writing to a lady who at that time was the object of my devotion. Naturally I brought considerable of the writer's art into telling her this. I was called to the telephone for a few minutes. When I returned, Morris was sitting on my desk reading the letter. At least, he was staring down at it, looking a little ill. He gave me that long, baffled look of which cats are capable, and immediately meowed to be let out. He didn't come back for three days. Thereafter I kept my private correspondence locked up.

The incident reminds me of another highly discriminating cat I had down on the farm by the name of Tante Hedwig. One Sunday a guest asked me whether I could make a cocktail called a Mexican.

I said I thought I could, and proceeded to blend a horror of gin, pineapple juice, vermouth, bitters and other ill-assorted ingredients. Pouring out a trial glass, I spilled it on the grass. Tante Hedwig came over, sniffed and, with a look of shameful embarrassment, solicitously covered it over. Everybody agreed later that she had something there.

Let me warn you not to put too much stock in the theory that animals do not think and that they act only by instinct. Did you ever try to keep a cat out that wanted to come in, or vice versa? I once locked a cat in the cellar. *He* climbed a straight, smooth cement wall, hung on with his paws (I saw the claw marks to prove it) ; unfastened the window hook with his nose; and climbed out.

Cats have fabulous memories, I maintain, and also the ability to measure and evaluate what they remember. Take, for instance, our two Ukrainian grays, Chin and Chilla. My wife brought them up on a medicine dropper. We gave them love and care and a good home on a farm in New Jersey.

Eventually we had to travel abroad, so Chin and Chilla went to live with friends in Glenview, Ill., a pretty, snazzy place. Back in the

P.B.

United States, we went out to spend Thanksgiving in Glenview. We looked forward, among other things, to seeing our two cats. When we arrived at the house, Chin and Chilla were squatting at the top of a broad flight of stairs. As we called up a tender greeting to them, we saw an expression of horror come over both their faces. "Great heavens! It's those *paupers!* Run!" With that, they vanished and could not be found for five hours. They were frightened to death we had come to take them back to the squalor of a country estate in New Jersey, and deprive them of a room of their own in Illinois, with glassed-in sun porch, screens for their toilets and similar super-luxuries.

After a time they made a grudging appearance and consented to play the old games and talk over old times, guardedly. But when the hour arrived for our departure, they vanished once more. Our hostess wrote us that apparently they got hold of a timetable somewhere and waited until our train was past Elkhart before coming out.

It was this same Chilla who, one day on the farm, after our big ginger cat, Wuzzy, had been missing for 48 hours led us to where he was, a half mile away, out of sight and out of hearing, caught in a trap. Every so often Chilla would look back to see if we were coming. Old Wuz was half dead when we got there, but when he saw Chilla he started to purr.

Two-Timing, or Leading the Double Life, is something you may be called upon to face with your cat. It means simply that Kitty manages to divide her time between two homes sufficiently far apart that each homeowner thinks she is his.

I discovered this when trying to check up on the unaccountable absences of Lulu II, a seal-point Siamese. I finally located her at the other end of the bay, mooching on an amiable spinster. When I said, "Oh, I hope that my Lulu hasn't been imposing on you," she replied indignantly, "*Your* Lulu! You mean *our* dear little Pitipoo! We've been wondering where she went when she disappeared occasionally. We do hope she hasn't been annoying *you*."

The shocking part of this story, of course, is that, for the sake of a handout, Lulu, with a pedigree as long as your arm, was willing to submit to being called Pitipoo.

Of all things a smart cat does to whip you into line, the gift of the captured mouse is the cleverest and most touching. There was Limpy, the wild barn cat down on the farm who lived off what she caught in the fields. We were already supporting four cats, but in the winter, when we went to town, we brought her along.

We had not been inside the apartment ten minutes before Limpy caught a mouse, or probably *the* mouse, and at once brought it over and laid it at our feet. Now, as indicated before, Limpy had hunted to survive. To Limpy, a dead mouse was Big and Little Casino, touchdown, home run and Grand Slam. Yet this one she gave to us.

How can you mark it up except as rent, or thanks, or "Here, looka; this is the most important thing I do. You take it because I like you"? You can teach a dog to retrieve and bring you game, but only a cat will voluntarily hand over its kill to you as an unsolicited gift.

How come Kitty acts not like the beast of prey she is but like a better-class human being? I don't know the answer. The point is, she does it—and makes you her slave ever after. Once you have been presented with a mouse by your cat, you will never be the same again. She can use you for a door mat. And she will, too.

Calvin

CHARLES DUDLEY WARNER

CALVIN is dead. His life, long to him, but short for the rest of us, was not marked by startling adventures, but his character was so uncommon and his qualities were so worthy of imitation, that I have been asked by those who personally knew him to set down my recollections of his career.

His origin and ancestry were shrouded in mystery; even his age was a matter of pure conjecture. Although he was of the Maltese race, I have reason to suppose that he was American by birth as he certainly was in sympathy. Calvin was given to me eight years ago by Mrs. Stowe, but she knew nothing of his age or origin. He walked into her house one day out of the great unknown and became at once at home, as if he had been always a friend of the family. He appeared to have artistic and literary tastes, and it was as if he had inquired at the door if that was the residence of the author of *Uncle Tom's Cabin,* and, upon being assured that it was, had decided to dwell there. This is, of course, fanciful, for his antecedents were wholly unknown, but in his time he could hardly have been in any household where he would not have heard *Uncle Tom's Cabin* talked about. When he came to Mrs. Stowe, he was as large as he ever was, and apparently as old as he ever became. Yet there was in him no appearance of age; he was in the happy maturity of all his powers, and you would have said in that maturity he had found the secret of perpetual youth. And it was as difficult to believe that he would ever be aged as it was to imagine that he had ever been in immature youth. There was in him a mysterious perpetuity.

After some years, when Mrs. Stowe made her winter home in Florida, Calvin came to live with us. From the first moment, he fell into the ways of the house and assumed a recognized position in the family,—I say recognized, because after he became known he was always inquired for by visitors, and in the letters to the other mem-

P. B.

bers of the family he always received a message. Although the least obtrusive of beings, his individuality always made itself felt.

His personal appearance had much to do with this, for he was of royal mould, and had an air of high breeding. He was large, but he had nothing of the fat grossness of the celebrated Angora family; though powerful, he was exquisitely proportioned, and as graceful in every movement as a young leopard. When he stood up to open a door—he opened all the doors with old-fashioned latches—he was portentously tall, and when stretched on the rug before the fire he seemed too long for this world—as indeed he was. His coat was the finest and softest I have ever seen, a shade of quiet Maltese; and from his throat downward, underneath, to the tips of his feet, he wore the whitest and most delicate ermine; and no person was ever more fastidiously neat. In his finely formed head you saw something of his aristocratic character; the ears were small and cleanly cut, there was a tinge of pink in the nostrils, his face was handsome, and the expression of his countenance exceedingly intelligent—I should call it even a sweet expression if the term were not inconsistent with his look of alertness and sagacity.

It is difficult to convey a just idea of his gaiety in connection with his dignity and gravity, which his name expressed. As we know nothing of his family, of course it will be understood that Calvin was his Christian name. He had times of relaxation into utter playfulness, delighting in a ball of yarn, catching sportively at stray ribbons when his mistress was at her toilet, and pursuing his own tail, with hilarity, for lack of anything better. He could amuse himself by the hour, and he did not care for children; perhaps something in his past was present to his memory. He had absolutely no bad habits, and his disposition was perfect, I never saw him exactly angry, though I have seen his tail grow to an enormous size when a strange cat appeared upon his lawn. He disliked cats, evidently regarding them as feline and treacherous, and he had no association with them. Occasionally there would be heard a night concert in the shrubbery. Calvin would ask to have the door opened, and you would hear a rush and a "pestzt," and the concert would explode, and Calvin would quietly come in and resume his seat on the hearth. There was no trace of anger in his manner, but he wouldn't have any of that about the house. He had the rare virtue of magnanimity. Although he had fixed notions about his own rights, and extraordinary persistency in getting them, he never showed temper at a repulse; he simply and firmly persisted till he had what he wanted. His diet was one point; his idea was that of the scholars about dictionaries,—to "get the best." He knew as well as anyone what was in the house, and would refuse beef if turkey was to be had; and if there were oysters, he would wait over the turkey to see if the oysters would not be forthcoming. And yet he was not a gross gourmand; he would eat bread if he saw me eating it, and thought he was not being imposed on. His habits of feeding, also, were refined; he never used a knife, and he would put up his hand and draw the fork down to his mouth as gracefully as a grown person. Unless necessity compelled, he would not eat in the kitchen, but insisted upon his meals in the dining room, and would wait patiently, unless a stranger were present; and then he was sure to importune the visitor, hoping that the latter was ignorant of the rule of the house, and would give him something. They used to say that he preferred as his table-cloth on the floor a certain well-known church journal; but this was said by an Episcopalian. So far as I know, he had no religious prejudices, except that he did not like the association with Romanists. He tolerated the servants, because they belonged to the house, and would sometimes linger by the kitchen stove; but the moment visitors came in he rose, opened the door, and marched into the drawing-room. Yet he enjoyed the company of his equals, and never withdrew, no matter how many callers—whom he recognized as of his society—might come into the drawing-room. Calvin was fond of company, but he wanted to choose it; and I have no doubt that his was an aristocratic fastidiousness rather than one of faith. It is so with most people.

The intelligence of Calvin was something phenomenal, in his rank of life. He established a method of communicating his wants, and even some of his sentiments; and he would help himself in many things. There was a furnace register in a retired room, where he used to go when he wished to be alone, that he always opened when he desired more heat; but never shut it, any more than he shut the door after himself. He could do almost everything but speak; and you would declare sometimes that you could see a pathetic longing to do that in his intelligent face. I have no desire to overdraw his qualities, but if there was one thing in him more noticeable than another, it was his fondness for nature. He could content himself for hours at a low window, looking into the ravine and at the great trees, noting the smallest stir there; he delighted, above all things, to accompany me walking about the garden, hearing the birds, getting the smell of the fresh earth, and rejoicing in the sunshine. He followed me and gambolled like a dog, rolling over on the turf and exhibiting his delight in a hundred ways. If I worked, he sat and watched me, or looked off over the bank, and kept his ear open to the twitter in the cherry-trees. When it stormed, he was sure to sit at the window, keenly watching the rain or the snow, glancing up and down at its falling; and a winter tempest always delighted him. I think he was genuinely fond of birds, but, so far as I know, he usually confined himself to one a day; he never killed, as some sportsmen do, for the sake of killing, but only as civilized people do,—from necessity. He was intimate with the flying-squirrels who dwell in the chestnut-trees,—too intimate, for almost every day in the summer he would bring in one, until he nearly discouraged them. He was, indeed, a superb hunter, and would have been a devastating one, if his bump of destructiveness had not been offset by a bump of moderation. There was very little of the brutality of the lower animals about him; I don't think he enjoyed rats for themselves, but he knew his business, and for the first few months of his residence with us he waged an awful campaign against the horde, and after that his simple presence was sufficient to deter them from coming on the premises. Mice amused him, but he usually considered them too small game to be taken seriously; I have seen him play for an hour with a mouse, and then let him go with a royal condescension. In this whole matter of "getting a living," Calvin was a great contrast to the rapacity of the age in which he lived.

I hesitate a little to speak of his capacity for friendship and the affectionateness of his nature, for I know from his own reserve that he would not care to have it much talked about. We understood each other perfectly but we never made any fuss about it; when I spoke his name and snapped my fingers, he came to me; when I returned home at night, he was pretty sure to be waiting for me near the gate, and would rise and saunter along the walk, as if his being there were purely accidental,—so shy was he commonly of showing feeling; and when I opened the door he never rushed in, like a cat, but loitered, and lounged, as if he had had no intention of going in, but would condescend to. And yet, the fact was, he knew dinner was ready, and he was bound to be there. He kept the run of dinner-time. It happened sometimes, during our absence in the summer, that dinner would be early, and Calvin, walking about the grounds, missed it and came in late. But he never made a mistake the second day. There was one thing he never did,—he never rushed through an open doorway. He never forgot his dignity. If he had asked to have the door opened, and was eager to go out, he always went deliberately; I can see him now, standing on the sill, looking about at the sky as if he was thinking whether it were worth while to take an umbrella, until he was near having his tail shut in.

His friendship was rather constant than demonstrative. When we returned from an absence of nearly two years, Calvin welcomed us with evident pleasure, but showed his satisfaction rather by tranquil happiness than by fuming about. He had the faculty of making us glad to get home. It was his constancy that was so attractive. He liked companionship, but he wouldn't be petted, or fussed over, or sit in anyone's lap a moment; he always extricated himself from such familiarity with dignity and with no show of temper. If there was any petting to be done, however, he chose to do it. Often he would sit looking at me, and then, moved by a delicate affection, come and pull at my coat and sleeve until he could touch my face with his nose, and then go away contented. He had a habit of coming to my study in the morning, sitting quietly by my side or on the table for hours, watching the pen run over the paper, occasionally swinging his tail round for a blotter, and then going to sleep among the papers by the inkstand. Or, more rarely, he would watch the writing from a perch on my shoulder. Writing always interested him, and, until he understood it, he wanted to hold the pen.

He always held himself in a kind of reserve with his friend, as if he had said, "Let us respect our personality, and not make a 'mess' of friendship." He saw, with Emerson, the risk of degrading it to trivial conveniency. "Why insist on rash personal relations with your friend?" "Leave this touching and clawing." Yet I would not give an unfair notion of his aloofness, his fine sense of the sacredness of the me and the not-me. And, at the risk of not being believed, I will relate an incident, which was often repeated. Calvin had the practice of passing a portion of the night in the contemplation of its beauties, and would come into our chamber over the roof of the conservatory through the open window, summer and winter, and go to sleep on the foot of my bed. He would do this always exactly in this way; he never was content to stay in the chamber if we compelled him to go upstairs and through the door. He had the obstinacy of General Grant. But this is by the way. In the morning, he performed his toilet and went down to breakfast with the rest of the family. Now, when the mistress was absent from home, and at no other time, Calvin would come in the morning, when the bell rang, to the head of the bed, put up his feet and look into my face, follow me about when I rose, "assist" at the dressing, and in many purring ways show his fondness, as if he had plainly said, "I know that she has gone away, but I am here." Such was Calvin in rare moments.

He had his limitations. Whatever passion he had for nature, he had no conception of art. There was sent to him once a fine and very expressive cat's head in bronze, by Frémiet. I placed it on the floor. He regarded it intently, approached it cautiously and crouchingly, touched it with his nose, perceived the fraud, turned away abruptly, and never would notice it afterward. On the whole, his life was not only a successful one, but a happy one. He never had but one fear, so far as I know: he had a mortal and a reasonable terror of plumbers. He would never stay in the house when they were here. No coaxing could quiet him. Of course he didn't share our fear about their charges, but he must have had some dreadful experience with them in that portion of his life which is unknown to us. A plumber was to him the devil, and I have no doubt that, in his scheme, plumbers were foreordained to do him mischief.

In speaking of his worth, it has never occurred to me to estimate Calvin by the worldly standard. I know that it is customary now, when anyone dies, to ask how much he was worth, and that no obituary in the newspapers is considered complete without such an estimate. The plumbers in our house were one day overheard to say that, "They say that *she* says that *he* says that he wouldn't take a hundred dollars for him." It is unnecessary to say that I never made such a remark, and that, so far as Calvin was concerned, there was no purchase in money.

As I look back upon it, Calvin's life seems to me a fortunate one, for it was natural and unforced. He ate when he was hungry, slept when he was sleepy, and enjoyed existence to the very tip of his toes and the end of his expressive and slow-moving tail. He delighted to roam about the garden, and stroll among the trees, and to lie on the green grass and luxuriate in all the sweet influences of summer. You could never accuse him of idleness, and yet he knew the secret of repose. The poet who wrote so prettily of him that his little life was rounded with a sleep understated his felicity; it was rounded with a good many. His conscience never seemed to interfere with his slumbers. In fact, he had good habits and a contented mind. I can see him now walk in at the study door, sit down by my chair, bring his tail artistically about his feet, and look up at me with unspeakable happiness in his handsome face. I often thought that he felt the dumb limitation which denied him the power of language. But since he was denied speech, he scorned the inarticulate mouthings of the lower animals. The vulgar mewing and yowling of the cat species was beneath him; he sometimes uttered a sort of articulate and well-bred ejaculation, when he wished to call attention to something that he considered remarkable, or to some want of his, but he never went whining about. He would sit for hours at a closed window, when he desired to enter, without a murmur, and when it was opened he never admitted that he had been impatient by "bolting" in. Though speech he had not, and the unpleasant kind of utterance given to his race he would not use, he had a mighty power of purr to express his measureless content with congenial society. There was in him a musical organ with stops of varied power and expression, upon which I have no doubt he could have performed Scarlatti's celebrated cat's-fugue.

Whether Calvin died of old age, or was carried off by one of the diseases incident to youth, it is impossible to say; for his departure was as quiet as his advent was mysterious. I only know that he appeared to us in this world in his perfect stature and beauty, and that after a time, like Lohengrin, he withdrew. In his illness there was nothing more to be regretted than in all his blameless life. I suppose there never was an illness that had more of dignity and sweetness and resignation in it. It came on gradually, in a kind of listlessness and want of appetite. An alarming symptom was his preference for the warmth of a furnace-register to the lively sparkle of the open wood-fire. Whatever pain he suffered, he bore it in silence, and seemed only anxious not to obtrude his malady. We tempted him with the delicacies of the season, but it soon became impossible for him to eat, and for two weeks he ate or drank scarcely anything. Sometimes he made the effort to take something, but it was evident that he made the effort to please us. The neighbors—and I am convinced that the advice of neighbors is never good for anything— suggested catnip. He wouldn't even smell it. We had the attendance of an amateur practitioner of medicine, whose real office was the cure of souls, but nothing touched his case. He took what was offered, but it was with the air of one to whom the time for pellets was passed. He sat or lay day after day almost motionless, never once making a display of those vulgar convulsions or contortions of pain which are so disagreeable to society. His favorite place was on the brightest spot of a Smyrna rug by the conservatory, where the sunlight fell and he could hear the fountain play. If we went to him and exhibited our interest in his condition, he always purred in recognition of our sympathy. And when I spoke his name, he looked up with an expression that said, "I understand it, old fellow, but it's no use." He was to all who came to visit him a model of calmness and patience in affliction.

I was absent from home at the last, but heard by daily postal-card of his failing condition; and never again saw him alive. One sunny morning, he rose from his rug, went into the conservatory (he was very thin then), walked around it deliberately, looking at all the plants he knew, and then went to the bay-window in the dining room, and stood a long time looking out upon the little field, now brown and sere, and toward the garden, where perhaps the happiest hours of his life had been spent. It was a last look. He turned and walked away, laid himself down upon the bright spot in the rug, and quietly died.

It is not too much to say that a little shock went through the neighborhood when it was known that Calvin was dead, so marked was his individuality; and his friends, one after another, came to see him. There was no sentimental nonsense about his obsequies; it was felt that any parade would have been distasteful to him. John, who acted as undertaker, prepared a candle-box for him, and I believe assumed a professional decorum; but there may have been the usual levity underneath, for I heard that he remarked in the kitchen that it was the "dryest wake he ever attended." Everybody, however, felt a fondness for Calvin, and regarded him with a certain respect. Between him and Bertha there existed a great friendship, and she apprehended his nature; she used to say that sometimes she was afraid of him, he looked at her so intelligently; she was never certain that he was what he appeared to be.

When I returned, they had laid Calvin on a table in an upper chamber by an open window. It was February. He reposed in a candle-box, lined about the edge with evergreen, and at his head stood a little wine-glass with flowers. He lay with his head tucked down in his arms—a favorite position of his before the fire,—as if asleep in the comfort of his soft and exquisite fur. It was the involuntary exclamation of those who saw him, "How natural he looks!" As for myself, I said nothing. John buried him under the twin hawthorn-trees,—one white and the other pink,—in a spot where Calvin was fond of lying and listening to the hum of summer insects and the twitter of birds.

Perhaps I have failed to make appear the individuality of character that was so evident to those who knew him. At any rate, I have set down nothing concerning him but the literal truth. He was always a mystery. I do not know whence he came; I do not know whither he has gone. I would not weave one spray of falsehood in the wreath I lay upon his grave.

The Fat Cat

Q. PATRICK

THE MARINES found her when they finally captured the old mission house at Fufa. After two days of relentless pounding, they hadn't expected to find anything alive there—least of all a fat cat.

And she was a very fat cat, sandy as a Scotchman, with enormous agate eyes and a fat amiable face. She sat there on the mat—or rather what was left of the mat—in front of what had been the mission porch, licking her paws as placidly as if the shell-blasted jungle were a summer lawn in New Jersey.

One of the men, remembering his childhood primer, quoted: "The fat cat sat on the mat."

The other men laughed; not that the remark was really funny; but laughter broke the tension and expressed their relief at having at last reached their objective, after two days of bitter fighting.

The fat cat, still sitting on the mat, smiled at them, as if to show she didn't mind the joke being on her. Then she saw Corporal Randy Jones, and for some reason known only to herself ran toward him as though he was her long-lost master. With a refrigerator purr, she weaved in and out of his muddy legs.

Everyone laughed again as Randy picked her up and pushed his ugly face against the sleek fur. It was funny to see any living thing show a preference for the dour, solitary Randy.

A sergeant flicked his fingers. "Kitty. Come here. We'll make you B Company mascot."

But the cat, perched on Randy's shoulder like a queen on her throne, merely smiled down majestically as much as to say: "You can be my subjects if you like. But this is my man—my royal consort."

And never for a second did she swerve from her devotion. She lived with Randy, slept with him, ate only food provided by him. Almost every man in Co. B tried to seduce her with caresses and morsels of canned ration, but all advances were met with a yawn of contempt.

49

For Randy this new love was ecstasy. He guarded her with the possessive tenderness of a mother. He combed her fur sleek; he almost starved himself to maintain her fatness. And all the time there was a strange wonder in him. The homeliest and ungainliest of ten in a West Virginia mining family, he had never before aroused affection in man or woman. No one had counted for him until the fat cat.

*   *   *

Randy's felicity, however, was short-lived. In a few days B Company was selected to carry out a flanking movement to surprise and possibly capture the enemy's headquarters, known to be twenty miles away through dense, sniper-infested jungle. The going would be rugged. Each man would carry his own supply of food and water, and sleep in foxholes with no support from the base.

The C.O. was definite about the fat cat: the stricken Randy was informed that the presence of a cat would seriously endanger the safety of the whole company. If it were seen following him, it would be shot on sight. Just before their scheduled departure, Randy carried the fat cat over to the mess of Co. H, where she was enthusiastically received by an equally fat cook. Randy could not bring himself to look back at the reproachful stare which he knew would be in the cat's agate eyes.

But all through that first day of perilous jungle travel, the thought of the cat's stare haunted him, and he was prey to all the heartache of parting; in leaving the cat, he had left behind wife, mother and child.

Darkness, like an immense black parachute, had descended hours ago on the jungle, when Randy was awakened from exhausted sleep. Something soft and warm was brushing his cheek; and his foxhole resounded to a symphony of purring. He stretched out an incredulous hand, but this was no dream. Real and solid, the cat was curled in a contented ball at his shoulder.

His first rush of pleasure was chilled as he remembered his C.O.'s words. The cat, spurning the blandishments of H Co.'s cuisine, had followed him through miles of treacherous jungle, only to face death the moment daylight revealed her presence. Randy was in an agony of uncertainty. To carry her back to the base would be desertion. To beat and drive her away was beyond the power of his simple nature.

The cat nuzzled his face again and breathed a mournful meow. She was hungry, of course, after her desperate trek. Suddenly Randy saw what he must do. If he could bring himself not to feed her, hunger would surely drive her back to the sanctuary of the cook.

She meowed again. He shushed her and gave her a half-hearted slap. "Ain't got nothing for you, honey. Scram. Go home. Scat!"

To his mingled pleasure and disappointment, she leaped silently out of the foxhole. When morning came there was no sign of her.

As B Company inched its furtive advance through the dense undergrowth, Randy felt the visit from the cat must have been a dream. But on the third night it came again. It brushed against his cheek and daintily took his ear in its teeth. When it meowed, the sound was still soft and cautious, but held a pitiful quaver of beseechment which cut through Randy like a Jap bayonet.

On its first visit, Randy had not seen the cat, but tonight some impulse made him reach for his flashlight. Holding it carefully downward, he turned it on. What he saw was the ultimate ordeal. The fat cat was fat no longer. Her body sagged; her sleek fur was matted and mud-stained, her paws torn and bloody. But it was the eyes, blinking up at him, that were the worst. There was no hint of reproach in them, only an expression of infinite trust and pleading.

Forgetting everything but those eyes, Randy tugged out one of his few remaining cans of ration. At sight of it, the cat weakly licked its lips. Randy moved to open the can. Then the realization that he would be signing the cat's death warrant surged over him. And, because the pent-up emotion in him had to have some outlet, it turned into unreasoning anger against this animal whose suffering had become more than he could bear. "Skat," he hissed. But the cat did not move.

He lashed out at her with the heavy flashlight. For a second she lay motionless under the blow. Then with a little moan she fled.

The next night she did not come back and Randy did not sleep.

* * *

On the fifth day they reached really dangerous territory. Randy and another marine, Joe, were sent forward to scout for the Jap command headquarters. Suddenly, weaving through the jungle, they came upon it.

A profound silence hung over the glade, with its two hastily erected shacks. Peering through dense foliage, they saw traces of recent evacuation—waste paper scattered on the grass, a pile of fresh garbage, a Jap army shirt flapping on a tree. Outside one of the shacks, under an awning, stretched a rough table strewn with the remains of a meal. "They must have got wind of us and scrammed," breathed Joe.

Randy edged forward—then froze as something stirred in the long grasses near the door of the first shack. As he watched, the once fat cat hobbled out into the sunlight.

A sense of heightened danger warred with Randy's pride that she had not abandoned him. Stiff with suspense, he watched it disappear into the shack. Soon it padded out.

"No Japs," said Joe. "That cat'd have raised 'em sure as shooting."

He started boldly into the glade. "Hey, Randy, there's a whole chicken on that table. Chicken's going to taste good after K ration."

He broke off, for the cat had seen the chicken too, and with pitiful clumsiness had leaped onto the table. With an angry yell Joe stooped for a rock and threw it.

Indignation blazed in Randy. He'd starved and spurned the cat, and yet she'd followed him with blind devotion. The chicken, surely, should be her reward. In his slow, simple mind it seemed the most important thing in the world for his beloved to have her fair share of the booty.

The cat, seeing the rock coming, lumbered off the table just in time, for the rock struck the chicken squarely, knocking it off its plate.

Randy leaped into the clearing. As he did so, a deafening explosion made him drop to the ground. A few seconds later, when he raised himself, there was no table, no shack, nothing but blazing wreckage of wood.

Dazedly he heard Joe's voice: "Booby trap under that chicken. Gee, if that cat hadn't jumped for it, I wouldn't have hurled the rock; we'd have grabbed it ourselves—and we'd be in heaven now." His voice dropped to an awed whisper. "That cat. I guess it's blown to hell . . . But it saved our lives." Randy couldn't speak. There was a constriction in his throat. He lay there, feeling more desolate than he'd ever felt in his life before.

Then from behind him came a contented purr.

He spun round. Freakishly, the explosion had hurled a crude rush mat out of the shack. It had come to rest on the grass behind him.

And, seated serenely on the mat, the cat was smiling at him.

The Immortal Cat

KAREL CAPEK

THIS story about a cat (with the inconsequence which is the very characteristic of reality) is at the beginning about a tomcat, in fact, about a tomcat which was presented to me. Every gift has about it something supernatural; each comes, so to speak, from another world, it drops from heaven, is sent upon us, invades our lives independently of its own and with some kind of exuberance, especially if it happens to be a particular tomcat with a blue ribbon round his neck. And he was called Philip, Percy, Scamp, and Rogue, in accordance with his various moral qualities; he was an Angora kitten, but dishevelled and carrotty like any other Christian scamp. One day on a tour of exploration he fell from the balcony onto the head of some female person; on the one hand she was scratched by it, on the other deeply offended, and she brought out a charge against my cat as a dangerous animal which springs from balconies onto people's heads. As a matter of fact I established the innocence of this Seraphic little beast; but three days later the little animal breathed his last, poisoned with arsenic and human malice. Just as through a strange mist I saw how with his last tremor his hips had sunken in, there was a mew on my doorstep; a stray brindled kitten was trembling there, as scraggy as a ridge-tile, and as frightened as a wandering child. Well, come here, Pussy; perhaps it is the finger of God, the will of Fate, a mysterious sign or whatever it is called; most probably the departed has sent you in his place; unfathomable is the continuity of life.

Such then was the first arrival of a cat which for her modesty was given the name of Pudlenka; as you see, she came from the Unknown, but I bear witness that she in no way puffed herself up on account of her mysterious and perhaps even supernatural origin. On the contrary, she behaved like every normal cat: she drank milk and stole the meat, she slept in one's lap and roamed in the night; and when her time had come, she gave birth to five kittens of which one

55

was red, one black, one mixed, one brindled, and one Angora. And I began to accost all the people I knew. "Listen," I began magnanimously, "I've got a marvellous kitten for you." Some of them (out of extreme modesty, very likely) managed to extricate themselves, saying that they would love to, but that unfortunately they couldn't, and so on; but others were so taken by surprise that before they could utter a word I had pressed their hand, and declared that it was settled then, they needn't worry, I was going to send them that kitten in due course; and already I was off after the next. Nothing is more charming than such a cat's maternal happiness; you ought to have a cat for yourself, if for nothing else but for those kittens. After six weeks Pudlenka let the kittens be kittens, and went to listen at first hand to the heroic baritone of the tomcat from the adjoining street. In fifty-three days she delivered six young ones. In a year and a day they added up to seventeen. Most probably that miraculous fertility was a legacy and post-mortem mission of the deceased bachelor little cat.

I always used to be of the opinion, may the deuce take them, that I had heaps of acquaintances, but from the time that Pudlenka threw herself into producing kittens, I found that in this life of ours I was terribly alone; for instance, I had no one to present with the twenty-sixth kitten. When I had to make myself known to someone I mumbled my name, and said: "Don't you want a kitten?" "What kitten?" they enquired dubiously. "I don't know yet," was my general answer; "but I think that I shall be having some kittens again." Soon I began to have the feeling that people were avoiding me; perhaps it was out of envy because I had such luck with kittens. According to Brehm cats bear young twice a year; Pudlenka had them three to four times a year without any regard to the seasons; she was a supernatural cat—apparently she had a higher mission, to revenge and replace a hundredfold the life of that tomcat which was done to death.

After three years of fertile vigour Pudlenka suddenly perished; some caretaker broke her back on the undignified pretext that according to him she had eaten a goose in his larder. The very same day that Pudlenka disappeared, her youngest daughter came back to us, a cat which I had pressed onto the people next door; and she lived with us under the name of Pudlenka II as a direct continuation of her deceased mother. She continued her to perfection; she was still a girlish adolescent when she began to swell, and then brought into the world four kittens. One was black, and had a noble, carrotty colour of the Vršovice race, one the elongated nose of the Strašnice cats, while the fourth was spotty like a bean, as the cats of Malâ Strana are. Pudlenka II produced kittens three times a year with the regularity of a law of Nature; in two and a quarter years she enriched the world with one and twenty kittens, of all colours and breeds, except that of the cats of the Isle of Man which are born without tails. For the twenty-first kitten I really had no market. I was just making up my mind that I ought to join the Free Thought or the Rosary Brotherhood, to gain a new circle of acquaintances when our neighbour's Rolf bit to death Pudlenka II. We carried her home and laid her on the bed; her chin still was trembling. Then the chin stopped shaking and from her dense coat fleas rapidly crawled away; this is the unmistakable sign of death with a cat. So then her surviving kitten for whom there was no market remained with us as Pudlenka III. In four months' time Pudlenka III gave birth to five kittens; from that time on she has conscientiously fulfilled her task of this life at regular intervals of fifteen weeks; only during those great frosts of this year did she miss one term.

You might not perhaps say of her that she had such a big and immortal mission; to look at, she seems an ordinary, many-coloured democratic puss, who spends the whole day long dozing on the family patriarch's lap, or on the bed. She has a highly-developed sense for her personal comfort, maintains a healthy distrust of men and animals, and when it comes to it she can defend her interests *dente unguibusque*. But when her fifteen weeks are over she begins to be excited and restless, and she sits nervously by the door giving one to understand: "Man, let me out quickly, I have got the tummy ache." After this, she dashes out like an arrow into the evening darkness, and doesn't return till morning, with a drawn face and rings round her eyes. At such times a huge black tomcat comes from the North, where the Olšany Cemeteries are; from the South, where Vršovice is, appears a carrotty and one-eyed fighter; from the West, the seat of civilization, arrives an Angora cat, with a bush of ostrich feathers; from the East, where there is nothing, a mysterious white animal appears with a curved-up tail. In their midst sits the simple many-coloured Pudlenka III, and with burning fascinated eyes she listens to their howling, stifled exclamations, screams as of murdered children, roar of drunken mariners, saxophones, roll of drums and other instruments in the Cats' Symphony. To put it clearly, not only are strength and courage necessary for a tomcat, but also perseverance; sometimes for a week at a time these four tomcats of the Apocalypse besiege Pudlenka's home, blockade the gate, make their way through the windows into the house, and leave

behind them merely a hellish stench. At last the night arrives when
Pudlenka III no longer has any desire to go out. "Let me sleep," she
says. "Let me sleep, sleep for ever. Sleep, dream. . . . Ah, I'm so
unhappy!" After this, at the proper time, she delivers five kittens.
On this question I have already had a certain amount of experience: there will be five of them. I already see them, those dear,
sweet little lumps, stumping, and padding about over the house,
pulling over electric lamps, making little puddles in slippers, crawling up my legs, onto my lap (my legs are scratched by them, like
Lazarus's), I see myself finding a kitten in the sleeve when I'm
putting on my coat, and my tie under the bed when I want to put it
on—Children are worrying, everybody will tell you that. It isn't
enough just to bring them up; you have to ensure their future.

In the editorial office everybody now has got a kitten from me; very
well, I shall have to get taken on at another place. I am ready to put
my name down for any society, or organization, if they will assure me
of the disposal of at least twenty-one kittens. While I shall be
struggling along in a hostile world to find room for more generations,
Pudlenka III, or Pudlenka IV, will be purring, her paws folded up
beneath her, and spinning the immortal thread of cat life. She will
dream of the cats' world, of the hosts of cats, of cats, when there will
be enough of them, seizing power to rule over the universe. For it is a
Great Task which was imposed upon her by the little Angora tomcat,
innocently done to death.

Seriously, now, wouldn't you like a kitten?

Alice and the Cheshire Cat

LEWIS CARROLL

ALICE was just beginning to think to herself, "Now, what am I to do with this creature when I get it home?" when it grunted again, so violently, that she looked down into its face in some alarm. This time there could be *no* mistake about it: it was neither more nor less than a pig, and she felt that it would be quite absurd for her to carry it any further.

So she set the little creature down, and felt quite relieved to see it trot away quietly into the wood. "If it had grown up," she said to herself, "it would have been a dreadfully ugly child: but it makes rather a handsome pig, I think." And she began thinking over other children she knew, who might do very well as pigs, and was just saying to herself, "if one only knew the right way to change them—" when she was a little startled by seeing the Cheshire Cat sitting on a bough of a tree a few yards off.

The Cat only grinned when it saw Alice. It looked good-natured, she thought: still it had *very* long claws and a great many teeth, so she felt it ought to be treated with respect.

"Cheshire Puss," she began, rather timidly, as she did not at all know whether it would like the name: however, it only grinned a little wider. "Come, it's pleased so far," thought Alice, and she went on, "Would you tell me, please, which way I ought to walk from here?"

"That depends a good deal on where you want to get to," said the Cat.

"I don't much care where—" said Alice.

"Then it doesn't matter which way you walk," said the Cat.

"—so long as I get *somewhere*," Alice added as an explanation.

"Oh, you're sure to do that," said the Cat, "if you only walk long enough."

Alice felt that this could not be denied, so she tried another question. "What sort of people live about here?"

"In *that* direction," the Cat said, waving its right paw round, "lives a Hatter: and in *that* direction," waving the other paw, "lives a March Hare. Visit either you like: they're both mad."

"But I don't want to go among mad people," Alice remarked.

"Oh, you can't help that," said the Cat: "we're all mad here. I'm mad. You're mad."

"How do you know I'm mad?" said Alice.

"You must be," said the Cat, "or you wouldn't have come here."

Alice didn't think that proved it at all; however, she went on: "and how do you know that you're mad?"

"To begin with," said the Cat, "a dog's not mad. You grant that?"

"I suppose so," said Alice.

"Well then," the Cat went on, "you see a dog growls when it's angry, and wags its tail when it's pleased. Now I growl when I'm pleased, and wag my tail when I'm angry. Therefore I'm mad."

"I call it purring, not growling," said Alice.

"Call it what you like," said the Cat. "Do you play croquet with the Queen to-day?"

"I should like it very much," said Alice, "but I haven't been invited yet."

"You'll see me there," said the Cat, and vanished.

Alice was not much surprised at this, she was getting so well used to queer things happening. While she was still looking at the place where it had been, it suddenly appeared again.

"By-the-bye, what became of the baby?" said the Cat. "I'd nearly forgotten to ask."

"It turned into a pig," Alice answered very quietly, just as if the Cat had come back in a natural way.

"I thought it would," said the Cat, and vanished again.

Alice waited a little, half expecting to see it again, but it did not appear, and after a minute or two she walked on in the direction in which the March Hare was said to live. "I've seen hatters before," she said to herself: "the March Hare will be much the most interesting, and perhaps as this is May it won't be raving mad—at least not so mad as it was in March." As she said this, she looked up, and there was the Cat again, sitting on a branch of a tree.

"Did you say pig, or fig?" said the Cat.

"I said pig," replied Alice; "and I wish you wouldn't keep appearing and vanishing so suddenly: you make one quite giddy."

"All right," said the Cat; and this time it vanished quite slowly, beginning with the end of the tail, and ending with the grin, which remained some time after the rest of it had gone.

"Well! I've often seen a cat without a grin," thought Alice; "but a grin without a cat! It's the most curious thing I ever saw in all my life!"

The players all played at once without waiting for turns, quarrelling all the while, and fighting for the hedgehogs; and in a very short time the Queen was in a furious passion, and went stamping about, and shouting, "Off with his head!" about once in a minute.

Alice began to feel uneasy: to be sure, she had not as yet had any dispute with the queen, but she knew that it might happen any minute, "and then," thought she, "what would become of me? They're dreadfully fond of beheading people here: the great wonder is, that there's any one left alive!"

She was looking about for some way of escape, and wondering whether she could get away without being seen, when she noticed a curious appearance in the air: it puzzled her very much at first, but after watching it a minute or two she made it out to be a grin, and she said to herself, "It's the Cheshire Cat: now I shall have somebody to talk to."

"How are you getting on?" said the Cat, as soon as there was mouth enough for it to speak with.

Alice waited till the eyes appeared, and then nodded. "It's no use speaking to it," she thought, "till its ears have come, or at least one of them." In another minute the whole head appeared, and then Alice put down her flamingo, and began an account of the game, feeling very glad she had some one to listen to her. The Cat seemed to think that there was enough of it now in sight, and no more of it appeared.

"I don't think they play at all fairly," Alice began, in rather a complaining tone, "and they all quarrel so dreadfully one can't hear one's-self speak—and they don't seem to have any rules in particular; at least, if there are, nobody attends to them—and you've no idea how confusing it is all the things being alive; for instance, there's the arch I've got to go through next walking about at the other end of the ground—and I should have croqueted the Queen's hedgehog just now, only it ran away when it saw mine coming!"

"How do you like the Queen?" said the Cat in a low voice.

"Not at all," said Alice: "she's so extremely—" Just then she noticed that the Queen was close behind her, listening: so she went on "—likely to win, that it's hardly worth while finishing the game."

The Queen smiled and passed on.

"Who *are* you talking to?" said the King, coming up to Alice, and looking at the Cat's head with great curiosity.

"It's a friend of mine—a Cheshire Cat," said Alice: "allow me to introduce it."

"I don't like the look of it at all," said the King: "however, it may kiss my hand if it likes."

"I'd rather not," the Cat remarked.

"Don't be impertinent," said the King, "and don't look at me like that!" He got behind Alice as he spoke.

"A cat may look at a king," said Alice. "I've read that in some book, but I don't remember where."

"Well, it must be removed," said the King very decidedly, and he called to the Queen, who was passing at the moment, "My dear! I wish you would have this cat removed!"

The Queen had only one way of settling all difficulties, great or small. "Off with his head!" she said without even looking round.

"I'll fetch the executioner myself," said the King eagerly, and he hurried off.

Alice thought she might as well go back and see how the game was going on, as she heard the Queen's voice in the distance, screaming with passion. She had already heard her sentence three of the players to be executed for having missed their turns, and she did not like the look of things at all, as the game was in such confusion that she never knew whether it was her turn or not. So she went off in search of her hedgehog.

The hedgehog was engaged in a fight with another hedgehog, which seemed to Alice an excellent opportunity for croqueting one of them with the other: the only difficulty was, that her flamingo was gone across to the other side of the garden, where Alice could see it trying in a helpless sort of way to fly up into a tree.

By the time she had caught the flamingo and brought it back, the fight was over, and both the hedgehogs were out of sight: "but it doesn't matter much," thought Alice, "as all the arches are gone from this side of the ground." So she tucked it away under her arm, that it might not escape again, and went back to have a little more conversation with her friend.

When she got back to the Cheshire Cat, she was surprised to find quite a large crowd collected round it: there was a dispute going on between the executioner, the King, and the Queen, who were all talking at once, while all the rest were quite silent, and looked very uncomfortable.

The moment Alice appeared, she was appealed to by all three to settle the question, and they repeated their arguments to her, though, as they all spoke at once, she found it very hard to make out exactly what they said.

The executioner's argument was, that you couldn't cut off a head unless there was a body to cut it off from: that he had never had to do such a thing before, and he wasn't going to begin at his time of life.

The King's argument was, that anything that had a head could be beheaded, and that you weren't to talk nonsense.

The Queen's argument was, that if something wasn't done about it in less than no time, she'd have everybody executed, all round. (It was this last remark that had made the whole party look so grave and anxious.)

Alice could think of nothing else to say but "It belongs to the Duchess: you'd better ask *her* about it."

"She's in prison," the Queen said to the executioner: "fetch her here." And the executioner went off like an arrow.

The Cat's head began fading away the moment he was gone, and, by the time he had come back with the Duchess, it had entirely disappeared: so the King and the executioner ran wildly up and down looking for it, while the rest of the party went back to the game.

The Cats

ADRIAAN MORRIËN

WHEN the war was over we all discovered, as if intuitively, that there were no cats left in our ill-treated town. What had become of them? They had vanished from the scene just as, in more peaceful times, they used to slip out of a living room: noiselessly—that is, if the door was open. Now, too, a door must have been open, for nobody had heard them meow. Had people eaten them? Had they starved to death or failed to reproduce themselves? Nobody knew. But everybody longed for them, once it was summer and there was no lack of milk. They were part of the furniture; they added the finishing touch to a cozy home; they were a solace to old folk, an example to young married couples awaiting the arrival of their first child. The milk saucers in the kitchens of many families stood conspicuously empty. The rats and mice grew bolder and bolder so that one almost felt impelled to offer these voracious creatures a seat at the table, which was once again well laden, or to apologize for the appetite of one's family. A balance had been upset—in the lower regions of domestic economy, it is true—but none the less it was intolerable. For even the gutter and the sewer have their rights.

Articles on the cat problem appeared in the newspapers. Conversations would begin with the statement that someone had seen a cat. In the afternoons, when the men were still at work in offices or factories, the women had nothing to pet or to talk to. But most to be pitied were the old people, who with a black or spotted tomcat in their lap found it easier to face the end. Never had it been so clearly appreciated that heads being rubbed, paws sticking out, and tails curled high were part of the indispensable décor of our lives. If only there had been a rationing of cats! Many a person would willingly have sacrificed his candy coupons.

Gradually details about the disappearance of the cats became

known, though for the time being statistics on feline mortality during the last winter of the war were lacking. With tears in their eyes
and remorse in their hearts, many people had eaten their pets—
melancholy meals by the light of a candle or an oil lamp, with everyone imagining he heard a meow. Other cats had died of hunger. Mis-
led by their fur, their friends had often not noticed till after their
death how badly off the poor animals had been, for it is deceptive
to go around in a fur coat when one is down and out.

Cats had fled in bewilderment from the houses where they were
born and bred—where they had become mother, grandmother,
great-grandmother, and great-great-grandmother—in search of the
food that no one could give them; they were lost in the snow that
then lay on the streets; hunted perhaps; frozen to death, and
amazed at what was happening to them. At the time, nobody took
any notice of them except for some sentimental girl or short-sighted
old gentleman. Now, they were lamented by everyone. The burgomaster turned his attention to them. A new political party, cutting
across the traditional party lines, came close to being formed. But
after a short period of vacillation which we referred to as "mature
consideration," politics reverted to its usual concerns.

Not all the cats had died out, however. Here and there one still
lived, unconscious of the general pity its species had aroused. When
they, too, had taken the edge off their hunger—at first with bread
and diluted milk, but presently with chitterlings and heads of fish—
they emerged from their anonymity and became individuals. They
rediscovered the world one radiant summer morning in the sunshine
near a window, or some evening on the eaves where the last damp-
ness had been evaporating, while people were once more going for
walks and children were playing in the streets. A solitary cat's head
would suddenly be filled with cherished memories. Peace had actually come, and spring and summer had been selected for the purpose. A cat does not have much difficulty in recognizing that life is
touching and beautiful. Furthermore, it has more opportunities for
changing its point of view. A cat looks at the world from between
trouser legs and women's stockings, then it looks down from a roof at
the tree-tops, with the street lights burning between them, and the
water of the canal glistening far below. A cat outlives all noise in the
still of the night, when it is alone with its fellow cats and the fine
game of chimneys and fences begins. More than once, coming home
late, I have caught the surprised look of a tomcat interrupting his
nightly task to watch me putting my key in the lock; and I would
compare my sleepiness with his robust, pungent lust for life.

ii

The tomcats were pretty busy that summer. Females being scarce, they often had to go far afield, crossing a street, a square, or a bridge to pay their visits. They developed an intimate knowledge of a part of the town's layout. People would sometimes come across their tomcat in some distant street, apparently ashamed of its presence there; occasionally the animal would forget all its intentions in joyful recognition of its master and would go home feigning hunger or a need for companionship. It would lie in a chair throughout the evening, full of magnanimous indolence, but become restless as soon as the family began to get ready for bed.

Anyone with a tabby-cat might at any moment of the day find a band of tomcats sitting in front of his house—a strange mixed company, evidently not related by ties of blood; moody, jealous, but at the same time trustful or full of misplaced faith; melancholy and resigned. Tomcats are not at their best in company. At night the house would seem surrounded by cats, with a cordon of tomcats across the street as though some strange sort of maneuver were being held. Traffic was heavy along the eaves. A lot of worldly wisdom was wasted unseen or, at best, glimpsed by a sleepless lodger from an attic window. Was there a special shortage of females, or were the males so faithless?

The news of the cat shortage in our country had traveled abroad, even across the ocean; and with the first parcels of food and clothing there also arrived small shipments of cats. They were unloaded at one of the ports in the south of the country, and were welcomed by a committee headed by the burgomaster, hat in hand. The cats were housed in oblong baskets partitioned off into little pens. If you lifted the lid, you could see them sitting under a wicker latticework—cats of all shades standing on their hind legs to rub their heads against the warmly responsive fingers of the committee members. One old lady went around with a bag of smoked sprats. There was passionate meowing beneath the blue sky. The same angelic smile played about everyone's mouth; and even the stevedores, strong matter-of-fact characters, interrupted their work to gaze affectionately at the animals and the people welcoming them. In the tepid air of morning there floated over the wharf the pungent smell of cat's urine, which, to the people sniffing it, was a reminder that their freedom had been regained and a promise of renewed domesticity.

That same day the cats lapped their first taste of our country's milk from white and flowered saucers, while parents and children observed this solemn performance through which a corner of the kitchen was consecrated. Slowly, gingerly, sniffing all over the place, pussy would make its way to the living room followed by the family, which had to adapt its movements to the animal's fancy. Once more there was the sound of purring in the room, a sound that is talking, laughing, and singing all in one. Cats lay in cherished places, curled up like a horn, rustling in their sleep.

As soon as the foreign cats had got settled, they went reconnoitering the neighborhood. Even while they were still shut up, nocturnal meowing from neighboring roofs had already given them warning that for them the world held no frontiers. One day they would come out and trot shivering over the damp stones of the street. There was always one of their kind who had been waiting for this moment and would open its eyes wide, petrified in an expectation which we take for enmity. Unhampered by language barriers, considerations of decency, or all-too-human shyness, they would recognize one another as street urchins do, but with the patience of their species that makes summer afternoons endless. The consequences were soon noticeable. Even before summer was over, kittens were born: a new generation which had not known the war or the distant country its parents came from, and which appropriated the world as its inalienable domain.

Meanwhile the unknown donors overseas had been requested not to send any more cats. The shortage threatened to turn into overpopulation; instinct does not need encouragement. The cat committee suspended its activities reluctantly, for an organization had been created, and it is hard to abandon a task even when it has become pointless.

Presently an old lady, perhaps the dispenser of the sprats, hit upon a charming idea. A monument should be erected in our town in honor of the cats who, albeit unintentionally, had given their lives in the liberation of our country. At first it was considered an idiotic, irreverent suggestion. But when one wants something, one has only to think about it, to want it more and more passionately. There were many who wanted the monument, and were still capable of surrendering to these crazy impulses that can make our lives so much more beautiful.

The committee resumed its work, somewhat hesitant at first because its purpose had been altered, but a fluent fountain pen can rid us of all our hesitations. Circulars were drawn up and money was collected—banknotes from rich eccentrics, but also unsightly prewar coins conscientiously hoarded in old-fashioned purses. Even the children donated their pennies. A small but moving justification had been added to the machinery of our lives.

The town council approved the erection of the monument in the largest park in town. This decision was preceded by a stormy council meeting, at which even the basic problems of life entered into the discussion.

The following summer, on a Saturday afternoon, the monument was unveiled. The ceremony came a year too late; for in almost every family, kittens were once more being drowned in kitchen pails or simply thrown into the canal. Even rationing was coming to an end. You could drink as much milk as you wanted.

It was raining, and the rain on the jasmine bushes in bloom and the well-kept lawns somehow reminded us, by the very contrast, of the war years. Somebody made a speech, standing under an umbrella —a speech ridiculous to anyone who could not switch off his intellect. It was a remarkable gathering of people who could not otherwise have been brought together outdoors so easily—inveterate stay-at-homes who think about a fire even in summer; meditative pipe-smokers and dreamers; old women as full of worries as though there would never be an end to their lives; lame children; bachelors with water on the brain; cripples too poor to buy an artificial leg; and an occasional blind person with a smile on his face as though his eyesight had been restored. But also a beautiful young woman with luxurious clothes, jewelry, and shoes of fine, expensive leather, shaking her damp curls.

A pious mischief was in the air; a feeling that for a moment one had left the earth, just as at meetings of spiritualists, vegetarians, novices in politics, and magazine editors. This impression was confirmed by the clothing—cloth caps and leather jackets, a nineteenth-century shawl, a peasant brooch on an urban bosom. There were beards, mustaches, powder and lipstick on withered faces, unwashed hands, and a vague smell of cats that hovered over the scent of the jasmine. The monument was simple—a pedestal with a bronze cat reclining on it.

Whenever I go walking in the park with my children, I never fail to go past it. The monument is already beginning to lose its color to the weather and turn gray. My children look at it with cheerful innocence and wonder, not having learned yet to count back to the war years when the snow refused to melt and when getting from the warm bed to the frozen kitchen was like traveling across the world.

It is good to live in a town where a statue has been erected to the cats. May the rats and mice forgive us.

The Paradise of Cats

EMILE ZOLA

An aunt bequeathed me an Angora cat, which is certainly the most stupid animal I know of. This is what my cat related to me, one winter night, before the warm embers.

i

I was then two years old, and I was certainly the fattest and most simple cat any one could have seen. Even at that tender age I displayed all the presumption of an animal that scorns the attractions of the fireside. And yet what gratitude I owed to Providence for having placed me with your aunt! The worthy woman idolised me. I had a regular bedroom at the bottom of a cupboard, with a feather pillow and a triple-folded rug. The food was as good as the bed; no bread or soup, nothing but meat, good underdone meat.

Well! amidst all these comforts, I had but one wish, but one dream, to slip out by the half-open window, and run away on to the tiles. Caresses appeared to me insipid, the softness of my bed disgusted me, I was so fat that I felt sick, and from morn till eve I experienced the weariness of being happy.

I must tell you that by straining my neck I had perceived the opposite roof from the window. That day four cats were fighting there. With bristling coats and tails in the air, they were rolling on the blue slates, in the full sun, amidst oaths of joy. I had never witnessed such an extraordinary sight. From that moment my convictions were settled. Real happiness was upon that roof, in front of that window which the people of the house so carefully closed. I found the proof of this in the way in which they shut the doors of the cupboards where the meat was hidden.

I made up my mind to fly. I felt sure there were other things in life than underdone meat. There was the unknown, the ideal. One day they forgot to close the kitchen window. I sprang on to a small roof beneath it.

ii

How beautiful the roofs were! They were bordered by broad gutters exhaling delicious odours. I followed those gutters in raptures of delight, my feet sinking into fine mud, which was deliciously warm and soft. I fancied I was walking on velvet. And the generous heat of the sun melted my fat.

I will not conceal from you the fact that I was trembling in every limb. My delight was mingled with terror. I remember, particularly, experiencing a terrible shock that almost made me tumble down into the street. Three cats came rolling over from the top of a house towards me, mewing most frightfully, and as I was on the point of fainting away, they called me a silly thing, and said they were mewing for fun. I began mewing with them. It was charming. The jolly fellows had none of my stupid fat. When I slipped on the sheets of zinc heated by the burning sun, they laughed at me. An old tom, who was one of the band, showed me particular friendship. He offered to teach me a thing or two, and I gratefully accepted. Ah! your aunt's cat's meat was far from my thoughts! I drank in the gutters, and never had sugared milk seemed so sweet to me. Everything appeared nice and beautiful. A she-cat passed by, a charming she-cat, the sight of her gave me a feeling I had never experienced before. Hitherto, I had only seen these exquisite creatures, with such delightfully supple backbones, in my dreams. I and my three companions rushed forward to meet the newcomer. I was in front of the others, and was about to pay my respects to the bewitching thing, when one of my comrades cruelly bit my neck. I cried out with pain.

"Bah!" said the old tom, leading me away; "you will meet with stranger adventures than that."

iii

After an hour's walk I felt as hungry as a wolf.

"What do you eat on the roofs?" I inquired of my friend the tom.

"What you can find," he answered shrewdly.

This reply caused me some embarrassment, for though I carefully searched I found nothing. At last I perceived a young work-girl in a garret preparing her lunch. A beautiful chop of a tasty red colour was lying on a table under the window.

"There's the very thing I want," I thought, in all simplicity.

And I sprang on to the table and took the chop. But the work-girl,

having seen me, struck me a fearful blow with a broom on the spine, and I fled, uttering a dreadful oath.

"You are fresh from your village then?" said the tom. "Meat that is on tables is there for the purpose of being longed for at a distance. You must search in the gutters."

I could never understand that kitchen meat did not belong to cats. My stomach was beginning to get seriously angry. The tom put me completely to despair by telling me it would be necessary to wait until night. Then we would go down into the street and turn over the heaps of muck. Wait until night! He said it quietly, like a hardened philosopher. I felt myself fainting at the mere thought of this prolonged fast.

iv

Night came slowly, a foggy night that chilled me to the bones. It soon began to rain, a fine, penetrating rain, driven by sudden gusts of wind. We went down along the glazed roof of a staircase. How ugly the street appeared to me! It was no longer that nice heat, that beautiful sun, those roofs white with light where one rolled about so deliciously. My paws slipped on the greasy stones. I sorrowfully recalled to memory my triple blanket and feather pillow.

We were hardly in the street when my friend the tom began to tremble. He made himself small, very small, and ran stealthily along beside the houses, telling me to follow as rapidly as possible. He rushed in at the first street door he came to, and purred with satisfaction as he sought refuge there. When I questioned him as to the motive of his flight, he answered:

"Did you see that man with a basket on his back and a stick with an iron hook at the end?"

"Yes."

"Well! if he had seen us he would have knocked us on the heads and roasted us!"

"Roasted us!" I exclaimed. "Then the street is not ours? One can't eat, but one's eaten!"

v

However, the boxes of kitchen refuse had been emptied before the street doors. I rummaged in the heaps in despair. I came across two or three bare bones that had been lying among the cinders, and I then understood what a succulent dish fresh cat's meat made. My friend the tom scratched artistically among the muck. He made me run about until morning, inspecting each heap, and without showing the least hurry. I was out in the rain for more than ten hours, shivering in every limb. Cursed street, cursed liberty, and how I regretted my prison!

At dawn the tom, seeing I was staggering said to me with a strange air:

"Have you had enough of it?"

"Oh yes," I answered.

"Do you want to go home?"

"I do, indeed; but how shall I find the house?"

"Come along. This morning, when I saw you come out, I understood that a fat cat like you was not made for the lively delights of liberty. I know your place of abode and will take you to the door."

The worthy tom said this very quietly. When we had arrived, he bid me "Good-bye," without betraying the least emotion.

"No," I exclaimed, "we will not leave each other so. You must accompany me. We will share the same bed and the same food. My mistress is a good woman—"

He would not allow me to finish my sentence.

"Hold your tongue," he said sharply, "you are a simpleton. Your effeminate existence would kill me. Your life of plenty is good for bastard cats. Free cats would never purchase your cat's meat and feather pillow at the price of a prison. Good-bye."

And he returned up on to the roofs, where I saw his long outline quiver with joy in the rays of the rising sun.

When I got in, your aunt took the whip and gave me a thrashing which I received with profound delight. I tasted in full measure the pleasure of being beaten and being warm. Whilst she was striking me, I thought with rapture of the meat she would give me afterwards.

Puss in Boots

CHARLES PERRAULT

ONCE upon a time there was a miller who left no more riches to the three sons he had than his mill, his ass, and his cat. The division was soon made. Neither the lawyer nor the attorney was sent for. They would soon have eaten up all the poor property. The eldest had the mill, the second the ass, and the youngest nothing but the cat.

The youngest, as we can understand, was quite unhappy at having so poor a share.

"My brothers," said he, "may get their living handsomely enough by joining their stocks together; but, for my part, when I have eaten up my cat, and made me a muff of his skin, I must die of hunger."

The Cat, who heard all this, without appearing to take any notice, said to him with a grave and serious air:—

"Do not thus afflict yourself, my master; you have nothing else to do but to give me a bag, and get a pair of boots made for me, that I may scamper through the brambles, and you shall see that you have not so poor a portion in me as you think."

Though the Cat's master did not think much of what he said, he had seen him play such cunning tricks to catch rats and mice—hanging himself by the heels, or hiding himself in the meal, to make believe he was dead—that he did not altogether despair of his helping him in his misery. When the Cat had what he asked for, he booted himself very gallantly, and putting his bag about his neck, he held the strings of it in his two forepaws, and went into a warren where was a great number of rabbits. He put bran and sow-thistle into his bag, and, stretching out at length, as if he were dead, he waited for some young rabbits, not yet acquainted with the deceits of the world, to come and rummage his bag for what he had put into it.

Scarcely was he settled but he had what he wanted. A rash and

foolish young rabbit jumped into his bag, and Monsieur Puss, immediately drawing close the strings, took him and killed him at once.
Proud of his prey, he went with it to the palace, and asked to speak
with the King. He was shown upstairs into his Majesty's apartment,
and, making a low bow to the King, he said:—

"I have brought you, sire, a rabbit which my noble Lord, the Master of Carabas" (for that was the title which Puss was pleased to
give his master) "has commanded me to present to your Majesty
from him."

"Tell thy master," said the King, "that I thank him, and that I
am pleased with his gift."

Another time he went and hid himself among some standing corn,
still holding his bag open; and when a brace of partridges ran into it,
he drew the strings, and so caught them both. He then went and
made a present of these to the King, as he had done before of the
rabbit which he took in the warren. The King, in like manner, received the partridges with great pleasure, and ordered his servants to
reward him.

The Cat continued for two or three months thus to carry his Majesty, from time to time, some of his master's game. One day when he
knew that the King was to take the air along the riverside, with his
daughter, the most beautiful princess in the world, he said to his
master:—

"If you will follow my advice, your fortune is made. You have nothing else to do but go and bathe in the river, just at the spot I shall show you, and leave the rest to me."

The Marquis of Carabas did what the Cat advised him to, without knowing what could be the use of doing it. While he was bathing, the King passed by, and the Cat cried out with all his might:—

"Help, help! My Lord the Marquis of Carabas is drowning!"

At this noise the King put his head out of the coach window, and seeing the Cat who had so often brought him game, he commanded his guards to run immediately to the assistance of his Lordship the Marquis of Carabas.

While they were drawing the poor Marquis out of the river, the Cat came up to the coach and told the King that, while his master was bathing, there came by some rogues, who ran off with his clothes, though he had cried out, "Thieves! thieves!" several times, as loud as he could. The cunning Cat had hidden the clothes under a great stone. The King immediately commanded the officers of his wardrobe to run and fetch one of his best suits for the Lord Marquis of Carabas.

The King was extremely polite to him, and as the fine clothes he had given him set off his good looks (for he was well made and handsome) , the King's daughter found him very much to her liking, and the Marquis of Carabas had no sooner cast two or three respectful and somewhat tender glances than she fell in love with him to distraction. The King would have him come into the coach and take part in the airing. The Cat, overjoyed to see his plan begin to succeed, marched on before, and, meeting with some countrymen, who were mowing a meadow, he said to them:—

"Good people, you who are mowing, if you do not tell the King that the meadow you mow belongs to my Lord Marquis of Carabas, you shall be chopped as small as herbs for the pot."

The King did not fail to ask the mowers to whom the meadow they were mowing belonged.

"To my Lord Marquis of Carabas," answered they all together, for the Cat's threat had made them afraid.

"You have a good property there," said the King to the Marquis of Carabas.

"You see, sire," said the Marquis, "this is a meadow which never fails to yield a plentiful harvest every year."

The Master Cat, who went still on before, met with some reapers, and said to them:—

"Good people, you who are reaping, if you do not say that all this corn belongs to the Marquis of Carabas, you shall be chopped as small as herbs for the pot."

The King, who passed by a moment after, wished to know to whom belonged all that corn, which he then saw.

"To my Lord Marquis of Carabas," replied the reapers, and the King was very well pleased with it, as well as the Marquis, whom he congratulated thereupon. The Master Cat, who went always before, said the same thing to all he met, and the King was astonished at the vast estates of my Lord Marquis of Carabas.

Monsieur Puss came at last to a stately castle, the master of which was an Ogre, the richest ever known; for all the lands which the King had then passed through belonged to this castle. The Cat, who had taken care to inform himself who this Ogre was and what he could do, asked to speak with him, saying he could not pass so near his castle without having the honor of paying his respects to him.

The Ogre received him as civilly as an Ogre could do, and made him sit down.

"I have been assured," said the Cat, "that you have the gift of being able to change yourself into all sorts of creatures you have a mind to; that you can, for example, transform yourself into a lion, or elephant, and the like."

"That is true," answered the Ogre, roughly; "and to convince you, you shall see me now become a lion."

Puss was so terrified at the sight of a lion so near him that he immediately climbed into the gutter, not without much trouble and danger, because of his boots, which were of no use at all to him for walking upon the tiles. A little while after, when Puss saw that the Ogre had resumed his natural form, he came down, and owned he had been very much frightened.

"I have, moreover, been informed," said the Cat, "but I know not how to believe it, that you have also the power to take on you the shape of the smallest animals; for example, to change yourself into a rat or a mouse, but I must own to you I take this to be impossible."

"Impossible!" cried the Ogre; "you shall see." And at the same time he changed himself into a mouse, and began to run about the floor. Puss no sooner perceived this than he fell upon him and ate him up.

Meanwhile, the King, who saw, as he passed, this fine castle of the Ogre's, had a mind to go into it. Puss, who heard the noise of his Majesty's coach coming over the drawbridge, ran out, and said to the King, "Your Majesty is welcome to this castle of my Lord Marquis of Carabas."

"What! my Lord Marquis," cried the King, "and does this castle also belong to you? There can be nothing finer than this courtyard and all the stately buildings which surround it; let us see the interior, if you please."

The Marquis gave his hand to the young Princess, and followed the King, who went first. They passed into the great hall, where they found a magnificent collation, which the Ogre had prepared for his friends, who were that very day to visit him, but dared not to enter, knowing the King was there. His Majesty, charmed with the good qualities of my Lord of Carabas, as was also his daughter, who had fallen violently in love with him, and seeing the vast estate he possessed, said to him:—

"It will be owing to yourself only, my Lord Marquis, if you are not my son-in-law."

The Marquis, with low bows, accepted the honor which his Majesty conferred upon him, and forthwith that very same day married the Princess.

Puss became a great lord, and never ran after mice any more except for his diversion.

Hurrli, Bold, Proud, and Amiable Master of the Elk House

PAUL EIPPER

HURRLI lived at the refuge for not quite two years. Then the spreading colossus of the city reached out inexorably for our little world, no longer peaceful as it had once been; the trees around us were felled more and more ruthlessly week by week, and so we built a new house deep in the Grunewald, at a point where, on a ramble one spring, I had once seen, with happy surprise, a tall, double-stemmed birch tree standing alone between fen and conifers.

We left the Happy Refuge in the autumn. Our son Herbert drove the family out of town to the Elk House; between my wife and me stood a covered basket on the floor of the car, and in it sat the tomcat, growling.

"Patience, my conquering hero! The lid will be off in another twenty minutes' time. You have no idea of all the wonderful things waiting for you. In your place I'd be ashamed to make that noise," said my wife. "Aren't we together, after all?" Herbert echoed her words by sounding the horn in a way that Hurrli knew full well—three blows, short-long-short—and the tom was entirely reassured. He had not lived with us three weeks before he discovered that this was how all the members of the family announced their return from a trip to town, and he would always come, tail waving joyfully in the air, to welcome us at the front door, even before it was opened to us. Another thing that never failed to amaze me as an achievement of animal intelligence was the way in which Hurrli was able not only to express his wishes to us but also to show exactly how we might help him. For instance, he would appear in the garden making his special cooing noise, prod me several times with his head, and trip off in the direction of the veranda door; then come back again, a second and a third time, until I followed him. He would go straight to the umbrella-stand in the hall and rub his head against my walking stick, which I would take, anxious to execute his wish but still uncomprehending. Then Hurrli would run to the dining-room and crouch down by the glass china-cupboard, staring intently into the empty space between the cupboard and the floor. After a time, the dull creature that I am realized what was wanted, and poked my stick under the cupboard. Hurrli's ping-pong ball would emerge; it had rolled all the way to the wall, and could not be extracted by the cat's paw, even when extended to full length. Hurrli would seize the celluloid ball between his teeth and walk away in silent satisfaction. Another time we would hear the clatter of dishes in the kitchen. My wife, fearing mischief, would run to see what was happening. Hurrli had rolled his enamelled drinking bowl into the middle of the floor, and was sitting with an expectant eye cocked at the kitchen tap. "Perfectly clear," says the understanding cat-expert, "our poor boy is thirsty."

The companionship of this perfectly ordinary, common-or-garden stray added a great deal to the range of our knowledge. I believe that unprejudiced observation of an untrained animal brings you closer to understanding the mystery of the animal soul than elaborate experiments and logical reasoning. Generally speaking, we humans ought not to try to be too clever about animals; if we do, we erect artificial barriers between them and ourselves and create a rigid system of classification which remains intact only so long as we believe in it. People say, for instance, that dogs live by their noses, while cats rely almost entirely on their visual sense. Also that cats are far less attached to people than to their accustomed surroundings, furniture, kitchen and living-room. And then an ordinary tomcat like Hurrli comes along and quietly proves the exact opposite.

Let me now return to the beginning: we had travelled with Hurrli about fifteen kilometres from the Refuge to the Elk House. On the morning of our move I, in my wisdom, had given orders that special care should be taken of the cat. "The best thing would be to keep him locked on the first floor of the new house for the first five days, to give him a chance to get used to the new surroundings. If he runs out into the garden (which was then not yet fenced in) and into the wood, that will be the last we shall ever see of him; he will never find his way back to the strange house."

Well, it is easy enough for the head of the family to issue orders of this kind; but who can keep a constant eye on a freedom-loving cat that has never been locked up before, in the midst of unpacking endless trunks and boxes, especially when there is a constant flow of strangers through every room of the house? Briefly, in the afternoon of the third day Hurrli had vanished.

"Well, that's that. We shall never see him again," said I. "Most likely he will get shot by a gamekeeper for poaching." Great agitation, and much conscience-searching all round. In spite of all the piled-up work, my wife found time every so often to go out and sadly call her darling cat; but all in vain. Evening came, and not a trace of Hurrli. . . .

We went to bed late, partly on account of the unpacking, partly in the hope that we might still hear the familiar mew at the front door.

Towards five o'clock in the morning I suddenly awoke. The new day was beginning to dawn faintly through the wide open window, and outside there was a scratching on the level of the window-sill. "Impossible," said my reason, "this is the first floor, fifteen feet above the ground."

"And yet there's something scratching," said my hearing, "and now it has moved higher still."

As I sat up, I heard my wife whisper: "Can you hear it, too?" And in the same instant there was a despairing yowl from outside, and a dark body shot like a torpedo, twisting round to the left, through the open window and landed with a bounce on my blankets: Hurrli, our tom, not in the least contrite at having startled us so. For a few moments he twisted and turned, trying to find the most comfortable position, then fell cosily asleep at once.

Only the next morning, taking stock of the situation outside the house, was I able to understand exactly what had happened and what must have gone on in our pussy's mind.

Of course, I am only human, and I may be wrong: but this is what I *think* occurred.

Hurrli, accustomed to the peace and quiet of our old house, had been thoroughly upset by the noise of the removal men and his imprisonment in the new unfamiliar-smelling rooms. The fact that one or another of his human friends looked in to see him every now and then was no comfort. His instinct told him to get away, as quickly and as far as possible: the fundamental urge of his cave-dwelling, solitary, wild forebears.

And so, when at some point one of us had carelessly neglected to shut the door properly, the tabby slipped quickly and noiselessly down the stairs and out into the open. There, between the garden and the wood, many novelties awaited him: flying birds and rustling leaves, hiding-places in the grass, perhaps a mouse's track. The hours passed quickly; evening came, and all was quiet. 'This is the time to

be sitting in the living-room, with the mistress: that is where I want to be.' And so Hurrli sets out to find his way back. His own tracks on the ground have long since disappeared; but the general direction must have remained in his memory, and he soon found himself back among the houses. But that is where the trouble began. Where is the home of his choice, where is his human family, his beloved mistress? There are three houses within an area of a hundred yards in the clearing, and all three are entirely strange to Hurrli.

There will have been a long period of indecision, of running this way and that, until at last, in the middle of the night, Hurrli found the house to which he had been brought three days earlier in his closed basket. I could see later from the round footmarks in the sand that Hurrli had approached the house from many different directions, circling it again and again. Everywhere he tried to find a way in, but in vain: the big front door and all the windows on the ground floor were shut.

Perhaps the poor little creature in its homesickness will have looked longingly up the four walls of the house, and its sharp night-eyes will have noticed the windows on the upper floor were open. But I think it is much more likely that the sense of smell played the decisive part on that occasion; for in the end Hurrli stopped below the window from which a familiar human scent was wafted by the still night air. 'Up there are my friends,' he will have said to himself, and he was right, for he was standing directly beneath our bedroom window. (He could not have known it; he had never been inside that room, which in addition, faced towards the east, i.e., almost 180 degrees from the north-west room in which Hurrli had been locked up for three days.)

The cat's next actions were extraordinarily courageous and intelligent. He overcame all difficulties by his brain, and found his way home without help from anyone.

Two yards away from the front wall of my house stands the old, straight birch tree; the trunk is divided, so that one-half rises vertically about a yard and a half from the bedroom window. That is where Hurrli climbed in the early dawn; that is how he came closer and closer to the scent of 'his' humans; but he climbed on, past the window, until at last he made up his mind to hurl himself downwards and sideways through the dark shaft of the window. It must have been terribly hard, suddenly to disengage all four clawed feet from the birch bark, to push off for the jump, and to take threefold, unerringly accurate aim: downwards, to the left, and forwards from the window-sill into the room. Hence the long, scratching hesitation and, at last, the despairing cry. Hurrli had staked everything on a single chance.

And I believe that only one motive force could have been strong enough in the little animal's soul: love of us, his human friends.

That was in the late summer. Winter came, and at last another spring. Hurrli had long ago settled down in his new home; he knew every corner inside and outside the house, as far as the boundary of our property, and he demanded strict observance of that boundary from all strange animals. "Really, we don't need a watchdog," my wife would often say; "just look how our proud squire is patrolling his land. All that's missing is the bark."

Hurrli was very fond of the garden, my highly unprofessional mixed forest plantation with the dense network of paths trodden by our feet. Whenever, as a change from travelling, I was able to stay and work at my desk, and if my thinking suddenly came to a halt, I would walk quietly up and down between the young leafy trees, the bushes, flowers and herbs.

Only a few minutes of solitude: then, as if conjured up from the earth, there stands my pussy by my side. At home, Hurrli is always communicative; but now he does not make a sound and expects no words from me. With his tail high in the air he follows me wherever I go (the paths are not wide enough for two abreast) and I feel very strongly that he is happy now, although I never bend down to stroke him. And Hurrli goes for such companionable walks with other members of my household, too, particularly with my wife, who is the first favourite of his manly heart.

He loves her so much that he will even tolerate the grave faults which—so he thinks—mar her character. For the truth is that she loves all animals and has a kind word for all, even the strangers; she actually goes so far as to feed the white hens and the coloured rooster belonging to some distant neighbours.

Oh, how fiercely, with what a dangerous passion does Hurrli hate these impudent fowls that go scratching and clucking all day in search of nourishment in the wood! When he goes hunting in his turn, he stalks stiffly and with averted eyes (I might almost say contemptuously) through the midst of this noisy company: disapproval personified!

Once, and only once, did the rooster dare to assault him. The tomcat hissed, briefly, but so angrily that the bird learnt his lesson once and for all. Since then he has been wise enough to walk behind a solid advance guard of hens whenever he sees Hurrli coming.

Yes, a cat has plenty of trouble with his humans. If Hurrli could speak in our fashion, he would surely utter many reproachful words; for, to his visible annoyance, the mistress throws vegetable scraps over the fence, day after day. That is why all the fowls in the neighbourhood come waddling and squawking through the wood whenever my wife appears on the terrace. Sometimes they even wait for her to come out, clucking and calling, spread out in a long line. 'A disgusting spectacle,' thinks Hurrli no doubt, profoundly indignant, as he emerges from the house with his mistress; but he refrains from any action, for the other day he had to listen to a long severe scolding and was not allowed into the dining-room for a whole evening. And all he had done was to pull out a miserable couple of feathers out of the cheekiest hen's tail, as a warning, no more!

But there is one point on which Hurrli will not yield even to my wife. That is the matter of distance, of physical distance between the fowls and our house. Not even at feeding times are they allowed within more than a couple of human paces from the fence. If ever a young cockerel crosses the invisible boundary in his uncontrollable greed, Hurrli jumps up—with a single, infinitely graceful movement —on top of a pointed five-foot fence pole, keeping balance precariously on all four paws between the rows of barbed wire, and looks down so threateningly that the cockerel withdraws at once, followed by all the hens.

Then Hurrli turns his head to look at his beloved mistress, coos softly, and disappears among the trees, deeply satisfied. 'There must be a boundary between the neighbours and ourselves; I hope you will not deny it, woman.'

This grey tabby possessed a nature of extraordinary variety, proud yet affectionate, brimful with tenderness, absolutely motionless in the dreamy hours, then again bursting with life.

Once Hurrli bitterly fought and completely demolished a large squirrel who also had failed to observe the boundary of our garden: and, after he had devoured the vanquished adversary, bushy tail and all, he went on at once to play gracefully with a faded leaf. His life with us seemed to be the fulfillment of every imaginable wish; Hurrli remained splendidly natural and free, even as a domestic pet; all his surroundings, near and far, remained open to him at every hour.

Until one day a speeding motor-cycle in the woodland lane ran him down, pressing the little ribs into his lungs and heart. Now only a memory remains to us of all Hurrli's sweetness.

He lies buried in the garden, under a young birch tree; many bright wild flowers grow from the soil that covers Hurrli's body.

Whenever we passed the spot during the remainder of our time at the Elk House, we would repeat his special sound in melancholy greeting: "Urr-urrh!" Yet at the same time we were glad that his short life had been so rich in happiness, and that he had been spared the infirmities, the powerlessness of old age. With every breath he drew, our house cat Hurrli had enjoyed the full freedom of his wild nature and, equally, the love of human beings.

'Do you remember still, proud companion and prince, how once you came to our door, a wretched, skinny foundling, and begged your first bowl of milk from us? How long ago it is . . .'

The Mysterious Ra

MARGARET BENSON

RA had three periods of development. In the first, he showed himself cowardly and colorless; in the second, he sowed his wild oats with a mild and sparing paw; and in the third period it was borne in on us that whatever qualities of heart and head he displayed were but superficial manifestations, while the inner being of Ra, the why and wherefore of his actions, must forever remain shrouded in mystery.

We might have guessed this, had we been wise enough, from his appearance. His very color was uncertain. His mistress could see that he was blue—a very dark, handsome, blue Persian. Those who knew less than she did about cats called him black. One, as rash as she was ignorant, said he was brown; but as there are no brown cats Ra could not have been brown. Finally, a so-called friend named him "The Incredible Blue."

When the Incredible Blue sat at a little distance two large green eyes were all that could be discerned of his features. The blue hair was so extremely dark that it could be hardly distinguished from his black nose and mouth. This gave him an inexpressibly serious appearance.

The solemnity of his aspect was well borne out by the stolidity of his behavior. There is little to record during his youth except an unrequited attachment to a fox-terrier. In earlier days Ra's grandmother had been devoted to the same dog—a devotion as little desired and as entirely unreciprocated.

But it was necessary that Ra should leave the object of his devotion and come with us to live in a town; and now it became apparent that his affections had been somehow nipped in the bud. Whether it was the loss of the fox-terrier, the new fear of Taffy's boisterous pursuits, or the severity of his grandmother's treatment,—for the first time he came into close contact with that formidable lady,—whatever the reason may have been, it was plain that Ra's heart was a guarded fortress. He set himself with steady appetite to rid the house of mice, but he neither gave nor wanted affection.

He would accept a momentary caress delicately offered; but if one stroked him an instant too long, sharp, needle-like teeth took a firm hold of the hand. We apologized once to a cat-lover for the sharpness of Ra's teeth. "I think the claws are worse," was all he said.

Ra was an arrant coward. If a wild scuffle of feet was heard overhead we were certain that it was the small, agile grandmother in pursuit of Ra. If Taffy were seen careering over the lawn and leaping into the first fork of the mulberry-tree, it was because Ra had not faced him out for a moment, but was peering with dusky face and wide emerald eyes between the leaves.

Once or twice there was an atmosphere of tension in the house, no movement of cat or dog, and it was found that the three were fixed on the staircase unable to move—Taffy looking up from below with gleaming eyes, Granny malevolently scowling from above, and Ra in sight like Bagheera, in heart like a frightened mouse protected by the very fact that he was between the devil and the deep sea. Taffy did not dare to chase Ra for fear of the claws of the cat above; Granny did not care to begin a scrimmage downstairs, which would land them both under the dog's nose. So they sat, free but enthralled, till human hands carried them simultaneously away.

But the general tension of feeling grew too great. Ra's life was a burden through fear, Granny's through jealousy, Taffy's through scolding. Ra was sent off to a little house in London, and here his second stage of development began.

He had always been pompous, now he grew grand. It took ten minutes to get him through the door, so measured were his steps, so ceremonious the waving of his tail. He sat in the drawing-room in the largest armchair. Then it irked him that there was no garden, so he searched the street until he discovered a house with a garden, and he went to stay there for days together. A house opposite was being rebuilt, and Ra surveyed the premises and overlooked the workmen, sliding through empty window-frames and prowling along scaffolding with a weight of disapproval in his expression.

Thus Ra, who had hitherto caused no anxiety to his family, now became a growing responsibility; visions of cat stealers, of skin-dealers, of cat's-meat men, of policemen, and lethal chambers began to flit through the imagination whenever Ra was missing—which was almost always. So to save the nerves and sanity of his friends Ra left London.

We had now removed to the country, and greatly to our regret, though little to that of Ra, his ancient foe had passed from the scene; and although he felt it better to decline the challenges of the sandy kitten, yet he no longer believed his safety and his life to be in the balance; it was plain that he had realized his freedom, and would assume for himself a certain position in the household.

The house was a very old one; but Ra had been not long employed before the scurrying of feet over the ceiling was perceptibly lessened, and behind the mouldering wainscot the mouse no longer shrieked. That, indeed, is a lame, conventional way of describing the previous doings of the mice. Rather let us say that the mice no longer danced in the washing basins at night, nor ran races over the beds, not bit the unsheltered finger of the sleeper, nor left the row of jam-pots clean and empty.

If Ra had confined himself to this small game all would have been well, but he proceeded to clear the garden of rabbits. Day by day he went out and fetched a rabbit, plump and tender, and ate it for his dinner. It must at least be recorded that at this time he was practically self-supporting.

Three he brought to me. The first was dead, and I let him eat it; the second showed the brightness of a patient brown eye, and while I held Ra an instant from his prey, the little thing had cleared the lawn like a duck-and-drake shot from a skillful hand, and disappeared in the hedgerow.

The third was dead. I took it and shut up Ra. We "devilled" the rabbit hot and strong; we positively filled it with mustard, and returned it. Ra ate half with the utmost enjoyment, and the sandy kitten finished the rest.

Then came Ra's final aspiration. Unwitting of strings of cats' tails, dead stoats, and the gay feathers of the jay with which the woodland was adorned, he took to the preserves. We have no reason to think he hunted anything but the innocent field mouse or a plump rabbit for us to season; but with a deadly confidence he crossed the fields evening by evening in sight of the keeper's cottage.

If we had all been ancient Egyptians we should have developed his talent. The keeper would have trained him to retrieve, and he would gayly have accompanied the shooting parties. If I had even been the Marchioness of Carabas I should have turned the talent to account, and Ra, clad in a neat pair of Wellingtons, would have left my compliments and a pair of rabbits at all the principal houses in the neighborhood.

Prejudice was too strong for us. I won a truce for Ra until we could find a new home for him, and he departed in safety. I heard, to my relief, that he seemed quite happy and settled, and had bitten and scratched a large number of Eton boys.

Now up to his departure we had at once admired and despised Ra, but no one understood him. His appearance was so dignified, his spirit seemed so mean. He lent a silky head to be caressed, and while you still stroked him, without a sign of warning except the heavy thud of the last joint of his tail, he turned and bit. He addressed one in a small, delicate voice of complaint, yet wanted nothing. He followed me up and down in the garden with a sedate step; there were no foolish games in bushes, pretence of escape, hope of chase and capture. Happy or fearful, sociable or solitary, Ra was utterly self-contained.

Now hear the last act.

Ra began paying calls from his new home, and was established on a footing of intimacy at a neighboring house. As he sat in the drawing-room window there one morning, he watched the gardener planting bulbs. The gardener planted a hundred crocus bulbs and went home to dinner. No sooner was he gone than Ra descended, went to the bed, and dug up the bulbs from first to last. Then he returned to the drawing-room window.

The gardener came back, and lo! his hundred bulbs lay exposed. Nothing moved; no creature was to be seen but a cat with solemn face and green, disapproving eyes, who glared at him from the window.

The gardener replanted half his bulbs and went to fetch some tool; when he returned he seemed to himself to be toiling in a weird dream, for the bulbs he had replanted lay again exposed and the cat still sat like an image in the window.

Again he toiled at his replanting, and finally left the garden.

In a moment Ra descended upon it; with hasty paws he disinterred the crocuses, and laid the hundred on the earth. Then, shrouded still in impenetrable mystery, Ra returned home.

History does not relate whether or no the gardener consulted a brain specialist the following day.

Cat's Cruise

MAZO DE LA ROCHE

CAT was as black as a crow. This very blackness made her presence desired by sailors, who were sure it brought them good luck. She was not pretty, but she had charm which she had spent her life in exercising, to get what she wanted. She was eight years old, and she had woven into that eight years more travel and more adventure than most humans achieve in eighty. She had also brought forty-five kittens into the world.

She had been born on board a coaling vessel, the *Sultara,* in the midst of a terrible storm when the crew thought that every moment would be their last. Her mother was ginger-colored; and she had, while the vessel floundered in distress, produced three ginger-colored kittens besides this last one, black as the coal which formed the cargo. The stoker, looking gloomily at their squirming bodies, had growled:

"There'll be no need for us to drown *them*. The bloomin' sea'll do it!"

He picked up the black midget and held it in his hand. He felt an instant's compassion for it. It had come out of darkness and was so soon to return; yet there it lay, curved in his palm, bullet-headed, its intricate mechanism of tiny organs and delicate bones padded with good flesh, the flesh covered by thick silky fur, the whole animated by a spirit so vigorous that already ten little claws made themselves felt on his palm.

"If I could find a bottle the right size," he said, "I'd put you into it and chuck you into the sea. I'll bet you'd get to land!"

But there was no need to try the experiment. Miraculously, it seemed, the storm began to abate. The waves subsided; the vessel was got under control. One and all declared that they had been saved by the timely birth of the black kitten. It became the mascot, the idol of the ship.

They could not agree on a name for it. Some wanted a simple one, easy to say and descriptive of its color, such as Smut, Darkie, Jet or Nigger. Others insisted on some name which would suggest the rescue of their lives by the kitten's timely birth. One offered Nick-o'-Time, with Nick for short. But they could not agree. Then someone called her simply "Cat," and the others, in spite of themselves, acquiesced, as is often the case with names. From then on she was proudly, affectionately, known as "Cat" wherever she went.

She had a very round head, with small ears and narrow, clear green eyes. She had exceptionally long, glossy whiskers above a large mouth that displayed needle-sharp teeth in a three-cornered smile or a ferocious grin when her emotions were stirred. Her tail was sleek and sinuous and almost never still. Happy was the sailor round whose neck she wound it. Her attentions were known to bring good luck.

As she grew up she reigned supreme on the vessel. Nothing was too good for her. If what she wanted was not given her at once, she climbed on to the neck of the man who withheld it and put both arms (you could not call them forelegs, because she used them ex-

actly like arms) round his neck and peered into his eyes out of the
narrow green slits of her own. If he did not at once surrender, she
pressed her stubby nose on first one side of his face, then on the other,
while with her claws she massaged the weather-beaten back of his
neck. If he were still obdurate, or perhaps mischievous enough still
to deny her, she reversed her position and put her claws into his
thigh. Gladly he gave her then whatever she desired.

She had a loud vibrant purr, and when she moved gracefully along
whatever deck she was favoring with her presence, purring and swaying her long tail, a feeling of reassurance and tranquility came to all
on board . . . It was a bitter thing to the crew of the coaling vessel
on which she had been born when, at the time of her first litter, she
deserted them for a Norwegian schooner. The captain could scarcely
persuade the crew to sail. The docks at Liverpool were combed for
her without success. The voyage was one of rough weather and general dissatisfaction.

At that time the Norwegians had not heard of her. They had their
own cat, and did not want another. But she soon won them over, and
they had the most successful voyage they had ever known. When they
next called at Liverpool, the mate boasted of Cat in the hearing of
one of the crew of the *Sultara*. He boasted of her intelligence, of her
blackness, of the luck she brought.

On board the *Sultara* there was joy when they learned that she was
safe, rage when they heard that she was living with the Norwegians.
They visited the foreigners and saw for themselves the cat was "Cat."
They found that she had a litter of ginger-colored kittens. But the
Norwegians would not give her up. They would give up one or all
of her ginger-colored litter, but they would not give up "Katt."

The crew of the *Sultara* hung about the docks with scraps of kipper
in their pockets, because Cat had a weakness for kippers; but the
Norwegians guarded Katt with terrible efficiency. When, however,
she chose to go ashore, nothing could stop her. A morsel of kipper
was proffered her at the right moment. She mounted the shoulder of
the giver, and was borne in triumph to her birthplace. She gave evidence of the greatest pleasure in her reunion with the crew, who
were ready to weep with joy at recovering her.

Cat remained with them for two voyages. Then again she disappeared, this time in favor of an oil tanker bound for the East . . .
And so it went on, this life of change and adventure. She chose her
ships. She remained on them till her love of variety prompted her to
seek another lodging. But wherever she sailed, she brought good
luck, and at regular intervals, she returned to the *Sultara*. On all the

Seven Seas she produced litters of ginger or gray kittens, but never one of her own glittering black. She held herself unique. She was Cat.

Now, on a morning in late February, she glided down the gangway of the *Greyhound,* which had just limped into port after an Antarctic relief expedition. The voyage had lasted for six months, and had been one of the mistakes of Cat's life, so far as her own pleasure was concerned.

The captain and crew of the *Greyhound* had been delighted when she sauntered aboard. The seal of success, they felt, had been set on the expedition. And they were right. The lost explorers had been discovered, living, though in desperate plight. Cat's reputation was still more enhanced.

But she herself was disgruntled, through and through. She had never, in all her years of travel, experienced such a voyage. She felt disillusioned; she felt ill. She felt like scratching the first hand that was stretched out to pat her.

"Hullo, Cat!" exclaimed a burly dock-hand. "So you're back from the Pole? And what captain are you going to sign up with next?" He bent to scratch her neck, but she eluded him and glided off with waving tail.

"Cat don't look very bright," observed another dock-hand.

"She's fed up, I expect, with the length of the last voyage," said the first speaker, staring after her. "She don't generally go for such long one. *And* the weather! *And* the grub! She could have done much better for herself, and she knows it."

He turned to one of a crew which was about to sail for Norway.

"Hi, Bob! Here's Cat! Just back from the South Pole. P'raps you can make up to her."

Bob approached, grinning. He planted himself in Cat's way, and held two thick tarry hands down to her.

"Puss, puss!" he wheedled. "Coom along wi' us. Tha can have whativer tha wants. Tha knaws me, Cat."

She knew Bob well, and liked him. She suffered herself to be laid across his breast and she gave him a long look out of her narrow green eyes. He felt her ribs with his blunt fingers.

"She's naught but fur and bone," he declared.

"Her's been frettin' fer home," said the first.

"The sea is her home," said Bob. "But she's a dainty feeder. S'll I carry thee off, Cat?"

She began softly to purr. She relaxed in every fiber. The tip of her tongue showed between her lips. She closed her eyes.

"She'll go with you," said the dock-hand, and Bob began to pick his way among the crates and bales, carrying Cat hopefully in his arms.

She heard the varied sounds of the docks, the shouts, the hoarse whistles of ships, the rattle of chains, smelled the familiar smells. It was music and sweetness to her after her long absence. She surrendered herself to the rhythmic movement of Bob's big chest.

In triumph he deposited her on his own deck. The rest of the crew stopped in their work for a moment to welcome her. The cook brought her a brace of sardines.

For politeness' sake she ate one; but left the other on the deck. She arched herself against the legs of the first mate and gave her three-cornered smile. A ray of feeble sunlight struggled through the wintry fog and fell across her. She began to think she might sail with this crew.

"Keep an eye on her," said the mate to a cabin-boy. "Don't let her out of your sight till we're away."

All about was hurry and noise. Cat sat on the deck washing the oil of the sardine from her whiskers. The pale sunshine surrounded her, but deep within her, there was dissatisfaction growing. This was not what she wanted, and soon it would be too late to return to the docks. She would be in for another long, cold voyage.

Her little round black head looked very innocent. Her eyes were tight shut. Methodically she moved her curved paw over her face.

Someone called the boy, and forgetting the earlier order, he ran off. Cat was galvanized into life and movement. She flew along the deck. In another instant she would be on the docks. But Bob saw her, and caught her in his huge hands. She liked him; still she did not weaken. She thrust her claws into his hands, and with a yell of triumph and every hair erect, escaped.

It was some time before she regained her calm. She slunk among legs, among trucks, through scattered straw and trampled mud. The fog thickened again, settling clammily on her fur. It was bitterly cold. What she wanted was solitude. She was sick of the sight and sound of men and their doings.

She entered a warehouse and passed between tiers of wooden boxes and bales, stopping to sniff now and again when some smell attracted her. The cold in this building was very penetrating. Was she never to know warmth again?

In a dim shed she found stalls, all empty except one in which a prize ram was awaiting shipment to America, where he was to be used for breeding. She clambered up the partition of the stall and perched there, gazing down at him. She did not remember having seen anything like him before. His yellow gaze was as inscrutable as hers.

With paws tucked under her breast she sat enjoying the sight of him. She stared at his massive wooly shoulders, his curly horns, his restless pawing hoofs. He lowered his head and butted the manger in front of him with his hard skull. Cat felt that she could watch him forever.

The gruff whistles of the ships shook the hoary air. The faint sunlight coming in at the cobwebbed window was shut off by a curtain of gray dusk. Cat and the ram were wrapped about by a strange intimacy. The chill increased. The docks became almost silent. The ram gave a bereft *baa* and sank to his knees.

Now he was only a pale mound in the dusk, but Cat still stared at him. He was conscious of her too; and like some earth-bound spirit, he raised his yellow gaze to the glimmering stars of her eyes.

Toward midnight the cold became unbearable to her. On the Antarctic expedition she had slept in the bunk with a well-fleshed sailor. Now a thin rime was stiffening every hair of her coat. She rose stiffly and stretched. Her tail hung powerless. Some message, some understanding, passed between her and the ram.

She leaped from the partition and landed between his shoulders. She sank into the deep oily warmth of his wool. He remained motionless, silent as the hill where he had pastured.

She stretched herself out on him with a purr of delight. She sought to feel his flesh with the fine points of her claws through the depth of his wool. A smell new to her rose from his body, and the beginning of a *baa* stirred in his throat. Their two bodies united in the quiet breathing of sleep. Her sleep was light, of a pale luminous quality, always just on the edge of waking; but his was dark and heavy, as though he were surrounded by shaggy furze and thick heather.

A dense fog rose from the sea at dawn and pressed thickly into the stall. With it crept a long gray cat with a white blaze on his face, and his ears torn by fighting. He scrambled up the partition of the stall and peered down at the two below. He dropped to the manger, and from there to the straw. He touched Cat tentatively.

She had been conscious of his approach. It had brought into her dreams a vague vision of a tawny striped cat she had met in Rio de Janeiro, where the relief ship had called. But the touch of the paw galvanized her. She gave a shriek and driving her hind paws into the ram's back, she reared herself and struck at the intruder's face as though she would put her mark on it forever.

But he was not easily frightened off. He sprang to the ram's back also, and through the fog Cat saw his white face grinning at her. He set his teeth in the back of her neck. They both shrieked.

The ram's deep, dark, warm slumber was shattered into fright. He bounded up, with a clatter of hoofs, overthrowing the cats. His white eyelashes flickered. He glared in primeval rage and lowered his head to charge.

The cats scrambled agilely over the partition and dropped to the stone floor outside, their tails enormous. They sped in opposite directions into dim corners of the shed. The battering of the ram's head against the door of the stall echoed through the fog.

As Cat reached her corner, a mouse flickered out of the gloom, squeaking in an agony of fear, and shot past her. With a graceful flourish of her limber body she turned completely round and captured the mouse with that one effective movement. She picked it up delicately in her teeth and crouched in the corner.

After a time the door opened and two men came in. They turned on a light, and the interior of the shed was revealed in foggy pallor. The men entered the stall where the ram was. There came strange bumping sounds. The men cursed. Then they appeared leading the ram, roped by the horns. He was led out helpless, his little hoofs pattering on the stone floor. He uttered a plaintive, lamblike *baa*. The men left the door open behind them.

Cat discovered the body of the mouse. It now meant nothing to her. She glided out onto the docks, wondering what ship she would sail in. She passed among them as they were dimly revealed, cargoes being loaded or unloaded, men working like ants. She felt a dim wonder at their activity, a faint disdain for their heaving bodies.

Toward noon, when a shabby blurred disk showed where the sun was, she came upon a passenger-ship just departing on a West India cruise. She had never sailed on a passenger-ship. They were an untrustworthy and strange world, and she hated the sight of women.

As she stood pessimistically surveying it, a kitchen worker tossed a slice of chicken-breast through a porthole to her. She crouched on the pier devouring it, while shivers of delight made her separate hairs quiver. She had not known that such food existed. After it was gone, she sat beaming toward the porthole, but nothing more was thrown out.

Luggage was being loaded onto the ship, and a throng of people of a sort she had never before seen, hastened up the gangway. One of them, a man, bent and gently massaged the muscles in the back of her neck, before he passed on. She beamed after him. She had not known such hands existed, so smooth, so tender. They were like the breast of chicken she had just devoured.

She rose, chilled by the clammy cold, and glided up the gangway onto the ship.

She knew that she was a stranger here, and some instinct told her that quite possibly she might not be welcome. She slunk along the innumerable white passages, making herself as nearly invisible as possible. She glanced in at the doors of staterooms, as she passed. Generally there were women inside, and sometimes the rather disgusting smell of flowers was in the air.

Cat heard the thunder of the whistle. She felt a quiver go through the ship. She had a mind to get off it while there was yet time, but she felt powerless to turn herself away from the delicious warmth that was radiated from every corner of the liner. It made her feel yielding, soft. She wanted something cozy to lie down on.

She paused at the door of a cabin that was empty except for the promise of a man's coat and hat thrown on the berth. She went in and walked round it, purring. She held her tail stiffly erect, all but the tip, which moved constantly as though it were, in some subtle way, gauging the spiritual atmosphere of the cabin.

Gregg, the swimming-instructor, found her there, curled up on his coat. They had left the docks, so she could not be put ashore. He recognized her as the cat he had caressed and supposed that she belonged on the liner. He tucked her under his arm and carried her to the kitchen quarters. The boy who had thrown her the morsel of chicken recognized her. He had once been galley-boy on an oil tanker she had favored with her presence.

"It's Cat," he explained. " 'Aven't yer never 'eard tell of Cat? W'y, we're in luck, mister! And yer ought to be proud to share your berth wiv 'er!"

But Gregg did not want to share his berth with Cat, even after he had heard her history and virtues. He dumped her down and rather glumly retraced his steps. He felt a shrinking from the long cruise that stretched ahead of him. To be sociable was a part of his job, and he hated the thought of sociability.

He had, in fact, seen too much of people. He had had more experience of society than was good for him. He was not yet thirty, but he had lost a fair-sized fortune, the woman he loved, and worst of all, his hope and his fortitude. He had been at his wits' end to find a job, when a friend had got him this post as swimming-instructor. He was in a state bordering on despair, but here he was bound to seem cheerful and gay, to take a passionate interest in the flounderings of fat passengers in the pool.

No one on board was so out of sympathy with the cruise as was he. Indeed, everyone on board was in sympathy with the cruise but Gregg and Cat, who did not at all understand cruising for pleasure.

She was there in his berth waiting for him when he returned to his cabin that night, having found her way through all the intricacy of glittering passages. He was a little drunk, for he was very attractive, and people insisted on treating him. The sight of Cat lying there on his bed angered him. He was about to put her out roughly, when she rolled over on her back, turned up her black velvet belly and round little face with the glittering eyes narrowed and the three-cornered smile showing her pink tongue. He bent over her, pleased in spite of himself.

"You're a rogue," he said. "But you can't get around me like that."

For answer she clasped her forepaws round his neck and with her hind paws clawed gently on his shirt front. She pressed her face on his, and purred loudly in his ear.

"Cheek to cheek, eh?" said Gregg, and gave himself up to her hypnotic overtures.

Morning found them snuggled close together. He sent the steward for a dish of milk for her. He appeared at the swimming-pool with her on his shoulder. She basked in the heavenly warmth of the place.

From that time, she spent her days by the pool. Tolerantly, almost benignly, she watched the skill or awkwardness of the swimmers. When the pool was deserted, she crouched by its brink gazing at her reflection, dreaming of lovely fish that might have graced it. At night she slept with Gregg. She thrived immensely.

When they were in sparkling southern waters, Cat disappeared early one evening. She met Gregg at the door of his cabin with a tremulously excited air. She advanced toward him, purring, then turned her back and flaunted her sinuous black tail. She looked back at him over her shoulder. Her head and tail met. She caught the tip of it in her mouth and lay down on her back, rolling coyly from side to side. She looked strangely slender.

"So you've been and gone and done it," said Gregg. "Not on the bed, I hope!"

No, not on the bed. In the wardrobe, where Gregg's soft dressing-gown had somehow fallen from the peg. There were three of them, all plump, all tawny, like the gentleman in Rio de Janeiro.

Next day Gregg got a nice box with a cushion and put the kittens in it. He carried them to the balmy warmth of the air that surrounded the swimming-pool, and all the bathers gathered to admire and stroke them. They were the pets of the ship. But Cat cared only for Gregg. She fussed over him far more than she did over her kittens. She refused to stay with them by the pool at night, so the box had to be carried to his cabin. There she would sit waiting for him, her glowing eyes fixed on the door, every nerve tuned for his coming.

But on one night, he did not come. She waited and waited, but he did not come. At last she sprang up from suckling her kittens, and they fell back like three tawny balls. The door was fixed ajar. She glided through the opening and began her search for him.

The smoke-room was closed; the lounge was empty, the decks deserted except for a pacing figure in uniform. At last Cat saw Gregg standing, still as a statue, in a secluded corner where a lifeboat hung. Silent as the shadows cast by moonlight, she drew near to him. But she did not rub herself against his leg as usual. She climbed into the lifeboat, and over its edge, peered down into his face.

That night Gregg felt alone—lost. In spite of the moonlight, the myriad glittering waves, the world was black to him. The life on this luxurious liner, among these spoiled shallow people, was suffocating him; he could not breathe. He looked back on his own life as a waste, on his future with despair. He had made up his mind to end it all.

Cat watched him intently as he leaned against the rail. If he had been her prey, she could not have observed him with more meticulous concentration as he mounted it. Just before he would have leaped over the side, she sprang onto his shoulders with a shriek that curdled the blood of those whose staterooms gave on that deck. She not only shrieked, but she drove every claw into Gregg. She turned herself into a black fury whose every hair stood on end, whose eyes glared with hate and fear at that gulf below . . .

"I don't know what the devil is the matter with her," Gregg said to the officer who hastened up. "She's as temperamental as a prima donna." His hand shook as he stroked her.

But she had saved him from his black mood, saved him from his despairing self. When he was undressed, he looked with wonder at the little bloody spots on his shoulders . . . Cat slept on his chest.

He made up his mind that he would never part with her. He owed her a debt which could only be repaid by the certainty of affection and gentle living for the rest of her days. He would find lodgings where she would be welcome.

But Gregg reckoned without Cat. By the time they reached port, she was sick to death of the luxury liner. There was not a smell on board that pleased her. She liked Gregg, but she could do without him. She liked her three plump kittens, but the quality of real mother love did not exist in her. She loved the sea and the men who spent their days in strenuous work on the sea. She disliked women and scent and all daintiness. She was Cat; she could not change herself.

In the confusion of landing, no one saw her slip ashore. She vanished like a puff of black smoke. It was as lovely a morning as any they had seen on the cruise. The air was balmy, the sky above the docks blue as a periwinkle. When Cat reached the places she was accustomed to, she purred loudly and rubbed herself against tarry trouser-legs, arched her neck to horny hands. But she was coy. She would not commit herself. For a fortnight she lived on the dock, absorbing the satisfying smells of fresh timber, straw, tar, salt fish, hemp, beer, oil and sweat. She even renewed acquaintance, this time more amiably though with loud screams, with the gray-furred gentleman who had called on her in the ram's stall.

At last she sailed on a cattle-ship, and all her past was as nothing to her!

James Goes Serenading

JENNIE LAIRD

"The Devil hath not, in all his quiver's choice,
An arrow for the heart like a sweet voice."
BYRON

LATE that night Muffet sat on the top of her bicycle shed, looking out over the neighboring gardens. All around her the white world was at peace. Asleep in their beds, the flowers were folded tight, wet-headed with dew, while in their nests the smaller birds lay silent; though the hunting owl that lived in Muffet's own elm tree was awake and hooting. Huddled in their houses, the human beings breathed heavily, some too heavily, in preparation for another day's toil in the service of those who own the earth and stalk it fearlessly at night.

Only the Armstrongs' rough-haired buffoon seemed disconsolate, as he sat outside his kennel and mourned. Perhaps, poor fool, he longed for the pale-gold moon that hung in the clear night sky. Or regretted, perhaps, the bareness of the bone that lay before him, gnawed and polished into ivory.

As Muffet sat ghostly white on her bicycle shed, she became aware of stealthy agitation in the gardens all around her. Dark shapes were moving, dark shadows were gathering, and where a few moments ago all had been pale and still, the earth was opening and giving forth multiple living forms that slid soundlessly along the paths, walls and fences. Expressionlessly she stared down at the shifting scene, noting with little surprise that out of the many furtive shapes the majority were headed in the direction of the Andersons' dustbin. . . . Black, tawny and striped, old, middling and young, one-eyed, battle-scarred or sound of limb, a spectral army thronged to answer the summons of the young spring night.

On other roof tops, shed tops, fences and back porches lesser and plainer Helens sat waiting for the tournament to begin. The yellow-and-green jewels of their eyes were dotted in an irregular string through the dark-blue air. Mothers of families many of them, as well as inexperienced girls and their elderly chaperones—all were young at heart, all inwardly illumined by the white-hot flame of anticipation, and they took their breath deliberately to steady the speed of their heartbeats.

But among them Muffet was queen. She shone in the palm of the moon's hand, softer than snow dust, whiter than nougat. . . . Her wide eyes gave forth a sea-blue incandescence. As the heroes silently assembled, she noted with satisfaction that those whose ears, eyes and limbs appeared the most intact were moving toward the Andersons' dustbin, and presently she stood up, arched her back, and began to make her way thither.

> "How shall I woo thee, O beautiful she-cat
> Piercing my soul with the spears of thy glances?
> How can I tell thee the tale of my love?
> Queen Cleopatra looks under thine eyelids,
> Venus anew in thy person advances,
> Come to me, come, my Medusa, my dove."

James was rehearsing his serenade as he trotted along the road toward the Anderson establishment. His heart was full of love and expectation, and as he padded along the shining road, inhaling the fragrance of the Garden City spring, he ignored the scurrying snacks that bolted across the road in front of him. Small mice, adolescent rabbits—various little rodents suffered unnecessary palpitations as he passed, singlehearted, murmuring to himself, "Come to me, come, my Medusa."

It was the custom for a suitor to compose a song for his ladylove. He would rough it out beforehand, and relying on the inspiration of the moment, half remember, half improvise when the time came for him to sing it. The merit of the song was as important a factor in courtship as the power of one's personality or the beauty of one's physique. Some overromantic shes could be won by a male of quite miserable appearance, as long as he possessed a full, rich voice and the gift of fluency. Ah, yes, with the willful blindness of her sex, many a she would ignore the merits of some fine, steady cat who unfortunately could not sing a note, and cast herself upon the bosom of a tuneful seducer who desired no more than a moment's pleasure.

James himself sang very well, and up to now would have frankly placed himself in the second category. But as he thought of the charms of Muffet, he felt more than ordinarily moved; indeed, he

could almost imagine her forever lovely and himself forever faithful
—he quickened his pace, for here was Westward Ho.

He entered the front garden through a gap in the hedge and followed the crazy paving around to the back of the house. Where was
she, where, the adorable, the white one? Clearing his throat in readiness, he sang a few notes to get the pitch; and even as he did so the
song died in his throat. At a glance, he knew that he was betrayed.

There she sat, the Queen of Perfidy, enthroned on the dustbin;

not for him alone, but holding court. She was surrounded by a semicircle of silent, motionless figures, and other figures were spaced at
intervals over the garden. The air was charged with tension. Every
ear was pricked up to its most acute, every brain alert, and every
furred chest contained a strongly determined heart. This was no love
tryst, as he had expected, but a tournament, a public contest for a she,
a ceremony ranking in importance second only to the Council. James
took the scene in at a glance; and even as he watched, the tournament
began.

A low, throaty cry two gardens away gave the signal, and one of Muffet's company—a sturdy ginger with white whiskers, diabolically slanting eyes and a crescent-shaped scar on his nose—lifted up his slightly nasal tenor in the first round of the competition. He was followed by a heavy black basso profundo, whose rich cadences began to swell forth with such fruity ardor that feminine hearts gave a bound, and a young she-tabby whispered on a roof top, "Who is that handsome black male with the beautiful voice?"

"Oh, he lives at Singapore," replied her neighbor. "Not a bad type, but rather pompous. I knew him rather well last year," she added nonchalantly. "What was that?" They listened attentively. James had suddenly come to his senses. He flung back his head, and even as the third competitor was opening his mouth to begin, James's full baritone forestalled him. Hot with anger and determination, he stood where he was and sang out to the stars with all the passion in his nature. As the wild notes pealed forth, all heads swung in his direction, and Muffet laid back her ears to listen. In the garden of Aburi, the Armstrongs' buffoon moaned and rattled his chains.

Two competitors rose and walked away, overcome by James's technique. But a bold and brindled suitor was not afraid to open his mouth, and after him two more—one of whom, being tone-deaf, was immediately counted out by a low, disapproving chorus of moans and hisses from all sides. Muffet stood up, stretched, turned sideways to the assembly to show her profile, and the second round began.

Rising to his feet and moving a few paces forward, the ginger cat again opened his mouth and let inspiration carry him away. So far did it carry him that before long a window was flung open, a head protruded, and the raucous voice of Mr. Anderson cried, "Aaaaaaahh! Get away!" Unhesitatingly, the ginger cat swallowed his uprising notes and side-stepped, avoiding the splash of cold water which his instinct told him would follow. As he expected, it fell on his neighbor, the basso profundo, who gave a high-pitched scream and shot behind a lavender bush. The assembly froze into position. Silence reigned, save for an occasional ejaculation from behind the lavender bush, where a frantic toilet was being performed.

"Geeeeeeertcha!" repeated the domestic threateningly, and hearing no more, shut the window and went back to bed.

The vulgar interruption was no surprise to the competitors, familiar as they were with human nature. Persecution of the sublime by the ridiculous was to them an everyday occurrence, and after the usual ninety-six seconds' pause the contest was fearlessly resumed. It was not long before James's turn came around again. He took a deep breath, closed his eyes, and once more summoned Apollo to his aid.

He sang in a tender, throaty voice that made the sleeping flowers unconsciously unfold their leaves, and Muffet's chilly little heart begin to grow warm. . . . Tears welled up in the spectators' eyes. . . . But the slant-eyed ginger tenor sat, with offensive indifference, washing his feet. This did not escape James, who when he had finished, stalked to the foot of the dustbin, seated himself and glared a challenge at the reduced semicircle. A fortunate move, for at that very moment half a dozen windows were flung up, and half a dozen voices bellowed in fury, and half a dozen arms hurled assorted missiles at the place where he had been standing. An article of footwear narrowly missed Muffet, bouncing off the dustbin with a clang. She looked at it scornfully and did not budge. As the bombardment continued, the cavaliers leaped to their feet, but not in flight. Skillfully they dodged, crouched and side-stepped, avoiding the hurtling objects as narrowly as possible, for coolness and daring in the face of danger was one of their knightly virtues.

Conspicuous in the moonlight and exquisitely groomed, the basso profundo reappeared from behind the lavender bush, and strolled down the middle of the lawn toward the rockery, daring Fate. But alas! It was his unlucky night. A piece of hard fruit struck him on the side of the head, and staggering slightly, he moved to the side and sat down. Presently he quitted the scene. But he need not have despaired. Her heart brimming with love and pity, the young shetabby slipped down from the roof and made her way softly toward him. . . .

Then James arose, advanced to the dustbin and, looking Muffet straight in the eyes, lifted up his heavenly voice. Her gaze fell before the meaning in his. Nervously dabbing at a fern, she averted her head and listened while he sang. Three more competitors threw up the sponge and walked away.

But the red knight had also advanced to the foot of the rock, and sat grimly waiting. The remaining competitors gave up hope and settled down to watch.

Hardly had James uttered the last note when it was taken up and derisively repeated in a voice that made the moon rock in the sky. The Armstrongs' buffoon bellowed more loudly than ever, many human voices joined in, the owl hooted, a young domestic cried, a gun went off, and there were sounds of breaking crockery, and of boots thudding on wooden sheds, and windows were noisily opened and closed, and competitors from other gardens all around fell silent in order to listen to the tremendous din. Higher and higher, louder and louder in admirable counterpoint strove the alternating voices of James and his rival, paying no heed to the whizzing missiles nor to the cries of despair from the servants' quarters. Pandemonium reigned, and sleep fled precipitate from the Garden City.

Now James reached the climax of his song. Quivering from head to foot, his eyes fixed on Muffet, his haunches tensed, he crouched ready to spring and claim her under the very nose of the other.

> *"Now comes thine hour, O thou frozen enchantress,*
> *Now shalt thou yield, for thy fate is pursuing,*
>   *Now is the union of Venus and Mars.*
> *Vain are thy prayers and thy loud lamentations,*
> *Beautiful she, thou hast met thine undoing—*
>   *Now art thou mine in the sight of the stars!"*

As the verse ended the red one sensed James's intention, and sprang even as he sprang, and turned to face him with snarl and uplifted paw. James paused to calculate his aim, and struck!

This was no hasty battle, but one of few blows, carefully timed and unexpectedly aimed. The two were expert strategists; a feint with a left paw, a dab with the right, and then a long sweep at the face with the left. Suddenly they would clinch, and clasping each other around the neck, sway as if in a dance, seeking to bite each other's throat or ear. Absorbed in the struggle, they soon forgot about the white shape crouching on the rockery and fought on for the wild pleasure alone. It was a strange, nightmarish performance, with all the controlled grace of ballet and all the menace of death. Silently, like shadows on a screen, the two dark figures bobbed and swayed, anonymous in the uncertain light, and all around them a ring of colored pinpricks blinked attentively. Save for low murmurs from the spectators' throats and an occasional stifled cry from one of the combatants as he lunged or parried, there was no sound. Mr. Anderson took the cotton wool out of his ears and sighed with relief, then felt for the rubber hot-water bottle with his feet. It was cold, and he kicked it out of bed, then settled down to sleep again, under the impression that all was over.

He was mistaken. A second later there came a wild squawk from outside, where the young she-tabby, though still full of admiration for the basso profundo, was finding his behavior a little unnerving. Mr. Anderson leaped out of bed, flung up the window, seized the hot-water bottle and hurled it from him with all his force. Alas! It landed fair and square on James, knocking him off his balance, bursting open at the seam and soaking him with water. He turned his head, dazed and unwary, and unscrupulously the red one fell on him, bit his ear, tore his face open, dealt him a couple of violent blows and leaped victoriously up onto the dustbin. James shut his eyes. His senses left him in a blind, whirling flash. . . . Thirty seconds elapsed before he could focus—to discover that Muffet, the red cat, and all the spectators had disappeared.

When he left the garden a little later, all was quiet, save for a rustling and a whispering among the bushes, which swayed a little, perhaps with the night wind. No voice spoke, and it must have been in his imagination that he heard, mockingly repeated, the last line of the last verse of his own love song—

"Now art thou mine in the sight of the stars!"

With a wail of despair, he turned and made off, dripping, down the road for home.

Birl Forms a Friendship

ALEXANDER M. FREY

BIRL hurried down the ladder, stepping from one rung to the next with the elegant agility of a cat, and never missing a single one of the thin rounds. She was in haste because she wanted to be at her post. If it should happen to be George coming home she felt it her duty to hand over the estate of which she had been unofficial caretaker.

The door opened—and it was George who came in. Birl did not know him, for she had not yet been born when he departed. But she found out at once that it was he, for behind him entered the two men who had come after the old woman's death, and the one rattling the bunch of keys boomed: "Well, Mr. Trumm, we hereby faithfully hand over your house to you. It is just as your deceased mother left it."

Birl heard George reply in a low, sad voice. "Alas that my mother is dead," he said. "Through many a long and cold night in foreign parts I thought of her. I was often warmed by the thought of sitting with her again in this room."

"Sorrowing won't help," the gruff man answered. "What's gone is gone. . . . Let's open the shutters." And he pulled the shutters roughly apart, letting in the light.

Birl watched while George stood shivering in the bare and dusty room and looking around him—George, the son of the kind old woman with whom she had lived happily for so many years. Would she not also get on well with the son? He was pale and thin and there were lines of grief around his youthful mouth. But although he now seemed distant and unhappy, Birl felt instantly drawn to him.

However, she did not like these two men who had made such grand and boastful gestures and had said, "We hereby hand over your house to you, Mr. Trumm." What had they done for the house? They had made it dark, locked it up and left it to its fate—the sad

fate of all deserted houses: gradual decay and ruin. No one had stirred a hand to replace a rotting board here or a broken roof slate there. The mice would long since have chewed hundreds upon hundreds of holes in everything, perhaps would have brought down the whole trembling structure, if she, Birl, had not been there. But these two men who had done nothing at all for Master George's house were now saying with hypocritical pompousness: "We have taken good care of your property."

But if Birl did not like them, the two men had no liking for her either. In the bright daylight that now flooded into the room they caught sight of Birl, and they began to bellow: "There's that worthless beast, still here. It isn't our fault, Mr. Trumm. We took care to chase her out before we locked the place up. Take our word for it, we were unremitting in our care for your property. But the vile creature must have crept in again through one of the holes in the wall or the roof—there are lots of them. And of course, Mr. Trumm, we couldn't do anything about that; we couldn't be expected to make repairs."

After repeating these assurances several times, they tried to make Birl responsible for the deplorable state of things which was now revealed. "Look at that!" they exclaimed. "The filthy cat has dragged all the straw out of the mattress, and she's gnawed a huge hole in the cupboard over here. Horrible beast!"

In George's heart sorrow over this sad homecoming was mingled with a mounting rage. The two men succeeded in their purpose; they turned his mind from the thought that possibly it was the fault of human beings that his house now presented such a shabby appearance. They had diverted him very cunningly, and now they cast all the blame for neglect and damage upon Birl.

For the moment at least George believed them. "Get out!" he too shouted, and kicked out at the cat. Birl realized that he was so angry and depressed that he could not think clearly, and therefore she decided that it was best to abandon the field for the present. Without a sound, and before the heavy boots of her two enemies started to swing toward her, she slipped out of the room. Behind her she heard one of the men reviling her: "The ugly beast must be always getting into fights. Her nose is all torn up and the whole floor is stained with spots of blood."

Birl left the three men to themselves. There was no chance of reasoning with them, since two were hardhearted and bad men who did not want to be different and the third had been deceived and roused to anger by the other two. But she did not feel that George was lost to her. She hoped he would soon come to his senses and examine the house. Then he would see whether or not Birl was really a good-for-nothing.

She sat down on the plank over the stream and watched the little fish. But none of them was inclined to swim near her paw today. And so she passed the time reflecting on the ways of men. People are always accusing cats of being deceitful, she thought. And of course, any cat treated as I have just been treated would have to become deceitful. Bad treatment creates badness. That is true of men and no less true of cats. How unjust human beings tend to be. Their observation of animals is shoddy and often they don't understand at all what we really want. When our claws sometimes hook a bit of their skin while we're playing with their fingers, they ought to realize that we never meant to hurt them. Anyway, why do they have such a tender skin instead of a pelt? If they had fur our sharp claws would slip off without hiding them. It isn't our fault that they're so unformed.

It is a sad truth, Birl reflected further, that people know so little about us animals. George is really a good man at heart—I can sense that with my feline intuition. But those two nasty hypocrites have talked him into believing something utterly stupid. He *is* gullible to believe that I made that hole in the cupboard. Do those idiots really imagine we cats can gnaw holes in wooden boards? We certainly couldn't, even if we wanted to. My dear George, you might have spent dull moments in that forest of yours, meditating whether cats enjoy gnawing round holes in the doors of cupboards. If you'd thought about it, you might have realized that such things are done by quite another kind of creature. It's really insulting to have men in their ignorance lump us together with rats and other rodents.

Amid such musings the afternoon passed. When dusk fell, a strong breeze sprang up over the stream, parting Birl's white fur in places so that her pink skin was exposed to the cool air. Then Birl decided to risk a visit to the house.

The two bad men had gone long ago. Birl squeezed in through the tiniest of her loop-holes. We'll see what mood he's in, she thought wisely. She waited in the farthest corner of the kitchen until she saw that George continued to sit motionless at the table, staring at the flame of a candle which was again burning tonight, after so long a time. Then, moving with graceful diffidence, Birl emerged from her corner.

The man looked very lonesome; although the room was small, he seemed to be surrounded by vast areas of solitude.

Birl saw that he had before him the letter her old mistress had been writing when she died. The paper still lay on the same spot. The overturned ink had long since dried on the page and on the table around it. The great blot of ink was already covered with a thick layer of dust.

Now George picked up the letter, brushed away the dust, and brought the paper toward the light of the candle. But his efforts to decipher the writing were in vain. All he could make out was the salutation, which read: "My dear son." Shaking his head, he finally gave up the attempt to read the remainder of the letter. He looked at the salutation once more, and in a low voice he repeated the words to the empty room: "My dear son." Then he fell silent, sat woodenly hunched in his chair, and stared into the night.

Birl saw that he was weeping silently. He sat stiffly in his chair while the tears of sorrow, glittering as if they had caught up all the feeble candlelight, rolled down his cheeks. Then Birl knew that the moment had come for her to make the bold venture.

She uttered a chirping sound, a kind of purring twitter to which she owed her name, that bespoke sympathy and an attempt to encourage him. She could, her voice promised, drive away the terrible solitude around him and replace it by the solidarity of companionship. And suiting the action to her words, she approached with a confident and confiding air and rubbed up against the man's feet.

Do not drive me away, not now; don't do that to yourself, don't shut yourself off in your loneliness, her chirping voice begged.

Every human being who can still listen to the promptings of his heart is conquered when a cat volunteers such a graceful and tender caress, and George too was moved. He stooped, lifted the happy puss, and set her before him in the middle of the table.

"Are you Birl whom my mother used to write about all the time?" he asked her. "Look here!"—he picked up the illegible letter—"here is a word, and here's another, and here and here, and all of them might be 'Birl.' Sometimes your name was all I could decipher in her letters. . . . You were named after your voice. . . . Yes, of course, you must be the one. . . . Your white fur fits her description. But you've certainly got very lean. Well, then, we suit each other pretty well. . . . Did I kick you this afternoon? Forgive me. Those two fools tried to make me believe that black is white, I mean that rats are cats and that you gnawed holes in the cupboard door. But after you left I threw the hypocrites out. I know cats don't do that sort of thing. I was just weak and helpless and so confused by sorrow that I couldn't think clearly, and they took advantage of me."

While George murmured this apology he stroked Birl gently. And Birl felt wonderfully contented and proud—proud not so much because she was now being caressed as because George, her new master, was a good man.

Purring, she lay down close to his elbow which was propped on the table, and George pressed his cheek against her warm white coat. And so the two of them found shelter in one another and overcame the loneliness of the night.

The Cat

MARY E. WILKINS

THE SNOW was falling, and the Cat's fur was stiffly pointed with it, but he was imperturbable. He sat crouched, ready for the death-spring, as he had sat for hours. It was night—but that made no difference—all times were as one to the Cat when he was in wait for prey. Then, too, he was under no constraint of human will, for he was living alone that winter. Nowhere in the world was any voice calling him; on no hearth was there a waiting dish. He was quite free except for his own desires, which tyrannized over him when unsatisfied as now. The Cat was very hungry—almost famished, in fact. For days the weather had been very bitter, and all the feebler wild things which were his prey by inheritance, the born serfs to his family, had kept, for the most part, in their burrows and nests, and the Cat's long hunt had availed him nothing. But he waited with the inconceivable patience and persistency of his race; besides, he was certain. The Cat was a creature of absolute convictions, and his faith in his deductions never wavered. The rabbit had gone in there between those low-hung pine boughs. Now her little doorway had before it a shaggy curtain of snow, but in there she was. The Cat had seen her enter, so like a swift gray shadow that even his sharp and practised eyes had glanced back for the substance following, and then she was gone. So he sat down and waited, and he waited still in the white night, listening angrily to the north wind starting in the upper heights of the mountains with distant screams, then swelling into an awful crescendo of rage, and swooping down with furious white wings of snow like a flock of fierce eagles into the valleys and ravines. The Cat was on the side of a mountain, on a wooded terrace. Above him a few feet away towered the rock ascent as steep as the wall of a cathedral. The Cat had never climbed it—trees were the ladders to his heights of life. He had often looked with wonder at the rock, and miauled bitterly and resentfully as man does in the face of a forbidding Providence. At his left was the sheer precipice. Behind him, with a short stretch of woody growth between, was the frozen perpendicular fall of a mountain stream. Before him was the way to his home. When the rabbit came out she was trapped; her little cloven feet could not scale such unbroken steeps. So the Cat waited. The place in which he was looked like a maelstrom of the wood. The tangle of trees and bushes clinging to the mountain-side with a stern clutch of roots, the prostrate trunks and branches, the vines embracing everything with strong knots and coils of growth, had a curious effect, as of things which had whirled for ages in a current of raging water, only it was not water, but wind, which had disposed everything in circling lines of yielding to its fiercest points of onset. And now over all this whirl of wood and rock and dead trunks and branches and vines descended the snow. It blew down like smoke over the rock-crest above; it stood in a gyrating column like some death-wraith of nature, on the level, than it broke over the edge of the precipice, and the Cat cowered before the fierce backward set of it. It was as if ice needles pricked his skin through his beautiful thick fur, but he never faltered and never once cried. He had nothing to gain from crying, and everything to lose; the rabbit would hear him cry and know he was waiting.

It grew darker and darker, with a strange white smother, instead of the natural blackness of night. It was a night of storm and death superadded to the night of nature. The mountains were all hidden, wrapped about, overawed, and tumultuously overborne by it, but in the midst of it waited, quite unconquered, this little, unswerving, living patience and power under a little coat of gray fur.

A fiercer blast swept over the rock, spun on one mighty foot of whirlwind athwart the level, then was over the precipice.

Then the Cat saw two eyes luminous with terror, frantic with the impulse of flight, he saw a little, quivering, dilating nose, he saw two pointing ears, and he kept still, with every one of his fine nerves and muscles strained like wires. Then the rabbit was out—there was one long line of incarnate flight and terror—and the Cat had her.

Then the Cat went home, trailing his prey through the snow.

The Cat lived in the house which his master had built, as rudely as a child's blockhouse, but stanchly enough. The snow was heavy on the low slant of its roof, but it would not settle under it. The two windows and the door were made fast, but the Cat knew a way in. Up a pine-tree behind the house he scuttled, though it was hard work with his heavy rabbit, and was in his little window under the eaves, then down through the trap to the room below, and on his master's bed with a spring and a great cry of triumph, rabbit and all. But his master was not there; he had been gone since early fall, and it was now February. He would not return until spring, for he was an old man, and the cruel cold of the mountains clutched at his vitals like a panther, and he had gone to the village to winter. The Cat had known for a long time that his master was gone, but his reasoning was always sequential and circuitous; always for him what had been would be, and the more easily for his marvellous waiting powers, so he always came home expecting to find his master.

When he saw that he was still gone, he dragged the rabbit off the rude couch which was the bed to the floor, put one little paw on the carcass to keep it steady, and began gnawing with head to one side to bring his strongest teeth to bear.

It was darker in the house than it had been in the wood, and the cold was as deadly, though not so fierce. If the Cat had not received his fur coat unquestioningly of Providence, he would have been thankful that he had it. It was a mottled gray, white on the face and breast, and thick as fur could grow.

The wind drove the snow on the windows with such force that it rattled like sleet, and the house trembled a little. Then all at once the Cat heard a noise, and stopped gnawing his rabbit and listened, his shining green eyes fixed upon a window. Then he heard a hoarse shout, a halloo of despair and entreaty; but he knew that it was not his master come home, and he waited, one paw still on the rabbit. Then the halloo came again, and then the Cat answered. He said all that was essential quite plainly to his own comprehension. There was in his cry of response inquiry, information, warning, terror, and finally, the offer of comradeship; but the man outside did not hear him, because of the howling of the storm.

Then there was a great battering pound at the door, then another, and another. The Cat dragged his rabbit under the bed. The blows came thicker and faster. It was a weak arm which gave them, but it was nerved by desperation. Finally the lock yielded, and the stranger came in. Then the Cat, peering from under the bed, blinked with a sudden light, and his green eyes narrowed. The stranger struck a match and looked about. The Cat saw a face wild and blue with hunger and cold, and a man who looked poorer and older than his poor old master, who was an outcast among men for his poverty and lowly mystery of antecedents; and he heard a muttered, unintelligible voicing of distress from the harsh, piteous mouth. There was in it both profanity and prayer, but the Cat knew nothing of that.

The stranger braced the door which he had forced, got some wood from the stock in the corner, and kindled a fire in the old stove as quickly as his half-frozen hands would allow. He shook so pitiably as he worked that the Cat under the bed felt the tremor of it. Then the man, who was small and feeble and marked with the scars of suffering which he had pulled down upon his head, sat down in one of the old chairs and crouched over the fire as if it were the one love and desire of his soul, holding out his yellow hands like yellow claws, and he groaned. The Cat came out from under the bed and leaped up on his lap with the rabbit. The man gave a great shout and start of terror, and sprang, and the Cat slid clawing to the floor, and the rabbit fell inertly, and the man leaned, gasping with fright, and ghastly, against the wall. The Cat grabbed the rabbit by the slack of its neck and dragged it to the man's feet. Then he raised his shrill, insistent cry, he arched his back high, his tail was a splendid waving plume. He rubbed against the man's feet, which were bursting out of their torn shoes.

The man pushed the Cat away, gently enough, and began searching about the little cabin. He even climbed painfully the ladder to the loft, lit a match, and peered up in the darkness with straining eyes. He feared lest there might be a man, since there was a cat. His experience with men had not been pleasant, and neither had the experience of men been pleasant with him. He was an old wandering Ishmael among his kind; he had stumbled upon the house of a brother, and the brother was not at home, and he was glad.

He returned to the Cat, and stooped stiffly and stroked his back, which the animal arched like the spring of a bow.

Then he took up the rabbit and looked at it eagerly by the firelight. His jaws worked. He could almost have devoured it raw. He fumbled—the Cat close at his heels—around some rude shelves and a table, and found, with a grunt of self-gratulation, a lamp with oil in it. That he lighted; then he found a frying-pan and a knife, and skinned the rabbit, and prepared it for cooking, the Cat always at his feet.

When the odor of the cooking flesh filled the cabin, both the man and the Cat looked wolfish. The man turned the rabbit with one hand, and stooped to pat the Cat with the other. The Cat thought him a fine man. He loved him with all his heart, though he had known him such a short time, and though the man had a face both pitiful and sharply set at variance with the best of things.

It was a face with the grimy grizzle of age upon it, with fever hollows in the cheeks, and the memories of wrong in the dim eyes, but the Cat accepted the man unquestioningly and loved him. When the rabbit was half cooked, neither the man nor the Cat could wait any longer. The man took it from the fire, divided it exactly in halves, gave the Cat one, and took the other himself. Then they ate.

Then the man blew out the light, called the Cat to him, got on the bed, drew up the ragged coverings, and fell asleep with the Cat in his bosom.

The man was the Cat's guest all the rest of the winter, and the winter is long in the mountains. The rightful owner of the little hut did not return until May. All that time the Cat toiled hard, and he grew rather thin himself, for he shared everything except mice with his guest; and sometimes game was wary, and the fruit of the patience of days was very little for two. The man was ill and weak, however, and unable to eat much, which was fortunate, since he could not hunt for himself. All day long he lay on the bed, or else sat crouched over the fire. It was a good thing that firewood was ready at hand for the picking up, not a stone's throw from the door, for that he had to attend to himself.

The Cat foraged tirelessly. Sometimes he was gone for days together, and at first the man used to be terrified, thinking he would never return; then he would hear the familiar cry at the door, and stumble to his feet and let him in. Then the two would dine together, sharing equally; then the Cat would rest and purr, and finally sleep in the man's arms.

Towards spring the game grew plentiful; more wild little quarry were tempted out of their homes, in search of love as well as food. One day the Cat had luck—a rabbit, a partridge, and a mouse. He could not carry them all at once, but finally he had them together at the house door. Then he cried, but no one answered. All the mountain streams were loosened, and the air was full of the gurgle of many waters, occasionally pierced by a bird whistle. The trees rustled with a new sound to the spring wind; there was a flush of rose and gold-green on the breasting surface of a distant mountain seen through an opening in the wood. The tips of the bushes were swollen and glistening red, and now and then there was a flower; but the Cat had nothing to do with flowers. He stood beside his booty at the house door, and cried and cried with his insistent triumph and complaint and pleading, but no one came to let him in. Then the Cat left his little treasures at the door, and went around to the back of the house to the pine-tree, and was up the trunk with a wild scramble, and in through his little window, and down through the trap to the room, and the man was gone.

The Cat cried again—that cry of the animal for human companionship which is one of the sad notes of the world; he looked in all the corners; he sprang to the chair at the window and looked out; but no one came. The man was gone, and he never came again.

The Cat ate his mouse out on the turf beside the house; the rabbit and the partridge he carried painfully into the house, but the man did not come to share them. Finally, in the course of a day or two, he ate them up himself; then he slept a long time on the bed, and when he waked the man was not there.

Then the Cat went forth to his hunting-grounds again, and came home at night with a plump bird, reasoning with his tireless persistency in expectancy that the man would be there; and there was a light in the window, and when he cried his old master opened the door and let him in.

His master had strong comradeship with the Cat, but not affection. He never patted him like that gentler outcast, but he had a pride in him and an anxiety for his welfare, though he had left him alone all winter without scruple. He feared lest some misfortune might have come to the Cat, though he was so large of his kind, and a mighty hunter. Therefore, when he saw him at the door in all the glory of his winter coat, his white breast and face shining like snow in the sun, his own face lit up with welcome, and the Cat embraced his feet with his sinuous body vibrant with rejoicing purrs.

The Cat had his bird to himself, for his master had his own supper already cooking on the stove. After supper the Cat's master took his pipe, and sought a small store of tobacco which he had left in his hut over winter. He had thought often of it; that and the Cat seemed something to come home to in the spring. But the tobacco was gone; not a dust left. The man swore a little in a grim monotone, which made the profanity lose its customary effect. He had been, and was, a hard drinker; he had knocked about the world until the marks of its sharp corners were on his very soul, which was thereby calloused, until his very sensibility to loss was dulled. He was a very old man.

He searched for the tobacco with a sort of dull combativeness of persistency; then he stared with stupid wonder around the room. Suddenly many features struck him as being changed. Another stove-lid was broken; an old piece of carpet was tacked up over a window to keep out the cold; his fire-wood was gone. He looked, and there was no oil left in his can. He looked at the coverings on his bed; he took them up, and again he made that strange remonstrant noise in his throat. Then he looked again for his tobacco.

Finally he gave it up. He sat down beside the fire, for May in the mountains is cold; he held his empty pipe in his mouth, his rough forehead knitted, and he and the Cat looked at each other across that impassable barrier of silence which has been set between man and beast from the creation of the world.

The Ninth Life

MAZO DE LA ROCHE

"Harriet! Harriet! Harriet!" Her name echoed through the pine woods. It echoed across the water to the next island, was flung back from its precipitous shore in a mournful echo. Still she did not come.

The launch stood waiting at the wharf, laden with the luggage attendant on the breaking up of the holiday season. Summer was past, October almost gone, wild geese were mirrored in the lake in their flight southward. Now, for eight months the Indians and the wild deer would have the islands to themselves.

The Boyds were the last of the summer people to go. They enjoyed the month of freedom at the end of the season, when tourists were gone. They were country people themselves, bred in the district. When they were not living on their island they lived in a small town at the foot of the lake, thirty miles away. The year was marked for them by their migration to the island in the middle of June and their return to winter habitation in October.

They were well-to-do. They owned their launch which now stood waiting at the wharf, with the Indian, John Nanabush, at the wheel. He stood, dark and imperturbable, while Mrs. Boyd, her daughter and her cook raised their voices for Harriet. Mr. Boyd prowled about at the back of the cottage, peering into the workshop, the icehouse, behind the woodpile, where freshly cut birch logs lay waiting for next year's fires. Now and again he gave a stentorian shout for Harriet.

They had delayed their departure for hours because of her. Now they must go without her. Mrs. Boyd came to the wide veranda where the canoe lay covered by canvas. She lifted the edge of the canvas and peered under it.

"Why, mother, what a place to look!" said her husband. "The cat wouldn't be in there."

"I know," said Mrs. Boyd. "But I just feel so desperate!"

"Well, we've got to go without her."

"And it's getting so cold!"

On the wharf the girls wailed, "Oh, father, we can't leave Harriet on the island!"

"Find her, Pat! Find Harriet!" said Mr. Boyd to the Irish terrier.

Pat leaped from the launch, where he was investigating the hamper of eatables, and raced up the rocky shore. In his own fashion he shouted for the cat. A chipmunk darted from the trunk of a jack pine, sped across a large flat rock, ran halfway up a flaming red maple and paused, upside down, to stare at the group on the wharf.

John Nanabush raised his soft, thick, Indian voice. "You folks go along home. I'll find Horriet. I'll keep her for you."

"That's a good idea," said Mr. Boyd.

"Harriet would never stay with John," said Mrs. Boyd. "She's devoted to us."

"Guess she'd rather stay with me than freeze," said the Indian.

"Will you promise to come back to the island tomorrow and search till you find her?"

"Oh, I'll find her," said Nanabush, in his comforting, sly voice. "We ought to be gettin' on now, if you folks want to be home before dark."

"Pat! Pat! Oh, where is Pat gone?" cried the young girls.

Pat came bounding out of the woods, rushed at the launch, scrambled on board, and sat there grinning.

"He's got some sense, anyhow," said the Indian.

"Sound the whistle, John," said Mrs. Boyd. "That might fetch her."

"What if she's dead!" cried the younger girl.

"You can't kill a cat," said Nanabush. He stretched out his dark hand and blew the whistle.

All eyes were turned to the woods.

The cook said, "I left a bowl of bread and milk for her, by the back door."

"Come, mother," said Mr. Boyd, "it's no use. We can't wait any longer."

The launch looked like a toy boat as it moved among the islands. The reflection of the islands lay on the dark blue lake, more perfect than the reality. They were deserted.

It was only an hour later when Harriet came back. She was tired and hungry, for she had been on a more strenuous hunt than usual. She had cut one of her feet and the hunt had been unsuccessful. She had curled up in the hollow of a tree and slept long, on the far side of the island. She had heard faint shouts for her, but feline perversity had made her curl herself closer.

Now she circled the cottage, meowed outside the doors, leaped to the window sills and peered into the rooms. There was a desolate air about it. She went to the wharf and saw that the launch was not there. The family would return in the launch.

She glided back to the cottage and found the bowl of bread and milk. She attacked it greedily, but after a few mouthfuls her appetite left her. She began to wash her face, then to lick her coat to cleanliness and luster. Her coat was a pleasing combination of tawny yellow and brown. She had a hard, shrewd face, but there was affection in her.

The October sun sank in spectacular grandeur among the islands. There was no twilight. A blue, cold evening took possession. A few glittering stars were reflected in the lake. The air became bitterly cold, and a white furry frost rimed the grass. Harriet crept into the canoe where Mrs. Boyd had lifted the canvas. There was a cushion in it. She curled herself up and slept.

At sunrise she leaped from the canoe and ran to the kitchen window. From its ledge she peered into the room. There was no fire. There was no cook. Harriet gave a faint meow of disappointment. She bent her acute sense of hearing to catch a sound of life in the cottage. All she heard was the whisper of little waves against the shore. Pointed leaves from the silver birches drifted in the golden air. It was very cold.

Harriet went to the bowl of bread and milk and began to eat it. She discovered that she was ravenous. But there was so much of it that she had to take breath before she could finish it. Even in her repletion she muttered a meow of longing. She was four years old, and she had never been separated from the Boyds before. Her mother and her grandmother had belonged to the Boyds. She knew their movements and their life as she knew the pads of her own paw.

The bowl was emptied. As empty and hollow as the world in which she now found herself. Mechanically she began to wash her face, groom the fine hair behind her ears till it was erect as the pile of fine velvet. She stretched out her hind leg and swiftly licked the fur on the rim of her thigh. In this attitude it could be seen that she was with young. Her little teats showed rosy and fresh.

She heard a rustle in the fallen leaves and turned her green eyes defensively, fearfully, in that direction. A pair of porcupines stood staring at her, side by side, their quills upright, their yellow teeth showing in their trepidation. They had come to investigate the empty cottage.

Harriet gave a hissing scream at them, making her face as horrify-

ing as she could. She stared with her back to the kitchen door, screaming and making faces. The porcupines turned and ambled away,
pushing into a dense growth of junipers.

An acorn clattered across the roof of the cottage and fell close to
Harriet. She stood up, wondering what was coming next. The chipmunk that had watched the departure yesterday now looked over
the eave at her. He knew she could not get at him where he was, but
he longed to retrieve his acorn. His neat striped head darted from
side to side, his eyes questioned her. Her tail lashed its implacable
answer. He put his little paw against the side of his face and settled
down to watch her.

With a sudden leap she sprang toward the acorn, curved her paw
about it, toyed with it. Beneath her fur her muscles flowed as she
bent low over the acorn as though loving it, leaped back from it in
disdain.

Paw to cheek, the chipmunk watched her.

Then, from all the empty world about her, her misery came to
taunt her. She was alone, except for the helpless kittens that stirred
inside her. She sank to her belly and gave a plaintive meow.

For a long while she lay with closed eyes. The chipmunk longed for
his acorn. No other acorn could take its place. He kept elongating
his neck to see into Harriet's face. She seemed oblivious of everything, but he was not deceived. Still he could not resist. He darted
down the wall of the cottage, made a dash for the acorn, snatched it.

He almost succeeded. But his nearness electrified her. In a flowing curve she sprang at him. He dropped the acorn and turned himself into wind and blew back against the wall of the cottage. From
the eaves he chattered at her. She stared out across the lake, ignoring
him.

As the sun neared the tops of the pines she heard the delicate approach of a canoe. She ran to a point of rock and crouched there,
among the junipers watching.

It was John Nanabush come to look for her. The lake was very still
and the reflection of canoe and Indian lay on the glassy water, in silent companionship. He dipped and raised his paddle, as though
caressing the lake. He gave glittering diamonds to it from the tip of
his paddle. He called, in his indifferent Indian voice: "Horriet!
Horriet! You there?"

She crouched, staring at him. She watched him with acute but contemptuous interest.

"Horriet! Horriet!" The canoe moved on, out of sight, behind a
tumble of rocks, but the Indian's voice still echoed dreamily.

She would not go with him! She would not go. Surely there was a mistake! If she ran very fast to the house, she would find the family there. Harriet ran, in swift undulations, up the rocky, shaggy steep to the cottage.

The chipmunk watched her approach from the eave, his little paws pressed together as though in prayer. But he reviled her shrilly.

She ran along the veranda and sprang to the sill of the kitchen window. Inside it was almost dark. There was no cook. The frying pan hung against the wall. She heard the chipmunk scampering across the roof, in haste to get a good view of her. She sat down on the sill and opened her mouth, but no sound came.

The chipmunk peered down at her, turning his striped head this way and that, quivering in his excitement. She lashed her tail, but she would not look up at him. She began to lick her sore paw.

The red of the sky turned to a clear lemon color. There was an exquisite stillness, as the trees awaited the first hard frost. An icy fear, a terrible loneliness, descended on Harriet. She would not spend another night on the island.

As she ran to the water's edge she meowed without ceasing, as in protest against what she must do. A wedge-shaped flock of wild geese flew strong and sure against the yellow sky.

Before her the lake stretched dark blue, crisping in its coldness, lapping icily at her paws. She cried loudly in her protest as she walked into it. A few steps and she was out of her depth.

She had never swum before, but she could do it. She moved her paws knowingly, treading the icy water in fear and hate. A loon skimming the lake was startled by her stark cat's head rising out of the water, and swung away, uttering his loud, wild laugh.

The next island was half a mile away. The last sunlight was held in the topmost branches of its pines. It seemed almost unattainable to Harriet, swimming in bitter stubbornness toward it. Sometimes she felt that she was sinking. The chill all but reached her heart, still she struggled toward the blackness of the rocks.

At last the island loomed above her. She smelled the scents of the land. All her hate of the water and her longing for home tautened her muscles. She swam fiercely and, before she was quite exhausted, clambered up on the rocks.

Once there, she was done. She lay flattened, a bit of wet draggled fur. But her heaving sides and gasping mouth showed that life was in her. The wet hairs of her fur began to crisp whitely in the frost. Her tail began to look stiff and brittle. She felt the spirit going out

of her and the bitter cold coming in. The red afterglow on the black horizon was fading. It would soon be dark.

Harriet had a curious feeling of life somewhere near. Not stirring, just sending its prickly essence, in a thin current, toward her. Her eyes flew open in horror of being attacked in her weak state. She looked straight into the eyes of a wild goose, spread on the rock near her.

One of his wings had been injured and he had been left behind, by the flock, to die. He was large and strong, but young. This had been his first flight southward. His injured wing lay spread on the rock like a fan. He rested his glossy head on it.

They stared at each other, fascinated, while the current of his fear pricked her to life. She tightened the muscles of her belly and pressed her claws against the rock. Their eyes communed, each to each, like instruments in tune. She drew her chin against her frosty breast, while her eyes became balls of fire, glaring into his.

He raised himself above his broken wing and reared his strong other wing, as though to fly. But she held him with her eyes. He opened his long beak, but the cry died in his throat. He got onto his webbed feet and stood, with trailing wing, facing her. He moved a step nearer.

So, they stared and stared, till he wanted her to take him. He had no will but hers. Now her blood was moving quickly. She felt strong and fierce. His long neck, his big downy breast, were defenseless. She sprang, sunk her teeth in his neck, tore his breast with her hind claws, clung to him. His strong wing beat the air, even after he knew himself dying.

It was dark when she had finished her meal. She sat on the rock, washing her face, attending to her sore paw. The air had grown even colder, and snowflakes drifted on the darkness. The water in pools and shallows began to freeze. Harriet crept close to the body of the goose, snuggling warmly in its down. She pressed under its wing, which spread above her, as though in protection.

She meowed plaintively as she prowled about the island next morning. The people who owned it had gone to their home, in a distant American city, many weeks ago. The windows of the cottage were boarded up. The flagstaff, where the big American flag had floated, was bare. Harriet prowled about the island, looking longingly at the mainland, filled with loathing of the icy water.

As she crept to its frozen rim she lifted her lip in loathing. A bit of down from the goose clung to her cheek. She crept onto the thin ice and, as it crackled beneath her, she meowed as in pain. At last, with a despairing lash of her tail, she went into the lake and set her face toward the mainland. It was three quarters of a mile away.

This ordeal was worse than last night's. The lake was more cruelly cold. But it was smooth, stretched like cold steel beneath the drifting snowflakes. Harriet's four paws went up and down, as though the lake were a great barrier of ice she was mounting. Her head looked small and sleek as a rat's. Her green eyes were unwinking. Like a lodestone, the house at the foot of the lake drew her. Her spirit drew courage from the fire of its hearth.

A snake also was swimming to the mainland. Its cold blood felt no chill. Its ebony head arched above the steel of the lake. A delicate flourish on the steely surface followed it. The two swimmers were acutely conscious of each other, but their cold eyes ignored.

Harriet scrambled onto the crackling ice at the shore and lay prone. The life was all but gone from her. She remembered neither food nor fire nor shelter. The snake glided over the stones near her, slippery and secure. She tried to rise but could not.

The flurry of snow passed. A wind from the southwest made a scatteration among the clouds. They moved north and east, settling in gray and purple on the horizon. The sun shone out strongly, turning the October foliage to a blaze of scarlet and gold. The sunlight lay warm on Harriet's sagging sides.

She felt new life creeping into her. She raised her head and began to lick her sore paw. Then she ran her tongue, in long eager strokes, across her flanks. Her fur stood upright. Her flesh grew warm and supple.

She crept out on a rock, from whose crevices hardy ferns and huckleberry bushes grew. A few huckleberries glimmered frostily blue among the russet leaves. Harriet peered into the pool below the rock. She saw some small bass resting there in the watered sunshine.

She crouched, watching them intently. Her colors mingled with the frost-browned fern and bronzed leaves. She settled herself on her breast, as though to rest, then her paws shot into the pool, her claws like fishhooks drove into the bright scales. The bass lay on the rock, its golden eye staring up at her.

Now she felt refreshed and strong. She found the sandy track through the woods and trotted along it toward the foot of the lake. All day she pressed forward, meeting no one. She stopped only to catch a little mouse and eat it and rest after the meal.

At sundown a deer stepped out of a thicket and stood before her, his antlers arching like the branches of a tree, his great eyes glowing.

He looked at her, then bent his antlers, listening. He raised a shapely hoof and stood poised. Harriet saw something shining among the leaves. There was a sharp noise. The shock of it lifted Harriet from her feet, made every hair of her tail vibrant.

The tall deer sank to his knees. He laid the side of his head on the ground and his great eyes were raised imploringly to the face of the hunter who came out of the wood. The hunter knelt by him, as though in compassion. Then a stream of red gushed from the deer's throat. A dog came and sniffed his flank. Harriet peered down from a tree where she had hid. It was long before she dared to go on.

She had gone only a short way when she saw a doe and a fawn, standing as though waiting. The doe lowered her head at Harriet, but the fawn looked proudly aloof, holding its head, with the face innocent as a little child's, high on its strong neck. Harriet glided away, her paws brushing the snow from the dead leaves. She curled herself in a hollow in a tree and lay licking her sore paw. She thought of the dead deer's great body and the large pieces of flesh she had seen cut from it.

In the morning she was very hungry, but there was nothing to eat. The sky was dark, the snow had turned to a rain that dripped from the trees and soaked her fur till it clung to her. But she ran steadily along the track, always drawn by the lodestone of the house at the foot of the lake. Passing toward it, she sometimes gave a meow as faint and thin as the fall of a pine needle. She ate a few blueberries from the dried bushes. She came to a space carpeted by glossy wintergreen leaves. She even ate some of the scarlet berries, eating them with distaste and curling lip, but she was so hungry because of the kittens she carried. There seemed nothing living abroad except her.

The path crossed a swamp dense with a growth of cranberries. Beyond this she came to a settler's cottage, clean and neat, with poultry in a wire run. There was a hen turkey in the yard, followed by three daintily moving poults. A girl was milking a cow in an open shed. Harriet stood staring, lonely, hungry. She felt weighted down, almost too tired to go on.

A man came out of the house with a bucket. He saw her, and a piercing whistle brought two hounds. He picked up a stone and threw it. It struck her side.

Harriet turned into a fury, an elongated, arched, fiery-eyed, sneering fury. The hounds hesitated before her claws that reached for their eyes. She whirled and flew down the path. They came after her, baying, sending up the volume of their voices in the rain. They urged each other on with loud cries. With her last strength she clambered into a tree and sat sneering down at them, her sides palpitating.

The hounds stood with their paws against the trunk of the tree, baying up at her. They changed places, as though that would help them. They flung themselves down, panting beneath the tree, then sprang up again, baying. But when the shrill whistle sounded again they ran without hesitating back to their master.

On and on Harriet limped over the rock track. Sometimes she had a glimpse of the lake between trees, but she scarcely looked to right or left. The homeward cord drew her ever more strongly. One would scarcely have recognized the sleek pet in this draggled tramp, this limping, heavy-eyed, slinking cat.

She could see the twinkling lights of the town across the bay, when her pain came on. It was so piercing, so sudden, that she turned, with a savage cry, to face what seemed to be attacking her in the rear. But then she knew that the pain was inside her.

She lay writhing on the ground and before long gave birth to a kitten. She began to lick it, then realized that it was dead. She ran on toward the town as fast as she could.

She was still two miles from it when she had two more kittens. She lay beside them for a while, feeling weak and peaceful. Now the lights of the town were out. Harriet picked up one of the kittens and limped on. With it in her mouth she went along the paved street. She gave a meow of delight as she reached the back door of her own home.

She laid the kitten on the doorstep and herself began limping back and forth, the length of the step, rubbing her sides against the door. For the first time since she had been left on the island she purred. The purr bubbled in her throat, vibrating through her nerves in an ecstasy of home-coming. She caressed the back door with every bit of her. She stood on her hind legs and caressed the door handle with a loving paw. Only the weak cry of her kitten made her desist.

She carried it to the tool shed and laid it on the mat where the terrier slept in warm weather. She laid herself down beside it, trilling to it in love. It buried its sightless face against her lank belly. She lay flat on her side, weary to the bone.

But the shape of the kitten she had abandoned on the road now crept into her mind. It crept on silken paws, with its tail pointed like a rat's and its eyelids glued together. Round and round it crept in its agony of abandonment, tearing her mind as its birth had torn her body. She flung herself on her other side, trying to forget it, but she could not.

With a piteous meow of protest against the instinct that hounded her, she left the kitten's side and went out into the dawn. The rain had stopped and there was a sharp clear wind that drove the dead leaves scurrying across the frozen ruts.

The pain of her sore paw on the ice ruts was like fire, but she hurried on, draggled, hard-faced, with the thought of the bereft kitten prodding her.

The dreadful road unrolled itself before her in an endless scroll of horrible hieroglyphics. She meowed in hate of it, at every yard. She covered it, mile after mile, till she reached the spot where she had littered. There in the coarse wet grass, she found the kitten. She turned it over with her nose, sniffing it to see if it were worth taking home. She decided that it was.

Along and long the road she limped, the kitten dangling from her unloving mouth, the dead leaves whirling about her, as though they would bury her, the icy ruts biting her paw.

But the clouds had broken and the Indian-summer sun was leaping out. As she hobbled into her own yard her fur was warm and dry on her back. She laid the kitten beside the other and gave herself up to suckling them. And as they drew life from her, her love went out to them. She made soft trilling noises to them, threw her forelegs about them, lashed her tail about them, binding them close. She licked their fat bodies and their blunt heads till they shone.

Then suddenly a noise in the kitchen galvanized her. She leaped up, scattering the sucklings from her nipples. It was the rattle of a stove lid she had heard. She ran up the steps and meowed at the back door. It opened and the cook let out a scream of joy.

"Harriet! Harriet! Harriet's here!"

Pat ran to meet her, putting his paw on her back. She arched herself at him, giving a three-cornered smile. The cook ran to room after room, telling the news. The Boyds came from room after room to welcome Harriet, to marvel at her return.

"She must have come early last night," said the cook, "for she's had kittens in the tool shed."

"Well, they'll have to be drowned," said Mr. Boyd.

Harriet could not eat her bread and milk for purring. The purring sang in her throat, like a kettle. She had left her saucer and went to Mr. Boyd and thrust her head into his hand.

"Just listen how she purrs!" said Mrs. Boyd. "I've always said she was an affectionate cat."

Jennie's Lessons to Peter on How to Behave Like a Cat

PAUL GALLICO

ONCE aboard, Jennie's experience and knowledge of ships stood her in good stead. She called for the point-to-point method of procedure again, for she was particularly anxious not to encounter any human beings before the ship had cast off, and while she herself could melt and blend with the shadows in corners and behind things, she was worried over the conspicuousness of Peter's snow-white coat. But she followed her nose and her instincts as well as her memory of the other steamships on which she had served and soon was leading Peter down a narrow companionway that led to a small dining-saloon and thence to the galley.

Tea was long since over, all of the crew and officers were on deck engaged with the cargo and preparations for leaving, and Jennie counted on finding that part of the ship deserted. She was right. The galley fires were out and there was no immediate sign of cook or sculleryman. Also no doors were shut anywhere, which gave Jennie further indication of what kind of craft it was, and she led him from the galley through the pantry to the small storeroom where the immediate supplies were kept. At the end of this room was a doorway and a narrow iron staircase that descended to another passageway, on one side of which was the refrigeration room and on the other a large dry-stores enclosure where the ship's supplies in bulk were kept —sacks of flour and beans and dried peas, tins of fruit and vegetables, boxes of biscuits, tea, coffee, and so on.

The slatted door to this also stood wide open. It was dark, but an electric light burning far down the passageway shed sufficient light so that with their acute vision they soon accustomed themselves and could see their way about the boxes and cartons and barrels as well as though it were broad daylight.

And it was there in the storeroom, well concealed behind a case of tinned tomatoes, that Peter saw and missed his first mouse, revealing what might have been a fatal weakness in their plans. It had never dawned on him, and Jennie too had quite neglected to think about it and take into consideration that, for all his looking like and appearing to be a cat and learning to behave like one, Peter had not the faintest idea how to go about the difficult and important business of catching a mouse. Indeed, it was only through a lucky break that at the last moment more cargo arrived and the *Countess of Greenock* did not sail that night, nor the next night either, and that they were able to remedy their deficiency at least partly, for, superstition or no, a cat that proved itself wholly unable to catch marauding rodents might have received short shrift aboard such a craft.

The awkward discovery came when Jennie called Peter's attention to a little scratching, nibbling sort of noise from the other side of the storeroom, whispering: "Ssh! Mouse! There he is over by the biscuit box. Let's see you get him."

Peter concentrated, staring through the gloom, and there indeed he was, just edging round the corner of the large tin marked "HUNTLEY & PALMER LTD., READING," a long, grayish chap with a greedy face, impertinent whiskers, and beady black eyes.

Peter was so anxious to show off to Jennie what he could do as a cat if given the chance that he hardly even set himself to spring, or paused to measure the distance, the obstacles and the possible avenues of escape open to the mouse. Without a moment's thought or plan, he launched himself through the air in one terrific pounce, paws spread wide, jaws open to snatch him.

There was of course no mouse there when Peter landed.

And not only that, but his teeth clicked together on empty air, there was nothing beneath his paws, and in addition, having miscalculated his distance, or rather not having calculated it at all, he gave himself a nasty knock on the head against the side of the tin box, all of which did not help the feeling that he had made a perfect fool of himself.

But while the mouse had saved itself momentarily, it also committed a fatal error by failing to dodge back behind the tin. Instead, gripped by panic, it emitted a squeak and went the other way, and the next instant, like a streak of furred lightning, Jennie had hurled herself through the air, her front paws, talons bared and extended, striking from side to side in a series of short, sharp, stunning hooks, even while she was in passage. The blows, as she landed, caught the mouse, knocking him first to one side, then back to the other, dazed and bewildered, then tossed him up in the air and batted him a couple before he came down at which point Jennie seized him in her mouth and it was all over before Peter had even so much as recovered his balance as well as from his confusion.

"Oh dear," Jennie said, dropping the mouse. "I hadn't thought of that. Of course you wouldn't know how. Why should you? But we *shall* be in a pretty pickle if we're caught here before you know something about it. And I don't know how much time we shall have. Still—"

Peter at last found his tongue and emitted a cry of anger and mortification. "Goodness," he said, "isn't there *anything* I can do? Does *everything* have to be learned?"

"It's practice really," Jennie explained. "Even *we* have to keep practicing constantly. That, and while I hate to use the expression —know-how. It's like everything else. You find there's a right way and a wrong way. The right way is to catch them with your paws, not your mouth, and of course the preparation is *everything*. Look here, I'll show you what I mean."

Here she crouched down a few feet away from the dead mouse and then began a slow waggling of her hindquarters from side to side, gradually increasing the speed and shortening the distance of the waggle. "*That's* what you must try, to begin with," she explained. "We don't do that for fun, or because we're nervous, but to give ourselves motion. It's ever so much harder and less accurate to spring from a standing start than from a moving one. Try it now and see how much easier it is to take off than the other way."

Peter's rear-end waggle was awkward at first, but he soon began to find the rhythm of it—it was almost like the "One to get set, two to make ready, and *three* to go" in foot-racing, except that this was even better because he found that what Jennie said was quite true and that the slight bit of motion did start him off the mark like an arrow.

Next he had to learn to move his paws so that, as he flew through the air and landed, they were striking left, right, with incredible speed, a feat that was much more difficult than it sounds since he could not use his paws to land on, but had to bring up his hind part in time while lashing out with the front.

His second mouse he missed by a hair's breadth due to overanxiousness, but Jennie praised his paw-work and spring, criticizing only his judgment of distance and haste. "You rarely lose a mouse by waiting just a little longer," she explained, "because a mouse has a one-track mind and will keep on doing what it started out to do provided it isn't disturbed; and if it is disturbed, it will just sit there and quake, so that you have all the time in the world really. . . ."

But his third mouse Peter caught and killed, one-two-three, just like that. Jennie said that she could not have done it better herself, and when Peter made her a present of it she accepted it graciously and with evident pleasure and ate it. But the others they saved because Jennie said that when they came to be discovered, it would be a good thing to have some samples of their type of work about them.

And so, for the rest, Peter practiced and hunted busily, and Jennie advised him to keep the mouse alive and in the air as long as possible, not to torture it, but to gain in skill and accuracy and train his muscles to react swiftly at the slightest movement.

It was the second night before they sailed that Peter awoke to an uncomfortable feeling. There was a new and unpleasant odor in the storeroom, one that tended to make him a little sick. And suddenly from a far corner he saw glowing two evil-looking red eyes. Before he could stir he sensed through his whiskers that Jennie was awake too; and for the first time using this means of communication with him so that there should not be a sound, she warned: "Rat! It is serious, Peter, and very dangerous. This is something I cannot teach you or help you with. You'll just have to watch me and try to learn as best you can. And, above all, now whatever happens, don't move a muscle, don't stir, and don't make a sound, even if you want to. Now remember. I'm off."

Through the shadowing gloom Peter watched the stalk, his heart thumping in his chest, for this was different from the gay, almost light-hearted hunt of mice. Jennie's entire approach and attitude were those of complete concentration—the carriage of her body, the expression of her head, flattened forward, the glitter in her eyes, and the slow, fluid, amazingly controlled movement of her body. There was a care, caution, and deadly earnestness about her that Peter had never seen before, and his own throat felt dry and his skin and mustache twitched nervously. But he did his best to hold himself rigid and motionless as she had told him, lest some slip of his might bring her into trouble.

The wicked red eyes were glowing like two hot coals now, and Peter's acute hearing could make out the nasty sniffling noises of the rat, and the dry scrabbling of its toes on the storeroom floor. Jennie had gone quite flat now and was crawling along the boards on her belly. She stopped and held herself long and rigid for a moment, her eyes intent upon her prey, measuring, measuring. . . .

Then, inch by inch, she began to draw herself up into a little ball of fur-covered steel muscles for the spring. The rat was broadside to her. She took only two waggles, one to the left, one to the right, and then she was in the air aimed at the flank of the rat.

But lightning-fast as she was, the rodent seemed to be even faster, for his head came around over his shoulder, and his white teeth were bared in a wicked slashing movement and Peter wanted to shout to his friend: "Jennie, *look out!*" but just in time he remembered her admonition under no circumstances to make a sound, and he choked it down.

And then he saw what seemed to him to be a miracle, for launched as she was and in mir-air, Jennie saw the swift movement of the rat and, swifter herself, avoided the sharp ripping teeth; and making a turn in the air, a kind of half-twist such as Peter had seen the high divers do in the pool at Wembley one summer, she landed on the back of the rat and immediately sank her teeth in its spine just below the head.

Then followed a dreadful moment of banging and slamming and scraping and squealing and the sharp snick of teeth as the rat snapped viciously and fought to escape, while Jennie hung on for dear life, her jaws clamping deeper and deeper until there was a sharp click and the next moment the rat hung limp and paralyzed and a few seconds later it was all over.

Jennie came away from it a little shaken and agitated, saying: "Phew! Filthy, sickening beasts! I *hate* rats—next to people. . . .

They're all unclean and diseased, and if you let them bite you any-where, then *you* get sick, for their teeth are all poisoned, and some-times you die from it. I'm always afraid of that."

Peter said with deep sincerity: "Jennie, I think you are the bravest and most wonderful person—I mean cat—I ever saw. *Nobody* could have done that the way you did."

For once, Jennie did not preen herself or parade before Peter, for she was worried now since it was she who had coaxed him into this adventure. She said: "That's just it, Peter. We can't practice and learn on the rats the way we did on the mice, because it's too dan-gerous. One mistake and—well, I don't want it to happen. I *can* show you the twist, because you have to know how to do it to avoid the slash of theirs, but the spring, the distance, the timing, and, above all, just the exact place to bite them behind the neck to get at their spines—well, you must do it one hundred per cent right when the time comes, and that's all there is. If you get them too high on the head, they can kick loose or even shake you off. Some of the big fel-lows weigh almost as much as you do, and if you seize them too far down the back they can turn their heads and cut you."

"But how will I learn, then?" Peter asked.

"Let me handle them for the time being," she replied, "and watch me closely each time I kill one. You'll be learning something. Then if and when the moment comes when you have to do it yourself, you'll either do it right the first time and never forget it thereafter or—" Jennie did not finish the sentence but instead went into the washing routine, and Peter felt a little cold chill run down his spine.

When they were finally discovered, it was some seven hours after sailing, as the *Countess of Greenock* was thumping her slow, plod-ding way down the broad reaches of the Thames Estuary. When the cook, an oddly triangular-shaped Jamaican Negro by the name of Mealie, came into the storeroom for some tinned corned beef, they had a bag of eight mice and three rats lined up in lieu of references and transportation. Three of the mice were Peter's, and he felt in-ordinately proud of them and wished there could have been some way whereby he might have had his name on them, like autograph-ing a book perhaps—"Caught by Peter Brown, Storeroom, *Countess of Greenock,* April 15, 1949."

The Negro grinned widely, increasing the triangular effect, for his face and head were narrower at the top than at the bottom. He said: "By Jominy dat good. Hit pays to hodvertise. I tell dat to Cop-tain," and forthwith he went up on the bridge, taking Jennie's and Peter's samples with him. It was the kind of ship where the cook did go up on the bridge if he felt like having a word with the captain. There he told him the story of finding the two stowaways and then added: "But by Jominy they pay possage already. Look you dat!" and unrolling his apron, showed him the fruits of their industry.

The captain, whose name was Sourlies and who was that rare specimen, a fat Scotsman, looked and felt ill and commanded Mealie in no uncertain language to throw the mess over the side and go back to his galley. It was the beginning of his time of deep unhappiness anyway, for he hated the sea and everything connected with it and was reasonably contented only when in port, or near it, or proceeding up and down an estuary or river with plenty of land on both sides.

He carried this queer notion to the point of refusing even to dress the part of a ship's captain, and conducted the affairs of the *Countess of Greenock* wearing a tweed pepper-and-salt business suit with a gold watch chain across his large expanse of stomach and a mustard-colored fedora hat or trilby with the brim turned up all around.

As Mealie was leaving, however, he did decree that inasmuch as the cats seemed to have got aboard and appeared inclined to work their passage, they might remain, but told him to shift one of them to the fo'castle as the men had been complaining of the rats there.

Mealie took his time going aft and told his story and showed the bag to everyone he met, with the result that there arrived back in the storeroom quite a committee, consisting of Mr. Strachan, the first mate, Mr. Carluke, the second, Chief Engineer McDunkeld, and the bo'sun, whose name appeared to be only Angus.

They held a meeting, the gist of which Peter tried to translate rapidly for Jennie's benefit, and before they knew it, the two friends found themselves separated for the first time, Jennie being sent forward to live with the crew and Peter retained, chiefly through the insistence of Mr. Strachan, in the officers' quarters.

Jennie had only time to say to Peter: "Don't worry. We'll find ways to get together. Do your best. And if you come across a rat, don't hesitate and don't play. Kill!"

Then the bo'sun picked her up by the scruff of the neck and carried her forward.

Using the smooth sides of a huge packing case as a practice ground, Peter learned the secret of the double jump-up, or second lift; or rather, after long hours of trial with Jennie coaching, it suddenly came to him. One moment he had been slipping, sliding, and falling back as he essayed to scale the perpendicular sides, and the next he had achieved it, a lightning-like thrust with the hind legs, which somehow this time stuck to the sides of the case and gave him added impetus upwards, and thereafter he could always do it.

Jennie was most pleased with him, for as she explained it, this particular trick of leaping up the side of a blank wall without so much as a crack or an irregularity to give a toe-hold was peculiar to cats, and it was also one that could be neither wholly explained, demonstrated, or taught. The best she was able to tell him was: "You *think* you're 'way to the top, Peter. You just know you are going to be able to do it, and then you can."

Well, once the old *Countess* had taken a bit of a roll in the trough of a sea, and that helped Peter a little and gave him confidence. And the next time he felt certain he was going to be able to do it and he did.

Jennie was endlessly patient in teaching Peter control of his body in the air for she maintained that few things are of so much importance to cats. With her he studied the twist in mid-air from the spring so that, once he had left the ground, he could change his direction almost as in flying, and Peter loved the sense of power and freedom that came to him when he turned himself in the air like an acrobat, or a high diver, and this he practiced more than anything else. And he had to learn, too, how to drop from any normal height and twist in falling so that he would always land on his feet; and soon, with Jennie's help, he became so expert that he could roll off a case no more than a yard from the ground and still, turning like a flash, whip round so that his four paws touched the deck first, and that without a sound.

But their free time was not all devoted to hard work and practice. There were quiet hours when they rested side by side on a hatch coaming and Peter would ask Jennie questions—for instance, why she always preferred to perch on high things and look down—and she would explain about the deep instincts that survived from the days millions and millions of years ago when no doubt all cats were alike in size and shape and had to learn to protect themselves to survive. To escape the dangers that lurked on or near the ground from things that crawled, slithered, or trampled, they took to living high up in rocky caves, or perched along branches of trees where they could look down and see everything that approached them.

In the same manner, Jennie explained, cats liked to sleep in boxes, or bureau drawers, because they felt completely surrounded on all sides by high walls, as they were deep in their caves, and therefore felt relaxed and secure and able to sleep.

Or again, Peter would say: "Jennie, why when you are pleased and happy and relaxed, do your claws work in and out in that queer way? Once back home—I mean when we lived in the warehouse—I noticed that you were moving your paws up and down, almost as though you were making the bed. I never do that, though I do purr when I am happy."

Jennie was lying on her side on the canvas hatch cover when Peter asked that question, and she raised her head and gave him a most tender glance before she replied: "I know, Peter. And it is just another of those things that tell me that in spite of your shape and form, you are really human, and perhaps always will be. But maybe I can explain it to you. Peter, say something sweet to me."

The only thing Peter could think of to say was: "Oh, Jennie, I wish that I could be all cat—so that I might be more like you."

The most beatific smile stole over Jennie's face. Her throat throbbed with purring, and slowly her white paws began to work, the claws moving in and out as though she were kneading dough.

"You see?" she said to Peter. "It has to do with feeling happy. It goes all the way back to our being kittens and being nursed by our mothers. We cannot even see at first, but only feel, for when we are first born we are blind, and our eyes open only after a few weeks. But we can feel our way to our mother's breast and bury ourselves in her soft, sweet-smelling fur to find her milk, and when we are there, we work our paws gently up and down to help the food we want so much to flow more freely. Then when it does, we feel it in our throats, warm and satisfying; it stops our hunger and our thirst, it soothes our fears and desires, and oh, Peter, we are *so* blissful and contented at that moment, so secure and peaceful and—well, just happy. We never forget those moments with our mothers. They remain with us all the rest of our lives. And later on, long after we are grown, when something makes us very happy, our paws and claws go in and out the same way, in memory of those early times of our first real happiness. And that is all I can tell you about it."

Peter found that after this recital he had need to wash himself energetically for a few moments, and then he went over to where Jennie was lying and washed her face too, giving her several caresses beneath her soft chin and along the side of her muzzle that conveyed more to her than words. She made a little soft crooning sound in her throat, and her claws worked in and out, kneading the canvas hatch cover faster than ever.

But likewise during the long days of the leisurely voyage, and particularly when they were imprisoned in Dartmouth Harbor for two

days by pea-soup fog, there was mock fighting to teach Peter how to
take care of himself should he ever find himself in any trouble, as
well as all the feline sports and games for one or two that Jennie
knew or remembered and could teach him, and they spent hours
rolling about, growling and spitting, locked in play combat, waiting
in ambush to surprise each other, playing hide-seek-and-jump-out, or
chasing each other madly up and down the gangways and passages
below deck, their pads ringing oddly on the iron floors of the ancient
Countess, like the hoofs of tiny galloping horses.

And here again Peter was to learn not only that there were method
and strict rules that governed play as well as the more serious encounters between cat and cat but that he needed to study as well as
practice them with Jennie in order to acquire by repetition the feeling of the rhythms that were a part of these games.

Thus Jennie would coach him: "I make a move to attack you,
maybe a pass at your tail, or a feint at one of your legs; raise your left
paw and be ready to strike with it. That's it. That makes me think
twice before coming in. No, no, Peter, don't take your eyes off me
just because I've stopped. Be ready as long as I am tense. But you've
got to *feel* it when I've changed my mind and relaxed a little. You
can drop your left paw, but keep watching. There! *I've* looked away
for a moment—now *wash!* That stops everything. I can't do anything
until you've finished except wash too, and that puts the next move
up to you and it's your advantage."

Most difficult for him was the keeping of the upper hand by eye
and body position and acquiring by experience the feeling of when
it was safe to relax and turn away to rest, how to break up the other's
plans by washing, luring and drawing the opponent on by pretending
to look away and then timing his own attack to the split second when
the other was off balance and unprepared for it, and yet not violate
the rules, which often made no rhyme or reason to him at all.

None of these things Peter would have done instinctively as a boy,
and he had to learn them from Jennie by endless repetition. Often
he marveled at her patience as she drilled him over and over:
"Crouch, Peter. Now sit up quickly and look away. . . . *Wash!* Size
up the situation out of the corner of your eye as you wash. I'm waiting to jump you as soon as you stop washing. Then turn and get
ready. Here I come. Roll with it, onto your back. Hold me with
your forepaws and kick with the hind legs. Harder—harder. . . .
No, stay there, Peter. I'm coming back for a second try. Chin down so
I can't get at your throat. Kick. Now roll over and sit up, paw ready,
and threaten with it. If I blink my eyes and back away, *wash.* Now

pretend you are interested in something imaginary. That's it. If you make it real enough you can get me to look at it, and when I do, then you spring!"

Jennie had a system of scoring these bouts, so many points for buffets, so many for knockdowns and roll-overs, for break-aways and washes, for chases and ambushes, for the amount of fur that flew by tufts to be counted later, for numbers of back-kicks delivered, for bluffs and walk-aways, feints and ducking, with bonuses for position and length of time in control, and game plus one hundred points called any time one maneuvered into position to grip teeth on the throat of the other.

And gradually, almost imperceptibly at first, the scores drew nearer level and soon Peter found himself winning regularly over Jennie in the training ring they had arranged among the crates and boxes in the forward hold. And when this happened and Peter won almost every time, none was prouder and happier over it than Jennie. "Soon," she said with satisfaction, "you'll be cat through and through."

And yet when the tragedy happened, it was just as well that Peter was not all cat.

In a way it began when Peter caught his first rat. The *Countess of Greenock* was plowing the Irish Sea 'twixt the Isle of Man and the Cumberland coast, close enough inshore so that one could see the peaks of the Cumbrian Mountains inland, shining in the sun. The ocean was flat calm and glassy and the only cloud in the sky was the one made by the black smoke poured forth by the *Countess,* which owing to a following breeze over the surface, she carried along with her over her head like an untidy old charwoman shielding herself from the sun with an old black cotton umbrella. They were on the reach between Liverpool and Port Carlisle on the Scottish border and Captain Sourlies was in a great hurry to make it before nightfall. That was why the *Countess* was under forced draft, emitting volumes of soft-coal smoke and shuddering from the vibrations of her hurrying engines.

Peter had an appointment with Jennie on the afterdeck at six bells of the early afternoon watch, or three o'clock, for he had quickly learned to tell the ship's time from the strokes of the bell struck by the lookout on the bridge. This was always a kind of do-as-you-please time aboard the *Countess,* for then Captain Sourlies would be taking his afternoon nap in his cabin, Mr. Carluke, torn from his latest literary composition, which he was calling *The Bandit of Golden Gulch,* was on duty on the bridge, and everybody else followed his hobby or loafed by the rail or snoozed in the sun. And since Mr. Strachan, the first mate, still had a badly aching arm from the stitches taken in it, his dummy lurked in a corner in disgrace and the red-haired mate on this day was yarning with Mr. Box, the carpenter, about an episode that had happened to him in Gibraltar during the war and as proof produced an 1890 Queen Victoria copper penny that he had happened to be carrying on his person at the time of the adventure.

Jennie was already dozing in the soft spring sunshine, squatted down atop the stern rail. She liked to perch there because it was fairly high and gave her an over-all view, and also to show her superiority, for everyone was always prophesying that some day she would be knocked or fall off from there into the sea. But of course there never was a cat more certain or sure-footed than Jennie Baldrin.

Peter awoke promptly at ten minutes to three—he found that he could now awake at exactly any time he desired—and made a rough toilet with his tongue. He stretched and strolled casually from the lower storeroom, which was his quarters and which it was also his job to keep clear of vermin. Up to that moment there had been only mice, which Peter had kept down quite handily.

He should have smelled the rat long before he saw it, but although his smell senses were feline and quite sharp, his mind was still human and he had been thinking that he must tell Jennie about a member of the black gang, a stoker who fed the furnace, who was such an admirer of Winston Churchill that he had a picture of the former Prime Minister tattooed on his chest, cigar and all. And so he had not been alert. When he saw the rat he was in a very bad position.

The beast was almost as large as a fox terrier and it was cornered in a small alcove made by some piled-up wooden cases of tinned baked beans, from which several boxes had been removed from the center. Also it was daylight, Peter wasn't stalking, and the rat saw Peter at the same time that Peter saw the rat. It uttered an ugly squeal of rage and bared long, yellow teeth, teeth that Peter knew were so unclean that a single scratch from them might well poison him beyond help. And for the first time he really understood what people meant by the expression "fight like a cornered rat," or rather he was about to understand. For in spite of the fact that Jennie had warned him never to go after a rat except when it was out in the open, he meant to attack this one and prove himself.

He was surprised to find that now in this moment of danger he was not thinking of lessons he had learned, or what he had seen or heard or what Jennie had said, but that his mind seemed to be extraordinarily calm and clear and that, almost as though it had always been there ready and waiting, his plan unfolded itself in his mind. It was only much later he found out that this was the result of discipline, study, patience, and practice that he had put behind him at Jennie's behest.

His spring, seemingly launched directly at the foe, appeared to be sheer folly, and the rat rose up on its hind legs to meet him head on, slashing at him viciously. But not for nothing had Peter learned and practiced the secret of continuing on up a smooth wall from a single leap from the floor. A split second faster than the rat, his fore and hind legs touched the slippery sides of one of the piles of cases for an instant and propelled him high into the air so that the flashing incisors of the rodent, like two hideously curved yataghans, whizzed between his legs, missing him by the proverbial hair's breadth.

The extra impetus upwards now gave Peter the speed and energy to twist not half but the whole way around in a complete reverse and drop onto the back of the rat to sink his own teeth deep into its spine just behind the ears.

For one dreadful moment Peter felt that he might yet be beaten, for the rat gave such a mighty heave and surge and lashed so desperately to and fro that Peter was thumped and banged up against the sides of the boxes until he felt himself growing sick and dizzy and no longer certain whether he could hold on. And if once he let go, the big fellow would turn on him and cut him to ribbons.

In desperation he set his teeth with all his might and bit, one, two, three times, hard. At the third bite he felt the rat suddenly stiffen. The swaying and banging stopped. The rodent kicked twice with its hind legs and then was still. It never moved again. Peter unclamped his aching jaws and sat down quickly and did some washing. He was badly shaken and most emphatically needed to recover his composure.

Nevertheless it was exactly at six bells that he came trotting onto the afterdeck carrying the rat in his mouth, or rather dragging it, because it was so large that when he held it in the middle, its head and tail hung down to the deck. It was so heavy that he could barely lift it. But of course he managed because he simply had to show it off to Jennie and anyone else who happened to be around.

It was Mr. Box who saw him first and let out a yell: "Blimey, looka there! The white un's caught a bloomin' helephant."

Mr. Strachan also gave a shout, for Peter passed quite close to him and the rat dragged over his foot, causing him to jump as though he had been stung. The cries brought several deckhands over on the run to see. They also woke up Jennie Baldrin.

She had not meant to fall so soundly asleep, but the peaceful sea and the warm afternoon sun had lulled her deeper than she had intended, and now the sudden cries sent alarms tingling down her spine. And when she opened her eyes they fell on Peter and his rat and in the first confusion she was not certain whether the rat was carrying Peter or vice versa, whether it was alive or dead, whether Peter was still engaged in fighting it. The sound of running feet added to her confusion, and she recoiled from the unknown and the uncertain and the thought of possible danger to Peter.

But there was no place to recoil to from her precarious perch on the ship's rail, and with an awful cry, her four paws widespread, and turning over once in the air, she fell into the sea and was swept away in the white salt froth of propeller wash.

"Cat overboard!" a deckhand cried, and then laughed.

"Good-by, pussy," said Mr. Box. "Arskin' for it, she was, perched up there loike that."

Mr. Strachan stared with his mouth open.

The sailor who had been a hermit said to Peter: "There goes yer pal, Whitey. Ye'll no see Coptain Sourlies tairnen his ship aboot to rrrrrrescue a wee puss baldrin."

But Peter was no longer there. There was only a white streak of fur as he dropped the rat, leaped to the rail, and from it, long and low, shot straight into the sea after Jennie.

(*Ed. note: Jennie and Peter were saved, needless to say, and continued their travels.*)

It was only half true that Peter wanted to go home. For boy and cat were becoming so intermingled that Peter was not at all certain any longer which he really was.

More than once during his voyage aboard the *Countess of Greenock* and the subsequent adventures Peter had thought of his mother and father and Scotch Nanny and wondered how they were, if they were missing him, and whether they had any explanation for his mysterious disappearance. For certainly none of them, not even Nanny, who had been right there at the time, could be expected to guess that he had changed suddenly from a boy into a snow-white tomcat under her very eyes almost and had been pitched out into the street by her as a stray.

He thought it was probable that they would have notified the police, or perhaps, believing that he had run away, placed an advertisement in the "Personal" columns of the *Times* saying: "Peter: Come home, all is forgiven—Mummy, Daddy, and Nanny," or possibly it might have been more formally worded: "Will anyone who can give information as to the whereabouts of Master Peter Brown, vanished from No. 1A Cavendish Mews, London, W.C. 2, kindly communicate with Colonel and Mrs. Alastair Brown of that address. Reward!"

But, in the main, when he thought of those at home he did not believe that he was much missed except by Nanny, who of course had been busy with him almost from morning until night, leaving out the hours when he was at school, and now that he was gone would have nothing to do. His father was away from home so much of the time that except for their occasional evening romps he could hardly be expected to notice the difference. And as for his mother—Peter always felt sad and heavy-hearted when he thought about his mother, because she had been so beautiful and he had loved her so much. But it was the kind of sadness that is connected with a memory of something long ago. Looking back to what life had been like in those now but dimly recollected days, he felt certain that his mother had been a little unhappy herself at first when he was missed, but then, after all, she never seemed to have much time, and now that he was gone, perhaps it would not have taken her long to get used to it.

Really it was Jennie who had come more and more to mean family to him and upon whom he leaned for advice, help, companionship, trust, and even affection. It was true she talked a great deal and was not the most beautiful cat in the world, but there was an endearing and ingratiating warmth and grace about her that made Peter feel comfortable and happy when they slept coiled up close to each other, or even when he only looked at her sometimes and saw her sweet attitudes, kindly eyes, gamin-wise face, and soft white throat.

The world was full of all kinds of beautiful cats, prize specimens whose pictures he had seen in the illustrated magazines during the times of the cat shows. Compared with them, Jennie was rather plain, but it was an appealing plainness he would not have exchanged for all the beauty in the world.

Nor was it his newly acquired cat-self that was seeking a return to Cavendish Mews in quest of a home, though to some extent the cat in him was now prey to curiosity about how things were there without him and what everyone was doing. But he knew quite definitely that his mother and father were people who had little or no interest in animals and appeared to have no need of them and hence would be hardly likely to offer a haven to a pair of stray cats come wandering in off the streets—namely, Jennie and himself.

Peter's suggestion that Jennie accompany him on a trip home to

Cavendish Mews was perhaps more than anything born out of the memory that when he had been unhappy and upset about their treatment of Mr. Grims at the time of their first encounter with him, *she* had managed to interest and distract him by proposing the journey to Scotland. When he saw her sunk in the depths of grief and guilt over the fate of the poor old man, Peter had plucked a leaf out of her book of experience in the hope that it would take her mind off the tragedy and particularly what she considered her share in it. By instinct he seemed to have known that nothing actually would have moved her from the spot but his expression of his need for her.

Anyway, it was clear after they had set out for Cavendish Mews that she was in a more cheerful frame of mind and anxious to help him achieve his objective.

It is not easy for cats to move about in a big city, particularly on long journeys, and Jennie could be of no assistance to Peter in finding his way back to Cavendish Mews, since she had never lived or even been there and hence could not use her homing instinct, a kind of automatic direction-finder that communicated itself through her sensitive whiskers and enabled her to travel unerringly to any place where she had once spent some time.

Peter at least had the unique—from a cat's point of view—ability to know what people around him were saying, as well as being able to read signs, such as for instance appeared on the front of omnibuses and in general terms announced where they were going. One then had but to keep going in that direction and eventually one would arrive at the same destination or vicinity. In his first panic at finding himself a cat and out in the street, Peter had fled far from his home, with never any account taken of the twistings and turnings he had made. He was quite familiar with his own neighborhood, however, and knew if he could once reach Oxford and Regent streets he would find his way. But when it came to the lore of the city and knowing how to preserve one's skin whole, eat, drink, and sleep, Jennie as usual proved invaluable.

En route he learned from her all the important things there were to know about dogs and how to handle them—that, for instance, he must beware of terriers of every kind, that the average street mongrel was to be despised. Dogs on leashes could be ignored even though they put up a terrific fuss and roared, threatened, growled, and strained. They only did it because they *were* on the leash, which of course injured their dignity, and they had to put up a big show of what they would do if they were free. They behaved exactly the same when sighting another dog, and the whole thing, according to Jennie, was nothing but a lot of bluff. She, for one, never paid the slightest attention to them.

"Never run from a dog if you can control it," she admonished Peter, "because most of them are half blind anyway, and inclined to be hysterical. They will chase anything that moves. But if you stand your ground and don't run, chances are he will go right by you and pretend he neither sees you nor smells you, particularly if he has tangled with one of us before. Dogs have long memories.

"Small dogs you can keep in their places by swatting them the way we do when we play-box, only you run your claws out and hit fast and hard, because most of them are scared of having their eyes scratched and they don't like their noses clawed either, because they are tender. Here, for instance, is one looking for trouble and I'll show you what I mean."

They were walking through Settle Street near Whitechapel, looking for a meal, when a fat, overfed Scotty ran barking from a doorway and made a good deal of attacking them, barking, yelping, and charging in short rushes, with an amount of snapping its teeth, bullying, and bravado.

Jennie calmly squatted down on the pavement facing the foe with a kind of humiliating disinterest, which he mistook for fear and abject cringing and which gave him sufficient courage to close in and risk a real bite at Jennie's flank. Like lightning flashes her left paw shot out three times, while she leaned away from the attack just enough to let the Scotty miss her. The next moment, cut on the end of the nose and just below the right eye, he was legging it for the cover and safety of the doorway, screaming: "Help! Murder! Watch!!"

"Come on," Jennie said to Peter. "Now *we've* got to move out. You'll see why in a minute." Peter had long since learned not to question her, particularly about anything that called for split-second timing, and he quickly ran after her out of range, just as the owner of the dog, a slatternly woman, evidently the proprietress of the dingy greengrocery, came out and threw a dishpanful of water after them, but missed, thanks to Jennie's wisdom and speedy action.

"I'm out of practice," Jennie said with just a touch of her old-time showing off for Peter. "I missed him with my third. Still—They'll run off screaming for help, and if you stay around you're likely to catch it, as you saw, though not from *them*. . . . And you don't always have to do that. Quite often they've been brought up with cats or are used to them and are just curious or want to play, and come sniffing and snuffling and smelling around with their tails wagging, which, as you know, means that *they* are pleased and friendly, and not angry or agitated or nervous over something, as it does with us. Then you can either bear up under it and pretend not to notice it, or try to walk away or get up on top of something they can't reach. I, for one, just don't care for a wet, cold, drooly nose messing about in my fur, so I usually give them just a little tap with the paw, unloaded, as a reminder that we are after all quite totally different species and their way of playing isn't ours."

"But supposing it's a bigger dog," Peter said, "like the ones in Glasgow."

Jennie gave a little shudder. "Ugh!" she said. "Don't remind me of those. As I told you then, any time you see a bull terrier, run, or, better still, start climbing. But a great many of the others you can bluff and scare by swelling up and pretending to be bigger than you actually are. Let me show you. You should have been taught this long ago, because you can never tell when you are going to need it."

They were walking near Paternoster Row in the wide-open spaces created by the bombs before St. Paul's Cathedral, and Jennie went over a low coping and into some weeds and fireflowers that were growing there. "Now," she said, "do just as I do. Take a deep breath—that's it, 'way in. Now blow, but hold your breath at the same time. Hard! There you go."

And, as she said, there indeed Peter went, swelling up to nearly twice his size, just as Jennie was, all puffed out into a kind of lopsided fur ball. He was sure that he was looking perfectly enormous and quite out of plumb, and he felt rather foolish. He said as much to Jennie, adding: "I think that's silly."

She answered: "Not at all. You don't realize it, but you really looked quite alarming. It's sort of preventive warfare, and it makes a good deal of sense. If you can win a battle without having to fight it, or the enemy is so scared of you that he won't even start it and goes away and there is no battle at all, that's better than anything. It doesn't do any harm, and it's always worth trying, even with other cats. For in spite of the fact that you know it's all wind and fur, it will still give you the creeps when someone does it to you."

Peter suddenly thought back to Dempsey and how truly terrifying the battle-scarred veteran of a thousand fights had looked when he had swelled up and gone all crooked and menacing on him.

"And anyway," Jennie concluded the lesson, "if it shouldn't happen to work, it's just as well to be filled up with air, because then you are ready to let out a perfect rouser of a battle cry, and very often that *does* work, provided you can get it out of your system before the other one does. A dog will usually back away from that and remember another engagement."

In the main, on this walk across a portion of London, Peter found cats to be very like people. Some were mean and small and persnickety and insisted upon all their rights even when asked politely to share; others were broad-minded and hospitable, with a cheery, "Certainly, do come right in. There's plenty of room here," before Jennie had even so much as finished her gentle request for permission to remain. Some were snobs who refused to associate with them because they were strays; others had once been strays themselves, remembered their hardships, and were sympathetic. There were cantankerous cats always spoiling for a fight, and others who fought just for the fun of fighting and asserting their superiority; and many a good-natured cat belonging to a butcher, or a pub, or a snack bar or greengrocer would steer them toward a meal, or share what they had, or give them a tip on where to get a bite.

Also Peter learned, not only from Jennie, but from bitter experience, to be wary of children and particularly those not old enough to understand cats, or even older ones with a streak of cruelty. And since one could not tell in advance what they would be like, or whether they would fondle or tease, one had no choice, if one was a London stray, but to act in the interest of one's own safety.

This sad piece of knowledge Peter acquired in a most distressful manner as they threaded their way past Petticoat Lane in Whitechapel, where a grubby little boy was playing in the gutter outside a fish-and-chips bar. He was about Peter's age, or at least the age Peter had been before the astonishing transformation had happened to him, and about his height, and he called to them as they hurried by: "Here, puss. Come here, Whitey. . . ."

Before ever Jennie could warn him or breathe a "Peter, be careful!" he went to him trustingly, because in a way the boy reminded him of himself and he remembered how much he had loved every cat he saw in the streets, and particularly the strays and wanderers. He went over and held up his head and face to be rubbed. The next moment the most sharp and agonizing pain shot through his body from head to foot so that he thought he would die on the spot. He cried out half with hurt and half with fear, for he did not know yet what had happened to him.

Then he realized that the boy had twined his fingers firmly about his tail and was pulling. *Pulling* HIS *tail*. Nothing had ever hurt him so much or so excruciatingly.

"Nah, then," laughed the boy, nastily, "let's see yer get away."

With a cry of horror and outrage, and digging his claws into the cracks in the pavement, Peter made a supreme effort and managed to break loose, certain that he had left his tail behind him in the hand of the boy, and only after he had run half a block did he determine that it was still streaming out behind and safely attached to him.

And here Peter discovered yet another thing about cats that he had never known before. There was involved not only the pain of having his tail pulled, but the humiliation. Never had he felt so small, ashamed, outraged, and dishonored. And all in front of Jennie. He felt that he would not be able to look at her again. It was much worse than being stood in a corner when he had been a boy, or being spoken to harshly, or having his ear tweaked or knuckles cracked in front of company.

What served to make it endurable was that Jennie seemed to understand. She neither spoke to him sympathizingly, which at that moment Peter felt he would not have been able to bear, nor even so much as glanced at him, but simply trotted alongside, minding her own business and pretending in a way that he was not there at all, which was a great help. Gradually the pain and the memory began to fade, and finally, after a long while, when Jennie turned to him and out of a clear sky said: "Do you know, I think it might rain tonight. What do *your* whiskers say?" he was able to thrust his mustache forward and wrinkle the skin on his back to the weather-forecasting position and reply:

"There might be a shower or two. We'd better hurry if we want to reach Cavendish Square before it starts. Oh, look there! There's the proper bus just going by now. We can't go wrong if we keep in the same direction."

It was a Number 7, and the sign on the front of it read: "Oxford Street and Marble Arch."

"For Oxford Street crosses Regent, and then comes Princes, and if we turn up Princes, we can't help coming into Cavendish Square," Peter explained, "and then it's only a short step to the Mews and home."

Jennie echoed the word "home" in so sad and wistful a voice that Peter looked at her sharply, but she said nothing more, and proceeding quickly by little short rushes from shop door to shop door, as it were, the two soon had passed from Holborn through New Oxford into Oxford Street and across Regent to Princes, where they turned up to the right for Cavendish Square.

The Cat That Was Fey

ARTHUR STANLEY RIGGS

SECOND OFFICER HENDERSON had the duty when Peter came aboard.

The rusty, wheezy, foul smelling tramp *Calyx* lay alongside the Shrub Terminal Stores loading machinery for Callao. A week before she had come in from Iloilo and Manila with a full cargo of copra—and copra bugs. Between the bugs that were everywhere, even in the java, and the gritty cinders and dust from her poor steam coal, there was reason enough for Mr. Henderson's dark mood. Nothing the war had done to him as a BM/2c under an unfit young skipper compared with this. He sat in the opened door of the charthouse sucking on a dead pipe and staring at the starboard gangway without seeing anything. Then *he* hove in sight.

"Holy St. Peter!" exclaimed the Second, shivering.

Marching with complete assurance up the gangway was the animated skeleton of what at second appraisal proved to be somewhat like a cat. He was as desolate and disreputable in appearance as the ship he was invading. Once evidently black, his fur was so matted, dirty, touseled and gouged out in spots that the washboard of ribs down each side made him something for a caricaturist's delight. His tail rose into a perfect question mark astern; the knot on its tip marked clearly some adventure with a door. One ear had been chewed into complete distortion; the other was ragged but cocked well forward.

The expression on his scarred, wicked and hungry face defied anything Mr. Henderson could find on his tongue. Straight up the gangplank without haste or hesitation, straight along the well-deck, up the ladder and straight to Mr. Henderson he came. A foot away he paused. Man and cat eyed each other in appraising silence. "Miaouw!" finally remarked the animal, and set a tentative paw against Mr. Henderson's near leg.

156

A deep sigh escaped the man. He could feel the sharp claws against his own tough hide. His relief was genuine. "Holy St. Peter," he murmured. "Cat, I swear you're real! I'm not—not just seein'—."

Two calculating green eyes peered anxiously at the shaken Second Officer, and from the scrawny throat of the creature came a harsh sound like an echo of the *Calyx's* gears grinding ominously in a quartering sea. Five needle sharp claws pricked gently a trifle deeper.

"Hah! Purr at me, will ye? An' hungry! Well, come along, fellah. Ought to be somethin' in the galley y' c'n eat."

There was. Cook Swensen and Second Officer Henderson watched amazed as the starveling snatched and gulped, choked and bolted, until his ribs bulged and he could not down another bite. He sighed profoundly as he backed away from his plate, his tail flicking. Slowly he came to Henderson, fixed him with unblinking eyes, rubbed against his leg and purred again, more grindingly than before. The cook grumbled.

"Likely he ain't et good f'r a week. S'pose we'll have to feed him now till we shove off. I git him the grub, and the beggar thanks you!"

"Sure. That's all right. He come to me first. I knew where the grub was an' brung him here. Y' know, Cookie," he added, transfixed by one of his rare ideas, "we ain't got no cat since Nig jumped ship in Manila. I think this here beauty's a-goin' with us."

Swensen looked sourly at the over-stuffed animal already half asleep at Henderson's feet. "If he's a ratter we c'n use him all right. Stores are so full o' them big brown devils boarded us in Iloilo we won't have no stores pretty soon. Cat!" he barked, bending over and shaking a thick finger at him. "Go git me a rat. Show some gratitude. Pay for your dinner!"

With dignity the stray rose, flexed his muscles, gave the cook a green glare and vanished. Swensen chuckled. "Goo'bye, pussy! Smart lad. He got me aw ri'. That's the last we'll see of him."

Mr. Henderson shook his head. A searching look through the galley port discovered no signs of life down the long pier, and though he should have been topside, he settled down again and he filled his pipe. The match he lighted never reached the tobacco. As he raised it, in staggered the cat, his jaws firmly clamped on a still struggling monster rat almost as large as himself. Scornfully he dropped it at Swensen's feet, gave it the *coup de grâce* with one ferocious crunch, crossed to Mr. Henderson and gazed up for approval.

"Holy St. Peter!" gasped that officer, burning his fingers.

Swensen laughed. "Some name y' got yourself, pussy!"

Gently the dazed Henderson took him on his muscular lap. Peter liked it. The man's legs were softer than dock planks, and warm and dry. The man's caressing hand was not too clumsy or heavy. Peter squirmed into a comfortable position, closed his eyes and again purred raucously. Both men stared at him silently. Henderson dropped his pipe and made no effort to pick it up. Too many hitherto unimagined things were stirring in his hardened soul to make even a pipe of importance. At last he said, a trifle huskily: "Cookie, this here's the first time anybody ever thought I was somethin'. Never a soul since I was confirmed, until a cat—an' Gawd, what a cat! But now . . . Say, this Peter's my cat. Him an' me, just him an' me. I can beat the ears off'n anybody says no."

"Includin' me?" gibed the burly Swensen.

"Includin' you, an' the Skipper, an' Mr. Blain!"

"The First, he don't like cats. He'll kick the guts outa him."

Mr. Henderson lowered his face over the drowsy animal and

tweaked an ear. "Hear that, Peter? You sheer off whenever the First Officer heaves in sight."

One green eye opened. Peter yawned prodigiously and turned his head under his paws. Mr. Henderson approved. "Don't try to tell me animals don't think an' can't savvy talk. Didn't he go git you the rat you ast for? We'll be the lucky ship with him aboard."

Exactly how lucky did not appear for some time. Mr. Henderson felt sure Peter knew all the answers, and his behavior was such that even the dour Mr. Blain failed to aim a single kick at him. Certainly the rats were no longer a nuisance. But when, the day before sailing, the owners picked up a good additional freight for Havana, Peter came to Mr. Henderson as soon as he knew of the change in orders, and protested vehemently.

Something was wrong, but what it could be the bewildered Henderson could not imagine. The extra freight was harmless enough; a deckload of sugar mill grinding machinery and the copper tubing for some rum stills. Nothing in that to worry about. And the change in course from the Old Bahama Channel and Mona Passage to the Yucatán Channel was nothing—only about six, seven hundred miles farther to Colón. Unless—. He suddenly wondered what courses the Old Man would order.

Peter continued objecting, his battle scarred face grim. He watched the deck load stowed and lashed, battened in with special timbers that secured it against anything but sheer disaster, and miaouwed his disapproval in tones so ominous everybody who heard them shuddered. "Murphy," a Polish oiler with a name so unpronounceable the ashcats had promptly dubbed him "Irish" and then "Murphy," crossed himself and shivered. Chief Engineer MacNab, sober for the moment because he was overhauling his ramshackle engines, also heard, and wagged his gray head.

"Trrouble be a-coomin', an' the beastie kens it weel. 'Tis fey he is. Betterr we a' watch oot. Peterr," he said gently to the uneasy cat, "coom tell ut me, a guid Scot, an' fey like yersel. Be ther' ony pixies wi' yon machinery?"

Peter rubbed against his legs and purred, but there was no conviction in the harsh rattle of his throat. Mr. Henderson, who was supervising the stowage, laughed sourly. "Pixies or no, Peter'll smell it afore it strikes, Chief. Him an' me are mates. I'll be waitin' for his warning. You just give us steam."

Chief MacNab grunted and vanished below. When the fasts were cast off a few hours later and the *Calyx* wheezed out into the stream, her engines were in better condition than they had known for a long time. The engine and firerooms, however, were not comfortable. The bridge was even less so. Old Captain Grant, a Scot like the Chief, and equally bibulous, confided his worries to the pilot who took the ship to sea.

"A beastie, a domned, worrthless, pierrheid-joomper of a strray cat, to upset a whole ship's coompany like he's doin'! Firrst thing ye know the whole blurry lot'll get rreligion. Whoosh! Aiblins they'll even stop off the'r whuskey. I'm no so guid as a navigator masel; the Firrst, he can't find any fix wi'in aboot a degree, the Second's not much betterr—him that claims yon beastie," pointing at the uneasy Peter, maintaining a sharp lookout forward—"an' ma Chief's soberr forr the firrst time in yearrs! He's got real steam on her this time. Arrrgh!"

The trim pilot snickered. "Looks like you'll have to keep sober yourself this trip, Captain," he grinned.

"Aye, that wull I, wi' such a lot o' maunderrin' ijits. An' that Peterr!"

A light southwest breeze, the barometer high, and only a touch of groundswell sped the rheumatic *Calyx* on her course to Havana. That Peter was a veteran seafarer was immediately evident. He had his sea legs, he showed his familiarity with the devious bowels of a ship, and he grew fat and clean and glossy, but not lazy. In his brilliant green eyes there was a concentration, a strange appearance of seeing beyond the visible. He talked a lot to Mr. Henderson, who worried a lot because he could not understand cat speech.

The men quickly forgot their initial forebodings, stuffed Peter outrageously, laughed at him, teased him with rough good humor, and complained only that he hated his job as much as any of them. Eat a rat he would not. And torment one he would not. Tigerish in his attack, he finished the vermin as quickly as possible and dropped each still warm carcass beside the nearest man and miaouwed fiercely if it were not hove overside promptly.

A day in hot and sticky Havana was enough to get rid of the deck-load of machinery and tubing; and the *Calyx* wheezed out to sea again, squared off for about 86° west, and churned along at her best eight knots without a cloud in her sky. Captain Grant breathed more easily. Only Peter, Henderson and MacNab continued alert. When they had made sufficient westing and turned sharply southeast on the

Old Man's order to save coal by threading the maze of banks and islands between them and the Panama Canal, Mr. Henderson did not need Peter's irritable restlessness to warn him of the danger.

There were islands and shoals all the way from Swan, past Old Providence right down to Colón. He pored over his charts, checked his plotting and fixes under Peter's warning gaze, and sweated freely. Occasionally the cat descended to the engineroom and tried to tell Chief MacNab something that not even the old Scot was fey enough to understand. But he always managed to have a bit of steak or liver somewhere about, and Peter accepted the titbit graciously.

Nothing happened. The voyage droned on under perfect conditions. Swan was sighted and passed safely to port. Thus far the navigation was correct. Ahead lay Old Providence and before that a series of reefs and cays, Christmas Eve, and a falling barometer. His fears gone now that the voyage was so well advanced and everything so apparently well in hand, Captain Grant gave permission for a mild celebration of the holiday.

"Peter," asked Mr. Henderson apprehensively, as the cat leaped to his table and stared down at the much soiled chart the Second was studying, "is this it? What will it be: snorter, shoals, leak, collision, Christmas—what?"

"Miaouw," replied the animal in his most beseeching tone. He set a paw firmly on the chart, but Henderson, however superstitiously he believed in the cat's prescience, could not make up his mind whether the paw's position denoted anything or was a mere gesture.

The barometer went slowly, steadily down, but there was nothing to indicate that a snorter, one of those terrific winds that develop Caribbean hurricanes, was in the making. Chief MacNab reported his domain in perfect order, the carpenter tested his wells and found nothing by way of leakage. Reluctantly, for Henderson had begun to consider himself distinctly important since Peter appeared to rely upon him so completely, surrendered his fears for the moment and entered into the Christmas jollifications as heartily as anyone. With everything secure, and no banks or cays to beware of for at least another twelve hours, the old *Calyx* gave herself over, fore and aft, above and below decks, to the sort of roistering that has sent many a stout ship to Davy Jones.

By the time a staggering hand made eight bells midnight, and Christmas was upon them, Captain Grant was in a happy fog partly slumber, largely Jamaica rum, the Chief was snoring in stentorian gasps and gurgles, the watch on deck was "singing" in the lee of the forward starboard lifeboat, Mr. Henderson was unable to focus his sextant to get a star sight, and Peter was snarling at him, switching his tail and venting strange sounds, half miaowing, half growls. In the fireroom the coal passers were over-firing, and the *Calyx's* rusty stack belched like a small volcano.

Steadily the old bucket rolled along, a fine bone in her teeth, doing better than her accustomed speed, while the drowsy quartermaster at the wheel kept only half an eye on the card. At five bells the horizon began to close in, wet and thick as a blanket.

In fifteen minutes all Mr. Henderson could see as he laid his sextant away was the glare of two green lights dead ahead: Peter's reproving eyes. He laughed, with a hiccup, and began mechanically to check his dead reckoning with his last position. Four days and nights had passed since they left Havana, and they must be getting very close to the 80th meridian and a change of course.

Before he could determine anything, Peter was upon him with a wicked miaouw. Sharp claws pressed through his trousers deep into his leg. He looked down. The cat stiffened, tense in a listening attitude. Again he laid a paw on the officer's leg, purred as loud and harsh as his throat permitted, stopped, and again took the listening pose.

"What ye want, Peter?" queried the startled Henderson, slightly sobered. "I don't hear anything. What it is?" The thought of fire flashed into his mind, and he turned to inspect the old-fashioned telltale on the after bulkhead of the charthouse. Tubes clear; not a sign of anything. He called the engineroom; nothing there.

Again Peter pressed close, and this time drove his claws deep, miaowing horribly. He sprang up on the chest abaft the wheel and stared out ahead, his head cocked to one side, every nerve and muscle tense. Henderson stared at him, then searched the wet fog blanket ahead. Except for the faintly bright spot aloft forward where his running light was evidently burning, there was nothing. And then, with the cat almost in hysterics, he too, heard it.

At intervals out of the soggy darkness came a long, low, soul chilling snore. It sounded like all the giants of all time rolled into one, rasping out a troubled dream of terror and destruction. As he leaped at the wheel and spun it hard over before the astonished quartermaster could wake up enough to know what he was doing, Henderson saw that every hair on Peter's back was stiffly erect.

Under the stress of the sudden turn, the old *Calyx* careened wildly in the heavy swell, groaned in every plate and rivet, and thrust her blunt nose into a sea that all but capsized her. A thunderous crash and clatter from the galley told of crockery tossed about by the lurch. Everything not secured carried away. In an instant the ship was wide-awake. Up from his bunk ran Mr. Blain, barefoot and with only his pajama trousers on, crying out to know what was wrong.

"Roncador Reef!" gasped Henderson, completely sober and more frightened than the rest. "Roncador, the Old Snorer! We just missed it. I got the wheel over just in time. Listen!"

Again and again through the fog came that ominous gurgling, gasping warning as the seas thrust through the vast hole in the reef at tide level, sucking air in with them to make the blood freezing snore that set men to crossing themselves and mumbling prayers of thanks for their salvation. One touch of the thin-sided old tramp on those jagged rocks, and the *Calyx* would have become a ghost.

"Phoooo!" breathed Mr. Blain at last.

Chief MacNab had burst furiously in a moment before. Now he was as scornful as only a Scots engineer can be of navigators. "Ye rruint me wi' yer twisty hellum," he growled. "Crracked ma bedplate, an' nearr took ma low pressure ingine off the strruts. Rroncadorr, is ut? Losh, Peterr," he said to the now quiet beastie, stroking his head, "if I didna keep ma ingines betterr than they topsides keep the'r navigation, whaur'd we a' be the noo?"

Peter arched his back, rose, turned as if to go below, thought better of it. Jumping down from the chart chest, he walked deliberately over to the binnacle, sniffed, pawed at something just forward of it, and came to Henderson with a heavy seaman's knife in his mouth. Before anyone could speak, the quartermaster cried out sharply. "Sir! Look! We were three points off course! That knife!"

Henderson stood with it in his hand, looking at it dumbly. Blain and the Chief stared. It was the Skipper's knife, evidently dropped after he had shaved off some plug to fill his pipe. Nobody spoke. Peter finally said softly: "Miaouw—ouw!"

Everyone but Henderson went out. Hastily he checked his plot, ordered half speed, set the new course. Satisfied that he had done everything he could, he looked at Peter, again comfortably sprawled on the bulkhead chest. For a long moment the man stared. Then he went over and knelt, taking the drowsy cat in his arms. His voice was shaky as he whispered, but the fear was out of him. "Peter! Peter! You saved the ship. You've—made me."

Soberly enough the *Calyx* anchored in Colón harbor, took her Canal pilot aboard, and soon was fast to the electric mules that would tow her through the Gatun locks. Mr. Blain was on the bridge, Mr. Henderson in the bows, Chief MacNab at the throttle below. Peter was everywhere. He purred at Mr. MacNab and was brusquely ordered out of the engineroom; he disdained Captain Grant, who stood beside the Canal pilot, and dropped down to Henderson, who did not notice him for a moment. The Canal auxiliary crew had his entire attention. Inch by inch the *Calyx* was nosing into the great lower lock.

Peter eyed the proceedings approvingly, calculated the side walls, and finally placed a paw against Henderson's leg. Without taking his eyes from the Canal men, the Second stooped and took the cat in his arms. This was as it should be. Peter purred and flicked his battered tail about. Made fast to the mules ahead, alongside and astern, the ship rose slowly as the lock filled, until her bridge was level with the central pier. Peter struggled, jumped from Henderson's grasp and leaped upon the ship's rail.

Poised there, he calculated the distance between himself and land, turned his head enough to give Henderson a loud, farewell hail, and with a prodigious leap, landed safely. Everyone shouted. Peter gave the ship one last searching survey, turned and marched away, tail erect. His work was done; he was back home.

The Best Bed

SYLVIA TOWNSEND WARNER

THE cat had known many winters, but none like this. Through two slow darkening months it had rained, and now, on the eve of Christmas, the wind had gone round to the east and instead of rain, sleet and hail fell.

The hard pellets hit his drenched sides and bruised them. He ran faster. When boys threw stones at him he could escape by running; but from this heavenly lapidation there was no escape. He was hungry, for he had had no food since he had happened upon a dead sparrow, dead of cold, three days ago. It had not been the cat's habit to eat dead meat, but having fallen upon evil days he had been thankful even for that unhealthy-tasting flesh. Thirst tormented him, worse than hunger. Every now and then he would stop, and scrape the frozen gutters with his tongue. He had given up all hope now, he had forgotten all his wiles. He despaired, and ran on.

The lights, the footsteps on the pavements, the crashing buses, the swift cars like the monster cats whose eyes could outstar his own, daunted him. Though a Londoner, he was not used to these things, for he was born by Thames' side, and had spent his days among the docks, a modest useful life of rat-catching and secure slumbers upon flour sacks. But one night the wharf where he lived had caught fire; and terrified by flames, and smoke, and uproar, he had begun to run, till by the morning he was far from the river, and homeless, and too unversed in the ways of the world to find himself another home.

A street door opened, and he flinched aside, and turned a corner. But in that street, doors were opening too, every door letting out horror. For it was closing-time. Once, earlier in his wanderings, he had crouched in by such a door, thinking that any shelter would be better than the rainy street. Before he had time to escape, a hand snatched him up and a voice shouted above his head. "Gorblime if the cat hasn't come in for a drink," the voice said. And the cat felt his nose thrust into a puddle of something fiery and stinking, that burned on in his nostrils and eyes for hours afterwards.

He flattened himself against the wall, and lay motionless until the last door should have swung open for the last time. Only when someone walked by, bearing that smell with him, did the cat stir. Then his nose quivered with invincible disgust, his large ears pressed back upon his head, and the tip of his tail beat stiffly upon the pavement. A dog, with its faculty of conscious despair, would have abandoned itself, and lain down to await death; but when the streets were quiet once more the cat ran on.

There had been a time when he ran and leaped for the pleasure of the thing, rejoicing in his strength like an athlete. The resources of that lean, sinewy body, disciplined in the hunting days of his youth, had served him well in the first days of his wandering; then, speeding before some barking terrier, he had hugged amidst his terrors a compact and haughty joy in the knowledge that he could so surely outstrip the pursuer; but now his strength would only serve to prolong his torment. Though an accumulated fatigue smouldered in every nerve, the obdurate limbs carried him on, and would carry him on still, a captive to himself, meekly trotting to the place of his death.

He ran as the wind directed, turning this way and that to avoid the gusts, spiked with hail, that ravened through the streets. His eyes were closed, but suddenly at a familiar sound he stopped and stiffened with fear. It was the sound of a door swinging on its hinges. He sniffed apprehensively. There was a smell, puffed out with every swinging-to of the door, but it was not the smell he abhorred; and though he waited in the shadow of a buttress, no sounds of jangling voices came to confirm his fears, and though the door continued to open and shut, no footsteps came from it. He stepped cautiously from his buttress into a porch. The smell was stronger here. It was aromatic, rich, and a little smoky. It tickled his nose and made him sneeze.

The door was swinging with the wind. The aperture was small, too small for anything to be seen through it, save only a darkness that was not quite dark. With a sudden determination the cat flitted through.

Of his first sensations, one overpowered all the others. Warmth! It poured over him, it penetrated his being, and confused his angular physical consciousness of cold and hunger and fatigue into something rounded and indistinct. Flooded with weariness, he sank down on the stone flags.

Another sneezing-fit roused him. He jumped up, and began to explore.

The building he was in reminded him of home. Often, hunting the riverside, he had strayed into places like this—lifty and dusky, stone-floored and securely uninhabited. But they had smelt of corn, of linseed, of tallow, of sugar; none of them had smelt as this did, smokily sweet. They had been cold. Here it was warm. They had been dark; and here the dusk was mellowed with one red star, burning in mid-air, and with the glimmer of a few tapers, that added to the smoky sweetness their smell of warm wax.

His curiosity growing with his confidence, the cat ran eagerly about the church. He rubbed his back against the font, he examined into the varying smell of the hassocks, he trotted up the pulpit stairs, sprang on the ledge, and sharpened his claws in the cushion. Outside the wind boomed, and the hail clattered against the windows, but within the air was warm and still, and the red star burned mildly on. Over against the pulpit the cat came on something that reminded him even more of home—a wisp of hay, lying on the flags. He had often seen hay; sometimes borne towering above the greasy tide on barges, sometimes fallen from the nosebags of the great draught horses who waited so peacefully in the wharfingers' yards.

The hay seemed to have fallen from a box on trestles, cut out of unstained wood. The cat stood on his hind legs, and tried to look in, but it was too high for him. He turned about, but his curiosity brought him back again; and poising himself on his clustered paws he rocked slightly, gauging his spring, and then jumped, alighting softly in a bed of hay. He landed so delicately that though the two kneeling figures at either end of the crib swayed forward for a moment, they did not topple over. The cat sniffed them, a trifle suspiciously, but they did not hold his attention long. It was the hay that interested him. A drowsy scent rose out of the deep, warm bed as he kneaded and shuffled it with his forepaws. This, this, promised him what he had so long yearned for; sound sleep, an enfolding in warmth and softness, a nourishing forgetfulness. He paced round in a small circle, burrowing himself a close nest, purring with a harsh note of joy. As he turned he brushed against a third figure in the crib; but he scarcely noticed it. Already a rapture of sleepiness was overcoming him; the two kneeling figures had done him no harm, nor would this reposing one. Soon the bed was made to his measure. Bowing his head upon his paws, he abandoned himself.

Another onslaught of hail dashed against the windows, the door creaked, and at a gust of wind entering the church the candle-flames wavered, as though they were nodding their heads in assent; but though the cat's ears flicked once or twice against the feet of the plaster Jesus, he was too securely asleep to know or heed.

The Cat That Walked by Himself

RUDYARD KIPLING

This befel and behappened and became and was, O, my Best Be-loved, when the tame animals were wild. The Dog was wild, and the Horse was wild, and the Cow was wild, and the Sheep was wild, and the Pig was wild—as wild as could be—and they walked in the wet wild woods by their wild lones, but the wildest of all the wild animals was the Cat. He walked by himself, and all places were alike to him.

Of course the Man was wild too. He was dreadfully wild. He didn't even begin to be tame till he met the Woman and she did not like living in his wild ways. She picked out a nice dry cave, instead of a heap of wet leaves, to lie down in, and she strewed clean sand on the floor, and she lit a nice fire of wood at the back of the cave, and she hung a dried Wild Horse skin, tail down, across the opening of the cave, and she said: "Wipe your feet when you come in, and now we'll keep house."

That night, Best Beloved, they ate Wild Sheep roasted on the hot stones and flavored with wild garlic and wild pepper, and Wild Duck stuffed with wild rice, and wild fenugreek and wild coriander, and marrow-bones of Wild Oxen, and wild cherries and wild granadillas. Then the Man went to sleep in front of the fire ever so happy, but the Woman sat up, combing. She took the bone of the shoulder of mutton, the big flat blade-bone and she looked at the wonderful marks on it, and she threw more wood on the fire and she made a magic. She made the first Singing Magic in the world.

Out in the wet wild woods all the wild animals gathered together where they could see the light of the fire a long way off, and they wondered what it meant.

Then Wild Horse stamped with his foot and said: "O, my friends and my enemies, why have the Man and the Woman made that great light in that great cave, and what harm will it do us?"

Wild Dog lifted up his nose and smelled the smell of the roast mutton and said: "I will go up and see and look and stay: for I think it is good. Cat, come with me."

"Nenni," said the Cat. "I am the Cat who walks by himself, and all places are alike to me. I will not come."

"Then we will never be friends again," said Wild Dog, and he trotted off to the cave.

But when he had gone a little way the Cat said to himself: "All places are alike to me. Why should I not go too and see and look and come away?" So he slipped after Wild Dog softly, very softly, and hid himself where he could hear everything.

When Wild Dog reached the mouth of the cave he lifted up the dried Horse skin with his nose a little bit and sniffed the beautiful smell of the roast mutton, and the Woman heard him and laughed and said: "Here comes the First wild thing out of the wild woods. What do you want?"

Wild Dog said: "O, my enemy and wife of my enemy, what is this that smells so good in the wild woods?"

Then the Woman picked up a roasted mutton bone and threw it to Wild Dog and said: "Wild thing out of the wild woods, taste and try." Wild Dog gnawed the bone and it was more delicious than anything he had ever tasted, and he said: "O, my enemy and wife of my enemy, give me another."

The Woman said: "Wild thing out of the wild woods, help my Man to hunt through the day and guard this cave at night and I will give you as many roast bones as you need."

"Ah!" said the Cat listening, "this is a very wise Woman, but she is not so wise as I am."

Wild Dog crawled into the cave and laid his head on the Woman's lap and said: "O, my friend and wife of my friend, I will help your Man to hunt through the day, and at night I will guard your cave."

"Ah!" said the Cat listening, "that is a very foolish Dog." And he went back through the wet wild woods waving his tail and walking by his wild lone. But he never told anybody.

When the Man waked up he said: "What is Wild Dog doing here?" And the Woman said: "His name is not Wild Dog any more, but the First Friend because he will be our friend for always and always and always. Take him with you when you go hunting."

Next night the Woman cut great green armfuls of fresh grass from the water-meadows and dried it before the fire so that it smelt like new-mown hay, and she sat at the mouth of the cave and plaited a halter out of Horse-hide, and she looked at the shoulder of mutton bone—at the big broad blade-bone—and she made a magic. She made the second Singing Magic in the world.

Out in the wild woods all the wild animals wondered what had happened to Wild Dog, and at last Wild Horse stamped with his foot and said: "I will go and see why Wild Dog has not returned. Cat, come with me."

"Nenni," said the Cat. "I am the Cat who walks by himself, and all places are alike to me. I will not come." But all the same he followed Wild Horse softly, very softly, and hid himself where he could hear everything.

When the Woman heard Wild Horse tripping and stumbling on his long mane she laughed and said: "Here comes the Second wild thing out of the wild woods. What do you want?"

Wild Horse said: "O, my enemy and wife of my enemy, where is Wild Dog?"

The Woman laughed and picked up the blade-bone and looked at it and said: "Wild thing out of the wild woods, you did not come here for Wild Dog, but for the sake of this good grass."

And Wild Horse, tripping and stumbling on his long mane, said: "That is true, give it me to eat."

The Woman said: "Wild thing out of the wild woods, bend your wild head and wear what I give you and you shall eat the wonderful grass three times a day."

"Ah," said the Cat listening, "this is a clever Woman, but she is not so clever as I am."

Wild Horse bent his wild head and the Woman slipped the plaited hide halter over it, and Wild Horse breathed on the woman's feet and said: "O, my mistress and wife of my master, I will be your servant for the sake of the wonderful grass."

"Ah," said the Cat listening, "that is a very foolish Horse." And he went back through the wet wild woods, waving his wild tail and walking by his wild lone.

When the Man and the Dog came back from hunting the Man said: "What is Wild Horse doing here?" And the Woman said: "His name is not Wild Horse any more, but the First Servant because he will carry us from place to place for always and always and always. Take him with you when you go hunting."

Next day, holding her wild head high that her wild horns should not catch in the wild trees, Wild Cow came up to the cave, and the Cat followed and hid himself just the same as before; and everything happened just the same as before; and the Cat said the same things as before, and when Wild Cow had promised to give her milk to the Woman every day in exchange for the wonderful grass, the Cat went back through the wet wild woods walking by his lone just the same as before.

And when the Man and the Horse and the Dog came home from hunting and asked the same questions, same as before, the Woman said: "Her name is not Wild Cow any more, but the Giver of Good Things. She will give us the warm white milk for always and always and always, and I will take care of her while you three go hunting."

Next day the Cat waited to see if any other wild thing would go up to the cave, but no one moved, so the Cat walked there by himself, and he saw the Woman milking the Cow, and he saw the light of the fire in the cave, and he smelt the smell of the warm white milk.

Cat said: "O, my enemy and wife of my enemy, where did Wild Cow go?"

The Woman laughed and said: "Wild thing out of the wild woods, go back to the woods again for I have braided up my hair and I have put away the blade-bone, and we have no more need of either friends or servants in our cave."

Cat said: "I am not a friend and I am not a servant. I am the Cat who walks by himself and I want to come into your cave."

The Woman said: "Then why did you not come with First Friend on the first night?"

Cat grew very angry and said: "Has Wild Dog told tales of me?"

Then the Woman laughed and said: "You are the Cat who walks by himself and all places are alike to you. You are neither a friend nor a servant. You have said it yourself. Go away and walk by yourself in all places alike."

Then the Cat pretended to be sorry and said: "Must I never come into the cave? Must I never sit by the warm fire? Must I never drink the warm white milk? You are very wise and very beautiful. You should not be cruel even to a Cat."

Then the Woman said: "I knew I was wise but I did not know I was beautiful. So I will make a bargain with you. If ever I say one word in your praise you may come into the cave."

"And if you say two words in my praise?" said the Cat.

"I never shall," said the Woman, "but if I say two words you may sit by the fire in the cave."

"And if you say three words?" said the Cat.

"I never shall," said the Woman, "but if I do you may drink the warm white milk three times a day for always and always and always."

Then the Cat arched his back and said: "Now let the curtain at the mouth of the cave, and the fire at the back of the cave, and the milk-pots that stand beside the fire remember what my enemy and the wife of my enemy has said." And he went away through the wet wild woods waving his wild tail and walking by his wild lone.

That night when the Man and the Horse and the Dog came home from hunting, the Woman did not tell them of the bargain that she had made because she was afraid that they might not like it.

Cat went far and far away and hid himself in the wet wild woods by his wild lone for a long time till the Woman forgot all about him. Only the Bat—the little upside-down Bat—that hung inside the cave knew where Cat hid, and every evening he would fly to Cat with the news.

One evening the Bat said: "There is a Baby in the cave. He is new and pink and fat and small, and the Woman is very fond of him."

"Ah," said the Cat listening, "but what is the Baby fond of?"

"He is fond of things that are soft and tickle," said the Bat. "He is fond of warm things to hold in his arms when he goes to sleep. He is fond of being played with. He is fond of all those things."

"Ah," said the Cat, "then my time has come."

Next night Cat walked through the wet wild woods and hid very near the cave till morning-time. The woman was very busy cooking, and the Baby cried and interrupted; so she carried him outside the cave and gave him a handful of pebbles to play with. But still the Baby cried.

Then the Cat put out his paddy-paw and patted the Baby on the cheek, and it cooed; and the Cat rubbed against its fat knees and tickled it under its fat chin with his tail. And the Baby laughed; and the Woman heard him and smiled.

Then the Bat—the little upside-down Bat—that hung in the mouth of the cave said: "O, my hostess and wife of my host and mother of my host, a wild thing from the wild woods is most beautifully playing with your Baby."

"A blessing on that wild thing whoever he may be," said the Woman straightening her back, "for I was a busy Woman this morning and he has done me a service."

That very minute and second, Best Beloved, the dried Horse-skin curtain that was stretched tail-down at the mouth of the cave fell down—*So!*—because it remembered the bargain, and when the Woman went to pick it up—lo and behold!—the Cat was sitting quite comfy inside the cave.

"O, my enemy and wife of my enemy and mother of my enemy," said the Cat, "it is I, for you have spoken a word in my praise, and now I can sit within the cave for always and always and always. But still I am the Cat who walks by himself and all places are alike to me."

The Woman was very angry and shut her lips tight and took up her spinning-wheel and began to spin.

But the Baby cried because the Cat had gone away, and the Woman could not hush him for he struggled and kicked and grew black in the face.

"O, my enemy and wife of my enemy and mother of my enemy," said the Cat, "take a strand of the thread that you are spinning and tie it to your spindle-wheel and drag it on the floor and I will show you a magic that shall make your Baby laugh as loudly as he is now crying."

"I will do so," said the Woman, "because I am at my wits' end, but I will not thank you for it."

She tied the thread to the little pot spindle-wheel and drew it across the floor and the Cat ran after it and patted it with his paws, and rolled head over heels, and tossed it backward over his shoulder, and chased it between his hindlegs, and pretended to lose it, and pounced down upon it again till the Baby laughed as loudly as he had been crying, and scrambled after the Cat and frolicked all over the cave till he grew tired and settled down to sleep with the Cat in his arms.

"Now," said the Cat, "I will sing the Baby a song that shall keep him asleep for an hour." And he began to purr loud and low, low and loud, till the Baby fell fast asleep. The Woman smiled as she looked down upon the two of them and said: "That was wonderfully done. Surely you are very clever, O, Cat."

That very minute and second, Best Beloved, the smoke of the fire at the back of the cave came down in clouds from the roof because it remembered the bargain, and when it had cleared away—lo and behold!—the Cat was sitting, quite comfy, close to the fire.

"O, my enemy and wife of my enemy and mother of my enemy," said the Cat, "it is I, for you have spoken a second word in my praise, and now I can sit by the warm fire at the back of the cave for always and always and always. But still I am the Cat who walks by himself and all places are alike to me."

Then the Woman was very, very angry and let down her hair and put more wood on the fire and brought out the broad blade-bone of the shoulder of mutton and began to make a magic that should prevent her from saying a third word in praise of the Cat. It was not a Singing Magic, Best Beloved, it was a Still Magic; and by and by the cave grew so still that a little we-wee Mouse crept out of a corner and ran across the floor.

"O, my enemy and wife of my enemy and mother of my enemy," said the Cat, "is that little Mouse part of your magic?"

"No," said the Woman, and she dropped the blade-bone and jumped upon a footstool in front of the fire and braided up her hair very quick for fear that the Mouse should run up it.

"Ah," said the Cat listening, "then the Mouse will do me no harm if I eat it?"

"No," said the Woman, braiding up her hair; "eat it quick and I will always be grateful to you."

Cat made one jump and caught the little Mouse, and the Woman said: "A hundred thanks to you, O, Cat. Even the First Friend is not quick enough to catch little Mice as you have done. You must be very wise."

That very moment and second, O, Best Beloved, the milkpot that stood by the fire cracked in two pieces—*So!*—because it remembered the bargain, and when the Woman jumped down from the footstool —lo and behold!—the Cat was lapping up the warm white milk that lay in one of the broken pieces.

"O, my enemy and wife of my enemy and mother of my enemy," said the Cat, "it is I, for you have spoken three words in my praise, and now I can drink the warm white milk three times a day for always and always and always. But *still* I am the Cat who walks by himself and all places are alike to me."

Then the Woman laughed and set him a bowl of the warm white milk and said: "O, Cat, you are as clever as a Man, but remember that the bargain was not made with the Man or the Dog, and I do not know what they will do when they come home."

"What is that to me?" said the Cat. "If I have my place by the fire and my milk three times a day I do not care what the Man or the Dog can do."

That evening when the Man and the Dog came into the cave the Woman told them all the story of the bargain, and the Man said: "Yes, but he has not made a bargain with me or with all proper Men after me." And he took off his two leather boots and he took up his little stone axe (that makes three) and he fetched a piece of wood and a hatchet (that is five altogether), and he set them out in a row, and he said: "Now we will make a bargain. If you do not catch Mice when you are in the cave, for always and always and always, I will throw these five things at you whenever I see you, and so shall all proper Men do after me."

"Ah," said the Woman listening. "This is a very clever Cat, but he is not so clever as my Man."

The Cat counted the five things (and they looked very knobby) and he said: "I will catch Mice when I am in the cave for always and always and always: but still I am the Cat that walks by himself and all places are alike to me."

"Not when I am near," said the Man. "If you had not said that I would have put all these things away (for always and always and always), but now I am going to throw my two boots and my little stone axe (that makes three) at you whenever I meet you, and so shall all proper Men do after me."

Then the Dog said: "Wait a minute. He has not made a bargain with me." And he sat down and growled dreadfully and showed all his teeth and said: "If you are not kind to the Baby while I am in the cave for always and always and always I will chase you till I catch you, and when I catch you I will bite you, and so shall all proper Dogs do after me."

"Ah," said the Woman listening. "This is a very clever Cat, but he is not so clever as the Dog."

Cat counted the Dog's teeth (and they looked very pointed) and he said: "I will be kind to the Baby while I am in the cave as long as he does not pull my tail too hard for always and always and always. But still I am the Cat that walks by himself and all places are alike to me."

"Not when I am near," said the Dog. "If you had not said that I would have shut my mouth for always and always and always, but now I am going to chase you up a tree whenever I meet you, and so shall all proper Dogs do after me."

Then the Man threw his two boots and his little stone axe (that makes three) at the Cat, and the Cat ran out of the cave and the Dog chased him up a tree, and from that day to this, Best Beloved, three proper Men out of five will always throw things at a Cat whenever they meet him, and all proper Dogs will chase him up a tree. But the Cat keeps his side of the bargain too. He will kill Mice and he will be kind to Babies when he is in the house, as long as they do not pull his tail too hard. But when he has done that, and between times, he is the Cat that walks by himself and all places are alike to him, and if you look out at nights you can see him waving his wild tail and walking by his wild lone—just the same as before.

The Long-Cat

COLETTE

A SHORT-HAIRED black cat always looks longer than any other cat. But this particular one, Babou, nicknamed the Long-cat, really did measure, stretched right out flat, well over a yard and a quarter. If you did not arrange him properly, he was not much more than a yard. I used to measure him sometimes.

"He's stopped growing longer," I said one day to my mother. "Isn't it a pity?"

"Why a pity? He's too long as it is. I can't understand why you want everything to grow bigger. It's bad to grow too much, very bad indeed!"

It's true that it always worried her when she thought that children were growing too fast, and she had good cause to be anxious about my elder half-brother, who went on growing until he was twenty-four.

"But I'd love to grow a bit taller."

"D'you mean you'd like to be like that Brisedoux girl, five-foot-seven tall at twelve years old? A midget can always make herself liked. But what can you do with a gigantic beauty? Who would want to marry her?"

"Couldn't Babou get married, then?"

"Oh, a cat's a cat. Babou's only too long when he really wants to be. Are we even sure he's black? He's probably white in snowy weather, dark blue at night, and red when he goes to steal strawberries. He's very light when he lies on your knees, and very heavy when I carry him into the kitchen in the evenings to prevent him from sleeping on my bed. I think he's too much of a vegetarian to be a real cat."

For the Long-cat really did steal strawberries, picking out the ripest of the variety called Docteur-Morère which are so sweet, and of the white Hautboys which taste faintly of ants. According to the season he would also go for the tender tips of the asparagus, and when it came to melons his choice was not so much for cantaloups as for the kind called Noir-des-Carmes whose rind, marbled light and dark like the skin of a salamander, he knew how to rip open. In all this he was not at all exceptional. I once had a she-cat who used to crunch rings of raw onion, provided they were the sweet onions of the South. There are cats who set great store by oysters, snails, and clams.

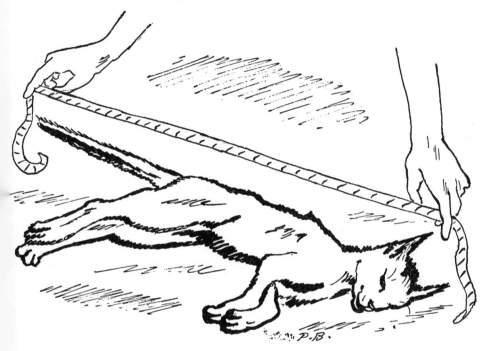

When the Long-cat went off to poach strawberries from our next-door neighbour, Monsieur Pomié, he went by way of the wall, which was covered with such dense ivy that the cats could walk along under cover, their presence revealed only by the quivering of the leaves, the mist of yellow pollen and the golden cloud of bees.

He loved this leafy tunnel but, do what he would, he had to come out of it at the end since Madame Pomié kept the top of the wall bare where it overlooked her garden. Once out in the open, he adopted a very off-hand manner, especially if he met Madame de Saint-Aubin's beautiful cat, who was black, with a white face and belly. I found this wall a good place to study tomcats, not so much their habits as their ceremonial procedure, governed by a kind of choreography. Unlike the females, they are more noisy than warlike and they try to gain

time by palavers. Hence all the snarling preambles. Not that they do
not know how to fight cruelly once they come to grips; but as a rule
they are far removed from the silent and furious grapplings of the females. The she-cat we had at the same time as the Long-cat literally
flew into battle if a female ventured into her haunts. Barely touching
the ground, she would pounce on the enemy, even if it were her own
offspring. She fought as a bird does, going for her adversary's head. I
never saw her chastise a male, except for a few cuffs, for as soon as the
males saw her they fled, while she followed them with a look of in-
expressible contempt. When July and January came, she settled her
amorous encounters in forty-eight hours. On the morning of the third
day, when the chosen partner, in fine fettle and with renewed appetite, approached her with a self-confident, prancing gait and a deep-
throated song, she would root him to the spot with a mere look.

"I've come," he would begin, "I . . . I came to resume our agreeable conversation of yesterday . . ."

"Excuse me," the she-cat interrupted, "you were saying? I didn't
quite catch. What agreeable conversation?"

"Why . . . the one we had at ten o'clock in the morning . . . and
the one at five in the afternoon . . . and especially our conversation
at ten in the evening, near the well."

The she-cat, perched on top of the pergola, raised herself a little on
her delicately-boned paws.

"Near the well, a conversation, you, with ME? Who do you suppose
is going to believe that? You don't expect ME to! Take yourself off!
It'll be the worse for you if you don't, I can tell you. Take yourself
off!"

"But . . . but I love you. And I'm ready to prove it to you again."

Standing upright there the she-cat towered over the tom as Satan,
jutting out from Notre Dame, broods over Paris. The look she cast on
him from her tawny-gold eyes was such as he could not long endure;
and the outcast would make off with the shambling gait of someone
who has been driven away.

As I was saying then, the Long-cat, impelled by a vegetarian craving which those who have not experienced it can never understand,
would go after the strawberries, the melons and the asparagus. On his
return, a little green or rosy pulp remained, as evidence of his pillag-
ings, in the grooves between his curved claws, and this he licked
casually during his siesta.

"Show your hands!" my mother used to say to him, and thereupon
he surrendered to her a long front paw, adept at every kind of mischief, with pads as hard as a road parched with drought.

"Have you been opening a melon?"

I dare say he understood. His gentle yellow eyes met Sido's penetrating look, but since his innocence was only assumed, he could not help squinting a little.

"Yes, you *have* opened a melon. And I expect it was the pretty little one I had my eye on, the one that looked like a globe with yellow continents and green seas." She released the long paw which fell back limp and expressionless.

"That deserves a good slap," said I.

"I know. But just think that instead of a melon he might have slit open a bird, or a little rabbit, or have eaten a chick."

She scratched the flat skull which he stretched up against her hand, and the half-bald temples which showed bluish between the sparse black hairs. A tremendous purring rose from his thick neck with its white patch under the chin. The Long-cat loved no one but my mother, followed no one but her and looked to her for everything. If I took him in my arms he would imperceptibly glide out of them as though he were melting away. Except for the ritual battles and during the brief seasons of love-making, the Long-cat was nothing but silence, sleep and nonchalant night-prowlings.

I naturally preferred our she-cats to him. The females of the feline tribe are so unlike the males that they seem to regard the tom as a stranger and often as an enemy. The only exceptions are the cats of Siam who live in couples like the wild beasts. Perhaps it is because the cats in our countries are such a hybrid collection of every coat and colour that they develop a taste for change and fickleness. In my home we were never without two or three she-cats who graced the lawns, crowned the pump and slept in the wistaria, which they had hollowed into a hammock. They confined their charming sociability to my mother and myself. As soon as January and July, the compulsory seasons of love, were over, they regarded the male once again as a suspect, a lout, and a wicked devourer of newly-born kittens, and their conversations with the Long-cat consisted chiefly of crisp insults, whenever he assumed the bland, gentle manner and the innocent smile of the cat who has never harboured any evil intentions, or even thoughts. Sometimes they seemed about to play, but this never came to anything. The females took fright at the strength of the male, and at that furious excitement which, in an uncastrated cat, turns playfulness into a murderous combat.

By virtue of his serpent-like build, the Long-cat excelled at strange leaps in which he nearly twisted himself into a figure of eight. In full sunlight his winter coat, which was longer and more satiny than in summer, revealed the waterings and markings of his far-off tabby ancestor. A tom will remain playful until he is quite old; but even in play his face never loses the gravity that is stamped on it. The Long-cat's expression softened only when he looked at my mother. Then his white whiskers would bristle powerfully, while into his eyes crept the smile of an innocent little boy. He used to follow her when she went to pick violets along the wall that separated M. de Fourolles' garden from ours. The close-set border provided every day a big bunch which my mother let fade, either pinned to her bodice or in an empty glass, because violets in water lose all their scent. Step by step the Long-cat followed his stooping mistress, sometimes imitating with his paw the gesture of her hand groping among the leaves, and imitating her discoveries also. "Ha, ha!" he would cry, "me too!" and thereupon show his prize: a bombardier beetle, a pink worm or a shrivelled cockchafer.

"My goodness, how silly you are," Sido would say to him, affectionately. "Never mind, what you've found is very pretty."

When we rejoined my elder brother in the Loiret, we took with us our favourite she-cat and the Long-cat. Both of them seemed to mind much less than I did exchanging a lovely house for a small cottage, and the vast grounds of our family property for a narrow garden. I have referred elsewhere to the stream which danced at the end of this garden. Left to itself, it was sufficiently clear and sparkling, and had enough soap-wort and wild radishes clinging to the walls which hemmed it in, to beautify any village, if the village had respected it. But those who lived on its banks polluted it.

At the end of our new garden there was a little wash-house which protected the straw palliasse on which the washerwomen knelt, the sloping board, white as a scraped bone, where they pressed the frothing linen, the washerwomen's battledores, the brushes made of couch-grass and the sprinklers. Soon after our arrival the she-cat laid claim to the palliasse, gave birth to her litter on it, and brought up there the one little tabby which we left her. Whenever the sun shone I joined her there and sat on the soaping-board. The tabby kitten, soft and heavy with milk, watched the reflections of the little river forming broken rings, gold serpents and wavelets on the tiled roof of the penthouse. At six weeks he was already trotting, and following the flight of the flies with eyes that were still blue, while his mother, with a coat as finely marked as his, saw herself mirrored in the beauty of her son.

Excluded though he was from this family happiness, the Long-cat for all that adopted an air of serenity that was vaguely patriarchal, the detached bearing of those fathers who are content to leave the care of their offspring to their worthy spouse. He confined himself to the parsley bed which the she-cat let him have, and there he would sprawl, warming his long belly, with its withered teats, in the sun. Or else he would drape himself over the heap of firewood, as if the spiky faggots were wool and down. For a cat's idea of what is comfortable and what is not is incomprehensible to a human.

Spring drenched our retreat with precocious warmth, and in the light air of May the scents of lilac, young tarragon and red-brown wallflower intermingled. I was at that time a prey to homesickness for my native village, and this I nursed in silence in the new village, amidst the bitterness of spring and its first flowers. There I sat, an anæmic young girl, leaning my cheeks and my little waxen ears against a wall already warm, the end of one of my over-long plaits always trailing far from me over the fine, sieved leaf-mould of a seed-bed.

One day when we were all dozing, the she-cat on her palliasse, the tom on his couch of spiky firewood-bundles, and I at the foot of the wall where the sun lingered longest, the little cat, who was wide awake and busy chasing flies on the edge of the river, fell into the water. True to the code of his tribe, he uttered no cry and began to swim by instinct as soon as he came to the surface. I happened to see him tumble in, and just as I was setting off for the house to seize the butterfly net, run down the road, and rejoin the river at the first little bridge, where I could have fished out the swimming kitten, the Long-cat threw himself into the water. He swam like an otter, ears flat and only his nostrils out of the water.

It is not every day that one sees a cat swim, swim of his own free will, I mean. He can glide unerringly through water like a serpent, but he never makes use of this gift except to save his life if he is in danger of drowning. Helped by the current, the Long-cat forged ahead strongly in pursuit of the kitten, the swift, transparent waters of the pent-up river on its bed of pebbles and broken shards making his long body look like a leech. I lost half a minute through stopping to watch him.

He seized the little cat by the scruff of its neck, turned right round and set off upstream, not without effort, for the current was strong and the kitten, inert like all little cats when you hold them by the scruff of their necks, weighed his full weight. The sight of the Long-cat struggling nearly made me jump into the water too. But the rescuer clambered up on to the washing-board and laid his dripping burden on the bank, after which he shook himself and looked in stupefaction at the drenched kitten. That was the moment when the rescued one, silent hitherto, elected to cough and sneeze and set up a terrific shrill lamentation which awoke the mother cat.

"Horrors!" she cried. "What do I see? You baby-snatcher! You wrecker, you devourer of infants, you stinking beast, what have you done to my son?"

Even as she jerked out these insults at the top of her voice, she was already encircling the little cat with her own body and sniffing him, finding time too to turn him all over and lick the river water off his coat.

"But," ventured the Long-cat, "but . . . but on the contrary, I jumped into the water to get him. Now I come to think of it, I don't know what made me do it!"

"Out of my sight! Or in another moment I'll bite your nose off and crush the breath out of you! I'll blind you, I'll slit your throat, I'll . . ."

She made ready to suit the action to the word, and I admired the furious beauty which animates a female when she pits herself against danger or an adversary bigger than herself.

The Long-cat took to his heels and, still dripping, gained the ladder leading to the cosy hay-loft warm under its tiled roof. The she-cat, changing her tone, led her son to the palliasse where he found once again the warm maternal belly with its milk, healing care and restoring sleep.

But the she-cat never forgave the Long-cat. Whenever she met him she never forgot to call him "baby-snatcher, drowner of little cats, assassin," accompanying this with snarls and yells, while the Long-cat strove each time to clear himself: "Now look here! I tell you that, on the contrary, it was I who, obeying only my own heart, overcame my loathing for cold water . . ."

I genuinely pitied him and used to call him "poor, misunderstood Long-cat."

"Misunderstood," said my mother, "that remains to be seen."

She could see deep into souls; and she was not one to be taken in by the equivocal meekness, the flickering yellow gleam in the eye of a tomcat, whenever it lights on tender, defenseless flesh.

Tobermory

SAKI (H. H. MUNRO)

IT WAS a chill, rain-washed afternoon of a late August day, that indefinite season when partridges are still in the security of cold storage, and there is nothing to hunt—unless one is bounded on the north by the Bristol Channel, in which case one may lawfully gallop after fat red stags. Lady Blemley's house-party was not bounded on the north by the Bristol Channel, hence there was a full gathering of her guests round the tea-table on this particular afternoon. And, in spite of the blankness of the season and the triteness of the occasion, there was no trace in the company of that fatigued restlessness which means a dread of the pianola and a subdued hankering for auction bridge. The undisguised, open-mouthed attention of the entire party was fixed on the homely, negative personality of Mr. Cornelius Appin. Of all her guests, he was the one who had come to Lady Blemley with the vaguest reputation. Someone had said he was "clever," and he had got his invitation in the moderate expectation, on the part of his hostess, that some portion at least of his cleverness would be contributed to the general entertainment. Until tea-time that day she had been unable to discover in what direction, if any, his cleverness lay. He was neither a wit nor a croquet champion, a hypnotic force nor a begetter of amateur theatricals. Neither did his exterior suggest the sort of man in whom women are willing to pardon a generous measure of mental deficiency. He had subsided into mere Mr. Appin, and the Cornelius seemed a piece of transparent baptismal bluff. And now he was claiming to have launched on the world a discovery beside which the invention of gun powder, of the printing-press, and of steam locomotion were inconsiderable trifles. Science had made bewildering strides in many directions during recent decades, but this thing seemed to belong to the domain of miracle rather than to scientific achievement.

"And do you really ask us to believe," Sir Wilfrid was saying, "that you have discovered a means for instructing animals in the art of human speech, and that dear old Tobermory has proved your first successful pupil?"

"It is a problem at which I have worked for the last seventeen years," said Mr. Appin, "but only during the last eight or nine months have I been rewarded with glimmerings of success. Of course I have experimented with thousands of animals, but latterly only with cats, those wonderful creatures which have assimilated themselves so marvelously with our civilization while retaining all their highly developed feral instincts. Here and there among cats one comes across an outstanding superior intellect, just as one does among the ruck of human beings, and when I made the acquaintance of Tobermory a week ago I saw at once that I was in contact with a 'Beyond-cat' of extraordinary intelligence. I had gone far along the road

to success in recent experiments; with Tobermory, as you call him, I have reached the goal."

Mr. Appin concluded his remarkable statement in a voice which he strove to divest of a triumphant inflexion. No one said "Rats," though Clovis's lips moved in a monosyllabic contortion which probably invoked those rodents of disbelief.

"And do you mean to say," asked Miss Resker, after a slight pause, "that you have taught Tobermory to say and understand easy sentences of one syllable?"

"My dear Miss Resker," said the wonder-worker patiently, "one teaches little children and savages and backward adults in that piecemeal fashion; when one has once solved the problem of making a beginning with an animal of highly developed intelligence one has no need for those halting methods. Tobermory can speak our language with perfect correctness."

This time Clovis very distinctly said, "Beyond-rats!" Sir Wilfrid was more polite, but equally sceptical.

"Hadn't we better have the cat in and judge for ourselves?" suggested Lady Blemley.

Sir Wilfrid went in search of the animal, and the company settled themselves down to the languid expectation of witnessing some more or less adroit drawing-room ventriloquism.

In a minute Sir Wilfrid was back in the room, his face white beneath its tan and his eyes dilated with excitement.

"By Gad, it's true!"

His agitation was unmistakably genuine, and his hearers started forward in a thrill of awakened interest.

Collapsing into an armchair he continued breathlessly: "I found him dozing in the smoking-room, and called after him to come for his tea. He blinked at me in his usual way, and I said, 'Come on, Toby; don't keep us waiting'; and, by Gad! he drawled out in a most horribly natural voice, that he'd come when he dashed well pleased! I nearly jumped out of my skin!"

Appin had preached to absolutely incredulous hearers; Sir Wilfrid's statement carried instant conviction. A Babel-like chorus of startled exclamation arose, amid which the scientist sat mutely enjoying the first fruit of his stupendous discovery.

In the midst of the clamour Tobermory entered the room and made his way with velvet tread and studied unconcern across to the group seated round the tea-table.

A sudden hush of awkwardness and constraint fell on the company. Somehow there seemed an element of embarrassment in addressing on equal terms a domestic cat of acknowledged mental ability.

"Will you have some milk, Tobermory?" asked Lady Blemley in a rather strained voice.

"I don't mind if I do," was the response, couched in a tone of even indifference. A shiver of suppressed excitement went through the listeners, and Lady Blemley might be excused for pouring out the saucerful of milk rather unsteadily.

"I am afraid I have spilt a good deal of it," she said apologetically.

"After all, it's not my Axminster," was Tobermory's rejoinder.

Another silence fell on the group, and then Miss Resker, in her best district-visitor manner, asked if the human language had been difficult to learn. Tobermory looked squarely at her for a moment and then fixed his gaze serenely on the middle distance. It was obvious that boring questions lay outside his scheme of life.

"What do you think of human intelligence?" asked Mavis Pellington lamely.

"Of whose intelligence in particular?" asked Tobermory coldly.

"Oh, well, mine for instance," said Mavis, with a feeble laugh.

"You put me in an embarrassing position," said Tobermory, whose tone and attitude certainly did not suggest a shred of embarrassment. "When your inclusion in this house party was suggested, Sir Wilfrid protested that you were the most brainless woman of his acquaintance, and that there was a wide distinction between hospitality and the care of the feeble-minded. Lady Blemley replied that your lack of brain-power was the precise quality which had earned you your invitation, as you were the only person she could think of who might be idiotic enough to buy their old car. You know, the one they call 'The Envy of Sisyphus,' because it goes quite nicely up-hill if you push it."

Lady Blemley's protestations would have had greater effect if she had not casually suggested to Mavis only that morning that the car in question would be just the thing for her down at her Devonshire home.

Major Barfield plunged in heavily to effect a diversion.

"How about your carryings-on with the tortoise-shell puss up at the stables, eh?"

The moment he had said it every one realized the blunder.

"One does not usually discuss these matters in public," said Tobermory frigidly. "From a slight observation of your ways since you've been in the house I should imagine you'd find it inconvenient if I were to shift the conversation on to your own little affairs."

The panic which ensued was not confined to the Major.

"Would you like to go and see if cook has got your dinner ready?" suggested Lady Blemley hurriedly, affecting to ignore the fact that it wanted at least two hours to Tobermory's dinner-time.

"Thanks," said Tobermory, "not quite so soon after my tea. I don't want to die of indigestion."

"Cats have nine lives, you know," said Sir Wilfrid heartily.

"Possibly," answered Tobermory; "but only one liver."

"Adelaide!" said Mrs. Cornett, "do you mean to encourage that cat to go out and gossip about us in the servants' hall?"

The panic had indeed become general. A narrow ornamental balustrade ran in front of most of the bedroom windows at the Towers, and it was recalled with dismay that this had formed a favourite promenade for Tobermory at all hours, whence he could watch the pigeons—and heaven knew what else besides. If he intended to become reminiscent in his present outspoken strain the effect would be something more than disconcerting. Mrs. Cornett, who spent much time at her toilet table, and whose complexion was reputed to be of a nomadic though punctual disposition, looked as ill at ease as the Major. Miss Scrawen, who wrote fiercely sensuous poetry and led a blameless life, merely displayed irritation; if you are methodical and virtuous in private you don't necessarily want every one to know it. Bertie van Tahn, who was so depraved at seventeen that he had long ago given up trying to be any worse, turned a dull shade of gardenia white, but he did not commit the error of dashing out of the room like Odo Finsberry, a young gentleman who was understood to be reading for the Church and who was possibly disturbed at the thought of scandals he might hear concerning other people. Clovis had the presence of mind to maintain a composed exterior; privately he was calculating how long it would take to procure a box of fancy mice through the agency of the *Exchange and Mart* as a species of hush-money.

Even in a delicate situation like the present, Agnes Resker could not endure to remain too long in the background.

"Why did I ever come down here?" she asked dramatically. Tobermory immediately accepted the opening.

"Judging by what you said to Mrs. Cornett on the croquet-lawn yesterday, you were out for food. You described the Blemleys as the dullest people to stay with that you knew, but said they were clever enough to employ a first-rate cook; otherwise they'd find it difficult to get any one to come down a second time."

"There's not a word of truth in it! I appeal to Mrs. Cornett—" exclaimed the discomfited Agnes.

"Mrs. Cornett repeated your remark afterwards to Bertie van Tahn," continued Tobermory, "and said, 'That woman is a regular Hunger Marcher; she'd go anywhere for four square meals a day,' and Bertie van Tahn said—"

At this point the chronicle mercifully ceased. Tobermory had caught a glimpse of the big yellow Tom from the Rectory working his way through the shrubbery towards the stable wing. In a flash he had vanished through the open French window.

With the disappearance of his too brilliant pupil Cornelius Appin found himself beset by a hurricane of bitter upbraiding, anxious inquiry, and frightened entreaty. The responsibility for the situation lay with him, and he must prevent matters from becoming worse. Could Tobermory impart his dangerous gift to other cats? was the first question he had to answer. It was possible, he replied, that he might have initiated his intimate friend the stable puss into his new accomplishment, but it was unlikely that his teaching could have taken a wider range as yet.

"Then," said Mrs. Cornett, "Tobermory may be a valuable cat and a great pet; but I'm sure you'll agree, Adelaide, that both he and the stable cat must be done away with without delay."

"You don't suppose I've enjoyed the last quarter of an hour, do you?" said Lady Blemley bitterly. "My husband and I are very fond of Tobermory—at least, we were before this horrible accomplishment was infused into him; but now, of course, the only thing is to have him destroyed as soon as possible."

"We can put some strychnine in the scraps he always gets at dinnertime," said Sir Wilfrid, "and I will go and drown the stable cat myself. The coachman will be very sore at losing his pet, but I'll say a very catching form of mange has broken out in both cats and we're afraid of it spreading to the kennels."

"But my great discovery!" expostulated Mr. Appin; "after all my years of research and experiment—"

"You can go and experiment on the short-horns at the farm, who are under proper control," said Mrs. Cornett, "or the elephants at the Zoological Gardens. They're said to be highly intelligent, and they have this recommendation, that they don't come creeping about our bedrooms and under chairs, and so forth."

An archangel ecstatically proclaiming the Millennium, and then finding that it clashed unpardonably with Henley and would have to be indefinitely postponed, could hardly have felt more crestfallen than Cornelius Appin at the reception of his wonderful achievement. Public opinion, however, was against him—in fact, had the general voice been consulted on the subject it is probable that a strong minority vote would have been in favour of including him in the strychnine diet.

Defective train arrangements and a nervous desire to see matters brought to a finish prevented an immediate dispersal of the party, but dinner that evening was not a social success. Sir Wilfrid had had rather a trying time with the stable cat and subsequently with the coachman. Agnes Resker ostentatiously limited her repast to a morsel of dry toast, which she bit as though it were a personal enemy; while Mavis Pellington maintained a vindictive silence throughout the meal. Lady Blemley kept up a flow of what she hoped was conversation, but her attention was fixed on the doorway. A plateful of carefully dosed fish scraps was in readiness on the sideboard, but sweets and savoury and dessert went their way, and no Tobermory appeared either in the dining-room or kitchen.

The sepulchral dinner was cheerful compared with the subsequent vigil in the smoking-room. Eating and drinking had at least supplied a distraction and cloak to the prevailing embarrassment. Bridge was out of the question in the general tension of nerves and tempers, and after Odo Finsberry had given a lugubrious rendering of "Melisande in the Wood" to a frigid audience, music was tacitly avoided. At eleven the servants went to bed, announcing that the small window in the pantry had been left open as usual for Tobermory's private use. The guests read steadily through the current batch of magazines, and fell back gradually on the "Badminton Library" and bound volumes of *Punch*. Lady Blemley made periodic visits to the pantry, returning each time with an expression of listless depression which forestalled questioning.

At two o'clock Clovis broke the dominating silence.

"He won't turn up tonight. He's probably in the local newspaper office at the present moment, dictating the first instalment of his reminiscences. Lady What's-her-name's book won't be in it. It will be the event of the day."

Having made this contribution to the general cheerfulness, Clovis went to bed. At long intervals the various members of the house followed his example.

The servants taking round the early tea made a uniform announcement in reply to a uniform question. Tobermory had not returned.

Breakfast was, if anything, a more unpleasant function than dinner had been, but before its conclusion the situation was relieved. Tobermory's corpse was brought in from the shrubbery, where a gardener had just discovered it. From the bites on his throat and the yellow fur which coated his claws it was evident that he had fallen in unequal combat with the big Tom from the Rectory.

By midday most of the guests had quitted the Towers, and after lunch Lady Blemley had sufficiently recovered her spirits to write an extremely nasty letter to the Rectory about the loss of her valuable pet.

Tobermory had been Appin's one successful pupil, and he was destined to have no successor. A few weeks later an elephant in the Dresden Zoological Garden, which had shown no previous signs of irritability, broke loose and killed an Englishman who had apparently been teasing it. The victim's name was variously reported in the papers as Oppin and Eppelin, but his front name was faithfully rendered Cornelius.

"If he was trying German irregular verbs on the poor beast," said Clovis, "he deserved all he got."

Tom Ivory, the Cat

MARY-CARTER ROBERTS

WHEN my Irish setter, Bill, died two years ago, I told myself that I would never own another animal unless I acquired the creature as I had acquired him—which means I intended never to own another animal unless the animal acquired me. For that is what Bill did. He had a good home. He relinquished it of his own accord to become my dog. I considered this an experience unlikely to be repeated. Notwithstanding, I have now been acquired by a cat.

Last year I went to spend the winter and spring in the lake region of Florida. I had a house there beside a county road and I had one near neighbor. Around the house was a small orange grove. Beyond that, on every side, was the matted waste characteristic of that part of the state—a stunted jungle of innumerable plants, all of which are scratchy. Out of this rasping tangle there came to my grove one morning in March a large tom, utterly unkempt, in color a singularly ugly gray.

When I first noticed him, he was sitting against the foundation of the back wall of the house, gathered down into himself in the mufflike feline attitude. I thought, a stray, said, "Hello, kitty," and kept on my way. He rose when I spoke to him and, standing where he was, lifted his front paws one after the other, curling and spreading the toes. It is a movement cats make when they are pleased—pleased, that is, in relation to a human being, not to one another—and to see this fellow perform it was to be virtually sure that he accompanied the gesture by breaking into a private purr. He gave it just so much of an extra edge of graciousness.

I was according him the most superficial attention, but what I saw I recognized as unique. Stray cats, as I knew them, did not return strangers' greetings with any such uncomplicated readiness; they were impervious, they were edgily suspicious, or they were desperately

affectionate. My visitor let me have the impression that, as well as being receptive to me, he was cheerful in himself. But positive cheerfulness is not a quality that one associates with cats—even playful cats. It is on the canine rather than the feline side.

The stranger stayed about the grove for several days, and in that time I offered no advance other than occasionally to repeat my "hello." He preserved his side of the balance. He would stand up and make his purr-suggestive gesture—and that would be all. He did not come on the porch, although its door was often ajar. Kitchen smells floated out of my windows; they brought from him no plaintive sound or other symptom of interest. It followed that recognition of his material independence was my next step in making his acquaintance.

His indifference to food—or to food that belonged to me—caused me to wonder about him. I could not doubt that he was a stray; there was too much evidence that he was. For instance, his light gray ears were oddly bordered with black. I took the line to be an unusual natural marking until I happened to pass very close to him one day; then (if this can be borne) I saw that it was simply a rim of ticks, the ticks of that locality being tiny and dark-colored, but otherwise—ticks. Obviously no one was looking after that cat. Yet he was not thin, and I never saw him display anxiety.

I told myself presently that he was an old fellow whose homelessness was of recent date. "He has been cared for all his life," I decided, "and now his people have gone off and left him, and he has too much a feeling of being theirs to look for a new owner. But he likes to be near human beings, so he comes here. He knows how to hunt and gets a living out there in the jungle. He will drift along this way a little longer and then be gone." I was mistaken in every one of these assumptions.

He disappeared from my grove for about two weeks, and I forgot about him. When I next saw him, he was in his customary place against the foundation, sitting in his old attitude, but obviously the worse for wear. He had a long scratch across his nose, and one ear was battered. He stood up to receive my greeting, and I realized that he was also crippled. His left back leg from the mid-joint down was hugely swollen. Looking out my window a little later, I saw him crossing the grove; he did not put the hurt paw down at all, but went on a rabbity, three-footed hop. I still felt no concern about him.

A day or two later, my neighbor complained that he was taking the food she put out for her cat, a muscular, aggressive young tom named Smoky. She spoke out of the context of morality and fair dealing. I listened in quite a different quarter: I had to admire the adjustment my visitor had made. He had not turned to stealing until he was hurt. Smoky, who was in the pink of condition, had not been able to withstand him. He might have taken to begging; he had not. Still, this was a change of habit, a departure from the way of independence, and I looked him over more attentively the next time I saw him. His leg was worse. It had become a great shapeless lump, and several wounds were to be seen on its surface. Those were jagged cuts and they were in bad shape indeed.

I thought: "He has been bitten by a snake or chewed by a dog—his leg must be either poisoned or crushed to swell so. It will gangrene. He will die in great misery. He is old. Mercy indicates that he be given an easy death."

I told this to my sister, Ruth, who lived a few miles away and has had a great career in helping unhappy cats. She agreed. As she owned a "cat carrier" satchel, she said she would come and get my poor acquaintance and convey him to the veterinarian.

I accompanied her into the grove when she came to fetch him up. My sister reached for him. He did not move. She picked him up and slid him into the carrier. He made no objection. She looked at me with a kind of indignant astonishment. She said, "He *purred*."

She telephoned me later that evening. She had been to the vet, and here was his report: the cat should not be killed. Far from being old, he was barely full-grown; except for his injury, he was in excellent health; he was a mixture of Siamese and Angora; he was an extraordinarily good cat.

"I never saw anything like it," continued my sister, whose experience in feline succor is, as I said, extensive. "The doctor probed and cleaned and bandaged those open cuts, and that chap lay perfectly still. He not only lay still, he purred."

"What made him look so old?" I asked.

"Dirt," said Ruth. She added in a mysterious tone. "He's had a bath now. You'd better come and see for yourself."

"Of course," I answered hastily. "But, after all, he seems to have no people. What is to become of him?"

She inquired, in the forbearing tone of one who has been through that gambit with the weak of heart many times, whether I wanted *her* to look after him. I said unhappily, "Well, you know how I feel about owning animals."

She replied, "All right. I'll find him a home."

"What was wrong with the leg?" I asked.

"It had been caught in a trap," she answered, "and he lost two toes.

The doctor says he must have pulled them off himself. In order to get free."

That bit of information crystallized my impressions of my visitor into something positive at last. I sat looking at my own foot, wondering if I would pull off two toes—in order to get free. I knew I would not. He would. If thy right eye offend thee . . . ? If thy left hind foot . . . ? How could a foot offend more culpably than by rendering one a prisoner? The cat had seen what had to be done, and did it.

Even so, I had no idea of owning him. I had never in my life wanted a "pet." Bill had not been one. He and I had lived together precisely as equals, and only on that basis could I imagine sharing my home with another animal. As I said, I did not think this experience likely to be repeated.

So, though I stopped at my sister's home the next evening, it was not primarily to see the rescued cat. We had some business and we first talked it over. Then she started to lead me to her screened back porch where the invalid was.

She snapped on the porch light and I saw lying with a bandaged leg on pillows in the corner what seemed to be a completely unfamiliar cat. Left to myself, I would not have recognized the creature as my acquaintance of the orange grove.

His coat, being washed, showed itself to be not gray at all. It varied from gleaming white to old ivory and, on the forelegs and shoulders, was faintly banded with gold. His tail was an impressively thick cylinder. His nose was pink. His ears were pink. His three visible paws were pink. He was elegantly beautiful. And he had lost his cheerfulness.

The change in his outward appearance was evidently matched by a change within. The self-reliant nomad of the grove looked remote and devoid of interest. "He wants something," my sister said matter-of-factly. "What?" I inquired. "I can't tell until I know him better," she replied. I bowed to her lore and went away.

Two evenings later she phoned to report that the cat had eaten nothing. "I took off the bandages," she said, "because I thought the wounds might be hurting him. But they're healing very well. Still, he won't eat. He can't go on this way."

I had nothing to offer, and she continued, "He misses something. And when cats feel that way, they will usually start out to find whatever it is they want. So I'm afraid this fellow will watch his chance and run off. I think you'd better take him back to where you found him."

I duly returned him to my residence. His leg was still badly swollen and the cuts, though on the mend, were open. I did not like to think of turning him out into the wilderness in such a state, so I released him from the carrier in my back porch. It was the first time I had touched him—his lightness astonished me. He *looked* huge and unquestionably he *was* remarkably long and high, but when I grasped him, I found that his bulk was chiefly fur. My fingers sank down and down into silkiness. His coat, which was very thick, normally stood on end; it did not, as do the coats of most short-haired cats, lie flat against him.

I put him on the porch floor and sat down in a chair near-by. He looked frankly around the place, hopped to the outside door, which was slightly ajar, seemingly assured himself that he was not shut up, then returned to me and leaped into my lap. He sat erect on my knee and looked into my face. After a moment he lifted his front paws and curled and spread them. I stroked his head. He purred. I offered him some food. He ate. On this occasion I also bestowed a name on him— Tom Ivory.

My sister, apprised of these events, said, "He wants to be your cat. He thinks he is. He's been waiting for you to find out about it."

I could not accept this conclusion. My own was that Tom Ivory wanted a peaceful place to rest until he was well, when—confirmed tramp that he seemed to be—he would resume his wanderings. Looking no farther ahead than that, I said I would feed him while he stayed with me. Then I began to learn his history.

Some things were known about him in the neighborhood. Residents told me that he was the son of a Siamese mother who had belonged to a northern family vacationing there the year before. The Siamese had made a mésalliance and her people, taking her home, had abandoned the kittens, "at that time," my informants said, "very little." This meant that Tom Ivory had fended for himself throughout virtually his whole life. He had gone into the jungle and there he had lived. "What became of the others?" I inquired. Nobody knew.

I gave the jungle some consideration. It was well supplied with game—also with hunters. Only the week before, the local bread-truck man had casually shown me the tail of an eleven-year-old rattlesnake; he had killed the creature as he was driving through. The moccasin lived out there. The coral snake, the black snake, foxes, bobcats, wild pig, hawks and owls. Where the jungle impinged on the swamps, there were alligators. Along the trails roamed packs of half-wild curs. The "very little" kitten, though, had survived.

That was extraordinary. But more than extraordinary—downright mysterious—was the fact that, with no experience behind him but fang and claw, he had not become wild himself. Carried, a prisoner in a dark bag, to a strange place, subjected arbitrarily to pain, he had been unresisting and good-tempered. This, I thought, was not due to any latent instinct for domestication. Domesticated cats did not behave so: they went panic-wild at imprisonment and pain.

The submissiveness of my guest was clearly an individual quality. Submissiveness? I put it beside the cold nerve that had sustained him to pull off his toes. The essential quality of this cat was intelligence—intelligence directed (intelligently) toward self-discipline. He could see what had to be done, whether that was to exercise courage or take refuge in patience, and, having seen it, he would do it. It sounded simple but I knew it was not.

Claiming no rarer endowment than this for him, I come now to the story of how he conducted himself in my home, which to all practical purposes was the first human residence he had known. He was an exemplary domestic cat.

I never had to train him. From the first he eschewed the traditional privileges of the feline pet—pre-empted no easy chair, sprang on no bed, uttered no begging cries beside the dining table. In one day he learned the location of his dish and the hours the dish would be filled. With that knowledge in his possession, he broke, then and there, his most profoundly physical habit—he had been a lifelong hunter and he ceased to hunt. Simply ceased. Twice, to be sure, he sinned in another manner in relation to food—there was meat on the kitchen table and he leaped up and began to eat. He did that without furtiveness; I was close by; he merely knew no better. I scolded him the first time. The second, I reinforced my voice with a cuff. I report the blow for the sake of truth; also for truth, however, I have to discount the blow's disciplinary effect, for it was evident to me that Tom Ivory did not consider that he was being punished—he pushed his head into my slapping hand and purred. But he learned what I was trying to teach him. He never stole again.

The exercise of his intelligence in these matters was, I believe, based on the following principle—he ignored my chairs and beds not from any impossible, super-feline considerateness, but simply because he did not care for the part of the house where the chairs and beds were located. That first morning, after I had accepted him to his satisfaction, he promptly set out on a tour of investigation, going on a brisk trot, bearing himself with a sort of prudent alertness. He entered every room, looked into closets, behind doors and under furniture—and returned to the back porch. From then on, he took the porch for his quarters.

It was a cushionless place and as to why he preferred it above the inner rooms (cats being famously addicted to comfort) I offer the idea that he was abiding by the lessons he had learned in his jungle days. He would have had two occupations out there—getting food and keeping safe. Food ceased to be his concern when he acquired an owner, and he relinquished his responsibility for it. He did not relinquish his responsibility for keeping safe. From what grim experiences I can only guess, he had become positive that safety ranks all other considerations, and he could not lay so great and plain a fact aside. He trusted me; he did not trust the world. So he maintained certain personal precautions.

The porch was screened and that, I believe, gave him a pleasurably unaccustomed sense of secure advantage. He could see the outdoors, whence came enemies, without needing to expose himself. Yet he did not put his whole faith in wire meshes. He also displayed a sense of over-all strategy that delighted me, since it proved, to my contentment at least, that brains rather than a prodigal luck had accounted for Tom Ivory's survival. As far as I could judge, he had viewed self-preservation as a science and had sought its basic principles, which, for his requirements, were—first, a high place where he could lie and overlook without being overlooked; second, a den into which he could dive and disappear. The back porch supplied him with these defenses.

Its furniture provided not one high place but two—the tops of a table and an ironing board. Immediately outside its door was the den, an opening between two foundation stones just wide enough to admit him. Between the refuges, to be sure, stood the door itself, and the door opened *inward*, but Tom Ivory mastered that obstacle before he had been my guest half a day. I watched him do it. He first tried to insert his claws between door and frame. Then he discovered a better method: he hooked the nails of one front paw into the screen meshes, pulled until the door opened a crack, jerked his paw free and shoved his head quickly into the aperture. It took what we speak of in human beings as co-ordination and timing. I may add that I presently gave him a mattress. I put this on the porch floor. It was certainly a comfort—and he ignored it. He continued to jump to his elevated vantage points, both of which were bare timber.

With his world established thus to suit him—allowing him the pleasure of a human friend and also according with the independence that was basic to him—Tom Ivory soon settled into a routine. He spent his days stretched out on his high places. At night he came into the house and entered the room where, at night, I always was. I would be at my desk, starting to work. He would lie down against my foot. There he would stay until I went to bed—perhaps five or six hours. At times, of course, I would move my foot; he would change his position accordingly. Or I might sit for long periods staring at my papers; that seemed to disturb him and he would make inquiring murmurs. When I retired, he would go back to his porch, but not to stay. I would hear him open the door and know that my cat, as is proper for cats, had gone forth into the dark. But in the morning when I opened the back door he always made his appearance from his den. This was the whole of our life, except as he carried on a mischievously one-sided war with the luckless Smoky.

He harried that arrogantly four-footed tom outrageously. Perhaps he remembered the days when he was a stray with ticks and Smoky the owner of a personal dish. I do not know. I know only that he would not let Smoky set paw on our ground. He was still lame, he went on a rabbity gallop, but he went fast and hard. How hard Smoky never delayed to discover. Tom Ivory let it be known that he was the cat of the orange grove.

So we lived until the first of June, when I had to return to Maryland. And still I did not think of Tom Ivory as my cat. Uneasy under my sister's eyes, I made some tentative arrangements for taking him with me, but the hard truth is that when I drove away I left him. I had asked my neighbor to give him temporary care, and to Ruth I entrusted the finding of a permanent home for him, with the result that he was presently taken to a place about fifteen miles away.

His injured leg was still distinctly out of commission. The surface wounds had healed, but the great wound in the paw, where the offending toes had been plucked out, would break and bleed if the foot was given more than light usage. It was bleeding pretty freely, I was told, when Tom Ivory finished his trek back to my empty house. He came into the grove, he went to the back steps, he tried to open the locked door of his one-time porch, and at every step he left a little wet print behind him. He was taken to the new place a second time and a second time he returned—came to the grove, went to the steps, tried to open the door. My sister telephoned me that same day.

She said, "He thinks he is your cat."

He arrived in Maryland by railroad express the following week. It was July and appallingly hot. I went to the station fearfully, expecting to find him wrought up in the extreme. He was lying on the floor of his little wire crate—asleep.

However, apart from his old quietude, he was so changed that I might have been excused for not recognizing him. He was terribly thin. His coat, for the first time in my knowledge of him, lay on him like the coats of common cats—lank and flat. I spoke to him but he gave me no response.

He had not forgotten me, but he did not remember me either. His mind just then was not working. Setting out on this new journey— imprisoned and launched once more, helpless, into the unknown— he had by habit imposed his old rule of patience on himself, since his intelligence told him that there was nothing else he could do. And he had been patient, confined in heat, hunger, dark and hurly-burly, for three days. The state of mind had taken on a sort of hypnotic rigidity, not subject to normal reaction. When I carried the crate out to my car, I believe he simply supposed that he was being taken on one more stage of the same inexplicable travel.

I talked to him as I drove along, and the sound of my voice or the fresh air—something—gradually brought him out of his trance. I noticed no change in him, however, until I took a hand from the steering wheel and held it to the side of his crate. He sat up then. He gave a meow. He looked around him. He pushed his cheek against the spot where my hand was. He purred.

We had a great day after we got home. Then it was night, and I put him out of doors. I thought: "He will stay here or he will not; there is no point in putting off the test."

The next morning when I opened the door, Tom Ivory emerged from under the front porch. There was a little break in the foundation wall there. He had found it. He had a den. He came hopping up the steps toward me, and I thought, quite as a matter of course, that as my porch was furnished with a table he would have a high place, too.

Biography

ERA ZISTEL

CHRIS was a small part of the litter borne by the big black cat in the fruit store. Indeed, he was the smallest part, the runt of the lot, the last of it, made up of leftovers. He didn't look like much, lying there gasping for breath, his skinny rat's tail inert, the wet black and white fur plastered on his scrawny little body.

Evidently his mother didn't think he looked like much either, for she gave him no more attention than a few licks that sent him sprawling over on his back with his helpless sticks of legs kicking feebly against the empty inhospitality of the new world. She was a wise mother, for this was her fourth litter. By this time she knew all about the survival of the fittest, and how useless it was to try to violate that law. So if this little one wanted to get back to the warmth of her, let him fight to get there—if he could. If he wanted food, let him fight for it—if he could. And if he could not, then let him die. There were plenty more fine strong ones snuggled against her belly. She would not miss him.

Chris did fight, and he did get back to her, but he was soon thrust aside again by his stronger brothers and sisters. So he did not get any food, and finally gave up struggling for it. Crawling around blindly, he found a spot where there was plenty of room, between his mother's front paws, and there he rested, with his head tucked under her chin.

The only time he ever got anything to eat was after the others had finished. He would wait until they had fallen asleep and dropped away from their mother like ripe fruit, then work his way cautiously among them and take what they had left. Sometimes he forgot to be cautious and nudged against one of them only half asleep; then there was a brief battle that woke all the rest and he was left waiting again. Sometimes there was no food left.

He didn't grow much. It was a miracle that he lived at all. Perhaps it was only because he used so little energy that he managed to make his inheritance from a healthy mother last over such an inconceivably long time; for he was very quiet. As his brothers and sisters gained strength and sight they played more and more wildly, kicking, biting, rolling over and over, chasing each other, engaging finally in a contest that none could win, scrabbling up the walls of their home to try to lift themselves over the top of it. During all these games Chris sat to one side, his paws tucked neatly under him, watching, occasionally being knocked over when one of them flew at a tangent, occasionally having to move to another spot when the battle shifted to his neutral ground.

That was how he managed to live. It was his way of fighting.

One day, while they were playing thus, terror came among them. A strange thing crept into their home, seized them one by one to hold them high above it, then dropped them down again. Chris was the last to be disturbed. He was wondering what was happening to the rest of them, not expecting it to happen to him, because nothing ever did, when the thing clutched at the back of his neck and lifted him up. He squealed once with surprise, paddled the air trying to find a foothold in it, then hung down quietly and waited for the end. But a moment later he was back with his brothers and sisters again, none the worse for the adventure.

The others were very excited. They hissed and spat when he joined them, as if he himself were the stranger; then went round and round their home, inspecting every inch of it. When at last they were satisfied that all was as it should be, they huddled up to let sleep rid them of the unpleasant experience. Chris crawled on the top of the pile, where he always slept, and at once found a dream that pleased him, in which he had all that he wanted to eat, but he was awakened again almost immediately by the thing at the back of his neck. This time it lifted him over the edge of his world, dropped him dizzily downward until he was caught and held by another thing. He looked at what was holding him, and thus for the first time in his life saw a Human Being.

She held him close, so that he could feel Her warmth and the movement of Her breathing. She spoke to him, and he stared at Her, his eyes round with wonder. It was as if he had heard that voice before, had known and loved it for a long time. He dug his claws in to get closer to Her, crawled up and at last found a place to rest with his head tucked under Her chin.

But he was not allowed to stay there long. Soon he was snatched

away and swung through the air down into a new world with high
walls. In a corner of it he crouched, shrinking away from its unfamil-
iarity. Then darkness closed around him. The world began to tip
and sway, so that he slid helplessly from one side to the other, while
from beyond came terrible noises, as if the darkness were full of roaring, battling monsters. He was frightened and cried for his mother,
but she did not come.

Finally the noises died down and the world became steady and the
darkness opened, and in the light above him he saw Her again. She
lifted him out of the little world and put him down in a bigger one.
It was bigger than he had thought any world could be, the walls of it
being quite beyond his vision. Cautiously he crept around in it, sniff-

ing, memorizing all the strange smells, and hunting for his mother.

After a while she put something in front of him that smelled like
his mother. He approached it eagerly and nuzzled against it. It was
warm, like his mother, but this warmth suddenly spread all over his
face, flooded into his mouth and nose and choked him. He stared at
it reproachfully for a moment, shook his head so vigorously that he
upset himself, then got up and licked the sticky sweetness from
around his mouth. It was good. It was like his mother.

He went back to it. Again he was repulsed and retreated coughing
and sneezing. But the accumulated hunger of his whole short life
urged him to keep on trying. So at last he found a way to manage this
vicarious mother. All he had to do was hold his breath, dip his mouth
in and out and then lick off the sweetness. This, with some practice,
he succeeded in doing quite rapidly. It was some time before he discovered another method that was much more efficient.

When he had finished, She picked him up. In Her lap he washed
himself sketchily, hampered by his new rotundity, until the pleasant
warmth of Her brought idleness to his tongue. He closed his eyes and

purred, nudged against Her questingly, trying to find his favorite spot under his mother's chin. Then the memory of his mother mingled with a comfortable awareness of Her, and at last he fell asleep.

The substitute for his mother was called "milk." Other names for it were "Areyouhungry" and "Doyouwantsomethingtoeat." These, in turn, became the names for other things as well. It was very confusing, but he managed to learn it eventually, and a great deal more besides: that "naughty" meant he had done something wrong, that "bad Chris" accompanied by a spanking meant a second offense. He learned that Chris was his name; indeed, he learned that too well, for sometimes when She mentioned him in conversation he jumped up and trotted over to Her. But above and beyond everything else was the way he learned to love Her.

When She was gone he crouched on the floor near the door that separated them and no matter how long it might be, waited for Her return, listening for Her footsteps and hating whatever it was that had taken Her away from him. So he hated Her friends when they came, because although he could still see Her and touch Her, She was gone from him then, too, only in another way. In the beginning he had tried scratching and biting them, but that made Her angry. So then he tried to lure Her away from them, going through, with grim abandon, all the antics that usually made Her laugh. And if that failed, then he simply made more noise than they, his rivals. For he, too, could talk.

Only they never understood him. They spoke a different language. Sometimes he even tried to imitate the sound of Her voice, using the same inflections and saying a great deal all at once, the way She did. But it was no use. Not even She ever really understood.

When he told Her friends how much he hated them, they laughed and petted him. When he told Her, in a long, elaborate sentence, of how much he loved Her, She was displeased and sent him away. Once when he complained to Her about the weather, which he was sure She controlled, as She did everything concerning his comfort, She answered by offering him something to eat!

Nor, for that matter, did he understand Her much better. Sometimes She would repeat the same thing over and over in Her language, saying it slowly and carefully and earnestly, and yet he could not comprehend. Sometimes then they would look at each other in a silence that was as immeasurable as all eternity holding them apart, until finally She would put Her hand down to stroke his head and he would rise to meet it halfway, and that became their common tongue.

But it wasn't until Ginger came that he really gave up trying. Ginger couldn't speak Her language either—and didn't even care; probably no one could but She and Her friends.

Ginger changed his ideas about a lot of things. In fact, Ginger changed his whole life.

She went away, and when She came back She was carrying a box. Chris liked boxes very much, and always welcomed them with eagerness. For each one, having been in many places, was like a new world to explore. And after he had become thoroughly familiar with the box itself, there was still what was inside it to be looked over and approved or rejected, as the case might be. All in all, it was one of his most agreeable tasks, especially if the box happened to contain, as it so frequently did, the things that She called "books"; because each one of these was a new world also, pungent with the memory of strange lands and distant places. Often he went over to where She had them lined up against the wall, to consult them and ponder over what they told him.

So when he saw this box She was carrying, he ran over to greet it joyfully, but at once withdrew again, overcome by distaste. It was an entirely different kind of box; it rustled, and a strong animal smell came from it. Horrified, he backed away until he found refuge under a chair, where he crouched and peered out anxiously. The box rustled again. He opened his mouth, and out came a rasping sound that startled him, it was so unlike anything he had ever said before. But there was comfort and confidence in it, so he repeated it. The box answered with a piercing shriek, and danced about so wildly that it almost tore itself out of Her hands.

She laughed and began to talk to him. She said a great deal, but he could understand only one word, and it was "kitty." Kitty? That was another name for him.

She put the box on the floor. It shrieked and danced and bulged at the top. Then She opened it. Out shot something yellow, across the room and under a chair in one long arc of fury. Fiery eyes glinted in the dimness there, and from the vague shadow came the same hiss of wrath and fear that was in his own voice.

After a while She went to the other one and tried to pick it up. With a swift glide it eluded Her and made its home under another chair, where the gleam of its eyes shifted rapidly from Chris to Her and back again. Then She came over and picked him up. He trusted Her. But when She tried to put him down in front of the other one a bright whirl of utter madness took possession of him. Only after She had released him and he was once more safe under his chair did he come to his senses again; it was only then that he heard the sharp exclamation of pain and reproach his claws had drawn from Her.

She went away, and he was miserable, listening to the echo of that reproach.

The gleaming yellow eyes regarded him with impersonal, menacing calm. They were alone together.

After a while the other one lifted its head. It looked around tentatively, swiftly back at Chris, then raised an experimental paw. Nothing happened. It slipped the paw forward and stood transfixed.

Chris did not move. The other eased out from under its chair, made a cautious tour of its own half of the room, then, having tested all things there and found them harmless, glanced past that known safety. Casually it padded out a circle in the middle of the room. Chris retreated. The other one promptly took possession of his shelter and gazed out triumphantly.

For a while it stayed there busily inspecting and approving of what had been his, but then, elaborately unaware of him, it made straight for him again. He managed to sidestep and selected a corner to sit in. The other immediately found something interesting, not in him, but in that very corner. So it went on, until at last She came back and the other one was subdued.

She called him, but although the fur on his back quivered, he would not go to Her. She called again and he answered with a high complaint. Then She talked to him, and he could not resist. Once he was in Her lap, nothing else mattered.

The eyes of the lonely, wild other one under the chair stared at them with a blazing intensity, then grew dim and disappeared.

Ginger was queer, shy and aggressive at the same time, bold but mistrustful, hungry for affection, but afraid of it when it was offered. Soon She gave up trying to make friends with her, and then Chris suffered her presence without protest. He was willing to give up anything but that magic circle in which She moved; and Ginger seemed to find that quite satisfactory. She had her own magic circle.

Up and down she raced, pursuing imaginary flies, escaping from imaginary foes, or chasing Chris' very own paper balls. She sunned herself in Chris' favorite place on the window ledge, padded about gravely inspecting his home that had now become all hers, slept first here, then there, her choice always being that spot he had chosen for himself. Yet there were times when she looked thoughtfully, perhaps longingly, at Her and at Chris curled up in Her lap.

One day, after Ginger had been there quite a while, something strange happened.

The wind was blowing through the open window, billowing out the curtains that Ginger played with and ruffling the fur of Chris as he sat on the window ledge. It was one of those days when sky and air and earth keep drawing together tighter and tighter, until the pressure is unbearable and a blinding flash of light tears them apart again.

Chris sat on the ledge and felt the excitement that was in the air tingle in his body. The fur along his back rippled in a series of delicious shudders. Ginger played wildly, leaping at the curtains and away again, drawing a series of quick eccentric circles in the fading light, scrambling madly on the polished floor without getting anywhere, then up the back of a chair and after the curtains again. She seemed to have gone insane.

Chris watched her, and something stirred in him. He had never felt it before, and did not know what it was. Suddenly a bright light from the sky questioned, and the earth roared back an answer. He started, and involuntarily his head jerked around. As the rumble died away he got up, stretched, and yawned, as if to prove to himself that he had not lost his customary poise. But just then Ginger inscribed a graceful circle through the air and landed on the ledge beside him. They had never been so close to each other before.

Chris recoiled from her sharply and jumped to the floor, but instead of stopping there and after a decorous pause walking away with seemly dignity, he kept on bounding across the room and when he was on the far side of it opened his mouth to utter a peculiar wail that made his fur bristle.

Ginger looked at him, tossed her head mischievously, leaped upward to trace another half circle against the light, then ran lightly toward him. With a vehement hiss he drew back, but she was away at once—and he was pursuing her! Again the anguished wail escaped from his throat. Ginger stopped abruptly to listen to it, and he stopped, too, close beside her. They stood very still staring at each other, as if they were seeing each other for the first time. Another flash of light burned briefly in her yellow eyes and disclosed the wild tenderness there. Without moving she began to croon to him. Then all at once, like the bursting of the light and the roaring of the earth, he knew what it was that he felt.

For days he forgot everything but Ginger, forgot to eat, forgot to wash himself, forgot even Her. And then he slept, and when he awoke the interlude was no more than a dream. But he was painfully aware of the fact that he had deserted Her in that dream, and tried as best he could to erase it from Her memory. Wherever She went he was at Her heels, begging humbly, persistently for Her forgiveness, telling Her over and over that the infatuation for Ginger could not be compared with his deep and undying affection for Her, that it had been an incomprehensible lapse, that it would never happen again.

Nevertheless he and Ginger were good friends now, sharing food and bed and window ledge, and sometimes Her lap, too.

The days passed, one much like another, and the change in Ginger was so gradual that he scarcely noticed it. Yet the time came when she seemed displeased with him again, and with everything else, for that matter, and kept going around restlessly as if she were searching for something.

Finally She brought home a large box and put something soft into it, and with eager satisfaction Ginger accepted it, scratching in the corners and digging her claws into the soft stuff. Chris sniffed at the box and also found it satisfactory, but when he tried to join her Ginger at once made it clear that it was her box and that she wished to be alone.

Yet it would be pleasant to lie there, curled up snugly, with the soft stuff billowing around on all sides. So while Ginger sunned herself on the window ledge he would steal into it and have a fine nap there; but the moment she jumped off the ledge he was out of it again.

Thus everything went well until the morning the box started making a noise. Faintly, almost inaudibly, it rustled and squeaked. There was something new about it, but in that newness was something strangely familiar, too. Chris peered in cautiously. The soft stuff was moving.

Ginger was away, so he jumped in. Immediately there was a terrible commotion, squealing and undulating all around his feet, and Ginger returning full of anxiety to fling herself down on her side and stare at him accusingly. With a disgusted grunt he retired. He would never go near that box again!

All of that day he spent sulking in a corner. He was even displeased with Her. Whatever it was, She should not have allowed it to happen. He refused to speak to Her, refused to go to Her, refused to eat, slept sitting in the corner until She made a bed for him there and he collapsed on it in weary gratitude.

The next day, however, was an entirely different day. No doubt the box had returned to normal again. So, as soon as Ginger left it, he began pacing around the room aimlessly, until quite accidentally he came close enough to look in. Nothing moved. With light and delicate tread he stepped in on the soft stuff.

Then the whole unpleasant procedure repeated itself, the squealing and upheaval, and Ginger returning, and his retiring to the corner to mope. It couldn't go on like that. Something would have to be done. Finally he went to Her and appealed to Her in a long, breathless sentence of complaint and entreaty. She gave him an absentminded pat, made a bed for him in the corner again, then went to fuss over Ginger and those new things.

That was more than he could bear. At once he went back, got into the box and waited for the commotion. It came, but he stayed. As soon as the little new things had gathered around Ginger and were quiet again he settled down, tucked his paws under him and stared at Ginger defiantly. She stared back, sleepily. Finally her eyes closed, and his head began to nod. The last thing he heard was Her laugh, and the last thing he felt was Her hand on his head, and that made everything all right.

When Ginger left the box he awoke with a start. The new ones were tumbling all around him, wailing noisily. Blindly seeking, they came over to him and snuggled against his belly. There was something very undignified and embarrassing about having them there, but no one seemed to be watching, and the warmth of them was not unpleasant, and the box with the soft stuff was comfortable. So he slept again, and the new ones were part of his sleep.

After that he didn't mind them. After that he lay there with them often, talking to them sometimes and washing their immaculate fur with an inept, affectionate tongue.

Even when they grew strong and bold and at last managed to scramble out of the box, so that from then on there was no peace anywhere, he really didn't mind having them around. When they awakened him by pouncing sharp-clawed on his tail an ill-timed dream had caused him to wave in his sleep, he did no more than stretch and yawn and lazily try to catch the next one to come flying past.

But once, while he was absent-mindedly twitching his tail to amuse them, he heard Her laugh, and that made all the difference in the world. He pricked up his ears and looked at Her. She was not laughing at him, She was laughing at *them*. There was no doubt about it. She was watching them, not him. He got up quickly and walked away. She did not even notice that he had left. He waited a moment, then, having made a swift decision as to which of his tricks She seemed to like the best, made a sudden leap and executed a beautiful slide across the polished floor. She paid no attention to him. But the little ones did! They all came chasing after, half mad with glee. And

She laughed twice as hard, and there was really no way of telling just what She was laughing at. So he did it again.

From then on he played earnestly, with a business-like zest, repeating the special slide performance over and over, until She turned away.

That was his way of fighting for Her.

He didn't notice when one of them was missing, nor even when two were gone, but finally there was only a lonely little pattering of feet following him, and it seemed to him something was wrong. Where were all the rest? He played with the one that was left, and kept expecting the others to rush out at him from somewhere at almost any moment, but they did not come, and the game petered out with the one that was left wandering off somewhere on its own.

It stayed with them a while longer. Then one day when Ginger called to it, there was no scrambling out of the box, no rustling from some remote corner, no answering squeak and pattering of feet. As quietly and mysteriously as the others, it had disappeared.

In a way, it was better that they were gone. Now he was sure that Her laugh belonged only to him. But She did not laugh so much, and an almost deafening silence lay everywhere, even in his dreams.

It occurred to him that it might amuse Her if he played with Ginger a bit. But he soon found out that Ginger would not play.

There was evidently something the matter with her. Not only did she refuse to play, but she seemed to have lost interest in everything. Each day she became less active, until at last she spent most of her time on the window ledge, her eyes wide open, staring at nothing.

Sometimes she would get up wearily and go to their plate of food, but she never touched anything. Sometimes she would wander pensively around the room, stopping to look for a long time at each place where she had lain contented, then turn away as if she had been refused the aid she had hoped might be given her.

Back on the ledge, in the sun, she would slowly settle herself in passive acceptance. And often, although she remained quite still, it seemed that she was going away.

Then one morning she was not there, not on the window ledge, not on any of the chairs, nor anywhere else in the room. Silently and persistently Chris searched for her, until at last She took him to a small room where he had never been before. The air in it was heavy with a sharp, sweet scent that terrified him. For although he had never met it before, he knew what it was. It was death.

Ginger was lying there on the floor in a patch of slanting sunlight. He went over to her slowly, bent his head to greet her, then recoiled.

The death was with her. Slowly he backed away. She picked him up and carried him out of the room and closed the door.

He did not search for her after that, but in his own way he grieved for her. Often he would go to the chair that was her favorite bed, or to the window ledge where the memory of her lingered for a while, and put his head down flat against it to be with her. But at last even that memory of her faded and was gone, and he was alone again.

So, just as Ginger had changed everything when she came, everything was changed to what it had been now that she was gone.

He went back to waiting at the door for Her again, while She was away, and hating whatever it was that kept Her from him. He even hated the door itself, and sometimes tore at it with his claws. But the noise that made only brought the silence crowding closer around him when he stopped. It never brought Her.

No matter how long She might be away, he never slept during those hours, so that by the time She returned he was usually worn out. Yet he had to coax Her somehow into never leaving him again. So, in spite of his weariness, he would sing for Her and dance for Her, and slide across the floor and chase paper balls, until at last She would stoop down and let him put his paws on Her shoulder. Then followed the good, quiet part of Her return. She would lift him and carry him over to the window, and they would spend some time there, while he purred and dug his claws into Her shoulder and, with his ears tipped forward, pretended each day to see for the first time the tiny golden things that danced in the sunlight, and a great many other things that weren't there at all.

At first it was no more than this restlessness that kept him awake all the time. It seemed that, although he was very tired and wanted more than anything else to have a good long nap, he must be constantly getting up and stretching himself and washing his fur, not with his usual vigorous efficiency, but with a nervous haste and lack of system that in itself irritated him. What he felt in his legs was in the beginning laziness, then a strange singing, as if they were made up of hundreds of little wires being played upon, then a numbness accompanied by a cold, remote pain.

He continued to play for Her, but each time it became more of an effort. Then one day something happened that made them both realize something was wrong, had been wrong for a long time.

She had just come home, and after his usual prancing, just a bit more stiff-legged than usual, that was all, he tried one of his slides across the floor. Suddenly his back legs refused to hold him up, splayed out, and forced him to complete the slide by ignominiously coasting along on his belly. It lasted no more than a moment, that weakness. Before She had even stopped laughing he was up and defiantly sliding back to Her again.

But She had noticed. He knew She had noticed because She picked him up quickly and then just stood there for a long time holding him tight, as if She thought he wanted to go away, so tight that he could not tell whether the trembling was in his body or Her hands.

She brought a box and put him into it and shut out the light, and in the darkness around him a dim memory seemed to stir uneasily. He cried, and She answered. Then he was quiet. The box began to tip and sway, so that he could not keep his balance, and the darkness seemed all at once to turn into a roaring inferno, filled with the memory of terrible monsters hurling themselves against each other.

But after a while these noises subsided, and were replaced by others, and a strong animal smell came sweeping in; then almost immediately that was cut off also, as if something solid had been closed against it. He heard Her voice again, and the darkness opened. She was there bending over him, and a stranger was beside Her, looking at him too.

She put him on the floor and the stranger stooped over to stroke him. The hand was firm and friendly, and when the stranger spoke Chris responded as he had never done before to any of Her friends, he rubbed himself a little against the stranger's leg. Here was another Human Being he felt he might love.

So when he was offered a piece of string to play with, he hopped after it obediently. But he could not make the stranger laugh, nor Her, and he tired quickly. Then the stranger patted a smooth chair without any soft stuff on it. Chris stared at the hand doubtfully, then looked from one to the other of them. He knew what they wanted him to do, but he did not think he could do it.

After a time She also began to plead and pat the chair; so he jumped, scrabbled helplessly for a moment with the claws of his front paws caught on the edge of the chair, then fell heavily to the floor. There he lay, with the cold gray pain whirling around him faster and faster, until there was nothing left but that.

When he became aware of Her again, She was putting him back into the box. He tried to cling to Her, but the pain carried him away. It made him indifferent to everything, to all the smells and all the sounds and even to his own fear, until his nostrils caught the scent of home again. Home! That got him to his feet, and set him to scratching away at the darkness to try to get through to it. Home! When She let in the light and he saw everything familiar and beloved around him just as always, he gave a cry of joy and sprang out of the box.

Only it was just his imagination that leapt so happily into the room. All his body did was lurch over on its side.

He was in the little room where he had last seen Ginger. He could not walk any longer. There was no pain now, only a cold gray lifelessness. His legs were stretched out stiff and were no longer a part of him. His whole body was really no longer a part of him. It lay heavy, inert, useless, while he floated above it, held to it only by a thread so slight that the next breath, the next instant dropping into eternity might break it apart.

His eyes were wide open, and through the mists he could see Her sitting there beside him. She did not touch him. Remotely, from the height where he watched, he was grateful to Her for not stroking that body to which he was still attached. For he was too far away to respond with any sign of pleasure. But he was glad that She was there. He would not be so frightened when the thread snapped and the thickening mists whirled him away.

He did not want to go away. He wanted to stay with her. Up above he began struggling violently to get closer to Her, and down there his body twitched a little. She bent over it, carefully lifted it and turned it on its other side. That was good. There was peace for a moment, the thread became slack, his eyes closed. But only for a moment. In the thick whirling mists he was alone and afraid. He opened them again.

She was still there.

All through this long night that was so close to the night that would never end, and through the many that followed, he fought with his eyes on Her, fought to get nearer to Her. Then one morning when the sun rose he thought he could feel the warmth of it on his body again. Slowly he descended through the cold mists to rest in it. At last his eyes closed, and he slept.

That battle they fought together seemed to change their relationship with each other. It was no longer love he felt as much now as a sense of *belonging* to Her. It was as if, having saved him from becoming part of that endless night, She had made him a part of Herself instead. He was Hers now so completely that nothing, not even another Ginger, could ever for a moment make him forget Her again.

Although he could walk in an awkward, stiff-legged fashion, he was not yet entirely well when She began to do strange things. First She brought home a great many boxes; but She took nothing out of them, She put things into them instead: all the books, and all the other small things in their home, until the whole place seemed to ring with emptiness. And then, even before he got used to having it like that, something even worse happened.

Early one morning She opened the door and let in three giant Human Beings. He did not like them and hissed at them, but they only roared and pushed him aside and then, to his horror, began taking all Her boxes away. He went to Her at once and reported them, but She paid little attention, and later amidst the growing confusion he actually saw Her talking to them and helping them. It was utterly incredible, but She was allowing them to carry off their home. Bit by bit it disappeared, the place where She slept, his favorite chair, his second best chair, everything, until there was nothing left but the memory of familiarity and the sound of his steps crossing the bare floor loud and sad with emptiness.

He was surprised when the giants came back again. They had taken everything, what else could they want? They stood there looking at him and he stared back at them defiantly, and still it did not occur to him what they wanted; not until She brought in another box and put it on the floor and then began to talk to him. There was something in Her voice that told him. But no! He would not let them take him away from Her, too!

He crouched down and moaned. One of the giants strode over and reached out a hand. He backed away hissing and spitting. Then She picked him up. He trusted Her. He did not think She would do it. How could She?

But She handed him over to the giant, and the giant put him into the box and closed it around him, and that was the end of everything. She had betrayed him.

This box was different from the other one he had been in; it had a small opening at one end. He put his nose to it and caught the odor of the giant and retreated; but then in spite of himself he had to return to look out, for he was being taken into the inferno again. Now he saw what made all the noise: big, swiftly moving evil creatures gliding around everywhere and hooting at each other; really monsters much as he had imagined them, but not fighting, only dodging about avoiding each other with marvelous agility, considering their bulk.

The box he was in stopped moving, then suddenly was raised and flung directly into the jaws of one of the monsters standing nearby. Chris shut his eyes and waited for the great teeth to crush him, but nothing happened.

After a while he got up courage enough to look out of his small window again, and discovered he could see right through the monster. Perhaps he was just behind one of its eyes. And what he saw seemed quite incredible, for She was standing there! Apparently She was waking the monster, for a moment later it began to move.

First it swayed and sighed, and then it shuddered and coughed, and then it began to purr. Gliding over to join a lot of others of its kind, it became a part of a procession, with another procession going in the opposite direction. For some time they all kept together like that, but then one by one the others turned aside and vanished, until at last the one Chris was in was the only one left. But still it kept on going.

It was going into a new world, a very fine world, from what Chris could see of it, all broad and flat, stretching out endlessly and shimmering in the sun. What a joy it would be to get out and run in it! But still they went on, until they came to a place where the world rose sharply and they had to climb its sides. Evidently the monster found that very hard to do, for it went slower now and began to wheeze.

Yet on they went, and on, until all at once something terrible happened. The monster began to falter. Its purr was choked off, it gave a sickening lurch and with a groan of exhaustion came to a stop.

The sudden silence was intolerable. Chris clawed frantically at his window, trying to enlarge it. He cried out to the monster to awake, to go on, to purr again, or bellow—anything to let him know that it was still alive. It stirred slightly and moaned. Its bones creaked. Then it gasped, and suddenly Chris felt his box lifted and lowered again. He looked through his window. He was outside the monster.

Then he heard Her voice. She had not betrayed him after all, of course She had not! The box opened and She was bending over to stroke him, talking to him with a joy and excitement in Her voice that was as new as the sharp, clear air that he breathed. He felt the intoxication of it, too, yet when She walked away and called to him to follow, he hesitated. So many unknown smells, such strange soft stuff to walk upon! Did he dare?

He put out a tentative paw. The soft stuff cushioned it pleasantly and caressed his leg. It was agreeable. It made him want to leap into it, roll in it, go bounding after Her, then back again and round and round in a wide circle of abandon. He put out another timid paw, then crawled from the box, distrust making his stiff legs even more awkward than usual. The soft stuff whispered around his feet, the gentle wind brought hundreds of strange odors to his nostrils.

He stood still and sniffed thoughtfully. Back there in the old world he believed he had learned all there was to know. But now here was another world, much larger, so large that he could not see its walls, and everything in it still to be learned: the source of each of those smells, the identification of all he saw around him, and its relation to himself. What part of it would bring him pleasure, and what pain? Even in the soft stuff there might be danger as well as delight. But where? Near or far? From what must he run to safety, and safety, where was that?

She called, and he made a wayward path toward Her, detouring to inspect this and that, stopping, turning back to catch again that whiff of something interesting, preoccupied, excited, and worried. At last he caught up with Her. She was standing in front of an immense box, and now She opened a door into it and they went inside. It was as empty as that place they had left so long ago, before the monster had swallowed him. But She was putting something on the floor of it, a box that She had been carrying. He went over to it. It was his old box, and inside it was the soft stuff that had been his bed ever since he could remember. He climbed into it and snuffed and snuffed, as if he could not get enough of the smell of it. Then he stopped trembling. Here was the safety, here was home. After a while he settled down, and then he slept, dreaming of the past, while the future waited for him to awake.

It had no walls. Each day he tried to find them, going a little farther to look for them, anxious to know how far he might go from Her and still be with Her. But no matter which way he went, or how far he went, it continued past seeing, without any walls to shut him in. It would have terrified him if it hadn't been for Her. But he knew nothing would ever happen to him, nothing *could* ever happen to him, as long as She was there, and of course She always was there, when he needed Her.

She was there that time when he first met the water and thought he could walk on it and sank into it instead; She pulled him out and dried him off and laughed a little, too. She was there to snatch him out of the way when the huge animal with horns lowered its head to answer his challenging hiss with an angry bellow. She was there to chase away the other one who tried to annoy him by darting out from ambush to attack him and sprint lithely away again too swiftly for his sluggish legs to follow. She came running to his rescue the evening the snarling red beast that barked and prowled around each night—the "fox," She called it—surprised him on the way home and very nearly caught him. She was always there. He had no need to fear.

In all his life that now seemed so long to him, he had never been so happy as this. There were no hours spent waiting for Her behind a closed door; there were no friends to hate, no need to worry about when She would leave, when She would return, or what She was planning to do next. For each day was exactly like the one before, and their very sameness made them perfect.

In the morning, soon after the rising of the sun, he would awake and ask Her to let him out into the cool, new air. She would open the door, then close it again between them, and he would stand there for a while just on the other side of it, savoring the confidence that he could have it opened and go right back in again if he wished, and surveying the territory he must explore.

For it was during the morning that he tried to find the walls; climbing over rocks, scrambling through brush, padding noiselessly on the clean soft carpet under old trees, sinking into deep leaf mold, leaping over the running water and skirting the still pools and making a wide detour around the big boxes in which other Humans lived. But always, at a certain time, he turned and started back home again. It was so that he would be there when She lay in the sun and seemed to have nothing to do but listen to him relate the story of his morning's adventures.

This was the best part of the day. He would tell Her of everything he had seen, of everything that had happened, and end up with his usual complaint that, in spite of all his seeking, he had not yet found the walls. And She would lie there quietly and listen and stroke his head and sometimes laugh at just the right moment, so that he was almost sure that She had understood.

Then, in a little while, when he could think of nothing more to say, and the sun on his fur became too hot, he would go away again, but not very far. In the shade nearby was his favorite rock, and there he settled down, his head between his paws, his eyes half closed, to watch with lazy interest the busy life that buzzed and crawled and whirred and leaped and floated and sang all around him. Sometimes he put out a paw to catch one of the jumping things that never ceased to startle him when they snapped just beneath his nose and then floated away in long arcs into invisibility. Sometimes, by accident, he did catch one. It wriggled deliciously, and for a while he would keep it imprisoned, appreciating its attempts to escape with ears tilted forward and eyes bright with excitement. But at last he would tire of it, and with a pretended fumble release it, to watch sleepily as it righted itself and poised for the spring. Then, just as always, it would snap under his nose and make him jump, and go sailing off through the air.

After that he would stretch out full length to sleep for a while, and in his dreams live through the morning walk all over again, and catch any number of jumping things between his paws that twitched a little while he slept. But he never failed to wake before She left. When She went away he was always there to watch Her go. He did not follow Her, but after She was gone he would go part way up the path that She had taken, and on a flat rock close by, keep a sharp lookout for Her return.

Perhaps this was really the best part of the day, for he knew She would not be gone long, and that when She came back She would bring him something to eat. Yes, surely it was, because then they played the Game. She would call to him, and he would not go to Her or answer. Instead he would crouch behind the tall grass at the edge of the path and wait until She was quite near, then with a cry leap out at Her so that She jumped back, startled, and then they would race each other home, and of course he always won.

Yes, that was the best part of the day—although maybe the afternoons were better still. That was when they went for a walk together, deep into the woods. And as soon as he got tired all he had to do was tell Her so; She would stoop down so that he could put his paws on Her shoulder, and thus he would go riding back again, like a king.

Only if the sky was gray and the world outside wet and dismal, they stayed at home instead. Then She did things with Her hands, or spent hours looking at one of the books he could read in a sniff, and he lay on Her lap dreaming. And that was good, too, for they were together.

There was no part of it, not one small second of any day that he would have changed. But it changed itself.

She changed.

At first he thought the fault was his when She no longer listened attentively to the narration of his morning's adventures. So he began to stay away longer and longer, going farther and farther afield, not searching for walls now, but for something that might interest Her, fighting through thorny tangles and dense woods, going over swamps and into caves where the smell of other animals was terrifyingly strong, coming home worn out, dirty and desperate to tell Her how desperate he was. But still She did not listen.

Then one morning She was not there. He went to the place where he should find her lying in the patch of sunlight, where the grass was flat and brown from Her lying on it, and She was not there. He lay down for a while there and waited for Her, his sides still heaving from the exertion of his walk, his head flat against the earth where he could first hear Her footsteps approaching; but she did not come.

Then, when the sun on his fur became too hot, he moved to his rock in the shade, paying no attention to the busy life that buzzed and crawled and whirred and leaped and floated and sang around him, but keeping his eyes fixed on that spot of brown, flattened grass where She should be.

The time came for Her to go away, and still She had not come. He went up the path as far as the flat rock where he always waited for Her and sat there alert and watchful, ready to leap behind the clump of grass the moment She should appear in the distance. But She did not come.

The hour for his dinner passed. It was time for their afternoon walk. While he sat waiting on the rock part of him took the walk with Her, telling Her soon how tired he was, so that he might ride home on Her shoulder. For a moment it seemed so real that he could almost feel the security and comfort of Her arms holding him. A short wail escaped from his throat. He was very hungry.

At last he saw Her, just when the shadows were lengthening. She was quite far away, but still he had to leap at once behind the clump of grass, wriggling with joy, getting ready to pounce out in front of Her. But then he had to wait too long. By the time She came he was tired again. And the pounce was somehow mismanaged, for it did not surprise Her and didn't make Her laugh. There was no race home. She seemed to have forgotten it. He followed her slowly and went inside with Her and ate the dinner She gave him, and that was all there was to the beautiful day.

Because he did not want to miss Her again, he went for only a short walk the following morning and came back very early. Yet She was not on Her patch of grass when he got there. Of course he had never been there that early before. Perhaps it was too early. He waited as he had the day before, moved to the shade, got up and walked along the path to his rock and waited for Her there.

Again the time for his dinner came and passed. He was not hungry today. He did not go on the afternoon walk with Her. He did not feel the comfort of Her arms holding him. He did not cry. And when he saw Her in the distance, he did not hide behind the clump of grass to surprise Her as She came by.

She was not alone.

With Her was another Human Being. They came up the path talking and laughing together, and they went by the clump of grass where he should be hiding without a pause. He looked after them and watched them go inside and stayed where he was, sitting on the rock where he always waited for Her to come home.

After a while She called him. He went to Her and followed Her inside. The Other One put down a hand to stroke him. It was a good hand, one that he would have liked if it had not touched Her. He allowed it to glide over his back, then slipped from under it and went away. The hand that had stroked him was raised to join Hers.

He knew it would not do any good now to make a lot of noise, or slide across the floor, or chase a paper ball. This was different.

Finally She remembered his dinner. She put it down on the floor and called him, and he went over to it but turned away without touching any of it. She did not notice.

He asked to be let out again, hoping She would refuse, as She had so often before, and take him on Her lap and talk to him instead. She did not even seem to hear him. But when he kept on asking, the Other One told Her. Then She got up and opened the door. For a while he stood just outside, with the door closed between them again, not knowing what to do. At last he went to the rock where he always waited for Her.

She did not come.

He waited until the shadows lengthened and he knew it was time for him to go in. He got up and stretched, turned away from watching the place where She always appeared in the distance and looked toward home. Then he sat down again.

The shadows darkened and thickened and closed around him. He shuddered, although he was not cold, and bunched himself together tighter, crouching low. The rock beneath him began to glow a little, as if the ghost of a sun were shining on it. From the grass came stealthy rustlings and squeakings and chirpings. Far away the fox was barking.

She did not come.

He should be inside now lying in his box, dreaming of the good day that had just passed, or in Her lap, purring, with Her hand stroking him. It was so vivid for a moment that he could see Her looking down at him and smiling, and feel the touch of Her hand. He stood up suddenly and let the short, sharp cry of anguish pierce the darkness between them.

Would She hear that? It was as if his body itself had escaped along with that cry, had sped swiftly home to Her and was now lying warm and contented in Her arms, with the Other One gone away.

From not quite so far away there was an answer. The fox barked.

Would She hear that? Would She come? Always when he needed Her She was there. And yet he was trembling.

The rustling and squeaking and chirping around his feet grew bolder. The ghostly light on the rock grew brighter, carving his figure out of the blackness of the night like a cameo. A moisture began to coat his fur, the rock on which he sat, and dropped on the grass like reluctant rain.

He raised his head, listened intently, searched the air with his nostrils.

Would She come now? There was still time. Would She come?

Just behind him there was a louder rustling in the grass, a stealthy gliding through it. He did not look toward the sound. He looked toward home.

Would She come? Would She miraculously appear at his side, just when he needed Her?

He heard the breathing close, creeping up on him, and turned to face the two points of fire gleaming through the grass. He had scarcely time to brace himself before the silent rushing mass of shadow was upon him. The impact threw him over on his back. He kicked wildly against the heavy body, dug his claws into the matted fur.

Sharp teeth fastened on his throat. There was only a moment to think of Her, to realize She had not come. Then the white light of pain shot through Her image and broke it into a thousand shivering splinters. Mist whirled above him, thickened and descended to crush him into itself. The night that was endless swept over everything.

Lillian

DAMON RUNYON

WHAT I always say is that Wilbur Willard is nothing but a very lucky guy, because what is it but luck that has him teetering along Forty-ninth Street one cold snowy morning when Lillian is mer-ow-ing around the sidewalk looking for her mamma?

And what is it but luck that has Wilbur Willard all mulled up to a million, what with him having been sitting out a few seidels of Scotch with a friend by the name of Haggerty in an apartment over in Fifty-ninth Street? Because if Wilbur Willard is not mulled up he will see Lillian as nothing but a little black cat, and give her plenty of room, for everybody knows that black cats are terribly bad luck, even when they are only kittens.

But being mulled up like I tell you, things look very different to Wilbur Willard, and he does not see Lillian as a little black kitten scrabbling around in the snow. He sees a beautiful leopard, because a copper by the name of O'Hara, who is walking past about then, and who knows Wilbur Willard, hears him say:

"Oh, you beautiful leopard!"

The copper takes a quick peek himself, because he does not wish any leopards running around his beat, it being against the law, but all he sees, as he tells me afterwards, is this rumpot ham, Wilbur Willard, picking up a scrawny little black kitten and shoving it in his overcoat pocket, and he also hears Wilbur say:

"Your name is Lillian."

Then Wilbur teeters on up to his room on the top floor of an old fleabag in Eighth Avenue that is called the Hotel de Brussels, where he lives quite a while, because the management does not mind actors, the management of the Hotel de Brussels being very broadminded, indeed.

There is some complaint this same morning from one of Wilbur's neighbors, an old burlesque doll by the name of Minnie Madigan, who is not working since Abraham Lincoln is assassinated, because she hears Wilbur going on in his room about a beautiful leopard, and calls up the clerk to say that a hotel which allows wild animals is not respectable. But the clerk looks in on Wilbur and finds him playing with nothing but a harmless-looking little black kitten, and nothing comes of the old doll's beef, especially as nobody ever claims the Hotel de Brussels is respectable anyway, or at least not much.

Of course when Wilbur comes out from under the ether next afternoon he can see Lillian is not a leopard, and in fact Wilbur is quite astonished to find himself in bed with a little black kitten, because it seems Lillian is sleeping on Wilbur's chest to keep warm. At first Wilbur does not believe what he sees, and puts it down to

Haggerty's Scotch, but finally he is convinced, and so he puts Lillian in his pocket, and takes her over to the Hot Box night club and gives her some milk, of which Lillian is very fond.

Now where Lillian comes from in the first place of course nobody knows. The chances are somebody chucks her out of a window into the snow, because people are always chucking kittens, and one thing and another, out of windows in New York. In fact, if there is one thing this town has plenty of, it is kittens, which finally grow up to be cats, and go snooping around ash cans, and mer-owing on roofs, and keeping people from sleeping good.

Personally, I have no use for cats, including kittens, because I never see one that has any too much sense, although I know a guy by the name of Pussy McGuire who makes a first-rate living doing nothing but stealing cats, and sometimes dogs, and selling them to old dolls who like such things for company. But Pussy only steals Persian and Angora cats, which are very fine cats, and of course Lillian is no such cat as this. Lillian is nothing but a black cat, and nobody will give you a dime a dozen for black cats in this town, as they are generally regarded as very bad jinxes.

Furthermore, it comes out in a few weeks that Wilbur Willard can just as well name her Herman, or Sidney, as not, but Wilbur sticks to Lillian, because this is the name of his partner when he is in vaudeville years ago. He often tells me about Lillian Withington when he is mulled up, which is more often than somewhat, for Wilbur is a great hand for drinking Scotch, or rye, or bourbon, or gin, or whatever else there is around for drinking, except water. In fact, Wilbur Willard is a high-class drinking man, and it does no good to tell him it is against the law to drink in this country, because it only makes him mad, and he says to the dickens with the law, only Wilbur uses a much rougher word than dickens.

"She is like a beautiful leopard," Wilbur says to me about Lillian Withington. "Black-haired, and black-eyed, and all ripply, like a leopard I see in an animal act on the same bill at the Palace with us once. We are headliners then," he says, "Willard and Withington, the best singing and dancing act in the country.

"I pick her up in San Antonio, which is a spot in Texas," Wilbur says. "She is not long out of a convent, and I just lose my old partner, Mary McGee, who ups and dies on me of pneumonia down there. Lillian wishes to go on the stage, and joins me. A natural-born actress with a great voice. But like a leopard," Wilbur says, "like a leopard. There is cat in her, no doubt of this, and cats and women are both ungrateful. I love Lillian Withington. I wish to marry her. But she is cold to me. She says she is not going to follow the stage all her life. She says she wishes money, and luxury, and a fine home, and of course a guy like me cannot give a doll such things.

"I wait on her hand and foot," Wilbur says. "I am her slave. There is nothing I will not do for her. Then one day she walks in on me in Boston very cool and says she is quitting me. She says she is marrying a rich guy there. Well, naturally it busts up the act and I never have the heart to look for another partner, and then I get to belting that old black bottle around, and now what am I but a cabaret performer?"

Then sometimes he will bust out crying, and sometimes I will cry with him, although the way I look at it, Wilbur gets a pretty fair break, at that, in getting rid of a doll who wishes things he cannot give her. Many a guy in this town is tangled up with a doll who wishes things he cannot give her, but keeps him tangled up just the same and busting himself trying to keep her quiet.

Wilbur makes pretty fair money as an entertainer in the Hot Box, though he spends most of it for Scotch, and he is not a bad entertainer, either. I often go to the Hot Box when I am feeling blue to hear him sing Melancholy Baby, and Moonshine Valley, and other sad songs which break my heart. Personally, I do not see why any doll cannot love Wilbur, especially if they listen to him sing such songs as Melancholy Baby when he is mulled up good, because he is a tall, nice-looking guy with long eyelashes, and sleepy brown eyes, and his voice has a low moaning sound that usually goes very big with the dolls. In fact, many a doll does do some pitching to Wilbur when he is singing in the Hot Box, but somehow Wilbur never gives them a tumble, which I suppose is because he is thinking only of Lillian Withington.

Well, after he gets Lillian, the black kitten, Wilbur seems to find a new interest in life, and Lillian turns out to be right cute, and not bad-looking after Wilbur gets her fed up good. She is blacker than a yard up a chimney, with not a white spot on her, and she grows so fast that by and by Wilbur cannot carry her in his pocket any more, so he puts a collar on her and leads her around. So Lillian becomes very well known on Broadway, what with Wilbur taking her many places, and finally she does not even have to be led around by Willard, but follows him like a pooch. And in all the Roaring Forties there is no pooch that cares to have any truck with Lillian, for she will leap aboard them quicker than you can say scat, and scratch and bite them until they are very glad indeed to get away from her.

But of course the pooches in the Forties are mainly nothing but

Chows, and Pekes, and Poms, or little woolly white poodles, which are led around by blond dolls, and are not fit to take their own part against a smart cat. In fact, Wilbur Willard is finally not on speaking terms with any doll that owns a pooch between Times Square and Columbus Circle, and they are all hoping that both Wilbur and Lillian will go lay down and die somewhere. Furthermore, Wilbur has a couple of battles with guys who also belong to the dolls, but Wilbur is no sucker in a battle if he is not mulled up too much and leg-weary.

After he is through entertaining people in the Hot Box, Wilbur generally goes around to any speakeasies which may still be open, and does a little offhand drinking on top of what he already drinks down in the Hot Box, which is plenty, and although it is considered very risky in this town to mix Hot Box liquor with any other, it never seems to bother Wilbur. Along toward daylight he takes a couple of bottles of Scotch over to his room in the Hotel de Brussels and uses them for a nightcap, so by the time Wilbur Willard is ready to slide off to sleep he has plenty of liquor of one kind and another inside him, and he sleeps pretty good.

Of course nobody on Broadway blames Wilbur so very much for being such a rumpot, because they know about him loving Lillian Withington, and losing her, and it is considered a reasonable excuse in this town for a guy to do some drinking when he loses a doll, which is why there is so much drinking here, but it is a mystery to one and all how Wilbur stands off all this liquor without croaking. The cemeteries are full of guys who do a lot less drinking then Wilbur, but he never even seems to feel extra tough, or if he does he keeps it to himself and does not go around saying it is the kind of liquor you get nowadays.

He costs some of the boys around Mindy's plenty of dough one winter, because he starts in doing most of his drinking after hours in Good Time Charley's speakeasy, and the boys lay a price of four to one against him lasting until spring, never figuring a guy can drink very much of Good Time Charley's liquor and keep on living. But Wilbur Willard does it just the same, so everybody says the guy is just naturally superhuman, and lets it go at that.

Sometimes Wilbur drops into Mindy's with Lillian following him on the lookout for pooches, or riding on his shoulder if the weather is bad, and the two of them will sit with us for hours chewing the rag about one thing and another. At such times Wilbur generally has a bottle on his hip and takes a shot now and then, but of course this does not come under the head of serious drinking with him. When Lillian is with Wilbur she always lays as close to him as she can get and anybody can see that she seems to be very fond of Wilbur, and that he is very fond of her, although he sometimes forgets himself and speaks of her as a beautiful leopard. But of course this is only a slip of the tongue, and anyway if Wilbur gets any pleasure out of thinking Lillian is a leopard, it is nobody's business but his own.

"I suppose she will run away from me some day," Wilbur says, running his hand over Lillian's back until her fur crackles. "Yes, although I give her plenty of liver and catnip, and one thing and another, and all my affection, she will probably give me the shake. Cats are like women, and women are like cats. They are both very ungrateful."

"They are both generally bad luck," Big Nig, the crap shooter, says. "Especially cats, and most especially black cats."

Many other guys tell Wilbur about black cats being bad luck, and advise him to slip Lillian into the North River some night with a sinker on her, but Wilbur claims he already has all the bad luck in the world when he loses Lillian Withington, and that Lillian, the cat, cannot make it any worse, so he goes on taking extra good care of her, and Lillian goes on getting bigger and bigger until I commence thinking maybe there is some St. Bernard in her.

Finally I commence to notice something funny about Lillian. Sometimes she will be acting very loving toward Wilbur, and then again she will be very unfriendly to him, and will spit at him, and snatch at him with her claws, very hostile. It seems to me that she is all right when Willard is mulled up, but is as sad and fretful as he is himself when he is only a little bit mulled. And when Lillian is sad and fretful she makes it very tough indeed on the pooches in the neighborhood of the Brussels.

In fact, Lillian takes to pooch-hunting, sneaking off when Wilbur is getting his rest, and running pooches bow-legged, especially when she finds one that is not on a leash. A loose pooch is just naturally cherry pie for Lillian.

Well, of course this causes great indignation among the dolls who own the pooches, particularly when Lillian comes home one day carrying a Peke as big as she is herself by the scruff of the neck, and with a very excited blond doll following her and yelling bloody murder outside Wilbur Willard's door when Lillian pops into Wilbur's room through a hole he cuts in the door for her, still lugging the Peke. But it seems that instead of being mad at Lillian and giving her a pasting for such goings on, Wilbur is somewhat pleased, because he happens to be still in a fog when Lillian arrives with the Peke, and is thinking of Lillian as a beautiful leopard.

"Why," Wilbur says, "this is devotion, indeed. My beautiful leopard goes off into the jungle and fetches me an antelope for dinner."

Now of course there is no sense whatever to this, because a Peke is certainly not anything like an antelope, but the blond doll outside Wilbur's door hears Wilbur mumble, and gets the idea that he is going to eat her Peke for dinner and the squawk she puts up is very terrible. There is plenty of trouble around the Brussels in chilling the blond doll's beef over Lillian snagging her Peke, and what is more the blond doll's ever-loving guy, who turns out to be a tough Ginney bootlegger by the name of Gregorio, shows up at the Hot Box the next night and wishes to put the slug on Wilbur Willard.

But Wilbur rounds him up with a few drinks and by singing Melancholy Baby to him, and before he leaves the Ginney gets very sentimental towards Wilbur, and Lillian, too, and wishes to give Wilbur five bucks to let Lillian grab the Peke again, if Lillian will promise not to bring it back. It seems Gregorio does not care for the Peke, and is only acting quarrelsome to please the blond doll and make her think he loves her dearly.

But I can see Lillian is having different moods, and finally I ask Wilbur if he notices it.

"Yes," he says very sad, "I do not seem to be holding her love. She is getting very fickle. A guy moves onto my floor at the Brussels the other day with a little boy, and Lillian becomes very fond of this kid at once. In fact, they are great friends. Ah, well," Wilbur says, "cats are like women. Their affection does not last."

I happen to go over to the Brussels a few days later to explain to a guy by the name of Crutchy, who lives on the same floor as Wilbur Willard, that some of our citizens do not like his face and that it may be a good idea for him to leave town, especially if he insists on bringing ale into their territory, and I see Lillian out in the hall with a youngster which I judge is the kid Wilbur is talking about. The kid is maybe three years old, and very cute, what with black hair, and black eyes, and he is wooling Lillian around the hall in a way that is most surprising, for Lillian is not such a cat as will stand for much wooling around, not even from Wilbur Willard.

I am wondering how anybody comes to take such a kid to a joint like the Brussels, but I figure it is some actor's kid, and that maybe there is no mamma for it. Later I am talking to Wilbur about this, and he says:

"Well, if the kid's old man is an actor, he is not working at it. He sticks close to his room all the time, and he does not allow the kid to go anywhere but in the hall, and I feel sorry for the little guy, which is why I allow Lillian to play with him."

Now it comes on a very cold spell, and a bunch of us are sitting in Mindy's along toward five o'clock in the morning when we hear fire engines going past. By and by in comes a guy by the name of Kansas, who is named Kansas because he comes from Kansas, and who is a crap shooter by trade.

"The old Brussels is on fire," this guy Kansas says.

"She is always on fire," Big Nig says, meaning there is always plenty of hot stuff going on around the Brussels.

About this time who walks in but Wilbur Willard, and anybody can see he is just naturally floating. The chances are he comes from Good Time Charley's, and he is certainly carrying plenty of pressure. I never see Wilbur Willard mulled up more. He does not have Lillian with him, but then he never takes Lillian to Good Time Charley's, because Charley hates cats.

"Hey, Wilbur," Big Nig says, "your joint, the Brussels, is on fire."

"Well," Wilbur says, "I am a little firefly, and I need a light. Let us go where there is fire."

The Brussels is only a few blocks from Mindy's, and there is nothing else to do just then, so some of us walk over to Eighth Avenue with Wilbur teetering along ahead of us. The old shack is certainly roaring good when we get in sight of it, and the firemen are tossing water into it, and the coppers have the fire lines out to keep the crowd back, although there is not much of a crowd at such an hour in the morning.

"Is it not beautiful?" Wilbur Willard says, looking up at the flames. "Is it not like a fairy palace all lighted up this way?"

You see, Wilbur does not realize the joint is on fire, although guys and dolls are running out of it every which way, most of them half dressed, or not dressed at all, and the firemen are getting out the life nets in case anybody wishes to hop out of the windows.

"It is certainly beautiful," Wilbur says. "I must get Lillian so she can see this."

And before anybody has time to think, there is Wilbur Willard walking into the front door of the Brussels as if nothing happens. The firemen and the coppers are so astonished all they can do is holler at Wilbur, but he pays no attention whatever. Well, naturally everybody figures Wilbur is a gone gosling, but in about ten minutes he comes walking out of this same door through the fire and smoke as cool as you please, and he has Lillian in his arms.

"You know," Wilbur says, coming over to where we are standing with our eyes popping out, "I have to walk all the way up to my floor because the elevators seem to be out of commission. The service is getting terrible in this hotel. I will certainly make a strong beef to the management about it as soon as I pay something on my account."

Then what happens but Lillian lets out a big mer-ow, and hops out of Wilbur's arms and skips past the coppers and the firemen with her back all humped up, and the next thing anybody knows she is tearing through the front door of the old hotel and making plenty of speed.

"Well, well," Wilbur says, looking much surprised, "there goes Lillian."

And what does this daffy Wilbur Willard do but turn and go marching back into the Brussels again, and by this time the smoke is pouring out of the front doors so thick he is out of sight in a second. Naturally he takes the coppers and firemen by surprise, because they are not used to guys walking in and out of fires on them.

This time anybody standing around will lay you plenty of odds— two and a half and maybe three to one that Wilbur never shows up again, because the old Brussels is now just popping with fire and smoke from the lower windows, although there does not seem to be quite so much fire in the upper story. Everybody seems to be out of the joint, and even the firemen are fighting the blaze from the outside because the Brussels is so old and ramshackly there is no sense in them risking the floors.

I mean everybody is out of the joint except Wilbur Willard and Lillian, and we figure they are getting a good frying somewhere inside, although Feet Samuels is around offering to take thirteen to five for a few small bets that Lillian comes out okay, because Feet claims that a cat had nine lives and that is a fair bet at the price.

Well, up comes a swell-looking doll all heated up about something and pushing and clawing her way through the crowd up to the ropes and screaming until you can hardly hear yourself think, and about this same minute everybody hears a voice going ai-lee-hi-hee-hoo, like a Swiss yodeler, which comes from the roof of the Brussels, and looking up what do we see but Wilbur Willard standing up there on the edge of the roof, high above the fire and smoke, and yodeling very loud.

Under one arm he has a big bundle of some kind, and under the other he has the little kid I see playing in the hall with Lillian. As he stands up there going ai-lee-hi-hee-hoo, the swell-dressed doll near us begins yipping louder than Wilbur is yodeling, and the firemen rush over under him with a life net.

Wilbur lets out another ai-lee-hi-hee-hoo, and down he comes all spraddled out, with the bundle and the kid, but he hits the net sitting down and bounces up and back again for a couple of minutes before he finally settles. In fact, Wilbur is enjoying the bouncing, and the chances are he will be bouncing yet if the firemen do not drop their hold on the net and let him fall to the ground.

Then Wilbur steps out of the net, and I can see the bundle is a rolled-up blanket with Lillian's eyes peeking out of one end. He still has the kid under the other arm with his head stuck out in front, and his legs stuck out behind, and it does not seem to me that Wilbur is handling the kid as careful as he is handling Lillian. He stands there looking at the firemen with a sneering look, and finally he says:

"Do not think you can catch me in your net unless I wish to be caught. I am a butterfly, and very hard to overtake."

Then all of a sudden the swell-dressed doll, who is doing so much hollering, piles on top of Wilbur and grabs the kid from him and begins hugging and kissing it.

"Wilbur," she says, "God bless you, Wilbur, for saving my baby! Oh, thank you, Wilbur, thank you! My wretched husband kidnaps and runs away with him, and it is only a few hours ago that my detectives find out where he is."

Wilbur gives the doll a funny look for about half a minute and starts to walk away, but Lillian comes wiggling out of the blanket, looking and smelling pretty much singed up, and the kid sees Lillian and begins hollering for her, so Wilbur finally hands Lillian over to the kid. And not wishing to leave Lillian, Wilbur stands around somewhat confused, and the doll gets talking to him, and finally they go away together, and as they go Wilbur is carrying the kid, and the kid is carrying Lillian, and Lillian is not feeling so good from her burns.

Furthermore, Wilbur is probably more sober than he ever is before in years at this hour in the morning, but before they go I get a chance to talk some to Wilbur when he is still rambling somewhat, and I make out from what he says that the first time he goes to get Lillian he finds her in his room and does not see hide or hair of the little kid and does not even think of him, because he does not know what room the kid is in, anyway, having never noticed such a thing.

But the second time he goes up, Lillian is sniffing at the crack under the door of a room down the hall from Wilbur's and Wilbur says he seems to remember seeing a trickle of something like water coming out of the crack.

"And," Wilbur says, "as I am looking for a blanket for Lillian, and it will be a bother to go back to my room, I figure I will get one out of this room. I try the knob but the door is locked, so I kick it in, and walk in to find the room is full of smoke, and fire is shooting through the windows very lovely, and when I grab a blanket off the bed for Lillian, what is under the blanket but the kid?

"Well," Wilbur says, "the kid is squawking, and Lillian is mer-owing, and there is so much confusion generally that it makes me nervous, so I figure we better go up on the roof and let the stink blow off us, and look at the fire from there. It seems there is a guy stretched out on the floor of the room alongside an upset table between the door and the bed. He has a bottle in one hand, and he is dead. Well, naturally there is no percentage in lugging a dead guy along, so I take Lillian and the kid and go up on the roof, and we just naturally fly off like humming birds. Now I must get a drink," Wilbur says. "I wonder if anybody has anything on their hip."

Well, the papers are certainly full of Wilbur and Lillian the next day, especially Lillian, and they are both great heroes.

But Wilbur cannot stand the publicity very long, because he never has no time to himself for his drinking, what with the scribes and the photographers hopping on him every few minutes wishing to hear his story, and to take more pictures of him and Lillian, so one night he disappears and Lillian disappears with him.

About a year later it comes out that he marries his old doll, Lillian Withington-Harmon, and falls into a lot of dough, and what is more he cuts out the liquor and becomes quite a useful citizen one way and another. So everybody has to admit that black cats are not always bad luck, although I say Wilbur's case is a little exceptional because he does not start out knowing Lillian is a black cat, but thinking she is a leopard.

I happen to run into Wilbur one day all dressed up in good clothes and jewelry and chucking quite a swell.

"Wilbur," I say to him, "I often think how remarkable it is the way Lillian suddenly gets such an attachment for the little kid and remembers about him being in the hotel and leads you back there a second time to the right room. If I do not see this come off with my own eyes. I will never believe a cat has brains enough to do such a thing, because I consider cats extra dumb."

"Brains nothing," Wilbur says. "Lillian does not have brains enough to grease a gimlet. And what is more she has no more attach-ment for the kid than a jack rabbit. The time has come," Wilbur says, "to expose Lillian. She gets a lot of credit which is never coming to her. I will now tell you about Lillian, and nobody knows this but me.

"You see," Wilbur says, "when Lillian is a little kitten I always put a little Scotch in her milk, partly to help make her good and strong and partly because I am never no hand to drink alone, unless there is nobody with me. Well, at first Lillian does not care so much for this Scotch in her milk, but finally she takes a liking to it, and I keep making her toddy stronger until in the end she will lap up a good big snort without any milk for a chaser, and yell for more. In fact, I suddenly realize that Lillian becomes a rumpot, just as I am in those days, and simply must have her grog, and it is when she is good and rummed up that Lillian goes off snatching Pekes, and acting tough generally.

"Now," Wilbur says, "the time of the fire is about the time I get home every morning and give Lillian her schnapps. But when I go into the hotel and get her the first time I forget to Scotch her up, and the reason she runs back into the hotel is because she is looking for her shot. And the reason she is sniffing at the kid's door is not because the kid is in there but because the trickle that is coming through the crack under the door is nothing but Scotch that is running out of the bottle in the dead guy's hand. I never mention this before because I figure it may be a knock to a dead guy's memory," Wilbur says. "Drinking is certainly a disgusting thing, especially secret drinking."

"But how is Lillian getting along these days?" I ask Wilbur Willard.

"I am greatly disappointed in Lillian," he says. "She refuses to reform when I do and the last I hear of her she takes up with Gregorio, the Ginney bootlegger, who keeps her well Scotched up all the time so she will lead his blond doll's Peke a dog's life."

Nellie and Tom

MARVIN R. CLARK

I WAS a boy of eighteen years of age when my mother brought home with her, all the way from the State of Maine, a Maltese Pussy, of full breed. We called her "Nellie." After mother had buttered Nellie's feet, a process which she said would always keep a cat from running away from home, the aristocratic Nellie became an important member of our household, and never deserted us.

One day I brought home to Nellie a companion who had been presented to me by a friend. "Tom," as we called the boy, was a pure Maltese, and a giant of his kind, a cheerful, clever and peaceable fellow and an ornament and pet, for he was admired by everybody who saw him. His feet were also buttered, and after a little spat with Nellie, who, at first, could see no just reason why Tom should encroach upon her domain, the two became fast friends, and finally married and raised several litters of pure Maltese kittens, all of whom we gave to longing friends save one, which we kept for Nellie's sake.

Tom remained true to his marriage vows for a long time, but one day, about six months after his advent in the household, he was missing, and the neighborhood was searched for Tom. He remained away until the following afternoon, when he returned, looking sheepish, while his appearance bore unmistakable evidence of his having been indulging in a debauch. Tom was very crestfallen and expressed his sorrow to his spouse Nellie, who would have nothing to do with him for several days. Poor Tom was disconsolate, and applied to me for sympathy. Of course every member of the family reproved Tom for his waywardness, but the story of the "Prodigal Son" and his return, in tatters, was not forgotten, although the fatted calf was omitted, and I was the first to forgive and console Tom. I used my influence so successfully with Nellie, who was very fond of me, that once more Tom was taken into Nellie's favor and everything went on as usual, excepting that Nellie gave every evidence of keeping a close eye upon her erring liege-lord, who was not fully restored to her confidence.

Some five weeks after, while Nellie was nursing a new brood of kittens, Tom turned up missing again. We did not go to any trouble that time to search for him, nor did we feel any anxiety concerning the wandering minstrel, knowing from our former experience that he was big enough and old enough to take care of himself. Three weary weeks for Nellie went by while she was worrying for her Romeo, although she tried to conceal her anxiety behind an appearance of unconcern, while lavishing her affections upon her infants. At the end of the third week Tom leisurely strolled into the house and sought Nellie's presence. He bore an air of bravado which seemed to say that he was lord and master of his own family, that he had a right to go whither, and stay there as long as he pleased. But he was battered and torn, almost beyond recognition. One eye was completely closed, much of his fur was gone, he limped when he walked, one ear was entirely bitten through and a portion of it missing, and his head was covered with bloody wounds, while his general appearance was emaciated, tattered and forlorn. Nellie's tail was a sight to behold when she spied Tom, and she raised herself to a

sitting posture and threw upon the debauchee a withering look of contempt which sent his tail between his legs in less time than it takes to tell it, while he completely lost his braggadocio air and slunk off to a corner of the room and Nellie returned to her babies.

After the tramp had received a scolding from each one of the family, and been thoroughly cleansed and his wounds dressed, he sat down a few feet from his lawful wife and moaned and cried for an hour or more, without once attracting a look of pity from her. After that he approached Nellie and attempted to ask her forgiveness for his absence upon some fictitous ground, but that faithful one raised herself upon her hind legs, spat upon the battered tramp and then deliberately beat him with her paws and scratched him with her claws until he slunk out of the room, a well reproved if not a better Cat. For more than a week, every time Tom made overtures looking toward a reconciliation, Nellie repeated his chastisement, and I fully believe if any other Maltese Tom had presented himself during that time, she would have taught Tom a lesson which he would have remembered to the end of his life, by adopting him in Tom's place, and, with his assistance, driven out upon the charity of a cold world, her wayward and presumably unfaithful consort. But, although we refused to intercede for him with Nellie, in the course of time Tom was partly forgiven and was again kept under the watchful eye of Nellie.

Three months later the vagabond again forgot his marriage vows and disappeared. This time we gave him up for lost, as he did not return for a month. Considering him a thing of the beautiful past, I bought another Tom and brought him home to Nellie. Singularly enough, the two did not fraternize, although it was not the fault of the new Tom, and Nellie remained, as she supposed, a widow, with her kittens as her constant care. Upon them she lavished all of her affections, spitting at and boxing the new Tom whenever he approached them.

One fine day, to our utter astonishment, the scoundrel, Tom strolled in upon the scene as nonchalantly as if he had not been off on a long protracted cruise. But this time he was covered with sores, and had, in addition, the mange. He was a sorry-looking Tom, and an animal to avoid. Even in that condition, I am sure, Nellie would have nursed him and doctored him until he recovered, had he been faithful to her. But there was no hope of it now. She had evidently been thinking deeply about the newcomer, and was making comparisons.

At first he showed contrition, but when he discovered the new

Tom, who he supposed had assumed his duties in the household, he did not become an Enoch Arden, but, with fire in his evil eye and without making proper inquiries concerning Nellie's unexceptionable conduct, with a great bologna sausage of a fuzzy tail and a fearful shriek for vengeance, he made for Tom Number Two with the speed of lightning, in the stereotyped manner of an outraged husband whose lapses of fealty and so on are forgotten in the greater sin of an interloper.

What might have become of the innocent new fellow was illustrated in the story of the Kilkenny cats, with this difference, that one of the two would have been left on the earth, and it wouldn't have been the new fellow, for Tom was the maddest Cat you ever saw. When the tocsin of war was sounded by the mangy deserter, Nellie sprang for him and there ensued a battle royal. There was war to the knife, from the point to the hilt. The screams of the combatants were terrific, and the dining-room floor was covered with a constantly accumulating mass of Maltese fur. In both the new Tom and Nellie, who, alone, was a host in herself, the mangy Tom found more than his match, and he was beaten, torn, wounded at every point, and a total wreck when he scurried out of the house and took his sorrowful way down the street, toward the dock at the foot of Hubert street. Whether or not he did the best thing he could have done under the circumstances, and went and drowned himself, is unknown, but Nellie never knew him more, for the new fellow thereafter succeeded to his lares and penates and Nellie and he lived happily together until Tom Number Two was shot by some cruel person. After that Nellie mourned his loss and refused to be comforted with another, although, of course, there were many Toms who would have lain down and died for her. She lived but a short time after the death of her second husband, and died regretted by all of us.

'Corban'

EDEN PHILLPOTTS

" 'Tis a question which to drown," said Mr. Sage. He smoked his churchwarden and looked down between his knees where a mother cat was gazing up at him with green eyes. She purred, rolled half on her back and opened and contracted her forepaws with pleasure, while she suckled two kittens.

Mr. Sage's daughter—a maiden of twelve—begged him to spare both squeaking dabs of life.

"They'm so like as two peas, faither—brave li'l chets both. Don't 'e drown one of 'em," she said.

"Thicky cat's been very generous of chets in her time," declared Mr. Sage. "If such things had ghostesses, you might see a whole regiment of 'em—black an' white, tabby an' tortoise-shell—down-along by the river come dark."

"Even I shouldn't be feared of a chet's ghostie," declared little Milly Sage.

But she had her way. One kitten, when it could face the world alone, was given to a friend who dwelt some miles distant at Princetown; the other grew into a noble tom of large tabby design and genial disposition. His mother, feeling him to be her masterpiece, passed gently out of life soon after her son reached cat's estate. She had done her duty to the feline community, and Milly mourned for her a whole week. But Mr. Sage did not mourn. He preferred the young tom, and between the cat and the old man, as years passed by, there waxed a friendship of remarkable character.

"I call un 'Corban,'" said Mr. Sage, " 'cause he was a gift—a gift from my girl when she was a little 'un. 'Twas her own ram cat, you mind, but as the creature growed up, it took that tender to me that Milly said it must be mine; an' mine 'tis; an' what he'd do wi' out me, or what I'd do wi' out he, be blessed if I know."

He spoke to his next-door neighbour and personal crony, Amos Oldreive, a gamekeeper and river-watcher for many years. Now this man was honorably retired, with a small pension and a great rheumatism, the reward of many a damp night on behalf of the salmon by Dart's ancient stream.

At Postbridge these old people dwelt—a hamlet in the heart of Dartmoor—a cluster of straggling cots beside the name-river of that region, where its eastern branch comes tumbling through the shaggy fens beneath Cut Hill. Here a disused pack-horse bridge crosses Dart, but the main road spans the stream upon a modern arch hard by. The lives of Sage and Oldreive had passed within twenty miles of this spot. The keeper knew every tor of the waste, together with the phases of the seasons, and the natural history of each bird and beast and fish sacred to sporting. His friend's days were also spent in this region, and both ancients, when necessity or occasion drove them into towns, felt the houses pressing upon their eyes and crushing their foreheads and the air choking them. At such times they did their business with all speed, and so returned in thankfulness to the beech-tree grove, the cottages and those meadow-lands of Postbridge by Dart, all circled and cradled in the hills.

Noah Sage and his next-door neighbour quarrelled thrice daily, and once daily made up their differences over a glass of spirit and water, sometimes consumed in one cottage, sometimes in the other. Their conditions were similar. Noah had only one daughter; Amos, an only son; and each old man, though both had married late in life, was a widower.

The lad and lass, thus thrown together, came naturally to courtship, and it was a matter understood and accepted that they should marry when young Ted Oldreive could show a pound a week. The course of true love progressed uneventfully. Milly was plain, if good health, good temper, and happy, honest eyes can be plain; while Ted, a sand-coloured and steady youth of a humble nature, leaning naturally upon distinction of classes for his peace of mind, had not a rival or an enemy in the world. Mr. Sage held him a promising husband for Milly, and Ted's master, appreciating the man's steadfast qualities, gave promise of the desired number of shillings weekly when Ted should have laboured for another six months at the Vitifer tin mines near his home.

Little of a sort to set down concerning these admirable folks had arisen but for the circumstance of the cat 'Corban.' Yet, when that beast had reached the ripe age of eight years and was still a thing of beauty and a cat of mark at Postbridge, he sowed the seeds of strife, wrecked two homes, and threatened seriously to interfere with the foundation of a third.

It happened like this: gaffer Oldreive, by reason of increasing infirmities, found it necessary to abandon those tramps on the high Moor that he loved, and to occupy his time and his energies nearer home. Therefore he started the rearing of young pheasants upon half an acre of land pertaining to his leasehold cottage. The old man built his own coops and bred his own hens, as he proudly declared. Good money was to be made by one who knew how to solve the difficulties of the business, and with revived interest in life, Amos bought pheasants' eggs and henceforth spent his time among his coops and foster-mothers. The occupation rendered him egotistical, and Noah secretly regretted it, nor would he do likewise when urged to make a similar experiment.

"Don't want no birds my side the wall," he said. "I've got a brave pig or two as'll goody into near so much money as your phaysants; an' there's 'Corban,' he'd make short work of any such things as chicks."

Oldreive nodded over the party wall and glanced, not without suspicion, at the cat, who chanced to be present.

"Let 'em taste game an' it grows 'pon 'em like drink 'pon a human," he said.

'Corban' stretched his thighs, cleaned his claws on a block of fire-wood, and feigned indifference. But he knew all about the young pheasants; and Mr. Oldreive knew that he knew.

Sage, on the other hand, with an experience of his cat extending from infancy, through green youth to ripe prime, took it upon him to say that the creature was trustworthy, high-minded and actuated by motives he had never seen equalled for loftiness even in a dog.

The old keeper snorted from his side of the wall.

"A dog! You wouldn't compare thicky green-eyed snake wi' a dog, would 'e?"

"Not me," answered the other. "No dog ever I knowed was worthy to wash his face for un. An' he'm no more a green-eyed snake than your spaniel, though a good deal more of a gen'leman."

"Us won't argue it then, for I never knowed any use for cats my-self but to plant at the root of a fruit-bearin' tree," said Mr. Oldreive cynically.

"An' I never seed no use for dogs, 'cept to keep gen'lefolks out of mischief," answered Sage, who was a Radical and no sportsman. He puffed, and grew a little red as he spoke.

Here, and thus, arose a cloud no bigger than a man's hand.

Noah Sage stumped indoors to his daughter, while 'Corban' fol-lowed with pensive step and a general air as though one should say, "I forgive, but I shan't forget."

Three days later Mr. Oldreive looked over the wall, and his neigh-bour saw him, and put a hasty foot on some feathers.

"Marnin', Sage. Look here—what I wants to know be, whether your blasted cat have took wan o' my phaysant chicks, or whether he haven't?"

"Might have, might not, Amos. Better ax un. Here he be."

Green-eyed innocence marked the fat round face of 'Corban.' He leapt upon the wall and saluted the breeder of game with open-hearted friendship.

"What be onder your heel, neighbour?"

"Why—a bit of rabbit's flax 'twas, I think. My sight ban't so good as of old nowadays."

"Rabbit's flax! 'Tis a phaysant's feathers! Get away, you hookem-snivey Judas, or I'll hit 'e over the chops!"

The last threat concerned 'Corban,' who was rubbing his whiskers against Mr. Oldreive's waistcoat.

The ancient Sage puffed out his cheeks and grew as red as a rose.

"Ban't the way to speak to any respectably domestic animal, an' you know it, Amos."

"Domestic!" echoed Mr. Oldreive bitterly. "About so domestic as old red fox I sent off wi' a flea in his ear two nights since. Domestic! He pretends to be to gain his private ends. Just a savage, cruel awnself beast of prey, an' no better. Can't shoot foxes, 'cause they'm the backbone of England; but I can shoot cats an'—an'—"

"Stop there!" roared the other ancient. He trembled with passion; his under jaw chattered; he lifted his legs up and down and cracked the joints of his fingers.

"To think I've knowed 'e all these years an' never seed through to the devilish nature of 'e! 'Tis sporting as makes men all the same— no better'n heathen savages."

The other kept calm before this shattering criticism.

"Whether or no, I don't breed these here phaysants for fun nor yet for your cat's belly. No call to quarrel, I should hope. But keep un his own side the wall, if you please, else he's like to have an onrestful time. I give 'e fair warning."

"Perhaps you'd wish for me to chain un up?"

"Might be better—for him—if you did."

"I don't want you in my house to-night," said the owner of 'Corban' suddenly. "You've shook me. You've shook a friendship of more'n fifty years' standing, Amos Oldreive, an' I can't abear to look upon your face again to-day."

"More shame to you, Noah Sage! If you recken your mangy cat be more to you than a good Christian neighbour, say so. But I ban't gwaine to fall down an' worship thicky varmint—no, not for twenty men, so now you know."

"So much for friendship, then," answered Noah Sage, wagging his head.

"So much for a silly fool," replied Amos Oldreive rudely, and they left it at that, and each turned his back upon his neighbour.

Not a word was exchanged between them for three days; then the keeper sent in a message by Milly, who trembled before her parent as she delivered it.

"Mr. Oldreive sez that 'Corban' have killed two more of his li'l game-birds, faither. An' he sez that if so be as he goes for to catch puss in there again, he'll shoot un! Don't 'e look so grievous gallied, dear faither! I'm sure he never could do it after bein' your friend fifty year, though certainly he was cleanin' his gun when he spoke to me."

"Shoot the cat! If he do, the world shall ring with it, God's my judge! Shoot my cat—red-handed, blood-sucking ruffian! Slay my cat; and then think to marry his ginger-headed son to my darter! Never! the bald pelican. You tell him that if a hair o' my cat be singed by his

beastly fowling-piece, I'll blaze it from here to Moretonhampstead—
ess fay, I will, an' lock him up, an' you shan't marry his Ted neither.
Shoot my—Hell! to think as that man had been trusted by me for
half a century! I cream all down my spine to picture his black heart.
Guy Fawkes be a Christian gen'leman to un. Here! 'Corban'! 'Corban'! 'Corban'! Where be you to, cat! Come here, can't 'e, my old
dear?"

He stormed off, and Milly, her grey eyes grown troubled and red
lips drawn down somewhat, hastened to tell Ted Oldreive the nature
of this dreadful discourse.

"He took it very unkind," she said. "Can't deny as poor faither was
strung up to a high pitch by it. Such obstinate, saucy old sillies as
both be. An' if faither's cat do come to harm, worse will follow, for
he swears I shan't have 'e if Mr. Oldreive does anything short an'
sharp wi' 'Corban.' "

Ted scratched his sandy locks as a way to let in light upon slow
brains.

" 'Tis very ill-convenient as your cat will eat faither's game-
birds," he said; "but knowin' the store your old man sets by the beast,
I'm sure my old man never would ackshually go for to shoot un."

"If he does, 'tis all off betwixt you an' me—gospel truth. Faither's a
man as stands to his word through thunder," declared Milly. "An' I
ban't of age yet, so he can keep me from you, an' he will if Mr.
Oldreive murders 'Corban.' "

"Too late for that," answered Ted, very positively. "The banns
was up last Sunday, as your father well knows. Us was axed out to
Princetown for the first time last Sunday; an' I get my pound a week
after midsummer, as I've told your faither. Then us'll take that cottage 'pon top of Merripit Hill, an' they must fight their own battles,
an' us shall be out o' earshot, thank God."

"I'll keep a eye 'pon 'Corban' day an' night so far as I can," she
promised, "but you know what a cat is. They've got their own ideas
an' their own affairs to look arter. 'Corban's' a cat as be that independent in his ways. He'll brook no meddlin' with—'specially of a
night."

"Well, caution un, for he've got a mazin' deal of sense. I hope he
won't be overbold for his skin's sake, 'cause my faither's every bit so
much a man of his word as Mr. Sage; an' what he says he'll stick to.
He've had to shoot scores o' cats in his business; an he'll add your
tabby to the reckoning, sure as Judgement, if any more of his phaysants be took."

Thus, with common gloom of mind, the lovers separated and the clouds thickened around them. Their parents were no longer upon speaking terms, and tragedy hung heavy on the air. Then, in the deep and dewy silence of a June night, with Dart murmuring under the moon and the new-born foliage of the beech trees whispering their silky song, there burst upon the nocturnal peace uproar of gunpowder. Somebody had fired a gun, and the noise of it woke a thousand echoes and leapt with reverberations thrice repeated along the stone crowns of Hartland and Stannon and huge Broad Down.

Gaffer Sage rushed to his window, but could see nothing more than a puff of white smoke rising lazily under the moon. Trembling with dark misgivings, he crept back to bed, but slept no more. 'Corban' usually came to the old man's chamber at dawn, when Milly opened the house; but though she was stirring before five o'clock on the following morning, no 'Corban' bolted into the cottage when she unbarred the door; no familiar friend padded and purred 'Good-morning' to Mr. Sage; neither did 'Corban' appear at breakfast—a course very unusual with him.

Noah could not eat his meal for anxiety. He pushed away his tea, rose and walked into the garden. Upon the other side of the wall Amos Oldreive was casting grain to his young pheasants.

"Where's my cat to?" asked Noah Sage bluntly. "I heard your gun explode last night. Did you shoot un? I've a right to know."

Mr. Oldreive was clearly nervous and ill at ease, his sallow face needing wiping before he replied. But his eyes shone defiance; he pointed at the pheasants ere he answered.

"A month ago there was four dozen of 'em," he said; "now there be ezacally three dozen an' two. An' as for your cat, maybe I have shot un, an' maybe I have not, so now."

"You ought to be stringed up for it, you grizzly, crook-back coward! I know very well you done it; an' you'll only be sorry once, and that's for ever. Don't suppose you've heard the last of this. I'll get upsides with you, God's my judge!"

He turned, went into the house and spoke to Milly. The man had aged strangely in five minutes, his voice grew squeaky and unsteady.

"He've—he've shot un. He've shot my cat!"

Then Mr. Sage took his stick and walked out upon the Moor to reflect and to consider what his life would be without his treasure. He wept a little, for he was not a man of strong intellect. But soon his painful tears were scorched up and he breathed threatenings and slaughter.

He tramped back to Postbridge with a mind made up, and bawled his determination over the party wall at Amos Oldreive's back.

"Your son shan't have my darter now—not if he travels on his naked knees from here to Exeter for her. No darter of mine shall marry the child of a dirty murderer! That's what you be; an' all men shall know it; an' I pray God your birds'll get the pip to the last one among 'em, an' come they grows, I pray God they'll choke the man as eats 'em; an' if I weren't so old an' so weak in the loins, be gormed if I wouldn't come over the wall this minute an' wring your skinny neck, you cruel, unlawful beast!"

Mr. Oldreive looked round and cast one glance at a spot ten yards distant, where the black earth looked as though newly upturned, near an apple tree. But he said not a word, only spat on his hands and proceeded with his digging.

A dreadful week passed, and Mr. Sage's mingled emotions and misfortunes resulted in an attack of gout. He remained singularly silent under his trial, but once broke into activity and his usual vigour of speech when his old friend sent him a dozen good trout from Dart, and a hope that his neighbour would let bygones be bygones. These excellent fish, despite his foot, Mr. Sage flung one by one through his bedroom window into Amos Oldreive's front garden; for what were trout to him with no 'Corban' to share them?

Behind the scenes of this tragedy Ted and Milly dwelt dismally on their own future. He clung to it that if the banns could but be asked a third time without interference, Mr. Sage was powerless; Milly, however, believed that she knew better.

"I be only eighteen," she explained, "an' faither's my guardian to do as he will with me until I come of age."

So they were troubled in secret until a sudden and amazing solution to the great problem came within a week of 'Corban's' exit. The only apparent way to be Ted's wife was opened through lying, and Milly rose to the necessary heights of untruth without a pang. She felt that good must come to her evil conduct—good not only to herself, but to her unhappy father. His bereavement had cost him dear. He still preserved a great tragical silence, but from time to time hinted of far-reaching deeds when his foot should be strong enough to bear him up.

There came a day when Milly walked to Princetown, and entering into the house of certain friends there, rubbed her eyes and stood astounded and open-mouthed before the spectacle of 'Corban.' It was no feline apparition that she saw, but a live cat, with bold tabby markings of alternate rabbit-brown and black—a cat with a strong, flat nose, cold and healthy; four good, well-defined tiers of whiskers on either side of his countenance; green eyes, that twinkled like the twin lamps of a little train when seen by night, and a tail of just proportion and brave carriage.

"Lord save us!" cried Milly; "however did 'e come by this here cat, Mrs. Veale? I had Mr. Oldreive's own sacred word as he'd shot un dead an' buried un under his apple tree."

"That's our butival puss; an' you should know how us come by it if anybody do, my dear, for you bringed it here in a basket from Post-bridge when you was a li'l maid seven year agone."

Milly's active mind was working too rapidly to allow of any reply for some moments. Then she told Mrs. Veale of the recent tribula-tion at home, and in ten minutes an obvious plot was hatched be-tween them.

" 'Tis a peace-loving cat, an' if you butter its paws an' treat it a bit generous in the matter of food 'twill very likely settle down along with you. Of course, you shall have un for such a Christian purpose as to bring them two dear old men together again. An' the more cheese you can spare un, the more like he is to bide with you."

So Mrs. Veale; and Milly answered:

" 'Corban' was fond of cheese too, an' his mother afore him! 'Twas a family failing, no doubt."

She scanned the cat narrowly and it mistook her attention for ad-miration, and purred in a soft, guttural, elderly way, and bent itself into a bow against her knee and snowed much natural goodness.

"So like t'other as two peas!" declared Milly, not remembering that she had made exactly the same remark when this cat and its late brother were born. "Faither's sight ban't strong enough to part 'em if only this one behaves well," she added.

It was decided that the girl should come early on Sunday morning for her tabby peacemaker, and meantime Mr. Oldreive and his son were to be acquainted with the plot. As for Amos, he was an easy man, and had not slain his neighbour's cat excepting under great provoca-tion. Ever since the deed he had regretted it, but had never confessed to the actual crime excepting in the ears of Milly and Ted. Nobody had officially announced the death of his cat to Mr. Sage. Therefore Milly hoped he would accept the stranger as his own, and suffer peace to return amongst them. The Oldreives, much cowed by Noah's atti-tude and frightened by his illness, gladly promised to do all they might for his daughter, and when Sunday came she started for Prince-town after an early breakfast and left her father behind her. He was in better health again, and she noticed, as an unusual circumstance, that he appeared very full of his own affairs upon that morning, and clearly desired her room more than her company.

With a heavy basket she set off homewards by nine o'clock. Inside the wickerwork a new 'Corban,' after protesting once or twice at the narrowness of its quarters, curled round nose to tail, abandoned itself to the mysteries of life and digested an ample breakfast.

But midway between Princetown and Postbridge, where the road traversed the high Moor and stretched like a white thread between granite hills and glimmering marsh-lands, from whence the breeding plover called, Milly nearly dropped her basket. For along the way, in a borrowed market-cart behind his own brown pony, came her father.

"Why, where on airth be you drivin' to, my old dear?" she asked; and Mr. Sage, puffing and growing very red, made answer:

"I be gwaine up-long to Princetown to holy worship."

Now this was an action absolutely unparalleled.

"To church! What for?"

"If you must know, 'tis that I may forbid your banns wi' Ted Oldreive. No use to fret nor cry. I be firm as a rock 'pon it; an' I be gwaine to deny them banns afore the face of the Lord an' the people."

"Why ever should 'e do such a cruel thing, dear faither?"

"Because no blood o' mine be gwaine to mix wi' that murdering villain's."

"He never told you he shot 'Corban.' "

"D'you doubt it? Don't the whole of Dartmoor know it?"

"Let me get up in the cart an' sit beside you," said Milly. "I want for you to look in this here basket."

She leapt from the step to the driving-seat beside her father, then opened the basket. Grateful for this sudden light and air, her burden gazed out, yawned, showed perfect teeth, black lips, and a pink mouth; then jumping boldly on to Mr. Sage's scanty lap, rubbed against him and purred deeply, while its upright tail brushed his chin.

"God's goodness!" cried the old man, and nearly fell out into the road.

"Somebody must have took un to Princetown," said Milly, outwardly calm though her heart beat hard. "There I found un none the worse, poor chap. Now he's twice 'Corban,' dear faither, an' twice my gift to 'e."

The old man was entirely deceived, as anybody even of keen sight might well have been. The friendship of the cat also aided his delusion. He stroked it, and it stood up, put its front paws upon his necktie and rubbed noses.

"Glory be to God! Now us'll go home-along," said Mr. Sage.

His dim eyes were dimmer for tears; but he could not take them off the creature. His hands held it close. Milly picked up the reins and turned the brown pony homeward.

And 'Corban' II, as though specially directed by Providence, played its part nobly, and maintained the imposition. Mr. Sage begged Amos Oldreive's pardon, and Amos, for his part, calmed his conscience by assuring Noah that henceforth his cat was more than welcome to a young pheasant whenever it had a mind to one. A little strangeness on the part of the returned wanderer seemed natural in Mr. Sage's opinion. That he had apparently developed one or two new habits was also reasonable in a cat with such increased experience of the world. And meantime the wedding preparations were pushed on.

At the end of the week Ted Oldreive came home from Vitifer for Sunday; and he expressed joy at the sight of 'Corban,' once more the glory of his old haunts.

But the young man's face changed when Noah and the cat had departed in company, and a look of wild alarm made Milly tremble before danger.

"Why, what's amiss?" she asked nervously. "All danger be past now, an' the creature's settled down so homely as need be."

"Matter enough," said Ted; " 'tis a ewe cat!"

"A ewe cat! Oh, Ted, don't say that!"

" 'Tis so; an' God send her don't have chets 'fore we'm married, else Postbridge won't hold your dear faither—nor Dartymoor neither."

The Slum Cat

ERNEST THOMPSON SETON

THE LITTLE SLUM KITTEN was not six weeks old yet, but she was alone in the old junk-yard. Her mother had gone to seek food among the garbage-boxes the night before, and had never returned, so when the second evening came she was very hungry. A deep-laid instinct drove her forth from the old cracker-box to seek something to eat. Feeling her way silently among the rubbish she smelt everything that seemed eatable, but without finding food. At length she reached the wooden steps leading down into Jap Malee's bird store underground at the far end of the yard. The door was open a little, and she walked in. A Negro sitting idly on a box in a corner watched her curiously. She wandered past some Rabbits; they paid no heed. She came to a wide-barred cage in which was a Fox. She gave a frightened "mew," and the Negro also sprang forward, spitting with such copious vigor in the Fox's face that he dropped the Kitten and returned to the corner, there to sit blinking his eyes in sullen fear.

The Negro pulled the Kitten out. She tottered in a circle a few times, then revived, and a few minutes later, when Jap Malee came back, she was purring in the Negro's lap, apparently none the worse.

Jap was not an Oriental: he was a full-blooded Cockney; but his eyes were such little accidental slits aslant in his round, flat face that his first name was forgotten in the highly descriptive title of "Jap." He was not especially unkind to the birds and beasts which furnished his living, but he did not want the Slum Kitten.

The Negro gave her all the food she could eat, and then carried her to a distant block and dropped her in an iron-yard. Here she lived and somehow found food enough to grow till, weeks later, an extended exploration brought her back to her old quarters in the junk-yard, and glad to be at home she at once settled down.

Kitty was now fully grown. She was a striking-looking Cat of the

251

Tiger type. Her marks were black on a pale gray, and the four beauty spots of white, on nose, ears and tail-tip, lent a certain distinction. She was expert now at getting a living, yet she had some days of starvation, and had so far failed in her ambition to catch a Sparrow. She was quite alone, but a new force was coming into her life.

She was lying in the sun one September day when a large black Cat came walking along the top of a wall in her direction. By his torn ear she recognized him at once as an old enemy. She slunk into her box and hid. He picked his way gingerly, bounded lightly to a shed that was at the end of the yard, and was crossing the roof when a yellow Cat rose up. The black Tom glared and growled; so did the yellow Tom. Their tails lashed from side to side. Strong throats growled and yowled. They approached with ears laid back, with muscles a-tense.

"Yow—yow—ow," said the Black one.

"Wow—w—w—" was the slightly deeper answer.

"Ya—wow—wow—wow—" said the Black one, edging up an inch nearer.

"Yow—w—w—" was the Yellow answer, as the blond Cat rose to full height and stepped with vast dignity a whole inch forward. "Yow—w," and he went another inch, while his tail went swish, thump, from one side to the other.

"Ya—wow—yow—w," screamed the Black in a rising tone, and he

backed an eighth of an inch as he marked the broad, unshrinking beast before him.

Windows opened all around, human voices were heard, but the Cat scene went on.

"Yow—yow—ow," rumbled the Yellow peril, his voice deepening as the other's rose. "Yow," and he advanced another step.

Now their noses were but three inches apart; they stood sidewise, both ready to clinch, but each waiting for the other. They glared at each other for three minutes in silence, and like statues, except that each tail-tip was twisting.

The Yellow began again. "Yow—ow—ow," in deep tone.

"Ya-a-a-a-a," screamed the Black with intent to strike terror by his yell, but he retreated one-sixteenth of an inch. The Yellow walked up a whole long inch; their whiskers were mixing now; another advance, and their noses almost touched.

"Yo—w—w," said Yellow, like a deep moan.

"Ya-a-a-a-a," screamed Black, but he retreated a thirty-second of an inch, and the Yellow warrior closed and clinched like a demon.

Oh, how they rolled and bit and tore—especially the Yellow one!

How they pitched and gripped and hugged—but especially the Yellow one!

Over and over, sometimes one on top, sometimes the other, but usually the Yellow one, and over they rolled till off the roof, amid cheers from all the windows. They lost not a second in that fall into the junk-yard; they tore and clawed all the way down, but especially the Yellow one; and when they struck the ground, still fighting, the one on top was chiefly the Yellow one; and before they separated both had had as much as they wanted, especially the Black one! He scaled the wall, and, bleeding and growling, disappeared, while the news was passed from window to window that Cayley's "Nig" had been licked by "Orange Billy."

Either the yellow Cat was a very clever seeker, or else Slum Kitty did not hide very hard, for he discovered her among the boxes and she made no attempt to get away, probably because she had witnessed the fight. There is nothing like success in warfare to win the female heart, and thereafter the yellow Tom and Kitty became very good friends, not sharing each other's lives or food—Cats do not do that much—but recognizing each other as entitled to special friendly privileges.

When October's shortening days were on an event took place in the old cracker-box. If "Orange Billy" had come he would have seen five little Kittens curled up in the embrace of their mother, the little

Slum Kitty. It was a wonderful thing for her. She felt all the elation an animal mother can feel—all the delight—as she tenderly loved them and licked them.

She had added a joy to her joyless life, but she had also added a heavy burden. All her strength was taken now to find food. And one day, led by a tempting smell, she wandered into the bird cellar and into an open cage. Everything was still, there was meat ahead, and she reached forward to seize it; the cage door fell with a snap, and she was a prisoner. That night the Negro put an end to the Kittens and was about to do the same with the mother when her unusual markings attracted the attention of the bird man, who decided to keep her.

Jap Malee was as disreputable a little Cockney bantam as ever sold cheap Canary birds in a cellar. He was extremely poor, and the Negro lived with him because the "Henglishman" was willing to share bed and board. Jap was perfectly honest according to his lights, but he had no lights, and there is little doubt that his chief revenue was derived from storing and restoring stolen Dogs and Cats. The Fox and the half a dozen Canaries were mere blinds. The "Lost and Found" columns of the papers were the only ones of interest to Jap, but he noticed and saved a clipping about breeding for fur. This was stuck on the wall of his den, and under its influence he set about making an experiment with the Slum Cat. First he soaked her dirty fur with stuff to kill the two or three kinds of creepers she wore, and when it had done its work he washed her thoroughly. Kitty was savagely indignant, but a warm and happy glow spread over her as she dried off in a cage near the stove, and her fur began to fluff out with wonderful softness and whiteness. Jap and his assistant were much pleased. But this was preparatory. "Nothing is so good for growing fur as plenty of oily food and continued exposure to cold weather," said the clipping. Winter was at hand, and Jap Malee put Kitty's cage out in the yard, protected only from the rain and the direct wind, and fed her all the oil cake and fish heads she could eat. In a week the change began to show. She was rapidly getting fat. She had nothing to do but get fat and dress her fur. Her cage was kept clean, and Nature responded to the chill weather and oily food by making Kitty's coat thicker and glossier every day, so that by Christmas she was an unusually beautiful Cat in the fullest and finest of fur with markings that were at least a rarity.

Why not send the Slum Cat to the show now coming on?

" 'Twon't do, ye kneow, Sammy, to henter 'er as a Tramp Cat, ye kneow," Jap observed to his helper, "but it kin be arranged to suit;

the Knickerbockers like 'Royal' anythink. Now, 'Royal Dick' or 'Royal Sam': 'ow's that? But 'owld on: them's Tom names. Oi say, Sammy, wot's the noime of that island where you were born?"

"Analostan Island, sah, was my native vicinity, sah."

"Oi say, now, that's good, ye kneow. 'Royal Analostan,' by Jove! The onliest pedigreed Royal Analostan in the howle sheow, ye kneow. Ain't that capital?" And they mingled their cackles.

"But we'll 'ave to 'ave a pedigree, ye kneow," so a very long fake pedigree on the recognized lines was prepared.

One afternoon Sam, in a borrowed silk hat, delivered the Cat and the pedigree at the show door. He had been a barber, and he could put on more pomp in five minutes than Jap Malee could have displayed in a lifetime, and this, doubtless, was one reason for the respectful reception awarded the Royal Analostan at the Cat show.

Jap had all a Cockney's reverence for the upper class. He was proud to be an exhibitor, but when, on the opening day, he went to the door he was overpowered to see the array of carriages and silk hats. The gateman looked at him sharply but passed him on his ticket, doubtless taking him for a stable boy to some exhibitor. The hall had velvet carpets before the long rows of cages. Jap was sneaking down the side row, glancing at the Cats of all kinds, noting the blue ribbons and the reds, glancing about but not daring to ask for his own exhibit, inwardly trembling to think what the gorgeous gathering of fashion would say if they discovered the trick he was playing on them. But he saw no sign of Slum Kitty.

In the middle of the center aisle were the high-class Cats. A great throng was there. The passage was roped and two policemen were there to keep the crowd moving. Jap wriggled in among them: he was too short to see over, but he gathered from the remarks that the gem of the show was there.

"Oh, isn't she a beauty!" said one tall woman.

"Ah, what distinction!" was the reply.

"One cannot mistake the air that comes only from ages of the most refined surroundings."

"How I should like to own that superb creature!"

Jap pushed near enough to get a glimpse of the cage and read a placard which announced that "The Blue Ribbon and Gold Medal of the Knickerbocker High Society Cat and Pet Show had been awarded to the thoroughbred pedigreed Royal Analostan, imported and exhibited by J. Malee, Esquire, the well-known fancier. Not for sale." Jap caught his breath; he stared—yes, surely, there, high in a gilded cage on velvet cushions, with two policemen for guards, her fur bright black and pale gray, her bluish eyes slightly closed, was his Slum Kitty, looking the picture of a Cat that was bored to death.

Jap Malee lingered around that cage for hours, drinking a draught of glory such as he had never before known. But he saw that it would be wise for him to remain unknown; his "butler" must do all the business.

It was Slum Kitty who made that show a success. Each day her value went up in the owner's eye. He did not know what prices had been given for Cats and thought that he was touching a record pitch when his "butler" gave the director authority to sell the Cat for one hundred dollars.

This is how it came about that the Slum Cat found herself transferred to a Fifth Avenue mansion. She showed a most unaccountable wildness as well as other peculiarities. Her retreat from the Lap Dog to the center of the dinner-table was understood to express a deep-rooted though mistaken idea of avoiding a defiling touch. The patrician way in which she would get the cover off a milk-can was especially applauded, while her frequent wallowings in the garbage-pail were understood to be the manifestation of a little pardonable high-born eccentricity. She was fed and pampered, shown and praised, but she was not happy. She clawed at that blue ribbon around her neck till she got it off; she jumped against the plate glass because that seemed the road to outside; and she would sit and gaze out on the roofs and back yards at the other side of the window and wish she could be among them for a change.

She was strictly watched—was never allowed outside—so that all the happy garbage-pail moments occurred while these receptacles of joy were indoors. But one night in March, as they were being set out a-row for the early scavenger, the Royal Analostan saw her chance, slipped out the door, and was lost to view.

Of course there was a grand stir, but Pussy neither knew nor cared anything about that. Her one thought was to go home. A raw east wind had been rising, and now it came to her with a particularly friendly message. Man would have called it an unpleasant smell of the docks, but to Pussy it was a welcome message from her own country. She trotted on down the long street due east, threading the rails of front gardens, stopping like a statue for an instant, or crossing the street in search of the darkest side. She came at length to the docks and to the water, but the place was strange. She could go north or south; something turned her southward, and dodging among docks and Dogs, carts and Cats, crooked arms of the bay and straight board fences, she got in an hour or two into familiar scenes and smells, and before the sun came up she crawled back, weary and footsore, through the same old hole in the same old fence, and over a wall into her junk-yard back of the bird cellar, yes, back into the very cracker-box where she was born.

After a long rest she came quietly down from the cracker-box toward the steps leading to the cellar, and engaged in her old-time pursuit of seeking for eatables. The door opened, and there stood the Negro. He shouted to the bird-man inside:

"Say, Boss, come hyar! Ef dere ain't dat dar Royal Analostan comed back!"

Jap came in time to see the Cat jumping the wall. The Royal Analostan had been a windfall for him; had been the means of adding many comforts to the cellar and several prisoners to the cages. It was now of the utmost importance to recapture Her Majesty. Stale fish heads and other infallible lures were put out till Pussy was induced to chew at a large fish head in a box trap. The Negro in watching pulled the string that dropped the lid, and a minute later the Analostan was again in a cage in the cellar. Meanwhile Jap had been watching the "Lost and Found" column. There it was: "Twenty-five dollars reward," etc. That night Mr. Malee's "butler" called at the Fifth Avenue mansion with the missing Cat. "Mr. Malee's compliments, sah." Of course, Mr. Malee would not be rewarded, but the "butler" was evidently open to any offer.

Kitty was guarded carefully after that, but far from being disgusted with the old life of starving and glad of her care, she became wilder and more dissatisfied.

The spring was on in full power now, and the Fifth Avenue family were thinking of their country residence. They packed up, closed house, and moved off to the summer home some fifty miles away, and Pussy, in a basket, went with them.

The basket was put on the back seat of a carriage. New sounds and passing smells were entered and left. Then a roaring of many feet, more swinging of the basket, then some clicks, some bangs, a long, shrill whistle, and door-bells of a very big front door, a rumbling and more smells. When at last it all stopped the sun came twinkling through the basket lid. The Royal Cat was lifted into another carriage and they turned aside from their past course. Very soon the carriage swerved, the noises of its wheels were grittings and rattlings, a new and horrible sound was added—the barking of Dogs, big and little, and dreadfully close. The basket was lifted, and Slum Kitty had reached her country home.

Everyone was officiously kind. All wanted to please the Royal Cat, but, somehow, none of them did, except possibly the big, fat cook that Kitty discovered on wandering into the kitchen. That greasy woman smelt more like a slum than anything she had met for months, and the Royal Analostan was proportionately attracted. The cook, when she learned that fears were entertained about the Cat's staying, said: "Shure, she'd 'tind to thot; wanst a Cat licks her futs shure she's at home." So she deftly caught the unapproachable Royalty in her apron and committed the horrible sacrilege of greasing the soles of her feet with pot grease. Of course, Kitty resented it: she resented everything in the place; but on being set down she began to dress her paws, and found evident satisfaction in that grease. She licked all four feet for an hour, and the cook triumphantly announced that now "shure she's apt to shtay"; and stay she did, but she showed a most surprising and disgusting preference for the kitchen and the cook and the garbage-pail.

The family, though distressed by these high-born eccentricities, were glad to see the Royal Analostan more contented and approachable. They gave her more liberty after a week or two. They guarded her from every menace. The Dogs were taught to respect her; no man or boy about the place would have dreamed of throwing a stone at the famous pedigreed Cat, and she had all the food she wanted, but still she was not happy. She was hankering for many things, she scarcely knew what. She had everything—yes, but she wanted something else. Plenty to eat and drink—yes, but milk does not taste the same when you can go and drink all you want from a saucer; it has to be stolen out of a tin pail when one is pinched with hunger, or it does not have the tang—it is not milk.

How Pussy did hate it all! True, there was one sweet-smelling shrub in the whole horrible place—one that she did enjoy nipping and rubbing against; it was the only bright spot in her country life.

One day, after a summer of discontent, a succession of things happened that stirred anew the slum instincts of the Royal prisoner. A great bundle of stuff from the docks had reached the country mansion. What it contained was of little moment, but it was rich with the most piquant of slum smells. The chords of memory surely dwell in the nose, and Pussy's past was conjured up with dangerous force. Next day the cook left through some trouble. That evening the youngest boy of the house, a horrid little American with no proper appreciation of Royalty, was tying a tin to the blue-blooded one's tail, doubtless in furtherance of some altruistic project, when Pussy resented it with a paw that wore five big fish-hooks for the occasion.

The howl of woe-trodden America roused America's mother; the deft and womanly blow she aimed with her book was miraculously avoided, and Pussy took flight, upstairs, of course. A hunted Rat runs downstairs, a hunted Dog goes on the level, a hunted Cat runs up. She hid in the garret and waited till night came. Then, gliding downstairs, she tried the screen doors, found one unlatched, and escaped into the black August night. Pitch black to man's eyes, it was simply gray to her, and she glided through the disgusting shrubbery and flower-beds, had a final nip at that one little bush that had been an attractive spot in the garden, and boldly took her back track of the spring.

How could she take a back track that she never saw? There is in all animals some sense of direction. It is low in man and high in Horses, but Cats have a large gift, and this mysterious guide took her westward, not clearly and definitely, but with a general impulse that was made definite because the easiest travel was on the road. In an hour she had reached the Hudson River. Her nose had told her many times that the course was true. Smell after smell came back.

At the river was the railroad. She could not go on the water; she must go north or south. This was a case where her sense of direction was clear: it said "go south"; and Kitty trotted down the footpath between the iron rails and the fence.

Cats can go very fast up a tree or over a wall, but when it comes to the long, steady trot that reels off mile after mile, hour after hour, it is not the Cat-hop, but the Dog-trot, that counts. She became tired and a little footsore. She was thinking of a rest when a Dog came running to the fence near by and broke out into such a horrible barking close to her ear that Pussy leaped in terror. She ran as hard as she could down the path. The barking seemed to grow into a low rumble—a louder rumble and roaring—a terrifying thunder. A light shone; Kitty glanced back to see, not the Dog, but a huge black thing with a blazing eye, coming on yowling and spitting like a yard full of Tom Cats. She put forth all her power to run, made such time as she never had made before, but dared not leap the fence. She was running like a Dog—was flying, but all in vain: the monstrous pursuer overtook her, but missed her in the darkness, and hurried past to be lost in the night, while Kitty sat gasping for breath.

This was only the first encounter with the strange monsters—strange to her eyes—her nose seemed to know them, and told her that this was another landmark on the home trail. But Pussy learned that they were very stupid and could not find her at all if she hid by slipping quietly under a fence and lying still. Before morning she had encountered many of them, but escaped unharmed from all.

About sunrise she reached a nice little slum on her home trail and was lucky enough to find several unsterilized eatables in an ash-heap. She spent the day around a stable. It was very like home, but she had no idea of staying there. She was driven by an inner craving that was neither hunger nor fear, and next evening set out as before. She had seen the "One-eyed Thunder-rollers" all day going by, and was getting used to them. That night passed much like the first one. The days went by in skulking in barns, hiding from Dogs and small boys, and the nights in limping along the track, for she was getting footsore; but on she went, mile after mile, southward, ever southward—Dogs, boys, roarers, hunger—Dogs, boys, roarers, hunger—but day after day with increasing weariness on she went, and her nose from time to time cheered her by confidently reporting, "This surely is a smell we passed last spring."

So week after week went by, and Pussy, dirty, ribbonless, footsore and weary, arrived at the Harlem Bridge. Though it was enveloped in delicious smells she did not like the look of that bridge. For half the night she wandered up and down the shore without discovering any other means of going south except some other bridges. Somehow she had to come back to it; not only its smells were familiar, but from time to time when a "One-eye" ran over it there was the peculiar rumbling roar that was a sensation in the springtime trip. She leaped to the timber stringer and glided out over the water. She had got less than a third of the way over when a "Thundering One-eye" came roaring at her from the opposite end. She was much frightened, but knowing their blindness she dropped to a low side beam and there crouched in hiding. Of course, the stupid monster missed her and passed on, and all would have been well, but it turned back, or another just like it, and came suddenly roaring behind her. Pussy leaped to the long track and made for the home shore. She might have got there but a third of the red-eye terrors came roaring down at her from that side. She was running her hardest, but was caught between two foes. There was nothing for it but a desperate leap from the timbers into—she did not know what. Down—down—down—plop! splash! plunge—into the deep water, not cold, for it was August, but oh! so horrible. She spluttered and coughed and struck out for the shore. She had never learned to swim, and yet she swam, for the simple reason that a Cat's position and attitude in swimming are the same as her position and attitude in walking. She had fallen into a place she did not like; naturally she tried to walk out, and the result was that she swam ashore. Which shore? It never fails—the south—the shore nearest home. She scrambled out all dripping wet, up the muddy bank and through coal-piles and dust-heaps, looking as black, dirty and unroyal as it was possible for a Cat to look.

Once the shock was over the Royal pedigreed slummer began to feel better for the plunge. A genial glow without from the bath, a genial sense of triumph within, for had she not outwitted three of the big terrors?

Her nose, her memory and her instinct of direction inclined her to get on the track again, but the place was infested with the big thunder-rollers, and prudence led her to turn aside and follow the river bank with its musky home reminders.

She was more than two days learning the infinite dangers and complexities of the East River docks, and at length, on the third night, she reached familiar ground, the place she had passed the night of her first escape. From that her course was sure and rapid. She knew just where she was going and how to get there. She knew even the most prominent features in the Dogscape now. She went faster, felt happier. In a little while she would be curled up in the old junkyard. Another turn and the block was in sight—

But—what!—it was gone. Kitty could not believe her eyes. There, where had stood, or leaned, or slouched, or straggled—the houses of the block—was a great broken wilderness of stone, lumber and holes in the ground.

Kitty walked all around it. She knew by the bearings and by the local color of the pavement that she was in her home; that there had lived the bird-man, and there was the old junk-yard; but all were gone, completely gone, taking the familiar odors with them; and Pussy turned sick at heart in the utter hopelessness of the case. Her home love was her master mood. She had given up all to come to a home that no longer existed, and for once her brave little spirit was cast down. She wandered over the silent heaps of rubbish and found neither consolation nor eatables. The ruin had covered several of the blocks and reached back from the water. It was not a fire. Kitty had seen one of these things once. Pussy knew nothing of the great bridge that was to rise from this very spot.

When the sun came up Kitty sought for cover. An adjoining block still stood with little change, and the Royal Analostan retired to that. She knew some of its trails, but once there was unpleasantly surprised to find the place swarming with Cats that, like herself, were driven from their old grounds, and when the garbage-cans came out there were several Cats to each. It meant a famine in the land, and Pussy, after standing it a few days, set out to find her other home on Fifth Avenue. She got there to find it shut up and deserted, and the next night she returned to the crowded slum.

September and October wore away. Many of the Cats died of starvation or were too weak to escape their natural enemies. But Kitty, young and strong, still lived.

Great changes had come over the ruined blocks. Though silent the night she saw them, they were crowded with noisy workmen all day. A tall building was completed by the end of October, and Slum Kitty, driven by hunger, went sneaking up to a pail that a Negro had set outside. The pail, unfortunately, was not garbage, but a new thing in that region, a scrubbing-pail—a sad disappointment, but it had a sense of comfort: there was a trace of a familiar touch on the handle. While she was studying it the Negro elevator boy came out again. In spite of his blue clothes his odorous person confirmed the good impression of the handle. Kitty had retreated across the street. He gazed at her.

"Sho ef dat don't like de Royal Analostan—Hya, Pussy—Pussy—Pussy—Pus-s-s-y, co-o-ome—Pus-s-sy, hya! I specs she's sho hungry."

Hungry! She had not had a real meal for a month. The Negro went into the hall and reappeared with a portion of his own lunch.

"Hya, Pussy, Puss—Puss—Puss." At length he laid the meat on the pavement and went back to the door. Slum Kitty came, found it savory, sniffed at the meat, seized it, and fled like a little Tigress to eat her prize in peace.

This was the beginning of a new era. Pussy came to the door of the building now when pinched by hunger, and the good feeling for the Negro grew. She had never understood that man before. Now he was her friend, the only one she had.

One week Pussy caught a Rat. She was crossing the street in front of the new building when her friend opened the door for a well-dressed man to come out.

"Hello, look at that for a Cat," said the man.

"Yes, sah," answered the Negro, "dat's ma Cat, sah; she's a terror on Rats, sah. Hez'em 'bout cleaned up, sah; dat's why she so thin."

"Well, don't let her starve," said the man, with the air of a landlord. "Can't you feed her?"

"De liver-meat man comes reg'lar, sah; quatah dollar a week, sah," said the Negro, realizing that he was entitled to the extra fifteen cents for "the idea."

"That's all right; I'll stand it."

Since then the Negro has sold her a number of times with a perfectly clear conscience, because he knows quite well that it is only a question of a few days before the Royal Analostan comes back again. She has learned to tolerate the elevator and even to ride up and down on it. The Negro stoutly maintains that once she heard the meat man while she was on the top floor and managed to press the button that called the elevator to take her down.

She is sleek and beautiful again. She is not only one of four hundred that form the inner circle about the liverman's barrow, but she is recognized as the star pensioner as well.

But in spite of her prosperity, her social position, her Royal name and fake pedigree, the greatest pleasure of her life is to slip out and go a-slumming in the gloaming, for now, as in her previous lives, she is at heart, and likely to be, nothing but a dirty little Slum Cat.

Mister Youth

SOPHIE KERR

MR. GEORGE WASHINGTON ODGER lay on his bed, expecting and expected to die. He did not object to the situation, for he found the business of living unsatisfactory and he had been sick so long that his body had no more resistance. His mind was clear, and active enough, but slow because of his weakness. Still he could think, and he did so. He thought of the words of M. Brillat-Savarin's great-aunt who had said at the last, "There comes a time when death is as necessary as sleep," and Mr. Odger paid a tribute to the lady's economy and exactness with words, a French characteristic he had always admired, though he conceded that exactness exceeded economy in most French phrases.

Having dismissed M. Brillat-Savarin's great-aunt with this qualified compliment, Mr. Odger looked about his room, at the back of a very fine old New York house. He had always enjoyed it. It did not incline to the gloomy and austere in the effort to avoid any feminine effect, as so many men's rooms do. The walls were ivory, the curtains blue and gold damask, the furniture walnut. There was a high walnut chest inlaid with marquetry ovals, and there were built-in bookshelves at one side, on which were set his treasures, a couple of Goya etchings of bloody bullfights, lithographs of Daumier and Forain in their most sophisticated moments, and George Bellows' "A Stag at Sharkey's," "Both Members of This Club" and the "Dempsey-Firpo" classic. It pleased Mr. Odger to see how the American matched the Frenchman and the old Spaniard in technique, in impersonal brutality. Mr. Odger hoped faintly that at his executor's sale someone would buy his prints who would like them as much as he had. Not that it mattered.

Then he began to wonder how long it would be before he was dead. The doctor had intimated that a week was the most he could expect, and had added, being a long-time friend and intimate, "You damned fool, you could just as easily get well, but you want to make them call me an old buzzard at the Club."

"So you are an old buzzard, Raymond—you even look like one with that beaky nose and bald head," responded Mr. Odger. "And if you can tell me one good reason why I should bother to get well, I might make the effort. Of course you can't."

"You're a useful man in the community—" began Dr. Raymond, but his friend's smile checked him.

"Don't be an ass as well as a buzzard. To wish to live, Raymond, implies an interest in life. I am no longer interested."

"You're only posing and trying to talk smart stuff," said Dr. Raymond. "You ought to have more sense." He looked at his watch and rose. A popular skillful physician cannot stop to administer soul-medicine when innumerable other patients who need only pills and powders are waiting. "I must go; got a consultation uptown in ten minutes. Brace up, we could have a rubber of bridge at the Club in a month's time—if you'd only rally yourself."

Mr. Odger's smile flickered again. A rubber of bridge at the Club, with Raymond and Barton and Green, all snarling over points, and postmorteming every hand to nausea, that was hardly an inducement to turn his acquiescent will to rebellion, to force further endurance upon his reluctant pain-torn body. No use fighting without an object. He watched Raymond's back through the door and would have grinned at it if he had had the strength. The old buzzard, the old dimwit! He might know a lot about humanity's vital organs, but he didn't know one item about their spirits.

His slight penciling of thought continued, with pauses and intervals, little blank spaces in the pattern which might have been sleep or unconsciousness, he did not know which, but he rather enjoyed speculating about them. He could not tell how long such intervals lasted, perhaps moments, perhaps hours. Any one of them, he knew, might be prolonged into the great unconsciousness he was awaiting. So, each fading out, each coming back was an adventure. Perhaps the next one—

It didn't matter. He had, indeed, no interest in living, no zest to acquire, to explore, to experience. He had no wife, no child, no near kin, and he disliked the few far-removed cousins he had with an unreasoning intensity such as we only bestow on our own blood. His business associates, excellent legal men like himself, in an excellent firm of which the chief business was handling excellent estates, meant nothing to him except reliable parts of a mechanism which supplied his income. They would come to his funeral and look conventionally serious, and they would administer his own estate excellently.

There was not one tendril, not one irrational warm little wisp of affection to hold and hinder his willing meeting of his last hour, not one hand to grip his in a passion of agony and drag him back from the unknown shadow which he was so ready to enter. He had always been afraid of human affection, distrustful of the value of human emotion. The first he had avoided, the second he had suppressed knowingly, without the least regret. He did not regret it now, but he wondered, in the quiet spaces between his intervals of sleep—or unconsciousness —whether he might perhaps have enjoyed life more if he had lived it at a tearing disorderly pace, if he had wallowed in sensibility and let his heart and nerves go bare for every greedy hand to pluck at. It might have been rather fun, he thought. Instead he had deliberately armor-plated his existence against anyone getting at him anywhere, through his sympathies, his love, his pity, his ambition, his acquisitiveness; none of man's usual weaknesses were allowed to sway him. "Life is the art of selection," was his motto, and "Organize your life for definite ends" his only bit of advice to younger men, and he had always been sufficiently tolerant and wise to add no suggestion of what he thought the best end might be.

It occurred to him now that a graph of his life would show surprisingly little variation, none of the dizzy peaks and sickening drops that make most life-graphs diverting contemplation. But maybe he ought to have had some peaks and drops—maybe it was amusing to swing up, away up, gulping for air, and then down, down, down, with the pit of your stomach—Mr. Odger meant his emotional stomach, not his actual physical stomach which had always given him thorough satisfaction—sickeningly tremulous. To know utter despair and sublime joy might possibly be, meditated Mr. Odger, as amusing as an even, unshaken, tasteful self-control. Once again he reminded himself that all this didn't matter. Really there was no use speculating, for speculation was apt to lead to regret, and regret was another thing he did not allow himself.

It was at this moment that he became aware of a presence in the room, a light and cautious step that was but a mere breath of a step, a step in quick broken rhythm with no implication of humanity. Mr. Odger could see no one, nothing. He knew that Miss Pendle, the day nurse, had not come in, for the door had not opened, and she was, he felt sure, pursuing the determined flirtation with his secretary which she had begun on the moment of her entry into the house. And anyway, this step wasn't the step of a nurse.

The step continued, very softly, very delicately, sometimes he lost it, but then it would start again. It seemed to be going about the room, close to the wall, an investigating sort of step. Mr. Odger took no stock in supernatural manifestations, so he did not for a moment imagine that the step was that of an angel who had been sent for him. But it puzzled him. There was a bell beside his hand, responsive to the slightest pressure. One touch of it and Miss Pendle would forsake her coquetry and be ready to hunt down the step. But he did not ring. Instead he lay still and listened.

The step seemed approaching. He could not lift his head, but it was propped high enough so that he had a good view of the expanse of the coverlet and the footboard, his bedside table, and anything else that was not too close to the floor. But the step was close to the floor, and though he looked directly toward the place whence the sound of it came again, he could see nothing. But it was getting very near.

Then, with a sudden silent leap, the visitor revealed himself. A small black cat with a very round head and short ears, black aigrette whiskers, with very round yellow eyes and velvet fur stood on the bed and stared at Mr. Odger, surprised and fearless. He was saying plainly, "Somebody here! What d'you think of that!"

Mr. Odger said nothing. He did not know any appropriate greeting for cats and he had always remained silent when he was ignorant of the correct thing to say. But he looked at the animal not unkindly. It would have been impossible for anyone, not a confirmed ailurophobe, to be indifferent to a cat so poised in manner, so elegant in person. This was no ragged cringing alley cat. This cat was a well-kept, well-bred and intelligent cat, a cat of subtlety and charm. With light short steps he advanced toward Mr. Odger and when he reached his hand he stopped and laid his paw upon it in the fashion of courteous greeting to an equal.

'How do you do, cat," said Mr. Odger.

The cat raised his tail and waved it like a banner, he arched his back slightly and widened and narrowed the slits of his eyes, as one making conversation. Again he advanced, and as he did so he stepped upon the satin-covered down quilt which had been but half pulled over Mr. Odger, and as his paws came in contact with the silk fabric he quivered in ecstasy. He padded it, alternately raising and lowering his paws, unsheathing and sheathing his claws so that the very tips of them went into the satin with a sleek little ripping sound which added to his keen pleasure. He opened and shut his eyes, and regarded Mr. Odger as one far away, while he himself was lost in a vale of delight.

"Your sense of touch is evidently highly developed," murmured Mr. Odger.

At the sound of his voice the cat stopped padding, removed his paws from the satin and sat down, swinging his tail round him and over his fore-paws, in a satisfied way. He had had a glorious sensation, but he was enough of an epicure to end it while it was still glorious. Mr. Odger applauded this move.

"You are a very clever cat. I wonder where you came from?"

The cat yawned, showing an arched pink mouth, white teeth. The gesture indicated to Mr. Odger that he was a very stupid human if he didn't know there was an extension roof, just below the one opened window, which was repeated on the house next door, with merely an iron grill for a division.

Mr. Odger followed the cat's hint. "Of course you belong to the McIntoshes."

The cat cocked his head sidewise, unconcerned. Now he began to lower himself, until he sat flat, his fore-paws neatly turned in, his hind legs drawn up, a compact black cat, all lovely curves and softnesses. And he purred.

There was an exquisite finish, a completeness about the cat which held Mr. Odger's eyes, always eager for beauty. And there was a sense of personality, of entity, which, though it might be on a different plane, was not inferior—and this piqued Mr. Odger's intellect, always eager for distinction in being—and lastly, there was a calm friendliness, a graciousness in the cat's behavior which demanded nothing, and thereby delighted Mr. Odger's social sense, always eager for freedom from petty conventional claims.

Involuntarily Mr. Odger's hand raised itself from the bed, and very weakly and gently patted the cat's head. The warm soft fur was delicious under his chilly thin fingers. Moreover, where the cat was sitting, close to his side, there began to be a warm sensation, more agreeable than hot water bottles can give, because it was a living warmth. And at Mr. Odger's touch, the cat's purr grew a little louder. He opened his mouth the least bit and protruded the tip of his rose-leaf tongue, giving to his mask a touch of color, a touch of whimsy.

"We cannot go on like this," said Mr. Odger. "You are my guest and I do not know your name, and I do not like to call you merely cat. Since you are a serious cat, and a charming cat, and a cat of fine manners, and a handsome cat, it is fitting that you should have a Spanish name, and since you are a young cat I believe I shall call you Señor Joven, which means, my dear sir, in our less euphonious language, Mr. Youth. Do you approve of this title?"

The cat had stopped purring while Mr. Odger spoke, but as he concluded, he arched his head under Mr. Odger's hand acquiescently and went on with his *rrrrrrronca*. At that moment Miss Pendle entered the room, very silently, and with the solemn expectant look which Mr. Odger had come to know so well. She thought to find him dead.

"Miss Pendle," asked Mr. Odger, "what do cats eat?"

Miss Pendle had not, for the moment, observed the presence of Señor Joven, so at this strange question her mouth and eyes flew open wide. She knew at once what had happened. The end was near and Mr. Odger's mind had gone. She approached the bed with a professional manner as good as Doctor Raymond's.

"There, there, Mr. Odger," she said soothingly. "Just lie still." She reached for his pulse—and her hand came in contact with Señor Joven. For once she was startled into naturalness. "Heavens!" she shrilled, jumping back. "There *is* a cat!"

"Certainly there is a cat. I want some lunch for him."

Miss Pendle recovered herself in scarlet vexation. "I beg your pardon, Mr. Odger—I didn't see the cat when I came in, and you spoke so oddly—"

"Please tell Warren to bring cream, and anything else a cat can eat that there is in the house, immediately." Mr. Odger did not like Miss Pendle, but he had enjoyed her outburst. Señor Joven did not like her either. He had sat straight at her sudden exclamation, prepared for departure. But at the word cream he paused, serenely expectant.

Miss Pendle tried to retrieve her lost dignity. "Wouldn't it be better if I took the cat downstairs and fed it?" She reached for Joven, as if to carry out her idea, but he moved himself deftly just beyond her reach.

"No," said Mr. Odger. "I wish to see him eat. Have the food

brought here at once, please." Weak as he was, there was an acid quality in his "please" which warned Miss Pendle to dally no longer.

When she had gone Joven walked back to his old place, treading on Mr. Odger's legs as he did so. The two creatures looked at each other understandingly. "Can you imagine such a simp?" asked Joven's yellow eyes.

"You know how it is with women, Señor," excused Mr. Odger. "In moments of excitement they seldom show good judgment."

Joven agreed. When Miss Pendle returned she had a tray. It contained the glass of milk, medicated, and laced with brandy, which was Mr. Odger's sole form of nourishment, and also a saucer of cream, and another saucer containing bits of boiled fish. In disapproving silence she swung Mr. Odger's bed-table around so that the drinking tube in his milk could be brought to his lips by his own hand. He had consistently refused to let her hold the glass, so this method had been evolved.

"What shall I do with this?" she asked, indicating the cream and the fish.

The aroma of the latter had reached Señor Joven, and he was now sitting straight, with whiskers quivering.

"Put them on the table, too," commanded Mr. Odger. "And then please go to your own luncheon. I will ring if I need anything."

Miss Pendle disappeared in an aura of starchy outrage. What could a nurse do with a patient like Mr. Odger! If it had not been that her duties were so very light, and Mr. Odger likely to pass away at any moment, and moreover, Mr. Odger's secretary such a, such a, well, *such* a—Miss Pendle would have asked Doctor Raymond to release her long ago.

"Will you partake, Señor?" asked Mr. Odger politely, as Miss Pendle shut the door.

Señor Joven looked at his host, then at the saucers of food, but he displayed no vulgar greed. He came toward the table as a gentleman should, promptly, but not hastily, and, with a questioning glance at Mr. Odger, placed his fore-paws upon it and inclined his head toward the delectable fish. "Help yourself, do," urged Mr. Odger.

Whereupon the Señor helped himself, but did not, in unmannerly fashion, drag the morsel of fish off the dish. Still standing he ate, in the Japanese manner of appreciative noise, to be sure, but not offensively loud. He did not hurry his meal. Having finished the fish he lapped up the cream, still standing with his paws on the table, chasing the last drop round the saucer with an almost comic determination. Mr. Odger, watching him, was moved to some slight appetite of his own. For the first time in many days he took more than half of his milk.

He found the presence of the cat oddly pleasant. How silent, how well-mannered, how unassuming was this animal! What a pattern for humanity, in taste and manners! If Miss Pendle, and Doctor Raymond, to name only two, had his attributes, how much more agreeable a dying man's last hours might be. So meditated Mr. Odger, and in the middle of his meditations, Señor Joven, satisfied and grateful, dropped down from the table, rubbed his furry head in a gracious and grateful gesture against Mr. Odger's hand, a gesture startling in its human quality.

"By George, he's thanking me," thought Mr. Odger. "He's saying his own *muchas gracias*. This is a damned fine young cat."

He watched the cat with new interest. Luncheon and gratitude over, Señor Joven retreated farther down the bed and washed his face, his paws, his ebon shirt front, rubbing behind his ears, cleaning himself with a meticulous, downright fussy thoroughness. He was satisfied with nothing less then perfection. His fur caught changing silvery lights; he was accurately graceful and assured in every move.

Mr. Odger observed and admired, but shortly he found himself dropping off into a soft sleep, a sleep in which there was no hint of the last unconsciousness which he had felt so close to him. He slept easily and naturally for two hours and when he woke it was mid-afternoon and Señor Joven had gone. Only Miss Pendle remained, keeping vigil by his bed. Mr. Odger's secretary was dismissed from duty at half past one, so Miss Pendle had now enough time to be attentive.

"Your pulse is stronger," she announced. "Let me take your temperature and I'll bring your milk."

"Where is the cat?" asked Mr. Odger, inattentive to the glad tidings of his pulse.

"He jumped out of the window when I came in. But I daresay he'll be back. Cats always come where they get fed." If the old boy was dotty over the cat, why she'd humor him, thought Miss Pendle. She always humored her patients on unessentials.

Mr. Odger was thinking also. "I believe I am better," he was thinking, with disgust. "And it comes from letting myself be interested in that insidious beast. This is absurd. I don't want to lie about dying for an indefinite period. I'd like to get it over."

He would not, however, do anything consciously to hasten his demise, such as refusing his milk. If he did, it might prove him a coward to himself, afraid to live. He was not a coward. He thought little of life, and little of death, but he was willing to accept either, and he would not tip the scales either way.

With such speculations, and with an occasional hour of sleep, the evening and night wore through for Mr. Odger. The night nurse, Miss Falt, who might have been Miss Pendle's twin in all save flirtatious tendencies, attended to him faithfully and marked his chart only with the dull record of his intervals of slumber, his quiet wakefulness, the amount of milk he had taken, but she told Miss Pendle, in the hall, as she left, "I think he's a little better, but he's so darn close with himself I can't be sure."

It was a gray day, with clouds that promised rain, and uneasy, gusty damp winds. Mr. Odger, washed, shaved—he insisted on a daily shaving, another of Miss Pendle's grievances—fed with his lacteal ration, gazed out on the clouds and waited to hear rain dash against the panes.

Suddenly, as if blown in, Señor Joven came over the sill in a scrambling crazy leap, no more the dignified and courteous gentleman of yesterday than Charlie Chaplin is Walter Hampden. The impending storm had made his kitten nerves as taut as fiddlestrings, and there was nothing for them but wild and rapid action. He sprang upon the bed, tail bushed like a squirrel, eyes gleaming wickedly—and he sprang down again, all in a breath! He pranced about the room, jumped to the top of chests, and vaulted over chairs, an acrobat, a clown, a rascally slum kid on the rampage. He smacked Mr. Odger's long unused shoehorn off the dresser with one swipe of a naughty paw, and pounced down on it, batted it swiftly over the floor hockey style, leaped up above it and down on it, threw it in the air, let it fall, and then abandoning it as suddenly as he had seized it, he careened wildly about the room again, landing in one giant leap on Mr. Odger's feet, and, as Mr. Odger naturally moved his feet hastily out of the way, Joven affected to believe this was a game of mouse, and he began pouncing and tumbling over Mr. Odger's feet, clawing them, biting them, rolling around and kicking them violently with his hind paws with such earnest make-believe that Mr. Odger burst into laughter!

At this unusual sound Señor Joven stopped his play, sat straight, and stared scornfully with his yellow eyes at Mr. Odger. His fur was fluffed out by his exertions, but he was as beautiful, as collected, as calm as yesterday.

"What's funny about it?" he asked silently. "A fine thing if a cat can't have his little before-the-storm excitement without some big dull human chortling at him."

"I ask your pardon, Señor," said Mr. Odger. "I myself am unable to move, as you see, and your unusual activity moved me to laughter merely as an indication of pleasure, not in derision, I assure you."

Señor Joven accepted the apology. His gayety disappeared, he became sedate and remembered his manners. He came forward amiably, and rubbed himself against Mr. Odger's body, that ingratiating movement by which a cat caresses himself as well as another being. And he spoke as he did so, not a loud boisterous meow, but the soft upward-inflected *"prrr-n-k"* with which well-behaved cats ask questions, or offer greeting.

"Would you like some fish again, and cream for luncheon?" asked Mr. Odger.

"Prrrr-n-k," said Señor Joven, meaning, yes, please.

Mr. Odger touched the bell—not so much of an effort as yesterday, he noticed. Fish and cream were ordered for the Señor's luncheon, and promptly brought, not by Miss Pendle, but by Warren, the butler-valet, who offered a comment on the situation.

"To have a black cat come to you's good luck, sir," he said.

Señor Joven, who had settled himself against Mr. Odger's side, looked up in approval of this sentiment. When the food was placed on the table he went and sniffed at it, but he was not hungry. He took a lap or two of the cream, and a bite of the fish, only as a token of his appreciation. Then he went back to Mr. Odger and curled himself with endearing confidence close at his side, lying like a warm black muff between Mr. Odger's right arm and his body. He was so little, so warm, so trusting in this attitude that Mr. Odger was moved to stroke him, and to rub him under the chin and about the ears. The Señor responded with sleepy, happy purrs.

"How do you know," asked Mr. Odger, "that I will not hand you over to Miss Pendle and thence to the lethal chamber of the S.P.C.A.? That is the proper fate of stray cats, is it not? But I am wrong—you are not a stray. You are a guest, uninvited, to be sure, but welcome, and you know that I will not betray the laws of hospitality. But how do you know it? I have never been a lover of cats, I have never had a pet of any kind since I was a little boy, and then I had a dog. What is it that has brought you to me, that urges you to offer me your friendship and your trust? In the obscure recesses of your youthful cat brain is there a challenge for my statement to Doctor Raymond, that I am interested in nothing? Do you want me to be interested in you? I wish you could talk, I'd like to hear a cat's-eye view of the world. I have a suspicion that you suffer from no sense of inferiority, though you are so small in stature you must look up even to a little child. Do you know, Señor Joven, that to animals men are gods, with power of life and death? There lies the tragedy of your life, Señor. Yet you are gifted with such instinct that you know perfectly I will be life for you, and you remove yourself beyond Miss Pendle's reach, because she might be death. Is not death preferable?"

Señor Joven stirred, rolled his head down a little further, pointed his nose at the ceiling, and opened a drowsy yellow eye, an eye so cynical, so amused, and so understanding that Mr. Odger was abashed. "Mr. Odger, you are absurd," said the eye. "You are not yet convinced of your insignificance. Be simple, as I am. While there is cream, while there is fish, while there are warm beds and hands that know the proper way to tickle a cat beneath the chin, I question nothing."

Mr. Odger found no more to say. Moreover, he, too, was sleepy, and the cat was gratefully warm to his chilled body. He dozed.

He woke stronger than before and actually with a glimmer of appetite. Doctor Raymond, coming in apprehensively, was greeted by a demand for a sliver of toast and a scrap of boiled breast of chicken. "I said so—if you want to live you can!" exclaimed the doctor. "Hey, what's this! A cat?"

He put out a brusque hand to Señor Joven and seized him. He was rewarded by five long bleeding scratches, and the transformation of the object of his rough attention into a spitting, defiant fury. Mr. Odger was delighted. Even Miss Pendle chuckled, though she brought instantly lotions and bandages and dressed the slight wound as though it were an amputation. The doctor cursed. "Get rid of that damned beast! He's dangerous." He made another menacing move toward the Señor, who did not retreat an inch, but laid back his ears and, crouching, growling, prepared to spring. "Take on something your own size, Raymond," advised Mr. Odger. "Don't trifle with my friend here."

After the doctor, still swearing, had gone, Mr. Odger congratulated the Señor. "Exactly the right thing to do, my dear sir. I wish you'd scratched both his hands." Joven listened and relaxed his tensity, but his eyes still flashed and he rolled a murmur of a growl in his throat. He was warning any possible bully of the neighborhood that they would get what he had given Doctor Raymond if they annoyed his sensibilities. Later, sharing the chicken breast with Mr. Odger, he returned to his usual placidity.

The little affair focused Mr. Odger's interest in the cat, raised it to affection. That the animal should keep anyone else at a distance, but should single him out, unsolicited, for trust and attention, was a flattery impossible to resist. He began to consider, seriously, what chance he had of securing Señor Joven's permanent residence. Those people next door—would they sell him? He couldn't ask them to give him. Perhaps they would lend, or share. Mr. Odger rang for Warren.

"Tell me about the people next door, at Number Twenty."

"A widow lady, Mrs. McIntosh and her daughter, very quiet, sir. Five servants and two cars, but very quiet. Good works, mostly, not pleasure."

The picture was complete. Mr. Odger wondered if his desire for the cat might be classed as good work. Perhaps the cat did not belong to Mrs. or Miss McIntosh, but to the McIntosh cook. But no—Señor Joven was no kitchen cat. Drawing-room or library, yes, but not among the pans and pots.

"Would you like to stay with me?" Mr. Odger asked him. The Señor Joven arched his back, executed a gentle spiral with his tail. It was assent.

"You are dragging me back, you know, to the tiresome business of living; it's only fair that you should take some of the responsibility." Again the Señor arched. Above all things, he said, he was a responsible cat.

Thereafter, day by day, he became the companion of Mr. Odger's tedious convalescence, which would have been far more tedious without his presence. He came in the morning and stayed until evening, going home for dinner. Sometimes he leaped through the window at night and slept for an hour or two beside Mr. Odger, only the warm softness of him revealing his presence, for his blackness made him part of the dark.

Mr. Odger discovered many moods in him. There was an obstinate Joven, who, having set his cat mind on doing any certain thing, such as sleeping directly on Mr. Odger's legs, or spending a delicious fifteen minutes sticking claws into the satin coverlet, or sitting on the dresser, or jumping to the mantelshelf and thence to the bookcase top, could not be persuaded otherwise by any threat, or any coaxing, or by any artful diversion of his attention.

There was a sensuous Joven who rolled and rollicked in the fresh catnip with which Miss Pendle tried to win his favor, poking out his nose amongst the green leaves and slavering, purring giant purrs of ecstasy, drugged with the strange joy which the green herb yields to all things feline. This same Joven loved the sunshine, sought it out, and now and then on dark days reproached Mr. Odger for not turning it on for him. He had an unfailing flair for warm places, soft places, cozy places.

There was an esthetic Joven who found his best background against fine color, chose a golden yellow cushion in preference to a brown, because his black fur would be more dramatic there; a Joven who posed in attitudes of conscious grace, a Mordkin before a mirror, stretched himself beautifully on waking, carried his tail in smart curved lines, and in his leapings and jumpings and runnings had a clear delight in his body.

There was a loving, doting Joven—this was very rare—whose kitten heart was near to bursting with devotion to Mr. Odger, who twined about him, rubbed him, purred at him, and swore eternal amity—amity, mind you, not faithfulness. Always, he was more demonstrative in the morning than at night but on some mornings he adored his friend and said so unmistakably. At night he became remote, listened for outside noises, was abstracted, absorbed in ancestral memories of stealthy stalking through dark jungles. At such times Mr. Odger did not exist for him.

There was the wild Joven of the second visit, the prancing, bounding, racing, gambolading Joven, who invariably anticipated the falling barometer in this manner. Joven before-a-storm was a mad creature, fluffed up to twice his size, full of the craziest pranks, the most fantastic capers. He would skip across Mr. Odger's pillows and climb Miss Pendle's starched back in one sweep of movement. At such times no small movable object on table or dresser was safe from his paws. Smack would go the bottles and the boxes, the brushes and bric-a-brac. Joven did not give a damn!

Then there was the dignified, gracious Joven, meticulously mannered, sedate as a cat of thrice his age, pacing through life with an air of proud reserve, slightly condescending to the poor mortals of his acquaintance who labor under such disadvantages as having to put on and take off clothes, instead of growing into them; who are unable to leap effortlessly ten times their height, who get no thrill from mice or catnip. "I pity you, Mr. Odger, indeed I do," was his manner at such times. And when he was in these moods he was fanciful and haughty about his food, sniffing at it and refusing it at first, pretending indifference to it and walking off and about the room for a careless promenade, coming back at last to his saucer with a simulation of surprise.

Another Joven who never failed to divert Mr. Odger was the Joven who loved boxes, preferring those large enough for him to climb in and sit, with his head sticking over the top in naïve rapture. Boxes and paper, tissue paper especially because it made a louder crinkling sound, never failed to allure him. He crawled into any open dresser drawer and he would remain for half an hour under an impromptu tent made of a newspaper and fancy himself a cat-Napoleon, conquering the world. Another sound besides the crisp noise of paper which he liked was the tick of the clock, though Mr. Odger surmised that curiosity rather than pleasure was his reason for listening to it so intently. But he detested the light whistling of tunes in which Mr. Odger sometimes indulged himself, and on such occasions would walk smartly up to Mr. Odger's face and bite him on the forehead, not viciously but with plain intent to enforce silence. Always he would do this, in an annoyed chiding way, first striding up and down in a state of nerves.

For Joven was given to nerves now and then, Mr. Odger observed. Too-sudden movements startled him, made him petulant and uneasy. A loud voice he detested. The bang of a piece of furniture knocked over, or a door closed with violence, would send him out of the window. Part of this sensitiveness to sound was easily attributable to his acute hearing. His ears were aware of the slightest noises, and he would wake, and turn his head watchfully toward the door when Miss Pendle or Warren were no farther than the foot of the stairs and thus tell Mr. Odger that someone was coming. Now and then he was sure that he heard a mouse in the wall, and on such occasions he was frenzied with desire, but supremely cautious, crouching stiffly with his nose to the baseboard, oblivious to all save the hunting call.

Besides an occasional indulgence in nerves, Joven was known to have fits of boredom, and these amused Mr. Odger exceedingly with their likeness to humanity. Joven would walk aimlessly around the room, the picture of listless ennui, thrusting a languid malicious paw at the electric lamp cord as he passed, jumping on a chair, sitting there for a moment or two, then jumping down with a despairing shrug, biting listlessly at a rose in the bowl of flowers on the table, knocking down the shoehorn (his favorite plaything) but not leaping after it; finding everything flat, stale and unprofitable. Sometimes, in such moods, he would come and sit before Mr. Odger and look at him with insolent accusation: "For heaven's sake, why don't you amuse me!"

There was the Joven of play, to whom a bit of string, a rolled scrap of woolly rag, a spool, a tiny ball (purchased at Mr. Odger's request by Miss Pendle) became a motive for a romp of extreme kittenishness, beneath which there was always the suggestion of ferocity. He would bite and toss and bat these objects about in tiger attitudes, and seeing him thus, Mr. Odger gave thanks that their respective sizes were not reversed. A Mr. Odger the size of Señor Joven, at the mercy of the paws and claws of a Señor Joven the size of Mr. Odger, would have short shrift from torture and annihilation.

Most agreeable of all these various Jovens was the sleeping, relaxed Joven, rolled on his back, belly up, paws tossed out carelessly, tail a limp black streak. In these deep slumbers he was not disturbed by Mr. Odger's caressing hand, would not open his eyes, and if he moved at all it was only to a more pliant, looser curve, a lazier ease. Sometimes he slept on his side, stretched to his full length, with four paws far extended to take up much more than his proper share of room, a dead cat to all appearances, and though Mr. Odger's attentions did not bring him to life, at the entrance of another person he would spring to his feet, wide awake, alert.

In all of these various phases of Joven's character and behavior, Mr. Odger constantly saw a self-respecting, independent personality, without servility, and without humbleness, asking little and giving nothing, save when the mood of generosity appeared. Joven treated humanity as equal, but never as superior. He would not fawn and beg, either for food or affection. His pride was as shining as his fur.

As Mr. Odger progressed from bed to easy chair, from pajamas to dressing gown to negligee, to shirt and real trousers, from slippers to shoes, so did his study of Señor Joven progress, and as his body strengthened and his vitality rose, so did his wish strengthen to keep this diverting companion and friend near him. He would not write to Mrs. McIntosh, he decided, because the written word is interpreted by the mind of the reader, and not the mind of the writer. Mr. Odger did not feel sufficiently acquainted with the convolutions of the mind of a woman given to good works, with five servants and two cars, to write a request for her cat which would be surely effective. When he was well enough he could call and state his case. The fact that the Señor spent so much time away from his home argued that no high value was placed on his society. No such value, for instance, as Mr. Odger placed on it. The cat had won a place in his esteem never before occupied by any living creature, human or beast; the place of being necessary to his heart and his brain. He wanted him, very much.

He believed, did Mr. Odger, that he knew the Señor well, and that his desire was reciprocated. He believed that he was as agreeable to the cat as the cat was agreeable to him. He was certain that Señor Joven's esteem for Mr. Odger was no less than Mr. Odger's esteem for Señor Joven. He was pleasantly certain that Señor Joven would welcome a change in habitat, would enjoy living beneath his roof far more than under that of the good workers.

Secure in these beliefs and certainties Mr. Odger prepared his argument for Señor Joven's transferal to him and his domicile. He was prepared to offer a magnificent donation to the chief of Mrs. McIntosh's good works, should she prove willing to part with Señor Joven, as earnest of his gratitude.

So, on the first day that he felt able to undertake so serious and important a mission, Mr. Odger prepared for an afternoon call in his most correct raiment. Being an old-fashioned man he wore a Prince Albert instead of a cut-away, but it was a Prince Albert of superb tailoring. His trousers were gray-striped, his scarf a French importation of conservative, but rich colors, his pin a lustrous black pearl. He took his silkiest silk hat and his best stick, of snakewood and rhinoceros horn. His black shoes, his gray gloves and lightweight gray overcoat completed an impressive ensemble. Miss Pendle, whose last day of attendance it was, suggested a flower for his buttonhole, but this he felt might strike the lady of good works as frivolous.

So attired, and feeling uncommonly jaunty, what with being dressed up and getting well and acquiring a pet cat, he descended his own front steps and walked the short distance to the steps of the McIntosh residence. These he ascended and put out his hand to the bell, when he saw a gentle stirring of the draperies of the window nearest the front door, and the head of Señor Joven appear. After the head came his whole sleek body, and he sat down deliberately, with the soft lace behind him, and the glass before, and prepared to survey the street.

"Joven," said Mr. Odger softly, with a joyous gesture of greeting.

Señor Joven turned slightly, fixed his yellow eyes on Mr. Odger, and cut him dead! There could be no mistake about it. He chose, at this crucial moment, to ignore and snub his friend, to put him coldly in his place. Indifferent, contemptuous, Señor Joven denied that he had ever known the person on the steps.

For a moment Mr. Odger stood, wounded to the quick. Then he understood. The Señor wished him to know that he was no cat to be bartered about between families! That the favor of his presence was bestowed by himself, at his pleasure and convenience, and not to be acquired by gift or purchase, direct or indirect. That Mr. Odger in this call on Mrs. McIntosh was violating the finer laws of courtesy, was offending against the one assumption which made his acquaintance with Joven possible—equality of being.

Mr. Odger's hand fell away from the bell, he turned and went down the steps. He was abashed, rebuked. He was ashamed, repentant. He could only hope that in the course of time his offense might be forgotten and forgiven.

Señor Joven, sitting in the late afternoon sunshine, turned his head away from the departing Mr. Odger, and gazed placidly up the street. And in his throat rumbled a faint triumphant purr.

The Totem of Amarillo

EMMA-LINDSAY SQUIER

PERHAPS you have heard me speak of Amarillo before. He was a yellow cat who came to us from out of the woods when Brother and I still lived in the little log cabin on the shores of Puget Sound. And he was, in those days, our very special friend. His coming to our home was most spectacular, and his departure was equally dramatic. As for the grand finale of his story, as I learned it from those who cared for him in his last years, it is so curious and hints so much of melodrama that I am afraid that some will doubt it. I offer in explanation of my belief that it is true, only the fact that Amarillo was always a most unusual cat. And the proof of it is that he is perpetuated forever in the village of Old Man House in a totem pole, carved and painted. Only the truly great are thus honored by the tribe of Skokomish.

Amarillo, the yellow one, was born, I think, in the woods. And I further believe that complete savagery was only a short generation behind him. For his ears were tufted as are the ears of a bobcat, and his eyes were slanted and amber, so that in moments of complete repose he resembled a Chinese mandarin pleasantly absorbed in thought.

He had grown up in a region where the law was that only the strongest survived. He had fought many battles and won them, and so had grown to a size unbelievable in an ordinary cat, another fact which hinted strongly at a parentage having nothing to do with domesticity and quiet firesides.

Still, he had within him the instinct of association with man. For when he first came to us, his lovely fur all draggled and covered with blood, he was sorely hurt and dragged a torn and wounded leg. He mewed pitifully and crawled to us, yet was afraid to let us touch him, and sprang back spitting venomously. But the instinct that had brought him down from the woods to the little cabin, where he knew he would find succor for his hurt, finally made him accept us. He let us examine the wounded leg, suffered us to bathe it and anoint it with salve. Then, being completely unble to hunt or care for himself, he allowed us to extend to him the hospitality of our home. He came to love us, and adopted us, and when he was well, he stayed with us and became our friend.

Now Brother and I were so fond of Amarillo, the yellow cat, that we saw none of his faults; and when they were called to our attention by the grown-ups, we made excuses for them and pretended that they did not matter. For he was our constant companion during the day, and when I slept out of doors on the camp bed, I would, sometimes during the night, hear his soft "Prr-t," which signified that he was about to jump up beside me, and then feel the thud of his soft, heavy body, as he leaped. But the grown-ups did not share our un-qualified approval of Amarillo and his ways. For he, never having had any knowledge of civilization, did not know, and could not be taught, that chickens were to be respected, and not stalked and de-voured whenever he happened to be hungry. Neither was it permis-sible that he should molest the pigeons, climb up to the nests and kill their young. So, after all persuasion had failed and many attempts at discipline, it was decreed that Amarillo must go. And Brother and I were very sad because of it.

It was not hard to find a new home for him. He was admired by all who saw him, and many places were open to our choosing. But it was deemed best that he be given into the kindly care of a fisherman friend of ours. A huge, dark man with kindly smiling eyes, a man whose descent was traced from Indian and Spanish blood, and whose wife and kinsfolk were of the tribe of Skokomish. They lived in the far-off village of Old Man House, called by the Indians, Suquamish.

They would, we knew, be kind to Amarillo. They had no chickens or pigeons for him to kill unlawfully, and there were rats and much small game in the woods to satisfy his hunting instincts.

So, on the day set for his departure, we took our friend, the Yellow One, down to the fishing launch which anchored at our float, and it was with heavy hearts that we set a dish of milk for him upon the deck. We hoped that eating would occupy his attention and that he would not realize until too late that he was going away from us. The Indian Fisherman shoved off very gently from the wharf and did not start the engine until the launch had drifted for a hundred feet or more. But when the whirring of the fly wheel startled Amarillo, and the churning of the propeller whirled the water into eddies of white and green—then he knew that he was being taken away without his will or knowledge.

He sprang to the gunwale and stood, for an instant, gazing out at us, his slanted, amber eyes wide with alarm. The Indian Fisherman spoke to him soothingly and moved toward him with friendly hand outstretched. But it was too late. For Amarillo, without an instant's hesitation, had leaped. We saw the flash of his yellow body as he sprang and the splash as he sank from sight. We cried out, because we thought he would drown. But he had no idea of coming to such an inglorious end. For the next instant he was swimming toward us, easily, powerfully, his tufted ears flattened back on his head, his body a lithe, yellow streak in the blueness of the water. When he reached the float, he climbed up on it, sat down with perfect composure, and commenced to wash himself with great earnestness and poise. He appeared to think nothing whatsoever of the swim he had taken. And that day, because of our entreaties, he was allowed to remain with us.

But it was, we knew, only a stay of sentence. On the next day we bade our friend good-by once more. This time the Yellow One was fastened in a sack, and when the launch started its chugging way out into the blueness of the bay, we saw the frenzied contortions of the burlap bag, and dimly heard protesting yowls above the throbbing of the engine. We watched sadly from the float until the fishing launch was but a speck of black athwart the jutting greenery of the Point. Then it was lost to sight, and we knew that Amarillo had gone from us forever.

In the years that followed, we heard of our yellow friend from time to time. Once the Indian Fisherman chugged around the Point and into our tiny cove specially to give us news of him. And once the Old Fisherman, who made his home with us, put into the village of Suquamish to learn at first hand of Amarillo's welfare. We were assured, each time, that the Yellow One was well and happy, and that he had established a kingship among the lesser cats of the village so that there was none to dispute his authority. But the details of his tempestous life I did not fully learn until, grown out of childhood, and many years away from the country of gray waters and singing pine trees, I came back to the woods and waters of Puget Sound; found at Suquamish our beloved Old Fisherman, with no trace of time upon the pinkness of his cheeks or within the clear twinkling of his eyes; found, too, the Indian Fisherman and his wife who had given Amarillo shelter; and learned from him, and from the Blind Boy who was their son, the story of the Yellow One's tragic, triumphant career.

Now, the Blind Boy was a carver of totems. And in the great darkness where there was no light, he found solace in bringing to remembrance the strange, almost forgotten tales of the Indians of the Sound. He made them live again, cunningly carved into symbols upon pine poles, and he painted them carefully, under the watchful eye of those who could see. There is today, in the open square of the village, a totem pole that the Blind Boy made. Upon it is depicted the story of how Teet' Motl, with his sweetheart Hoo Han Hoo, rode upon a dolphin's back toward a far country where the Great Spirit promised them rest and prosperity. Their progress was barred by a school of blackfish, those tigers of the water called by the Indians "killers." But the brave dolphin, with a word of encouragement to those upon his back, dove into the depths of the sea, scraping up pebbles in his mouth. Then there came a great storm, and Teet' Motl and Hoo Han Hoo crept into the dolphin's mouth for safety. Inside they found the shining pebbles scraped up by the giant fish. And when at last the storm abated, the dolphin had indeed brought them safely to a pleasant country, green with trees and fruitful with berries. The Indians who inhabited the country used for currency shining pebbles. And Teet' Motl and Hoo Han Hoo, having many of them, were rich and forever prosperous. Even to this day, said the Blind Boy, when the killers come from the south, then a storm will rise. So he portrayed upon the totem Teet' Motl and his sweetheart safe in the belly of the dolphin.

It was while the Blind Boy still carved the story upon the totem pole that Amarillo was brought into the household. And curiously enough, it was to the child who lived in darkness that the Yellow One gave his love and never-ending loyalty. He liked very well indeed the Indian Fisherman and his wife, who was of the tribe of Skokomish. He obligingly caught the rats that had formerly made merry under the cabin, and once in the dead of night he gave alarm of fire that had started from a chance spark, by mewing and rubbing his cold nose against the Indian Fisherman's face. He repaid the hospitality they offered him with a friendship that was staunch and true. But it was only the Blind Boy that he loved—and I believe, and would have you believe, that it was because he knew of the darkness in which the Blind Boy lived, and because he knew that in some ways his friend was helpless.

But because he loved the little Blind Boy so well, Amarillo was jealous of everything to which he gave his attention. During the long evenings, when the Blind Boy carved the totem pole, the Yellow One would sit on the table beside him, watching with slanted amber eyes, while the childish, sensitive fingers crept over the long pine pole, feeling out with a sharp knife the contours of the dolphin, the killer blackfish, and the rude figures of Teet' Motl and his sweetheart. When Amarillo thought his friend had given too much attention to the work of carving, he would reach out a padded, yellow paw and pat the Blind Boy's hand. If there was no response, he would yawn prodigiously, get up and stretch, and rub his broad back against the Blind Boy's face, deliberately walking on the pole, so that he could not carve. Then, if his friend persisted in his work, Amarillo would mew sharply, a little angry sound that ended in a snarl. He would switch his tail violently, jump down from the table with a loud thump, and sulk under the stove, refusing to come out for commands or cajoling words.

Now, Amarillo was not the only four-footed guest in the household of the Indian Fisherman and his wife. The hospitality of their little cabin was offered freely to any living thing that needed shelter or aid, and there was rarely a time when they were not caring for some boarder from the woods who had come to grief. Once they found a pheasant's nest with the mother's dead body beside it, bullet-riddled, and the tiny, brown chicks scarcely out of their shells. They took the tiny things to their cabin and fed them so carefully that all of them lived, and would have grown eventually to adult pheasanthood—had it not been for Amarillo.

At first, it was not difficult to keep the wee brown pheasant chicks secluded. They learned very soon to run briskly to the door of their wire coop when they heard a footstep approaching, and they were as friendly as if their parents had never lived in the wilds. Amarillo watched them with sullen, amber eyes, his tail twitching ever so little, his shoulder muscles moving slightly whenever he saw the baby pheasants running about in the safety of the wire enclosure. But he never attempted to molest them. And even when they grew so large that the coop was deemed too small to hold them comfortably, and so were permitted to roam at liberty, he did not try to pounce upon them—having perhaps in mind the punishment meted out to him at our cabin the day when he tried to kill the chickens.

But upon the day when the little Blind Boy made his way out to the wire enclosure and called to the pheasants, who came running to peck at the crumbs he held in his hand—upon that day did Amarillo declare war upon the brown intruders. Never did the Indian Fisherman or his wife actually catch him doing violence to the pheasant boarders, but one by one they disappeared with only a bunch of feathers left to tell of their passing. And once the Yellow One came into the cabin with one tiny feather still hanging from his whiskers—he had forgotten to remove the evidence. It was the last feather of the last pheasant. So they spanked him soundly, and he snarled, and spat, and ran away into the woods, and did not come back for two days, during which time the Blind Boy missed him sorely. When he returned, it was with sullen, padding steps, and his amber eyes were rather furtive, as if he doubted whether he would be welcomed. But the family forgave him the pheasants, and made much of him, and the Blind Boy cried, holding the yellow cat close against his cheek. So Amarillo purred deeply, like an organ, and dug his toes comfortably into his friend's shoulders, and that night slept upon the Blind Boy's bed, unrebuked. For a week he would not let the child go out of his sight, but followed him like a dog, and every evening sat near him when he carved upon the totem pole.

It was soon after the incident of the pheasants that another woods friend was brought into the kindly care of the Indian Fisherman and his wife. One day the Indian Fisherman saw in the woods, near the village of Suquamish, a little lady racoon who had been caught in a trap such as they set for racoons on the Puget Sound country. A hole had been bored in a small log, and honey-comb had been put deep inside it. Then nails had been set in such a way that a racoon hand, reaching inside for the honey-comb, could not pull itself out without tearing the skin completely away. So the Indian Fisherman found the racoon lady with one arm inside the hole, her bright eyes blinking worriedly through the black markings that ran completely across her face like a highwayman's mask. She was really very foolish to have kept her clutch on the honey-comb, for by realeasing it and squeezing her little black hand together, she could have brought it through the nail barricade without mishap. But she wanted the honey-comb, and so she kept her hold of it, thus keeping herself prisoner—as indeed, those who set the trap knew she would do.

But the Indian Fisherman could not bear to see the little lady racoon thus a captive. For she was soon to have babies. He drew out the nails, very carefully, while she stood rigidly alert to all he was doing, but stubbornly refusing to let go her hold on the sweetness that was in the hole. He slipped his hat over her, then in her sudden alarm she withdrew her hand, all sticky with honey-comb, and the Indian Fisherman brought her to the cabin, wriggling and squeaking in protest.

He saw to it that she had a comfortable pen to live in, and all the family made much of her. By the time her tiny children were born, she was quite at home in her new environment, and accepted philosophically all the kindly attentions bestowed upon her.

They named her Betty, and her children were born in a box behind the kitchen stove. Soon afterward she was put into a comfortable cage in the woodshed. But one day she escaped from the pen and came into the house, with her three babies following her in single file, their tails curled up high over their backs, as if they had been taught just the correct way of holding them thus, and on every tiny face was a black mask through which bright eyes blinked in friendly curiosity at the new world in which they found themselves.

Now, Amarillo saw this strange procession with astonishment not unmixed with alarm. He had been away hunting in the woods when Betty was brought to the cabin, and the Indian Fisherman had taken care that he had had no access to her cage or to her box behind the kitchen stove. Certainly he had never seen a racoon baby, with a black mask on its face, and its tail curling up neatly over its head. He leaped upon a chair and spat vigorously as the little procession trundled across the kitchen floor to a saucer of milk behind the stove.

Betty took no notice of him and pursued her even course, her three babies following in a line, one directly behind the other.

Amarillo leaned over the edge of the chair and growled terrifically. Betty looked up at him from behind her highwayman's mask, and her eyes glittered at him. She showed a line of white, menacing teeth. The Yellow One continued to snarl deep in his throat, but made no move, except to settle down on his haunches and watch and speculate. If Betty and her babies had been out in the open, he would have set upon them without delay. But their presence in the kitchen disturbed him, made him vaguely uncertain as to their standing. For he had been punished many times for interfering with domestic friends. He licked his chops and continued to growl.

Then, suddenly, his temper getting the better of him—he sprang. The Indian Fisherman moved to protect the racoon lady whose life he thought in peril. But Betty was quite capable of defending herself and her family. Although she had apparently given no heed to the yellow cat, yet she was ready for his pounce. She gave a shrill squeal and darted to one side so quickly that even Amarillo's swiftness was not equaled by it. Before the yellow cat could realize what had happened, she was upon him, her black, little hands clutching at his neck, her sharp teeth digging through his thick fur and into the flesh beneath. Amarillo snarled and yowled with pain. He rolled over and over, seeking vainly to fasten his claws on the alert, darting body of the lady racoon. The racoon babies scuttled under the stove, where they sat and peeped with bright, inquisitive eyes at the rolling, scrambling whirlwind of fur—yellow fur and brown. It was Amarillo who finally cried "enough" in the unequal battle. His authority had been undisputed for such a long time that it made his surrender the more complete. He bolted for the open door, yowling in wholehearted terror, with Betty astride him like a jockey, her hands deep in his fur, her eyes viciously sardonic through the black highwayman's mask.

Amarillo finally rid himself of his unwelcome rider by rolling with despairing energy. Having freed himself, he climbed a tree, spitting at every step, and found shelter on a limb, very high above the ground, where he snarled, and spat, and licked his wounds, and had many harsh and bitter thoughts toward racoons and the world in general.

Betty, on the other hand, took her victory with modest simplicity. She curled her tail high over her head and marched sedately back to the kitchen and her babies. And after taking a refreshing drink of milk from the saucer, proceeded to give her children their lunch, while she tidied her disordered coat, pulling from it the bits of twigs and tufts of yellow fur that had clung to it in the battle.

Amarillo went away into the woods, as was his custom when insulted, and he stayed so long that the family feared that his nose had been put permanently out of joint. But he came back at last, very sulky and bad-tempered until he found that he was really welcomed, especially by the Blind Boy who had missed him greatly. So he purred, and rolled on the floor like a kitten, and slept at night on the little boy's bed. The racoon family—who now lived under the house—he did not molest. Betty and her children came at will into the kitchen and the room adjoining, they even received food from the hand of the Blind Boy—and Amarillo did not seek to prevent them. Sometimes he would growl and spit softly, but when Betty glanced at him sharply from behind her menacing mask, he would blink, and look away, and pretend that he had not said a word.

The racoons were very cleanly folk. There was a big pan of water for them always upon the back porch, and into it they would dip every morsel of food before they ate it. They would bathe regularly, too, sitting up around the pan like little, furry toys, dipping their black hands in the water and washing their faces and necks very daintily and properly. They knew where the Indian Fisherman beached the flat-bottomed boat in which he carried fish to sell. It was his custom to leave a few small fish in it after the day's work, just for the pleasure of seeing Betty lead her children down through the woods to the graveled shore, the four of them in single file, with their tails curled over their heads, and all of them humming a curious, little monotone of a song, such as racoons sing when they are journeying and are contented with life.

When the fall came, the racoon babies, quite well grown by that time, went away into the woods, and later Betty, too, slipped away, to be gone for the whole winter. They expected that she would return in the spring. But she did not, and they never knew what became of the intrepid little lady.

Her absence, as you can readily imagine, was no grief at all to Amarillo. His kingship was once more undisputed, and he was happy in the friendship of the Indian Fisherman and his wife, and in the affection that the Blind Boy gave him. The two were more inseparable than ever. It was rarely now that the Yellow One went away to hunt in the woods. He preferred, instead, to remain with the little boy he loved, to follow when the child walked about in the yard with the halting, uncertain steps of those who cannot see, and to sleep on his bed at night.

In due course of time he found a lady cat to his liking, and he brought her to live at the cabin of the Indian Fisherman. Only one kitten did the lady cat give birth to, a kitten who was almost as golden in color as Amarillo himself. And Amarillo as a father, I am glad to say, emulated his savage ancestors rather than his immediate domestic forebears. He cared for the kitten much more tenderly than the mother cat did, for she proved after all to be a careless jade, totally unworthy of Amarillo's affections. Soon after her daughter was weaned she went away into the woods, and the kitten, to whom the Indian Fisherman gave the outrageous name of "Whiskey Susan," grew up entirely under her father's supervision.

Whiskey Susan was the only one beside himself whom Amarillo would suffer the family to pet. He was not jealous of the affection they gave her, and even the Blind Boy could hold the snuggling, yellow kitten in his lap while he carved upon the totem pole, and Amarillo would sit on the table beside him, purring deep in his throat, his eyes closed to mere slits of contentment.

But one day, many months later, there came another, and this time a final, disturbing factor in the life of the Yellow One. The Indian Fisherman had found a small mallard duck caught in the meshes of his nets, and one leg had been broken, so that he floundered there, helpless, beating the water with his wings. The Indian Fisherman released him gently and brought him to the cabin, where his wife took kindly charge of the invalid, set the hurt leg in splints, and tended to his wants. It was upon the first evening of his stay, that Amarillo, coming in from the out-of-doors, spied the newcomer. The Blind Boy, who could not see the Yellow One's approach, was bending over the wounded duck, stroking him gently. And at the sight Amarillo hissed sharply—and sprang. His leap did no more than knock the astonished duck over on the floor, but the Fisherman's wife was impatient that her invalid should be so treated. She cuffed Amarillo sharply, and he stared at her with furious, amber eyes, then laid his ears back on his head and trotted out of the house, his fur in thick, outraged ruffles, and headed straight for the woods.

He did not come back for one week, nor for two weeks. And the Blind Boy grew daily more worried and more lonely. He took to wandering about the yard, calling for Amarillo, and when his mother was busy, so that she could not prevent him, he would feel his way through the gate and set off up the trail that led into the deep woods, walking very slowly with his hands outstretched before him, calling

Amarillo's name, hoping that the yellow cat would hear and come to him.

Now, it was not safe to go alone or unarmed into the thickness of those forests, for many dangers lurked in the shadowed depths of them, and many were the tales told of bold attacks made by cougars and bobcats driven down from the high mountains by hunger or forest fires. Yet always the Blind Boy came back safely, for he ventured only a little way and returned before his absence could be noticed.

But one day he slipped away, having acquired some confidence in his knowledge of the trail. He went farther and farther, calling to Amarillo with louder tones as he felt himself out of hearing distance from the cabin. The trail became rougher and was unfamiliar to his feet. But still he went on, and at last he realized that there was a chill in the air that spoke of coming night. The woods were very still, with only the light dropping of pine needles to dot the silence, or the distant call of a heron flying to a tall pine-tree nest. A little frightened, the Blind Boy turned toward home. But his feet had lost their confidence. He turned into a ragged, wandering trail that led away from the true path. And as the night grew colder, and his feet stumbled over sprawling roots, and low-hanging branches struck his face, he knew that he was lost, lost and helpless.

Then he ceased to call for Amarillo, but sent up his voice in a thin, wavering cry such as the Indians use. It is a sound which carries clearly across great spaces, and the Indians know it for a signal of distress.

Down in the cabin it was nearly sunset before the absence of the Blind Boy had been discovered, for both the Indian Fisherman and his wife were at work mending nets upon the beach. When evening came, and they returned home, they looked at each other with startled eyes, and a great fear was in their hearts. For they knew the menace of the dark woods behind them.

The Indian Fisherman called the others of the tribe of Skokomish, and with that cunning that Indians possess, they found the child's light, halting footprints in the softness of the earth, and followed them into the forest, until it was too dark for them to see further.

They listened, and presently, from far away, a thin, wavering cry came to their ears. They responded mightily and plunged along the trail, the glimmering of their lanterns throwing dark, grotesque shadows on the path before them.

But suddenly they heard another cry, and they stood breathless for a moment, tingling cold with horror. For it was the savage, hunting cry of the bobcat—the cry he gives as he springs upon his prey.

Firing their guns and shouting fiercely, they set off at a run toward the direction from which the two cries—the call for help, and the call of death—had come. It was easy to guide themselves so, for the woods were alive with the savage sounds of fighting—eerie screams that set the birds to twittering nervously and made the men grit their teeth with fear at what they should find.

When they turned down the ragged, wandering trail, they heard above the snarls and shrieks a child's voice sobbing in fear. And the gleam of the lanterns caught a wild tangle of blazing eyes, white, snapping teeth, and rolling, twisting, furry bodies upon the ground. The Blind Boy crouched in the ferns at the side of the trail and crawled toward them, his arms lifted to the unseen rescuers. His father caught him up with a fierce sobbing of breath. And there came a fusillade of shots barking viciously into the whirl of writhing bodies. There was a sharp, sudden silence. The bodies dropped down loosely, twitched for a moment, then lay still.

Then the child screamed sharply. "Don't shoot," he cried, "don't shoot—you'll hurt Amarillo!"

The men stared. And for once the Indian Fisherman was glad that his child could not see. For there before them, in the trail, lay the tawny, dead body of a bobcat, its cruel claws clenched about the yellow body of a cat—the gallant body of Amarillo. The body of the Yellow One was torn almost to shreds, and he lay in a pool of blood. But the wildcat had suffered too. For Amarillo's teeth were buried in his throat, and even death had not sufficed to loosen the hold.

They carried the poor, torn body very tenderly back to the cabin, and the Blind Boy sobbed on his father's shoulder. He told them later how, in that cold darkness, he had heard a light swishing of leaves, and then a well known "Prr-t," which told him that Amarillo had heard him at last and was coming to him. But even as he had knelt, his arms outstretched to welcome the Yellow One to his heart, there had come a stirring in the branches over his head—and the wild, savage shriek of a bobcat. Then had come the leap that had knocked him upon his face. But before the bloodthirsty creature could spring again, Amarillo was upon him, fighting savagely, and the bobcat, surprised at the sudden attack, had fought back, for the moment forgetting the human prey whom he had stalked.

So it was that many years later, when I came to the village of Old Man House, known by the Indians as Suquamish, I found the Old Fisherman, and the Indian Fisherman, and his wife who was of the tribe of Skokomish. I met the Blind Boy, grown now almost to manhood, and I saw in the open square of the village the totem telling the story of how Teet' Motl and Hoo Han Hoo found the promised land.

There, in the cabin yard, is a little grave. It bears no headstone, such as a white man would erect to a well-remembered friend. It has a nobler, more fitting monument of gratitude and love—a carved and painted totem pole. At the bottom of the totem is the fierce, snarling face of a wildcat with white, cruel fangs displayed. Over the snarling face sits the stolid figure of a mallard duck, with one leg stiffly wrapped in splints. Above this are two closed eyes—eyes that cannot see the light. And at the very top, in the place of honor, is the carved portrait of Amarillo himself—his yellow face benign and almost smiling—his tufted ears erect and alert—

If he could know of this, I am sure he would be proud. For only the truly great are thus honored by the tribe of Skokomish.

How a Cat Played Robinson Crusoe

CHARLES G. D. ROBERTS

THE island was a mere sandbank off the low, flat coast. Not a tree broke its bleak levels—not even a shrub. But the long, gritty stalks of the marsh grass clothed it everywhere above tidemark; and a tiny rivulet of sweet water, flowing from a spring at its center, drew a ribbon of inland herbage and tenderer green across the harsh and somber yellow gray of the grass. Few would have chosen the island as a place to live, yet at its seaward end, where the changing tides were never still, stood a spacious, one-storied, wide-verandaed cottage, with a low shed behind it. The virtue of this lone plot of sand was coolness. When the neighbor mainland would be sweltering day and night alike under a breathless heat, out here on the island there was always a cool wind blowing. Therefore a wise city dweller had appropriated the sea waif and built his summer home thereon, where the tonic airs might bring back the rose to the pale cheeks of his children.

The family came to the island toward the end of June. In the first week of September they went away, leaving every door and window of house and shed securely shuttered, bolted or barred against the winter's storms. A roomy boat, rowed by two fishermen, carried them across the half mile of racing tides that separated them from the mainland. The elders of the household were not sorry to get back to the world of men, after two months of mere wind, and sun, and waves, and waving grass tops. But the children went with tear-stained faces. They were leaving behind them their favorite pet, the accustomed comrade of their migrations, a handsome, moon-faced cat, striped like a tiger. The animal had mysteriously disappeared two days before, vanishing from the face of the island without leaving a trace behind. The only reasonable explanation seemed to be that she had been snapped up by a passing eagle. The cat, meanwhile, was fast prisoner at the other end of the island, hidden beneath a broken barrel and some hundredweight of drifted sand.

The old barrel, with the staves battered out of one side, had stood, half buried, on the crest of a sand ridge raised by a long prevailing wind. Under its lee the cat had found a sheltered hollow, full of sun, where she had been wont to lie curled up for hours at a time, basking and sleeping. Meanwhile the sand had been steadily piling itself higher and higher behind the unstable barrier. At last it had piled too high; and suddenly, before a stronger gust, the barrel had come toppling over beneath a mass of sand, burying the sleeping cat out of sight and light. But at the same time the sound half of the barrel had formed a safe roof to her prison, and she was neither crushed nor smothered. When the children in their anxious search all over the island chanced upon the mound of fine, white sand they gave it but one careless look. They could not hear the faint cries that came, at intervals, from the close darkness within. So they went away sorrowfully, little dreaming that their friend was imprisoned almost beneath their feet.

For three days the prisoner kept up her appeals for help. On the third day the wind changed and presently blew up a gale. In a few hours it had uncovered the barrel. At one corner a tiny spot of light appeared.

Eagerly the cat stuck her paw through the hole. When she withdrew it again the hole was much enlarged. She took the hint and fell to scratching. At first her efforts were rather aimless; but presently, whether by good luck or quick sagacity, she learned to make her scratching more effective. The opening rapidly enlarged, and at last she was able to squeeze her way out.

The wind was tearing madly across the island, filled with flying sand. The seas hurled themselves trampling up the beach, with the uproar of a bombardment. The grasses lay bowed flat in long quivering ranks. Over the turmoil the sun stared down from a deep, unclouded blue. The cat, when first she met the full force of the gale, was fairly blown off her feet. As soon as she could recover herself she crouched low and darted into the grasses for shelter. But there was little shelter there, the long stalks being held down almost level. Through their lashed lines, however, she sped straight before the gale, making for the cottage at the other end of the island, where she would find, as she fondly imagined, not only food and shelter but also loving comfort to make her forget her terrors.

Still and desolate in the bright sunshine and the tearing wind the house frightened her. She could not understand the tight-closed shutters, the blind, unresponding doors that would no longer open to her anxious appeal. The wind swept her savagely across the naked veranda. Climbing with difficulty to the dining-room windowsill, where so often she had been let in, she clung there a few moments and yowled heartbrokenly. Then, in a sudden panic, she jumped down and ran to the shed. That, too, was closed. Never before had she seen the shed doors closed, and she could not understand it. Cautiously she crept around the foundations—but those had been built hon-

estly: there was no such thing as getting in that way. On every side it was nothing but a blank, forbidding face that the old familiar house confronted her with.

The cat had always been so coddled and pampered by the children that she had had no need to forage for herself; but, fortunately for her, she had learned to hunt the marsh mice and grass sparrows for amusement. So now, being ravenous from her long fast under the sand, she slunk mournfully away from the deserted house and crept along under the lee of a sand ridge to a little grassy hollow which she knew. Here the gale caught only the tops of the grasses; and here, in the warmth and comparative calm, the furry little marsh folk, mice and shrews, were going about their business undisturbed.

The cat, quick and stealthy, soon caught one and eased her hunger. She caught several. And then, making her way back to the house, she spent hours in heartsick prowling around it and around, sniffing and peering, yowling piteously on the threshold and windowsill; and every now and then being blown ignominiously across the smooth, naked expanse of the veranda floor. At last, hopelessly discouraged, she curled herself up beneath the children's window and went to sleep.

In spite of her loneliness and grief the life of the island prisoner during the next two or three weeks was by no means one of hardship. Besides her abundant food of birds and mice she quickly learned to catch tiny fish in the mouth of the rivulet, where salt water and fresh water met. It was an exciting game, and she became expert at dashing the gray tom-cod and blue-and-silver sand-lance far up the slope with a sweep of her armed paw. But when the equinoctial storms roared down upon the island, with furious rain, and low, black clouds torn to shreds, then life became more difficult for her. Game all took to cover, where it was hard to find. It was difficult to get around in the drenched and lashing grass; and, moreover, she loathed wet. Most of the time she went hungry, sitting sullen and desolate under the lee of the house, glaring out defiantly at the rush and battling tumult of the waves.

The storm lasted nearly ten days before it blew itself clean out. On the eighth day the abandoned wreck of a small Nova Scotia schooner drove ashore, battered out of all likeness to a ship. But hulk as it was it had passengers of a sort. A horde of rats got through the surf and scurried into the hiding of the grass roots. They promptly made themselves at home, burrowing under the grass and beneath old, half-buried timbers, and carrying panic into the ranks of the mice and shrews.

When the storm was over the cat had a decided surprise in her first long hunting expedition. Something had rustled the grass heavily and she trailed it, expecting a particularly large, fat marsh mouse. When she pounced and alighted up an immense old ship's rat, many-voyaged and many-battled, she got badly bitten. Such an experience had never before fallen to her lot. At first she felt so injured that she was on the point of backing out and running away. Then her latent pugnacity awoke, and the fire of far-off ancestors. She flung herself into the fight with a rage that took no accounting of the wounds she got; and the struggle was soon over. Her wounds, faithfully licked, quickly healed themselves in that clean and tonic air; and after that, having learned how to handle such big game, she no more got bitten.

During the first full moon after her abandonment—the first week in October—the island was visited by still weather with sharp night frosts. The cat discovered then that it was most exciting to hunt by night and do her sleeping in the daytime. She found that now, under the strange whiteness of the moon, all her game was astir—except the birds, which had fled to the mainland during the storm, gathering for the southward flight. The blanched grasses, she found, were now everywhere a-rustle; and everywhere dim little shapes went darting with thin squeaks across ghostly-white sands. Also she made the acquaintance of a new bird, which she regarded at first uneasily and then with vengeful wrath. This was the brown marsh owl, which came over from the mainland to do some autumn mouse hunting. There were two pairs of these big, downy-winged, round-eyed hunters, and they did not know there was a cat on the island.

The cat, spying one of them as it swooped soundlessly hither and thither over the silvered grass tops, crouched with flattened ears. With its wide spread of wing it looked bigger than herself; and the great round face, with hooked beak and wild, staring eyes, appeared extremely formidable. However, she was no coward; and presently, though not without reasonable caution, she went about her hunting. Suddenly the owl caught a partial glimpse of her in the grass—probably of her ears or head. He swooped; and at the same instant she sprang upward to meet the assault, spitting and growling harshly and striking with unsheathed claws. With a frantic flapping of his great wings the owl checked himself and drew back into the air, just escaping the clutch of those indignant claws. After that the marsh owls were careful to give her a wide berth. They realized that the black-striped animal with the quick spring and the clutching claws was not to be interfered with. They perceived that she was some relation to that ferocious prowler, the lynx.

In spite of all this hunting, however, the furry life of the marsh grass was so teeming, so inexhaustible, that the depredations of cat, rats and owls were powerless to make more than a passing impression upon it. So the hunting and the merrymaking went on side by side under the indifferent moon.

As the winter deepened—with bursts of sharp cold and changing winds that forced the cat to be continually changing her refuge— she grew more and more unhappy. She felt her homelessness keenly. Nowhere on the whole island could she find a nook where she might feel secure from both wind and rain. As for the old barrel, the first cause of her misfortunes, there was no help in that. The winds had long ago turned it completely over, open to the sky, then drifted it full of sand and reburied it. And in any case the cat would have been afraid to go near it again. So it came about that she alone of all the island dwellers had no shelter to turn to when the real winter arrived, with snows that smothered the grass tops out of sight, and frosts that lined the shore with grinding ice cakes. The rats had their holes under the buried fragments of wreckage; the mice and shrews had their deep, warm tunnels; the owls had nests in hollow trees far away in the forests of the mainland. But the cat, shivering and frightened, could do nothing but crouch against the blind walls of the unrelenting house and let the snow whirl itself and pile itself about her.

And now, in her misery, she found her food cut off. The mice ran secure in their hidden runways, where the grass roots on each side of them gave them easy and abundant provender. The rats, too, were out of sight—digging burrows themselves in the soft snow in the hope of intercepting some of the tunnels of the mice, and now and then snapping up an unwary passerby. The ice fringe, crumbling and heaving under the ruthless tide, put an end to her fishing. She would have tried to capture one of the formidable owls in her hunger, but the owls no longer came to the island. They would return, no doubt, later in the season when the snow had hardened and the mice had begun to come out and play on the surface. But for the present they were following an easier chase in the deeps of the upland forest.

When the snow stopped falling and the sun came out again there fell such keen cold as the cat had never felt before. The day, as it chanced, was Christmas; and if the cat had had any idea as to the calendar she would certainly have marked the day in her memory as it was an eventful one for her. Starving as she was she could not sleep, but kept ceaselessly on the prowl. This was fortunate, for had she gone to sleep without any more shelter than the wall of the house she would never have wakened again. In her restlessness she wandered to the farther side of the island where, in a somewaht sheltered and sunny recess of the shore facing the mainland, she found a patch of bare sand, free of ice cakes and just uncovered by the tide. Opening upon this recess were the tiny entrances to several of the mouse tunnels.

Close beside one of these holes in the snow the cat crouched, quiveringly intent. For ten minutes or more she waited, never so much as twitching a whisker. At last a mouse thrust out its little pointed head. Not daring to give it time to change its mind or take alarm she pounced. The mouse, glimpsing the doom ere it fell, doubled back upon itself in the narrow runway. Hardly realizing what she did in her desperation the cat plunged head and shoulders into the snow, reaching blindly after the vanished prize. By great good luck she caught it.

It was her first meal in four bitter days. The children had always tried to share with her their Christmas cheer and enthusiasm, and had usually succeeded in interesting her by an agreeable lavishness in the matter of cream; but never before had she found a Christmas feast so good.

Now she had learned a lesson. Being naturally clever and her wits sharpened by her fierce necessities, she had grasped the idea that it was possible to follow her prey a little way into the snow. She had not realized that the snow was so penetrable. She had quite wiped out the door of this particular runway; so she went and crouched beside a similar one, but here she had to wait a long time before an adventurous mouse came to peer out. But this time she showed that she had grasped her lesson. It was straight at the side of the entrance that she pounced, where instinct told her that the body of the mouse would be. One outstretched paw thus cut off the quarry's retreat. Her tactics were completely successful; and as her head went plunging into the fluffy whiteness she felt the prize between her paws.

Her hunger now fairly appeased, she found herself immensely excited over this new fashion of hunting. Often before had she waited at mouse holes, but never had she found it possible to break down the walls and invade the holes themselves. It was a thrilling idea. As she crept toward another hole a mouse scurried swiftly up the sand and darted into it. The cat, too late to catch him before he disappeared, tried to follow him. Scratching clumsily but hopefully she succeeded in forcing the full length of her body into the snow. She found no sign of the fugitive, which was by this time racing in safety down some dim transverse tunnel. Her eyes, mouth, whiskers and fur full of the powdery white particles, she backed out, much disappointed. But in that moment she had realized that it was much warmer in there beneath the snow than out in the stinging air. It was a second and vitally important lesson; and though she was probably unconscious of having learned it she instinctively put the new lore into practice a little while later.

Having succeeded in catching yet another mouse for which her appetite made no immediate demand, she carried it back to the house and laid it down in tribute on the veranda steps while she meowed and stared hopefully at the desolate, snow-draped door. Getting no response she carried the mouse down with her to the hollow behind the drift which had been caused by the bulging front of the bay-window on the end of the house. Here she curled herself up forlornly, thinking to have a wink of sleep.

But the still cold was too searching. She looked at the sloping wall of snow beside her and cautiously thrust her paw into it. It was very soft and light. It seemed to offer practically no resistance. She pawed away in an awkward fashion till she had scooped out a sort of tiny cave. Gently she pushed herself into it, pressing back the snow on every side till she had room to turn around.

Then turn around she did several times, as dogs do in getting their beds arranged to their liking. In this process she not only packed down the snow beneath her, but she also rounded out for herself a snug chamber with a comparatively narrow doorway. From this snowy retreat she gazed forth with a solemn air of possession; then she went to sleep with a sense of comfort, of "homeyness," such as she had never before felt since the disappearance of her friends.

Having thus conquered misfortune and won herself the freedom of the winter wild, her life though strenuous was no longer one of any terrible hardship. With patience at the mouse holes she could catch enough to eat; and in her snowy den she slept warm and secure. In a little while, when a crust had formed over the surface, the mice took to coming out at night and holding revels on the snow. Then the owls, too, came back; and the cat, having tried to catch one, got sharply bitten and clawed before she realized the propriety of letting it go. After this experience she decided that owls, on the whole, were meant to be let alone. But for all that she found it fine hunting, out there on the bleak, unfenced, white reaches of the snow.

Thus, mistress of the situation, she found the winter slipping by without further serious trials. Only once, toward the end of January, did Fate send her another bad quarter of an hour. On the heels of a peculiarly bitter cold snap a huge white owl from the Arctic Barrens came one night to the island. The cat, taking observations from the corner of the veranda, caught sight of him. One look was enough to assure her that this was a very different kind of visitor from the brown marsh owls. She slipped inconspicuously down into her burrow; and until the great white owl went away, some twenty-four hours later, she kept herself discreetly out of sight.

When spring came back to the island, with the nightly shrill chorus of fluting frogs in the shallow, sedgy pools and the young grass alive with nesting birds, the prisoner's life became almost luxurious in its easy abundance. But now she was once more homeless, since her snug den had vanished with the snow. This did not much matter to her, however, for the weather grew warmer and more tranquil day by day; and moreover, she herself, in being forced back upon her instincts, had learned to be as contented as a tramp. Nevertheless, with all her capacity for learning and adapting herself she had not forgotten anything. So when, one day in June, a crowded boat came over from the mainland, and children's voices, clamoring across the grass tops, broke the desolate silence of the island, the cat heard and sprang up out of her sleep on the veranda steps.

For one second she stood, listening intently. Then, almost as a dog would have done, and as few of her supercilious tribe ever condescend to do, she went racing across to the landing place—to be snatched up into the arms of four happy children at once, and to have her fine fur ruffled to a state which it would cost her an hour's assiduous toilet to put in order.

A Black Affair

W. W. JACOBS

"I DIDN'T want to bring it," said Captain Gubson, regarding somewhat unfavorably a grey parrot whose cage was hanging against the main-mast, "but my old uncle was so set on it I had to. He said a sea-voyage would set its 'elth up."

"It seems to be all right at present," said the mate, who was ten-derly sucking his forefinger; "best of spirits, I should say."

"It's playful," assented the skipper. "The old man thinks a rare lot of it. I think I shall have a little bit in that quarter, so keep your eye on the beggar."

"Scratch Poll!" said the parrot, giving its bill a preliminary strop on its perch. "Scratch poor Polly!"

It bent its head against the bars, and waited patiently to play off what it had always regarded as the most consummate practical joke in existence. The first doubt it had ever had about it occurred when the mate came forward and obligingly scratched it with the stem of his pipe. It was a wholly unforeseen development, and the parrot, ruffling its feathers, edged along its perch and brooded darkly at the other end of it.

Opinion before the mast was also against the new arrival, the gen-eral view being that the wild jealousy which raged in the bosom of the ship's cat would sooner or later lead to mischief.

"Old Satan don't like it," said the cook, shaking his head. "The blessed bird hadn't been aboard ten minutes before Satan was prowl-ing around. The blooming image waited till he was about a foot off the cage, and then he did the perlite and asked him whether he'd like a glass o' beer. *I* never see a cat so took aback in all my life. Never."

"There'll be trouble between 'em," said old Sam, who was the cat's special protector, "mark my words."

"I'd put my money on the parrot," said one of the men confidently. "It's 'ad a crool bit out of the mate's finger. Where 'ud the cat be again that beak?"

"Well, you'd lose your money," said Sam. "If you want to do the cat a kindness, every time you see him near that cage cuff his 'ed."

The crew being much attached to the cat, which had been presented to them when a kitten by the mate's wife, acted upon the advice with so much zest that for the next two days the indignant animal was like to have been killed with kindness. On the third day, however, the parrot's cage being on the cabin table, the cat stole furtively down, and, at the pressing request of the occupant itself, scratched its head for it.

The skipper was the first to discover the mischief, and he came on deck and published the news in a voice which struck a chill to all hearts.

"Where's that black devil got to?" he yelled.

"Anything wrong, sir?" asked Sam anxiously.

"Come and look here," said the skipper. He led the way to the cabin, where the mate and one of the crew were already standing, shaking their heads over the parrot.

"What do you make of that?" demanded the skipper fiercely.

"Too much dry food, sir," said Sam, after due deliberation.

"Too much what?" bellowed the skipper.

"Too much dry food," repeated Sam firmly. "A parrot—a grey parrot—wants plenty o' sop. If it don't get it, it moults."

"It's had too much *cat*," said the skipper fiercely, "and you know it, and overboard it goes."

"I don't believe it was the cat, sir," interposed the other man; "it's too soft-hearted to do a thing like that."

"You can shut your jaw," said the skipper, reddening. "Who asked you to come down here at all?"

"Nobody saw the cat do it," urged the mate.

The skipper said nothing, but, stooping down, picked up a tail feather from the floor, and laid it on the table. He then went on deck, followed by the others, and began calling, in seductive tones, for the cat. No reply forthcoming from the sagacious animal, which had gone into hiding, he turned to Sam, and bade him call it.

"No, sir, I won't 'ave no 'and in it," said the old man. "Putting aside my liking for the animal, *I'm* not going to 'ave anything to do with the killing of a black cat."

"Rubbish!" said the skipper.

"Very good, sir," said Sam, shrugging his shoulders, "you know best, o' course. You're eddicated and I'm not, an' p'raps you can afford to make a laugh o' such things. I knew one man who killed a black cat an' he went mad. There's something very pecooliar about that cat o' ours."

"It knows more than we do," said one of the crew, shaking his head. "That time you—I mean we—ran the smack down, that cat was expecting of it 'ours before. It was like a wild thing."

"Look at the weather we've 'ad—look at the trips we've made since he's been aboard," said the old man. "Tell me it's chance if you like, but I *know* better."

The skipper hesitated. He was a superstitious man even for a sailor, and his weakness was so well known that he had become a sympathetic receptacle for every ghost story which, by reason of its crudeness or lack of corroboration, had been rejected by other experts. He was a perfect reference library for omens, and his interpretations of dreams had gained for him a widespread reputation.

"That's all nonsense," he said, pausing uneasily; "still, I only want to be just. There's nothing vindictive about me, and I'll have no hand in it myself. Joe, just tie a lump of coal to that cat and heave it overboard."

"Not me," said the cook, following Sam's lead, and working up a shudder. "Not for fifty pun in gold. I don't want to be haunted."

"The parrot's a little better now, sir," said one of the men, taking advantage of his hesitation, "he's opened one eye."

"Well, I only want to be just," repeated the skipper. "I won't do anything in a hurry, but, mark my words, if the parrot dies that cat goes overboard."

Contrary to expectations, the bird was still alive when London was reached, though the cook, who from his connection with the cabin had suddenly reached a position of unusual importance, reported great loss of strength and irritability of temper. It was still alive, but failing fast on the day they were put to sea again; and the fo'c'sle, in preparation for the worst, stowed their pet away in the paint-locker, and discussed the situation.

Their council was interrupted by the mysterious behaviour of the cook, who, having gone out to lay in a stock of bread, suddenly broke in upon them more in the manner of a member of a secret society than a humble but useful unit of a ship's company.

"Where's the cap'n?" he asked in a hoarse whisper, as he took a seat on the locker with the sack of bread between his knees.

"In the cabin," said Sam, regarding his antics with some disfavour. "What's wrong, cookie?"

"What d' yer think I've got in here?" asked the cook, patting the bag.

The obvious reply to this question was, of course, bread; but as it was known that the cook had departed specially to buy some, and that he could hardly ask a question involving such a simple answer, nobody gave it.

"It come to me all of a sudden," said the cook, in a thrilling whisper. "I'd just bought the bread and left the shop, when I see a big black cat, the very image of ours, sitting on a doorstep. I just stooped down to stroke its 'ed, when it come to me."

"They will sometimes," said one of the seamen.

"I don't mean that," said the cook, with the contempt of genius. "I mean the idea did. Ses I to myself, 'You might be old Satan's brother by the look of you; an' if the cap'n wants to kill a cat, let it be you,' I ses. And with that, before it could say Jack Robinson, I picked it up by the scruff o' the neck and shoved it in the bag."

"What, all in along of our bread?" said the previous interrupter, in a pained voice.

"Some of yer are 'ard ter please," said the cook, deeply offended.

"Don't mind him, cook," said the admiring Sam. "You're a masterpiece, that's what you are."

"Of course, if any of you've got a better plan—" said the cook generously.

"Don't talk rubbish, cook," said Sam; "fetch the two cats out and put 'em together."

"Don't mix 'em," said the cook warningly; "for you'll never know which is which agin if you do."

He cautiously opened the top of the sack and produced his captive, and Satan, having been relieved from his prison, the two animals were carefully compared.

"They're as like as two lumps o' coal," said Sam slowly. "Lord, what a joke on the old man. I must tell the mate o' this; he'll enjoy it."

"It'll be all right if the parrot don't die," said the dainty pessimist, still harping on his pet theme. "All that bread spoilt, and two cats aboard."

"Don't mind what he ses," said Sam; "you're a brick, that's what you are. I'll just make a few holes on the lid o' the boy's chest, and pop old Satan in. You don't mind, do you, Billy?"

"Of course he don't," said the other men indignantly.

Matters being thus agreeably arranged, Sam got a gimlet, and prepared the chest for the reception of its tenant, who, convinced that he was being put out of the way to make room for a rival, made a frantic fight for freedom.

"Now get something 'eavy and put on the top of it," said Sam, having convinced himself that the lock was broken; "and, Billy, put the noo cat in the paint-locker till we start; it's home-sick."

The boy obeyed, and the understudy was kept in durance vile until they were off Limehouse, when he came on deck and nearly ended his career there and then by attempting to jump over the bulwark into the next garden. For some time he paced the deck in a perturbed fashion, and then, leaping on the stern, mewed plaintively as his native city receded farther and farther from his view.

"What's the matter with old Satan?" said the mate, who had been let into the secret. "He seems to have something on his mind."

"He'll have something round his neck presently," said the skipper grimly.

The prophecy was fulfilled some three hours later, when he came up on deck ruefully regarding the remains of a bird whose vocabulary had once been the pride of its native town. He threw it overboard without a word, and then, seizing the innocent cat, who had followed him under the impression that it was about to lunch, produced half a brick attached to a string, and tied it round his neck. The crew, who were enjoying the joke immensely, raised a howl of protest.

"The *Skylark*'ll never have another like it, sir," said Sam solemnly. "That cat was the luck of the ship."

"I don't want any of your old woman's yarns," said the skipper brutally. "If you want the cat, go and fetch it."

He stepped aft as he spoke, and sent the gentle stranger hurtling through the air. There was a "plomp" as it reached the water, a bubble or two came to the surface, and all was over.

"That's the last o' that," he said, turning away.

The old man shook his head. "You can't kill a black cat for nothing," said he, "mark my words!"

The skipper, who was in a temper at the time, thought little of them, but they recurred to him vividly the next day. The wind had freshened during the night, and rain was falling heavily. On deck the crew stood about in oilskins, while below, the boy, in his new capacity of gaoler, was ministering to the wants of an ungrateful prisoner, when the cook, happening to glance that way, was horrified to see the animal emerge from the fo'c'sle. It eluded easily the frantic clutch of the boy as he sprang up the ladder after it, and walked leisurely along the deck in the direction of the cabin. Just as the crew had given it up for lost it encountered Sam, and the next moment, despite its cries, was caught up and huddled away beneath his stiff clammy oilskins. At the noise the skipper, who was talking to the mate, turned as though he had been shot, and gazed wildly round him.

"Dick," said he, "can you hear a cat?"

"Cat!" said the mate, in accents of great astonishment.

"I thought I heard it," said the puzzled skipper.

"Fancy, sir," said Dick firmly, as a mewing, appalling in its wrath, came from beneath Sam's coat.

"Did you hear it, Sam?" called the skipper, as the old man was moving off.

"Hear what, sir?" inquired Sam respectfully, without turning round.

"Nothing," said the skipper, collecting himself. "Nothing. All right."

The old man, hardly able to believe in his good fortune, made his way forward, and, seizing a favourable opportunity, handed his ungrateful burden back to the boy.

"Fancy you heard a cat just now?" inquired the mate casually.

"Well, between you an' me, Dick," said the skipper, in a mysterious voice, "I did, and it wasn't fancy neither. I heard that cat as plain as if it was alive."

"Well, I've heard of such things," said the other, "but I don't believe 'em. What a lark if the old cat comes back climbing up over the side out of the sea to-night, with the brick hanging round its neck."

The skipper stared at him for some time without speaking. "If that's your idea of a lark," he said at length, in a voice which betrayed traces of some emotion, "it ain't mine."

"Well, if you hear it again," said the mate cordially, "you might let me know. I'm rather interested in such things."

The skipper, hearing no more of it that day, tried hard to persuade himself that he was the victim of imagination, but, in spite of this, he was pleased at night, as he stood at the wheel, to reflect on the sense of companionship afforded by the look-out in the bows. On his part the look-out was quite charmed with the unwonted affability of the skipper, as he yelled out to him two or three times on matters only faintly connected with the progress of the schooner.

The night, which had been dirty, cleared somewhat, and the bright crescent of the moon appeared above a heavy bank of clouds, as the cat, which had by dint of using its back as a lever at length got free from that cursed chest, licked its shapely limbs, and came up on deck. After its stifling prison, the air was simply delicious.

"Bob!" yelled the skipper suddenly.

"Ay, ay, sir!" said the look-out, in a startled voice.

"Did you mew?" inquired the skipper.

"Did I *wot,* sir?" cried the astonished Bob.

"Mew," said the skipper sharply, "like a cat?"

"No, sir," said the offended seaman. "What 'ud I want to do that for?"

"I don't know what you want to for," said the skipper, looking round him uneasily. "There's some more rain coming, Bob."

"Ay, ay, sir," said Bob.

"Lot o' rain we've had this summer," said the skipper, in a meditative bawl.

"Ay, ay, sir," said Bob. "Sailing-ship on the port bow, sir."

The conversation dropped, the skipper, anxious to divert his thoughts, watching the dark mass of sail as it came plunging out of the darkness into the moonlight until it was abreast of his own craft. His eyes followed it as it passed his quarter, so that he saw not the stealthy approach of the cat which came from behind the companion, and sat down close by him. For over thirty hours the animal had been subjected to the grossest indignities at the hands of every man on board the ship except one. That one was the skipper, and there is no doubt but that its subsequent behaviour was a direct recognition of that fact. It rose to its feet, and crossing over to the unconscious skipper, rubbed its head affectionately and vigorously against his leg.

From simple causes great events do spring. The skipper sprang four yards, and let off a screech which was the subject of much comment on the barque which had just passed. When Bob, who came shuffling up at the double, reached him he was leaning against the side, incapable of speech, and shaking all over.

"Anything wrong, sir?" inquired the seaman anxiously, as he ran to the wheel.

The skipper pulled himself together a bit, and got closer to his companion.

"Believe me or not, Bob," he said at length, in trembling accents, "just as you please, but the ghost of that—cat, I mean the ghost of that poor affectionate animal which I drowned, and which I wish I hadn't, came and rubbed itself up against my leg."

"Which leg?" inquired Bob, who was ever careful about details.

"What the blazes does it matter which leg?" demanded the skipper, whose nerves were in a terrible state. "Ah, look—look there!"

The seaman followed his outstretched finger, and his heart failed him as he saw the cat, with its back arched, gingerly picking its way along the side of the vessel.

"I can't see nothing," he said doggedly.

"I don't suppose you can, Bob," said the skipper in a melancholy voice, as the cat vanished in the bows; "it's evidently only meant for me to see. What it means I don't know. I'm going down to turn in. I ain't fit for duty. You don't mind being left alone till the mate comes up, do you?"

"I ain't afraid," said Bob.

His superior officer disappeared below, and, shaking the sleepy mate, who protested strongly against the proceedings, narrated in trembling tones his horrible experiences.

"If I were you—" said the mate.

"Yes?" said the skipper, waiting a bit. Then he shook him again, roughly.

"What were you going to say?" he inquired.

"Say?" said the mate, rubbing his eyes. "Nothing."

"About the cat?" suggested the skipper.

"Cat?" said the mate, nestling lovingly down in the blankets again. "Wha' ca'—goo'ni'—"

Then the skipper drew the blankets from the mate's sleepy clutches, and, rolling him backwards and forwards in the bunk, patiently explained to him that he was very unwell, that he was going to have a drop of whiskey neat, and turn in, and that he, the mate, was to take the watch. From this moment the joke lost much of its savour for the mate.

"You can have a nip too, Dick," said the skipper, proffering him the whiskey, as the other sullenly dressed himself.

"It's all rot," said the mate, tossing the spirits down his throat, "and it's no use either; you can't run away from a ghost; it's just as likely to be in your bed as anywhere else. Good night."

He left the skipper pondering over his last words, and dubiously eyeing the piece of furniture in question. Nor did he retire until he had subjected it to an analysis of the most searching description, and then, leaving the lamp burning, he sprang hastily in, and forgot his troubles in sleep.

It was day when he awoke, and went on deck to find a heavy sea running, and just sufficient sail set to keep the schooner's head before the wind as she bobbed about on the waters. An exclamation from the skipper, as a wave broke against the side and flung a cloud of spray over him, brought the mate's head round.

"Why, you ain't going to get up?" he said, in tones of insincere surprise.

"Why not?" inquired the other gruffly.

"You go and lay down agin," said the mate, "and have a cup o' nice hot tea an' some toast."

"Clear out," said the skipper, making a dash for the wheel, and reaching it as the wet deck suddenly changed its angle. "I know you didn't like being woke up, Dick; but I got the horrors last night. Go below and turn in."

"All right," said the mollified mate.

"You didn't see anything?" inquired the skipper, as he took the wheel from him.

"Nothing at all," said the other.

The skipper shook his head thoughtfully, then shook it again vigorously, as another shower-bath put its head over the side and saluted him.

"I wish I hadn't drowned that cat, Dick," he said.

"You won't see it again," said Dick, with the confidence of a man who had taken every possible precaution to render the prophecy a safe one.

He went below, leaving the skipper at the wheel idly watching the cook as he performed marvellous feats of jugglery, between the galley and the fo'c'sle, with the men's breakfast.

A little while later, leaving the wheel to Sam, he went below him-

self and had his own, talking freely, to the discomfort of the con-
science-stricken cook, about his weird experiences of the night before.

"You won't see it no more, sir, I don't expect," he said faintly; "I
b'leeve it come and rubbed itself up agin your leg to show it forgave
you."

"Well, I hope it knows it's understood," said the other. "I don't
want it to take any more trouble."

He finished the breakfast in silence, and then went on deck again.
It was still blowing hard, and he went over to superintend the men
who were attempting to lash together some empties which were rolling about in all directions amidships. A violent roll set them free
again, and at the same time separated two chests in the fo'c'sle, which
were standing one on top of the other. This enabled Satan, who was
crouching in the lower one, half crazed with terror, to come flying
madly up on deck and give his feelings full vent. Three times in full
view of the horrified skipper he circled the deck at racing speed, and
had just started on the fourth when a heavy packing-case, which had
been temporarily set on end and abandoned by the men at his sudden appearance, fell over and caught him by the tail. Sam rushed to
the rescue.

"Stop!" yelled the skipper.

"Won't I put it up, sir?" inquired Sam.

"Do you see what's beneath it?" said the skipper, in a husky voice.

"Beneath it, sir?" said Sam, whose ideas were in a whirl.

"The cat, can't you see the cat?" said the skipper, whose eyes had
been riveted on the animal since its first appearance on deck.

Sam hesitated a moment, and then shook his head.

"The case has fallen on the cat," said the skipper, "I can see it
distinctly."

He might have said "heard it," too, for Satan was making frenzied
appeals to his sympathetic friends for assistance.

"Let me put the case back, sir," said one of the men, "then p'raps
the wision'll disappear."

"No, stop where you are," said the skipper. "I can stand it better
by daylight. It's the most wonderful and extraordinary thing I've
ever seen. Do you mean to say you can't see anything, Sam?"

"I can see a case, sir," said Sam, speaking slowly and carefully,
"with a bit of rusty iron band sticking out from it. That's what
you're mistaking for the cat, p'raps, sir."

"Can't you see anything, cook?" demanded the skipper.

"It may be fancy, sir," faltered the cook, lowering his eyes, "but it does seem to me as though I can see a little misty sort o' thing there. Ah, now it's gone."

"No, it ain't," said the skipper. "The ghost of Satan's sitting there. The case seems to have fallen on its tail. It appears to be howling something dreadful."

The men made a desperate effort to display the astonishment suitable to such a marvel, whilst Satan, who was trying all he knew to get his tail out, cursed freely. How long the superstitious captain of the *Skylark* would have let him remain there will never be known, for just then the mate came on deck and caught sight of it before he was quite aware of the part he was expected to play.

"Why the devil don't you lift the thing off the poor brute," he yelled, hurrying up towards the case.

"What, can *you* see it, Dick?" said the skipper impressively, laying his hand on his arm.

"*See* it?" retorted the mate, "D'ye think I'm blind? Listen to the poor brute. I should— Oh!"

He became conscious of the concentrated significant gaze of the crew. Five pairs of eyes speaking as one, all saying "idiot" plainly, the boy's eyes conveying an expression too great to be translated.

Turning, the skipper saw the byplay, and a light slowly dawned upon him. But he wanted more, and he wheeled suddenly to the cook for the required illumination.

The cook said it was a lark. Then he corrected himself and said it wasn't a lark, then he corrected himself again and became incoherent. Meantime the skipper eyed him stonily, while the mate released the cat and good-naturedly helped to straighten its tail.

It took fully five minutes of unwilling explanation before the skipper could grasp the situation. He did not appear to fairly understand it until he was shown the chest with the ventilated lid; then his countenance cleared, and, taking the unhappy Billy by the collar, he called sternly for a piece of rope.

By this statesmanlike handling of the subject a question of much delicacy and difficulty was solved, discipline was preserved, and a practical illustration of the perils of deceit afforded to a youngster who was at an age best suited to receive such impressions. That he should exhaust the resources of a youthful but powerful vocabulary upon the crew in general, and Sam in particular, was only to be expected. They bore him no malice for it, but, when he showed signs of going beyond his years, held a hasty consultation, and then stopped his mouth with sixpence-halfpenny and a broken jack-knife.

The Cat of the Cane-brake

FREDERICK STUART GREENE

SALLY! O-oh, Sally! I'm a-goin' now." Jim Gantt pushed back the limp brim of his rusty felt hat and turned colorless eyes toward the cabin.

A young woman came from around the corner of the house. From each hand dangled a bunch of squawking chickens. She did not speak until she had reached the wagon.

"Now, Jim, you ain't a-goin' to let them fellers down in Andalushy git you inter no blind tiger, air you?" The question came in a hopeless drawl; hopeless, too, her look into the man's sallow face.

"I ain't teched a drop in more'n three months, had I?" Jim's answer was in a sullen key.

"No, Jim, you bin doin' right well lately." She tossed the chickens into the wagon, thoughtless of the hurt to their tied and twisted legs. "They're worth two bits apiece, that comes to two dollars, Jim. Don't you take a nickel less'n that."

Jim gave a listless pull at the cotton rope that served as reins.

"Git up thar, mule!" he called, and the wagon creaked off on wobbling wheels down the hot, dusty road.

The woman looked scornfully at the man's humped-over back for a full minute, turned and walked to the house, a hard smile at her mouth.

Sally Gantt gave no heed to her drab surroundings as she crossed the short stretch from road to cabin. All her twenty-two years had been spent in this far end of Alabama, where one dreary, unkempt clearing in the pine-woods is as dismal as the next. Comparisons which might add their fuel to her smouldering discontent, were spared her. Yet, unconsciously, this bare, grassless country with its flat miles of monotonous pine forest, its flatter miles of rank cane-brake, served to distill a bitter gall, poisoning all her thoughts.

The double cabin of Jim Gantt, its two rooms separated by a "dog-trot"—an open porch cut through the center of the structure—was

313

counted a thing of luxury by his scattered neighbors. Gantt had built it four years before, when he took up the land as his homestead, and Sally for his wife. The labor of building this cabin had apparently drained his stock of energy to the dregs. Beyond the necessary toil of planting a small patch of corn, a smaller one of sweet potatoes and fishing in the sluggish water of Pigeon Creek, he now did nothing. Sally tended the chickens, their one source of money, and gave intermittent attention to the half-dozen razor-back hogs, which, with the scrubby mule, comprised their toll of livestock.

As the woman mounted the hewn log that answered as a step to the dog-trot she stopped to listen. From the kitchen came a faint noise; a sound of crunching. Sally went on silent feet to the door. On the table, littered with unwashed dishes, a cat was gnawing at a fish head; a gaunt beast, its lean flanks covered with wiry fur, except where ragged scars left exposed the bare hide. Its strong jaws crushed through the thick skullbone of the fish as if it were an empty bird's egg.

Sally sprang to the stove and seized a pine knot.

"Dog-gone your yaller hide!" she screamed. "Git out of hyar!"

The cat wheeled with a start and faced the woman, its evil eyes glittering.

"Git, you yaller devil!" the woman screamed again.

The cat sprang sidewise to the floor. Sally sent the jagged piece of wood spinning through the air. It crashed against the far wall, missing the beast by an inch. The animal arched its huge body and held its ground.

"You varmint, I'll git you this time!" Sally stooped for another piece of wood. The cat darted through the door ahead of the flying missile.

"I'll kill you yit!" Sally shouted after it. "An' he kain't hinder me neither!"

She sat down heavily and wiped the sweat from her forehead.

It was several minutes before the woman rose from the chair and crossed the dog-trot to the sleeping-room. Throwing her faded sun-bonnet into a corner, she loosened her hair and began to brush it.

Sally Gantt was neither pretty nor handsome. But in a country peopled solely by pine-woods Crackers, her black hair and eyes, clear skin and white teeth, made her stand out. She was a woman, and young. To a man, also young, who for two years had seen no face unpainted with the sallow hue of chills and fever, no eyes except faded blue ones framed by white, straggling lashes, no sound teeth, and the unsound ones stained always by the snuff stick, she might easily appear alluring.

With feminine deftness Sally recoiled her hair. She took from a wooden peg a blue calico dress, its printed pattern as yet unbleached by the fierce suns. It gave her slender figure some touch of grace. From beneath the bed she drew a pair of heavy brogans; a shoe fashioned, doubtless, to match the listless nature of the people who most use them; slipping on or off without hindrance from lace or buckle. As a final touch, she fastened about her head a piece of blue ribbon, the band of cheap silk making the flash in her black eyes the brighter.

Sally left the house and started across the rubbish-littered yard. A short distance from the cabin she stopped to look about her.

"I'm dog-tired of it all," she said fiercely. "I hates the house. I hates the whole place, an' more'n all I hates Jim."

She turned, scowling, and walked between the rows of growing corn that reached to the edge of the clearing. Here began the pine-woods, the one saving touch nature has given to this land. Beneath the grateful shade she hastened her steps. The trees stood in endless disordered ranks, rising straight and bare of branch until high aloft their spreading tops caught the sunlight.

A quarter of a mile brought her to the lowland. She went down the slight decline and stepped within the cane-brake. Here gloom closed about her, the thickly growing cane reached to twice her height. Above the cane the cypress spread its branches, draped with the sad, gray moss of the South. No sun's ray struggled through the rank foliage to lighten the sodden earth beneath. Sally picked her way slowly through the swamp, peering cautiously beyond each fallen log before venturing a further step. Crawfish scuttled backward from her path to slip down the mud chimneys of their homes. The black earth and decaying plants filled the hot, still air with noisome odors. Thousands of hidden insects sounded through the dank stretches their grating calls. Slimy water oozed from beneath the heavy soles of her brogans, green and purple bubbles were left in each footprint, bubbles with iridescent oily skins.

As she went around a sharp turn she was caught up and lifted clear from the ground in the arms of a young man—a boy of twenty or thereabout.

"Oh, Bob, you scairt me—you certainly air rough!"

Without words he kissed her again and again.

"Now, Bob, you quit! Ain't you had enough?"

"Could I ever have enough? Oh, Sally, I love you so!" The words trembled from the boy.

"You certainly ain't like none of 'em 'round hyar, Bob." There was some pride in Sally's drawling voice. "I never seed none of them menfolks act with gals like you does."

"There's no other girl like you to make them." Then holding her from him he went on fiercely, "You don't let any of them try it, do you?"

Sally smiled up into his glowing eyes.

"You knows I don't. They'd be afeard of Jim."

The blood rushed to the boy's cheeks, his arms dropped to his side —he stood sobered.

"Sally, we can't go on this way any longer, that's why I asked you to come to the river today."

"What's a-goin' to stop us?" A frightened look crossed the woman's face.

"I'm going away."

She made a quick step toward him.

"You ain't lost your job on the new railroad?"

"No—come down to the boat where we can talk this over."

He helped her down the bank of the creek to a flat-bottomed skiff, and seated her with a touch of courtesy in the stern before taking the cross seat facing her.

"No, I haven't lost my job," he began earnestly, "but my section of the road is about finished. They'll move me farther up the line in about a week."

She sat silent for a moment, her black eyes wide with question. He searched them for some sign of sorrow.

"What kin I do after you air gone?"

There was a hopeless note in her voice—it pleased the boy.

"That's the point—instead of letting them move me, I'm going to move myself."

He paused that she might get the full meaning of his coming words.

"I'm going away from here tonight, and I'm going to take you away with me."

"No, no! I dasn't!" She shrank before his steady gaze.

He moved swiftly across to her—throwing his arms around her, he poured out his words.

"Yes! You will! You must! You love me, don't you?"

Sally nodded in helpless assent.

"Better than anything in this world?"

Again Sally nodded. The boy kissed her.

"Then listen. Tonight at twelve you come to the river—I'll be waiting for you at the edge of the swamp. We'll row down to Brewton; we can easily catch the 6:20 to Mobile, and, once there, we'll begin to live," he finished grandly.

"But I can't! Air you crazy? How kin I git away an' Jim right in the house?"

"I've thought of all that; you just let him see this." From beneath the seat he drew a bottle. "You know what he'll do to this—it's the strongest corn whiskey I could find."

"Oh, Bob. I'm ascairt to."

"Don't you love me?" His young eyes looked reproach.

Sally threw both arms about the boy's neck and drew his head down to her lips. Then she pushed him from her.

"Bob, is it so what the menfolks all say, that the railroad gives you a hundred dollars every month?"

He laughed. "Yes, you darling girl, and more. I get a hundred and a quarter, and I've been getting it for two years in this God-forsaken country, and nothing to spend it on. I've got over a thousand dollars saved up."

The woman's eyes widened. She kissed the boy on the mouth.

"They 'lows as how you're the smartest engineer on the road."

The boy's head was held high.

Sally made some mental calculations before she spoke again.

"Oh, Bob, I jes' can't. I'm ascairt to."

He caught her to him. A man of longer experience might have noted the sham in her reluctance.

"My darling, what are you afraid of?" he cried.

"What air we a-goin' to do after we gits to Mobile?"

"Oh, I've thought of everything—they're building a new line down in Texas—we'll go there. I'll get another job as resident engineer. I have my profession," he ended proudly.

"You might git tired, and want to git shed of me, Bob."

He smothered her words under fierce kisses. His young heart beat at bursting pressure. In bright colors he pictured the glory of Mobile, New Orleans, and all the world that lay before them to love each other in.

When Sally left the boat she had promised to come. Where the pine trees meet the cane-brake he would be waiting for her, at midnight.

At the top of the bank she turned to wave.

"Wait! Wait!" called the boy. He rushed up the slope.

"Quit it, Bob, you're hurtin' me." She tore herself from his arms and hastened back alone the slimy path. When she reached the pinewood she paused.

"More'n a thousand dollars!" she murmured. And a slow, satisfied smile crossed her shrewd face.

The sun, now directly over the tops of the trees, shot its scorching rays through the foliage. They struck the earth in vertical shafts, heating it to the burning point. Not a breath stirred the glistening pine needles on the towering branches. It was one of those noon-times which, in the moisture-charged air of southern Alabama, makes life a steaming hell to all living things save reptiles and lovers.

Reaching the cabin, Sally went first to the kitchen room. She opened a cupboard and, taking the cork from the bottle, placed the whiskey on the top shelf and closed the wooden door.

She crossed the dog-trot to the sleeping-room—a spitting snarl greeted her entrance. In the center of the bed crouched the yellow cat, its eyes gleaming, every muscle over its bony frame drawn taut, ready for the spring. The woman, startled, drew back. The cat moved on stiff legs nearer. Unflinchingly they glared into each other's eyes.

"Git out of hyar afore I kill yer! You yaller devil!" Sally's voice rang hard as steel.

The cat stood poised at the edge of the bed, its glistening teeth showing in its wide mouth. Without an instant's shift of her defiant stare, Sally wrenched a shoe from her foot.

The animal with spread claws sprang straight for the woman's throat. The cat and the heavy brogan crashed together in mid-air. Together they fell to the floor—the cat landed lightly, silently, and bounded through the open door.

Sally fell back against the log wall, feeling her throat with trembling fingers.

"Jim! O-h, Jim!" Sally called from the cabin. "Come on in, yer supper's ready."

"He ain't took nothin' to drink today," she thought. "It's nigh three months now; he'll be 'most crazy."

The man took from the ground a few sticks of wood and came on dragging feet through the gloom. As Sally watched his listless approach, she felt in full force the oppressive melancholy of her dismal surroundings. Awakened by the boy's enthusiastic plans, imagination stirred within her. In the distance a girdled pine stood clear-cut against the horizon. Its bark, peeled and fallen, left the dead, naked trunk the color of dried bones. Near the stunted top one bare limb stretched out. Unnoticed a thousand times before, to the woman it looked, tonight, a ghostly gibbet against the black sky.

Sally shuddered and went into the lighted kitchen.

"I jes' kilt a rattler down by the wood-pile." Jim threw down his load and drew a splint-bottomed chair to the table.

"Ground-rattler, Jim?"

"Naw sir-ee! A hell-bendin' big diamond-back."

"Did you hurt the skin?" Sally asked quickly.

"Naw—I chopped his neck clean, short to the haid. An' I done it so durn quick his fangs is a-stickin' out yit, I reckon."

"Did he strike at you?"

"Yes sir-ee, an' the pizen came out of his mouth jes' like a fog."

"Ah, you're foolin' me!"

"No, I ain't neither. I've hearn tell of it but I never seed it afore. The ground was kinda black whar he lit, an' jes' as I brought the axe down on him, thar I seed a little puff like, same as white steam, in front of his mouth."

"How big was he, Jim?"

"'Leven rattles an' a button."

"Did you skin him?"

"Naw, it was too durn dark, but I hung him high up, so's the hawgs won't git at him. His skin'll fotch fo' bits down at Andalushy."

"Ax 'em six, Jim; them big ones gittin' kinda skeerce."

Jim finished his supper in silence—the killing of the snake had provided more conversation than was usual during three meals among pine-woods people.

As Sally was clearing away the dishes, the yellow cat came through the door. Slinking close to the wall, it avoided the woman, and sprang upon the knees of its master. Jim grinned into the eyes of the beast and began stroking its coarse hair. The cat set up a grating purr.

Sally looked at the two for a moment in silence.

"Jim, you gotta kill that cat."

Jim's grin widened, showing his tobacco-stained teeth.

"Jim, I'm a-tellin' you, you gotta kill that cat."

"An' I'm a-tellin' you I won't."

"Jim, it sprung at me today, an' would have hurt me somethin' turrible if I hadn't hit it over the haid with my shoe."

"Well, you must 'a' done somethin' to make him. You leave him alone, an' he won't pester you."

The woman hesitated; she looked at the man as yet undecided; after a moment she spoke again.

"Jim Gantt, I'm axin' you for the las' time, which does you think more'n of, me or that snarlin' varmint?"

"He don't snarl at me so much as you does," the man answered doggedly. "Anyway, I ain't a-goin' to kill him—an' you gotta leave him alone, too. You jes' mind you own business an' go tote the mattress out on the trot. It's too durn hot to sleep in the house."

The woman passed behind him to the cupboard, reached up, opened wide the wooden door and went out of the room.

Jim stoked the cat, its grating purr growing louder in the stillness.

A minute passed.

Into the dull eyes of the man a glitter came—and grew. Slowly he lifted his head. Farther and farther his chin drew up until the cords beneath the red skin of his neck stood out in ridges. The nostrils of his bony nose quivered, he sniffed the hot air like a dog straining to catch a distant scent. His tongue protruded and moved from side to side across his lips.

Standing in the darkness without, the woman smiled grimly.

Abruptly the man arose. The forgotten cat fell, twisted in the air and lighted on its feet. Jim wheeled and strode to the cupboard. As his hand closed about the bottle the gleam in his eyes became burning flames. He jerked the bottle from the shelf, threw his head far back. The fiery liquor ran down his throat. He returned to his seat, the cat rubbed its ribbed flank against his leg, he stooped and lifted it to the table. Waving the bottle in front of the yellow beast, he laughed:

"Here's to yer—an' to'ad yer!" and swallowed half a tumblerful of the colorless liquid.

Sally dragged the shuck mattress to the dog-trot. Fully dressed, she lay waiting for midnight.

An hour went by before Jim shivered the empty bottle against the log wall of the kitchen. Pressing both hands hard upon the table, he heaved himself to his feet, upsetting the candle in the effort. He leered at the flame and slapped his bare palm down on it; the hot, melted wax oozed up, unheeded, between his fingers. Clinging to the table top, he turned himself toward the open door, steadied his swaying body for an instant, then lurched forward. His shoulder crashed against the doorpost, his body spun halfway round. The man fell flat upon his back, missing the mattress by a yard, the back of his head struck hard on the rough boards of the porch floor. He lay motionless, his feet sticking straight up on the doorsill.

The yellow cat sprang lightly over the fallen body and went outside into the night.

Wide-eyed, the woman lay—watching. After moments of tense listening the sound of faint breathing came to her from the prone figure. Sally frowned. "He's too no 'count to git kilt," she said aloud, and turned on her side. She judged, from the stars, it was not yet eleven. Drowsiness came; she fell into uneasy slumber.

Out in the night the yellow cat was prowling. It stopped near the woodpile. With extended paw, it touched lightly something that lay on the ground. Its long teeth fastened upon it. The cat slunk off toward the house. Without sound it sprang to the floor of the dog-trot. Stealthily, its body crouched low, it started to cross through the open way. As it passed the woman she muttered and struck out in her sleep. The cat flattened to the floor. Near the moving arm, the thing it carried fell from its teeth. The beast scurried out across the opening.

The night marched on to the sound of a million voices calling shrilly through the gloom.

The woman woke. The stars glowed pale from a cloudy midnight sky. She reached out her right hand, palm down, to raise herself from the bed, throwing her full weight upon it. Two needle points pierced her wrist. A smothered cry was wrung from her lips. She reached with her left hand to pluck at the hurt place. It touched something cold, something hard and clammy, some dead thing. She jerked back the hand. A scream shivered through the still air. Pains, becoming instantly acute—unbearable—darted through her arm. Again she tried to pull away the torturing needle points. Her quiver-

ing hand groped aimlessly in the darkness. She could not force herself, a second time, to touch the dead, clinging thing at her wrist.
Screaming, she dragged herself to the man.

"Jim, I'm hurt; help me! Help me!"

The man did not move.

"Jim, wake up! Help me!" she wailed uselessly to the inert man.

The terrifying pain spurted from wrist to shoulder. With her
clenched left hand she beat against the man's upturned face.

"You drunken fool, help me! Take this thing away!" The man
lay torpid beneath her pounding fist.

Along the path of Pigeon Creek, where the pine-woods run into
the cane-brake, a boy waited—waited until the eastern sky grew
from black to gray. Then with cautious tread he began to move, his
face turned toward the cabin. As he neared the clearing the gray in
the east changed to red. He left the woods and entered the field of
corn.

At the cabin he drew close against the wall and listened. A man's
heavy breathing reached his straining ears. Slowly he moved toward
the opening in the middle of the house.

Above the breathing he heard a grating noise; between the deep
drawn breaths and the grating, another sound came to him; a harsh,
rhythmic scratching.

The edge of the sun rose abruptly above the flat earth.

The boy thrust his head around the angle. A yellow cat was sitting
at the foot of the mattress. From its throat grating purrs came in
regular measure; between each purr the beast's spread claws clutched
and released the stiff ticking.

Beyond lay the man.

Between the cat and the man, stretched across the shuck bed, was
the woman; her glassy eyes staring up into the grinning face of the
cat. From her shoulder, reaching out toward the boy was a living
turgid thing; a hand and arm, puffed beyond all human shape. From
the swollen wrist, its poisoned fangs sunk deep into an artery, hung
the mangled head of a snake.

The swaying corn blades whipped against the boy's white face as
he fled between the rows.

Sukey

ELEANOR BOOTH SIMMONS

IT WAS in May, on a day when the farmer's little girl found the first wind-flowers in the woods, and High Farm was buzzing with the activity of planting time, that Sukey was born. Of the four kittens in the litter she was the roundest and the silkiest, and when her nine days of blindness ended, and her blue eyes opened to the world, she became entrancingly jolly. Her three brothers were rather common. They had the drab coat, the narrow head and pointed nose of Old Tomas, a disreputable fellow who occasionally visited High Farm to beg a handout at the kitchen door and tell Mrs. Cat how beautiful she was. Mrs. Cat always swore at him, but as the farmer said, with these women you never could tell. Any way the boy kittens were so plainly Old Tomas that their careers were cut short in a pail of water, and the farmer's little girl had a nice funeral for them.

But Sukey was the image of her mother, who really was a beauty. From some unknown highborn strain in her ancestry she had inherited the soft coloring and exquisite markings of the pure silver tabby, and she had bequeathed them to Sukey, down to the smallest whorl of the butterflies on her hips. Sukey's gaze, like her mother's, was wide and innocent, and covered many things. She could sit on the farm-wife's knee looking like a cat angel, and all the time she would be plotting how to steal her knitting and tangle it in the blackberry bushes.

It was a good life, Sukey's life. Dancing leaves and her mother's tail to play with, tall nodding grass in which to get deliciously frightened at What-is-it that chased her, and sunny garden spots where a tired kitten could roll and stretch and slip off into forty winks. When the sun went away there was the snug box behind the kitchen stove, and her mother's breast was a soft pillow and a perpetual refreshment booth.

At mealtimes Mrs. Cat sat behind the farmer's chair, demure but alert, and Sukey learned that this was a good custom to copy. For the farmer was soft-hearted, and even the farmer's wife, who didn't believe in feeding cats at the table, succumbed to Sukey. For the kitten had witchery, and with all her mischief she was mannerly. Mrs. Cat took great pains with her education, and when she was still very young she knew that a spot on her coat was a disgrace, that the sandbox in the room where they were shut at night was for a purpose, and that baby chickens were only to be looked at, never to be chased.

It was a good life, even after Mrs. Cat turned peevish when Sukey tried to nurse her, and took to slipping away from the house at night to prowl and look at the moon. If the box behind the kitchen stove seemed lonely, there was the farm-wife's ample lap to lie in when the family sat out on the porch in the evening. She lay there, one night in August, when a noisy laughing party drove up in a touring car.

They had stopped, they said, to see if they could buy some eggs. There was a big man behind the wheel, and there were two girlish middle-aged women, one in pink and one in blue, and some children.

They crowded around to pet Sukey, and Sukey rose politely and made her little cat bow, murmuring "T-r-r, t-r-r-r!"

"What a beautiful cat!" cried the woman in blue.

"Real tortoise-shell, isn't he?" the woman in pink chimed in.

"She," said the farm-wife, "is a silver tabby."

"Tabby, of course," agreed the woman in blue. "We do love cats. We always go to the cat shows in New York. I'd just love to enter this cat in a show. I know she'd carry off all the prizes. We do miss our cat up here. I don't know why we didn't bring him. We've taken the Moxley place for the summer and fall. That old house, you know, in the woods on the other side of the hill, a dozen miles from anywhere."

She took a ribbon from the many that floated from her dress, and tied it around Sukey's neck.

"Dear me," she said, standing off to admire the effect, "how I would adore to have that little cat to fuss with."

"Perhaps the lady will sell you the cat," the big man suggested. "You've got others, haven't you?" he asked. "I saw a tom running across the road just now."

"Oh, Old Tomas just hangs around; he's a born tramp. Of course we've got Sukey's mother. But I couldn't sell Sukey."

"Hey!" said one of the spindling little boys. "You'll prob'bly have a lot o' kittens right away."

The farm-wife repeated that she didn't think she could spare Sukey. Her little girl would cry if she woke up in the morning to find Sukey gone. But the two women coaxed her till she could hardly think. She wished her husband were there to decide, but he had gone to the village. In the end she weakened. She refused the dollar bill that the big man held out to her, but she brought a basket and put Sukey in it. Sukey didn't want to go. She clung with all her little strength to the farm-wife's bosom, and when the lid of the basket closed over her she gave a desolate cry, and then was still. The farm-wife could hear that cry long after the car shot away with its laughing people.

The farmer was quite cut up when he came home and heard about the transaction. His wife said she didn't know, herself, why she let Sukey go, but the kitten would have a fine home. She reminded her husband that Old Tomas and Mrs. Cat had been flirting in the orchard the last few nights, but he said gloomily that there wasn't likely to be another Sukey in the next batch. He was right; Mrs. Cat's new kittens all looked like Old Tomas; not a silver Tabby among them. He saved the likeliest one when he drowned them, and it took its place in the household, but it was not Sukey. The little girl sometimes cried for Sukey, but her mother told her that she ought to be proud that her kitten had gone to New York to live in a grand apartment and be shown in cat shows. For the woman never doubted that Sukey's new friends had taken her home with them.

Christmas came, and the little girl tied red neck ribbons on Mrs. Cat and Young Tomas.

"If I knew where Sukey lived I'd send her a present," she said. "But I s'pose she's got a tree and everything."

"Why of course she has," said the mother. "Those people were just crazy about that little cat."

It was a hard winter. Day after day it snowed, and snowed again, and even when the clouds lifted and the sun came out the wind was bitter, and the snow drifted high in the forest. Deer came to the edge of the clearing to eat the hay the farmer carried there for them. Timid hares and rabbits forgot their fright in their desire for cabbage leaves and carrots scattered in the garden for them. Old Tomas, a mighty hunter in normal times, forsook the woods and took up his residence in the barn, and his handout at the kitchen door became a regular thing.

On a dreary day late in January the farmer, returned from a trip over the drifted roads to the village, brought out a letter from his pocket.

"It's from Alice," he said.

Alice was his niece in New York, and when he had put the team in the stable, and brought the groceries in from the sleigh, and eaten dinner, his wife read the letter to him while he popped corn for the child. It was a gay letter. Alice had had a raise at New Year's . . . her boss had praised her . . . the skating suit her aunt knitted her for Christmas was much admired when her beau took her to the rink . . . But here the farm-wife stopped, read silently for a minute.

"Well, for pity's sake!" she exclaimed. "Alice knows the people that took Sukey, and they didn't take her to the city. They left her at the Moxley place. They said their car was so full they didn't have room for her. They said a cat could look out for itself, and they thought Sukey'd be happier in the country."

The farmer snorted.

"How'd Alice come to know 'em?"

"They come to the store where she works. The boss's cat was on the counter, and they started talking about their vacation cat. Minute they mentioned the Moxley place and us, Alice knew, of course."

The little girl had dropped her doll and was listening.

"Is Sukey all alone?" she asked.

"Reckon so," her father said. He made some popcorn into a ball with maple sugar, and offered it to the child. She pushed it away.

"Wanta go get Sukey," she wailed.

"Dearie, the Moxley place is three miles away, and the road's full of snow," said her mother. She folded up the letter and knitted for a time, her eyes on the window.

"Henry," she finally said, "do you suppose we could get through? I'd feel easier in my mind—"

"No use bein' silly for a cat that's prob'bly dead anyhow," the farmer growled. But he got up, pulled on his boots, yanked his heavy coat from its nail, drew his fur cap down over his ears.

"You stay here," he told his wife. "No use two people gettin' froze."

The Moxley place looked dreary enough when after a long hard pull, getting out more than once to dig a way for his team, the farmer reached it. Snow weighted the boughs of the yew trees that stood around the house, snow lay against the shut doors and blank windows. There was not so much as the print of a paw to be seen, or a snow-bird fluttering. The farmer trampled a path to the outhouses. There might be a hole or a broken window through which Sukey could get inside and find shelter from the storms. He saw one at last, a jagged break in the woodhouse wall, and from a nail at one side hung some grey fur matted with frozen blood.

He wrenched a rail from the fence and beat the door down. Sukey was there. She lay in a corner, her glazed eyes staring at him. One paw held two starved kittens to her flat breast. The other front paw was only a stump, and there was a pool of clotted blood under it. The farmer stood a moment, shaking his head, then turned away, but at the door he turned back and looked for an empty box, found one, and placed Sukey and her kittens therein.

"I'll bury them at home," he muttered.

It was not hard to reconstruct Sukey's life as it must have gone after her false friends forsook her. The farmer, unimaginative man though he was, could see it. At first she must have felt a great loneliness and bewilderment. He could see her sitting outside the closed door, waiting . . . waiting . . . Then she became hungry. She had never been a hunter, but now she hunted, though unsuccessfully for the most part. Still she managed to keep herself alive, and in January Sukey, hardly more than a kitten herself, gave birth to her kittens.

Now the foraging must be redoubled. But game was scarce, and it was a very nice surprise when she discovered one day, in a wire box set in a thicket, a large lump of something that smelt good to eat. True, the thing looked suspicious, but her need was great, and she thrust her paw in to seize the food. And the steel jaws fastened upon it.

Only the trees and the snows were witnesses of the agony Sukey underwent while she freed her severed leg and crawled home to die with her kittens, but the farmer could picture it. His little girl was waiting at the window as he drove up in the twilight, and as he ate his supper he pacified her with a story of a beautiful home to which Sukey had gone. And when she was in bed and asleep he took his pickaxe and shovel and dug a grave for Sukey and her kittens, in the frozen earth of the garden where she had played so gayly a few months ago.

The Cat and the Cobra

A. W. SMITH

A FIVE-FOOT COBRA is a big one. A six-footer may exist. A seven-footer
is unheard of. This, of course, applies to the common cobra. The
hamadryad, or King Cobra, is known to exceed twelve feet in length.
He is really dangerous because he will attack at sight. The common
cobra will not. If he can he slips quietly away unless he thinks he is
cornered. Then you will hear what is to nearly all human beings one
of the most frightening sounds on earth—the hiss of an angry snake.

The inhuman "aah," low and throaty, of an angry mob, the drawn
"wheeow" of an approaching shell—these sounds are bad enough.
But for real blood-freezing paralysis go into a dark bathroom and
hear the sudden explosive hiss from the wet cement floor.

Perhaps it came from behind the tin bathtub . . . or from the
corner under the window . . .

Stand still—stand very still.

You thought you heard the dry whisper of coils across the floor?
The great earthenware *chatti* in the corner sweating cold water from
its porous sides does not sweat as coldly as you. It could not stand
more still.

The chink from the door ajar throws a shaft of friendly yellow
light on the wet shining floor. Faiz Ullah moving discreetly, laying
out shirt (click go studs into shirtfront) —wonders what it is that
keeps master . . .

Acutely conscious of bare ankles. Hair lifting on scalp, prickling
the skin. Move softly—very softly. Take the big bath towel—oh very
gently. Hold it loosely, making a curtain in front of your shins, so—

Back out . . . gently, I said. No king deserves more reverence.
. . . And don't cry out. As you value your life, don't cry out.

Wheew—

Once again in the warm yellow light of your room with bathroom
door slammed shut, feel brave again. Send Faiz Ullah flying for

something long and strong, light and whippy. A cut down polo stick, for instance—that is the best—

Ai, Faiz Ullah—polo lakri lao—Nag gussul khana men hai.

Shout and shout—send them running.

Ai, Maharaj, nag gussul khana men hai.

Slip feet into riding boots. Powder them first if feet are bare. You'll be late for dinner taking them off if you don't.

Ai, durwan! Hurricane lamp lao—Nag gussul khana men hai.

Wrapped discreetly in a heavy blanket, approach with caution—electric torch and stick of whippy cane in hand.

Butler, sweeper, *durwan, bhisti,* and the *bhisti's* son, *hamal, mali,* and *syces* two hang whispering at the verandah door.

Hold the dog, Faiz Ullah—Kuttha puckerao.

Fling wide the door, strike hard, cut just below the spectacles on the swaying swollen sac of the hood.

Shabash—Shabash, huzoor.

They will throw him out to the kites and crows, but not before the sweeper has removed the head in order to collect the Government reward.

"Sorry I'm late. I killed a cobra in my bathroom—eight feet at least." You may be nonchalant now over gin and bitters.

"More gin?"—"Thanks"—"No ice came up on the mail train"—
"Sorry."

India is not all cobras, as some people think, but they are common
enough—even in Calcutta. As a business we used to occupy one of
those gloomy fortresses of finance off Clive Street. It was an ancient
semiclassical affair of Corinthian columns and deep verandahs. The
outside was stucco which grew a green mossy beard every rains. The
inside was dark and cool with high ceilings and creaking floors. It
was so unpretentious and old-fashioned that only a firm of our re-
spectability and reputation could have risked its credit by occupy-
ing it.

Not one of us would ever think of changing. We took great pride
in our building—it had been ours for a hundred years—and we pro-
fessed to look down on those who occupied the newly risen steel and
concrete buildings which are so popular and cost so much.

The building was Jones' domain. As head accountant he was responsible, among other things, for its organization and upkeep, for
the hiring and firing of the subordinate staff and for generally making the way smooth for those of us who were solely concerned with
making profits. Jones, of course, had no more high office than to see
that our actions were properly recorded in terms of *rupees* and *annas*
and *pice*. His role was more or less automatic, in so far as anything
can be said to be automatic in India.

He was doubtless a good accountant, but he lacked above all things
that sweet nature and supreme tact which is necessary for the easy
handling of an Indian staff. He bewildered them. He tried to alter
age-old customs. In doing so he was always stubbing his toe. He might
just as well have tried to change the multiplication table.

Instead of accepting the order of things painstakingly built up on
a web of belief and precedent, he tried to treat everyone as a ra-
tional human being. From the head clerk down to the humblest
sweeper, he thought they could be persuaded by the validity of argument. With dogmatic thoroughness he tried to explain that so and
so was a better, a shorter, a quicker, and a less laborious way of doing
things—in short, that it was more efficient.

He was met with charming indulgent smiles and ready acquies-
cence—and nothing was done about it.

Moreover, he lacked understanding. He couldn't see why Rajah
Singh, the sepoy, must never be asked to touch a glass of water, or
why the waterman must never be told to carry a pair of shoes to be
mended, or quite why Shauqat Ali, one of the piece-goods bazaar

clerks, wouldn't move a plate of ham sandwiches. (Jones often had meals in the office—disgusting habit, but Efficiency was his watchword.)

All these things merely caused Jones to lose his temper, which didn't do a bit of good. By degrees he learned better, although it was a slow process. There was always something to send Jones into a fit of inarticulate rage. For instance, one day he took it into his head to go over the pay sheet. He checked it with a blue pencil, name by name, all the way from Ahmed Ali, Chittagonian driver of the office car, past the Bannerjis and Mukerjis, down to Xavier and Zachariah, the Indian Christian wharf clerks. At the very bottom of the pay roll Jones discovered—"Cats two—one *rupee* each."

He hammered his bell. The cashier was quite undisturbed.

"And why not—?" he asked in effect. Ever since Wilson Sahib's time there had always been two cats on the pay roll. First there had been only one and then two.

Now Wilson Sahib had retired somewhere back in the early nineties. Jones had met him in London—an elderly man in the middle eighties.

"But why—?" Jones almost frothed at the mouth.

"For forty years two *rupees* a month—nearly a thousand *rupees* on cats."

"It was the Sahib's order," purred the cashier.

Jones instituted an inquiry into the status of the office cats.

"I will make immediate inquisition," said the cashier.

"Not emolument for cats two, your honor," said the cashier later, "but subsistence allowance at *rupees* one *per mensem per capita*. How can cat get the salary, notwithstanding?"

He smiled gently at the whimsy. Jones found his smile particularly infuriating.

"I don't believe there are any cats," he said resentfully. "It's just another ramp. It simply means that the sweeper or someone gets two *rupees* a month extra because once someone was fool enough—"

"Wilson Sahib's order, your honor," said the cashier reprovingly, "but I will bring—"

In due course he brought—two meager gray cats who struggled in the arms of the head sweeper and his assistant and swore volubly when Jones was rash enough to put out a hand.

The head sweeper said something which Jones could not understand. Jones had never bothered to learn any language but his own.

"That is senior cat—ten years' service, your honor," translated the cashier. "Sweeper say please he must have more subsistence. The old age draws on and it cat must get milk, the bowls one *per diem*."

"Oh, shut up," said Jones. "I'm going to sack both. We can't have cats, of all things, on the pay roll—what with economy and jute prices and everything."

"But Wilson Sahib's order," protested the cashier, who could not connect jute with cats.

"Blow Wilson Sahib," said Jones.

With a lordly sweep of his blue pencil he struck the cats, two, senior and junior, from the pay roll.

Our building was old. It dated back to the eighteen twenties, to the palmy days of indigo and opium, when a fortune might be turned on a cargo. Into it poured rats like a plague of Egypt. They scuttered along the partition tops and swizzled their noses at us from the dusk of corners. There were great gray-scarred veterans who seemed to prefer a simple diet of paper and electric-light cords to the fat living of the docks and sewers. There were little brown tiddlers who nested in the cotton and jute samples.

We complained one at a time and all together, but on the subject of cats Jones was adamant.

"Ridiculous," he said. "Two *rupees* a month for cats—I ask you—"

He spent untold gold on traps and poison. He bought parched corn for bait by the sack load—enough to feed not only the whole corps of sweepers but the waterman also and the waterman's son, the godown staff, the driver of the office car and the man who sold betel nuts and pan leaves at the bottom of the stairs. There were queer smells in dark cupboards—rotten cheesy fish smells.

"Jones Sahib," explained the sepoys with a knowing leer.

But to all the wiles of Jones the rats seemed to prefer the great calfskin ledgers which it took two strong men to lift.

It was too much. Every plague of overpopulation is followed by its natural antidote.

A sepoy was sent down the rickety stairs to the jute sample room. He was a portly and dignified figure in his smart blue uniform and scarlet *pugri*. He did not hurry, not yet did he dawdle. He descended with measured stride, head up, well-brushed beard fluffed up to his ears.

He came up the stairs again in headlong flight. He had seen a fine cobra, he gibbered, playing with its tail at the bottom of the stairs. He positively refused to go down again.

"*Nag*—" the word spreads round the office like wildfire. The little clerks at their desks looked suspiciously at the floor. They hitched their bare toes more securely round the legs of their stools.

"Oh, yes—a cobra—" said the head sweeper cheerfully. "He guards the stairs—ever since the cats went. We sweeper folk don't use the stairs any more. I've seen it many times. It's so long—"

He indicated a strip of floor about fifteen or twenty feet to the wall.

"Nonsense," said Jones who was busy investigating the claims of a new kind of poison. "A cobra in the middle of Calcutta? Nonsense."

It did look odd with the tramcars clanging in the street and a row of taxis on the opposite corner.

"Nonsense," said Jones firmly.

But where there are rats there will be cobras, fulfilling the law of supply and demand. The office staff definitely refused to go up and down those stairs. They were perfectly good-natured about it and no amount of bullying by Jones made the least difference. To get at the samples we had to send a man all the way round by the street and in at the back door. It was a tedious process, but we accepted it, as one does in India, until the senior partner . . . He sent for Jones.

"What's all this," he said, "about the office being full of cobras?"

"Oh, nothing," said Jones a little uneasily. "Just a yarn."

"Well, everybody's complaining. You'd better do something about them—catch them or get the men to work properly—I don't care which. That's what you're here for."

Jones sent for the cashier.

"Kill it?" said the cashier in horror. "But your honor—" he lowered his voice to a whisper—"the snake is holy—Our Lord Krishna, your honor."

"Well, get rid of it," said Jones testily.

"As your honor wills," said the cashier. "I have a friend in Kuccha Bazaar who is a very holy man. A snake catcher. For two *rupees* the cash money he will catch—"

"Fetch him," rapped Jones.

Jones found most of the office staff gathered at the foot of the stairs. There was hardly one among them who did not believe that when a man died without an heir his soul returned in the form of a cobra. Didn't everyone know the supreme importance of getting himself a son? Aren't cobras holy? Well then—

There was an air of tension. Everyone felt that something exciting was going to happen. No one knew quite what. In the hot dusty dark among the packing cases and the pillars supporting the building it was pleasantly mysterious.

"Haven't any of you people got any work to do?" snapped Jones. "Go away—*Jao*—"

There was a shifting of feet, a shuffling of faces, a pretense of obeying the order. No one actually went. Jones decided to ignore his audience.

There was a ripple in the crowd and a little sigh went up.

"Are you the snake catcher?" asked Jones.

The newcomer walked past Jones as if he hadn't seen him. He settled himself comfortably on his heels and lighted a green *bidi*. He sucked in the evil-smelling smoke through cupped hands and coughed.

It wasn't the snake catcher—only someone from outside who had heard that there was free entertainment to be had.

The crowd squatted on its heels, chatting. The show was free. Who knew but that it mightn't be surprising.

Jones grew impatient.

"He comes, your honor," murmured the cashier soothingly. "He sees if the hour is auspicious."

Upstairs all work seemed to be over for the day.

"He comes," said someone. A hush fell. The silence was broken by the sudden outcry of the small son of a friend of the head sweeper. Dressed up in a round embroidered cap and a heart-shaped silver amulet, he had been brought to see the show. He bellowed, rubbing his small fists in his eyes.

"*Aiee—bawa sahib—durro mut—durro mut—* Hush thee, princeling, don't fear—" said the father, looking round proudly, hoping that everyone had seen his son and heir. "See the fat sahib perched on the railing. Soon he will blow fire from his lips and smoke and serpents will come forth."

"*Chup tum*. Shut up you," said the cashier rudely from a safe and lordly eminence on top of a packing case.

"*Ai, babuji*," said the head sweeper. "Oh, come, sir clerk—the fat sahib lacks understanding, and it is but speech to a child."

Jones found the big black eyes of the infant fastened on him. Their earnestness embarrassed him. He stamped the floor impatiently.

Again quiet. The snake catcher with due regard for the effect of his entrance, came slowly down the stairs, step by step.

He made a deep salaam. Jones replied with an indeterminate kind of salute, rather an awkward gesture which was supposed to be one of condescension.

"*Salaam, huzoor,*" said the snake catcher.

"Good morning," said Jones. "It's a fine day, isn't it?"

When this remark had been translated by the cashier the snake catcher had no hesitation in agreeing. The fact was sufficiently evident.

"Why does the fat sahib say that the sun shines?" piped the small son of the head sweeper's friend.

"It is the way of sahibs," said the head sweeper heavily. "As we say '*Ram Ram*'—so they say 'the day has well-dawned.' They find it auspicious no matter whether it is hot or wet or cold."

"Let's get on with it—" commanded Jones briskly.

"First, your honor," said the cashier, "first he do the *puja*. He very holy man. He must have money."

The crowd craned its necks as a silver *rupee* was handed over. This looked like big business. Money was being spent like water for their entertainment. Their whispering ceased as the snake catcher, seated crosslegged on the stone floor, erected copper coins and some pan leaves in a little pile before him. He drew diagrams, triangles and circles in the dust with a bit of iron. The point grated on the stone.

"That stick," whispered the cashier, "that iron stick very holy."

To Jones it looked like a simple piece of jute baling but he hesitated to say so. The cashier wriggled his bare toes apprehensively.

With a quick movement the holy man rose to his feet pointing dramatically with his rusty iron at a crevice in a dim corner under the stairs. Certain of his audience, he walked across the floor. He began to probe between the blocks of stone. The crowd sighed a deep "Aah—." Even Jones was a little impressed.

The holy stick was doing its work. Immediately there issued from the crevice a loud and angry hiss. It sent the watching crowd pressing back into the dusky recesses of the basement. Jones felt the hair rise on the back of his neck. He shared in common with the rest a general distrust of snakes. He wondered whether it would be dignified to retire a step or two up the stairs.

He hardly had time to think. Quick as light a fine five-foot cobra launched itself like a whiplash across the smooth stone floor. Quick as light—but quicker still the holy snake catcher made a leap for the staircase. And the crowd found points of security on packing cases and bales of cotton.

To Jones was left the sole possession of the floor.

Somewhat bewildered the cobra coiled. It raised a hooded head, barring Jones' exit to safety up the stairs.

"Stand still, your honor, stand still," admonished the cashier.

Jones needed no warning. Horror-struck he watched the swaying head—a blunt thimbleshaped object standing out from the distended hood. He did not dare move. He squinted down his nose in a painful effort to see.

"*Lathi lao,*" cried the cashier. "Bring a stick."

"*Lathi lao—maro maro,*" "Bring a stick and strike, strike," echoed the crowd.

The holiness of the cobra was forgotten.

"What is the fat sahib doing?" asked the infant son of the sweeper's friend.

"See the cobra," said his father.

"Did he spit that?" asked the childish voice.

Jones stood. He was fiercely conscious of ankles and lower legs. He wondered whether, as he had heard, a pair of trousers was enough to stop the poison. And would it hurt?

Through long tense seconds they eyed each other—when, from somewhere in the dark, crept the senior cat. He was light gray, thin and motheaten. Ears flattened to his head, body flattened to the floor, he slid, experienced warrior that he was, with stealthy stride.

The Indian cat is not like any other cat. The hand of man is more than usually turned against him. He is about as strokeable as a porcupine, and the snake is a traditional enemy.

The senior cat crept crouching past Jones' legs. The tip of his mangy tail flicked convulsively. It was this which caught the cobra's eye. His weaving head changed its direction. It increased in speed.

Jones, white as a sheet, squinted down his nose at the senior cat.

The cobra struck. In that split second a lot of things happened. The cat leaped lightly to land over the cobra's back. And Jones—Jones displayed an agility of which those who knew him best could hardly believe him capable. In one standing jump he landed about five steps up the stairs.

The son of the sweeper's friend crowed in delight, but the crowd was too intent on the senior cat's battle to notice Jones. Each time the cobra struck the senior cat jumped. To one side, to the other side—or merely straight up in the air so that the snake shot beneath him. Each time he jumped he dealt a vicious blow with clawed forepaw.

After each attack the cobra whirled round to set up on his coiled body, head swaying, hood extended, forked tongue flicking, and the senior cat crouched low to the floor, still but for the convulsive flicking of his tail. His growls were horrible.

Again the cobra struck with no loss of force. This time the senior cat leaped high, only to whirl around in midair. He dropped with all four feet extended, biting just where the head joined the spectacled hood. For a moment snake and cat lashed about the floor. The cat jumped clear. He left his enemy writhing.

For the cobra that was the end. The senior cat paraded stealthily round his victim. He waited only for a chance to close.

Jones mopped his brow. Fascinated, he watched the senior cat.

It was time now for the junior cat. With skill she sprang from behind a pillar. It was the turn, too, of Rajah Singh Sepoy, burly Rajputani from the fighting races of Lucknow. Black beard brushed up fiercely to his ears, waving a heavy bamboo *lathi,* he leaped into the arena.

"*Hut jao, billi*— Out of the way, cat—" he cried.

"*Shabash, maro, maro*—" "Well done, lay on, lay on—" chanted the crowd.

Rajah Singh laid on. The iron shoe of his staff struck sparks from the floor. The dust flew. The cobra was dead.

The senior and junior cat faded like lean gray shadows.

Of course, you may say it was a put-up job. If the cats were there all the time . . . you see what I mean.

Possibly.

This doubtless occurred to Jones who was always suspicious of human nature. He debated the question for a whole afternoon before signing a voucher for reinstatement of the cats and incidental expenses. (To cash—holy man for finding one cobra serpent . . . *et cetera.*)

Jones also sacked the head sweeper.

You see, one of his visitors during the afternoon was a dirty dishevelled gentleman who forced himself into Jones' office. He claimed to be the head sweeper's caste brother. He claimed also that he had not been paid. He demanded to be paid. He presented, in fact, a dirty bill, for one fine cobra from which the poison fangs had been removed.

"The Fat of the Cat"

GOTTFRIED KELLER

IN SELDWYLA, when someone has made a bad bargain, people say, "He has tried to buy the fat off the cat!" It is a queer saying and a puzzling one. But there is an old, half-forgotten story which tells how it first came to be used and what it really means.

Several hundred years ago, so runs the tale, there lived in Seldwyla an old, old lady whose only companion was a handsome gray cat. This fine creature was always to be seen with his mistress; he was quiet and clever, and never harmed anyone who let him alone. "Everything in moderation" was his motto—everything that is, except hunting, which was his one great enjoyment. But even in this sport he was never savage or cruel. He caught and killed only the most impudent and troublesome mice; the others he merely chased away. He left the small circle in which he hunted only once in a while, when some particularly bold mouse roused his anger. Then there was no stopping him! He would follow the foolhardy nibbler everywhere. And if the mouse tried to hide at some neighbor's place, the cat would walk up to the owner, make a deep bow and politely ask permission to hunt there. And you may be sure he was always allowed to do so, for he never disturbed anything in the house. He did not knock over the butter-crocks, never stole milk from pails, never sprang up on the sides of ham which hung against the wall. He went about his business very quietly, very carefully; and, after he had captured his mouse, disappeared just as quietly as he came. He was neither naughty nor wild, but friendly to everyone. He never ran away from well-behaved children and allowed them to pinch his ears a little without scratching them. Even when stupid people annoyed him, he would simply get out of their way or thump them over the hand if they tried to take liberties with him.

Glassy—for this was the name that was given him on account of his smooth and shiny fur—lived his days happily in comfort and modesty. He did not sit on his mistress's shoulder just to snatch a piece of food from her fork, but only when he saw that it pleased her to have him there. He was neither selfish nor lazy, but only too happy to go walking with his mistress along the little river that flowed into the lake near by. He did not sleep the whole day long on his warm pillow

behind the stove. Instead, he loved to lie wide-awake, thinking out his plans at the foot of the stairs, or prowling along the edge of the roof, considering the ways of the world like the gray-haired philosopher that he was. His calm life was interrupted only in spring, when the violets blossomed, and in autumn, when the warm days of Indian Summer imitated Maytime. At such times Glassy would stroll over the roofs like an inspired poet and sing the strangest and most beautiful songs. He had the wildest adventures during these nights, and when he would come home after his reckless wanderings, he looked so rough and towsled that his mistress used to say, "Glassy, how *can* you behave that way! Aren't you ashamed of yourself?" But Glassy felt no shame; he thought he was now a regular man-of-the-world. Never answering a word, he would sit quietly in his corner, smoothing his fur and washing himself behind the ears, as innocently as if he had never stirred from the fireside.

One day this pleasant manner of life came to an unhappy end. Just as Glassy became a full-grown cat, his mistress died of old age, leaving him an unprotected orphan. It was Glassy's first misfortune and his piercing cries and long wailing showed how deep was his grief. He followed the funeral part of the way down the street and then returned to the house, wandering helplessly from room to room. But his good sense told him he must serve the heirs of his mistress as faithfully as he did her—he must continue to keep the mice in their place, be ever watchful and ready, and (whenever necessary) give the new owners good advice. But these foolish people would not let Glassy get near them. On the contrary, whenever they saw him, they threw the slippers and the foot-stool of his departed mistress at his bewildered head. After eight days of quarreling among themselves, they boarded up the windows, closed the house, and—while they went to court to see who really owned it—no one was allowed to set foot inside the doors.

Poor Glassy, thrown into the street, sat on the doorstep of his old home and no one took the slightest notice of him. All day long he sat and he sat and he sat. At night he roamed about the roofs and, at first, he spent a great part of the time hidden and asleep, trying to forget his cares. But hunger drove him to people again, to be at hand whenever there might be a chance of getting a scrap of something to eat. As food grew scarcer, his eyes grew sharper; and, as his whole attention was given to this one thing, he ceased to look like his old self. He ran from door to door and stole about the streets, sometimes pouncing gladly upon a greasy morsel that, in the old days, he would never even have sniffed at. Often, indeed, he found nothing at all. He grew hungrier and thinner from day to day; he who was once so plump and proud became scraggy and timid. All his courage, his dignity, his wisdom and his philosophy vanished. When the boys came from school, he crawled behind a barrel or into an old can, daring to stick his head out only to see whether one of them would throw away a crust of bread. In the old days he could look the fiercest dog straight in the eye and many was the time he punished them severely. Now he ran away from the commonest cur. And while, in the times gone by, he used to run away from rough and unpleasant people, now he would let them come quite near, not because he liked them any better, but because—who knows?—they might toss him something to chew on. Even when, instead of feeding him, coarse men would strike him or twist his tail, still he would not cry. He would just sit there and look longingly at the hand which had hurt him, but which had such a heavenly smell of sausage or herring.

The wise and gentle Glassy had, indeed, come down in the world. He was starving as he sat one day, on his stone, dreaming and blinking in the sunlight. As he lay there, the town-wizard, a sly magician by the name of Pineiss, came that way, noticed the cat and stopped in front of him. Hoping for something good, Glassy sat meekly on his stone, waiting to see what Pineiss would do or say. At the first words, Glassy lost hope, for Pineiss said, "Well, cat, would you like to sell your fat?" He thought that the magician was only making fun of his skinny appearance. But still he answered demurely, "Ah, Master Pineiss likes to joke!"

"But I am serious!" the wizard replied, "I need cat's fat in my witchery; I work wonders with it. But it must be taken only if the cat is willing to give it—otherwise the magic will not work. I am thinking if ever a cat was in a position to make a good bargain, you're the very one! Come into my service; I'll feed you as you never have been fed. I'll give you the richest of warm milk and the sweetest of cakes. You will grow fat as a dumpling on juicy sausages, chicken livers and roast quail. On my enormous roof—which is well known as the greatest hunting-ground in the world for cats—there are hundreds of interesting corners and inviting dark holes. And there, on the top of that old roof, there grows a wonderful grass, green as an emerald. When you play in it, you will think you are a tiger in the jungle, and —if you have eaten too many rich things—a few nibbles of it will cure the worst stomach-ache. My mice are the tenderest—and the slowest—in the country, and catnip grows in the back of my garden. Thus, you see, *you* will be happy and healthy, and *I* will have a good supply of useful fat. What do you say?"

Glassy had listened to this speech with ears pricked up and his mouth watering. But he was so weak that he did not quite understand the bargain, and he said, "That isn't half bad, Master Pineiss. If I only understood how I could hold on to my reward! If I have to lose my life to give you my fat, how am I to enjoy all these fine things when I am dead?"

"Hold on to your reward?" answered the magician, impatiently. "Your reward is in the enjoyment of all you can eat and drink *while* you are alive. That ought to be clear enough. But I don't want to force you!" And he shrugged his shoulders and made as if he were going to walk off.

But Glassy cried, quickly and eagerly, "Wait! Wait! I will say yes on one condition. You must wait a few days *after* I have reached my roundest and fattest fullness before you take my life. I must have a little time so that I am not torn away too suddenly when I am so happy, so full of food and contentment."

"So be it!" said Pineiss with seeming generosity. "Until the next full-moon you shall enjoy yourself as much as you like. But it cannot last a minute longer than that. For, when the moon begins to wane, the fat will grow less powerful and my well-earned property will shrink."

So they came to an agreement. Pineiss disappeared for a moment. Then he came running back with a great quill-pen and an enormous roll of paper. This was the contract and it was so large because it was full of queer words that lawyers are fond of—words like "whereas" and "notwithstanding" and "hereinbefore" and "thereunto" and "party-of-the-second-part" and others too long and expensive to print here. Without stopping to read it through, Glassy signed his name neatly on the dotted line, which proved how well he had been brought up.

"Now you can come and have lunch with me," said the magician. "We dine at twelve, sharp." "Thanks," replied the famished cat, "I will be pleased to accept your invitation," and a few minutes before noon he was waiting at the table of Master Pineiss.

From that moment Glassy began to enjoy a wonderful month. He had nothing else to do but to eat all the delicate dishes that were put before him, to watch the magician at work and go climbing about the roof. It was really a most heavenly sort of roof—dark, high and pointed like a steeple—just the sort of a top for a house of magic and mystery.

ii

But you should know something about the town-magician. Master Pineiss was a jack-of-all-trades. He did a thousand different things. He cured sick people, removed warts, cleared houses of rats, drove out roaches, pulled teeth, loaned money, and collected bills. He took charge of all the orphans and widows, made black ink out of charcoal and, in his spare time, cut quill-pens, which he sold twelve for a penny. He sold ginger and pepper, candy and axle-grease, shoe-nails and perfume, books and button-hooks, sausages and string. He repaired clocks, extracted corns, painted signs, delivered papers, forecasted the weather, and prepared the farmer's almanac. He did a great many good things in the daytime very cheaply; and, for much higher prices, he did other things (which are not spoken about) after it grew dark. Although he was a magician, his principal business was not witchcraft; he made magic and worked spells only for household use. The people of Seldwyla needed *someone* who would do all sorts of unpleasant jobs and mysterious things for them, so they had elected him town-wizard. And, for many years, Pineiss had worked hard, early and late, to do whatever they wished—and a few things to please himself.

In this house, full of all sorts of curious objects, Glassy had plenty of time to see, smell, and taste everything. Tired out with doing nothing, he lay on large, soft cushions all day long. At first he paid attention to nothing else but eating. He devoured greedily whatever Pineiss offered him and could scarcely wait from one meal to the next. Often, indeed, he ate too much and then he would have to go and chew the green grass on the roof to be well enough—so he could eat still more. His master was well pleased with this hunger, and thought to himself, "That cat will soon be round and fat,—and the more I give him now the less he will be able to eat later."

So Pineiss built a little countryside for Glassy. He planted a tiny forest of a dozen baby pine-trees, made a few hills of stones and moss, and scooped out a hole with water so there would be a lake. In the trees he stuck sweet roast finches, stuffed larks, baked sparrows, and small potted pigeons. The hills were full of the most exciting mouse-holes; and inside of them Pineiss had hidden more than a hundred juicy mice, which had been fattened on wheat-flour and broiled in bacon. Some of these delicious mice were easily within reach of Glassy's paw; others (to give him more of an appetite) had to be dug for, but all were on strings so that Glassy could play he was chasing without losing them. The little lake was filled with fresh milk every morning and, as Glassy was fond of fishing, young sardines and tender gold-fish floated in that delightful pool.

It was Glassy's idea of Paradise, a cat's heaven on earth. He ate and ate and ate. And in between his meals, he nibbled. When he did not eat, he rested. And *how* he slept! It got so that the mice began to gather about his pillow where he lay and mock at him. And Glassy never stirred—not even when their tails whisked across his whiskers!

Now that Glassy could eat all he wanted and whenever he wished to, his whole appearance changed. He looked like his old self: his fur became glossy and smooth again, his eyes grew large and fiery, and his mind acted more cleverly than before. He stopped being greedy; he no longer stuffed himself just for the pleasure of eating. He began to think seriously about life in general—and about his own in particular. One day, as he was thoughtfully tearing apart a cooked quail, he saw that the little insides of the bird were packed with unspoilt food. Some green herbs, black and white seeds, a few crumbs, grains of corn and one bright red berry were crowded together— just as tight as a mother packs her boy's lunch-basket when he goes off for the day. As Glassy saw this, he grew still more thoughtful. And the more thoughtful he grew, the sadder he became. At last he began to think out loud. "Poor bird," he said, scratching his head, "what good did all this fine food do you? You had to search so hard for these crumbs, fly who knows how many miles to find those grains of corn. That red berry was snatched at great risk from the bird-catcher's trap. And all for what? You thought you ate to keep yourself alive, but the fatter you grew, the nearer you came to your end. . . . Ah, me," he sighed deeply, "why did I ever make such a wretched bargain! I did not think—I was too foolish with hunger. And now that I can think again, all I can see is that I will end like this poor quail. When I am fat enough, I will have to die—for no other reason except that I will be fat enough! A fine end for a lively and intelligent cat-of-the-world! Oh, if I could only get out of this fix!"

He kept on brooding and worrying, yet he could think of no way to escape his fate. But, like a wise man, he controlled himself and his appetite and tried to put off the final day as long as possible. He refused to lie on the great cushions, which Pineiss had placed all over so that he could sleep a great deal and get fat quicker. Instead of soft places, he rested himself on the cold sill or lay down on the hard stones whenever he was tired. Rather than munch the roasted birds and stuffed mice, he began to hunt in earnest on the tall roof-top. And the living mice he caught with his own efforts tasted far better to him than all the rich goodies from Pineiss's kitchen—especially since they did not make him so fat. The constant exercise made him strong and slender—much to Pineiss's astonishment. The magician could not understand how Glassy remained so active and healthy; he expected to see a great clumsy animal that never moved from its pillows and was just one enormous roll of fat.

After some time had passed and Glassy, instead of wallowing in fat, grew still stronger and handsomer without losing his slender figure, Pineiss determined to do something. "What is the matter, Glassy?" he harshly inquired one day. "What is wrong with you? Why don't you eat the good things that I prepare for you with such care? Why don't you fetch the roast birds down from the trees? Why don't you dig the dainty broiled mice out of their holes? Why have you stopped fishing in the milky sea? Why don't you take better care of yourself? Why do you refuse to lie on the nice, soft cushions? Why do you wear yourself out instead of resting comfortably and growing good and round?"

"Because, Master Pineiss," answered Glassy, "I feel much better this way! I have only a little while to live—and shouldn't I enjoy that short time in the way it suits me?"

"Not at all!" exclaimed Pineiss. "You should live the sort of life that will make you thick and soft! But I know what you are driving at! You think you'll make a monkey of me and prevent me from doing what we have agreed upon. You think I'll let you go on like this forever? Don't you believe it! I tell you it is your duty to eat and drink and take care of yourself so that you'll grow layer upon layer of fat! I tell you to stop behaving the way you have been doing! And if you don't act according to the contract, I'll have something still more serious to say!"

Glassy stopped purring (which he had begun only to show how calm he was) and said quietly "I don't remember a single word in the contract against my being healthy or living the kind of life I liked. There was nothing in the agreement that did not allow me to eat whatever food I wished, and even chase after it if I cared to! If the town-magician took it for granted that I was a lazy, greedy, good-for-nothing, that is not my fault! You do a thousand good things every day, so do this one also—let us remain good friends as we are. And don't forget that you can only use my fat if you get it by fair means!"

"Stop your chattering!" cried Pineiss angrily. "Don't you dare to lecture me! Perhaps I had better put an end to you at once!" He seized Glassy sharply, whereupon the surprised cat struck out and scratched him sharply on the hand. Pineiss looked thoughtful for a moment. Then he said, "Is that the way things are, you beast? Very well. Then I declare that, according to our agreement, I consider you fat enough. I am satisfied with the way you are, and I will act according to the contract. In five days the moon will be full, and until then you can live the way you wish, just as it is written down.

You can do exactly as you please until then—and not one minute longer!"

With this, he turned his back and left the cat to his own thoughts.

These thoughts, as you can believe, were painful and gloomy. Was the time really so near when Glassy would have to lose his skin? And, with all his cleverness, was there nothing he could do? What miracle could save him now? Sighing, he climbed up to the roof, whose pointed ridge rose like a threatening sign against the happy Autumn sky. It was early evening and the moon began to climb up the other side of the roof. Soon the whole town was flooded with blue light and a sweet song sounded in Glassy's ears. It was the voice of a snow-white puss whose body was shining like silver on a neighboring roof. Immediately Glassy forgot the thought of death and answered with his loudest and loveliest notes. Still singing, he hurried to her side and soon was engaged in the most terrific battle with three other gallant cats. After he had defeated his rivals, he turned to his lady, who met his ardent glance with a modest but encouraging miaow.

Glassy was charmed. He remained with the white stranger day and night, and was her devoted slave. Without giving a single thought to Pineiss, he never came home, but remained close to his lady-love. He sang like a nightingale every moonlight night, went on wild hunts with his fair companion, and was in continual fights with other tomcats who wanted to come too close. Many times he was almost clawed to pieces, many times he was tumbled from the roof; but he only shook his towsled fur and came back to the struggle as hardy as ever. All these adventures—moments of peaceful talk and hours of angry quarrels, love and jealousy, friendship and fights —all of these exciting days made a great change in Glassy. The wild life showed its effects. And finally when the moon was full, the poor animal looked wilder, tougher and thinner than ever.

At this moment, Pineiss (who had not seen his cat for almost a week) leaned out of the window and cried, "Glassy, Glassy! Where are you? Don't you know it's time to come home!" And Glassy, leaving his partner, who trotted off contentedly, came back to the magician's house. It was dark as he entered the kitchen and Pineiss came toward him, rustling the paper contract, and saying, "Come, Glassy, good Glassy." But as soon as the magician had struck a light and saw the cat sitting there defiantly, nothing but a bundle of bones and ragged hair, he flew into a terrible rage. Jumping up and down with anger, he screamed, "So that's the way you tried to cheat me! You villain, you ragamuffin! You evil parcel of bones! Wait! I'll show you!" Beside himself with fury, he seized a broom and sprang at Glassy. But the desperate cat was no longer frightened. With his back high in the air, he faced his maddened owner. His hair stood up straight, sparks flew from his green eyes, and his appearance was so terrifying that Pineiss retreated two or three steps. The town-wizard began to be afraid; for it suddenly struck him that this might also be a magician, and a more powerful one than himself. Uncertain and anxious, he asked in a low voice, "Is the honorable gentleman perhaps in the same profession as myself? Ah, it must be a very learned enchanter who can not only put on the appearance of a cat, but change his size whenever he wishes—large and strong one minute, then suddenly as skinny as a skeleton!"

Glassy calmed himself and spoke honestly. "No, Master Pineiss, I am no magician. It is nothing but my wildness, my love of life, which has taken away my, I mean your, fat. Let us start over again, and this time I promise you I will eat anything and everything you bring me. Fetch out your longest sausage—and you will see!"

Still angry, Pineiss picked Glassy up by his collar and threw him into the goose-pen, which was empty, and cried, "Now see if your love of life will help you. Let's see if your wildness is greater than my witchcraft! Now, my plucked bird, you'll remain in your cage—and there you will eat or die!"

Pineiss began at once to broil a huge sausage that had such a heavenly flavor that he himself had to taste it before he stuck it between the bars. Glassy finished it, skin and all, without stopping for breath. And, as he sat comfortably cleaning his whiskers and smoothing his fur, he said to himself, "Ah, this love of life is a fine thing, after all! Once again it has saved me from a cruel fate. Now I will rest a while and keep my wits about me. This prison is not so bad, and something good may come of having nothing to do but to think and eat for a change. Everything has its time. Yesterday a little trouble; to-day a little quiet; to-morrow something different. Yes, life is a very interesting affair."

Now Pineiss saw to it that no time was wasted. All day long he chopped and seasoned and mixed and boiled and basted and stewed and baked and broiled and roasted and fried. In short he cooked such delicious meals that Glassy simply could not resist. The delighted cat ate and ate until Pineiss was afraid that there would not be enough left in the house for the smallest mouse to nibble at.

When finally Glassy seemed fat enough, Pineiss did not delay a moment. Right in front of his victim's eyes, he set out pots and pans and made a great fire in the stove. Then he sharpened a large knife, lifted the latch of Glassy's cell, pulled the poor cat out (first taking care to lock the kitchen-door) and said cheerfully, "Come, my young friend. Now to business! First, we shall cut your head off; then, when that's done, we shall skin you. Your fur will make a nice warm cap for me and maybe even a pair of gloves. Or shall I skin you first and then cut off your head?"

"No," answered Glassy meekly, "if it's the same to you, I'd rather have my head off first."

"Right you are, poor fellow," said Pineiss, putting some more wood on the big fire, "I don't want to hurt you more than necessary. Let us do only what is right."

"That is a true saying," said Glassy, with a deep sigh and hung his head. "Oh, if I had only remembered that—if I only had done what was right, I could die with a clear conscience, for I die willingly. But a wrong which I have done makes it hard for me."

"What sort of a wrong?" asked Pineiss inquisitively.

"Ah, what's the use of talking about it now," sighed Glassy. "What's done is done and it's too late to cry over it."

"You rascal!" Pineiss went on. "You must indeed be a wicked scoundrel who richly deserves to die. But what did you really *do*? Tell me at once! Have you hid anything of mine? Or stolen something? Have you done me a great injury which I know nothing about? Confess your crimes immediately or I'll skin and boil you alive! Will you talk—or die a horrible death?"

"But you don't understand," said Glassy. "It isn't anything about you that troubles my conscience. It concerns the ten thousand gold guldens of my poor dear mistress. . . . But what's the sense of talking! Only—when I look at you, I think perhaps it is not too late, after all. When I look at you, I see a handsome man still in the prime of life, wise and active and . . . Tell me, Master Pineiss, have you never cared to marry—to come into a good family and a fortune? But what am I talking about! Such a smart and busy man as you has no time for such idle thoughts. Why should such a learned magician think about silly women! Of course, it's no good denying the fact that a woman is very comforting to have around the house. To be sure, a wife can be a great help to a busy man—obliging in her manner, careful about his tastes, sparing with his money and extravagant only in his praise. A good wife will do a thousand things to please her husband. When he is downcast, she will make him happy; when he is happy, she will make him happier. She will fetch his slippers when he wants to be comfortable, stroke his beard and kiss him when he wants to be petted. When he is working, she will let nobody disturb him, but go quietly about her household duties or tell the neighbors what a wonderful man she has. . . . But here I am talking like a fool at the very door of death! How could such a wise man care for such vanities! . . . Excuse me, Master Pineiss, and cut my head off."

But Pineiss spoke up quickly, "Wait a moment, can't you! Tell me, where is such a woman? And are you sure she has ten thousand gold guldens?"

"Ten thousand gold guldens?" asked Glassy.

"Yes," answered Pineiss, impatiently. "Isn't that what you were just talking about?"

"Oh, those are two separate things. The money lies buried in a certain place."

"And what is it doing there? Who does it belong to?" Pineiss asked eagerly.

"To nobody—that's just what is on my conscience! I should have seen to it that the money was put in good hands. Really, the guldens belong to the man who marries the woman I have described. But how is a person to bring those three things together in this stupid town: a fair white lady, ten thousand guldens, and a wise and upright man? That is too hard a task for one poor cat."

"Now listen," advised Pineiss. "If you don't tell me the whole story in the proper order, I'll cut off your tail and both your ears to start with! So begin!"

"Well, if you wish it, I will go ahead," said Glassy, and sat down on his haunches, "although this delay only makes my troubles worse. But still, I am willing to live a little longer—for your sake, Master Pineiss."

The magician stuck his sharp knife in the bare boards between Glassy and himself, sat down on a barrel, and the cat told the following story.

iii

"You may know, Master Pineiss," he began, "that the good lady who used to be my mistress died unmarried. She was a quiet person —people knew her only as an old maid who did good to a great many and harm to none. But she was not always so plain and quiet. As a young girl, she was the most beautiful creature for miles around and young men came flocking from far and wide. Everyone who saw her dancing eyes and laughing mouth fell in love with her at once. She had hundreds of offers of marriage and many a duel was fought on her account. She, too, had decided to marry—and she had enough candidates to choose from. There came bold suitors and shy ones, honest lovers and sly ones, merchants, cavaliers, landowners, loud wooers and silent adorers, suitors who were boastful, suitors who were bashful—in short, the lady had as great a choice as any girl could wish. But she had one great fault: she was suspicious of everybody. Besides her beauty, she had a fortune of many thousand gold guldens—and it was just because of this that she never could decide which man to marry. She had managed her affairs so shrewdly that her property had grown still larger, and (as people always judge others by themselves) she thought that the suitors only wanted her because of her fortune. If a man happened to be rich, she thought, 'Oh, he only wants to increase his wealth. He wouldn't look at me if I were poor.' If a poor man proposed to her, she would think, 'Ah, he's only after my gold guldens.' The foolish lady did not realize that she was thinking about her money much more than the suitors did and what she believed to be *their* greed for gold was really something in her own nature. Several times she was as good as engaged, but at the last minute something in her lover's face would convince her that he, too, was only after her wealth. And so, with a heavy heart, but a stubborn will, she would have no more to do with him.

"When they brought her presents or gave feasts in her honor, she would say, 'I am not so foolish a fish to be caught with such bait!' And she would give their gifts to the poor and send the givers off. In fact she put them to so many tests and treated them so badly that, after a time, all of the right sort of men stayed away. The only men that came to win her were sharp and cunning fellows, and this made her more suspicious than ever. So, in the end, she who was only looking for an honest heart, found herself surrounded by mean and dishonest persons. She could not bear it any longer. One day she sent all the grasping suitors from her doors, locked up the house and set out for Italy, for the city of Milan, where she had a cousin. Her thoughts were heavy and sorrowful as she travelled across the Alps and her eyes were blind to those great mountains, standing like proud kings with sunset crowning their happy heads. Even in Italy, beneath the bluest skies, she remained pale; no matter how light the heavens were, her thoughts were dark.

"But one day the clouds began to lift from her heart and the winds (which had never spoken to her before) whispered little songs in her ear. For a young man had come to visit at her cousin's house, a young man who looked so fair and talked so pleasantly that she fell in love with him at once. He was a handsome youngster, well educated and of fine family, not too rich and not too poor. He had just ten thousand guldens (which had been left to him by his parents) and with this sum he was going to start a silk business in Milan. Highly educated though he was, he seemed as innocent as a child, and, though only a merchant, he carried his sword with a knightly air. All of this so pleased the fair lady that she could scarcely contain herself. She was happy again—and if she had little moments of sadness, it was only when she feared that the young man might not return her affection. The lovelier she grew, the more she worried whether or not she made a good impression on him.

"As for the young merchant, he had never seen anyone so charming and (to tell the truth) he was even more in love with her than she was with him. But he was very shy and most modest. 'How can any man,' he said to his anxious heart, 'hope to win such beauty for himself? How can I expect one so far beyond me even to consider me? No, no, I must not think of it; it is impossible.' For several weeks he tried to conquer his love or, at least, to hide it from the world. But his nature was so warm and sincere he could not disguise it. Whenever he was near his adored one, or even when her name was mentioned, he trembled, grew confused; and it was easy to see where his thoughts were. His very timid manner made my mistress still fonder of him—especially since he was so different from all her other suitors of the past—and her love grew greater with every day.

"Here was a peculiar situation. Two hearts were on fire; cupids were fanning the blaze—and yet nothing happened. Here were two people head-over-heels in love with each other—and remaining as distant as strangers. He, for his part, was too bashful to declare his desire; she, naturally, was too modest to speak of hers. It was a curious comedy, and the people of Milan watched it being played with keen enjoyment. It must be confessed that she helped him a bit —not, of course, with words, but with smiles and little expressions of pleasure whenever he gave her some trifle, and with a hundred unspoken hints that women understand so well. Things could not go on like this much longer. Finally the day came. People were beginning to gossip and he felt it was not fair to her to let matters stand as they were. 'Better put an end to it,' he thought, 'even though it will kill my last hope!' So he came to her and, frightened but desperate, blurted out his love in a few words. He gave her little time to consider, his sentences came so fast. It never occurred to him that a young lady might like to delay the happy moment before answering; he did not know that women, even when they are most in love, say 'no' at first when they expect to say 'yes' afterwards. He just poured out his heart in one burst, ending with, 'Do not keep me in agony! If

I have spoken rashly, let the blow fall at once! With me it is one thing or the other: life or death, yes or no! Speak—which is it to be!'

"Just as she was about to open her arms to him as an answer, her old distrust overcame her. The old suspicion flashed on her that, maybe, like all the others, he only cared for her fortune. 'Possibly,' an evil thought nudged her, 'he is only saying this to get your money into his business. Don't yield to your impulse too quickly. Think it over. Test him first!' Therefore, instead of telling him the truth and completing her happiness, she listened to the voice of doubt and decided to put her lover to a severe test. As he stood waiting for her answer, she put a sad expression on her face and made up the following story.

"She was sorry, she said, that she could not say 'yes' to him because (here she blushed at her falsehood) because she was already engaged to marry a man in her own country. 'I am very fond of you, as you can tell,' she continued, 'and you see I confide in you. I regard you as a brother—but my heart belongs to the man who is waiting for me in my own land. It is a secret that nobody knows—how deeply I love this man and how impossible it would be for me to marry anyone else. We would have been married long ago, but my lover is a poor merchant and he expected to start in business with the money I was to bring him as a bridal gift. Everything was ready; he had started a shop; our wedding was to be celebrated in a few days—when hard times came and, overnight, most of my fortune was lost. My poor lover was beside himself; he did not know where to turn. As I said, he had already made preparations for a large business, had ordered supplies, had bought goods, and he owed for all of it, mostly to merchants in Italy. The day of payment is close at hand, and that is the reason I came here—in the hope of getting help from my relatives. But I see I have come at a bad time; nobody here can do anything for me—even my uncle will not risk his money. And if I return without assistance, I think I will die.'

"She finished and buried her face in her hands, but watched between her fingers to see what effect this tale would have on the young man. During her story, he had grown pale and, as she ended, he was as white as a new napkin. But he did not utter a sound of complaint or speak another word about himself or his love. He only asked, with a sadness he tried to hide, what was the amount of money owed by her fiancé? 'Ten thousand gold guldens,' she answered, in a still sadder voice. The young merchant stood up, advised her to be of good cheer and left the room without telling her how deeply her story had moved him. The poor fellow, of course, believed every word of it and his affection for her was so great that he made up his mind to help her, even though she was (as he thought) going to marry another. Her happiness—not his—was the only thing he now considered. So he gathered together everything he possessed—all the money with which he was going to start in business—and in a few hours' time he was back again. He offered the money and asked her, as a great favor to him, to accept it until things improved after her marriage and her husband could afford to pay it back.

"Her eyes danced and her heart beat faster with a joy such as she had never felt before. She did not doubt any longer. 'But where,' she inquired, as if she could not imagine, 'where did you get all this money?''

" 'Oh,' he replied, 'I have had a lot of luck lately. Business has been very good with me, and I can spare this amount without any trouble.'

"She looked closely at him and knew at once that he was lying; she realized it was his entire fortune he was sacrificing for her sake. Still, she pretended to believe him and thanked him heartily for his kindness. But, she said, she would accept his generous offer only on one condition: that, on a certain day, he would come to her wedding, as he was her best friend and, also, because he had made her marriage possible.

" 'No, no; do not ask me that,' he pleaded, 'ask me anything else!'

" 'And why not?' she inquired, looking offended.

"He grew red and could scarcely speak for a moment. Finally, he said, 'There are many reasons why I cannot come to your wedding. In the first place, my business demands me here. In the second place, I haven't the time to go to Switzerland. And,' he added honestly, 'there are other reasons.'

"But she would not listen to him. 'Unless you do as I ask, I will not accept a single one of these gold-pieces,' she said firmly, and pushed the money toward him.

"So finally he consented and she made him give her his hand in promise. As soon as he left her, she locked the treasure in her trunk and placed the key in the bosom of her dress. She did not stay in Milan more than a few days more, but travelled quickly back to Switzerland. Crossing the Alps was a far different experience than the first time; instead of shedding tears or carrying a dark expression, she laughed and sunshine leaped out of her eyes. It was a happy voyage and a happier home-coming. She aired the house from top to bottom, threw the doors wide open, had the floors polished and decorated the rooms as if she were expecting a royal prince. But at the head of her bed she placed the precious bag with the ten thousand gold gulden, and every night her happy head rested on it as comfortably as though the hard bundle were stuffed with the softest feathers. She could scarcely wait until the day came when he was expected, the day of beautiful surprises, when she would give him not only his own ten thousand guldens, but many times that amount, as well as her whole household and (here she must have blushed sweetly) herself. He would surely come; for she knew, no matter what happened, he would never break his word.

"But the day came and her belovèd did not appear. And many days passed and many weeks, and still he did not come. She began to tremble and all her hours were filled with fear. Her messengers searched for him on every highway. She stood at the window of her topmost balcony from daybreak till night blotted out the whitest roads. She sent despatches to Milan, letter after letter—to him, to relatives, to strangers—all without result. No answer came; no one could tell where he was to be found.

"At last, quite by accident," continued Glassy, taking a breath in the midst of his long story, "she learned that her belovèd had gone to the wars and that his body had been found, full of wounds, on the field of battle. Just before he died, he had turned to the man lying next to him—a Swiss soldier who happened to come from Seldwyla and who had not been so badly hurt—and had given him this message. 'If you ever return to Seldwyla,' he said, 'seek out my love and ask her to forgive me for breaking my word. Tell her I loved her so much that I could not bear to go to her wedding and see her married to another. She will forgive me, I know—if she still remembers me—for she has also suffered because of love. Tell her I wish her a long lifetime of happiness.'

"As soon as the soldier from Seldwyla reached home, he repeated these words (which, like a true Swiss, he had carefully put down in his note-book) to my mistress. The poor girl scarcely listened till he had finished the sad message. She beat her breast, tore her clothes and began to cry in such a loud voice that people far down the street thought that someone was being murdered. Her reason almost left her. She carried his bag of gold guldens about with her as tenderly as if it were a baby. At other times she would scatter the coins on the ground and throw herself, weeping, upon them. She lay there, day and night, without eating or drinking, kissing the cold metal, which was all she had left of him. Suddenly, one dark midnight, she gathered the treasure together, tied up the bag, and, carrying it into her garden, threw it down a deep well so that it should never belong to anyone else."

As soon as Glassy had finished this sorrowful tale, Pineiss broke in eagerly, "And is the money still there?"

"Yes," replied Glassy, "it is lying just where she dropped it. But don't forget that I am the person who was supposed to see that it was given to the right man—and my conscience is troubled because I have failed to do this."

"Quite right," Pineiss added hastily, "your interesting story made me forget all about you. What you say makes me feel that, after all, it might not be a bad thing to have a wife with ten thousand guldens around the house. But she would have to be very pretty! . . . But there must be more to your story. Go on with the rest of it so I can see how it hangs together."

Glassy continued, "It was many years later that I first came to know the unfortunate lady I have been telling you about. She was a lonely old maid when she took me into her household, and I allow myself to believe that I was her best friend and her only comfort to the end of her days. As she saw this end drawing near, she related the whole story of her youth to me and told me, with many tears, how she had lost her whole life's happiness because of suspicion and distrust. 'Let it be a warning to others,' she said to me. 'Ah, if I could only save some other girl from my fate!' It was then that she thought of a way to use the gold guldens lying in the well. 'Promise me, Glassy, you will do just what I tell you?' she said to me one day, as I sat perched on her work-basket. And when I had promised, she spoke as follows: 'Look around, keep your eyes open, until you find a beautiful girl who has no suitors because she is too poor. Then, if she should meet an honest, hard-working, handsome man—and the man loves her for herself alone—then you must help her. If the man will take an oath always to cherish and protect the girl, you are to give her the ten thousand gold guldens which are in the well; so that, on her wedding-day, the bride can surprise her husband by giving him this wedding-present.' Those were almost the last words of my dear mistress. She died soon after speaking them. And, because of my bad luck, I have never been able to carry out her wishes."

iv

There was a moment's silence as Glassy finished. Then Pineiss, with a greedy look and a distrustful voice, said, "I'd like to believe you were telling me the truth. And maybe I *would* believe it—if you could let me have a peep at the place."

"Why not?" answered Glassy. "Only I warn you not to try to take the treasure out of its hiding-place. In the first place, the gold can only be removed at the right time; in the second place, it lies in a very dangerous part and you would be sure to break your neck if you tried to go after it."

"Who said anything about taking it out?" protested Pineiss, somewhat frightened. "Just lead me there so I can see whether you are telling the truth. Or, better still, I will lead you on a stout string so that you won't try to run away."

"As you like!" replied Glassy. "But take a long rope and a lantern with you, for it's a very deep and dark well."

Pineiss followed this advice and led the cat to the garden of his dead mistress. They climbed over a crumbling wall and through an overgrown path which was almost blotted out by bushes and weeds. Finally they reached the spot. Pineiss tied the lantern to the rope and dropped it part of the way down the well, still holding Glassy with the other hand. Pineiss leaned over and trembled as he caught the glint of something shining in the depths.

"Sure enough!" he cried, excitedly. "I see it! It's there, all right! Glassy, you are a wonder!" Then, looking eagerly down again, "Are you sure there are ten thousand?"

"I can't swear to that," replied Glassy, "I have not been down there and I have never counted them! Also, the poor lady may have dropped a few when she carried them here, as she was so worried and nervous at the time."

"Well, if there are two or three less," said Pineiss, rubbing his chin, "I will have to be satisfied." He sat down on the rim of the well; Glassy also seated himself there and began to lick his paws. Pineiss scratched his head and began again, "There is the treasure, and here is the man. But where is the girl?"

"What do you mean?" inquired Glassy.

"I mean there is only one thing missing to fulfil the old lady's wishes—the girl who is to give her husband the ten thousand guldens as a wedding-present and who has also all the other good qualities you spoke about."

"Hum!" replied Glassy, with a wide yawn. "The facts are not exactly the way you state them. The treasure is there, as you have seen, and the girl is ready, for I have already found her. But where can I find the right man who will marry under such conditions? For he will come into a great deal of money, and money brings with it a lot of cares and troubles. The man who has such a fortune has so much to keep him busy. He will have fine horses and many servants. He will have velvet suits and fresh linen sheets, cattle and hunting-dogs, oak furniture and a kitchen full of copper pots. He will have to remember what to tell his gardner to plant, will have to think of his property, his flowers, his wife, his crops, his armour, his old wines, his carriages, his rare books, his games—always his and his and his, from dawn till dark. Yes, owning things is a lot of trouble for a wealthy man. Then there are his rich clothes, his fat cows, his—"

But Pineiss interrupted him. "Enough, you chatterbox! Will you ever stop babbling?" he cried, tugging at the string until Glassy miaowed with pain. For, you can imagine, Pineiss would gladly have had all these "troubles"—and the more he heard about what such a fortune would bring, the more his mouth watered. "Where is the young woman you have found?" he asked, suddenly.

Glassy acted as if he were astonished. "Would you really care to try it? Are you sure?"

"Of course, I am sure! Who else but *I* should have the fortune? Tell me, where is she?" demanded Pineiss.

"So that you can go there and be her suitor?" inquired Glassy. "Absolutely."

"Understand, then," Glassy declared, "the business can only be conducted through me. You must deal with *me* if you want the gold and the girl!"

"I see," said Pineiss slowly. "You are trying to get me to give up our contract so you can save your head?"

"Is that so unnatural?" inquired Glassy, and began to wash his ears with wet paws.

"You think, you sly scoundrel, you'll cheat me in the end!" cried Pineiss.

"Is that possible?" mocked Glassy.

"I tell you, don't you dare betray me!"

"All right, then I won't," said Glassy.

"If you do!" threatened Pineiss.

"Then I will."

"Don't torture me like this!" said the excited Pineiss, almost crying.

And Glassy answered seriously. "You are a remarkable man, Master Pineiss! You have me on a string and you pull on it until I can scarcely breathe. You have kept the sword of death hanging over me for two hours—what am I saying! —for two years, for two eternities! And now you say 'Don't torture me like this!' You ask that of *me!* . . . With your permission, let me tell you something," Glassy continued in a calmer key. "I would be only too happy to carry out the wishes of my late mistress and find the man fit for the lovely girl

I spoke of—and you seem to be the right sort in every way. But it will not be easy for me to persuade the young lady. It is a difficult task. And if I must die . . . ! No, I tell you frankly, Master Pineiss, I must have my freedom before I speak another word. Therefore, take the cord from my neck and lay the contract here on the well-curb, or cut my head off—one or the other!"

"Why so excited and hot-headed?" asked Pineiss. "Let us talk this thing over."

But Glassy sat there, motionless, and for three or four minutes neither uttered a word. Then Pineiss, afraid that he might lose the fortune, reached into his pocket, took out the precious piece of paper, unfolded it, read it through once more and put it slowly down in front of the cat. The paper had scarcely reached the stone-curb before Glassy pounced upon it, chewing up every morsel. And, although he almost choked on some of the large words, he still considered it the best, the most wholesome meal he had ever enjoyed—and hoped it would make him healthy and fat!

As he finished this very satisfying dish, he turned to the magician ceremoniously and said, "You will hear from me without fail, Master Pineiss. I promise to deliver the treasure as well as the lovely lady. Therefore, make yourself ready: prepare to receive your future wife, who is as good as yours already, and be happy. Finally, allow me to thank you for your care and hospitality, and kindly excuse me while I take leave of you for a little while."

So saying, Glassy went his way and rejoiced at the stupidity of the town-wizard who thought he could fool everyone. This man even tried to fool himself, thought Glassy, by declaring he was going to marry the girl for herself alone, whereas all he cared about was the sack of money. Glassy was already thinking of who the bride would be as he passed the street where the magician lived.

v

Across the way from the worker-in-magic, stood a house whose plaster front was whiter than milk and whose windows were always washed till they shone. The curtains were equally white and prim, and everything that one could see was as clean and stiffly ironed as the linen head-dress and collar worn by the woman who lived in this house. She was an old woman, very pious and very ugly. The starched edges and corners of her clothes were sharp; but they were no sharper than her long nose, her pointed chin, her spiteful tongue or her cutting glance. Yet she scarcely ever spoke to people, for she was so stingy she would not even spend her breath on them. Her neighbors disliked her intensely, but they had to admit she was religious—at least she seemed to be. Three times a day they watched her go to church; and every time the children saw her long nose coming down the street, they ran to get out of her way. Even the grown people ducked behind their doors if they had time. But still, even if nobody cared to go near her, she had a good reputation because of her continual prayers and church-going. So the strict old woman lived—never smiling, never mingling with other people—from one day to the other, at peace and utterly alone. And if the neighbors had nothing to do with her, she, for her part, never concerned herself about them. The only person she ever paid any attention to was Pineiss—and him she hated. Whenever he appeared, she would throw him a terrible look and pull her curtains together quickly; while he, who feared her like fire, hid himself away from her.

As I have said, the part of her house that faced the street was neat and clean. But as white as was the front, so dark, so gloomy, so queer and so evil-smelling was the back. Built in the corner of an old wall, it was so black and lost in shadows that it could only be seen by the birds in the air and the cats on the roof. Under the eaves, in a place that no one had ever seen, hung filthy bundles, torn scraps of clothing, ragged underwear, broken baskets, bags of strange herbs. On top of the roof was a little forest of thorn-bushes and mosses, from the centre of which a thin chimney stretched its length like a lean and wicked finger. And out of this chimney, when the nights were darkest, a witch would often rise—young and fair and without a stitch of clothing—and go riding about on a broom-stick. Thus, by the power of her secret magic, the old woman would disguise herself as a young girl. She would laugh lightly as she galloped through the air on her one-footed steed; her lips would shine like polished cherries and her long black hair would flutter in the night-wind like a flag.

In a hole in the chimney sat an old owl. And it was to this wise bird that Glassy came as soon as he was freed, carrying a fat mouse in his jaws.

"Good evening, dear Madam Owl," said Glassy. "Still busy keeping watch?"

"I have to," replied the owl. "And good evening to you. You have not given your friends the pleasure of your company for a long time."

"There were reasons, as I will tell you. Have you had your supper yet? No? Here is a mouse; nothing much, but it is all I could find on the way. I hope you won't refuse it. And has your mistress gone out riding?"

"Not yet," answered the owl. "She will wait another hour until it is almost morning. Thanks for the fine mouse. And here I have a small sparrow laid aside; it happened to fly too close to me. Try it, just to please me. And how have things gone with you?"

"Wonderfully. You would hardly believe it. If you care to listen, I'll tell you." And so, while the two good friends enjoyed their little meal, Glassy told the whole tale, how he came to make the fearful contract, how Pineiss had almost killed him and how, in the end, he had saved himself.

After Glassy had finished, the owl said, "Well, I congratulate you! And I wish you the best of luck. Now you are a free man again; you can go where you please and do whatever you wish!"

"But not right away," objected Glassy. "First, Pineiss must have his lady and the ten thousand gold guldens."

"Are you crazy?" screamed the owl. "Surely, you are only joking! You certainly are not going to reward the man who wanted to take the very skin off your back?"

"Yes, he was about to do that. But if I can pay him back in the same coin, why shouldn't I? The story I told him was a pure fairy-tale; I made the whole thing up myself from beginning to end. My mistress was a simple body; she was quite plain, had never been in love, and no suitors ever came near her all her life. As to the treasure, there really are some guldens at the bottom of the well. But it is stolen money and my mistress would never touch it. 'Let it lie there,' she used to say to me, 'for there is a curse on it. Whoever takes it out and uses it will be unlucky!' That shall be Master Pineiss's 'reward'!"

"Ah," the owl chuckled, "that's different! You're a deep one! But where is the promised lady going to come from?"

"From this chimney!" answered Glassy. "That is the reason I came here. Let us talk it over like two sensible people. Wouldn't you like to be free of this witch who is always making you work for her? And wouldn't it be a lovely thing to get these two old villains married to each other? But first, we must catch our witch. And that's no easy matter. Stir your brains; think how we can manage it!"

For a while there was nothing but silence in the night. Then the owl whispered, "I think I have it! As soon as you are here with me, my brain begins to work!"

"Good," said Glassy. "Soon we will have a plan."

"I have a plan already," continued the owl. "Everything joins together nicely."

"When do we begin?" asked Glassy, eagerly.

"At once!" said the owl.

"And how are we going to catch her?" inquired Glassy, with eyes that burned like green fire.

"With a net for catching snipe, a fine new net made of the toughest hemp. It must have been woven by a twenty-year-old hunter's son who has never once looked at a woman. The night-dew must have fallen three times upon it where it lay without having caught a single snipe. And it must have lain there because of three good deeds. Only such a net is strong enough to catch witches!"

"But I am curious to know where such a net can be found," said Glassy. "There must be one somewhere in the world, I suppose, because I have never known you to say a foolish thing. But where," repeated the puzzled animal, "are we ever to find such a remarkable affair?"

"It has been found already, just as if it were made for us," replied the owl. "Listen. In a wood, not far from here, there sits the twenty-year-old son of a hunter who has never looked at a woman as much as once. He was born blind. There's your first requirement. Being blind, he cannot do much except weave yarn and, a few days ago, he finished a fine net for catching snipe. As the old hunter was about to spread it out to trap the birds, a woman came along who wanted him to go with her and join a band of wealthy robbers. But she was so hideous that he dropped everything in fright and ran away. So the hempen net lay in the dew without catching a snipe and a good motive was the cause of it. The next day, as the old hunter returned to stretch the net, a horseman rode past carrying a heavy bundle behind him. In this bundle was a small hole and, from time to time, a gold-piece fell out of it. The hunter dropped the net again and ran hotly after the horseman, picking up the gold pieces and putting them in his own hat—until suddenly the horseman turned around, saw what the hunter had been doing, and charged angrily down upon him. Fearing for his life, the hunter bowed suddenly, snatched his cap from his head and said, 'Allow me—you have been losing your money, and I have run all the way after so I could give it back to you.' This was the second 'good' act and, as the hunter was by this time far away from the net, it lay a second night without being used as a trap. Finally on the third day, which was yesterday, as he came to the place, he met a young woman who carried a basketful of delicious home-cooked sausages and cakes. She was a pleasant girl and when she invited the hunter to come to her sister's wedding, where there was to be a great feast that evening, he accepted gladly and said, 'Oh, let the snipes go! One ought to take pity on the animals! Besides, who cares for snipes when there's a goose?' And because of these three good acts, the net has lain for three nights in the dew without being used—quite ready for us. All I have to do is fetch it."

"Fetch it quickly, then," cried Glassy. "It is the very thing we need!"

"I will get it at once," said the owl. "You keep watch for me here and if my mistress should call up the chimney asking if the coast is clear, answer her in my voice and say, 'No, it is not foul enough!'"

Glassy, thereupon, took his friend's place and the owl flew over the town toward the wood. In fifteen minutes she was back, carrying the snipe-net in her beak. "Has she called out?" asked the owl. "Not yet," said Glassy.

Then they stretched the closely woven trap over the chimney and sat down to wait for whatever might happen. The night was pitch dark and an early morning wind blew out two or three pale stars. Suddenly they heard the witch's voice: "Is the coast clear?" And the owl answered, "Quite clear. The air is fine and foul!"

As soon as the words were said, a white form rose from the chimney—and the next moment the witch was squirming in the snare, while the two animals pulled and tied it together. The witch raged and kicked and flopped and floundered like a gleaming fish in a net, but "Hold fast!" cried the owl, and "Tie it tight!" called Glassy. And the net held. Finally, seeing she was helpless, the witch grew quiet and asked, "What do you want of me, you strange creatures?"

"Let me leave your service and give me my freedom," said the owl.

"Such a great boast for such a little roast!" said the witch, using an old Swiss proverb. "Why all this trouble? You are free. Now open the net."

"Wait a moment," cried Glassy, "before we let you out you must promise to marry the town-wizard, Pineiss, in the way we shall explain to you."

"Marry that man? Never!" replied the witch, and began to fume again.

But Glassy continued quietly. "Would you like the whole town to know who you are? If you don't do exactly as we say, we will hang the net—and all that is inside of it—right under the part of your roof which faces the street. Tomorrow morning the villagers will pass this house on their way to work. When they look up, they'll see you caught here and everybody will know who the witch is! Besides," Glassy went on in a more persuading tone of voice, "just think how easy you will be able to rule Master Pineiss after you are his wife!"

It is hard to say which of these two arguments convinced the witch. At any rate, after a long pause, she said with a sigh, "Tell me, then, what you want me to do." And Glassy told her the plan he had in mind and explained to her exactly how it was to be carried out. "Very well, then, as I cannot help myself, I agree," said the sorceress, and pledged her word with the strongest magic known to witchcraft. Then she mounted her broom, the owl settled herself on the handle. Glassy perched securely behind on the straw bottom, and so they flew through the air to the old well. The witch descended it, took out the treasure and the three parted company for the time being.

Early next morning Glassy appeared before Pineiss and informed him that he could see the promised lady. She was so poor and lonely that she had no suitors and was sitting underneath a willow in front of the town-gate, crying bitterly. As soon as Pineiss heard this, he was overjoyed and his dark room seemed lighter. He ran to his mirror, took off his shabby working clothes, put on his yellow velvet doublet (which he only wore on holidays), his silk hose (which he always thought too good to wear), his best fur-cap, and stuck a colored handkerchief in his pocket. As if this were not enough, he sprinkled perfume on himself, sent a boy out for a big bouquet of flowers, carried a pair of green gloves and, thus magnificently attired, went with Glassy to the town-gate. There he saw a girl seated under a willow-tree weeping as if her heart would break. She was the loveliest person he had ever seen, even though her dress was so torn that it barely covered her. Pineiss could scarcely take his eyes off her and it was some time before he could speak. The girl was really too beautiful. But she dried her eyes as he comforted her and when he asked her to marry him, she even laughed in musical tones and said yes. Quickly Pineiss provided her with a wedding-dress and a bridal veil as long as a water-fall. She looked lovelier than ever, so radiant that when they passed the town the men sitting outside raised their glasses and cheered. Afraid that she might change her mind, Pineiss hurried to an old hermit and, within an hour, the town-magician and the fair unknown were made man and wife. Candles were lit, merry cupids seemed to be singing in the air and, with downcast eyes, the lovely bride entered her new home. The wedding-feast was celebrated in the wizard's house without any other guests except the owl and the cat, who had asked permission to come. The ten thousand gold guldens were in a bowl upon the table and Pineiss's greedy eyes kept looking from his beloved gold to the lovely girl and back again from the girl to the gold. She sat, in sea-blue velvet, with pearls around her slender neck and her eyes brighter than diamonds. But Pineiss cared most for her piled-up yellow hair, for it looked to him like a great mass of glittering gold-pieces.

It was a merry dinner, spiced with Glassy's witty remarks, flavored with the owl's wise sayings and sweetened with the smiles of the beautiful bride. When the meal was over, the two animals sang a few duets and, as it was beginning to grow dark, prepared to leave their host. Pineiss took them, with a light, to the door, thanked Glassy again and wished them both good-night. Then, gleefully rubbing his hands together, he went back to the room, congratulating himself on his clever bargain. He closed the door, letting his greedy eyes drink in the happy sight.

There, in the bowl, sparkled the yellow money. But, as his eyes went further, his heart almost stopped beating. Something had gone wrong! There, at the head of the table, instead of the young bride, sat his neighbor, the horrible old woman, frowning at him with a look of hate! She rose from her chair, picked up a broomstick and rode on it in all her hideousness. Imps and demons appeared in every corner, goblins ran about, kobolds sprang on top of the stove. The room was full of strange sounds and queer lights. The very air flickered. Dazzled and scarcely able to see, Pineiss let the candle fall and leaned, trembling, against the wall. His jaw dropped and his whole face grew as white and sharp as the old witch's. They were two of a kind—and the town-wizard richly deserved his "reward."

When the marriage became known, the townspeople said, "Still waters run deep! Who would have thought that the pious old lady would have married the master-magician! Well, they are a well-matched pair—if not very handsome!"

From that time on, Pineiss lived a hard life. His wife learned all his secrets and kept him busy from morning to night. She ruled him with an iron hand; there was not an idle minute he could call his own. And whenever Glassy happened to pass by, the cat would smile cheerfully and say, "Always busy—eh, Master Pineiss? That's the way—always keep busy!"

And so in Seldwyla, even to-day, whenever a person has made a bad bargain, they say, "Too bad! But he should never have tried to buy the fat off the cat!"

Broomsticks

WALTER DE LA MARE

Miss Chauncey's cat, Sam, had been with her many years before she noticed anything unusual, anything *disturbing*, in his conduct. Like most cats who live under the same roof with but one or two humans, he had always been more sagacious than cats of a common household. He had learned Miss Chauncey's ways. He acted, that is, as nearly like a small mortal dressed up in a hairy coat as one could expect a cat to act. He was what is called an "intelligent" cat.

But though Sam had learned much from Miss Chauncey, I am bound to say that Miss Chauncey had learned very little from Sam. She was a kind indulgent mistress; she could sew, and cook, and crochet, and make a bed, and read and write and cipher a little. And when she was a girl she used to sing "Kathleen Mavourneen" to the piano. Sam, of course, could do nothing of this kind.

But then, Miss Chauncey could no more have caught and killed a mouse or a blackbird with her five naked fingers than she could have been Pope of Rome. Nor could she run up a six-foot brick wall, or leap clean from the hearth-mat in her parlor on to the shelf of her chimney-piece without disturbing a single ornament, or even tinkle one crystal glass-drop against another. Unlike Sam, she could not find her way in the dark, or by her sense of smell; or keep in good health by merely nibbling grass in the garden. If, moreover, as a little girl she had been held up by her feet and hands two or three feet above the ground and then dropped, she would have at once fallen plump on her back, whereas when Sam was only a three-months-old, he could have managed to twist clean about in the air in twelve inches and come down on his four feet as firm as a table.

While Sam, then, had learned a good deal from Miss Chauncey, she had learned nothing from him. And even if she had been willing to be taught, it is doubtful if she would ever have proved even a promising pupil. What is more, she knew much less about Sam than he knew about his mistress—until, at least, that afternoon when she was doing her hair in the glass. And then she could hardly believe her own eyes. It was a moment that completely changed her views about Sam—and nothing after that experience was ever quite the same again.

Sam had always been a fine upstanding creature, his fur jet-black and silky, his eyes a lambent green, even in sunshine, and at night a-glow like green topazes. He was now full seven years of age, and had an unusually powerful miaou. Living as he did quite alone with Miss Chauncey at Post Houses, it was natural that he should become her constant companion. For Post Houses was a singularly solitary house, standing almost in the middle of Haggurdsdon Moor, just where two wandering byways cross each other like the half-closed blades of a pair of shears or scissors.

It was a mile and a half from its nearest neighbor, Mr. Cullings, the carrier; and yet another quarter of a mile from the village of Haggurdsdon. Its roads were extremely ancient. They had been sheep-tracks long before the Romans came to England and had cut *their* roads from shore to shore. But for many years past few travellers or carts or even sheep with their shepherd came Miss Chauncey's way. You could have gazed from her windows for hours together, even on a summer's day, without seeing so much as a tinker's barrow or a gipsy's van.

Post Houses, too, was perhaps the ugliest house there ever was. Its four corners stood straight up on the moor like a house of nursery bricks. From its flat roof on a clear day the eye could see for miles across the moor, Mr. Cullings' cottage being out of sight in a shallow hollow. It had belonged to Miss Chauncey's ancestors for numbers of generations. Many people in Haggurdsdon indeed called it Chauncey's. And though in a great wind it was almost as full of noises as an organ, though it was a cold barn in winter and though another branch of the family had as far back as the 'seventies gone to live in the Isle of Wight, Miss Chauncey still remained faithful to its four walls. In fact she loved the ugly old place, for she had lived in it ever since she was a little girl with knickerbockers showing under her skirts and pale-blue ribbon shoulder knots.

This fact alone made Sam's conduct the more reprehensible, for never cat had kinder mistress. Miss Chauncey herself was now about sixty years of age—fifty-three years older than Sam. She was five foot ten-and-a-half inches in height. On week-days she wore black alpaca, and on Sundays a watered silk. Her large round steel spectacles straddling across her high nose gave her a look of being keen as well as cold. But truly she was neither. For even so stupid a man as Mr.

Cullings could take her in over the cartage charge of a parcel—just by looking tired or sighing as he glanced at his rough-haired, knock-kneed mare. And there was the warmest of hearts under her stiff bodice.

Being so far from the village, milk and cream were a little difficult, of course. But Miss Chauncey could deny Sam nothing—in reason. She paid a whole sixpence a week to a little girl called Susan Ard who brought these dainties from the nearest farm. They were dainties indeed, for though the grasses on Haggurdsdon Moor were of dark sour green, the cows that grazed on it gave an uncommonly rich milk, and Sam flourished on it. Mr. Cullings called once a week on his round, and had a standing order to bring with him a few sprats or fresh herrings, or any other toothsome fish that was in season. Miss Chauncey would not even withhold her purse from expensive white-bait, if no other cheaper fish were procurable. And Mr. Cullings would eye Sam fawning about his cartwheel, or gloating up at his dish, and say, " 'Ee be a queer animal, shure enough; 'ee be a wunner-ful queer animal, 'ee be."

As for Miss Chauncey herself, she was a niggardly eater, though much attached to her tea. She made her own bread and cookies. On Saturday a butcher-boy drove up in a striped apron. Besides which she was a wonderful manager. Her cupboards were full of homemade jams and bottled fruits and dried herbs—everything of that kind, for Post Houses had a nice long strip of garden behind it, surrounded by a high old yellow brick wall.

Quite early in life Sam, of course, had learned to know his meal-time—though how he "told" it was known only to himself, for he never appeared even to glance at the face of the grandfather's clock on the staircase. He was punctual, particularly in his toilet, and a prodigious sleeper. He had learned to pull down the latch of the back door, if, in the months when an open window was not to be found, he wished to go out. Indeed at last he preferred the latch. He never slept on Miss Chauncey's patchwork quilt, unless his own had been placed over it. He was particular almost to a foppish degree in his habits, and he was no thief. He had a mew on one note to show when he wanted something to eat; a mew a semitone or two higher if he wanted drink (that is, cold water, for which he had a great taste) ; and yet another mew—gentle and sustained—when he wished, so to speak, to converse with his mistress.

Not, of course, that the creature talked *English*, but he liked to sit up on one chair by the fireside, especially in the kitchen—for he was no born parlor-cat—and to look up at the glinting glasses of Miss

Chauncey's spectacles, and then down awhile at the fire-flames (drawing his claws in and out as he did so, and purring the while), almost as if he might be preaching a sermon, or reciting a poem.

But this was in the happy days when all seemed well. This was in the days when Miss Chauncey's mind was innocent of all doubts and suspicions. Like others of his kind, too, Sam delighted to lie in the window and idly watch the birds in the apple-trees—tits and bull-finches and dunnocks—or to crouch over a mouse-hole for hours together. Such were his amusements (for he never ate his mice) while Miss Chauncey with cap and broom, duster and dishclout, went about her housework. But he also had a way of examining things in which cats are not generally interested. He as good as told Miss Chauncey one afternoon that a hole was coming in her parlor carpet. For he walked to and fro and back and forth with his tail up, until she attended to him. And he certainly warned her, with a yelp like an Amazonian monkey, when a red-hot coal had set her kitchen mat on fire.

He would lie or sit with his whiskers to the North before noonday, and due South afterwards. In general his manners were perfection. But occasionally when she called him, his face would appear to knot itself into a frown—at any rate to assume a low sullen look, as if he expostulated "Why must you be interrupting me, Madam, when I am thinking of something else?" And now and then, Miss Chauncey fancied he would deliberately secrete himself or steal out and in of Post Houses unbeknown.

Miss Chauncey, too, would sometimes find him trotting from room to room as if on a visit of inspection. On his fifth birthday he had brought an immense mouse and laid it beside the patent toe-cap of her boot, as she sat knitting by the fire. She smiled and nodded merrily at him, as usual, but on this occasion he had looked at her intently, and then deliberately shook his head. After that, he never paid the smallest attention to mouse or mouse-hole or mousery, and Miss Chauncey was obliged to purchase a cheese-bait trap, else she would have been overrun.

Almost any domestic cat may do things of this nature, and of course all this was solely on Sam's domestic side. For he shared a house with Miss Chauncey and, like any two beings that lived together, he was bound to keep up certain appearances. He met her half-way, as the saying goes. When, however, he was "on his own," he was no longer Miss Chauncey's Sam, he was no longer merely the cat at Post Houses, but just *himself*. He went back, that is, to his own free independent life; to his own private habits.

Then the moor on which he roved was his own country, and the humans and their houses on it were no more to him in his wild, privy existence than molehills or badgers' earths, or rabbits' mounds, are to us. On this side of his life his mistress knew practically nothing. She did not consider it. She supposed that Sam behaved like other cats, though it was evident that at times he went far abroad, for he now and then brought home a Cochin China chick, and the nearest Cochin China fowls were at the vicarage, a good four miles off. Sometimes of an evening, too, when Miss Chauncey was taking a little walk herself, she would see him—a swiftly-moving black speck—far along the road, hastening home. And there was more purpose expressed in his gait and appearance than ever Mr. Cullings showed!

It was pleasant to observe, too, when he came within miaouing distance how his manner changed. He turned at once from being a Cat into being a Domestic Cat. He was instantaneously no longer the Feline Adventurer, the Nocturnal Marauder and Haunter of Haggurdsdon Moor (though Miss Chauncey would not have so expressed it), but simply his mistress' spoiled pet, Sam. She loved him dearly. But, as again with human beings who are accustomed to live together, she did not *think* very much about him. It could not but be a shock then that latish afternoon, when without the slightest warning Miss Chauncey discovered that Sam was deliberately deceiving her!

She was brushing her thin brown front hair before her looking-glass. And this moment it hung down over her face like a fine loose veil. And as she always mused of other things when she was brushing her hair, she was somewhat absentminded the while. Then suddenly on raising her eyes behind this mesh of hair, she perceived not only that Sam's reflection was in sight of the looking-glass, but that something a little mysterious was happening. Sam was sitting up as if to beg. There was nothing in that. It had been a customary feat of his since he was six months old. Still, for what might he be begging, no one by?

Now the window to the right of the chintz-valanced dressing-table was open at the top. Without, it was beginning to grow dark. All Haggurdsdon Moor lay hushed and still in the evening's coming gloom. And apart from begging when there was nothing to beg for, Sam seemed, so to speak, to be gesticulating with his paws. He appeared, that is, to be making signs, just as if there were someone or something looking in at the window at him from out of the air— which was quite impossible. And there was a look upon his face that certainly Miss Chauncey had never seen before.

She stayed a moment with her hair-brush uplifted, her long lean arm at an angle with her head. On seeing this, Sam had instantly desisted from these motions. He had dropped to his fours again, and was now apparently composing himself for another nap. No; this too was a pretense, for presently as she watched, he turned restlessly about so that his whiskers were once again due South. His backward part toward the window, he was now gazing straight in front of him out of a far from friendly face. Far indeed from friendly for a creature that has lived with you ever since he opened the eyes of his first kittenhood.

As if he had read her thoughts, Sam at that moment lifted his head to look at his mistress; she withdrew her eyes to the glass only in the nick of time and when she turned from her toilet there sat he—so serene in appearance, so puss-like, so ordinary once more that Miss Chauncey could scarcely believe anything whatever had been amiss. Had her eyes deluded her—her glass? Was that peculiar motion of Sam's fore-paws (almost as if he were knitting), was that wide excited stare only due to the fact that he was catching what was, to her, an invisible fly?

Miss Chauncey having now neatly arranged her "window-curtains" —the sleek loops of hair she wore on either side her high forehead —glanced yet again at the window. Nothing there but the silence of the moor; nothing there but the faint pricking of a star as the evening darkened.

Sam's cream was waiting on the hearthrug in the parlor as usual at five o'clock. The lamp was lit. The red blinds were drawn. The fire crackled in the grate. There they sat, these two; the walls of the four-cornered house beside the cross-roads rising up above them like a huge oblong box under the immense starry sky that saucered in the wide darkness of the moor.

And while she so sat—with Sam there, seemingly fast asleep— Miss Chauncey was thinking. What had occurred in the bedroom that early evening had reminded her of other odd little bygone happenings. Trifles she had scarcely noticed but which now returned clearly to memory. How often in the past, for example, Sam at this hour would be sitting as if fast asleep (as now) his paws tucked neatly in, looking much like a stout alderman after a high dinner. And then suddenly, without warning, as if a distant voice had called him, he would leap to his feet and run straight out of the room. And somewhere in the house—door ajar or window agape, he would find his egress and be up and away into the night. This had been a common thing to happen.

Once, too, Miss Chauncey had found him squatting on his hind-quarters on the window-ledge of a little room that had been entirely disused since her fair little Cousin Milly had stayed at Post Houses when Miss Chauncey was a child of eight. She had cried out at sight of him, "You foolish Sam, you! Come in, sir. You will be tumbling out of the window next!" And she remembered as if it were yesterday that though at this he had stepped gingerly in at once from his dizzy perch, he had not looked at her. He had passed her without a sign.

On moonlight evenings, too—why, you could never be sure where he was. You could never be sure from what errand he had *returned*. Was she sure indeed where he was on *any* night? The longer she reflected, the deeper grew her doubts and misgivings. This night, at any rate, Miss Chauncey determined to keep watch. But she was not happy in doing so. She hated all manner of spying. They were old companions, Sam and she; and she, without him, in bleak Post Houses, would be sadly desolate. She loved Sam dearly. None the less, the spectacle of that afternoon haunted her, and it would be wiser to know all that there was to be known, even if for Sam's sake only.

Now Miss Chauncey always slept with her bedroom door ajar. She had slept so ever since her nursery days. Being a rather timid little girl, she liked in those far-away times to hear the grown-up voices downstairs and the spoons and forks clinking. As for Sam, he always slept in his basket beside her fireplace. Every morning there he would be, though on some mornings Miss Chauncey's eyes would open gently to find herself gazing steadily into his pale-green ones as he stood on his hind-paws, resting his front ones on her bed-side, and looking up into her face. "Time for your milk, Sam?" his mistress would murmur. And Sam would mew, as distantly almost as a sea-gull in the height of the sky.

To-night, however, Miss Chauncey only pretended to fall asleep. It was difficult, however, to keep wholly awake, and she was all but drowsing off when there came a faint squeak from the hinge of her door, and she realized that Sam was gone out. After waiting a moment or two, she struck a match. Yes, there was his empty basket in the dark silent room, and presently from far away—from the steeple at Haggurdsdon Village—came the knolling of midnight.

Miss Chauncey placed the dead end of the match in the saucer of her candlestick, and at that moment fancied she heard a faint *whssh* at her window, as of a sudden gust or scurry of wind, or the wings of a fast-flying bird—of a wild goose. It even reminded Miss Chauncey of half-forgotten Guy Fawkes Days and of the sound the stick of a rocket makes as it sweeps down through the air while its green and ruby lights die out in the immense heavens above. Miss Chauncey gathered up her long legs in the bed, drew on the flannel dressing-gown that always hung on her bed-rail, and lifting back the blind an inch or two, looked out of the window.

It was a high starry night, and a brightening in the sky above the roof seemed to betoken there must be a moon over the backward parts of the house. Even as she watched, a streak of pale silver descended swiftly out of the far spaces of the heavens where a few large stars were gathered as if in the shape of a sickle. It was a meteorite; and at that very instant Miss Chauncey fancied she heard a faint remote dwindling *whssh* in the air. Was *that* a meteor too? Could she have been deceived? Was she being deceived in everything? She drew back.

And then, as if in deliberate and defiant answer, out of the distance, from what appeared to be the extreme end of her long garden, where grew a tangle of sloe bushes, there followed a prolonged and as if half-secret caterwaul; very low—contralto, one might say—*Meea-rou-rou-rou-rou-rou.*

Heaven forbid! Was *that* Sam's tongue? The caterwauling ceased. Yet still Miss Chauncey could not suppress a shudder. She knew Sam's voice of old. But surely not that! Surely not that!

Strange and immodest, too, though it was to hear herself in that solitary place calling out in the dead of night, she none the less at once opened the window and summoned Sam by name. There was no response. The trees and bushes of the garden stood motionless; their faint shadows on the ground revealing how small a moon was actually in the sky, and how low it hung towards its setting. The vague undulations of the moor stretched into the distance. Not a light to be seen except those of the firmament. Again, and yet again, Miss Chauncey cried "Sam, Sam! Come away in! Come away in, sir, you bad creature!" Not a sound. Not the least stir of leaf or blade of grass.

When, after so broken a night, Miss Chauncey awoke a little late the next morning, the first thing her eyes beheld when she sat up in bed was Sam—couched as usual in his basket. It was a mystery, an uneasy one. After supping up his morning bowl, he slept steadily on until noonday. This happened to be the day of the week when Miss Chauncey made bread. On and on she steadily kneaded the dough with her knuckled hands, glancing ever and again towards the motionless creature. With fingers clotted from the great earthenware bowl, she stood over him at last for a few moments, and looked at him closely.

He was lying curled round with his whiskered face to one side towards the fire. And it seemed to Miss Chauncey that she had never noticed before that faint peculiar grin on his face. "Sam!" she cried sharply. An eye instantly opened, fiercely green as if a mouse had squeaked. He stared at her for an instant; then the lid narrowed. The gaze slunk away a little, but Sam began to purr.

The truth of it is, all this was making Miss Chauncey exceedingly unhappy. Mr. Cullings called that afternoon with a basket of some fine comely young sprats. "Them'll wake his Royal Highness up," he said. "They'm fresh as daisies. Lor, m'm, what a Nero that beast be!"

"Cats *are* strange creatures, Mr. Cullings," replied Miss Chauncey reflectively, complacently, supposing that Mr. Cullings had misplaced an *h* and had meant to say *an hero*. And Sam himself, with uplifted tail, and as if of the same opinion, was rubbing his head gently against her boot.

Mr. Cullings eyed her closely. "Why, yes, they be," he said. "What I says is, is that as soon as they're out of sight, you are out of their mind. There's no more gratitood nor affection in a cat than in a pump. Though so far as the pump is concerned, the gratitood should be on our side. I knew a Family of Cats once what fairly druv their mistress out of house and home."

"But you wouldn't have a cat *only* a pet?" said Miss Chauncey faintly; afraid to ask for further particulars of the peculiar occurrence.

"Why no, m'm," said the carrier. "As the Lord made 'em, so they be. But I'll be bound they could tell some knotty stories if they had a human tongue in their heads!"

Sam had ceased caressing his mistress's foot, and was looking steadily at Mr. Cullings, his hair roughed a little about the neck and shoulders. And the carrier looked back.

"No, m'm. We wouldn't keep 'em," he said at last, "if they was *four* times that size. Or, not for long!"

Having watched Mr. Cullings' little cart bowl away into the distance, Miss Chauncey returned into the house, more disturbed than ever. Nor did her uneasiness abate when Sam refused even to sniff at his sprats. Instead, he crawled under a low table in the kitchen, behind the old seaman's chest in which Miss Chauncey kept her kindling-wood. She fancied she heard his claws working in the wood now and again; once he seemed to be expressing his natural feelings in what vulgar people with little sympathy for animals describe as "swearing."

Her caressing "Sams," at any rate, were all in vain. His only reply was a kind of sneeze which uncomfortably resembled "spitting." Miss Chauncey's feelings had already been hurt. It was now her mind that suffered. Something the carrier had said, or the way he had said it, or the peculiar look she had noticed on his face when he was returning Sam's stare in the porch, haunted her thoughts. She was no longer young; was she becoming fanciful? Or must she indeed conclude that for weeks past Sam had been steadily deceiving her, or at any rate concealing his wanderings and his interests? What nonsense! Worse still:—Was she now so credulous as to believe that Sam had in actual fact been making signals—and secretly, behind her back—to some confederate that must either have been up in the sky, or in the moon!

Whether or not, Miss Chauncey determined to keep a sharper eye on him, if for his own sake only. She would at least make sure that he did not leave the house that night. But then: why not? she asked herself. Why shouldn't the creature choose his own hour and season? Cats, like owls, *see* best in the dark. They go best a-mousing in the dark, and may prefer the dark for their private, social, and even public affairs. Post Houses, after all, was only rather more than two miles from Haggurdsdon Village, and there were cats there in plenty. Poor fellow, her own dumb human company must sometimes be dull enough!

Such were Miss Chauncey's reflections; and as if to reassure her, Sam himself at that moment serenely entered the room and leapt up on to the empty chair beside her tea-table. As if, too, to prove that he had thought better of his evil temper, or to insinuate that there had been nothing amiss between himself and Mr. Cullings, he was licking his chops, and there was no mistaking the odor of fish which he brought in with him from his saucer.

"So you have thought better of it, my boy?" thought Miss Chauncey, though she did not utter the words aloud. And yet as she returned his steady feline gaze, she realized how difficult it was to read the intelligence behind those eyes. You might say that, Sam being only a cat, there was no meaning in them at all. But Miss Chauncey knew she couldn't have said it if such eyes had looked out of a *human* shape at her! She would have been acutely alarmed.

Unfortunately, and almost as if Sam had overheard his mistress's speculations regarding possible cat friends in the Village, there came at that moment a faint wambling mew beneath the open window. In a flash Sam was out of his chair and over the window ledge, and Miss Chauncey rose only just in time to see him in infuriated pursuit of a slim sleek tortoise-shell creature that had evidently come to Post Houses in hope of a friendlier reception, and was now fleeing in positive fear of its life.

Sam returned from his chase as fresh as paint, and Miss Chauncey was horrified to detect—caught up between the claws of his right foot —a tuft or two of tortoise-shell fur, which, having composed himself by the fire, he promptly removed by licking.

Still pondering on these disquieting events, Miss Chauncey took her usual evening walk in the garden. Candytuft and Virginia stock were blossoming along the shell-lined path, and roses were already beginning to blow on the high brick wall which shut off her narrow strip of land from the vast lap of the moor. Having come to the end of the path, Miss Chauncey pushed on a little farther than usual, to where the grasses grew more rampant, and where wild headlong weeds raised their heads beneath her few lichenous apple trees. Still farther down—for hers was a long, though narrow, garden—there grew straggling bushes of sloe, spiny white-thorn. These had blossomed there indeed in the moor's bleak springs long before Post Houses had raised its chimney-pots into the sky. Here, too, flourished a dense drift of dead nettles—their sour odor haunting the air.

And it was in this forlorn spot that—like Robinson Crusoe before her—Miss Chauncey was suddenly brought to a standstill by the sight of what appeared to be nothing else than a strange footprint in the mould. Nearby the footprint, moreover, showed what might be the impression of a walking-cane or possibly of something stouter and heavier—a crutch. Could she again be deceived? The footprint, it was true, was unlike most human footprints, the heel sunk low, the toe square. Might it be accidental? *Was* it a footprint?

Miss Chauncey glanced up across the bushes toward the house. It loomed gaunt and forbidding in the moorland dusk. And she fancied she could see, though the evening light might be deceiving her, the cowering shape of Sam looking out at her from the kitchen-window. To be watched! To be herself spied upon—and watched.

But then, of course, Sam was always watching her. What oddity was there in that? Where else would his sprats come from, his cream, his saucer of milk, his bowl of fresh well-water? Nevertheless Miss Chauncey returned to her parlor gravely discomposed.

It was an uncommonly still evening, and as she went from room to room locking the windows, she noticed there was already a moon in the sky. She eyed it with misgiving. And at last bed-time came, and when Sam, as usual, after a lick or two had composed himself in his basket, Miss Chauncey, holding the key almost challengingly within view, deliberately locked her bedroom door.

When she awoke next morning Sam was sleeping in his basket as usual, and during the day-time he kept pretty closely to the house. So, too, on the Wednesday and the Thursday. It was not until the following Friday that having occasion to go into an upper bedroom that had no fireplace, and being followed as usual by Sam, Miss Chauncey detected the faint rank smell of soot in the room. No chimney, and a smell of soot! She turned rapidly on her companion; he had already left the room.

And when that afternoon she discovered a black sooty smear upon her own patchwork quilt, she realized not only that her suspicions had been justified, but that for the first time in his life Sam had deliberately laid himself down there in her absence. At this act of sheer defiance, she was no longer so much hurt as exceedingly angry. There was no doubt now. Sam was deliberately defying her. No two companions could share a house on such terms as these. He must be taught a lesson.

That evening in full sight of the creature, having locked her bedroom door, she stuffed a large piece of mattress ticking into the mouth of her chimney and pulled down the register. Having watched these proceedings, Sam rose from his basket, and with an easy spring, leapt up on to the dressing-table. Beyond the window, the moor lay almost as bright as day. Ignoring Miss Chauncey, the creature squatted there steadily and openly staring into the empty skies, for a whole stretch of them was visible from where he sat.

Miss Chauncey proceeded to make her toilet for the night, trying in vain to pretend that she was entirely uninterested in what the animal was at. Faint sounds—not exactly mewings or growlings—but a kind of low inward caterwauling, hardly audible, was proceeding from his throat. But whatever these sounds might mean, Sam himself can have been the only listener. There was not a sign or movement at the window or in the world without. And then Miss Chauncey promptly drew down the blind. At this Sam at once raised his paw for all the world as if he were about to protest, and then, apparently thinking better of it, he pretended instead that the action had been only for the purpose of commencing his nightly wash.

Long after her candle had been extinguished, Miss Chauncey lay listening. Every stir and movement in the quiet darkness could be clearly followed. First there came a furtive footing and tapping at the register of the fireplace, so closely showing what was happening that Miss Chauncey could positively see in her imagination Sam on the hearth-stone, erecting himself there upon his hind-legs, vainly attempting to push the obstacle back.

This being in vain, he appeared to have dropped back on to his fours. Then came a pause. Had he given up his intention? No; now he was at the door, pawing, gently scratching. Then a leap, even towards the handle; but one only—the door was locked. Retiring from the door, he now sprang lightly again on to the dressing-table. What now was he at? By covertly raising her head a little from her pillow, Miss Chauncey could see him with paw thrust out, gently drawing back the blind from the moon-flooded window-pane. And even while she listened and watched, she heard yet again—and yet again—the faint *whssh* as of a wild swan cleaving the air; and then what might have been the cry of a bird, but which to Miss Chauncey's ears resembled a shrill cackle of laughter. At this Sam hastily turned from the window and without the least attempt at concealment pounced clean from the dressing-table on to the lower rail of her bed.

This unmannerly conduct could be ignored no longer. Poor Miss Chauncey raised herself in her sheets, pulled her night-cap a little closer down over her ears, and thrusting out her hand towards the chair beside the bed, struck a match and relit her candle. It was with a real effort that she then slowly turned her head and faced her night-companion. His hair was bristling about his body as if he had had an electric shock. His whiskers stood out at stiff angles with his jaws. He looked at least twice his usual size, and his eyes blazed in his head, as averting his face from her regard he gave vent to a low sustained *Miariou-rou-rou!*

"I say you shall *not*," cried Miss Chauncey at the creature. At the sound of her words, he turned slowly and confronted her. And it seemed that until that moment Miss Chauncey had never actually seen Sam's countenance as in actual fact it really was. It was not so much the grinning tigerish look it wore, but the sullen assurance upon it of what he wanted and that he meant to get it.

All thought of sleep was out of the question. Miss Chauncey could be obstinate too. The creature seemed to shed an influence on the very air which she could hardly resist. She rose from her bed and thrusting on her slippers made her way to the window. Once more a peculiar inward cry broke out from the bed-rail. She raised the blind and the light of the moon from over the moor swept in upon her little apartment. And when she turned to remonstrate with her pet at his ingratitude, and at all this unseemliness and the deceit of his ways, there was something so menacing and pitiless in his aspect that Miss Chauncey hesitated no more.

"Well, mark me!" she cried in a trembling voice, "go out of the *door* you shan't. But if you enjoy soot, soot it shall be."

With that she thrust back the register with the poker, and drew down the bundle of ticking with the tongs. And before the fit of coughing caused by the consequent smotheration that followed had ceased, the lithe black shape had sprung from the bed-rail, and with a scramble was into the hearth, over the fire-bars, up the chimney, and away.

Trembling from head to foot, Miss Chauncey sat down on a cane rocking-chair that stood nearby to reflect what next she must be doing. *Wh-ssh! Wh-ssh!* Again at the window came that mysterious rushing sound, but now the flurrying murmur as of a rocket shooting up with its fiery train of sparks thinning into space, rather than the sound of its descending stick. And then in the hush that followed, there sounded yet again, like a voice from the foot of the garden—a caterwauling piercing and sonorous enough to arouse the sleeping cocks in the Haggurdsdon hen-roosts and for miles around. Out of the distance their chanticleering broke shrill on the night air; to be followed a moment afterwards by the tardy clang of midnight from the church steeple. Then once more silence; utter quiet. Miss Chauncey returned to her bed, but that night she slept no more.

Her mind overflowed with unhappy thoughts. Her faith in Sam was gone. Far worse she had lost faith even in her affection for him. To have wasted that!—all the sprats, all the whitebait in the wide seas were as nothing by comparison. That Sam had wearied of her company was at least beyond question. It shamed her to think how much this meant to her—a mere animal! But she knew what was gone; knew how dull and spiritless in future the day's round would seem—the rising, the housework, the meals, a clean linen collar—the long, slow afternoon, forsaken and companionless! The solitary tea, her candle, prayers, bed—on and on. In what wild company was her cat Sam now? At her own refusal to face that horrid question it was as if she had heard the hollow clanging slam of an immense iron door.

Next morning—still ruminating on these strange events, grieved to the heart at this dreadful rift between herself and one who had been her honest companion of so many years; ashamed, too, that Sam should have had his way with her when she had determined not to allow him to go out during the night—the next morning Miss Chauncey, as if merely to take a little exercise, once again ventured down to the foot of her garden. A faint, blurred mark (such as she had seen on the previous evening) in the black mould of what *might* be a footprint is nothing very much.

But now—in the neglected patch beyond the bushes of white-thorn and bramble—there was no doubt in the world appeared the marks of many. And surely no cats' paw-prints these! Of what use, too, to a cat could a crutch or a staff be? A staff or crutch which—to judge from the impression it had left in the mould—must have been at least as thick as a broomstick.

More disquieted and alarmed than ever over this fresh mystery, Miss Chauncey glanced up and back towards the chimney-pots of the house, clearly and sharply fretted against the morning light of the

eastern skies. And she realized what perils even so sure-footed a creature as Sam had faced when he skirred up out of the chimney in his
wild effort to emerge into the night. Having thus astonishingly
reached the rim of the chimney-pot—the burning stars above and the
wilderness of the moor spread out far beneath and around him—he
must have leaped from the top of the pot to a narrow brick ledge not
three inches wide. Thence on to the peak of the roof and thence
down a steep slippery slope of slates to a leaden gutter.

And how then? The thick tod of ivy matting the walls of the house
reached hardly more than half-way up. Could Sam actually have
plunged from gutter to tod? The very thought of such peril drew
Miss Chauncey's steps towards the house again, in the sharpest
anxiety to assure herself that he was still in the land of the living.

And lo and behold, when she was but half-way on her journey, she
heard a succession of frenzied cries and catcalls in the air from over
the moor. Hastily placing a flower-pot by the wall, she stood on tiptoe and peered over. And even now, at this very moment, in full sight
across the nearer slope of the moor she descried her Sam, not now in
chase of a foolishly trustful visitor, but hotly pursued by what appeared to be the complete rabblement of Haggurdsdon's cats. Sore
spent though he showed himself to be, Sam was keeping his distance.
Only a few lank tabby gibs, and what appeared to be a gray-ginger
Manx (unless he was an ordinary cat with his tail chopped off) were
close behind.

"Sam! Sam!" Miss Chauncey cried, and yet again, "Sam!" but in
her excitement and anxiety her foot slipped on the flower-pot and in
an instant the feline chase had fallen out of sight. Gathering herself
together again, she clutched a long besom or garden broom that was
leaning against the wall, and rushed down to the point at which she
judged Sam would make his entrance into the garden. She was not
mistaken, nor an instant too soon. With a bound he was up and over,
and in three seconds the rabble had followed in frenzied pursuit.

What came after Miss Chauncey could never very clearly recall.
She could but remember plying her besom with might and main
amid the rabble and mellay of animals, while Sam, no longer a fugitive, turned on his enemies and fought them cat for cat. None the
less, it was by no means an easy victory. And had not the over-fatted
cur from the butcher's in Haggurdsdon—which had long since
started in pursuit of this congregation of his enemies—had he not at
last managed to overtake them, the contest might very well have had
a tragic ending. But at the sound of his baying and at sight of the cur's
teeth snapping at them as he vainly attempted to surmount the wall,

Sam's enemies turned and fled in all directions. And faint and panting, Miss Chauncey was able to fling down her besom and to lean for a brief respite against the trunk of a tree.

At last she opened her eyes again. "Well, Sam," she managed to mutter at last, "we got the best of them, then?"

But to her amazement she found herself uttering these friendly words into a complete vacancy. The creature was nowhere to be seen. His cream disappeared during the day, however, and by an occasional rasping sound Miss Chauncey knew that he once more lay hidden in his dingy resort behind the kindling-wood box. And there she did not disturb him.

Not until tea-time of the following day did Sam reappear. And then—after attending to his hurts—it was merely to sit with face towards the fire, sluggish and sullen and dumb as a dog. It was not Miss Chauncey's "place" to make advances, she thought. She took no notice of the beast except to rub in a little hog's fat on the raw places of his wounds. She was rejoiced to find, however, that he kept steadily to Post Houses for the next few days, though her dismay was reawakened at hearing on the third night a more dismal wailing and wauling than ever from the sloe-bushes, even while Sam himself sat motionless beside the fire. His ears twitched, his fur seemed to bristle; he sneezed or spat, but remained otherwise motionless.

When Mr. Cullings called again, Sam at once hid himself in the coal-cellar, but gradually his manners toward Miss Chauncey began to recover their usual suavity. And within a fortnight after the full-moon, the two of them had almost returned to their old friendly companionship. He was healed, sleek, confident and punctual. No intruder of his species had appeared from Haggurdsdon. The night noises had ceased; Post Houses to all appearances—apart from its strange ugliness—was as peaceful and calm as any other solitary domicile in the United Kingdom.

But alas and alas. With the very first peeping of the crescent moon, Sam's mood and habits began to change again. He mouched about with a sly and furtive eye. And when he fawned on her, purring and clawing, the whole look of him was full of deceit. If Miss Chauncey chanced softly to enter the room wherein he sat, he would at once leap down from the window at which he had been perched as if in the attempt to prove that he had *not* been looking out of it. And once, towards evening, though she was no spy, she could not but pause at the parlor door. She had peeped through its crack as it stood ajar. And there on the hard sharp back of an old prie-dieu chair that had belonged to her pious great-aunt Jemima, there sat Sam on his hindquarters. And without the least doubt in the world he was vigorously signalling to some observer outside with his forepaws. Miss Chauncey turned away sick at heart.

From that hour on Sam more and more steadily ignored and flouted his mistress, was openly insolent, shockingly audacious. Mr. Cullings gave her small help indeed. "If I had a cat, m'm, what had manners like that, after all your kindness, fresh fish and all every week, and cream, as I understand, not skim, I'd—I'd give him away."

"To whom?" said Miss Chauncey shortly.

"Well," said the carrier, "I don't know as how I'd much mind to who. Just a home, m'm."

"He seems to have no friends in the Village," said Miss Chauncey in as light a tone as she could manage.

"When they're as black as that, with them saucer eyes, you can never tell," said Mr. Cullings. "There's that old trollimog what lives in Hogges Bottom. She's got a cat that might be your Sam's twin."

"Indeed no, he has the mange," said Miss Chauncey, loyal to the end. The carrier shrugged his shoulders, climbed into his cart, and bowled away off over the moor. And Miss Chauncey returning into the house, laid the platter of silvery sprats on the table, sat down and burst into tears.

It was, then, in most ways a fortunate thing that the very next morning—three complete days, that is, before the next full-moon-tide—she received a letter from her sister-in-law in Shanklin, in the Isle of Wight, entreating her to pay them a long visit.

"My dear Emma, you must sometimes be feeling very lonely (it ran), shut up in that great house so far from any neighbors. We often think of you, and particularly these last few days. It's nice to have that Sam of yours for company, but after all, as George says, a pet is only a pet. And we do all think it's high time you took a little holiday with us. I am looking out of my window at this moment. The sea is as calm as a mill-pond, a solemn beautiful blue. The fishing boats are coming in with their brown sails. This is the best time of the year with us, because as it's not yet holy-day-time there are few of those horrid visitors to be seen, and no crowds. George says you *must* come. He joins with me in his love as would Maria if she weren't out shopping, and will meet you at the station in the trap. Emmie is now free of her cough, only whooping when the memory takes her and never sick. And we shall all be looking forward to seeing you in a few days."

At this kindness, and with all her anxieties, Miss Chauncey all but broke down. When the butcher drove up in his cart an hour or two afterwards, he took a telegram for her back to the Village, and on the

Monday her box was packed and all that remained was to put Sam in his basket in preparation for the journey. But I am bound to say it took more than the persuasion of his old protectress to accomplish this. Indeed Mr. Cullings had actually to hold the creature with his gloved hands and none too gently, while Miss Chauncey pressed down the lid and pushed the skewer in to hold it close.

"What's done's dumned done!" said the carrier, as he rubbed a pinch of earth into his scratches. "But what I say is, better done for-ever. Mark my words, m'm!"

Miss Chauncey took a shilling out of her large leather purse; but made no reply.

Indeed all this trouble proved at last in vain. Thirty miles distant from Haggurdsdon, at Blackmoor Junction, Miss Chauncey had to change trains. Her box and Sam's basket were placed together on the station platform beside half-a-dozen empty milkcans and some fowls in a crate, and Miss Chauncey went to enquire of the station-master to make sure of her platform.

It was the furious panic-stricken cackling of these fowls that brought her hastily back to her belongings, only to find that by hook or by crook Sam had managed to push the skewer of the basket out of its cane loops. The wicker lid yawned open—the basket was empty. Indeed one poor gaping hen, its life fluttering away from its helpless body, was proof not only of Sam's prowess but of his cowardly fe-rocity.

A few days afterwards, as Miss Chauncey sat in the very room to which her sister-in-law had referred in her invitation, looking over the placid surface of the English Channel, the sun gently shining in the sky, there came a letter from Mr. Cullings. It was in pencil and written upon the back of a baker's bag:

"Dear Madam, i take the libberty of riteing you in referense to the Animall as how i helped put in is bawskit which has cum back returned empty agenn by rail me having okashun to cart sum hop powles from Haggurdsdon late at nite ov Sunday. I seez him squattin at the parlor windy grimasin out at me fit to curdle your blood in your vanes and lights at the upper windies and a yowling and screetch-ing such as i never hopes to hear agen in a Christian lokalety. And that ole wumman from Hogges Botom sitting in the porch mi own vew being that there is no good in the place and the Animall be be-witched. Mr. Flint the fyshmunger agrees with me as how now only last mesures is of any use and as i have said afore i am wiling to take over the house the rent if so be being low and moddrate considering of the bad name it as in these parts around Haggurdsdon. I remain dear madam waitin your orders and oblidge yours truely William Cullings."

To look at Miss Chauncey you might have supposed she was a strong-minded woman. You might have supposed that this uncivil reference to the bad name her family house had won for itself would have mortified her beyond words. Whether or not, she neither showed this letter to her sister-in-law nor for many days together did she even answer it. Sitting on the Esplanade, and looking out to sea, she brooded on and on in the warm, salt, yet balmy air. It was a distressing problem. But "No, he must go his own way," she sighed to herself at last; "I have done my best for him."

What is more, Miss Chauncey never returned to Post Houses. She sold it at last, house and garden and for a pitiful sum, to the carrier, Mr. Cullings. By that time Sam had vanished, had been never seen again.

Not that Miss Chauncey was faithless of memory. Whenever the faint swish of a sea-gull's wing sounded in the air above her head; or the crackling of an ascending rocket for the amusement of the visitors broke the silence of the nearer heavens over the sea; whenever even she became conscious of the rustling frou-frou of her Sunday watered-silk gown as she sallied out to church from the neat little villa she now rented on the Shanklin Esplanade—she never noticed such things without being instantly transported back in imagination to her bedroom at Post Houses, to see again that strange deluded animal, once her Sam, squatting there on her patchwork counterpane, and as it were knitting with his fore-paws the while he stood erect upon his hind.

Feathers

CARL VAN VECHTEN

EVEN in babyhood it seems I had begun to love cats. My mother records the fact in her diary, such a diary as others plan to keep when their sons are born, in which at first a daily entry is made, but which soon dwindle through short weekly reports down to a sentence or two a month, and eventually to nothing. On September 25, 1881, when I was a little more than a year old, my mother wrote of me, He seems very bright in imitation: he will bleat like a lamb, bark like a dog, or mew like a kitten. I think of all the things he has ever played with or seen nothing pleases him so well as a cat. Grandma has an old tortoise-shell and she seems to be willing to have baby fondle her as much as he likes even if he does rub the fur the wrong way sometimes.

My talent for imitation does not appear to have developed, but my warm feeling for cats has intensified with the years. I recall a blue short-haired cat which I carried around the house as a child, and then for fifteen years I was not permitted to possess another. My family compromised on birds, canaries and thrushes, alligators, chameleons, field mice, and turtles. Once, even, the door was opened to a dog, a fox-terrier named Peg Woffington, but never again to a cat. My passion for animals was so strong that I think something living was always beside me, but it was only later in life, after I had left the home of my parents, that I became familiar with the animal I cared for most.

Since those early days a succession of cats has passed before me, cats who lived with others, cats in fiction and poetry. Some of these I have described, many I have not, for I hold a memory of many pleasant cats including Jessie Pickens's strange, brown tabby Persian, Dodo, with a snarl and a snap and a growl and a hiss for all the world, which terrified her, but always a kiss for Jessie. This puss crossed the Atlantic—in a cabin—seventeen times before she died. I cannot forget Anna Marble Pollock's dynasties of orange, white,

and smoke cats. When I passed a weekend at her place on Long Island, Inky, a cuddling smoke, used to sleep with me. For many years
two black cats lived together at a florist's in the Hippodrome building on Sixth Avenue. One, long since dead, was in existence when I
first came to New York, the other, much younger, is still living,
withal very old. When both were alive they were wont to lie together
in the window, under the bowls of roses or the pots of ferns, assum-

ing medieval attitudes, recalling the sleek, black cats with dilated
topaz eyes, which once frequented witches' hearths, or they would
sit in the doorway in the posture in which so many Egyptian cats
have been immortalized. I have never gone by this shop without
stopping to speak to these handsome ebony cats, abnormally large.
Cats, indeed, are as personal as people, and ordinarily more memorable, as far as I am concerned. How often I have visited Mabel
Reber to talk to her cats, the magnificent silver Jack Frost, twice
the size of the average cat, with the eyes of a Raphael cherub, eyes
of so frank and naïve a character that they seemed strangely perverse
in a cat. His companion, Comet, I believe was even larger, a mam-

moth cat, a great red tabby Persian with butterfly markings and copper eyes, who lived to be nearly fourteen years old, with all his teeth,
most of his energy, and the coat of a llama, a coat, indeed, which
seemed to grow thicker as the years went by. Jack and Comet are
angels now, hunting mice along the Milky Way, pursuing the shadows of phantom butterflies in the feline paradise. Then there was
Avery Hopwood's Abelard, our companion on many an automobile
drive, a friendly feline who purringly enjoyed the knee of any
stranger. So, indoors, he lacked mystery, but in the garden, wandering among the pink cosmos and the purple dahlias, waving his flaring
banner of a tail, he became a feral enigma of nature. There was Tom,
an ugly, gaunt, grey tabby with a white belly, who took refuge in
the cellar six stories below our garret on East Nineteenth Street,
merely tolerated for a year until a new janitor bought him a collar
and fed him liver. The metamorphosis was astounding, both physi-
cally and psychologically. As Tom's belly expanded, his coat growing
sleek and smooth, he began to pay an inordinate amount of attention
to his toilet, polishing his nails assiduously and flecking the tiniest
suspicion of dust from his whiskers. His walk became languid and
dandified, his manner somewhat arrogant. In preference to walking,
this cat employed the elevator and he would call out his floor in no
uncertain voice. Emerging from the opened car, he would pay a visit
to some favoured tenant, scratching on the door until he was admitted, when he would stroll around the apartment, examining new
objects or searching for mice, until his curiosity was satisfied, when
he requested permission to leave. Other cats of this period and locality come back to the memory: the cat next door, a handsome
brown tabby, with a coat which shone as if brilliantine had been applied to it, lying in the sun on the stucco wall, with the manner of a
breathing sphinx, never venturing into the street, not even so far as
the sidewalk, and permitting no alien hand to stroke his back. There
were the black and white cats of Giovanni Guidone, the grocer,
whose white faces were so curiously smudged with spots of black that
they resembled clowns, and indeed their behaviour intensified this
impression. Above all, there was the blue short-haired cat with the
white tip at the end of his tail who lived with a nearby delicatessen
dealer. This grimalkin had learned to roll eggs from the counter so
that they would break on the floor and he might eat the contents. He
unfailingly chose, the dealer informed me, the freshest and most
costly eggs.

As for my own cats, I still cherish an affection for the blue, short-
haired cat of my childhood, my Paris cat, bereft of his tail, and deli-

cate Ariel, an orange tabby Persian with a white belly, a soft, appealing cat who suffered from strange illnesses, an invalid from birth; but Feathers meant more to me than these others.

In the closing pages of "The Tiger in the House" I have drawn a picture of Feathers about to become a mother. These paragraphs were written in good faith. Feathers, about eighteen months old at the time, had passed a weekend on Long Island with an orange tabby male and I had every reason to believe that the usual result would follow. It did not. Feathers died without issue. I am convinced, indeed, that she died a virgin.

I had discovered her one day, a tiny kitten, at a pet shop. In a cage with ten or twelve companions, kinsmen or acquaintances, bouncing and rolling about like Andalusian dancers or miniature harlequins, she alone had chanced to please me. She gave me her absorbed attention when I entered the shop and she continued to gaze at me, a slight smile flickering about her eyes. As I gathered her into my arms, she playfully extended one padded paw, a paw out of all proportion to her diminutive size, and pressed it against my lips. This gesture won me so completely that after the fashion of a Roman gentleman acquiring a desirable slave in the public market, I purchased her at once. This simile cannot be carried further, for, after the manner of cats, she presently asserted her authority so impressively that in a few days such slaves as inhabited my garret were not garbed in fur. "It is certain," Claude Farrère has written in his biography of the Chat-Comme-ça, "that man is superior to the other animals, but it is also certain that the cat is superior to man."

She was a Persian pussy, but she never could have been exhibited at any cat show where the rules were strict, for she was the logical outcome of misalliances and miscegenation. Not alone her mother, but also her grandmothers for generations back, must have been easy going. The evidence went to prove that these loose ladies had received visits from black gentlemen, from yellow gentlemen, and from white gentlemen, indiscriminately, for Feathers had a coat of many colors and, had she been a male, Joseph would have been her suitable name. In the circumstances, she might reasonably have been christened Iris. Her own name, which fell to her naturally enough in a few weeks—I never hurry to identify a cat—was derived from the long hairs which protruded from her ears, long, curly hairs, technically known to cat-fanciers as feathers. She was, as you may have gathered, a tortoise-shell: her fur was marked with splotches of the richest orange, the deepest black, the palest tan, but the splotches were not well-defined in the manner that judges at cat-shows demand of prize-winning tortoise-shells. Moreover, she had other markings. Some of the black hairs were tipped with gold. Her breast and nose were white and so were her paws, but her legs were barred (sinisterly, no doubt) with tabby stripes. She belonged, as a matter of fact, to that unclassified variety, the tortoise-shell and white smoke tabbies! So far as I could ascertain, she had no silver or blue blood, but she atoned for this lack, in a measure, by another peculiarity: she had seven toes on each paw and these twenty-eight toes were all fitted with claws. Her eyes, rather indefinite in colour in the beginning, later became a pale yellow. They were large, round, and intelligent.

Nevertheless, in spite of her mixed breeding and her scarcity of "points," she was a picture cat, beautiful in her terato-logical manner. Any painter would have been delighted to ask her to sit for him. As a kitten she was a tawny, orange, and black ball of fur, an exasperatingly roguish, ambulatory chrysanthemum with a ridiculous Christmas tree for a tail. She had, of course, even then, her moments of repose, of pensive reflection. I can never forget how, on her arrival in our garret, after the inevitable tour of exploration which any cat, however young and inexperienced, however old and brave, always makes in a new environment, I say I cannot forget how, with quaint dignity and grace, she settled herself at last around her legs, and cocking her head at that angle which a robin often affects.

As she grew older, her grace and beauty developed and, very early in our acquaintanceship, she asserted her independence and displayed her character. Never seriously ill before her fatal sickness, she refused vehemently to take medicine when she suffered the minor ailments of kittenhood. Exerting all her strength to free herself, scratching the controlling hand, she would attempt to bite and, if still held, would growl and spit, as the hissing of cats is so cacophonously called. She possessed an extremely quick temper and any sort of restraint immediately infuriated her. Her growl was faint and rather ridiculous, but her spit, which required a considerable distortion of the jaw, was her last word, a word by no means to be taken lightly. On such occasions her face lost something of its ordinary beauty, a beauty which was never placid, which always included something of alertness in its makeup. Fortunately, she never sulked, never bore malice and, once restored to her liberty, forgave quickly. I do not think she would have forgiven a real insult or, from a stranger, even a fancied one, but she knew at heart that I was her devoted friend and presumably reasonably well-intentioned towards her. She indicated plainly, however, on more than one occasion, that even well-meaning attentions would not be tolerated when they involved sequestration of any variety. All cats—almost all cats, at any rate—are independent, but Feathers made a fetish of independence.

In her own way, she was affectionate. She soon learned to come to the door to greet us, my wife or myself; indeed, the sound of the ascending elevator, were one of us absent, was sufficient to send her flying to the door. She disliked solitude, even if she were asleep, and so passed most of her time, when circumstances permitted, in the same room with either Fania or me, but she usually did not care to lie on my knee when I was sitting, and she would soon contrive to extricate herself from any kind of vulgar embrace. When one of us was lying down, however, she often found the belly an excellent place to nap on, never, curiously enough, after we had gone to bed. She had one tender trick which was original with her: if held in the palms of the hands, she would lie, contentedly enough, on her back, with her great paws relaxed, or perhaps she would press one, padded and soft, the claws concealed and inactive, over an eye or over the lips, as she had done, indeed, on the day when I made her acquaintance. Occasionally she became paradoxically soft and yielding, lying on my knee in the most abandoned attitude, with one paw depending, limp, but she never liked to have her belly stroked and would use her claws vigorously to protect herself from this dishonour. Often she was feral. At times she seemed to fly from one end of the garret to the other, touching the floor as seldom as would Nijinsky or some flying-squirrel.

She never saw a mouse. Her hunting expeditions, there, were perforce directed against insects. She believed the airplane to be an insect. One of these giant craft flew frequently past my garret window and she never missed the whimpering buzz. Standing on her hind paws, she pressed her little rose nose eagerly against the pane and gave vent to the curious cry, so like the creaking of a rusty hinge, which always associated itself in my mind with her hunting. She never succeeded in bringing down an airplane, but she never missed a fly and she was expert at attacking moths. It was an aesthetic pleasure, a lesson in grace, to observe her catch one. Whenever I discovered a moth, I cried: "Feathers, come here!" The tone was sufficient. From a sound sleep in the farthest corner of my garret she would come bounding, expectant, alert, a feverish intensity in her eyes, her ears pointed back, and the faint quick mew of her hunting cry issuing from her throat. Then, as with my down-turned palm I would sweep the white, flying insect into her vision, she would leap for it, with one rapidly extended paw, sometimes following its flight

to the top of the piano or a shelf of books. It was a joy to observe her
perfect muscular control on such occasions. Once the moth was
stunned, she permitted it to escape to give herself the pleasure of re-
capturing it; eventually, with every appearance of pleasure, she
would eat it, and then she would purr.

She did not care much for toys; at any rate she soon tired of them.
A celluloid ball, which rattled, amused her for a few hours. She
leaped after it into the porcelain bathtub, following its clattering
bounds with wild celerity, but after a few repetitions of this exercise
she began to be bored. Presently, she was through and never con-
descended to notice the ball again. One object, however, invariably
entertained her, a silly, simulated strawberry, of a type once worn on
women's hats. She would carry this by the stem in her teeth from
place to place, pouncing upon it, pushing it from her, gathering it
towards her. If someone would play the game with her she would retrieve this strawberry. She also enjoyed another game which began by
her establishing herself behind the crack made by an open door,
lying in wait, and catching passing objects with her paw through the
space beneath the hinge.

She liked to lie on my knee while I sipped my coffee in the morning. Almost invariably—she was never entirely consistent about any
act—she came to me for a few moments after she had eaten her own
breakfast. It is possible that this gracious ceremony partook of the
nature of gratitude. Next, habitually, she took up her position on
the cover of the soiled-clothes basket, adjacent to the bathtub, and
appeared to be interested in our ablutions. This interest was not
feigned, but it was directed towards her personal ends. She was waiting until we had bathed and the tub was empty, so that she might
repose herself in its warm bottom. Sometimes when baths were un-
duly prolonged, in her impatience she encircled the ledge at the top
of the tub, waving her tail in annoyance and making faint mews, occasionally almost losing her footing on the narrow, perilous, slippery
path. As the last drop dribbled down the waste-pipe, she would leap
in, lie on her back, and roll luxuriously on the heated porcelain. A
few moments of this dissipation was enough to satisfy her. Leaping
out, she began to wash herself in preparation for her morning nap.
She honored no one spot: sometimes she slept on Fania's lap, sometimes on top of the piano, sometimes on the floor.

She was not afraid of strangers, but she took no particular interest
or pleasure in their presence. Her manner was perhaps more languid
than usual, as though she were assuming a special social grace. Indeed, she entertained but one fear—she was an exceedingly cour-

ageous cat—and that was for storms. An ordinary rainstorm terrified her, a thunderstorm unbalanced her reason.[1] While the bolts were flashing and booming, she was wont to hide herself under the bathtub, under a bed, or behind some door, quivering with nerves, her ears laid back almost flat on her head, her fur awry. Such comfort as we could give her was unavailing. Only with the ceasing of the storm did she regain self-control. This peculiarity she never conquered. Indeed, being a cat, she probably made no effort to conquer it.

Cats seldom break glass or china by accident, but it often amuses them to play with frail objects, pushing them off their foundations. Feathers never broke anything. Her grace was abundant and it was a pleasure akin to that of watching an expert trapezist to see her take a long and daring leap to a shelf on which reposed rows of glasses or cups without disturbing a single piece. One of these shelves, higher than my head, was ranged with unserried ranks of Venetian goblets. She was not destructive; neither was she secretive. Pens and keys might be left in plain view without arousing in her a desire to hide them. My Ariel, on the other hand, had caches under the corners of the rugs where she concealed every small object she could discover. Other habits of Feathers were less agreeable: she pulled the threads loose in a Daghestan rug and shredded the canvas backs of many scrap-books, sharpening her claws.

Like all well-bred cats, she was mostly mute. When she spoke, her voice was soft, almost, indeed, inaudible. Waiting in the morning outside our bedroom door for her breakfast, which she usually received at seven o'clock, she sat rigid and silent. When she was "calling," as the period of heat is poetically described by cat-breeders, her voice was as musical as the soft coo of a dove which it somewhat resembled. She was very sparing, too, with her purrs, only lavishing them on exceptional occasions. She never overdid anything.

She had a fascinating habit of looking at me, without speaking, when she wanted something. She expected me to divine her wish, and this was usually easy to do. It was as if she had reasoned, "It is absurd of me to try to make him comprehend my speech, although I understand very well what he says. I'll simply wish very hard what I want and he will probably understand it sooner and more completely than if I had asked for it."

She was right. We had a very profound understanding and neither of us imposed on the other. Within the boundaries of our garret walls she was permitted to do anything she liked—even to play the

[1] A later cat, Scheherazade, would sit on the window-ledge and placidly observe the course of the wildest storm.

piano at three o'clock in the morning, a pastime of which she never tired—and for the most part she generously allowed Fania and me the same privilege. In one respect, however, she was obstinate. She refused to tolerate the presence of a rival. This aversion manifested itself for the first time when I brought an orange kitten home. During the three days that the kitten remained in our garret she not only tortured him in countless complicated and subtle ways, but also she altered deeply in her attitude towards me. She refused, indeed, to be blamed until the cause of her perturbation was removed.

How adorable she was in the seasons when she yearned for love! Many female cats in this condition are over-obtrusive, objectionably salacious. She became more affectionate, more gracious, and her tender little love-signs were very ingratiating. The first time she "called" for a mate, a great tabby tom, the very fellow I have described as an elevator passenger, arrived from six flights below and began to scratch on the outer door. What instinct is this? How cats divine such a condition is more than I can guess. Felines are not supposed to enjoy a highly developed sense of smell and a calling female does not exude an odor which is obvious to humans. Nor, in this particular instance, so soft was her voice, could it be supposed that she had been overheard. It has been stated by lepidopterists that if a female butterfly of some rare species be exposed in a cage in an open window, before many hours have passed males of this species will present themselves. At this period another Persian cat resided in our apartment house. On the unique occasion on which he secured his liberty, like the tabby tom, he came directly to our door and endeavoured to effect an entrance. Feathers, ensconced behind the door, heard the scratching and challenged the invaders, her manner completely altered. She growled. She spat. The warmth of her nature had frozen. She was *chatte pour tout le monde, mais pour les chats tigresse!*

Still, she was a female and so manifestly destined for motherhood. In a basket, following the fashion of the aristocratic cat-world, in which the lady visits the gentleman, she was carried to a country-place on Long Island where she was gently inserted into a cage already containing a eupeptic orange tabby sire who must have been puzzled by her subsequent behavior. She remained with him for a week, during which period she fought off his attempted approaches with teeth and claws. Nevertheless, when she returned home I hoped for progeny. When it became evident that none might be expected, she was sent back to her consort, again with no result.

In the middle of the hot summer of 1920, stupidly I caused her to be sent back a third time. Yet I know very well a cat will never do anything she does not wish to do. She is quite willing to die to preserve her independence of thought and action. Perhaps, in previous incarnations, Feathers had done all the mating she considered necessary. Perhaps she held a racial memory of the dreadful misalliances, the social errors, the sexual loosenesses of her mother and grandmothers. At any rate, on this third visit, although exposed to the company of every male in the cattery—for it was possible, we thought, that her refusal had been dictated by her aversion for some particular cat—she continued to defend her chastity. Her period of calling passed and the lady in charge of the males asked me to come out. Feathers was imprisoned in a cage near a ferocious smoke who usually automatically dominated any cat to whom he was introduced. He was twice as large as Feathers. As I entered the room she was crouching on a shelf, but she rose, arched her back, waved her tail, and purred a greeting. She was begging me to take her away, but I did not understand. She was very thin: the most nervous cat I have ever known, she had not been eating well in this new environment. The smoke ventured a step towards her. With a well-aimed blow at his head she contrived to throw him off his balance and the shelf. Like a villain in a melodrama foiled in his peccancy, he cringed on the floor. Still I did not understand.

The woman, who seemed to feel that her breeder's honor was at stake, begged me—in complete good faith, I am sure—to leave Feathers with her for another two weeks. "If she remains with the cats until she calls again, she will perhaps learn to know them," was her specious argument. Unfortunately, I heeded it and bade farewell to Feathers. Did she plead with me with her eyes as I went away or, in recalling the scene later, did I imagine this? Rather, probably, she sank into a hopeless lassitude, hopeless of making any impression on my stupidity, hopeless of making me understand her at the crucial moment. Probably she turned her head away and resigned herself to her fate, dedicating herself to death.

The weather was cruelly warm, not hot and dry but unbearably humid. Showers were frequent, and one night, during a terrific thunderstorm, I lay awake, thinking how terrified Feathers must be. The end came a few days later, on a Sunday morning. In response to a telephone call, I hurried to her, a long, tedious journey of an hour. When I arrived, she was lying on her side, panting in the last breaths she was to take. A film was forming over her eyes.

For two years, save for those brief visits to Long Island, I had never been separated from Feathers. She had sat with me at breakfast and while I was writing. Her fine intelligent eyes, her repose, her graceful beauty, her silence, and her mystery had become a part of my life, a part that I found I could do very ill without, a part that no other creature has supplied.

More, she represented a period, a period of two years, and it became increasingly difficult to recall any episode of these years divorced from her personality. It is seemingly simple, such a companionship, depending on scarcely more than mere propinquity, a few actions, a touch of the cold, moist nose, a soft paw against the cheek, a greeting at the door, a few moments of romping, a warm soft ball of fur curled on the knee, or a long stare. It is thus that the sympathy between men and animals expresses itself, but interwoven, and collectively, these details evoke an emotion which it is very difficult even for time to destroy.

The Fur Person

MAY SARTON

ON HIS roves and rambles, on his rounds and travels, he had never found himself exactly where he now found himself, on the border of a dangerous street—very dangerous, he realized after a short exposure to the roar of cars, the squeaking of brakes, the lurching, weaving, rumbling, interspersed with loud bangs and horns of a really incredible amount of traffic. It was quite bewildering, and the Fur Person looked about for a place where he could withdraw and sit awhile. He was rather tired. It was time, he considered, for a short snooze, after which the question of Lunch might be approached in the proper frame of mind. And there, providentially indeed, he noticed that he was standing in front of a house bounded on one side by a porch with a very suitable railing running along it. He took the porch in one leap, sat for a second measuring the distance to the square platform on top of the railing post, then swung up to it rather casually, and there he was, safe and free as you please, in a little patch of sunlight which seemed to have been laid down there just for him. He tucked in his paws and closed his eyes. The sun was delicious on his back, so much so that he began to sing very softly, accompanying himself this time with one of his lighter purrs, just a tremolo to keep things going.

And there he sat for maybe an hour, or maybe even two, enjoying the peace and quiet, and restoring himself after the rather helter-skelter life he had been leading for two days, since his metamorphosis into a Gentleman Cat in search of a housekeeper. He was so deep down in the peace and the quiet that when a window went up right beside him on the porch, he did not jump into the air as he might have done had it not been such a very fine May morning or had he been a little less tired. As it was, he merely opened his eyes very wide and looked.

"Come here," a voice said inside the house, "there's a pussin on the porch."

The Fur Person waited politely, for he had rather enjoyed the timbre of the voice, quite low and sweet, and he was always prepared to be admired. Pretty soon two faces appeared in the window and looked at him, and he looked back.

"Well," said another voice, "perhaps he would like some lunch."

The Fur Person woke right up then, rose, and stretched on the tips of his toes, his tail making a wide arc to keep his balance.

"He is rather thin," said the first voice. "I wonder where he belongs. We've never seen him before, have we?"

"And what are we having for lunch?" said the second voice.

"There's that haddock left over—I could cream it."

The Fur Person pivoted on the fence post and stamped three times with his back feet, to show how dearly he loved the sound of haddock.

"What is he doing now?" said the first voice and chuckled.

"Saying he likes haddock, I expect."

Then, quite unexpectedly, the window was closed. Dear me, he thought, won't I do? For the first time, he began to be really anxious about his appearance. Was the tip of his tail as white as it could be? How about his shirt front? Dear me, he thought, won't I do? And his heart began to beat rather fast, for he was, after all, tired and empty and in a highly emotional state. This made him unusually impulsive. He jumped down to the porch and then to the ground below and trotted round to the back door, for as he expected, there was a garden at the back, with a pear tree at the end of it, and excellent posts for claw-sharpening in a small laundry yard. He could not resist casting a glance at the flower beds, nicely dug up and raked, in just the right condition for making holes, and in fact the thought of a neat little hole was quite irresistible, so he dug one there and then.

When he had finished, he saw that the crocuses were teeming with bees. His whiskers trembled. He crouched down in an ecstasy of impatience and coiled himself tight as a spring, lashed his tail, and before he knew it himself was in the air and down like lightning on an unsuspecting crocus. The bee escaped, though the crocus did not. Well, thought the Fur Person, a little madness in the spring is all very well, but I must remember that this is serious business and I must get down to it. So he sat and looked the house over. It was already evident that there were innumerable entrances and exits like the window opening to the porch, that there were places of safety in case he was locked out, and that (extraordinary bit of luck) he had found not one old maid with a garden and a house but *two*. Still, his hopes had been dashed rather often in the last twenty-four hours and he reminded himself this time to be circumspect and hummed a bit of the tune about being a free cat, just to give himself courage.

Then he walked very slowly, stopping to stretch out one back leg and lick it, for he remembered the Fifth Commandment: "Never hurry towards an objective, never look as if you had only one thing in mind, it is not polite." Just as he was nibbling the muscle in his back foot with considerable pleasure, for he was always discovering delightful things about himself, he heard the back door open. Cagey, now, he told himself. So he went on nibbling and even spread his toes and licked his foot quite thoroughly, and all this time, a very sweet voice was saying:

"Are you hungry, puss-cat? Come, pussin . . ."

And so at last he came, his tail tentatively raised in a question mark; he came slowly, picking up his paws with care, and gazing all the while in a quite romantic way (for he couldn't help it) at the saucer held in the old maid's hand. At the foot of the back stairs he sat down and waited the necessary interval.

"Well, come on," said the voice, a slightly impatient one, with a little roughness to it, a great relief after the syrupy lady in the hot apartment from which he had escaped.

At this the Fur Person bounded up the stairs, and at the very instant he entered the kitchen, the purrs began to swell inside him and he wound himself round and round two pairs of legs (for he must be impartial), his nose in the air, his tail straight up like a flag, on tiptoe, and roaring with thanks.

"He's awfully thin," said the first voice.

"And not very beautiful, I must say," said the second voice.

But the Fur Person fortunately was not listening. He was delicately and with great deliberation sniffing the plate of haddock; he was settling down; he was even winding his tail around him, because here at last was a meal worthy of a Gentleman Cat.

The most remarkable thing about the two kind ladies was that they left him to eat in peace and did not say one word. They had the tact to withdraw into the next room and to talk about other things, and leave him entirely to himself. It seemed to him that he had been looked up and down, remarked upon, and hugged and squeezed far too much in the last days, and now he was terribly grateful for the chance to savor this delicious meal with no exclaiming this or that, and without the slightest interruption. When he had finished every single scrap and then licked over the plate several times (For if a meal is Worthy, the Sixth Commandment says, "The plate must be left clean, so clean that a person might think it had been washed."), the Fur Person sat up and licked his chops. He licked them perhaps twenty or twenty-five times, maybe even fifty times, his raspberry-colored tongue devoting itself to each whisker, until his face was quite clean. Then he began on his front paws and rubbed his face gently with a nice wet piece of fur, and rubbed right over his ears, and all this took a considerable time. While he was doing it he could hear a steady gentle murmur of conversation in the next room and pretty soon, he stopped with one paw in the air, shook it once, shook his head the way a person does whose hair has just been washed in the bowl, and then took a discreet ramble.

"Just make yourself at home," said the voice he liked best. "Just look around."

His tail went straight up so they would understand that he was out for a rove and did not intend, at the moment, to catch a mouse, that in fact he was looking around, and not committing himself one way or another. The house, he discovered, was quite large enough, quite nice and dark, with a long hall for playing and at least three sleeping places. He preferred a bed, but there was a large comfortable armchair that would do in a pinch. Still, he reminded himself, one must not be hasty. Just then he walked into a rather small room lined with books and with (this was really splendid) a huge flat desk in it. There are times in a Gentleman Cat's life when what he likes best is to stretch out full length (and the Fur Person's length was considerable) on a clean hard place. The floor is apt to be dirty and to smell of old crumbs, but a desk, preferably with papers strewn across it, is quite the thing. The Fur Person felt a light elegant obbligato of purrs rising in his throat.

Neither of the old maids had, until now, touched him. And this, he felt, was a sign of understanding. They had given him a superior lunch and allowed him to rove and ramble in peace. Now he suddenly felt quite curious to discover what they were like. It is amazing how much a cat learns about life by the way he is stroked. His heart was beating rather fast as he approached the table. One of the two old maids had almost disappeared in a cloud of smoke, the brusque one; he did not like smoke, so he made a beeline toward the other, gazing out of wide-open eyes, preceded by his purrs.

"Well, old thing, do you want a lap?" the gentle voice inquired very politely. She did not reach down and gather him up. She leaned forward and ran one finger down his head and along his spine. Then she scratched him between the ears in a most delightful way. The purrs began to sound like bass drums very lightly drummed, and the Fur Person felt himself swell with pleasure. It was incredibly enjoyable, after all he had been through, to be handled with such *savoir-faire,* and before he knew it himself he had jumped up on this welcoming lap and begun to knead. The Fur Person, you remember, had lost his mother when he was such a small kitten that his ears were still buttoned down and his eyes quite blue, but when he jumped up onto this lady's lap, he seemed dimly to remember kneading his mother like this, with tiny starfish paws that went in and out, in and out.

"I wish he'd settle," the gentle voice said, "his claws are rather sharp."

But the Fur Person did not hear this for he was in a trance of homecoming and while he kneaded he composed a song, and while he composed it, it seemed as if every hair on his body tingled and was burnished, so happy was he at last.

"He actually looks fatter," the brusque voice said, "he must have been awfully hungry."

The Fur Person closed his eyes and sang his song and it went like this:

Thank you, thank you,
You and no other
Dear gentle voice,
Dear human mother,
For your delicate air,
For your savoir-faire
For your kind soft touch
Thank you very much.

He was so terribly sleepy that the last line became inextricably confused in a purr and in his suddenly making himself into a round circle of peace, all kneading spent, and one paw over his nose.

There was an indefinite interval of silence; but it must not be forgotten that the Fur Person had led a hectic and disillusioning life, and while he slept his nose twitched and his paws twitched and he imagined that he was caught and being smothered, and before he even quite woke up or had his eyes open he had leapt off the kind lap, in a great state of nerves.

It is all very well, he told himself severely, but this time you have to be careful. Remember Alexander, remember the grocer, remember the lady and her suffocating apartment. It was not easy to do, but without giving the old maids a parting look, he walked in great dignity down the long dark hall to the front door and sat down before it, wishing it to open. Pretty soon he heard footsteps, but he did not turn his head. I must have time to think this over, he was telling himself. Never be hasty when choosing a housekeeper. The door opened and he was outside. Never be hasty, he was telling himself, as he bounded down the steps and into the sweet May afternoon. But at the same time, quite without intending it, he found that he had composed a short poem, and as he sharpened his claws on the elm by the door and as he ran up it, just to show what a fine Gentleman Cat he was, he hummed it over. It was very short and sweet:

East and West
Home is best.

And though he spent several days coming and going, it was very queer how, wherever he went, he always found himself somehow coming back to the two old maids, just to be sure they were still there, and also, it must be confessed, to find out what they were having for supper. And on the fourth day it rained and that settled it: he spent the night. The next morning while he was washing his face after eating a nice little dish of stew beef cut up into small pieces, he made his decision. After all, if a Gentleman Cat spends the night, it is a kind of promise. I will be your cat, he said to himself, sitting on the desk with his paws tucked in and his eyes looking gravely at the two old maids standing in the doorway, if you will be my housekeepers. And of course they agreed, because of the white tip to his tail, because he hummed such a variety of purrs and songs, because he really was quite a handsome fellow, and because they had very soft hearts.

Little White King

MARGUERITE STEEN

THE Black One stirred, sat up and pricked her ears uneasily. It was just on midnight, and the bed lamp was still on, but I was asleep, a book, as usual, in my hand. The Black One advanced her nose to my hand and gave it a quick lick to rouse me. I opened my eyes, blinking through my glasses, and looked at the clock. Three minutes to twelve. By now certainly he would be in.

I got up, hushing the Black One, who pranced wildly at the door; as usual, she obeyed the gesture of silence, but as soon as I got the door open rushed past me down the stairs. I heard her fling herself against the door below and burst through into the kitchen. I followed, telling myself it was sure to be all right.

The light had been left on and the back door stood open to the rain. On the table, the papier mâché bowl and the cushion covered with its woollen square were still unoccupied.

I flashed the torch out into the slanting lines of rain and flicked it round the lawn, the hedge, the shrubbery at the top of the brick wall. Then I went through to the front of the house and repeated the manoeuvre. The Black One accompanied me nervously; stood out on the steps with pricked ears and sharp turns of the head to right and left. There was no sound but the lash of the rain, the gouts dropping from the sycamore branches; nothing to be seen but blackness and the long beam of the torch reflected from the wet flagstones leading towards the invisible lawn.

Cats are so sensible, I told the Black One; he's found some dry corner and settled in out of the wet. The Black One did not believe a word of it, nor did I. One says these things, as one whistles in the dark.

We had been playing cards. He, petulant at the postponement of his game, after a few dabs and antics through and round the back of the couch, went to the door; sat upright with his tail curled round

his feet in an attitude of deprecation, and finally let out a cry of protest.

'He wants to go out.'

But when I opened the parlor door and let him trot ahead of me,
he refused the exit into the pouring darkness, made for the kitchen
and insisted he was hungry.

He had had his full ration for the day, and I had always been firm
about not overfeeding him; but something had to be done to make
up for the way he had been ignored since we began the canasta game.
I looked in the refrigerator, found a little casserole with the delicious
remains of some pâté, and put it down. He settled to it, purring
through his mouthfuls; pausing now and then to look up at me as
though to say, '*Why* have I never had this before?'

The game of cards was resumed, and when it was finished we went
in search of him, and found him in the guest room, calling urgently to
be let out. He swept down the stairs, took one look through the open

door at the rain, and, accepting discomfort for the sake of decorum, vanished into the dark.

It was part of his nightly ritual. It aroused no misgivings. Every night, about this hour, he went out to perform his devoirs, take a look and a sniff round the garden, and perhaps the neighbors' garden, and returned within half an hour, or, on moonlight nights, perhaps an hour, smelling sweetly of earth and leaves; and allowed us to tuck him into his bowl for the night.

Cards were put away, the parlor tidied, hot bottles filled, stoves made up.

'Isn't he in yet?'

It was nearly eleven o'clock.

'He'll soon be back; I'll go down when I've undressed.'

Eleven fifteen.

'He's not there. What shall we do?'

'Leave the door open and the light on. I'll be reading a long time yet.'

It happened that night I was very tired. Pretending to read, I told myself all the sensible things I had learned over a lifetime as guardian of cats: their independence, their gift for making themselves comfortable in unusual places, their hatred of rain and mud and their readiness to seize on any shelter from bad weather. I knew that not one of these facts, which I had learned from my North Country kittens, applied to my little deaf cat, whose first thought would be to make for home. I reminded myself that he was known and adored by the neighbors, free of their outhouses and of their open windows. A personal friend would, of course, ring up to say he was there; but he might have found refuge with one of the cottagers. Anybody who loved animals might take in a beautiful, stray cat on a wet night.

I made, as best I could, an Act of Commonsense, and with one eye on the clock and an ear pricked for the familiar call on the stairs, affected to read my book.

At half-past two the Black One sat up suddenly, put her head on one side and fixed me with a stare of desperation.

'What is it, my little dog?'

She jumped off the bed and went silently to the door.

The Black One is seldom silent; apart from her distressingly shrill bark, she has a variety of little noises that she employs to communicate with human beings. She was silent, except for one deep bark, on the night she saved us from being burned to death when the house caught fire at Bagshot. If she had yapped I would have hushed her; but that one low note got me out of bed, to open the door and see flames roaring from floor to ceiling. While we struggled through smoke towards the telephone and the water supply, she settled down as guardian on my folded day clothes, where she remained immovable until the fire was beaten.

Now she stood by the door, facing towards me, with all of her desperate soul concentrated in her eyes. Come. Come. *Come.*

I got up and followed her down the stairs. She went to the front door, urging me to open it. I had a moment of hope as I switched on the porch light and lifted the latch. The Black One rushed out into the pouring rain and was lost in the darkness. Leaving her to her own devices, I went to the back and again shot the beam of the torch over the grass, the hedge, the outbuildings. I went out to the furnace room, with its comfortable glow of heat: just the place on a wet night for a sensible little cat. Shining the torch into packing cases, buckets and up on shelves, I could not believe I would not find him there—although he did not much care for the furnace room; it was too dusty for him.

The Black One flew back, her narrow feet, her frilled pantaloons soaked and dripping and allowed me to dry her. We went upstairs, past an open door and a light.

'Has he come in?'

'No.'

Half-past three. I put out my light. At any moment he'll come proudly in, a wet, white rag; he'll let out his cry . . . The Black One got off the bed. It was dark. She sniffed along the door. At the first inaudible pressure of his paws on the landing, I told myself, she'll burst out yapping. She made no sound. But again I got out of bed, and with a sickening kind of hope, opened the door. Nothing but the tick of clocks, like pins nailing the silence down over stairs and landing.

'Come to bed, my little dog.'

No answer. All through that dark, interminable night, she never returned.

At some moment I must have fallen asleep. When dawn came, my room was a shambles. The Black One, most scrupulous and well-mannered of beings, had suffered an emotional upheaval whose traces were all over the floor. She crept to lay her shamed head at my feet.

Leaving her home that morning, Alice said, 'I must go, "something's" waiting for me on the wall!'

She brought the tray into my devastated bedroom.

'Alice?—Bert's lost. He's not been home all night.'

The morning smile vanished, the pink drained from the flower-like face.

Soon after ten o'clock, a note was pinned up at the Post Office:

LOST
White, half-Persian Cat.

REWARD
For information leading to recovery.

A last, defiant gesture.

Somebody's picked him up and carried him off. He's got himself shut in somewhere and can't get out. (How many times had he been shut in cupboard or drawer, and 'lost' until his cries were heard?)

I shut myself into the work-room while the others went out in search of him. I knew there was no point in searching.

Half an hour after the notice went up in the Post Office, Alice was sobbing 'I *did* love him!' while I watched from my window the little grave being dug under the apple tree for him who would never again chase the falling blossoms; who had seen but one spring, one summer, one autumn and part of a winter.

When it happened, only the Black One knows. It was just before, or just after, she got off the bed for the last time.

The Black One's head rests on my foot. The Black One needs comfort, and reassurance. Something has vanished from the pattern of the Black One's life; she has lost, for the time, her sense of security, and she looks to the one who has always, to her, represented security, for its re-establishment.

For the present, she brings her habitual messages—'It's lunch time'—'Tea's ready'—'Come down for dinner'—'There's someone at the door'—not with her shrill voice, but with her willing feet, her urgent eyes. Soon, I hope, she will recover her bark. For the present, she is glad of bedtime, when she can push her small spine close to a human one, or her little head under a human chin. That part of the pattern, at least, is still unchanged.

In the course of forty years as a motorist, I have learned much about the ways of animals on the roads. I know, or think I know, more or less when to stand on the brake and when it is safe to keep up my cruising speed in open country. I can recognize, at a reasonable distance, a wary, road-wise dog or a flitter-headed youngster who only waits my approach to dash across the front wheels. Living in training country, I respect the strings, and hate those who don't, no less than any head lad or trainer; in common with all but a few of my country neighbors, I would rather risk missing a train than set fire to a line of nervy two-year-olds by pressing impatiently on.

After nightfall, these hazards are removed. The horses are safe in their boxes; the few amorous lurchers who have deserted their yards, their barns, the nondescript quarters they regard as 'home,' do not conduct their amours on the highroad; respectable dogs are on their rugs, in their baskets or kennels. But far ahead, picked up by the headlights, are two other little headlights, luminous, like sequins sewn on the dark hem of the hedgerow. *Cat.*

Slowing down, to wait for the safety signal, another car roars past me on the right. I close my eyes and hold my breath.

Some motorists appear to imagine that when the locals are shut, the villagers presumably indoors and abed, there is no need, even in or on the outskirts of a village, to abide by the thirty-mile limit. And the victims, too often, are cats.

By daylight, the growing volume of transport on the roads has taught the average cat road-wisdom it certainly did not possess twenty years ago; but the judgment of even the shrewdest tramp-cat is not always enough to protect it from the dazzle of head-lamps advancing at the speed of an express train down the lane it is proposing to cross. The sensible cat vanishes into the hedgerow until the danger is past, but many a dashing young spark—either losing its head, deliberately showing off, or in pursuit of some irresistible female— pays the toll of a broken shoulder or shattered pelvis to the petrol-driven pirates of darkness.

And supposing the car to be travelling at a civilized pace.

The first little pair of headlights crosses the road; but any cat-minded person can tell you that where one passes, at night, another is likely to follow. So you wait long enough, at least, for the escort to get safely across; or, allowing for indecision, you creep, your foot hovering over the brake, until the danger-point is passed.

If this unwritten rule of the road had been observed, le Petit Roi might be alive today. Deaf though he was, he was fearless, alert and sensible, but it was beyond reason to pit his speed and his strength against that of twelve horses, bearing down on him out of darkness at a pace he was incapable of calculating. Somewhere he was caught and thrown; his unmarked body was found in the gutter, with a few spots of blood on his little nose. Happily, he was not mutilated; he cannot have suffered, for death must have been instantaneous.

Bert, lovely and loving cat; stately, kindly, lordly friend . . .

He is the Last, as he was the Best, of all the cats I have ever known.

Lives of Two Cats

PIERRE LOTI

I HAVE often seen, with a questioning restlessness infinitely sad, the soul of animals meet mine from the depths of their eyes: the soul of a cat, the soul of a dog, the soul of a monkey, as pathetically, for an instant, as a human soul, revealing itself suddenly in a glance and seeking my own soul with tenderness, supplication, or terror; and I have felt perhaps more pity for these souls of animals than for those of my own brethren, because they are speechless, incapable of emerging from their semi-intelligence; above all, because they are more humble and despised.

The two cats whose histories I am about to write are associated in memory with comparatively happy years of my life,—years scarce past by the dates they bear, but years already seeming in the remote past, borne away by the frightfully accelerating speed of time, and which, placed beside the gray to-day, bear tints of early dawn or last rosy light of morning. So fast our days hasten to the twilight, so fast our fall to the night.

Pardon me that I call each of my cats Pussy. At first I had no idea of giving names to my pets. A cat was "Pussy," a kitten "Kitty"; and surely no names could be more expressive and tender than these. I shall call the poor little personages of my story by the names they bore in their real lives, Pussy White and Pussy Gray; the latter often known as Pussy Chinese.

As the oldest, allow me first to present the Angora, Pussy White. Her visiting card, by her desire, was thus inscribed—

MADAME MOUMOUTTE BLANCHE
PREMIÈRE CHATTE

Chez M. Pierre Loti.

On a memorable evening nearly twelve years ago, I saw her for the first time. It was a winter's evening, on one of my returns home at the close of some Eastern campaign. I had been in the house but a few moments, and was warming myself before a blazing wood fire, seated between my mother and my aunt Clara. Suddenly something appeared on the scene, bounding like a panther, and then rolling itself wildly on the hearth rug like a live snowball on its crimson ground. "Ah!" said Aunt Clara, "you don't know her; I will introduce her; this is our new inmate, Pussy White! We thought we would have another cat, for a mouse had found our closet in the saloon below."

The house had been catless for a long time; succeeding the mourning for a certain African cat that I had brought home from my first voyage and worshiped for two years, but who one fine morning, after a short illness, breathed out her little foreign soul, giving me her last conscious glance, and whom I had afterward buried beneath a tree in the garden.

I lifted for a closer view the roll of fur which lay so white on the crimson mat. I held her carefully with both hands, in a position cats immediately comprehend, and say to themselves, "Here is a man who understands us; his caresses we can gratefully condescend to receive."

The face of the new cat was very prepossessing. The young, brilliant eyes, the tip of a pink nose, and all else lost in a mass of silken Angora fur; white, warm, clean, exquisite to fondle and caress. Besides, she was marked nearly like her predecessor from Senegal, which fact probably decided the selection of my mother and aunt Clara,—to the end that I might finally regard the two as one, in my somewhat fickle affections. Above the cat's eyes, a capote shaped spot, jet black in color, was set straight, forming a band over the bright eyes; another and larger spot, shaped like a cape, lay over her shoulders; a plumy black tail, moving like a superb train or an animated fly-brush, completed the costume. Her breast, belly, and paws were white as the down of a swan; her "total" gave me the impression of a ball of animated fur; light, soft, and moved by some capricious hidden spring. After making my acquaintance, Pussy White left my arms to recommence her play. And in these first moments of arrival, inevitably melancholy, because they marked another epoch in my life, the new black and white obliged me to busy my thoughts with her, jumping on my knee to reiterate my welcome, or stretching herself with feigned weariness on the floor, that I might better admire the silken whiteness of her belly and neck. So she gambolled, the new cat, while my eyes rested with tender remembrances on the two dear faces which smiled on me, somewhat aged and framed in grayer curls; upon the family portraits which preserved their expression and age in their frames upon the walls; upon the thousand objects seen in their accustomed places; upon the well known furniture of this hereditary dwelling immovably fixed there, while my unquiet, restless, changing being had roamed over a changing world.

And this is the persistent, distinct image of our Pussy White, with me still, long after her death: an embodied frolic in fur, snowy white and bounding or rolling on the crimson rug between the sombre black robes of my mother and aunt Clara, in the evening of one of my great returns.

Poor Pussy! During the first winter of her life she was usually the familiar demon, the hearthstone imp, who enlivened the loneliness of the blessed guardians of my home, my mother and aunt Clara. While I sailed over distant seas, when the house resumed its grand emptiness, in sombre twilights and interminable December nights, she was their constant attendant, though often their tormentor; leaving upon their immaculate black gowns, precisely alike, tufts of her white fur. With reckless indiscretion she took forcible possession of a place on their laps, their work table, or in the centre of their work baskets, tangling beyond rearrangement their skeins of wool, their reels of silk. Then they would say with great pretense of anger, meanwhile longing to laugh, "Oh! that cat, that bad cat, she will never learn how to behave herself! Get out, miss! Get out! Were there ever such actions as these!" They busied themselves inventing methods for her amusement, even to keeping a jumping-jack, a ludicrous wooden toy, for her special edification.

She loved them cattishly, with indocility, but added thereto a touching constancy, for which alone her little incomplete and fantastic existence merits my lasting remembrance.

In springtime, when the March sun began to brighten our courtyard, she experienced new and endless surprises in seeing, awake and crawling from his winter retreat, our tortoise Suleïma, her fellow resident and friend.

During the beautiful month of May she seemed seized by yearnings for space and freedom; then she made excursions on the walls, the roof, through the lanes, in the neighboring gardens, and even nocturnal absences, which I should here state were unaccountable in the austere circle where fate had placed her.

In summer she was languid as a creole. For entire days she lay lazily in the sunshine on the old wall top among the honeysuckles and roses, or, extended on the tiled walks, turned her white belly to the sun amidst the pots of red or golden cacti.

Extremely careful of her little person, always neat, correct, aristocratic, even to the ends of her toes, she was haughtily disdainful of other cats, and conducted herself as if ill bred if any neighbor cat called on her. In this courtyard, which she considered her own domain, she conceded no right of entry. If, above the adjoining garden wall, two ear tips, a cat's nose, rose timidly, or if something stirred in the vines or moss, she upsprang like a young fury, bristling angrily to the tip of her tail, impossible to restrain, quite beside herself! Cries in harsh tones and bad taste followed, struggles, blows, and savage clawings.

In fact, our pet was ferociously independent. She was also extremely affectionate when so inclined, caressing, cajoling, uttering so gentle a cry of joy, a tremulous "miaou" every time she returned from one of her vagabond tramps in the vicinity.

She was then five years old, in the mature beauty of an Angora, with superb attitudes of dignity and the graces of a queen. I had become much attached to her in the course of my absences and returns, considering her one of our home treasures, when there appeared on the scene—three thousand miles afar in the Gulf of Pekin, and of a far less distinguished family than the Angoras—the kitten destined to become her inseparable friend, the most unique little personage I have yet known, "Pussy Gray" or "Pussy Chinese."

MADAME MOUMOUTTE CHINOISE
DEUXIÈME CHATTE

Chez M. Pierre Loti.

Most singular was the destiny which united to me this cat of the yellow race, progeny of obscure parentage and destitute of all beauty.

It was at the close of our last foreign war, one of those evenings of revelry which often occurred at that time. I know not how the little distraught creature, driven from some wrecked junk or sampan, came on board our warship, in great terror, seeking a refuge in my cabin beneath my berth. She was young, not half grown, thin and melancholy, having doubtless, like her relatives and masters subsisted meanly on fishes' heads with a bit of cooked rice. I pitied her much and bade my servant give her food and drink.

With an unmistakable air of humility and gratitude she accepted my kindness,—and I can see her now, creeping slowly toward the unhoped-for repast, advancing first one foot, then another, her clear eyes fixed on mine to assure herself that she was not deceived, that it was really intended for her.

In the morning I wished to turn her away. After giving her a farewell breakfast, I clapped my hands loudly, and stamping both feet together by way of emphasis, I said in a harsh tone, "Get out, go away, little Kitty!"

But no, she did not go, the little pagan. Evidently she felt no fear of me, intuitively certain that all this angry noise was a pretense. With an air that seemed to say, "I know very well that you will not harm me," she crouched silently in the corner, lying close to the floor in a supplicating attitude, fixing upon me two dilated eyes, alight with a human look that I have never seen except in hers.

What could I do? Impossible to domicile a cat in the contracted cabin of a warship. Besides, she was such a distressingly homely little creature, what an encumbrance by and by!

Then I lifted her carefully to my neck, saying to her, "I am very sorry, Kitty;" but I carried her resolutely the length of the deck, to the further end of the battery, to the sailors' quarters, who usually are both fond of and kind to cats of whatever age or pedigree.

Flattened close to the deck, her head imploringly turned towards me, she gave me one beseeching look; then rose and fled with a queer and swift gait in the direction of my cabin, where she arrived first in the race between us; when I entered I found her crouched obstinately in the corner from which I had taken her, with an expression, a remonstrance in her golden eyes, that deprived me of all courage to again take her away. And this is the way by which Pussy Chinese chose me for her owner and protector.

My servant, evidently on her side from the début of the contest, completed immediate preparations for her installment in my cabin, by placing beneath my bed a lined basket for her bed, and one of my large Chinese bowls, very practically filled with sand; an arrangement which froze me with fright.

Day and night she lived for seven months in the dim light and unceasing movement of my cabin, and gradually an intimacy was established between us, simultaneously with a faculty of mutual comprehension very rare between man and animal.

I recall the first day when our relations became truly affectionate. We were far out in the Yellow Sea, in gloomy September weather. The first autumnal fogs had gathered over the suddenly cooled and restless waters. In these latitudes cold and cloud come suddenly, bringing to us European voyagers a sadness whose intensity is proportioned to our distance from home. We were steaming eastward against a long swell which had arisen, and rocked in dismal monotony to the plaintive groans and creakings of the ship. It had become necessary to close my port, and the cabin received its sole light through the thick bull's-eye, past which the crests of the waves swept in green translucency, making intermittent obscurity. I had seated myself to write at the little sliding table, the same in all our cabins on board,—during one of those rare moments, when our service allows a complete freedom and peace, and when the longing comes to be alone as in a cloister.

Pussy Gray had lived under my berth for nearly two weeks. She had behaved with great circumspection; melancholy, showing herself seldom, keeping in darkest corners as if suffering from homesickness and pining for the land to which there was no return.

Suddenly she came forth from the shadows, stretched herself leisurely, as if giving time for farther reflection, then moved towards me, still hesitating with abrupt stops; at times affecting a peculiarly Chinese gesture, she raised a fore paw, holding it in the air some seconds before deciding to make another advancing step; and all this time her eyes were fixed on mine with infinite solicitude.

What did she want of me? She was evidently not hungry: suitable food was given her by my servant twice daily. What then could it be?

When she was sufficiently near to touch my leg, she sat down, curled her tail about her, and uttered a very low mew; and still looked directly in my eyes, as if they could communicate with hers, which showed a world of intelligent conception in her little brain. She must first have learned, like other superior animals, that I was not a thing, but a thinking being, capable of pity and influenced by the mute appeal of a look; besides, she felt that my eyes were for her eyes, that they were mirrors, where her little soul sought anxiously to seize a reflection of mine. Truly they are startlingly near us, when we reflect upon it, animals capable of such inferences.

As to myself, I studied for the first time the little visitor who for two weeks had shared my lodging: she was fawn-colored like a wild rabbit, mottled with darker spots like a tiger, her nose and neck were white; homely in effect, mainly consequent on her extremely thin and sickly condition, and really more odd looking than homely to a man freed like myself from all conventional ideas of beauty. Besides, she was quite unlike our French cats: low on the legs, very long bodied, a tail of unusual length, large upright ears, and a triangular face; all her charm was in the eyes, raised at the outer corners like all eyes of the extreme Orient, of a fine golden yellow instead of green, and ever changing, astonishingly expressive.

While examining her, I laid my hand gently upon her queer little head, stroking the brown fur in a first caress.

Whatever she experienced was an emotion beyond mere physical pleasure; she felt the sentiment of a protection, a pity for her condition of an abandoned foundling. This, then, was why she came out of her retreat, poor Pussy Gray; this was why she resolved, after so much hesitation, to beg from me not food or drink, but, for the solace of her lonely cat soul, a little friendly company and interest.

Where had she learned to know that, this miserable outcast, never stroked by a kind hand, never loved by any one,—if not perhaps in the paternal junk, by some poor Chinese child without playthings, and without caresses, thrown by chance like a useless weed in the immense yellow swarm, miserable and hungry as herself, and whose incomplete soul in departing, left behind no more trace than her own?

Then a frail paw was laid timidly upon me—oh! with so much delicacy, so much discretion!—and after looking at me a long time beseechingly, she decided to venture upon my knee. Jumping there lightly she curled herself in a light, small mass, making herself small as possible and almost without weight, never taking her eyes from me. She lay a long time thus, much in my way, but I had not the heart to dislodge her, which I should doubtless have done had she been a gay pretty kitten in the bloom of kittenhood. As if in fear at my least movement, she watched me incessantly, not fearing that I should harm her—she was too intelligent to think me capable of that—but with an air that seemed to ask: "Is it true that I do not weary you, that I do not trouble you?" and then, her eyes growing still more tender and expressive, saying to mine very plainly: "On this dismal autumn day, so depressing to the soul of cats, since we two are here so lonely, in this abode so strange, so unquiet, shaken and lost amid I know not what dangerous and endless space, can we not give to each other a little of that sweet thing, immaterial and beyond the power of death, which is called affection and which sometimes shows itself in a caress?"

As soon as the treaty of friendship was signed between this cat and myself, anxieties arose within me concerning her future. What could I do with her? Carry her to France over so many thousand miles and difficulties innumerable? To be sure, my home would be for her the unhoped-for asylum where the short mysterious dream of her little life would pass with least suffering and most peace. But I could not see, without forebodings, this sickly, illy-robed foreigner the fellow resident of our superb Pussy White, so jealous, who would certainly drive her from the premises as soon as she appeared. No, that was impossible.

On the other side, to abandon her at our next port of call, among chance new friends—that was equally impossible; I could have done so had she been vigorous and beautiful, but this melancholy little creature, with her human eyes, held me to her by a profound pity.

Our intimacy, founded on mutual loneliness, constantly increased. Weeks and months passed, on the never resting seas, while all remained the same in the obscure corner of the ship where Pussy had chosen her abode. For us men who sail the seas there are always the strong winds that buffet us, the starry nights on deck, and the goings on shore in foreign ports—always some event to break the monotony of sea life. She, on the contrary, knew nothing of the vast world over which her prison moved, nothing of her kindred, or of the sun, or of verdure, or of shade. And, never going outside, she lived in the solitude of my narrow cabin; it was a glacial place at times when the door swung open to the fierce wind sweeping the decks; oftener it was a hot and stifling furnace, where Chinese incense burned before the expatriated idols as if in a Buddhist temple. For companions in her musings she had monsters in wood or bronze, fixed to the walls, and grinning with malicious laughter; in the midst of a mass of relics of things sacred in her country, pillaged from dwellings and temples, she wasted away, without air, among the silken hangings that she loved to tear with her restless little claws.

As soon as I entered my cabin she would come forward with her soft welcoming cry of joy, springing like a jack in the box from behind some curtain, desk, or chest. If by chance I seated myself to write, she very slyly, very tenderly, seeking protection and caresses, would softly take her place on my knees and follow the comings and goings of my pen,—sometimes effacing, with an unintentional stroke of her paw, lines of whose tenor she disapproved.

The shocks, the pitchings of the ship in rough weather, the noise of our cannon, gave her great terror: at these times, she threw herself against the walls, spun around like a mad creature, after which she would stop breathless, and hide herself in the darkest corner, with a terrified and sad expression.

Her cloistered youth resulted in an unnatural state of invalidism, becoming daily more and more pronounced. Her appetite continued normal, but she was emaciated, her face grew, if possible, more triangular, her ears pointed sharply and bat-like, her large golden eyes sought mine with an air of distress, uncomfortably humanlike, or with questionings on the problem of life, perhaps equally troubling and far more unanswerable to her little intelligence than to my own.

She was very curious about outside matters, despite her unaccountable determination never to cross the threshold of my door, and never failed to examine with extreme attention any new object brought to our common lodging, probably giving her confused impressions of the foreign ports where our ship called. In India, for example, I remember she was once deeply interested, even to the total neglect of her breakfast, in a bouquet of fragrant orchids,—so extraordinary for her who had never known garden or forest, never seen other than the withered or dead flowers in my bronze vases. As an offset to her rough and discolored fur, which at first sight gave her a gutter-cat air, she was finely formed, and the least movement of her delicate paws was of patrician grace. While watching her, I sometimes fancied her some little enchanted princess, condemned by wicked fairies to share my solitude in this lowly guise; and I called to mind a story of the mother of the great Tchengiz-Khan, which an old Armenian priest of Constantinople, my teacher of the Turkish language, had given me to translate:

"The young princess Ulemalik-Kurekli, doomed before her birth to die if she beheld the light of day, lived shut up in an obscure dungeon. And she asked her servants: 'Is this what they call the world? Tell me, is there anything else outside these walls? is this tower in something?'

" 'No, princess, this is not the world: that is outside and very much larger. And there are also things they call stars, that they call sun and they call moon.'

" 'Oh!' replied Ulemalik, 'let me die, but let me see them!' "

It was at the close of winter, one of the first warm days of March, that Pussy Chinese made her début at my home in France. Pussy White still wore at that season her royal winter robe, and I had never seen her more imposing. The contrast would be the more overwhelming for my poor favorite, lean, lank, with her faded fawn-colored fur looking as if moth-eaten. I felt myself much embarrassed when our man Sylvester, returning with my pet from the ship, lifted, with a half disdainful air, the cover of the basket where he had placed her, and I saw, in the midst of the assembled family, my little Chinese friend creep tremblingly forth.

Most deplorable was her first appearance. I felt the impression of the group in Aunt Clara's simple exclamation: "Oh! my friend, how homely she is!"

Homely indeed! And in what way, under what pretense could I present her to the magnificent Pussy White? In utter helplessness I had her carried, for the time being, to an isolated granary,—that I might gain time to reflect on the situation.

Their first interview was certainly terrible. It was unpremeditated, a few days after, in the kichen (a locality of irresistible attractions, where the cats of the same household, do what one can to prevent, will some day meet). The servants summoned me hastily and I ran to the battlefield, where, uttering unearthly yells, a shapeless package of fur and claws formed of their closely clinched little bodies, rolled and bounded,—shattering glasses, plates, and dishes, while tufts of white fur, gray fur, black fur, and fawn fur flew and floated everywhere. It was necessary to interfere energetically and instantly: to separate them I threw upon them a whole carafe of water. I was at my wits' end.

Breathless, scratched, and bleeding, her heart beating as if it must break, Pussy Gray was gathered to my breast, where she clung closely, growing more quiet in the consciousness of sweet security; then she became less and less rigid and as limp and inert as if dying, which is a way cats have of showing entire confidence in one who holds them. Pussy White, seated thoughtful and gloomy in a corner, looked at us with surprised eyes, and a deduction from the view was formed in her little jealous brain; that she, who from one year's end to the other had driven from the neighboring walls all other cats, unwilling even to endure their presence, must acknowledge this ugly pagan as mine, since I held her so tenderly, so closely; then it became necessary that she, Pussy White, should tolerate her presence in the mansion and trouble her no more.

My surprise and admiration were great to see these two, an instant after, pass by each other, not merely with indifference but calmly, civilly,—and all was ended. During their lives they never quarreled again.

The springtime of the following year! How pleasant my reminiscences of its sunny days.

Very short as all seasons now seem, it was the last which held a charm for me, like the mysterious enchantment of childhood's days, passed in the same environment of verdure and bloom, in the midst of flowers blooming anew in their annual ranks, the same jasmines, the same roses. After my campaigns I joyfully returned there, to forget other continents and the immense seas; again, as in my infancy, I limited the exterior world to the old walls hung with vines and mosses, which bounded my rambles; the distant lands where I have since lived seeming unreal as those of which I dreamed, having never seen. The far horizons fade; they vanish imperceptibly and nothing is real to me save our mossy stones, our trees, our trellises, and our beloved white roses!

At that time, I had built in a corner of my mansion a Buddhist pagoda, the collected débris of original temples. From the large cases opened daily in the courtyard in the warm sunshine there arose that indefinable and mingled odor of China, from pedestals of columns, bas-reliefs of ceilings, carved altars, and mouldy old idols and vases. It was interesting and unique, this unpacking; to watch these grotesque objects reappearing one by one, arranging themselves, as it were, on the grass or the mossy pavement,—all this assembly of monsters of far Asia, bearing on their faces the same frowns and grimaces they had borne for ages. Occasionally my mother and Aunt Clara would come out to look at them, astonished at their overwhelming ugliness. Pussy Gray was the most interested spectator of these unpackings; recognizing her ocean surroundings, she sniffed all with confused memories of her native land; afterward, habituated to dwelling so long in semi-darkness, she would crawl into the boxes and hide herself in the empty spaces, under the exotic straw still smelling of sandal-wood and musk.

It was an exhilarating and beautiful springtime, bird songs filling the air; and Pussy Gray thought it marvelous. Poor little recluse, grown up in the stifling obscurity of my rolling home! Bright sunlight, balmy air, the vicinity of feline friends alike astonished and charmed her. She now made long and exhaustive explorations of the courtyard and garden, smelling every blade of grass, every new plant; in fact everything that sprang fresh and odorous from the awakened earth. These forms, these colors, old as the world, which plants unconsciously produce every succeeding spring, these immutable laws, perfectly and silently obeyed by unfolding leaf and bursting bud, were phenomena for her who had never known springtime or verdure. And Pussy White, formerly absolute and intolerant queen of the place, had deigned to share her domain with the forlorn stranger, allowing her to roam at will among the evergreens, the potted flowers, or along the promenade on the gray wall-top under the pendent boughs. Pussy Chinese was especially impressed by a miniature lake, so closely interwoven with my infantile memories, which fascinated her for a long time. There, in the grass each day higher and more luxuriant, she crouched close to the earth, like a panther intent on his prey (doubtless inheriting this movement from her ancestors, Mongolian cats with uncultivated manners). She hid behind the lilliputian rocks, buried herself beneath the vines like a little tiger in a miniature virgin forest.

I found great pleasure in watching her goings and comings, her sudden haltings, her surprises; when she realized that I was watching her, she in turn watched me, posing in an attitude peculiarly her own;—very graceful, but very like a Chinese belle, with a paw extended as if holding a fan, just as I have seen one holding an article raise coquettishly the little finger; and her droll golden eyes grew infinitely expressive, "speaking" to mine. "Please permit me to amuse myself? Does it incommode you in the least? Look! I walk with lightness, I play with extreme carefulness, I go about with discretion among these beautiful green things that smell so sweetly, and this good air is so refreshing in this wide, free space! And these other strange objects that I see in turn high over us, 'Things they call stars, that they call sun, and they call moon!' Oh! how different from our trembling lodging on the ship and how delightful to be here together in this happy place!"

This home, so new to her, was equally for me the oldest, the most familiar of all places on the earth; whose least details, whose feeblest blade of grass were known to me since the earliest and most impressible days of my existence. So dear to me that I am bound to it with all my being, so dear that I love with a love akin to idolatry the old vines and shrubs which are there, the jasmine, the honeysuckles, and a certain dielytra rose, which every returning March unfolds its precocious leaves, gives the same April roses, fades in the June sun, then burns in August heat and seems to perish.

And while Pussy Gray abandons herself to the joy of youth and springtime, I, on the contrary, knowing that all this will pass away,

feel for the first time in my life, shadows like those of evening stealing over my own life,—presages of the inexorable night, the morn-
ingless night of the final autumn,—never to be succeeded by spring.

And with profound sadness in this courtyard bright with sunshine,
I gaze upon the two dear ones, their silvery hair, their mourning
robes—my mother and Aunt Clara, going and coming, stooping
down as has been their wont for many springs, to discover what
flower seeds had come up, or raising their heads to see the buds of
honeysuckles and rose trees. And when their sombre robes vanished
from my view, at the end of the green avenue, which is the vesti-
bule of our family residence, I am forced to notice that their steps
are slower and less firm. Oh, time, perhaps near, when in the unchanging green avenue I shall behold them no more. Can it be
possible that time may arrive? If ever they shall be gone I have the
illusion that it will not be an entire departure, so long as I remain
there recalling their presence;—that in the quiet summer evenings
I shall sometimes see their spirits glide beneath the jasmine; that
something of their existence will still live in the plants they have
tended, and breathe from the falling honeysuckle, the old dielytra
rose.

Since her life in open air, my favorite flourished visibly. The bare
and unsightly spots in her rabbit-colored coat were covered with new
glossy fur; she was less thin, more careful of her little person, and
bore no longer the appearance of a witch's cat. My mother and Aunt
Clara often stopped to speak to her, interested in her odd ways, her
expressive eyes, and her soft responsive "Trr! trr! trr!" that she never
failed to utter when addressed.

"Certainly," they said, "this Chinese pussy seems very happy with
us; no cat's face could show greater content."

A happy look, in fact; even a look of gratitude to me, who had
brought her to her new home. And the happiness of young animals is
perfect, perhaps because they have not, like us, forebodings of the
inevitable future.

She passed deliciously dreamy days in most luxuriant idleness,
extended on the warm tiles or the soft moss, enjoying the silence—
somewhat depressing to me—of this abode where neither the con-
tention of wind and wave or the terrible shock of cannon troubled
her repose. She had reached the distant peaceful haven, the last port
in her short life's voyage, and rested happily unconscious of the end.

One fine day, without intervention, seized by some sudden whim,
the indifference of Pussy White changed to a tender friendship. She

came deliberately to Pussy Gray and rubbed her nose against her own affectionately, which is with her race the equivalent of a kiss. Sylvester, who was present at the performance, showed himself skeptical regarding its good intent. "Did you see," said I, "the kiss of peace?" "Oh no, sir!" he replied, in that tone of accomplished connoisseur, assumed whenever any question arises concerning my cats, dogs, horses, or any other animals; "Oh no, sir! it is simply that Pussy White wishes to ascertain if Pussy Gray has been stealing her meat."

He was mistaken for once nevertheless,—and from that hour they were fast friends. They could be seen sitting in the same chair, eating

the same food, even from the same plate, and every morning running to exchange salutations, rubbing together the tips of their soft noses, one yellow, the other pink.

After this we said, "The cats did this or that." They were an intimate and inseparable pair, taking counsel together, following each other in the least and most trivial actions of their lives; and making their toilets together, licking each other with mutual interest.

Pussy White maintained her position as the special cat of Aunt

Clara, while the Chinese continued my faithful little friend, holding fast to her old habits of following me with her speaking eyes, and replying in her expressive "Trr-trr-trr," whenever I spoke to her. Scarcely would I be seated before a light paw rested on me, as in the old evenings on the ship; two questioning eyes sought mine, then a bound and she was on my knees,—slowly making her preparations for a nap; plying her fore paws alternately, turning herself round to the right, then to the left, and usually finding the right position by the time I was ready to depart.

What a mystery! A soul's mystery perhaps, this constant affection of an animal and its unchanging gratitude.

They were much spoiled, the two cats; admitted to the dining-room at meal times; often seated one on my right and the other on my left; recalling to me, occasionally, their presence by a light stroke of the paw on my napkin, and watching for tit-bits that I fed them surreptitiously, like a guilty schoolboy, from the tip of my fork.

In recording this, I still farther darken my reputation, which, it seems, is already reputed incorrect and eccentric. I can however criticise a certain member of the Academy, who, having done me the honor of dining at my table, did not refrain from offering to our pussies, even in his own spoon, a little Chantilly cream.

The following summer was for Pussy Gray a period of absolutely delicious life. With her originality and her foreign air, she had grown almost beautiful, so finely reclad in glossy fawn color. All around, in the cat world, in the gardens and on the roofs, the news had circulated of the presence of this piquant stranger; and candidates for her smiles were numerous; they smirked and serenaded beneath her windows in the balmy nights filled with perfume of honeysuckle and rose.

During September, the two cats experienced, at almost the same time, the joy of motherhood.

Pussy White, it is needless to relate, was already a well known matron. As to Pussy Gray, when her first moments of surprise had passed, she tenderly licked the precious tiny gray kitten, spotted and mottled like a tiger,—her only son.

The reciprocal attachment of the two families was touching; the comical little Chinese and the little Angora, round as a powder puff, frolicking together, and nourished, washed, and watched by one or the other mother with an almost equal solicitude.

In the winter season pussy becomes peculiarly the hearthstone guest, constant companion of the fireside, sharing with us, before the flickering flames, vague melancholies and endless reveries of the long twilights.

Since the first frost Pussy Gray had lost all roughness of her mottled coat, and Pussy White had donned a most imposing cravat, a boa of snowy whiteness that framed her face like a Medici ruff. It is well known that in winter the cat attains its fullest perfection of flesh and fur. Their attachment grew as they warmed themselves together by the fireside; they slept entire days in each other's arms, on the cushions in the armchairs, rolled in a single ball where heads and tails were alike indistinguishable.

Pussy Gray could never get sufficiently close to her friend. Returning from some scamper in open air, if she perceived the Angora sleeping before the fire, she softly, very softly approached her, as if about to spring upon a mouse; the other, always nervous, whimsical, irritated at being disturbed, sometimes gave her a light cuff of disapproval. She never retaliated, the Chinese, but merely raising her little paw, as if quite ready to laugh, then saying to me from a corner of her eyes, "You must allow that she is rather cross! But I don't mind it at all, you may be sure!" Then, with redoubled precaution, she always attained her desired purpose, which was to lay herself completely upon the other, her head sunk in the silky snow,—and before sleeping she said to me, from half-closed eyes: "This is all I wanted! Here I am!"

Oh! our winter's evenings of that time! In the most sheltered corner of the mansion, elsewhere closed and left silent and dark, was a small and warm parlor facing the sun, the courtyard, and the gardens, where my mother and Aunt Clara sat beneath their hanging lamp, in their usual places where so many past and similar winters had found them. And, usually, I was there also, that I might not lose an hour of their presence on earth and of my days at home near them. On the other side of the mansion, far from us, I abandoned my study, leaving it dark and fireless that I might simply pass my evenings in their dear company, within the cosy room, innermost sanctuary of our family life, the home dearest to us all. (No other spot has given me a fuller, a sweeter impression of a nest; nowhere have I warmed myself with more tranquil melancholy than before the blaze in its small fireplace.) The windows, whose blinds were never closed, so confident were we in our security, the glass door, almost too summer-like, opened upon the desolation of naked trees and vines, brown leaves, and despoiled trellises often silvered by pale moonlight. Not a sound reached us from the street, which was some rods distant,—and besides a very quiet one, its silence rarely broken save by the songs of sailors celebrating, at long intervals, their safe returns. No, we had rather the sounds of the country, whose nearness was felt beyond the gardens and old ramparts of the city;—in summer, immense concerts of frogs in the marshes which surrounded us smooth as steppes, and the intermittent flutelike note of the owl; in the winter evenings of which I write, the shrill cry of the marsh bird, and above all, the long wail of the west wind coming from the sea.

Upon the round table, covered with a gayly flowered cloth, which I have known all my life, my mother and aunt Clara placed their workbaskets, containing articles that I would fain designate "fondamentales," if I dared employ that word which, in the present instance, will signify nothing save to myself; those trifles, now sacred relics, which hold in my eyes, in my memory, in my life, a supreme importance: embroidery scissors, heirlooms in the family, lent me rarely when a child, with manifold charges to carefulness, that I might amuse myself with paper cutting; winders for thread, in rare colonial woods, brought long years ago from over the oceans by sailors, and giving material for deep reveries; needlecases, thimbles, spectacles, and pocketbooks. How well I know and love every one of them, the trifles so precious, spread out every evening for so many years on the gay old tablecloth, by the hands of my mother and Aunt Clara; after each distant voyage with what tenderness I see them again and bid them my good-day of return! In writing of them I have used the word "fondamentale," so inappropriate I confess, but can only explain it thus: if they were destroyed, if they ceased to appear in their unchanged positions, I should feel as if I had taken a long step nearer the annihilation of my being, towards dust and oblivion.

And when they shall be gone, my mother and Aunt Clara, it seems to me that these precious little objects, religiously treasured after their departure, will recall their presence, will perhaps prolong their stay in our midst.

The cats, naturally, remained usually in our common room,—sleeping together, a warm, soft ball, upon some taboret or cushioned chair, the nearest to the fire. And their sudden awakenings, their musings, their droll ways, cheered our somewhat monotonous evenings.

Once it was Pussy White who, seized by a desire to be in our closer company, leaped upon the table and sat gravely down upon the sewing work of Aunt Clara, turning her back upon her mistress, after unceremoniously sweeping her plumy tail over her face; afterwards remaining there, obstinately indiscreet, and gazing abstractedly at the flame of the lamp. Once in a night of tingling frost, so excitable to a cat's nerves, we heard, in a near garden, an animated discussion: "Miaou! Miaraouraou!" Then from the mute fur ball, which slumbered so soundly, upsprang two heads, two pair of shining eyes. Again: "Miaraou! Miaraou!" The quarrel goes on! The Angora rose up resolutely, her fur bristling in anger, and ran from door to door, seeking an exit as if called outside by some imperative duty of great importance: "No, no, Pussy," said Aunt Clara, "believe me, there is no necessity for your interference; they will settle their quarrel without your help!" And the Chinese, on the contrary, always calm and averse to perilous adventure, contented herself by glancing at me with a knowing air, evidently regarding her friend's movements as ridiculous, and asking me, "Am I not right in keeping away from this fracas?"

A certain beatitude, profound and almost infantile, pervaded the silent little parlor where my mother and Aunt Clara sat at work. And if by turns I remembered, with a dull heart throb, having possessed an oriental soul, an African soul, and a number of other souls, of having indulged, under divers suns, in numberless fantasies and dreams, all that appeared to me as far distant and forever finished. And this roving past let me more thoroughly to enjoy the present hour, the side-scene in this interlude of my life, which is so unknown, so unsuspected, which would astonish many people, and perhaps make them smile. In all sincerity of purpose, I said to myself that nothing could again take me from my home, that nothing could be so precious as the peace of dwelling there, and finding again part of my first soul; to feel around me, in this nest of my infancy, I know not what benignant protection against worthlessness and death; to picture to myself through the window, in all the obscurity of dying foliage, beneath the winter moon, this courtyard which once held my entire world, which has remained the same all these years past, with its vines, its mimic rocks, its old walls, and which may perhaps resume its importance in my eyes, its former greatness, and repeople itself with the same dreams. Above all, I resolved that nothing in the wide world was worth the gentle bliss of watching mother and Aunt Clara sewing at the round table, bending toward the bright flowered cloth their caps of black lace, their coils of silvery hair.

Oh! one evening I will recall. There was a scene, a drama among the cats! Even now I cannot recall it without laughter.

It was a frosty night about Christmas time. In the deep silence we had heard passing above the roofs, through cold and cloudless skies, a flock of wild geese, emigrating to other climates: a sound of harsh voices, very numerous, wailing not too harmoniously together and soon lost in the infinite regions of the sky. "Do you hear? Do you hear?" said Aunt Clara with a slight smile and an anxious look to banter me; recalling the fact that in my childhood I was greatly alarmed by these nocturnal flights of birds. To hear their voices one should have a keen ear and listen in an otherwise silent place.

Our room then resumed its calm,—a calm so profound that I heard the complaint of the blazing wood on the hearth, and the regular breathing of our cats seated in the chimney corner.

Suddenly, a certain large yellow gentleman cat, held in horror by Pussy White, but persistently pursuing her with his declarations, appeared behind a window pane, showing in full relief against the background of dark foliage, looking at her with an impertinent and excited air and uttering a formidable "Miaou" of provocation. Then she sprang up at the window like a panther, or a ball deftly thrown, and there, nose to nose, on each side of the pane, there was a useless battle, a volley of unpardonable insults poured out in shrill, coarse tones; blows of unsheathed claws given with emphasis, vain scratchings across the glass, which made great noise and did nothing. Oh! the fright of my mother and Aunt Clara, starting from their chairs at the first alarm,—then their hearty laugh afterward, the ridiculousness of all this impetuous racket breaking in upon the intense silence,—and above all the visage of the visitor, the yellow cat, discomfited and breathless, whose eyes blazed so drolly behind the glass!

"Putting the pussies to bed" was in those evenings, one of the important events,—"primordiales" shall I call it?—of our daily existence. They were never allowed, as are many other cats, to roam all night among the vines and flowers, beneath the stars, or contemplating the moon; we held opinions upon that subject from which we never departed and made no compromises.

The going to bed was merely shutting them up in an old granary at the end of the courtyard, almost hidden under a growth of vines and honeysuckles; it was really in Sylvester's quarters, beside his chamber; so that every evening they said good-night together, the cats and he. When each one of these days—these unappreciated days now wept for—was ended, fallen in the abyss of time, Sylvester was called and my mother would say in a half solemn tone, as if fulfilling a religious duty, "Sylvester, it is time for the cats to go to bed."

At the first words of this phrase, uttered in ever so low a voice, Pussy White pricked up her ears; then knowing there was no mistake about it, jumped down from her cushion with an important though disturbed air, and ran to the door, that she might make her exit first, and on her own feet, unwilling to be carried, and determined to go of her own free will or not at all. The Chinese, on the contrary, endeavored to delay the inevitable change; reluctant to quit the warm room, she got down slyly, crouching very low on the carpet to be less in view, and glancing around to ascertain if any one had seen her, would hide under some article of furniture. The big Sylvester, accustomed to these subterfuges, called with his childlike tone and smile: "Where are you, Pussy Gray? I know you are not far off." Tenderly she responded "Trr! Trr! Trr!" knowing further pretense useless, and allowing herself to be lifted to the broad shoulder of her friend. The procession finally took up the line of march: at the head, Pussy White, independent and superb; behind followed Sylvester who said "Good-night," and who in one hand carried his lantern, and with the other grasped the long tail of Pussy Gray which hung pendent on his breast. The Angora usually proceeded resignedly to her proper sleeping place. Sometimes it happened, at certain phases of the moon, that vagabond fancies seized her, aspirations to play the truant and sleep at the angle of some roof, or at the summit of a solitary pear tree, in the bracing air of December, after having passed the entire day in an armchair by the fireside. On these occasions Sylvester soon reappeared with a drolly despondent face, still holding the tail of Pussy Gray who clung close to his neck: saying "Again that Pussy White will not go to bed!"—"Again! Ah! what actions!" replied Aunt Clara indignantly. And she stepped outside, herself, to try the effect of her authority, calling "Pussy, Pussy" in her dear, feeble voice which I can hear now, as it echoed then in the courtyard through the sonorous depth of the winter night. But no, Pussy obeyed not; from the height of a tree, from the top of a wall she gazed about her with a nonchalant air, seated at her ease on her chosen throne, her furry robe making a white spot in the darkness and her eyes emitting tiny phosphorescent gleams. "Pussy, Pussy! Oh you naughty creature! It is shameful, miss, such conduct, shameful!"

Then out in her turn came my mother, shivering in the cold, and trying to make Aunt Clara come in. An instant after, I follow to bring both indoors. And then to see ourselves gathered in the courtyard, in a freezing night, Sylvester also of the group and still holding his cat by the tail, and all this united authority set at defiance by a little cat perched high above us, gave an irresistible desire to laugh at ourselves, beginning with Aunt Clara, and in which we all joined. I have never believed there existed in the entire world two such blessed old ladies,—Oh, how old, alas!—capable of such hearty laughter with the young; knowing so well how to be amiable, how to be gay. Truly I have been happier with them than with any or all others; they always discovered in seemingly insignificant trifles an amusing or comical aspect. Pussy White decidedly had the best of the discussion! We re-entered, crestfallen and chilled, the little room too much cooled by the opened door, to gain our respective chambers by a series of stairways and sombre passages. And Aunt Clara, with a relapse of anger, when reaching her threshold, said to me, "Good-night; but, on the whole, what is your opinion of that cat?"

The life of a cat may extend over a period of twelve to fifteen years, if no accident occurs.

Our two pets lived to enjoy together the light and warmth of another delicious summer; they found again their days of blissful idleness, in company of the everlasting tortoise, Suleïma, whom the years forgot, between the blooming cacti, on the sun-heated pavements,—or stretched on the old wall amidst the profusion of jasmines and roses. They had many kittens, raised with tender care and afterward advantageously domiciled in the neighborhood; those of the Chinese were in great demand, being of a peculiar color and bearing distinctive race marks.

They lived another winter and recommenced their long naps in the chimney corner, their meditations before the changing aspect of the flame or embers of our wood fire.

But this was their last season of health and joy, and soon after, their decline began. In the succeeding spring some mysterious malady attacked their little bodies, which should have endured vigorous and sound for still some years.

Pussy Chinese, first attacked, seemed stricken by some mental trouble, a sombre melancholy,—regrets perhaps for her native Mongolia. Refusing both food and drink, she made long retreats to the wall top, lying there motionless for entire days; replying only to our appeals by a sorrowful glance and plaintive "Meaou."

The Angora also, from the first warm days, began to languish, and by April both were really ill.

Doctors, called in consultation, gravely prescribed absurd medicines and impossible treatments. For one, pills morning and evening and poultices applied to the belly! For the other, a hydropathic course, close shaving of the body, and a cold plunge bath twice daily! Sylvester himself, who adored the pussies, who obeyed him as they would no one else, declared all this impossible. We then tried the efficacy of domestic remedies; the mothers Michel were summoned, but their simple prescriptions were of no avail.

They were going from us, our beloved and cherished pets, filling our hearts with great compassion,—and neither the loveliness of spring nor its glory of returning sunshine could rouse them from the torpor of approaching death.

One morning as I arrived from a trip to Paris, Sylvester, while receiving my valise, said to me sadly, "Sir, the Chinese is dead."

She had disappeared for three days, she so orderly, so domestic, who never left our premises. Doubtless, feeling her end near, she had fled, obedient to an impulse or sentiment of extreme modesty which leads some animals to hide themselves to die. "She remained all the week," said Sylvester, "up on the high wall lying on the red jasmine vine, and would not come down to eat or drink; but she always answered when we spoke to her, in such a little feeble voice!"

Where then had she gone, poor Pussy Gray, to meet the terrible hour? Perhaps, in her ignorance of the world, to some strange house, where she was not allowed to die in peace, but was tormented, driven out,—and afterwards cast on the dunghill. Truly, I would have chosen that she might die at her home; my heart swelled a little at the remembrance of her strange human glances, so beseeching, so indicative of that need of affection which she could not otherwise express, seeking my own eyes with mute interrogation forever unutterable.—Who knows what mysterious agonies rend the little, disturbed souls of the lower animals in their dying hours?

As if a fatal spell had been cast upon our cats, Pussy White, also, seemed near her end.

By fantasy of the dying, she had selected her last lodging in my dressing-room,—upon a certain lounge whose rose color doubtless pleased her.

There we carried to her a little food, a little milk, which were alike untasted; she looked at us whenever we entered, with kind eyes, glad to see us, and still purred feebly when caressed.

Then, one pleasant morning, she also disappeared, and we thought she would return no more.

She did return, however, and I recall nothing more sad than her re-appearance. It was about three days after, in one of those delightful periods at the commencement of June, which shine and glow in the unclouded heavens,—deceivers with promises of eternal duration, woeful to beings born to die. Our courtyard displayed all its leaves, all its flowers, all its roses upon its walls, as in so many past Junes; the martinets, the swallows, exhilarated with light and life, darted about with songs of joy in the blue above us; there was a universal festival of things without Soul and gay animals unconscious of death.

Aunt Clara, walking there, watching the opening blossoms, called to me suddenly, and her voice showed that something unusual had occurred.

"Oh! come! look here.—Our poor Pussy has returned."

She was there indeed, reappearing as a wretched little phantom, emaciated, weak, her fur already discolored with earth;—she was half dead. Who knows what emotion led her home: an afterthought, a lack of courage at the last hour, a longing to see us once more!

With extreme exertion she had surmounted the lower wall, so familiar, which she was wont to cross in two bounds, when she re-turned from her beat of police guard, to cuff some acquaintance, to correct some neighbor. Breathless from her supreme effort, she lay extended on the new grass at the margin of the mimic lake, bending her poor head to lap a mouthful of fresh water. And her imploring eyes called for aid. "Do you not see that I am dying? Can you do nothing to help me live a little longer?"

Presages of death everywhere, this fair June morning, beneath its resplendent sky: Aunt Clara, leaning over her suffering favorite, seemed to me suddenly, so old, feebler than ever before, ready also to go from us.

We decided to carry Pussy White back to the dressing-room, and place her on the rose-colored lounge she herself had chosen the pre-ceding week, and which had seemed to please her. I resolved to watch carefully that she should not depart again, that at least her bones might rest in the earth of our courtyard, that she should not be thrown on some dunghill,—like that of my poor Chinese companion, whose anxious eyes still haunted me. I held her to my breast with careful tenderness, and, contrary to her habitude, she allowed herself to be carried, this time, in complete confidence, her drooping head leaning on my arm.

Upon the rose-colored lounge she struggled against death for three days, so great is a cat's vitality. The sun shone on the mansion and the gardens around us. We continued to visit her often, and she always endeavored to rise to greet us with a grateful and pathetic air, her eyes telling as plainly as those of a human being the presence and the distress of what we call the soul.

One morning I found her dead, rigid, her open eyes glassy, expressionless,—a corpse, a thing to be hidden from view. Then I bade Sylvester make a grave in a terrace of the courtyard, at the foot of a tree. Whither had fled that which I had seen shine forth from her dying eyes; the restless Spark within, whither had it gone?

The burial of Pussy White, in the quiet courtyard, under the blue sky of June, in the full sunlight of two o'clock!

At the chosen place Sylvester dug the grave,—then stopped, looking at the bottom of the excavation, and stooping to pick up something that surprised him. "What is this," said he, stirring the small white bones which he had discovered,—"a rabbit"?

The bones of an animal, indeed; those of my cat from Senegal, an old pussy, my companion in Africa, very much beloved long ago, that I had buried there a dozen years before, and then forgotten, in the abyss where beings and things that disappear forever accumulate. And while looking at these bones mingled with the earth, these tiny legs like white sticks, this collection still suggesting what was once the back and tail of an animal,—there arose before me, with an inclination to smile and a heavy heart-throb, a scene well-nigh forgotten, a certain occasion when I had seen this same posterior of a cat, clothed in agile muscles and in silky fur, fly before me comically, tail in air, in the very height of terror.

It was one day when, with the obstinacy natural to her race, she had climbed again on a piece of furniture twenty times forbidden, and had there broken a vase which I prized very highly. I had at first given her a cuff; then my temper rising, I followed it by a rather brutal kick. She, surprised only by the blow, realized by the succeeding kick that war was declared; it was then that she swiftly fled, her plumy tail in the air, and from her refuge beneath the sofa she turned to give me a reproachful and distressed look, believing herself lost, betrayed, assassinated by him she loved, and to whose hands she had confided her fate; and as my eyes still were angry she uttered finally her cry of surrender, of hopeless despair, that peculiar and sinister cry of animals that realize themselves on the verge of death. All my anger vanished; I called her, caressed her, still trembling and panting, upon my knees. Oh! the last agonized cry of an animal, be it that of the ox, drawn down to the abattoir, even that of the miserable rat held between the teeth of a bulldog; that hopeless appeal, addressed to no one, which seems a protest addressed to nature itself,—an appeal to an unknown, impersonal mercy, pervading all space.

Two or three bones sunken at the foot of a tree is all now remaining of the once cherished creature that I recall so living and so droll. And her flesh, her little person, her attachment to me, her intense terror on a certain occasion, her precipitate flight, her plaintive reproach, all finally that encompassed these bones,—has become a little earth. When the hole was sufficiently deep, I went upstairs where all that remained of our beautiful Angora lay rigid on the rose-colored lounge. And in descending with my light burden, I found, in the courtyard, my mother and Aunt Clara seated on a bench in the shade, assuming to be there by chance, and pretending to converse unconcernedly: that we should thus assemble expressly for this burial would seem rather ridiculous, and we perhaps should have smiled despite our grief.

There never glowed a brighter day; never was balmier silence, unbroken save by the hum of insects; the garden was in full bloom, the rose-trees white with their blossoms; the peace of the country brooded over the neighborhood, the martinets and swallows slept, the everlasting tortoise, most lively when the sun shone hotly, trotted aimlessly to and fro on the pavement. Everything was imbued with the melancholy of too tranquil skies, of a season too monotonous, of the oppression of noonday. Against the fresh green verdure, the dazzling brightness of color, the two similar robes of my mother and Aunt Clara formed two intensely black spots. Their silvery heads were bowed down as if somewhat weary of having seen and reseen so many times, almost eighty times, the deceitful renewal. Everything around them, trees, birds, insects, and flowers, seemed chanting the triumph of their perpetual resurrection, regardless of the fragile beings who listened, already agonized by the presage of their inevitable end.

I laid Pussy White in her grave, and the black and white fur disappeared under a falling mass of earth. I was glad that I had succeeded in keeping her in her last days with us, that she had not died elsewhere like the other; at least her body would decay in our courtyard, where for so long a period she had laid down the law for all cats of the neighborhood, where she had idled away the summer hours on the vine-covered wall, and where on winter nights, at her capricious hour for retiring, her name had resounded so many times in the silence, called by the failing voice of Aunt Clara.

It seemed to me that her death was the beginning of the end of the dwellers in our home; in my consciousness, this cat was bound like a long cherished plaything to the two well-beloved guardians of my hearthstone, seated there upon the bench, and to whom she had been a faithful companion in my absences afar. My sorrow was less for herself, inexplicable and uncertain little soul, than for her existence which had just finished. It was like ten years of our own life that we had buried there in the earth.

My First Tiger

LLOYD ALEXANDER

I was not always partial to cats. In my family, we kept dogs: of no particular breed, but usually several at a time. Since my parents looked after them, trained them, and worried over their illnesses, I can't claim the dogs as belonging exclusively to me. But they were my favorite animals, and I acquired my first cat reluctantly.

In Paris, where I met my wife after the war, we lived in a small apartment and looked forward to having our own house. When we came back to the United States we were able to find a place for ourselves in spite of the building shortage. Near Philadelphia, in an area rapidly being built up, our community still manages to remain countrified. We have some woods nearby, a creek, and our own property covers a tolerable amount of ground. Our house is the most ancient on the street, and looks it. The flooring has a tendency to sag. Doors and windows operate according to climatic conditions: immovable on a damp day, impossible to keep shut in fine weather. But the lawn and gardens make up for everything.

That first spring, while Janine set about getting the house in livable shape, I undertook to find a pet. Naturally, I chose a dog: an eight-months puppy from the local animal refuge. I named him Barkis—Barkis the Unwilling—and his conduct was enough to try the patience of the most unshakable dog-lover.

I forgave him for refusing to learn house manners, for pulling my books from the shelves and chewing the bindings. Even when he rummaged through neighborhood rubbish bins and brought home his loot, I overlooked it. Since he disdained the dog house I bought for him, and howled if I tied him up, I allowed him to ramble where he pleased. But his excursions took him farther and farther afield. One day he ran off and never came back.

My lack of success with Barkis disappointed me; but when Janine first suggested taking in a cat, I refused. I still preferred dogs. Cats seemed of little consequence. Outside of catching a few mice, they

437

performed no apparent work. They didn't guard your house or fetch your slippers. Under no circumstances would they shake hands, sit up, or play dead. As a supreme insult to their owners, they wouldn't come when you called.

These are the usual objections to a cat. They are true, in a way, and not true at all. For the pleasures of cat-keeping appeal directly to the heart, with no need for token gestures.

In any case, we found ourselves without a pet. The animal shelter had no dogs that appealed to me at the moment and once again Janine brought up the subject of a cat. A friend of ours had a six-weeks kitten available and, with much mental reservation, I agreed we could adopt it.

The kitten turned out to be a brown tabby, domestic short-hair—I called him an alley cat then. His white chest and paws made him look as if he were wearing a boiled shirt and gloves. The loops and whorls of a gigantic fingerprint covered his back. On his forehead he wore a mark in the shape of a scrawled capital "M": the badge of tabbies immemorial.

We named him Rabbit because of his coloring. Aside from his immediate appearance, I knew nothing about him; only that he had been born in a bath tub in a city apartment. I did notice that he came equipped with an efficient-looking set of claws and seemed capable of looking after his own interests.

In contrast to the roly-poly aspect of many puppies, Rabbit was surprisingly lean and wiry. And he looked at me more critically than any dog would dare.

He consented to sit on my lap for a little while and purred discreetly when Janine stroked him. I had always enjoyed the enthusiastic barking of a puppy, although I had to admit that Rabbit's buzz of satisfaction was not unpleasant.

But, as I was to realize, humans are not always the most important features in a cat's life. A strange kitten, in particular, has a number of affairs to settle. There are times, with cats, when we may only watch and try to understand.

On his first day, Rabbit performed the ceremony of taking possession. This ritual has followed the same pattern with each subsequent cat, so I should outline the main points of it here.

It begins with hiding, preferably underneath something. (In Rabbit's case, a living-room chair.) This spot becomes a general headquarters and all operations proceed from it.

A slight advance constitutes the next step. The kitten forms himself into a reconnaissance party and establishes an outpost a short distance from his base—at the leg of a coffee table, say. He sets up bridgeheads on either flank—possibly the bookshelves and the piano—until he attains something like a defense perimeter. There is a good bit of scuttling back and forth between these and the base camp. At a sudden noise or movement, he retreats immediately.

Gradually he enlarges the periphery until it includes the entire room. By now, he has various strong-points and low-echelon head-quarters here and there, the base camp functioning only in extreme emergencies. In this way, little by little, he explores the whole house.

Like any wild animal, the kitten must be sure of his ground from the beginning. He wants to know where he can fight and where he can hide; he likes to work out alternate routes between one place and another, long cuts, short cuts, and convenient spots for neat little ambushes. In a short while, the kitten learns the plan of the house by heart; from then on, he can rarely be taken unawares.

Nothing is sacred to an exploring cat. Rabbit poked into closets and cupboards, crawled into the kitchen cabinets, and tested out the living room chairs. He caught sight of me closing a bureau drawer and immediately wanted it opened again, standing on his hind legs and trying to slip his paws into the crack. He examined my shirts, my wife's linen, and even took a nap in the drawer, just to get the feel of things.

The second part of the ceremony occurs when the cat ventures out-doors. More caution is needed here. A new kitten sticks pretty close to the walls of the house and slides around corners like a trickle of water. The only part of the outside world that confused Rabbit was the grass. He walked on it very gingerly, raising his paws high at every step, as if he didn't like the sensation.

Finally, the kitten leaves the immediate premises: the last step in taking possession. How far he goes depends on his personality, but even the most adventurous cat reaches his limit. The more he branches out from his original base, the more tenuous become his lines of communication; and perhaps some instinct warns him not to overextend himself. And he settles down. It is just as well. With a cat's curiosity, he would explore to the horizon if nothing stopped him.

Although I don't lay this down as a rule, I believe you can get a good idea of a cat's general inclinations in this ritual of taking possession. A cat who requires a long time for it usually grows up to be a little shy. Rabbit, however, concluded the affair in record time.

For an inexperienced kitten, Rabbit held definite views about life and his own position in the scheme of things. First, he made it clear that cats like to choose their own sleeping quarters. From a grocery carton, I prepared what I judged to be a comfortable cat box, lining it carefully with an old blanket. I set it in a corner of the bedroom, where I imagined a kitten should like to be.

I was wrong. The only place a kitten likes is the one he finds for himself. Rabbit found our bed.

At first he seemed contented with his box, but he was only faking. As soon as we turned out the lights, I heard a scratching on the covers and saw a small, shadowy form struggling over the edge of the bed. I got up, returned him to his box and we played this game for about an hour. Rabbit won. He settled himself at my feet and rolled over on his back. He never used the box afterward.

Demanding our bed for serious sleeping, he preferred higher altitudes for his daytime naps. Small as he was, he painstakingly scaled the summit of the sofa cushions and by slow stages made his way to the top of the bookshelves. He had a fancy for an old Irish harp at one end of the shelf and liked to curl up at the bottom of it. On occasion, he would pluck the strings. The vibration tickled his paw and he would draw back suddenly to lick his pads. Since he appeared so interested in the harp, I took it down once and twanged a few notes. In his curiosity, he poked his nose against a string, sneezed and ran away. After that, he preferred the harp to be silent.

He reached another favorite spot, the top shelf of our bedroom closet, by crawling up my bathrobe. In relation to his size, I estimate the feat to correspond roughly to a man climbing a ten-floor building by means of a Jacob's ladder. Rabbit dug in his claws and hoisted himself, paw over paw, until he arrived at the shoulder of my robe. There he balanced between the clothes hangers and the wooden closet-bar, made a leap and came to rest in the middle of the shelf. This spectacular performance pleased him as much as it startled us, and he rolled triumphantly among the spare bedclothes.

Sometimes I felt Rabbit spent more time off the ground than on it. At meals, he insisted on being served at the drainboard of the kitchen sink, mewing and scratching the base cabinet until my wife picked him up.

He liked height even for his drinking water. Although I made sure he had a fresh bowl twice a day, he soon discovered the bathroom faucets provided the same liquid, and he took his drinks from the wash basin. He would come in as soon as he heard me getting ready to shave, jump to the rim of the tub, from there to the basin, and dip in his paw. To oblige him, I stopped shaving, drained the basin and filled it up again.

Rabbit also liked to make a game of fishing for the stopper. He never cared to dive deep enough to catch it for himself, so I had to assist by hauling up the chain and bringing it within easy reach— while the lather on my face dried to plaster.

Books and newspapers, he found, made excellent places on which to relax. There was no use trying to drive him off. He looked at us so reproachfully that we wished we hadn't mentioned it. I did little reading while Rabbit was in the house.

For an alley cat, Rabbit had the makings of an oriental despot. At meal time, he strode up and down in the kitchen, whisking his tail and muttering until Janine put him on the drainboard, where he ate promptly. Three things he demanded of food: regularity, quantity, and quality, although what constituted quality depended on his whim. He could look at a plate of excellent horsemeat and, if it didn't impress him for some reason, push it aside with an expression of haughty repugnance. He made the gesture of covering it up as if it were offal, and did so with such contempt that I almost lost my temper.

After eating, he retired to the living room, took his position under the harp, or on top of the piano, and gave out word that he didn't want to be disturbed. Then I could tempt him with catnip mice, with strings and crumpled paper to no avail. Rabbit's time was his own, and he noticed us only when he chose to do so.

This independence must not be confused with lack of affection. Rabbit could be charming when he felt like it. His advances were subtle: a movement of his head, a light grazing of our legs with his flank, a glance, a moment of purring. Unobvious things that we gradually learned to observe and interpret. The nearest Rabbit came to effusiveness was rolling—his specialty. He would sink down in a long, slow glide until his head touched the floor, then deftly throw himself over on his back, wiggling his hind paws in a supreme gesture of good will. But a cat usually writes his love notes in shorthand and reading them demands a certain amount of practice.

Most cats enjoy kneading—digging their claws into rugs, fabrics, or human arms and legs. It exercises certain muscles, but I think they do it for fun, too. Rabbit was also a past master in this art, a businesslike and competent baker. I have never seen a cat take such relish in his work. He always chose a wool shirt—whichever one I happened to be wearing. A spot above my belt made an ideal location, allowing him to sit at ease on my lap. Simultaneously, he pushed his nose under my sleeve and chewed along my arm as if it were an ear of corn. He would pump his claws in and out, purring all the while, for half an hour at a time.

At first, I thought he did this because he hadn't been properly weaned. So, each time he started I gave him a saucer of milk. Sometimes he drank it, sometimes not, but he always returned to me and my shirt. As he grew older, I expected him to lose the habit. He never did. Even as a full-grown, twelve-pound cat, Rabbit often curls on my lap like a kitten: purring, rolling out invisible biscuits and completely abandoning his dignity—at times when none of his subordinates are watching.

In addition to these idiosyncrasies, Rabbit had a wide repertoire of standard postures, and assumed them at suitable moments. A cat can put himself into more positions than a ballet dancer. Observing Rabbit, I was able to isolate a few basic ones.

First, the simplest and most typical: the Cat Couchant from which the Egyptians must have taken their model for the Sphinx. The cat lies on his stomach, four paws parallel to the ground, the front ones extended, the hind ones neatly tucked in at the sides. In a variation, the front paws are folded against the chest, mandarin style. The tail can be straight or curled around the hips, depending on the foot traffic. A good utilitarian pose for use on flat surfaces such as radiator covers, newly made beds, or even the floor.

Another posture with overtones of the ancient Egyptian is the Cat Regardant. A statuesque position, and in it the cat of the twentieth century recalls a sculpture from a thousand years ago. The seated attitude, back slightly curved, head erect, allows the cat to be at ease and alert at the same time. Good for looking out of windows on a rainy day and for general meditation. The tail, of course, must come forward until it reaches the front paws. Only an inexperienced kitten without a sense of style would let it dangle.

The Coiled Spring, or Accordion. Ideal for mouse stalking and bird watching. A wonderful demonstration of potential energy. The cat draws into himself, back strongly arched, one paw off the ground, hindquarters arched and wiggling. A vista of the jungle. Despite the evident strain, the cat can hold this pose for some time.

Also familiar is the Halloween position. Here the cat tries to imitate a crowd. The body is squeezed into the shape of an inverted "U," legs stiff, tail bristling; extremely warlike and ferocious—exactly the impression he wants to convey. Actually, he is probably scared himself and doesn't want to admit it. This is one of Rabbit's old standbys for use with new kittens. Effective for a while, but it doesn't take with the older hands.

I haven't mentioned the contortions involved in washing and scratching; the leg-over-elbow, 'cello-playing posture; and the doughnut, in which the cat curls up in a circle, much favored for sleeping. But a cat with ingenuity can ring changes on any of these.

Rabbit, of course, could execute them all, plus many others. But for informal relaxing at the foot of our bed, he usually lay on his side in simple elegance.

None of these positions takes into account one of the cat's most expressive features: his tail. Rabbit could point the tip of his in all directions, or crook it like an index finger. When pleased, he waved it back and forth, undulating it like the arms of a Balinese temple dancer. In anger, he gave beaver-like slaps on the floor. For inside purposes, he carried it upright, as a flagstaff; when stalking, it curved behind him like a saber.

His tail was Rabbit's regimental banner and I never knew him to lower it in defeat.

That spring we began gardening. The house had been empty for two years when we moved in. The hedges had gone wild, the lawn was a relief map of interlaced humps and hillocks. We had spading, cutting, raking and leveling to do. Rabbit supervised.

For a city cat, Rabbit took to nature with enthusiasm. He investigated the grounds thoroughly and set up an office under the barberry hedge. The branches curved down in a thorny screen and there he could be invisible and unassailable.

When the robins appeared, he developed a lively interest in ornithology. He pursued them relentlessly, implacably, and with remarkable lack of success.

After a long, roundabout creeping, starting from his office and proceeding behind the mulberry trees, advancing slowly, belly to the ground, Rabbit assumed the accordion position. He wiggled his rear end, leaped forward—and the robins flew away.

Either the birds were uncooperative or he had yet to learn the finer points of stalking. But he never let on that he missed his game. While the robins perched on the high branches and whistled at him, the infuriated Rabbit pounced on a bit of twig or leaf as if he had come for that in the first place.

His appearance changed remarkably during the first six weeks. His fuzziness wore off, leaving him sleek and efficient looking. His head and neck came into proportion with the rest of him, and his markings showed up handsomely. His white hind legs flashed like a pair of new gaiters against the dark volutions covering his body. When he wanted to camouflage himself, he tucked his legs under him and became indistinguishable from a bare spot on the lawn. As a result of his busy fashion of walking about, peering into things as if he were carrying a quizzing glass, we added the "Esquire" to his name, and prefaced it with a gentlemanly "Robert."

He enjoyed planting and when Janine set down flowers he amused himself by catching the dangling roots. He also used for his own purposes the holes my wife intended for rose bushes. Rabbit contributed to the heavy work by running beside the lawn roller, so closely that I feared he might be flattened along with the mole hills.

Rabbit felt the outdoors to be his special domain. As a human, he would have made a first-rate naturalist. Ant hills occupied him for hours, and he sat in front of them, his head cocked to one side, curving out a paw from time to time to scoop up the little creatures. Although he preferred animate objects, the motion of grass in the wind fascinated him; he played with old walnut shells, with dandelion puffs and feathers. Once he found a robin's discarded eggshell. He flicked at the shell with his paw, sniffed the hollow inside, and carried it in his mouth for a few moments before finally abandoning it as lacking interest.

As he became more at home outside, his sense of personal dignity increased. He refused to allow familiarities beyond the door. On the lawn, if we picked him up he kicked and struggled; he reminded me of a boy whose doting parents interrupt him at a game of marbles. He twisted himself out of our arms and dashed away to a hummock, where he sat and angrily smoothed away imaginary ruffles in his fur.

During this period of repairs and improvements, I smashed one of the cellar windows. Very little happens that a cat can't turn to advantage and Rabbit discovered he could jump through the window and enter the house via the basement. He hopped down to a storage barrel and from there to the cellar floor, making his way up the steps. He could push open the unbolted door with ease—although he never closed it behind him.

He appeared so pleased with this arrangement that I left the window broken. It proved to be the turning point in his career. Like a gentleman with his own flat, Rabbit became completely independent of us in the matter of going in and out.

His destiny, he realized, was to be a cat of the world. Instead of retiring to an armchair after meals, he took up a position on the cellar window ledge. I could usually find him there, evenings, sitting with his paws tucked around him, watching nothing and everything. He still used his office under the barberry hedge, but the cellar window offered other advantages. It provided him with an excellent escape hatch.

Not for defense against dogs. He was fearless in that matter. A band of canine delinquents roamed our neighborhood and from time to time one of the group would climb over our retaining wall.

The sight of Rabbit sunning himself on the lawn promised real sport, and the dog would come loping and hallooing across the grass. Rabbit held his ground. After a few moments' toleration of disrespectful yapping, Rabbit would swat the intruder on the nose. The dog would reconsider and fall back a little ways, puzzled. Rabbit then felt free to withdraw, which he did with dignity, scornfully turning his back and slowly walking to his window or to the cover of the hedge.

His main concern was other cats. I never realized there were so many in the vicinity until Rabbit came. Suddenly they materialized from nowhere, curious about the newcomer and rarely giving him cordial welcome. In the feline world, competition for females must be worse than our human competition for money; at least, I presume that sex jealousy accounts for the attitude of one tomcat toward another. From what I could observe, they all appeared to be on extremely bad terms among themselves and on worse ones with Rabbit. Hardly an evening passed without the noise of one quarrel or another, and I would race outside to find some huge old male skulking in the bushes, and to see Rabbit just vanishing through the cellar window. Their goal seemed to be his complete elimination, and the most persistent in this aim was Felix Cat.

The ferocious gray tom had no given name as far as we knew, so we called him after his owner. Felix, whose property adjoined ours, estimated the animal to be about eight years old. But considering the cat's enormous size, almost nonexistent ears, a head like a cabbage, and the accumulation of scar tissue around the eyes, I should have guessed a hundred and eight.

The worst thing about Felix Cat was his omnipresence. He made his legal residence in Felix' barn, where his early life among the worn-out tires and abandoned hardware accounted for his disposition. But he rarely stayed home. He preferred our grounds and spent his waking hours lurking in the gardens that marked the dividing line between properties. On a fine morning I could see him sitting in a corner of the flower bed, cleaning his paws in anticipation, waiting for Rabbit to appear. His favorite gambit was to spring out and seize our kitten by the neck before he had a chance to assume a defensive position. I have also seen him stalk Rabbit from behind, like an ordinary human cutthroat. In a face-to-face encounter, Felix Cat was everywhere at once, his powerful hind legs pedaling viciously. Whenever I heard the sounds of battle, I ran out of the house to break up the fight, usually finding Rabbit on his back, trying valiantly to get in a few good blows while Felix Cat pummeled him mercilessly. As soon as he saw me, the gangster departed hastily and I took Rabbit inside for repairs.

For his part, Rabbit never tried to avoid the old tom, no matter what the consequences. Sometimes I thought he even went out of his way to meet him. Perhaps from bravado. In any case, I blamed these duels for one of Rabbit's most serious injuries.

He came limping into our bedroom one night. At first I thought he had picked up a thorn in the foot, but when I examined him I saw that his left hind leg had been almost bitten off. Although it was late, I telephoned the vet who agreed to look at him immediately.

Rabbit made no complaint about going in the car. He lay on my wife's lap, his leg pitifully bent, and didn't struggle when the vet looked him over.

The vet was sure some animal (I judged Felix Cat guilty without further evidence) had sunk his teeth into the flesh just above the joint. A bad wound in itself, but in tearing himself free, Rabbit had severed the Achilles tendon. The vet had never known of anything healing after such a cut. He pointed the tendon out to me—an insignificant white thing that looked like a rubber band. The vet thought it probable that Rabbit would be crippled for life.

He etherized the cat and put a splint on the leg. A jury-rig at best. He warned us to keep the splint on for several days, but predicted that Rabbit would do his best to chew it off.

We took the unconscious Rabbit home. Several hours passed before he came out of the anesthetic. We stayed with him while he tried to raise himself, slipping, struggling, mewing faintly to ask what had happened. I made up a bed in his old grocery carton and he stayed there without protest.

Next day, as the vet foresaw, Rabbit set about removing the splint. He chewed systematically at the gauze. Even though we picked him up and tried to distract his attention he began again as soon as we let him go. Finally, he succeeded in ripping one end of the tight bandage. Shortly afterward, his toes swelled up to twice size. The splint had to be removed. I resigned myself to Rabbit's hopping about on three legs.

After a week, I noticed Rabbit tentatively putting weight on the damaged leg. Until then, it had jack-knifed every time he walked on it. This time it held—shaky but straight. The tendon had healed. Even the vet was surprised. Before long, Rabbit was back in business, daring Felix Cat and the rest of the competition to do their worst.

The beginning of winter marked Rabbit's coming of age, and he started keeping extremely late hours. The neighborhood cats gathered in a ramshackle outbuilding in a field near our house. There must have been a dozen members of this club, with Felix Cat surely the president. I believe the old tom fathered every mackerel tabby in the vicinity and packed the organization with his relatives so he couldn't be voted out. Rabbit joined, of course. In the evenings I would sometimes catch a glimpse of him tracking across the field to the shack. At two or three in the morning, I would hear a thump as he leaped from the storage barrel to the cellar floor, and the sound of his paws on the steps. I don't know what orgies took place in Rabbit's club but they must have been exceptionally interesting. On several occasions they kept him out all night and he arrived only in time for breakfast. Around Christmas, he disappeared altogether.

I hadn't seen him that day, but paid no great attention to it. He was in the habit of concealing himself for hours at a time, either in his main office or one of the subsidiaries among the bushes at the far end of the lawn. He was studying the habits of the winter grackle then, and it took a lot of time. But his absence at supper alarmed me. I went out calling for him. He usually answered to a "Psht! Psht!", especially if he hadn't eaten. There was no sign of him and the frozen turf stood deserted.

By nightfall, we grew more anxious. I dropped in at his office and found it closed. I walked across the field to the club house. Half a dozen of Felix Cat's offspring were entertaining there, but they ran away as soon as I approached. I poked around neighboring bushes without success.

All next day, I carried him as missing in action, and the following day as well. We drove to my parents' house for Christmas dinner, but it was a pretty glum affair. I told my wife that if Rabbit didn't have sense enough to stay around the house, he would have to take the consequences; that alley cats like him were common enough and we could get another without any trouble.

We went back home to a cheerless, cat-less Christmas night. I never imagined such a small animal could fill a house and leave such an enormous blank when he left it. Neither of us slept much. I had just dozed off when I heard a noise in the cellar. I went down immediately, only to find Felix Cat warming himself under the steps. He ran off, with what I interpreted as a guilty look.

At breakfast the next morning, the cellar door banged open. Rabbit walked into the kitchen, waving his tail and acting as if he had just stepped outside for a short turn around the lawn. He clucked at us and demanded something to eat.

Deservedly or not, he received a hero's welcome. Janine picked him up and carried him triumphantly, while I patted and scolded him at the same time. Rabbit briefly acknowledged the cheers of the crowd, but he had no mind for civilities. He wanted breakfast.

While he ate, I checked him over to estimate damages. I found none. His white gaiters were dingy and his shirtfront looked as if he had slept in it for three days. But nothing worse.

For the rest of the morning, he stayed around the house without begging to go out. Mostly he napped on a living room chair. At dinner, he roused himself to eat again and spent the evening doing his laundry. When he saw me, he rolled over on his back and stretched out his neck to be tickled.

That night I insisted he sleep on our bed. I knew then that he had really taken possession.

Plutarch's Lives

DONALD AND LOUISE PEATTIE

IT HAD been upon blue satin that Plutarch first opened his eyes. Luxury is a Persian kitten in a satin-lined basket. That was a soft and safe beginning; but the man gods are willful, and the war gods are greater than they. So it came to be that Linda Waverly, in earshot of the cannons of France, saw Jim Rand as the one thing worth wanting in an uncertain world; though had she met him first on the mountain trails of his Carolina, striding along with his long lope, she would have nodded regally down from her mount and cantered on, leaving only dust in his face. But that is not the story. This is Plutarch's story, and that he traveled with Linda, in his satin basket, to her new mountain home is all that he knew or cared about, for the selfishness of cats is magnificent.

Plutarch endured the train journey and the long jolting in the mule-drawn cart, assuaged by the familiar smell and circumscription of the blue-lined basket. Only the basket was home to him for weeks after he arrived, for this was a surrounding utterly alien. The towering blue mountains Plutarch disdained as only a cat would dare to; he picked his way with delicate scorn about the rude cabin that was never quite neat, never quite clean, for all the work of Linda's white hands. Only when those tired hands, idle for a rare hour, stroked him as he lay in her lap was Plutarch happy, yielding voluptuously, though with barely tolerant eyes, to the fingers that ran softly through his fur, under his chin, behind his ears—tickling, caressing, soothing. Very likely Plutarch, with fine feline discrimination, felt the fatigue and unhappiness of those fingers as he felt their love, but if he did he did not care; he only purred to himself and kneaded his claws on the homespun knee.

Things got worse when Plutarch outgrew the blue-lined basket. Then there was no place for him to sleep but an old carpet in the corner, and he spent less and less time in the cabin and came to prowl the hours away in the garden outside. For spring, the easy, prolific spring of the Southern mountains, was softening the earth, giving green hints all down the valley slope.

Like her cat, the woman came out of the cabin and spent her hours in the sunny plot in front of the house, on her knees digging, or sitting back on her heels to stare at the blue wall of mountains, while Plutarch rubbed himself undulately against her side. The dark cabin,

more untidy and dirty than before, had less appeal than ever to Plutarch, and sometimes he spent his nights out-of-doors, wandering through black shadow, or up in the crotch of the big maple by the gate of the snake fence guarding the garden plot. Very likely, observing his mistress' thin cheeks and dragging hair, he knew a flicker of disapproval, for his own coat, under the pink currycomb of his tongue, was always scrupulously neat.

Yet she was a good sort, he felt tolerantly when the hand with the saucer of milk descended and he approached to drink, curling his plumy tail about his side, purring an appreciation untouched by gratitude. He approved the garden, with the well-hoed earth between the rows soft under the pads of his feet, with the little poodle-faced Johnny-jump-ups looking up at him, and stocks and balsam and maiden pinks; the herb bed interested him, with its rank scents of dill, which is the symbol of flattery, and caraway, and sage that is for recollection, and he rather liked the smell of the gill-over-the-ground that grew in the trodden places by the door. He approved, too—aware that it was the fount of cream—the cow browsing just outside the fence on the weeds in the shadow of the crowding woods.

For the hot summer had come, the dry and burning summer of the South, and only the nights were livable, when Plutarch wandered under the remote stars and played in the shadows old savage games of quarry and pounce. August came, and outside the fence, in the shade of the trees where the cow browsed, the white snakeroot flowered in evil, foamy bloom. And in the garden corner under the maple was installed a new denizen of the garden, carefully patted in place and thriftily watered by Linda—catnip, filling the sunny heat with the giddy rank smell of mintiness. Plutarch the cryptic, the composed, yielded to intoxication. He rolled and frivoled there in the dull-green leaves, and went away sneezing and shaking his whiskers.

Yet, despite catnip and plenitude of cream, he began to feel discomfort.

He withdrew more than ever to himself, as all sick animals will do; he would not look at the cream saucer, but went away and sat on the fence, humped up in himself. It was the cream that was wrong, something told him, some wise beast knowledge that is better than logic.

One day when he followed the woman out of the cabin down the garden path he had to walk very slowly, putting down one soundless paw a long moment after another. That was not because he felt weak —for now he was better, living on an occasional field mouse and a few table scraps—it was because the woman's step was so slow and dragging. She leaned on her hoe as she went and in the middle of the garden stopped, staring with darkening eyes at the lovely white snakeroot that had pushed its way under the fence into the garden. "It's pretty, but I'd better get it out," she said aloud. "It's a weed— I'd better get it out."

And there in the bright safe sunlight she swayed, and toppled on the garden path, the hoe clattering, and lay there a long time, with Plutarch sitting motionless beside her, staring out of the narrow slits of his green eyes.

Jim Rand found her and carried her into the house. Plutarch mincing along behind them, waving a wise tail. He did not very much like the dark, dirty cabin; he came out again after a little while and prowled among the ragged robin and the bouncing Bet. He had the garden to himself; for days he had it to himself, for the woman never came out of that shadowed door, and the man only stumbled out and about his chores, forgetting sometimes even to put down the plate of scraps by the woodpile.

Plutarch got hungry; he curled up on the fence and glared at the cow, as though to demand what she had done to the milk that it was not fit for a cat to drink. But the poor cow only stood there, shaking strangely, her knees knocking together, her neck held stiffly, and her glazed eyes staring down unseeing. Plutarch jumped down and strolled away through the frothy snakeroot, to the house and into the cabin.

From the cot in the corner the woman's hand hung; Plutarch went over and rubbed himself against it; a faint warmth of affection stirred in his secretive heart. The fingers fumbled feebly, rubbing his fur the wrong way; it annoyed Plutarch, and he went and sat in the sun on the threshold. From there he observed that beyond the fence the cow lay stiffly on her side.

Plutarch was out in the valley meadow stalking field mice through the grasses when, two days later, Jim Rand dug a grave in the garden. Beyond the fence the cow had been roughly buried, and now the smiling snakeroot saw the clods turned again, saw them put back, with the little plants of rue still blooming upon them—rue, that's for sorrow. Plutarch later observed the grave indifferently; watched from the vantage of his top rail the man bundling things into the cart that stood at the gate, with the mule in the shafts. The man called him coaxingly; Plutarch got daintily down, expecting that it might be worth his while, and in a few more moments he was clawing, stifled, at the enveloping folds of a burlap bag. Meowing fiercely, he heard the crack of the whip, felt the jolting of the cart. Only the open, empty door watched them go, and the white snakeroot, ethereal in the dusk, the snakeroot that had carried fatal poison in its green juices.

In the night, when there was stillness over the deserted cabin and all the mountainside, a soft paw fell in the bed of catnip. It was Plutarch back again. He kneaded the claws that had ripped open the burlap, and crouched, staring at the dark with great yellow eyes. Plutarch, who had been born to blue satin, was back again, back to the primitive, perilous freedom that was his truer birthright.

Before man came, there was no one and no way to measure the passage of time. So it was with Plutarch in his wilderness. And why should he mark the days, he with nine lives to be lived, undisturbed in the sun by the doorway; in the night, under the house where the field mice hid?

Autumn was here, but the sun was still warm in the catnip bed, and there he rolled and stretched and napped, with pungent savor floating into his nostrils, and contented animal half dreams in his cat brain under the low furry skull. Obedient to no call but inner impulse, he would arise and shake himself and stalk up the path into the empty house, into the heretofore forbidden precincts of the pantry. There on the shelves stood a jumble of foodstuffs—cheese, rancid butter, a few cooked potatoes, and a mutton bone. Among them Plutarch prowled daintily, sniffing, biting tentatively, settling to eat with his tail curled around his forepaws and a deep vibration in his throat. Sometimes when a board creaked or a bough tapped on the window Plutarch would cast a fierce, suspicious glance over his hunched shoulder and leap down from the shelf, to pad back to the catnip bed, licking his chops and waving his tail as though nothing in the world could ever startle his poise.

But there came a day when the dishes on the pantry shelf were empty, and the mutton bone bare as polished stone. Plutarch, fumbling it hungrily, knocked it off the shelf, and then jumped after it, to turn it over with a disdainful paw, discontent gnawing him inwardly. But there was scarcely the smell of meat left on the bone, and Plutarch went out of the pantry, out of the house to the woodpile where the old scrap plate stood on the ground. Odors of mingled food were here, and hungrily he licked the bare china till it shone with polishing. He looked up and mewed a plaintive appeal, but half-heartedly, for he knew that no one would come.

The sun was gone and chill had fallen. There was no comfort in his inner self, and the wind blew coldly through his fur. He wandered to the hearth and sniffed at the cold ashes so that they rose in a fine cloud and tickled his nose. He sneezed disgustedly and turned away into the bedroom where lingered still, very faintly and sweetly, a familiar feminine odor.

Plutarch went to the bed and mewed softly. There was no answer.

Early, early in the dawn light, he slipped out and went a-birding. In the old days there had been malicious sport in stalking a robin, and then, when the bird flew up with a flirt of his tail, in walking away as though in boredom and scorn. There was no play in Plutarch now; this was hunger coldly raging in him. But the little juncos and chickadees, all that remained of the bird people, peeped and twittered alertly, and drifted like snow from weed to undercover, away from the enemy crouching and glaring in the grasses.

Plutarch returned to the woodpile and licked the old plate again, and mewed, and went into the cabin to curl up on the quilt edge and dream of tinned salmon. When he woke up, sleet pattered on the panes.

Out into the snow he went, Plutarch who had hated so to wet one fastidious paw, and floundered in the drifts. He could see the three-toed tracks of chickadees, and here a weasel track crossed them, all four paw marks close together; and there rank odor of skunk lingered on the snow. Plutarch sniffed at this and backed away sneezing and spitting, making a painful circuit through the snow to find the bird tracks again.

But because the wind blew noisily, and pressure of hunger may make even the wary careless, a junco hopping amid brown ragweed fell prey to Plutarch's taloned paw. With the fine drift of ice blowing into his ruffled fur Plutarch made his meal, all amid the snow, and went home, licking his sharp and shining teeth. Through the drifted leaves in the open cabin doorway, over the floor to his quilt limped Plutarch, and lay there crying softly to himself as he licked at the balls of ice that had wedged between his toe pads and stuck there, stinging.

There were burs in his tail. Every day there were more burs in that once immaculate gray fluff, every day his coat was wet with snow or rain, and not even sleep could shut out the misery of wet fur. Lean was the lone cat's hunting—a hapless bird now and then in the chilly woods; oftener a mouse after long hours of waiting at the mouse holes he learned to know wearily well.

Thaw came; soft days came; the birds drifted back from over the southward mountains. Scent of fresh earth was in Plutarch's nose, odor of catnip pushing up again. The sun was warm. Dogwood fluttered white in the woods, and Johnny-jump-up peeped up here and there along the garden path. Other plants rose there, elbowing, pushing the tenderer flowers from the beds. Ragweed and fennel and chickweed sent up coarse healthy leaves, and Linda's hoe rusted and rotted on the garden path where she had dropped it.

Inertia left Plutarch, and spring hunger rose in him. The jungle, pre-Adamite, primeval, was in the long howl he raised, he scarce knew why, these warm nights with restlessness abroad. In the woods he stretched up on his hind legs and sharpened his claws on the trunks of the mountain birch, leaving long scratches in the gleaming bark to show what a mighty sort of Tom he was. And then, infinitely pleased with himself, he went back to the catnip bed and danced a rigadoon on it in the moonlight and tossing shadows, and raised his voice again in a weird, passionate howl that rose a moment to the heights of melody and died away in an ambiguous, primitive hissing.

And then, out of the forest that had never answered him before, he heard a cry echoing his; not his own speech, but near it—a wild "yang-yang!" that made him whirl about with paw uplifted. Back and forth Plutarch and the voice from the forest tossed their messages, long yowls that meant nothing and hinted everything.

But it was the next night, when the mountain dusk was thick in the cabin, that his nose told him there was a stranger in the garden. Out of the cabin he prowled and saw in the catnip bed a shadowy figure. He stole closer and stared with luminous round eyes. She was bigger than the biggest tame Tom, long of leg, tufted of ear, with wild tangles of yellow hair striped black, white-throated, bob-tailed —a splendid savage. Plutarch paused, startled, attracted, reserved, and then he spoke—once, in a strange low voice. The Wild One leaped from her back to all four feet like a spring uncoiled and faced him, ferocity gleaming from her big eyes. Plutarch spoke again, and took a step nearer, and she did not move.

And that was how Plutarch and the Wild One came to hunt side by side in the soft April dusks, flank brushing flank as they loped along, breaths coming together, low voices speaking to each other. And that was how Plutarch came to leave the cabin and vanish into the depths of the forest with his mate, till the leaves closed around them, screening them, concealing their nights and days.

Strange things Plutarch learned from the Wild One—life in the tree tops, the hollow trees and their inhabitants. She showed him how to make a feint at one end of a hollow log and catch a hare as he sped out of the other, and she taught him how to catch mountain trout with his paw. And then, the wanderlust upon her, the Wild One led the way on longer raids, to mountain farms, where fat geese and foolish chickens slept unguarded.

Plutarch could smell Man on these forays. Man and the things that are Man's. He found, by a henhouse door, an empty saucer that the farm cat had eaten out of, and went away with strange conflicting feelings twitching in his nose. Man. Smell of wood smoke; smell of cream. Smell of the fur that petted tabby; smell of fish that he could not get at. Yet in the air the smell of fowl, and flank of his mate rubbing against his flank as they loped along together—wild beauty of his mate, rolling fire-opal eyes in the darkness!

Farther and farther went the two, down to the Cane Bottoms in the mountain valley, up the other side of the slopes of Chunky Gal Mountain, where the little farms stretched steeply up. And so one night they wandered to the Great Balds, where sheep grazed alone on the tangled grass and starry flowers of mountain meadows.

He watched her as she peered out on the sheep, her paw uplifted, passion shaking her tawny flanks. A new emotion had come over her; something alien to Plutarch. He saw her slowly push head and shoulders forward, throwing her weight on trembling foreshanks; he saw the swift and liquid run, the spring, the pounce, heard the sheep cry as it went down. Then while the terrified flock went clattering and bleating, Plutarch stared at the Wild One's dark form in the moonlight bent over the prostrate head, muzzle to woolly throat. Plutarch sat humped against the moon on an old snake rail fence, watching her. He could smell Man about, Man's touch strong on the rail where he sat. And the moveless cat thought strange confused things while he waited for his mate to come back to him from some other world.

Shouts tore the night, and the jagged glare of torches wavering, hurrying up the hillside. The Wild One lifted her head with a glittering glare; then she wheeled and sprang as a shot rang out, and fell. Plutarch had leaped from the fence top and crouched now in its shadow, his hair raised stiffly along his arched spine. Man smell came toward him on the wind, and calling, and the crashing of branches. From the hiding shadow of the old fence post he watched the figures moving darkly in the torchlight, and saw at last the file of them go past, over the hill, with what had been his mate and fellow swinging head down from a pole they carried, her wild hair in the mountain wind fluttering good-by to him.

It was day when Plutarch came again to the deserted cabin. Perhaps he did not grieve; it had been a strange mismating, and Plutarch, Oriental, enigmatic, seemed indifferent. But he walked solemnly in the catnip bed, and up and down the rows of garden flowers choked with weeds.

He belonged to no world now, wild or tame; weeds and flowers were alike to him; the house and its familiar odors sent him restless into the woods to stretch his mightiest and scratch his mark upon the birch, and the woods overpowered him and sent him disconsolate back to his cabin.

One day in autumn, when Plutarch sat humped on the threshold, paws folded under him, wheels rattled down the road; voices called; odor of man, horse, cow, came up to him along the deserted ruts long deep in leaves. He waited, timid as a hare, fierce as a lynx, lonely as only a neglected pet can be. One glance he shot at the caravan creaking into the sunlight of the clearing, and one glance the newcomers had of a magnificent unkempt creature loping for the woods.

From a cleft of the big maple outside the fence Plutarch watched them, and they had a glimpse of him as yellow eyes burning through the turning leaves. Dusk came; lights shone in the cabin; out through the door floated odors of cooking. Plutarch got down out of the tree.

Beside the door he found a saucer of milk. He sniffed it, the breath of his nostrils stirring a tiny whirlpool in it, took one tentative lap, and then drank with ravenous fury. Milk again! Soft clots of cream in it! Sweet sense of it slipping down his throat. Then there was a step on the threshold, and Plutarch was a dark streak of shadow down the garden path.

But daily he found the saucer filled. And so it was that, bit by bit, he learned the woman's step, the shape of her shoe coming out of the door, the smell of her skirt hem, and let kind fingers smooth his fur and pull the burs out of his hair. He took to washing himself again with a rough pink tongue, to sleeping fearlessly in the sun. He forgot all that for a lone year he had known. When winter came and fires were lit he slept on the hearth once more, and dreamed.

What did he dream? In waking hours he never could remember. But sometimes, in his sleep, under the triangular, elegantly furred head vague trouble stirred, and his nose twitched and twitched, and his plumy tail lashed, and tremors shook his fattened sides, and he would start up from his dream with a wild "Grrrrr-WHEEEESHT!" and spring into the air. And then he would stalk away like one who has been caught losing his dignity, or is wakened out of sleepwalking, and go to the door and roll wild eyes at the dark circle of the woods.

The Far-Sighted Cat

JOHN V. A. WEAVER AND PEGGY WOOD

HE SLUNK into alleyways, prowling from garbage can to garbage can, scuttled across streets seething with monsters on rubber tires that snorted foul-smelling gases and explosive yips. His coat was mangy from lack of proper food, his frame gaunt; and often, after some miraculous escape from the monsters, he hid in areaways for minutes, his heart hammering in weakness and fright against his too prominent ribs.

"Something ought to be done about stray cats," said a woman who saw him one day. "They are a menace—spread disease and all that sort of thing."

"Oh, the poor things," said her companion, "maybe it's not their fault they look so evil; cats are really clean by nature. Maybe some family went away. Here, kitty, kitty."

"Don't touch that wretched beast, Mary!"

Wretched beast, indeed! And "kitty" too! His name was Rupert, and he had been with a good family.

The tears sprang to his eyes. Quickly he wiped them away.

"There! You see?" cried the woman called Mary. "He's trying to clean up now!" But she was dragged on; the traffic had changed, and you know how it is.

"Rupert"—alas, no one called him that now. And the worst of it was he could never tell them that was his name. No tag on his collar was stamped with letters spelling Rupert; indeed, he had no collar. No advertisement in the New York *Times* had said "Answers to the name of Rupert," for none had been inserted. He was homeless and nameless, except for that horrid sexless appellation humans gave to all his tribe—"kitty."

Things had not always been so; time was when he had known the comforts of cushions, cream, liver, a smoothing hand and sometimes, on Fridays, an occasional sardine. But gone were those halcyon days. Gone forever.

What had he come to now? And why?

He could never figure it out. Many's the long hour he had mused upon this very problem, but the end was ever the same—an overwhelming wave of bitterness toward the human race. They were fickle. They played with you one minute, loved you, caressed you, and the next turned you out into the world without so much as "By your leave," slamming the door irrevocably and finally in your face.

And for no real reason.

The Taylors had apparently been nice people. His mother had sworn by them. She'd been in the family for years and years—would have been there yet if she hadn't been bitten by a rat she was chasing out of the Taylor cellar one night. She died in the cat and dog hospital of blood poisoning. An honorable and a noble death for any cat; chloroform and everything.

She had always brought up her kittens to respect the family and do all they could for them—amuse them and later, in the serious business of life, keep their house free from rats and mice.

Rupert had tried very hard to follow in his mother's footsteps—perhaps the more so because he knew the Taylors had kept him out of the litter for his resemblance to his mother. He had the same white shirt front, the same clean white paws, like gloves, and "such a nice face." The rest of him was tiger.

"Rupert—we'll call him Rupert," Mrs. Taylor had said, and all through his kittenhood he had answered gayly to that name.

Then the time came to put away kittenish things and settle down to mousing. But here, alas, Rupert's resemblance to his mother ceased. For some unaccountable reason he could not seem to catch a mouse. He could smell them, see them, watch at holes and pounce, but they always got away from him. He worried about it a good deal, tried all the tricks his mother had trained him in. Nothing seemed to work. The mouse tribe grew, and the smell maddened him.

One day he overheard a conversation. "He's a silly useless animal," Mr. Taylor was saying.

"He was such a dear little kitten," Mrs. Taylor objected.

"He's a silly useless animal," repeated her spouse.

"Of course, the mice are simply eating us up, and the butcher has one he says is a fine mouser."

"He's as useless as a dollar umbrella." Mr. Taylor warmed to his subject.

"And two cats in this little flat——"

"He's as obsolete as a crossword puzzle."

"I can't understand it. He's so like Tabby, and for her sake I've wanted to give him every chance; but truly we have been long-suffering, haven't we? And it isn't as if we were really turning him out. Old Miss Martin is very loving with cats, and she hasn't a thing to do but pet those seventeen—or maybe it's eighteen—and she begged me only yesterday again, so I suppose——"

"That's where he goes, and there's an end of it," shouted her husband. "I'll bring home the butcher's cat tonight."

And Mr. Taylor took him in a basket to old Miss Martin's, where he deposited him without a farewell of any kind. The door closed on that part of Rupert's life.

At Miss Martin's Rupert made the twenty-first cat to overflow the forlorn shack of the eccentric spinster. And while the grimy hostess lavished her tiny patrimony upon the creatures of her adoption, stinting her own table for their upkeep and allowing them unheard-of liberties, there was little pleasure for a decent individual among this mass of spoiled, shameless parasites.

They lay about and quarreled, lifting no paw in even a pretended gesture of feline skill.

A Byzantine existence, ruinous to morale and galling to the high soul of Rupert.

"But what do you do all the time?" he demanded of several contemptuous males who, shortly after his arrival, were cross-questioning him.

They nudged each other and smirked. "Do?" one of them repeated. "Why, nothing! Who cares?"

Rupert drew back. "But—but a life of nothing!" he cried.

A burst of raucous wailing greeted him.

"For cream's sake, sweetheart!"

"Listen to Saint Thomas!"

"Wait'll you've been around here awhile—you'll get to know your catnip!"

They retired, snickering, leaving him sick with longing for the clean integrity of his old home. For a week he crouched in the corner, lonely, frantic, only venturing into the mob when hunger drove him.

At last he found a friend. The patriarch, Elmer, old, decrepit and blind, groped his way through the night toward him and began a low conversation.

"You're the new one, ain't you?"

"Yes."

"I like you. Somethin' about your voice—there's a real spirit there. Since I lost my sight I'm sensitive, see? I can tell. You're worth savin'."

"Am I?" Rupert answered bitterly.

"I think so. The rest of 'em—this trash—" He was silent for a moment. Then he continued. "I'm helpless, of course. That's why I stay. My life's over. But do you think, if I had my youth and a chance — Get out! Tonight, this minute!"

"Get out? Where to?"

"Anywhere! It don't matter. Fight, work, run the streets, starve, if you have to! Anything's better than this horrible place! Look at these rotten creatures that once were cats! It gets you, this place. Get out before it's too late! Save yourself! Be a cat!"

Rupert felt a warmth of resolve surge through him. Suddenly he said, "I will! But how?"

Elmer spoke rapidly. "Creep under the old hag's bed. Halfway to the foot there's a hole in the floor. It's stuffed with rags, but the rags are loose. I'll help you pull 'em away. The hole ain't big; it'll take some squeezing. But you're lucky—you're not full-grown yet, and you're still in good shape. You can make it. Come. Follow me!"

Half an hour later, the breathless worming through the aperture, then the sharp freshness of the night air. Freedom! Opportunity! Life!

"I'll never forget you," he whispered back to the kindly blind face.

"Make good!" he heard faintly, and then came a sigh, "Oh, Youth!"

Freedom! But what had freedom brought him? And where? Sitting on the cold pavement of an areaway, his tail curled around those once-white gloves, his dirty shirt front but an inch from the icy stone, he thought over those dreadful weeks since his escape. He was out of the sinister house, yes, but now he had no home at all. An open doorway or a park bench for a bed, a garbage can for a larder. And where was he heading?

The flagging got colder and colder; he drowsed a little, too hungry and numb to move.

"Make good!" Elmer had said.

At what? Dodging trucks, stealing or just staying alive? He thought of the river but shuddered. No real cat would ever face such a death as that. Water—ugh! Better to freeze slowly here on the stones and be found in the morning stark and stiff.

A man came in the area—it was really the entrance to the basement of one of those old-fashioned brownstone houses. He fumbled for his key and tripped over Rupert.

Too cold to leap and run away, Rupert merely looked up and meowed.

"Oh, kitty, did I kick you? Well, that's a shame. You're a poor forlorn-looking thing. Here, let's go in and warm you up." He picked up an unresisting, almost rigid Rupert and carried him into the house and back to the kitchen, where a cook was getting dinner.

It was Friday, and the overpowering smell of frying mackerel caused Rupert, in his weakened condition, to swoon. Tenderly the man put him near the range and instructed the cook to warm some milk for him.

"Where did you get that awful-looking thing?" she demanded.

"I fell over him at the door. Can't let a poor animal freeze to death on my own doorstep. He doesn't look a bad sort, if he were cleaned up. Give him a chance. And didn't I hear you wailing for a cat to get at those mice in the pantry? Give him some milk when he thaws out."

The cook obeyed. Rupert lapped the warm soothing milk ravenously, and subconsciously he purred. He stopped a moment, surprised at himself. Why, he hadn't purred since he didn't know when!

After dinner the man came downstairs with his wife. "How's the cat?" he said. "Well, he doesn't look quite so forlorn now. Poor thing. I often wonder about animals—have they the different stages of society we have? Do the undercats get a chance? We know they suffer from toothache, tumors, deafness, blindness, but do they have the little handicaps we are learning about among ourselves these days? Suppose a cat has astigmatism, myopia or farsightedness; with no tests to apply except that of life or death, how would such an animal get along in life? Could he be a success?"

"Always thinking of your own profession!" laughed his wife. "Isn't it enough that practically everybody in the United States wears glasses, or must you wonder if the animals don't need them too?"

"How do we know? And suppose they were anemic or had adenoids. They surely are not more perfect than humans; and such little things make criminals and failures! It would be mighty interesting to know just how far these little handicaps which we control mean annihilation to the animals."

"The only annihilation I am interested in is that of mice, and I hope their faculties are all so badly impaired that this cat will rid us of the nasty things!"

So Rupert came into a home again.

But it was with sinking heart he heard his task. That mouse business again!

If there were only something else a cat could do! But no, they must all be in the same mold, cut from the same pattern, standardized.

Well, perhaps his luck would change—or maybe these uptown mice would be less wise.

But success eluded him as before, and the cook scolded at his inefficiency. She told her mistress, who reported it to her husband. So it happened that he came downstairs one evening with a trap in his hand in which something ran round and round.

"See this?" he demanded of Rupert. "This is your job, Mr. Cat, and you don't work at it. Aren't you ashamed?"

Rupert, smelling the mouse, stirred uneasily and looked about for it.

"Here! Here!"

But Rupert seemed bewildered.

"Oh, for heaven's sake!" said the man, exasperated. He opened the door of the trap and let the mouse out.

Madly it scuttled to the far corner of the room.

Rupert, now galvanized into action, pounced. But he planned his trajectory too short, as if the mouse were near him. Surprised at not finding his prey between his paws, he looked around. The mouse scrambled to another corner. Rupert leaped. But again he was far too short of the mark. The mouse made for behind the range. Rupert sprang again, but bumped his nose against the stove with such a whack that he was rolled completely over, yowling in pain.

The man watched the performance with growing interest. Slowly he sat down and stared at Rupert.

"I wonder," he said. "I wonder."

Next morning, after Rupert had spent an almost sleepless night, what with chagrin and his burned nose, the man came down into the kitchen.

The air was charged with something. Rupert, like all cats, sensed the electricity and stood tensely awaiting his fate. Was it to be the street again?

The man picked him up, and Rupert's heart sank. He knew it—this was the end.

But to his surprise the man carried him upstairs into the strangest room that Rupert had ever seen. There limply the poor cat gazed about trying to make out his queer surroundings.

The walls were bare except for some queer pictures.

There were extraordinary shiny mechanical contrivances all about. Rupert was bewildered, dazed.

The mistress entered the room as they arrived. "You know, you are perfectly crazy," she said.

"Perfectly. But I just want to find out. Will you hold him while I fix things?"

"Do get through before your office hours begin. I dread to think what your patients would say if they knew what you were about. You just wouldn't have any patients, that's all."

But the man was propping something against the wall. His wife sat on a chair about five feet away, holding Rupert and facing the man. Now he pulled the shade down. The room was quite dark. Suddenly he flashed on a torch which made a circle of light on a card where something black appeared. Rupert couldn't help seeing that.

The man waited. Rupert looked blank.

"Move back a little," said the man to his wife. "There!"

He turned off the light; once more the circle of light on the card appeared.

Rupert jumped automatically. There on the card was a large rat! He leaped, but as on the previous evening he fell short of his prey.

"Great!" said the man. "I thought as much."

Rupert ran around the room looking for the rat.

"Never mind, old man, you'll be getting a real one, one of these days, but first you've got to train on this cotton fellow. Anna, I'll rig up a sort of frame, and we'll try out lenses tomorrow. I am wondering about that—a cat's pupils, you see, are slits instead of holes. I may have a prescription for the optician to grind which will make his hair stand on end."

Rupert was taken to the basement again and spent the day at a mousehole, hoping by vigilance to make up for his two failures. Nothing appeared, but he was there just in case.

Next day his master took him again to the strange room, and this time had the woman hold a queer sort of frame before his eyes. Once more the light flashed. The woman did something with pieces of glass in the frame, and everthing blurred. Rupert drew back, frightened.

She calmed him, smoothed his head; the man came over and fooled with the pieces of glass. The light flashed on again; Rupert stiffened.

There on the wall in front of him was the big rat again; but now Rupert noticed he had beneath him two small fishes, and below that a row of fat, juicy mice.

The woman snapped the frame on his head and released him. He leaped straight to his mark, his paws slapping the counterfeit vermin.

Breathlessly the man and woman looked at each other. Rupert began to claw at the frame.

"Quick, before we lose the adjustment!" cried the man. His wife grabbed the cat, who fought desperately to get rid of her grasp and the annoying thing on his head. Suddenly his attention was diverted. The man was opening a trap, just as he had done in the kitchen that night. A live mouse popped out very near. The woman screamed and tucked her feet up.

In a flash Rupert struck. The mouse was transfixed in his claws. The oculist seized Rupert, removed his spectacles quickly and left him to his catch.

"But how on earth shall we fasten them so they will stay on?" asked the woman.

"Shut the cat in a closet; I have a plan."

She did, and there the alarmed animal was incarcerated for two long days unfed. Then he was taken once more to the strange room, where Anna held him and the man soothed his frantic struggles with gentle voice and hand while he adjusted the frame to Rupert's head. Only this time there were wire bands over his ears, which were fastened to a collar.

Those uncomfortable things on his nose! He clawed at them, tried to rub them off. They shifted, but nothing he could do dislodged them. He looked pitifully at the woman and meowed for help.

She burst into shrieks of laughter. "He looks like Eddie Ca-Cantor!"

Still soothing the poor cat the oculist picked him up and carried him to the cellar.

" 'Fraid I can't give you 20-20 sight, old man, but see if this isn't an improvement."

Still torn with the pangs of hunger and very low in his mind, Rupert made his way to the old rug which served as his bed.

The cellar was a place of torment to him, for the mice had long since learned he was harmless and frolicked gayly all over the place every night. And there was one he especially loathed who, bolder than the rest, even made so free as to creep up and nibble Rupert's tail! Rupert longed for the sweet oblivion of a dish of milk. That would make him forget.

Then all at once he saw it—a mouse emerging nonchalantly from a hole under the stairs; a mouse, confident of inviolability, coming to twit him.

Rupert padded with his back feet, crouched low—and sailed through the air. A few minutes later he crouched again on his rug, licking his chops.

Another small whiskered face appeared at the hole; a body followed. Pounce! . . . All was silent. There hadn't even been time to squeak.

Next morning the woman, calling "Kitty, kitty" without effect, came gingerly down the stairs.

She found Rupert, his spectacles a little awry, slumbering. Upon his face was a beatific smile, and his paunch was swollen as a basketball.

The work of ridding his own domicile of his enemies did not take Rupert long, and presently the word was passed among the better mice to avoid a certain cellar above all in the block, for Death stalked there—Death, with great round eyes.

The oculist was jubilant.

"For two pins I'd write it up for the medical journal," he exulted.

As soon as Rupert's efficiency was established the oculist visited a neighbor who had complained bitterly of infestation. After sundry leading remarks he made his proposition.

"My cat can clean 'em out," said he.

The neighbor did not even hesitate. "—twenty-five bucks that your cat can't clean us out in a week."

"Twenty-five that within two days there will not be a mouse in your basement."

The oculist made his conditions, and the terms of the wager were carried out. He brought Rupert to the scene of conflict, took him alone in the basement, adjusted the glasses, patted him, locked the doors and put the keys into his own pocket.

At the end of two days he returned, removed the spectacles from his gorged pet and fetched him home.

The neighbor appeared.

"Here y'are," he said. "I can't believe it, but it's true. Let me see that cat." Rupert was exhibited. "Why, he's just an ordinary sort of cat, to look at him. How did he do it?"

"I suppose that's his secret," said the oculist and laughed.

And a secret it remained. The same procedure was followed regularly, once a week. The oculist always won. And nobody found out about Rupert's specs.

His reputation spread throughout the community. He was written up in the papers as the feline Attila, while his master gained the name of the Pied Piper of Harlem. Among his fellows, of course, Rupert's publicity was superlative. Envy, adoration, jealousy, applause—these were now his daily lot. They fed his soul; he found life good.

Then one brimming June day Love, which had hitherto played a casual part in his existence, came tripping down the sidewalk.

He was out on one of his brisk training walks along the East River water front. His nostrils were filled with the fragrance of spring, mingled in the breeze with the enticing odor of the abattoir near Fiftieth Street. The nostalgia of the season, the old ache for someone dimly imagined but never perceived, saddened him delightfully. He stood still and closed his eyes for a moment, musing.

A catty altercation near at hand caused him to open them suddenly. There, twenty feet away, so that his far-sighted eyes could see quite clearly, was his dream incarnate, a white Persian, slender and beautiful as the first snowdrop; a dapper town cat with a smirk and a leer was making what was palpably an unwelcomed play for her.

All the teachings of his mother rose in Rupert's mind—"a lady in distress," and all that. His back arched, his tail bristled to the size of a bottle brush, and with a savage growl he walked stiffly toward the couple.

"Here, here," he snarled, "don't you know a lady when you see one? Quit that and get out of here!"

The town cat whirled, saw who it was—for Rupert was too well known not to be recognized at once by all his contemporaries—and cringed.

"So sorry, sir; I didn't know the lady was a friend of yours. Well, er—good-bye." And the town cat tore away.

"Sorry he troubled you—he should have known better; but then, the product of this part of town isn't long on etiquette."

"How can I ever thank you!" breathed the Persian. "I should never have come here, of course. It's my own fault, I suppose. Can you tell me where Fifth Avenue is?"

Fifth Avenue? Here *was* a swell. "Allow me to escort you there, er—madam?"

"Miss," she answered demurely.

"You're quite a ways from home," said he, walking proudly beside her, his white shirt front swelling.

"I suppose I am. And I am simply terrified of these cross streets. You'll protect me, won't you, and show me how to keep from being run over?"

Protect her? Rupert almost burst with masculine superiority. "Well, I know the town pretty well; and I guess"—he laughed fatuously—"it knows me too."

"You're an American, aren't you?" she purred. "You say 'I guess.' "

"I guess I do," agreed Rupert. "You're Persian."

"Persian descent, but our family have lived mostly in London. I moved here a fortnight ago with my mistress, and I've never been allowed out of the house. But the front door was open, and it was so lovely in the sunshine that I simply couldn't resist a tiny walk. And then the automobiles confused me, and I got quite turned around— panicky, don't you know?"

They had passed several cats during the course of the conversation, all of whom either turned and stared or spoke civilly to Rupert. "You do seem to be quite well known," said the Persian. "More so than any cat I ever saw."

"Maybe they've seen my picture in the paper," said Rupert.

"Gracious, are you a prize cat too?"

She was a thoroughbred, then; he knew it. Should he tell her it was not for blue ribbons he was known? Well, why not? Wasn't his an honorable profession, and very remunerative—to his master?

"Not in the way you mean," he said. "I suppose you'd call me the champion mouser of Greater New York."

"Oh!" said she, glancing sideways at him. "And they put your picture in the paper?"

"Of course I don't want to brag," he said, "but the circumstances are pretty unusual. Some day I'd like to show you the scrapbook of clippings my master has saved about me; then you'll understand. That is, of course," he added hastily, "if you are going to let me see you again. I hope this doesn't end our acquaintance."

They had reached the Avenue.

"Oh, there's the house—and the door's open. I must run. Thank you so much."

"Wait! You haven't said you would see me again."

"I don't know—it's so difficult."

"Haven't you got a back yard?"

"There *is* a garden back of the house, but it has an awfully high wall. Sometimes I am let out there after dinner. Thank you again. Good-bye!" She was gone in a flash of white.

Rupert walked on air all the way home.

He meowed at the back door to be let in, for it was near dinnertime. The cook opened the door, and Rupert walked to his saucer by the range hungry as a rat, for adventure gives one an appetite. It was empty! He stopped short. That meant but one thing—he was in for one of his fasts which preceded an expedition of demousing. No sir, he just wouldn't, that was all!

But how escape? He was never let out of the house at night. No, the thing to do was to get out in the daytime and stay out. But tonight—

As he was cogitating and conniving his master seized him. Rupert fought.

"Here! Here! What's the matter, old fellow? Did I frighten you? Come, there's a good cat—just a few hours now, and you'll have as pretty a mess of mice to clean out as a cat ever saw! Big fat ones. Win for me, and I'll get the missus that string of cat's-eyes I've been pricing."

Rupert gave in. How could he do otherwise? And anyway, maybe it was a good thing to let the Persian wait. Only not too long, of course. He ceased struggling, and the next day went to his task.

In two days he was home again, sleeping off one of the heaviest mouse barbecues he'd ever had, and the oculist was on his way downtown to buy the cat's-eyes.

When Rupert awoke at last it was not with the elation of former expeditions; he felt queer and heavy. Could he have had one mouse too many, or was something depressing him? What day was it? He couldn't remember. Then suddenly he thought of the Persian and groaned. She'd have forgotten him by now.

Oh, why had he ever come home that day? Why had he gone on this last mouse cleaning? A great wave of revulsion swept over him. He knew now what was the matter—he was nothing but a mouser after all. And yet that once had meant all the world to him.

Now he was ashamed. But toward late afternoon he perked up a bit. The lady called Anna had brought him some fresh catnip, which cheered him considerably.

He jumped to the kitchen window sill. It was a beautiful sunset. He wondered if there might not be a moon later. . . . The cook opened the back door for something, and Rupert was gone.

He found his way to the Avenue, scooted along some fences and finally reached a high garden wall. This would be it, he figured, dropping into the garden below.

Rupert looked around him. Always in strange places he longed for his glasses, but they were the last thing he wanted now. What if she should ever see him in his Eddie Cantor make-up!

A door was opened at the other end of the garden, and a beam of light fell across the grass. In that beam she stood, a soft-white cloud. Rupert's heart hammered as in those old days when he dodged trucks. She hesitated, then picked her delicate way through the grass, holding each paw high before placing it on the ground.

He came forward.

"Oh!" said she, frightened.

"It's me, miss," said he. "Don't you remember me?"

"Oh, yes—my American friend. I thought you had forgotten me."

She had looked for him, then!

"I couldn't get away; business, you know. This is the very first chance I've had. You should have known I'd come the minute I could."

"Why should I?"

"Because—because—oh, what's the use? I never saw anyone like you before. I think you're wonderful."

"You Americans are so impulsive."

"We say what we think, if that is what you mean. Say you'll allow a common mouser to come to see you."

"But you're not a common mouser."

("Estelle!" a commanding voice cut through the shadows.)

"For me," she murmured. "Quick, you must go! My people—if they saw me with a strange cat I'd never get out again."

"Shall I see you—"

"Yes. Tomorrow."

("Estelle!")

She ran swiftly toward the light.

Rupert watched her. The door closed. He leaped on the garden wall, his heart swelling. The moon came out, and for the first time in his life Rupert sang.

Next night he was there, waiting for her as she stepped along her pathway of light.

"I heard you last night," she said.

He was instantly embarrassed. "I guess it was pretty terrible," he said.

"Not at all. You have a naturally well-placed voice," she answered. "You ought to study."

"You make me feel so—so—oh, you've been abroad and everything. I feel like nothing at all beside you."

"Nonsense. Or—what is it you American cats say?—rats! I think you are quite—quite nice."

"Oh, this is great! And just as I'd always dreamed and planned— love at first sight. But I never hoped anything as beautiful as you would find me 'nice.' Do you know you are the loveliest, sweetest, dearest—"

"Aren't you taking a lot for granted, sir?" she demurred in her best English manner; but he could see she was pleased.

"I'm past that!" he shouted. "I'm crazy about you. Cats like me, once we make up our minds"—he waved a paw—"are like that."

("Estelle!")

"Oh, I must go. Come tomorrow night and tell me more. I—I think I like to hear myself talked about."

Rupert made the top of the wall in one leap that night and danced off home. Tomorrow night! How could he wait? He forgot the glasses, his false position; forgot all in an ecstasy of passion. She thought him "nice"!

Next day he noticed the oculist polishing up the spectacles, and his saucer was again empty. In agony of mind he determined not to be deterred this time, now that his romance showed real progress. He watched his chance and stole upstairs to the door where patients went in and out from the street. There he managed to sneak out and down the steps.

The oculist's preparations brought his infirmity close to his thoughts. What was he to do about that? Well, nothing now. After all, perhaps she need never know.

She met him again and breathlessly listened to his love-making, purring softly. This night he declared himself and waited for his answer.

Once more she repeated he hardly knew her, or she him; but impetuously he swept that aside.

"Come with me over the garden wall and see the world beyond," he cried.

"But I've already seen considerable of that," she answered.

Rupert's fine fervor was somewhat dampened. "Oh, I'm a fool," he exclaimed. "What have I to offer you anyhow? Luxury such as you've known? No; I can't even be sure you'd have a home." Disillusionment engulfed him. If he took her to the oculist's house she'd find out about his specs and perhaps hate him.

He drew himself together.

"Darling," he said, "perhaps I shan't be able to come to see you for several days. There may be business waiting for me; I can never tell. But when I return I shall ask you again to come with me. I'll have something to tell you then which may be a shock, but until then we won't decide anything. I love you—that is what I am really offering; but whether you can love me will remain to be seen."

"Let's not think of anything now but the moon," she murmured.

But Rupert knew the time had come, and slowly he groped his way home after Estelle had been called indoors.

Toward evening the following day he began dogging the oculist's every footstep. Somehow he had to get across his purpose, and his first job was to attract his master's attention. He meowed, he purred, he jumped up on the oculist's shoulder, rubbed against him.

"What is it you want, for the love of mud?" snorted the exasperated man after tumbling twice over the cat, and once shoving him off the papers on his desk. "What ails this cat, Anna?"

"Affection, perhaps," she replied.

"No, he seems to want something. Doggone it, why can't you talk? Although if you did it would have to be English. It always amazes me to think that French cats, for instance, understand what their masters say to them."

Now that he had their attention Rupert proceeded on a different tack. He knew his spectacles were kept in a little box on his master's bureau, and mewing insistently he made them follow him, as a dog does to his catch, up the stairs and over to the bureau. There he sprang to the top and nosed the box.

"He wants his specs!" cried the man.

"Maybe he's hungry for a mouse," said his wife.

"He's had food. No, I believe he likes 'em. Well, you shall have them, so you shall. Far be it from me to deny you full sight."

He removed them from the case and adjusted them, while Rupert purred his thanks. As soon as they were secure the cat dashed down to the kitchen and through the open back door.

He reached the garden wall and jumped carefully to the ground. After a long wait the door opened and the familiar stream of light fell across the grass. Estelle walked along that beam like a soft furry angel. He walked out and stood full in the path of light.

She saw him. She stopped in her tracks. She screamed. Rupert's heart sank. He knew it; he was a terrifying sight. It was over. He sprang to the top of the wall; the cobblestones of the alley far beneath loomed black.

Estelle screamed again.

He closed his eyes. He folded his paws under him and plunged headlong.

Pain, tearing pain in his head; but a voice in his ears, "My dear, my dear! Come back to me—come back!"

Estelle over the wall? Himself alive?

He opened his eyes, fighting against the soaring agony. Beside him lay the shattered fragments of the spectacles. He looked up.

Bending over him, almost touching him, was that exquisite face. She was crying. "How could you? Didn't you know I'd understand?"

From his racked lips he wrung the words, "I had to show you, to tell you I'm only a fraud, a—"

"Hush! Oh, hush, my sweetheart, my kitten," she crooned. "Nothing matters that you could tell; nothing. What do I care what you've done, what you will do? It's you I love, whatever you are!"

"Anna, come here and look at this cat! His glasses are busted, the frame's a mess, and he's a wreck!"

"Ralph, Ralph, where did this Persian come from? Did you ever see such a darling in all your days? Look how she goes to our cat and stands by him. Ralph, he wanted those spectacles to go a-wooing, I do believe. His 'dress-up' clothes. The darling! Oh, make him a new pair, dearest. And please let me keep the Persian."

"Wanted to get a good look at her, old boy? That's right. Sure, keep the white thing if you want to—you must have had some battle over her too."

But Rupert said nothing. They wouldn't have understood anyway.

There was an advertisement in *The New Gazette* for days for a white Persian female cat answering to the name of "Estelle," but the oculist and his wife read only *The Independent Courier*.

The Stuff of Dreams

HELEN DORE BOYLSTON

SHAH first met Sadie Thompson in the apple tree.

He was lying far out on a branch in the sun, his taffy-colored paws tucked under his chest, his golden ruff a halo around his flowerlike little face. The red-gold plume of his tail flowed back along the limb. In all the spring morning there was no sound except the twittering of birds. The warm sweetness of the earth drifted up to him. His eyes closed.

Something scrambled under the fence at the back of the garden. Shah's eyes flew open. He stared, incredulous. She was coming across the yard, Shah's *own* yard, invading it, mincing and dainty, a half-grown black kitten with high white boots and small yellow eyes, as expressionless as marbles. She was larger than Shah and her fur was very short and sleek.

She made straight for the tree, climbed it with impressive, ripping bounds, and approached Shah on his branch, heedless of his frightened hissing. He backed away as far as the limb would permit, but she came on steadily. The orange of Shah's eyes was drowned in black. He arched with enormous tail.

Reserve was unknown to Sadie. She loomed over him. She breathed on him. She sniffed along his quivering and appalled whiskers, her blackness very smooth beside his golden fluffiness. Her tongue rasped on his coral nose, worked along his cheek, and up to his tufted ear.

Somewhere, at some other time, another tongue had licked him so. Another paw had lain across his back. And it had been pleasant. His terror subsided and he relaxed, bowing his head to the onslaught.

When he had been washed until his bright fur stood up in long, damp spears all over his body, Sadie settled on the limb beside him and did her nails. Her tail hung down behind her, long, black, and elegant.

Shah looked at it. Sadie wasn't noticing. Her wrinkling nose was buried in the spread toes of a hind foot. Shah reached out a tentative claw and hooked the tail. Sadie nibbled on. Emboldened, Shah patted her face and shrank back when she put down her leg and rose. But she only moved along the limb, pausing to look over her shoulder at him.

"Prrrt!" she said.

Shah pattered after her, enchanted.

She dashed down the tree trunk, head first, and sprang to the ground. Shah was admiring but embarrassed. After a moment of indecision he peered down the vast wall of the trunk. It had a great many smooth places, and the ground was so far away! In sudden obstinacy Shah turned, lowered himself over the limb, and backed down ignominiously, clinging to the friendly bark, his furry stomach pressed close against it. The ground received him at last and he hurried after Sadie.

She ran along the garden path to a tangle of grass and bushes at the back—a dank, cool jungle. Shah's eyes were very big as he pushed through behind her. She squeezed under the fence, and Shah, following, entered a new world of space and sun and weeds.

While he hesitated, bewildered, Sadie made a black streak into the air after a bug, missed it, came down without a sound, and melted into nothing behind a clump of grass. Shah brightened and his whiskers moved forward. He crouched and sprang, his little body an orange flame in the sun. They met, head on, and, clutching each other, rolled among the weeds. Sadie's hind feet encountered Shah's chin and she kicked it with steady rhythm. Her fur filled his mouth.

Sadie tore herself free at last and fled. Shah bounded after her, tail high.

The grass blurred greenly past him and gave place to low, gray mounds. Shah halted with a little bounce. Gray dust settled on him and strange odors came to his nose. Sadie was prowling, long and sinuous, on top of one of the mounds. Her tail twitched, her whiskers quivered.

Shah sniffed and was backing away in distaste when a thin, sweet smell, drifting on a breeze, drew him forward again. He set his paws down carefully, avoiding bits of broken glass, a doll's wig, and a heap of lemon rinds. Flashes of sunlight jumped from tin can to tin can, and something stirred under his paws. He spat sharply, but the smell drew him on, up the mound, to where a condensed milk can lay on its side. A little trickle of milk came from it.

"Mrrrt!" Shah called.

Sadie came in a scrambling run. Her eyes glittered. Shah drew back graciously and waited until her round, black head was bent over the rich find. Then he joined her; red cheek against black, they lapped up the thick sweetness.

Shah withdrew first, leaving Sadie the last drop. He shook out his ruff, and, sitting down, was lifting a paw to his whiskers when his nose caught the first whiff of something which stirred him to the very tips of his toes. His paw dropped. He rose; moving with the stiffness of one hypnotized, he went straight up the mound of ashes and down the other side. His nose had not deceived him. There it lay, his for the taking, brown and shiny, dried by wind and sun, washed by rain, but still pungent—an exquisite fish head!

Shah gazed upon it in silent rapture. Never, in all his life, had such a gift been laid before him. Never before had his nose been blessed with such an odor—succulent, soul-stirring, beautiful. A high, tenor purr began in his little chest. Sadie was forgotten. His ears were deaf to the sound of a low, excited yowl. He realized nothing until Sadie shot under his chin and crouched, growling, over his treasure.

Shah's ears flattened against his head in shocked surprise. Then they lifted and he stepped forward, confidently, to share. It was over in an instant! Claws raked his nose and he fell back, blinded with pain, his mouth opening in a soundless shriek. He shook his head and wiped at his nose with a trembling paw, but the pain wouldn't come off. The sound of snarling continued.

When Shah could see, he moved a prudent distance away and sat down. His whiskers drooped miserably and his eyes were very big.

The change in Sadie was beyond belief. She was no longer the motherly little cat, nor the gay companion, but a stranger from whose body came a sickening, brassy odor of hatred. Her eyes blazed and her tail lashed the ashes into a semicircle of dust.

Even as Shah watched, her teeth sank deep into the fish head with a crackling sound. Shah's mouth watered. Outraged, he saw her lift his personal property from the ground, saw it sticking out on either side of her head, crisp and tempting. Its fragrance almost overcame him.

Still crouching, Sadie turned with a weaving motion of her head and was gone—back along the way they had come. Her tail was not jaunty now. It slithered behind her, close to the ground. Shah hurried after her, keeping at a safe distance. She darted under the fence into his own garden and Shah cried out at the added insult.

In the middle of the garden, on the new grass, Sadie laid Shah's fish head down with tenderness and gloating. Shah stood still. Sadie walked around the prize, glancing out of the corner of her eye at the anxious little figure beyond. Her whiskers twitched and the corners of her mouth curled upward. Then, elaborately unaware of him, she inserted a paw beneath the jewel, flipped it into the air, batted it a foot or two in Shah's direction, and when he stepped forward, all eagerness, she sprang upon it, growling.

The black pools of Shah's eyes blazed. His whiskers stood forward until they almost met before his stinging nose. The watered silk of his flanks, burning red and orange in the sun, trembled with the explosions of his breath.

Sadie danced before the fish head in curves and arabesques. She curled around it. She killed it with pomp, restored it to life with ceremony. She was a black feather, a drift of smoke, an exclamation point of delight. And all the while her eyes glittered at Shah's agony.

He was pacing back and forth now, unable to endure that sight, unable to tear his eyes from it. The brush of his tail drooped behind him. Another drop of blood was gathering on his nose.

At that moment George, Shah's own Scottie, came around a distant corner of the house. Shah's tail swept upward and the furrows of anxiety on his forehead were smooth stripes again. He opened his mouth in a long wail for help. George, always the gentleman, removed his nose from the trail of his own affairs and waved his tail in response, but he had not understood, and after a moment went on his way. Shah's tail dropped slowly down.

The noon sun shone in benign indifference. The little heat waves over the garden were saturated with the smell of fish, and insects, emerging from under stones, toiled through the wilderness of grass in search of it. Shah's tongue trembled over his lips as Sadie paused in her frolicking to bite into the dream of dreams. It crunched brownly, and Shah wailed aloud.

The door of Shah's kitchen opened and the cook's voice issued from it. Sadie, startled, turned to look, leaving the fish head unprotected for the briefest of moments. In that moment Shah was a silent golden streak across the grass. His teeth met between bones and he fled, straight for that open door, and through it into the warm kitchen. He crept into the steamy darkness under the stove and waited there, breathless.

Presently there was a commotion in the kitchen. Windows were thrown open and the cook's voice was shrill. Her lumps of feet shadowed back and forth in front of Shah's hiding place with increasing rapidity. They paused. There were grunts, a thump, and heavy breathing near the door. Shah's heart pounded in his throat, but he remained motionless. Then his eyes and the cook's met over the fish head.

A hand, at the end of a fat arm, came under the stove, groped, caught Shah by the scruff of the neck, and dragged him out. His treasure was wrenched from his jaws—though not before he had left long red marks on the cook's arm. He hit the floor, hard. The kitchen door was jerked open, and the fish head sailed through it in a splendid arc. Shah raced through the door after it, but he was too late. The triumphant Sadie was already climbing into the apple tree, carrying the fish head.

He followed her grimly, but without hope.

She clambered on, far up into the topmost branches, wedged the fish head into a little crotch, and bunched herself on a limb just below.

Shah began his vigil slightly farther down. Neither looked at the other. Above them the fish head was a brown triangle against the tender green of new leaves.

Shah had eaten nothing since the few drops of condensed milk that morning and his inside was a large and drafty emptiness, but he made no move to descend. One taffy paw was tucked under his chest. The other extended along the limb, and upon this, after a while, he rested his chin. His golden whiskers lay back along his cheeks until their curving tips touched his ruff. His tail hung down, and his orange eyes were fixed, unblinking, on the brown triangle above.

Sadie was two solid black circles melting together against the sky—a large one, and a small one with ears. Her yellow eyes stared at nothing.

The kitchen door opened and a familiar and beloved voice called out words that Shah knew. "Shah!" it said. "Come! *Dinner!*"

Shah's head lifted and the emptiness inside him began to ache, but he remained where he was. He gave one beseeching little cry when the door closed, but that was all.

The shadow of the tree trunk grew longer. A breeze stirred among the leaves and blew away a swarm of gnats which had been jigging around Shah's head. There was a sudden fluttering as a pair of robins invaded the tree, hopping from twig to twig, chattering. Shah and Sadie looked up hungrily, but continued glued to their branches. The leaves whispered above them. From far away a sound of hammering came to them on the wind. The air was sweet with the smell of grass and heavy with wood smoke. Shah's coral nose quivered. His emptiness was a sharp pain now, and he shifted uneasily on his branch. Sadie did not move.

The beloved voice called again, from an open window, and Shah called back desperately. The porch door opened at once, and She came out, hurrying across the garden to the apple tree. Shah's chest fur trembled with the hopeful beating of his heart. His little face, furrowed with hunger, peered down at Her.

"Shah—my foolish! What is it? Come down! Come, Shah, *dinner!*"

Shah didn't wail, this time. He squalled, pink mouth wide, ears back.

Sadie stared but said nothing.

"Come, Shah! Dinner!"

"Eee-yow!" Shah screamed, clinging to his branch. His emptiness roared in his ears.

After a time She went away.

The brown tree shadows slowly deepened to blue and a chill crept into the air. Shah wrapped his tail around him for warmth. The leaves hung motionless, and the robins, with a final twitter, swooped away. Sadie was a motionless black lump. In the west the wings of the sunset trailed scarlet across a lemon-yellow sky, and the breath of the fields was a white mist. Lights came on in Shah's house.

Something moved in the gloom below. She had returned—with a ladder. Shah mewed hysterically, peeking over his branch. The ladder scraped against the tree trunk and was still, but the tree shook a little, and Her voice came nearer, speaking to Shah. At the sound of it Sadie uncoiled and stretched upward, swift and black. Shah heard the lovely crunch as her teeth met in the fish head. Unseen leaves rustled violently, higher up. Shah followed instantly.

His heart sank as he climbed, for Her voice was suddenly angry. "*Bad!*" it said. But he went on up, little and orange and determined.

Sadie had settled down again, beside the fish head. There was no comfortable place for Shah and he was forced to lie upward along a branch and hold with his claws.

After a moment he looked down. She was on the ground again, and taking away the ladder in an unpleasant silence. Then Her feet swished across the grass. The kitchen door was a sudden oblong of light—then darkness.

The first stars were flaring above him when Shah heard, far in the distance, the terrifying wail of a fire siren. It grew louder every second. All the doors of his house opened and there was running in the driveway. Out in the road passing cars drew hastily to one side with a squealing of brakes; there was more running, and a babel of voices.

Two long cones of light swept down the highway and the screaming wail came with them. They swung ponderously at the driveway entrance and crept in, drawing behind them something long and high and red. It clattered. The wailing died away to a whine and ceased. An engine throbbed—stopped. In the silence Her voice spoke, alone, apologetic.

There was laughter, and more clattering. The cones of light moved, turned, and focused on the suddenly golden tree. Shah's claws almost lost their grip.

People tramped across the grass carrying another ladder, very long, very red. Other people made a semicircle of grinning faces on the edge of the light.

The ladder reared into the air and grew longer and longer. It squeaked, and Shah's ears pricked forward nervously. His eyes widened in terror as the uppermost prongs of it reached a level with his face and remained there, not resting against anything. A dark shape in a glaring red hat detached itself from the group below and began to mount the ladder, which swayed. The figure came steadily higher, nearer and nearer to the paralyzed Shah. It said something to the people below in a voice quite like George's—a definite bark— and the ladder squeaked again.

Just over Shah's head there was a stealthy, frightened movement. It was very slight, but Shah heard it and looked up. Sadie's branch was empty! She had gone only the night knew where—and she had left the fish head behind!

Everything else was forgotten. Shah was a whirlwind among the leaves.

When a large masculine hand closed on the scruff of his neck he scarcely knew it. Crisp brownness filled his mouth, pricked his throat until his eyes bulged, drowned his nostrils with its exquisite pun- gency. His teeth met in crackling succulence. His ecstatic purr was strained through scales and delicious, crumbling bones.

Shah came down the ladder dangling from the hand, not hearing the cheers which burst from the darkness. Into the circle of light Her hands reached to take him—Her dear hands that understood. He nestled into them, exhausted but trusting.

One of Her fingers touched his treasure gingerly. Her eyes were close, peering. Her voice said, "Good heavens! A *fish head!*"

There was a pause during which Shah's round eyes looked up at Her happily, glistening with pride.

"So that was it!" She said at last. And She laughed—an odd, quavering little laugh. Shah was lifted suddenly and held close under Her chin, and together they went away, out of the blinding light, to the warm shelter of the kitchen.

The fish head was buried in the hollow of Her neck—safe at last.

The Queen's Cat

PEGGY BACON

ONCE there was a great and powerful King who was as good as gold and as brave as a lion, but he had one weakness, which was a horror of cats. If he saw one through an open window he shuddered so that his medals jangled together and his crown fell off; if any one mentioned a cat at the table he instantly spilled his soup all down the front of his ermine; and if by any chance a cat happened to stroll into the audience chamber, he immediately jumped on to his throne, gathering his robes around him and shrieking at the top of his lungs.

Now this King was a bachelor and his people didn't like it; so being desirous of pleasing them, he looked around among the neighbouring royal families and hit upon a very sweet and beautiful princess, whom he asked in marriage without any delay, for he was a man of action.

Her parents giving their hearty consent, the pair were married at her father's palace; and after the festivities were over, the King sped home to see to the preparation of his wife's apartments. In due time she arrived, bringing with her a cat. When he saw her mounting the steps with the animal under her arm, the King, who was at the door to meet her, uttering a horrid yell, fell in a swoon and had to be revived with spirits of ammonia. The courtiers hastened to inform the Queen of her husband's failing, and when he came to, he found her in tears.

"I cannot exist without a cat!" she wept.

"And I, my love," replied the King, "cannot exist with one!"

"You must learn to bear it!" said she.

"You must learn to live without it!" said he.

"But life would not be worth living without a cat!" she wailed.

"Well, well, my love, we will see what we can do," sighed the King.

"Suppose," he went on, "you kept it in the round tower over there. Then you could go to see it."

"Shut up my cat that has been used to running around in the open air?" cried the Queen. "Never!"

"Suppose," suggested the King again, "we made an enclosure for it of wire netting."

"My dear," cried the Queen, "a good strong cat like mine could climb out in a minute."

"Well," said the King once more, "suppose we give it the palace roof, and I will keep out of the way."

"That is a good scheme," said his wife, drying her eyes.

P. B.

And they immediately fitted up the roof with a cushioned shelter, and a bed of catnip, and a bench where the Queen might sit. There the cat was left; and the Queen went up three times a day to feed it, and twice as many times to visit it, and for almost two days that seemed the solution of the problem. Then the cat discovered that by making a spring to the limb of an overhanging oak tree, it could climb down the trunk and go where it liked. This it did, making its appearance in the throne-room, where the King was giving audience to an important ambassador. Much to the amazement of the latter, the monarch leapt up screaming, and was moreover so upset, that the affairs of state had all to be postponed till the following day. The tree was, of course, cut down; and the next day the cat found crawling down the gutter to be just as easy, and jumped in the window while the court was at breakfast. The King scrambled on to the breakfast table, skilfully overturning the cream and the coffee with one foot, while planting the other in the poached eggs, and wreaking untold havoc among the teacups. Again the affairs of state were postponed while the gutter was ripped off the roof, to the fury of the head gardener, who had just planted his spring seeds in the beds around the palace walls. Of course the next rain washed them all away.

This sort of thing continued. The wistaria vine which had covered the front of the palace for centuries, was ruthlessly torn down, the trellises along the wings soon followed; and finally an ancient grape arbour had perforce to be removed as it proved a sure means of descent for that invincible cat. Even then, he cleverly utilized the balconies as a ladder to the ground; but by this time the poor King's nerves were quite shattered and the doctor was called in. All he could prescribe was a total abstinence from cat; and the Queen, tearfully finding a home for her pet, composed herself to live without one. The King, well cared for, soon revived and was himself again, placidly conducting the affairs of state, and happy in the society of his beloved wife. Not so the latter.

Before long it was noticed that the Queen grew wan, was often heard to sniff, and seen to wipe her eyes, would not eat, could not sleep,—in short, the doctor was again called in.

"Dear, dear," he said disconsolately, combing his long beard with his thin fingers. "This is a difficult situation indeed. There must not be a cat on the premises, or the King will assuredly have nervous prostration. Yet the Queen must have a cat or she will pine quite away with nostalgia."

"I think I had best return to my family," sobbed the poor Queen, dejectedly. "I bring you nothing but trouble, my own."

"That is impossible, my dearest love," said the King decidedly— "Here my people have so long desired me to marry, and now that I am at last settled in the matrimonial way, we must not disappoint them. They enjoy a Queen so much. It gives them something pretty to think about. Besides, my love, I am attached to you, myself, and could not possibly manage without you. No, my dear, there may be a way out of our difficulties, but that certainly is not it." Having delivered which speech the King lapsed again into gloom, and the doctor who was an old friend of the King's went away sadly.

He returned, however, the following day with a smile tangled somewhere in his long beard. He found the King sitting mournfully by the Queen's bed-side.

"Would your majesty," began the doctor, turning to the Queen, "object to a cat that did not look like a cat?"

"Oh, no," cried she, earnestly, "just so it's a *cat!*"

"Would your majesty," said the doctor again, turning to the King, "object to a cat that did not look like a cat?"

"Oh, no," cried he, "just so it doesn't *look* like a cat!"

"Well," said the doctor, beaming, "I have a cat that is a cat and that doesn't look any more like a cat than a skillet, and I should be only too honoured to present it to the Queen if she would be so gracious as to accept it."

Both the King and the Queen were overjoyed and thanked the doctor with tears in their eyes. So the cat—for it was a cat though you never would have known it—arrived and was duly presented to the Queen, who welcomed it with open arms and felt better immediately.

It was a thin, wiry, long-legged creature, with no tail at all, and large ears like sails, a face like a lean isosceles triangle with the nose as a very sharp apex, eyes small and yellow like flat buttons, brown fur short and coarse, and large floppy feet. It had a voice like a steam siren and its name was Rosamund.

The King and Queen were both devoted to it; she because it was a cat, he because it seemed anything but a cat. No one indeed could convince the King that it was not a beautiful animal, and he had made for it a handsome collar of gold and amber—"to match," he said, sentimentally, "its lovely eyes." In sooth so ugly a beast never had such a pampered and luxurious existence, certainly never so royal a one. Appreciating its wonderful good fortune, it never showed any inclination to depart; and the King, the Queen, and Rosamund lived happily ever after.

A Cat for Christmas

BETH BROWN

BRUISER pushed back the lid of the garbage can and crawled out into the day.

It was still very early of a cold blue morning. A soft film of snow had fallen through the night, transforming the ugly old gray sidewalk into a path of beauty. A flurry of fat flakes came flying through the air as if to make sure they were preparing the scene for the coming of a very special event here to Broadway.

Bruiser sampled a flake.

It was cold and dry and he was cold and hungry. He stood up, stretched north, south, east and west in worshipful genuflection to all four corners of the earth as a greeting from himself and his venerable ancestors. Then he peered up and down the street, primed for the day's adventure.

Every ash can was covered tight, according to the city regulations. But Bruiser made his own laws here in New York. He knew how to leap aboard, cross-wise, hitting the cover a smart blow and getting it to come off in the hope of finding table scraps as well as lumpy ashes.

The janitors and the street cleaners both knew who tossed the litter as carelessly as confetti in circles round the cans, and cursed him roundly for the crime.

But Bruiser's life was full of curses. A kind word from a human being was foreign to his mangled ears. He had never tasted either love or companionship. Yet he walked in pride, asking no quarter of life as a cat, hungry and homeless on the streets of New York. He gave no quarter either. He was heartless, insolent and intensely independent.

A mass of brown and yellow fur spun into sight and stopped like a striped ball on the far corner of Amsterdam Avenue.

"Hi, Bruiser!" came the familiar cat-waul.

Bruiser sketched a scowl into place through which he regarded his hated enemy Mustard. "Aw! Go lose yourself!" spat Bruiser. "Get killed!"

"The same to you!" returned Mustard warmly. "I hope you run into a great big chunk of good bad luck today!"

"I have already! I just met up with you!" sneered Bruiser. "Now beat it or I'll bite off that other ear of yours!"

"S'long, Hell-cat!"

The two cats arched their backs in parting. Mustard's beat was confined to Amsterdam Avenue. He knew better than to cross the line into Bruiser's territory which was Broadway, a block away.

Now another cat, a huge Tortoise shell known to the gang as Smoky, made his appearance on the chipped stoop of the old brownstone tenement beside the shoe shine parlor.

"Good morning, Bruiser!"

"What's good about it?"

"Don't you know what day this is?"

"Don't know and don't care!" Bruiser spat airily at a snow flake.

"Get off that sidewalk with those two front paws of yours. It's bad luck to step on a crack!"

"No bad luck can come to me, Smoky old boy!"

"That's what you think! I know a witch's chant that protects me. How about learning it, Bruiser? I see trouble hanging over you."

"Trouble is right—and it's coming your way! On the lam, you old buzzard! Get lost!"

Smoky bared his claws but thought better of it. He murmured an incantation against Bruiser and stalked off into space, his proud parading halted suddenly by an unexpected kick from the shoe shine man.

An iron cellar door clanged noisily down the street and a thin Tabby cat emerged timorously into the open. Spider made her residence with a shifty old character who did odd jobs around the neighborhood. Bruiser had a low regard for Mr. Bangs. He boozed all night and slept all day and was none too kind to Spider. Of all the cats in the community, Bruiser found the scrawny little Tabby the least obnoxious of his kin.

The cat stood still, her yellow eyes full of pleading. Spider never stopped hoping she could make a friend of Bruiser.

"I got a fish-head," she tempted.

"Fish-head!" echoed Bruiser. "Who cares?"

"And I'm getting liver for supper."

"Liar!"

"Mr. Bangs said so. He said it's a very special day."

"What's so special about it?"

"It's Christmas, Bruiser. Tonight is Christmas Eve. Didn't you know?"

"No. And I care less. I got things to do. I got places to go. I got a busy day ahead of me. S'long."

"Wait a minute, Bruiser."

"What is it?"

"Don't you want my fish-head? I'd like to give it to you."

Bruiser hesitated. In all the time he had known Spider, he had never been so tempted to accept an offer. Something must be wrong with him. Maybe something was wrong with the fish-head. Something was wrong somewhere.

The ugly street, for instance, looked so very showy in its dress of white. The early dawn was such a sudden blue. A man was coming toward him. The man was singing. And here was Spider fearlessly bearing the fish-head as a truce between them.

Bruiser was hungry. His taste buds watered. He darted his rough red tongue along his thin, dry lips. But Bruiser was proud. Besides, taking a gift from Spider would let down the barriers and all the cats on Amsterdam Avenue might decide to roam Bruiser's Broadway.

"For all I care," he declared defiantly, "you can keep your dead fish-head. And I hope tonight that you choke on liver with your Mr. Bangs, the old booze-hound!"

Spider's sigh was audible. "What if he takes a drink now and then? He's been a friend to me. At least we've got each other."

"Well, if I had a human being in my life, I wouldn't choose an old sot like him." Bruiser rocked a little, back and forth, cradling his black body on his velvet white paws. "I'd choose the doctor on the corner. He's rich. Or the blonde who operates the beauty parlor. She's beautiful."

"Mr. Bangs used to be rich once upon a time. He had a wife who was beautiful. He was a star performer, a song-and-dance man at the Palace Theatre. He's told me so. In fact, he showed me all the pictures—"

"But now what is he? Nothing! And where does he live? Down in a cellar with the coal!"

"It's warm down there. I sleep in bed with him."

"Well, for all I care, you can have each other forever and a day. And you can keep your old fish-head, too. S'long, Spider!"

"Merry Christmas, Bruiser!"

"Merry Christmas indeed!" he echoed as he turned on the gift and the giver and stalked haughtily away.

Danny's Fruit Market on the corner was his first stop.

This was more or less a perfunctory measure on his part since he did not consider Danny's place in the same light, say, as Willy's

Hamburger Heaven. The familiar clerks were busy setting the vegetable crates and bushels of fruit out on the sidewalk. He knew there was nothing here for him in the way of early morning nourishment and he was about to pass on to greener pastures when Danny called his name.

"Hey, Bruiser!" Danny was beaming. "Come back!"

Bruiser stopped short at the curb. He wheeled half of his body around. "What is it, Danny?" he meowed. "What do you want?"

"I want to give you something. Seeing how it's Christmas, I got a gift for you."

Bruiser waited to see what lay behind such an apparent subterfuge. True, he had caught a few rats every now and then for Danny but he had not expected to collect any pay for his services.

Danny dived deep into a big, wooden bin. "Here you are!" he announced. "Here's some catnip for you!"

A small bunch of green went winging through the air and fell at Bruiser's feet. Bruiser blinked in blind amazement. In all his years on Broadway, such a prize had never come his way. He picked it up and ran all the way home with it, slipping it safely under his garbage can cover. Catnip was wonderful dessert, he concluded. But some sort of solid food must come first.

The door of the fragrant delicatessen store flew ajar and there stood Benjy, the lanky delivery boy, wielding his early morning broom. Bruiser had often felt its harsh impact from either end. Once, Benjy had even flung a bucket of greasy hot water full in his face.

But now, strangely enough, he halted the broom in hand to call out a greeting to Bruiser. "Hello, Bruiser! How's the world been treating you?"

Bruiser thought of the catnip. "Fine!" he answered. "I just wish I wasn't so hungry."

"I got the cure for that," said Benjy. "Wait a minute, my friend."

Bruiser waited. Somehow the wait did not portend evil nor did it seem at all tedious. There was so much to see in the way of new sights here on the street. The sounds were new, too. The street itself was different today with its billowy banks of dark green Christmas trees and wreaths made bright with red ribbon and scarlet berries.

People seemed different, too. They smiled at each other and at Bruiser. A woman stooped to give him a pat. A boy stroked his tail without tugging it.

Then Benjy was back with a huge slab of sturgeon. "Here you are, Bruiser. It's from me to you with a Merry Christmas!"

Bruiser dragged the delicacy to the curb. He finished it down to the last crumb. Then he cleaned off his whiskers, waxed them with his tongue and sauntered off to his next port of call.

This was the dime store at 79th and Broadway.

He stopped to stare at the windows hung with silver and gold tinsel and brilliant with Christmas tree baubles. The sidewalks were crowded with people, coming and going through the big glass doors. In the past, he had tried more than once to venture inside the beckoning fairyland only to find himself being booted out clear into the ugly gutter.

Now to his surprise, the door opened as if just for him and a girl in white called out to him to follow her behind the counter. Her gift to him was a rubber mouse which he carried out to the street.

Well, here he was, full of good food, rich in possessions and ready for more adventure. He heard his name being called.

"Bruiser, Baby! Hey, Bruiser!"

He turned around to see who it was that knew him so intimately. Then he noticed the fat Santa Claus seated beside the black kettle. Santa was beckoning to him. Bruiser advanced very slowly, suspicion padding beside him.

Why, of course! Who else could it be but Mr. Bangs! So the old boozer was playing Santa Claus, was he, fooling all the people into thinking he was a Saint? Well, he couldn't fool Bruiser. Bruiser was too smart for that.

"You smell of fish," said Mr. Bangs, curling his cotton whiskers as he said it. "You must be thirsty. How about some mocha?" He opened a small paper cup full of coffee, took a swallow and offered the rest to Bruiser.

The cat was so stunned that before he knew what had happened, he found himself taking a sip. Then he leaped in the air at his folly. He raced to the other side of the street as if the devil were at his heels.

What in the world had come over him? What in the world was coming over all of humanity? Why was this day so different from any other day of the year? How was it that nobody had kicked him or cursed him or thrown something at him?

The fish-head. The catnip. The sturgeon. And now the gift of coffee at the hands of Mr. Bangs.

Why should Christmas make such a difference? The whole thing was incredible. Just for the fun of it, he would tempt the fates of darkness. He would challenge evil, defying a witch's chant.

He looked up at the traffic light. It sparkled green. A moving river of cars and trucks was roaring without ceasing. He stepped off the curb and began crossing the street. The line of cars stopped short in unaccustomed courtesy, marked by a reverence almost for his person. He reached the other side in safety.

He stood on the curb, secure yet confused. His feet moved him forward and backward, rocking his orderly mind into a turmoil that was foreign to him. Something beyond his usual ken, something deep within him, propelled him forward into the rest of the day. He was looking for something, something he could not name.

He slithered into Dubarry's on 77th Street. Alex, the proprietor, allowed him to warm himself. At Stark's, a diner seated in a window, brought him out a bit of hamburger. The cashier at the C. and L. was waiting with a banquet of salami. He ate it right down to the string.

His thoughts were still swimming round and round in his head. He was badly confused by the events of the day. Now he realized there was more than the semblance of truth in what Spider had said so very early that morning.

Yes, somehow this day was different. He had seen the difference for himself. He had heard the difference with his own ears.

He reached 72nd Street. Here was the end of his beat. People were pouring out of the subway kiosk, their arms full of packages, their lips full of chatter. Their words all had to do with giving something to someone. All this talk of giving, this business of gifts, began to have an odd effect on Bruiser. What did a cat have to give, a cat, say, such as Bruiser?

He was ugly. He was old. He had a bad temper. Besides, what did he own? What could he buy? All he had in the world was himself, he told himself. And then he answered himself, well, why not give himself? Someone—somewhere—was sure to want him. Who could it be? Where could he go?

He glanced up and down Broadway.

It had begun to snow again. The streets were becoming deserted. One by one, the lights in the shop windows were being turned out. One by one, the storekeepers were locking up for the night and heading for home.

He reached his corner and went straight to his garbage can cover. Someone had been here. Someone had moved it. The catnip was safe. And here beside it lay the familiar fish-head. Spider had come—left her gift—and gone.

Bruiser took a sniff or two but he did not touch the food. Another sort of hunger was gnawing at him now. He felt lonely and alone. He longed for the warmth of companionship.

Why not run over and pay Spider a visit under pretext of thanking her? Yes, why not bring her the catnip? The thought charged his being with a new emotion. He felt a new happiness. He had a sense of giving which brought a sense of belonging.

The thought made him leap into action. He crossed the street in a dozen flashes of black and white fur. Then, at the opposite curb only a few steps from Spider's home, he stopped so suddenly that he skidded in the snow.

A body was lying in the gutter, clotted with crimson and dirty white flakes. Bruiser recoiled in horror but he did not stir from the spot. He knew that body, so very still, so very cold. The scrawny little Tabby was the only friend in all his world—and now Bruiser had no one. Spider was gone. She must have been struck by a motorist when she was bringing him the fish-head.

Now Bruiser would not be able to thank her. It was too late for thanks. It was too late for anything. Mustard's curse had born its fruit. Bruiser had run into a great big chunk of good bad luck today. He placed the little bunch of catnip beside Spider like a wreath at the head of the great and said goodby in silence.

Aimlessly, he dragged himself back to the loneliness of his garbage can cover on the other side of the street. He sat down feeling mournful and desolate. All at once, he saw Mr. Bangs emerge from his cellar, lugging a wooden box. Bruiser watched him set it down beside the remains of Tabby. He saw the little cat being gathered up and put away to sleep. Now even the shadow of Mr. Bangs moved off and was gone in the distance.

A blue dawn announced Christmas morning. Bruiser awoke, empty and listless. He stretched, yawned, began his usual tour of the streets.

The sidewalks were full of people, their arms full of gifts. The air was full of laughter and singing, the voices of children raised in joyous regard for the day. Only Bruiser felt no joy. The memory of the still form in the gutter haunted his steps. The image of Mr. Bangs refused to fade from his mind.

Somehow—he did not know how—he found himself back on the familiar street. Now he was descending the cellar stairs to the place where Spider used to live. The narrow hall was dark and cold. The odor was dank. But the door was open.

Bruiser walked in.

The little room was small and shabby. Its only furniture were a table, a chair and a cot. Up on a shelf, a red votive candle flickered solemnly.

Bruiser's sharp eyes continued making their survey. Not a single detail was lost to his scrutiny.

He saw the Santa Claus suit, a tangle of flannel and whiskers, lying in a pool on the floor. He saw the one-burner stove and he caught the acrid odor of fish. He saw the wobbly kitchen table with its missing leg used for a window wedge. He saw the ten cent Christmas tree on a stool beside Spider's blanket. A rubber mouse lay beside it as well as a new rubber ball.

And there was Mr. Bangs, his head on his arms, his shoulders shaking. Drunk, no doubt. No. Mr. Bangs was sobbing softly.

He stopped sobbing. He looked up.

"Oh, hello, Bruiser!" he blubbered. "Spider's gone." He tried to smile at Bruiser. "I haven't got a cat any more." He picked up the little rubber mouse as if to give it back. "What brings you here to me?"

Bruiser's voice was hoarse with emotion. His heart was beating like a drum. The floor was ice under his feet.

"Would you like a cat for Christmas?" he inquired with an effort at casualness. "Of course, I know I could never replace Spider in your heart, but I could try." Bruiser arched his back and he waited. "Here I am—if you'll have me."

"We'll have each other, Bruiser!" said Mr. Bangs. "I got some nice fish for our dinner!"